LEON

THE EXTRAORDINARY

JAMAR NICHOLAS

WITH COLOR BY BONAIA ROSADO

graphix

An Imprint of
SCHOLASTIC

THANKS TO . . .

Darcy, for everything.

Raen Ngu, my tireless assistant. Bonaia Rosado for her marvelous colors. Mike Manley, L. Jamal Walton, Thom Zahler, Mike Hawthorne, and Ben Harvey for their art assists and kinship.

Friends and family, specifically the Russottos, Gallaghers, Hawthornes, Grahamnatows, Marianos, Kesilmans, Waters, Cheeks, and dear friends of Eula, Lurie Forney and Jon Schuyler.

Dan Lazar, my extraordinary agent.

My Scholastic family: David Saylor, Jonah Newman, Phil Falco, Steve Ponzo, Taylan Salvati, and Lizette Serrano.

To Marc & Shelly Nathan, Joe Murray, and everyone who has supported Leon along the way.

Nothing is impossible!

Library of Congress Control Number: 2021936599

ISBN 978-1-338-74416-3 (hardcover)
ISBN 978-1-338-74415-6 (paperback)

10 9 8 7 6 5 4 3 2 1   22 23 24 25 26

Printed in China   62
First edition, October 2022

Color by Bonaia Rosado
Lettering by EK Weaver

Edited by David Saylor and Jonah Newman
Book design by Steve Ponzo
Creative Director: Phil Falco
Publisher: David Saylor

I dedicate this book to the memory of
my mother, Eula Nicholas, my hero.

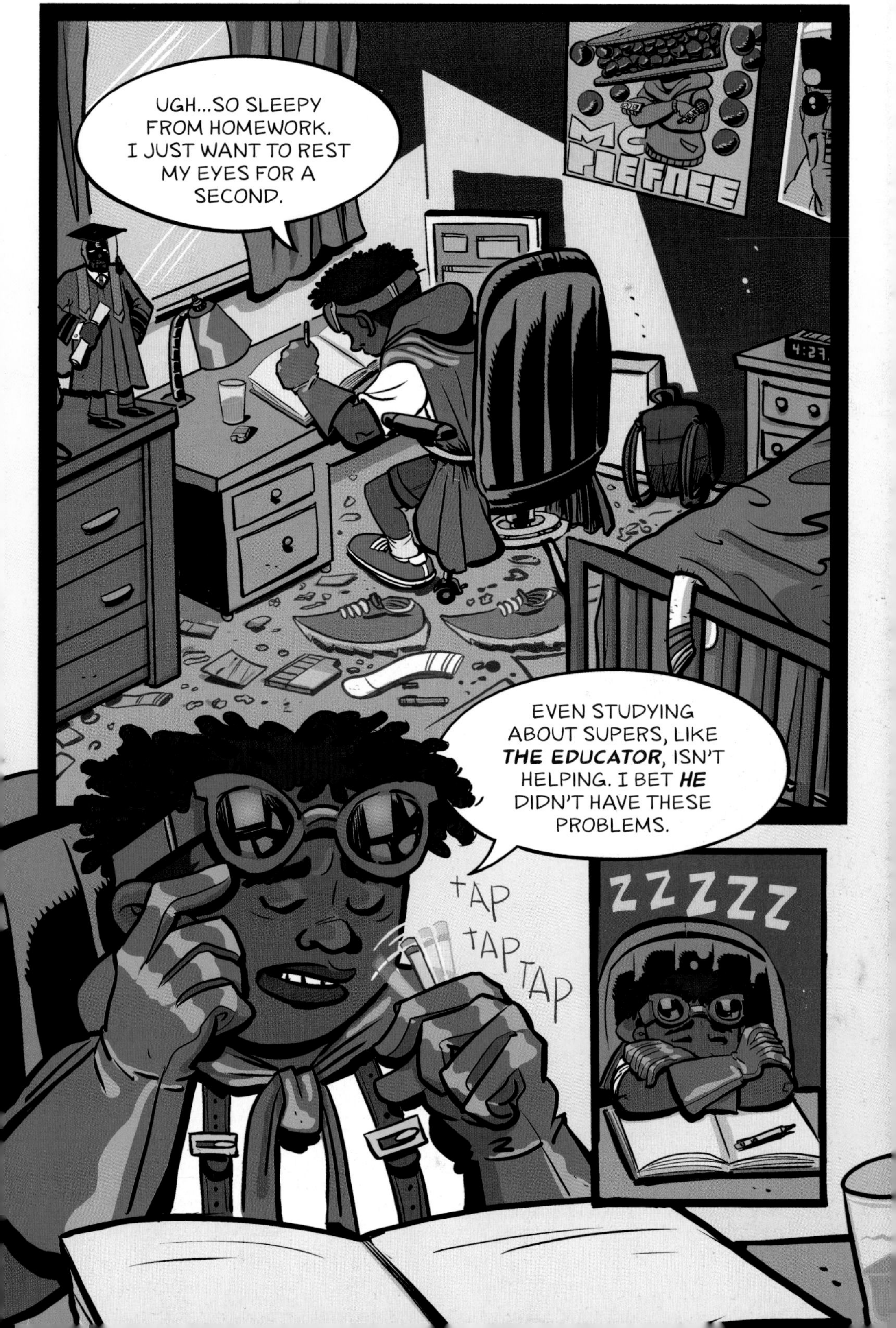
UGH...SO SLEEPY FROM HOMEWORK. I JUST WANT TO REST MY EYES FOR A SECOND.
MC PIEFACE
EVEN STUDYING ABOUT SUPERS, LIKE ***THE EDUCATOR***, ISN'T HELPING. I BET ***HE*** DIDN'T HAVE THESE PROBLEMS.
TAP TAP TAP
ZZZZZ

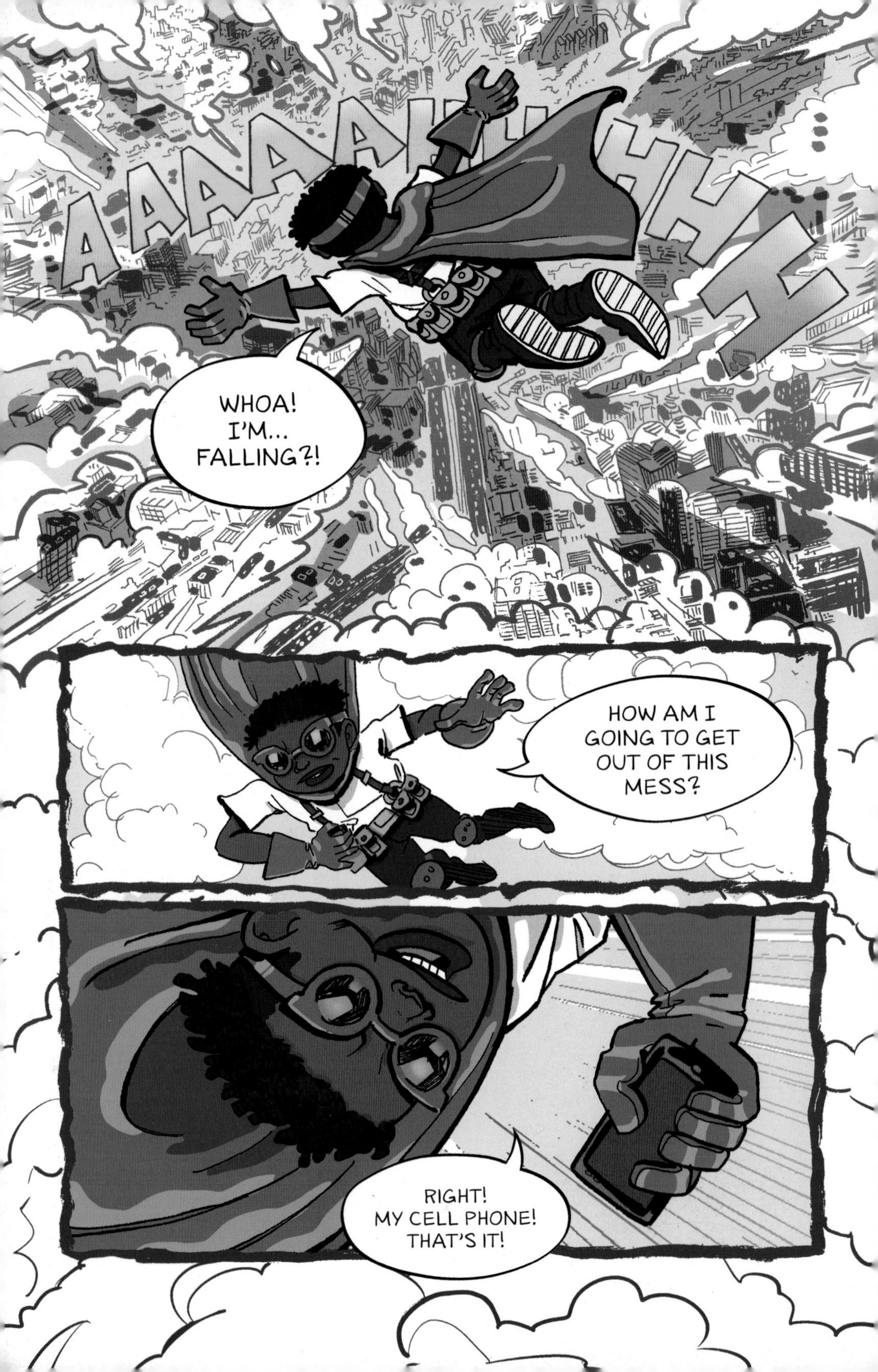
AAAAAHHHHHH!
WHOA! I'M... FALLING?!
HOW AM I GOING TO GET OUT OF THIS MESS?
RIGHT! MY CELL PHONE! THAT'S IT!

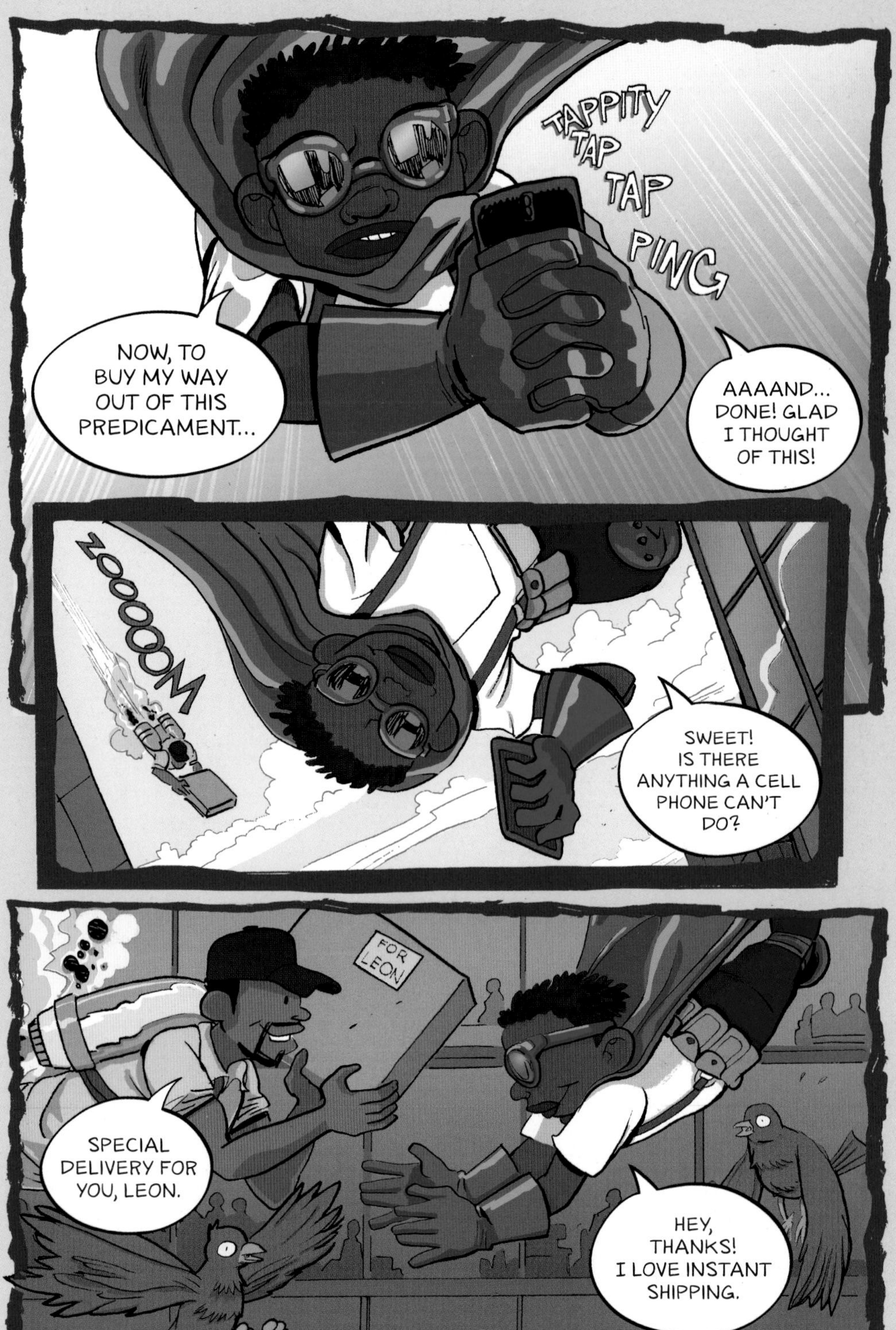
TAPPITY
TAP
TAP
PING
NOW, TO BUY MY WAY OUT OF THIS PREDICAMENT...
AAAAND... DONE! GLAD I THOUGHT OF THIS!
ZOOOOOM
SWEET! IS THERE ANYTHING A CELL PHONE CAN'T DO?
FOR LEON
SPECIAL DELIVERY FOR YOU, LEON.
HEY, THANKS! I LOVE INSTANT SHIPPING.

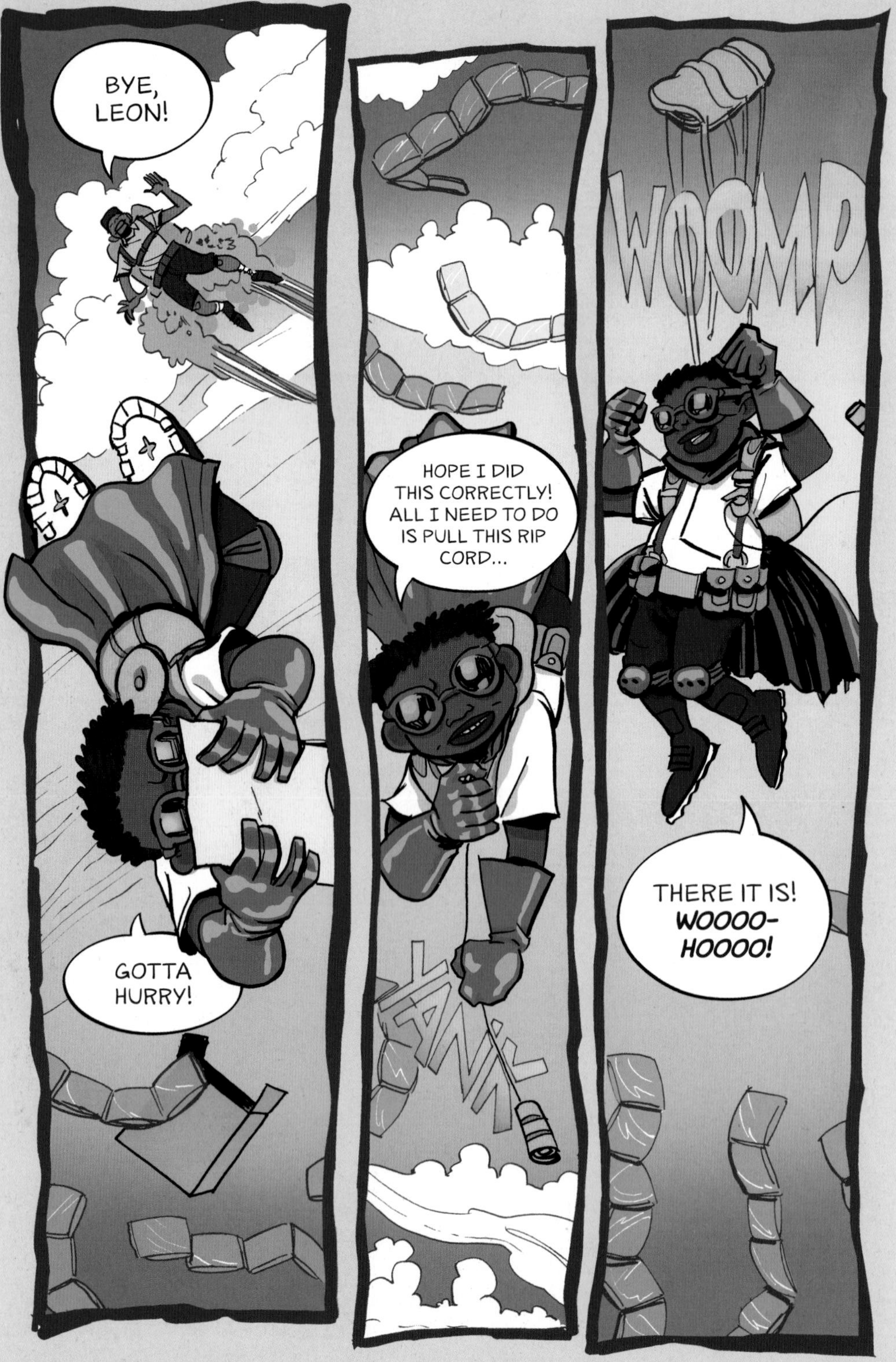
BYE, LEON!
GOTTA HURRY!
HOPE I DID THIS CORRECTLY! ALL I NEED TO DO IS PULL THIS RIP CORD...
YANK
WOOMP
THERE IT IS! **WOOOO-HOOOO!**

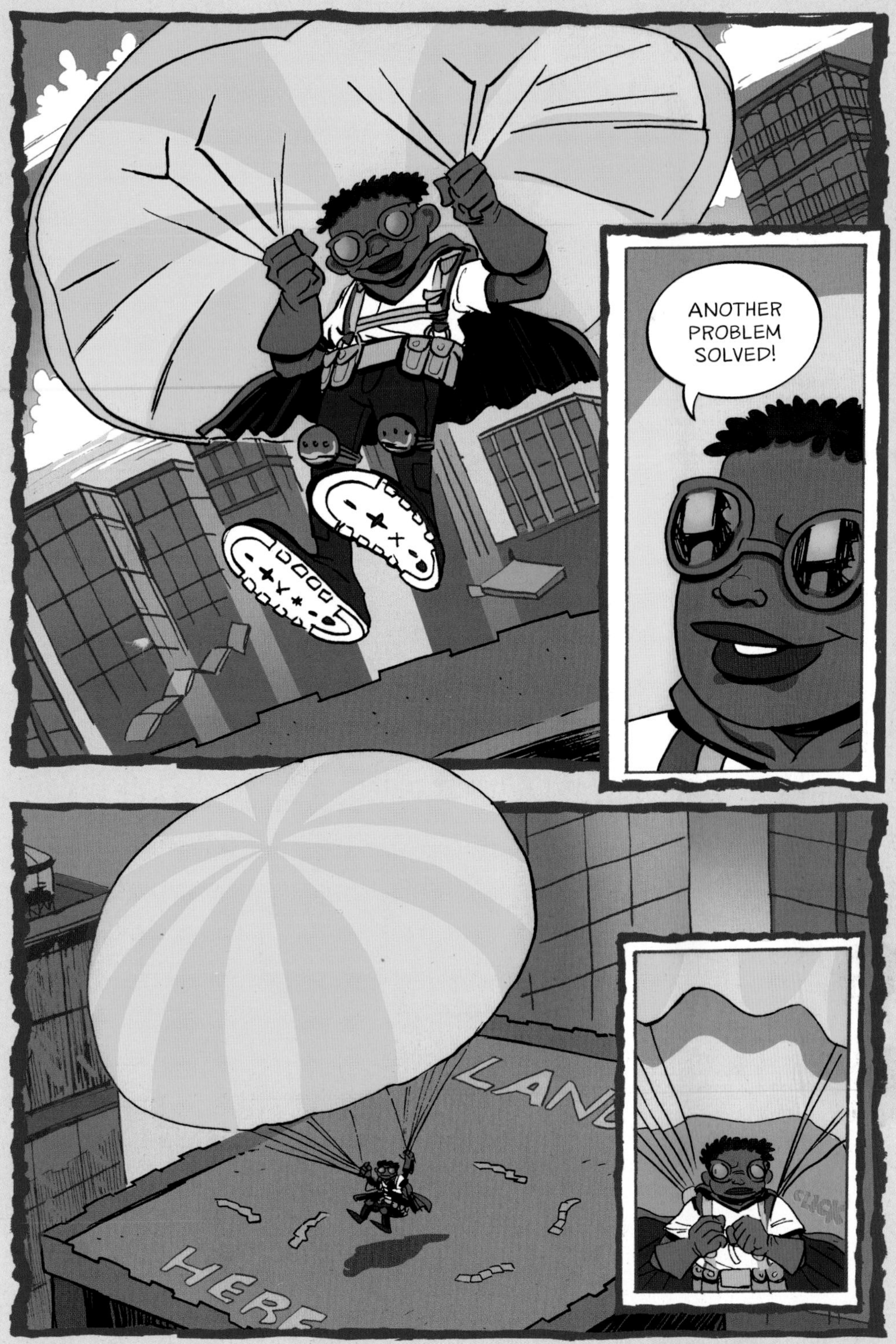
ANOTHER PROBLEM SOLVED!
CLICK

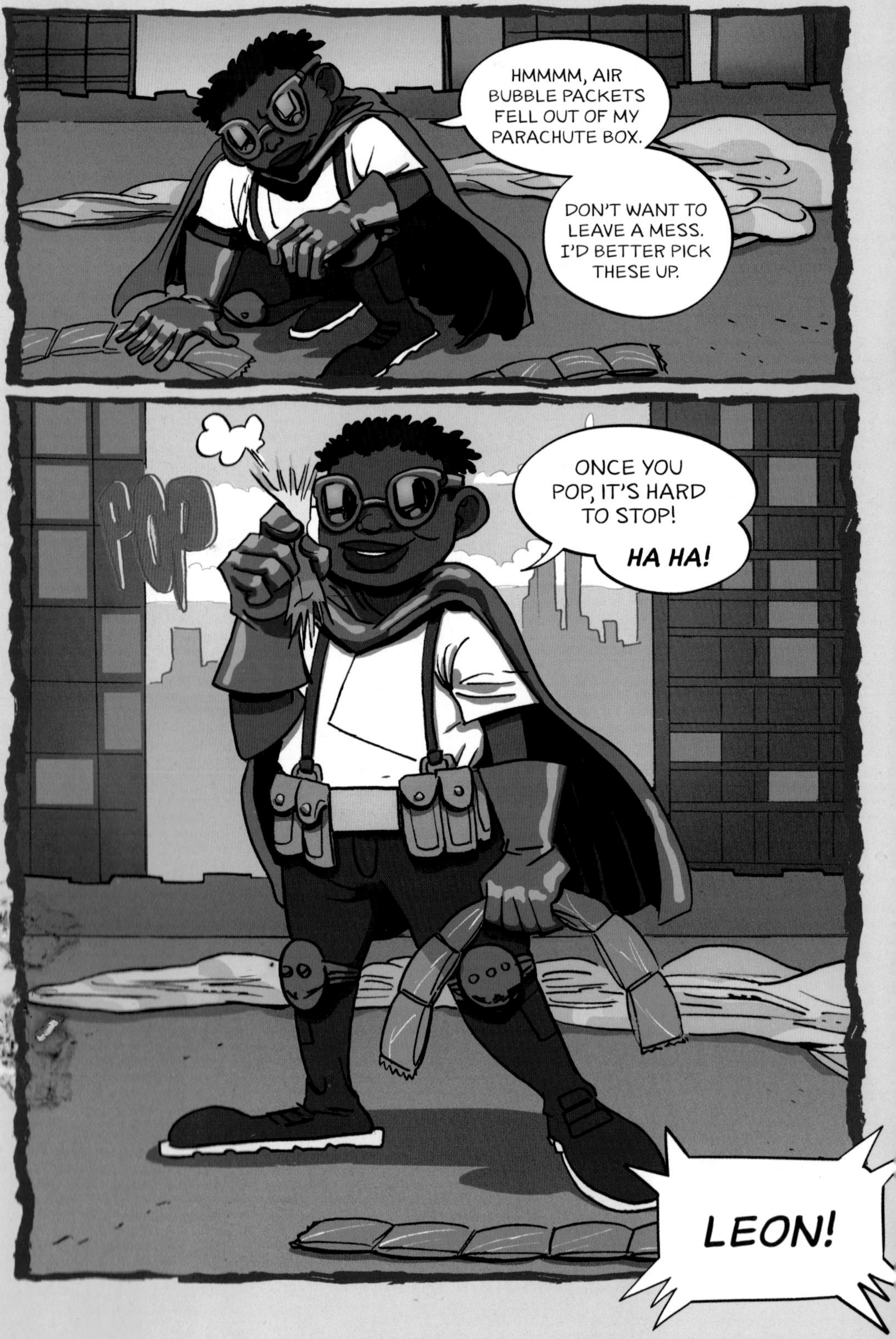
HMMMM, AIR BUBBLE PACKETS FELL OUT OF MY PARACHUTE BOX.
DON'T WANT TO LEAVE A MESS. I'D BETTER PICK THESE UP.
POP
ONCE YOU POP, IT'S HARD TO STOP!
HA HA!
LEON!

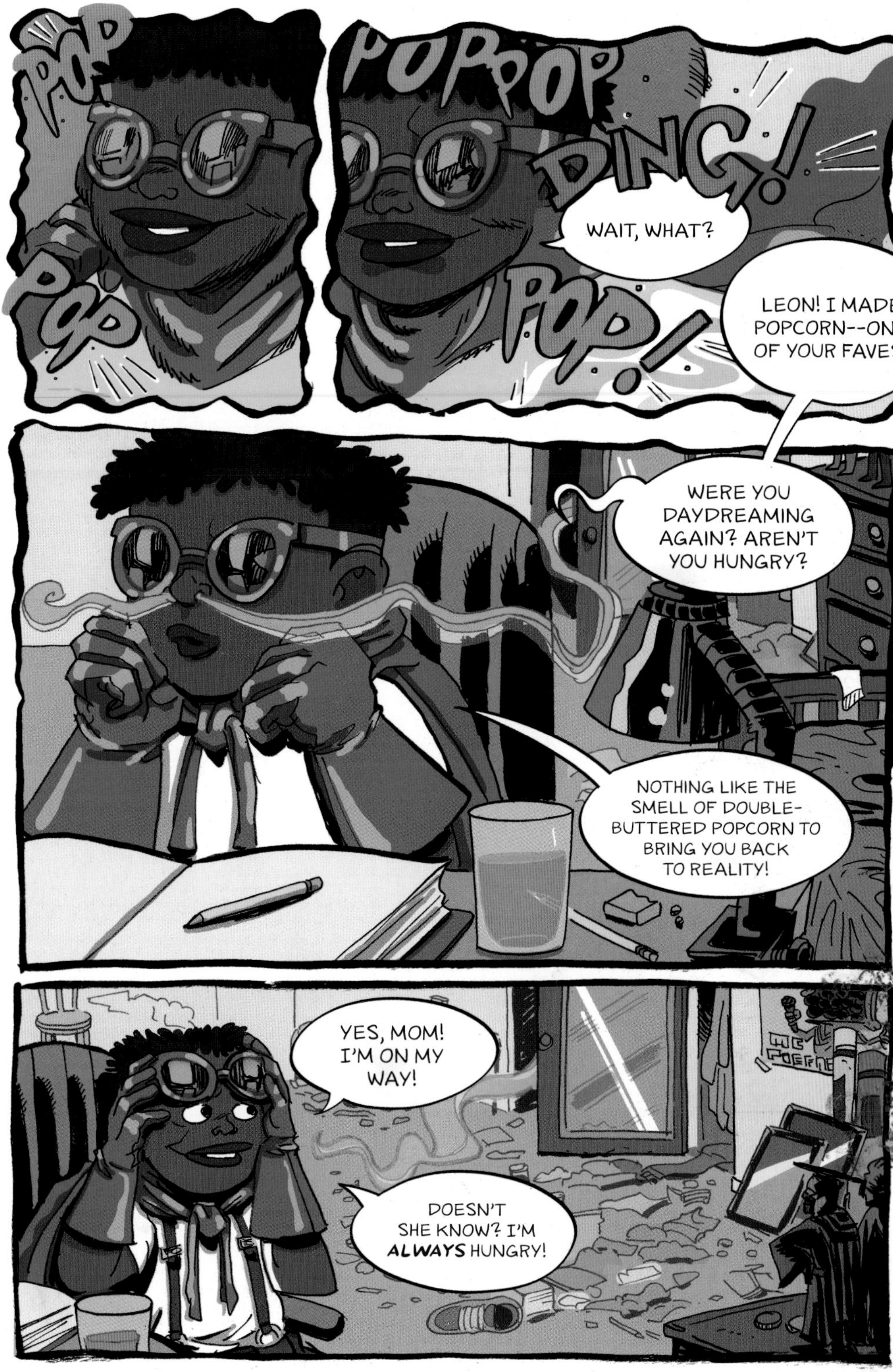
POP
POP
POPPOP
DING!
WAIT, WHAT?
POP!
LEON! I MADE POPCORN--ONE OF YOUR FAVES!
WERE YOU DAYDREAMING AGAIN? AREN'T YOU HUNGRY?
NOTHING LIKE THE SMELL OF DOUBLE-BUTTERED POPCORN TO BRING YOU BACK TO REALITY!
YES, MOM! I'M ON MY WAY!
DOESN'T SHE KNOW? I'M **ALWAYS** HUNGRY!

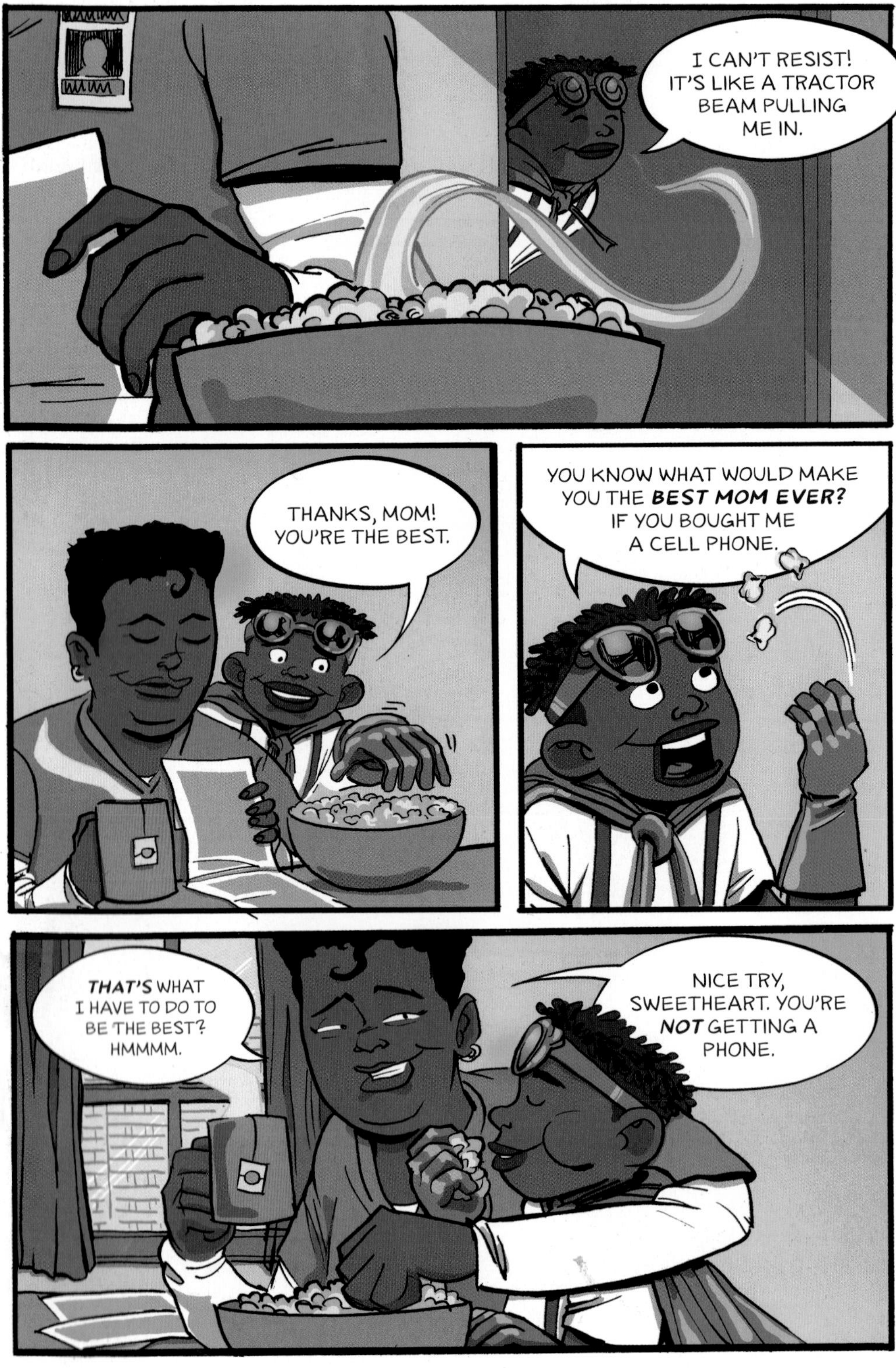
I CAN'T RESIST! IT'S LIKE A TRACTOR BEAM PULLING ME IN.
THANKS, MOM! YOU'RE THE BEST.
YOU KNOW WHAT WOULD MAKE YOU THE **BEST MOM EVER?** IF YOU BOUGHT ME A CELL PHONE.
NICE TRY, SWEETHEART. YOU'RE **NOT** GETTING A PHONE.
THAT'S WHAT I HAVE TO DO TO BE THE BEST? HMMMM.

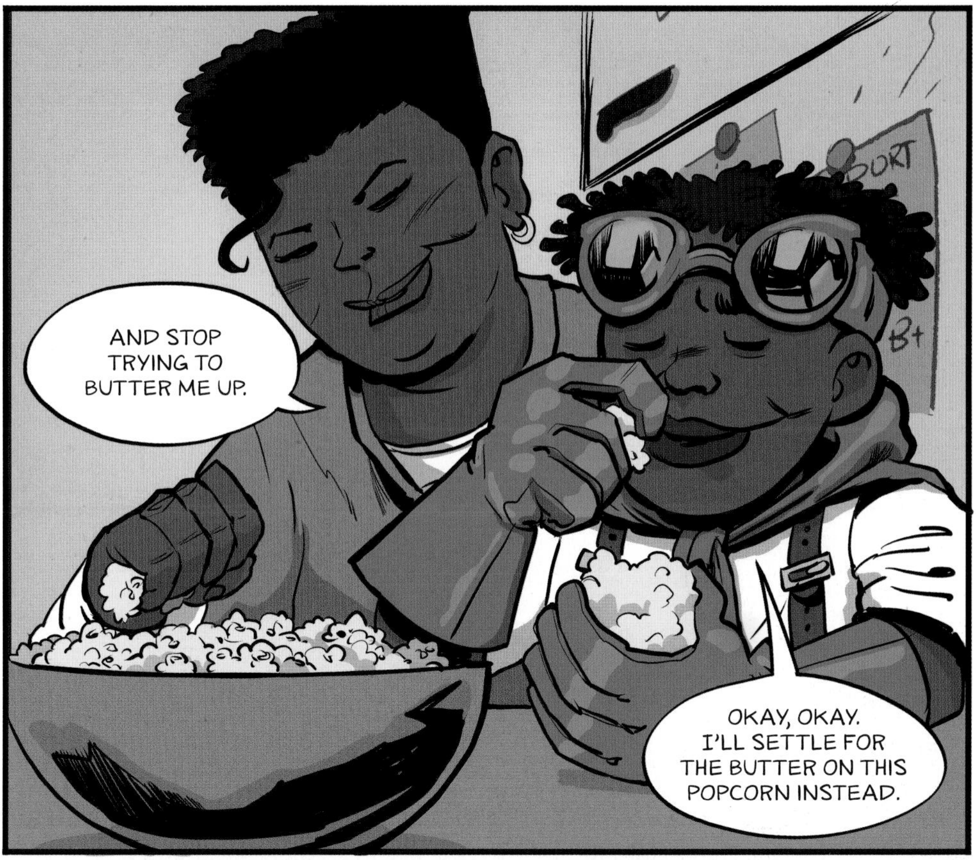
AND STOP TRYING TO BUTTER ME UP.
OKAY, OKAY. I'LL SETTLE FOR THE BUTTER ON THIS POPCORN INSTEAD.

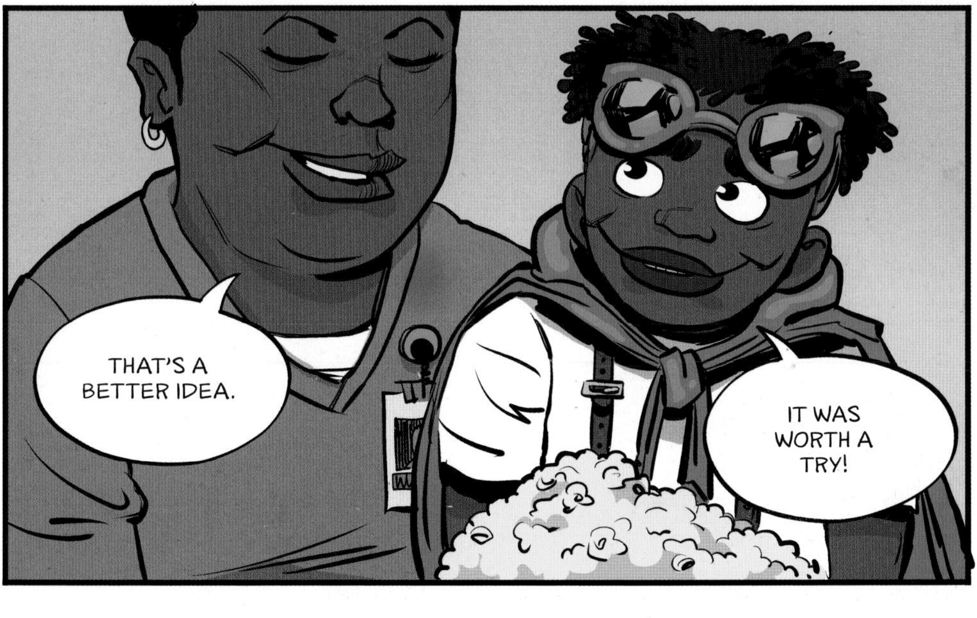
THAT'S A BETTER IDEA.
IT WAS WORTH A TRY!

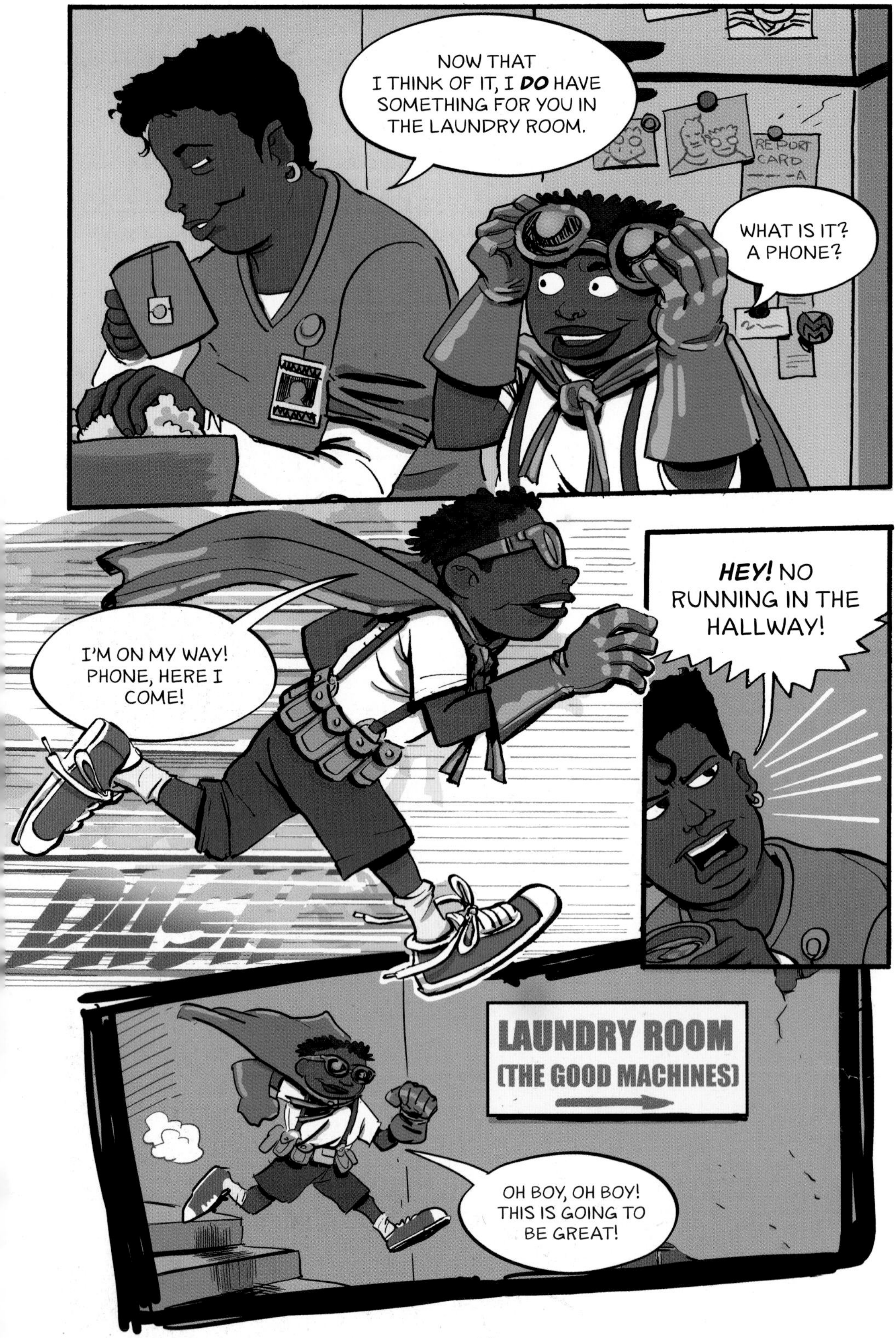
NOW THAT I THINK OF IT, I **DO** HAVE SOMETHING FOR YOU IN THE LAUNDRY ROOM.
REPORT CARD
WHAT IS IT? A PHONE?
I'M ON MY WAY! PHONE, HERE I COME!
HEY! NO RUNNING IN THE HALLWAY!
LAUNDRY ROOM (THE GOOD MACHINES)
OH BOY, OH BOY! THIS IS GOING TO BE GREAT!

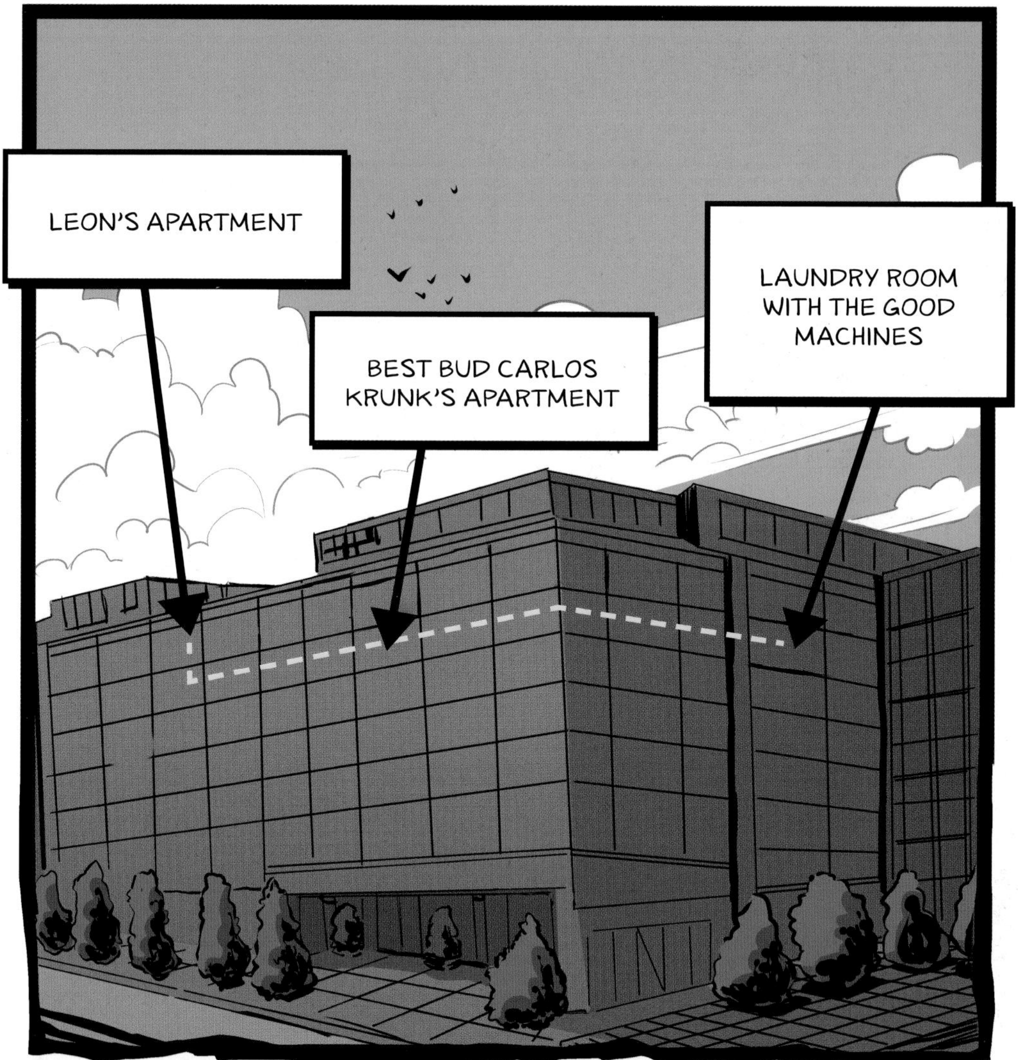
LEON'S APARTMENT
BEST BUD CARLOS KRUNK'S APARTMENT
LAUNDRY ROOM WITH THE GOOD MACHINES

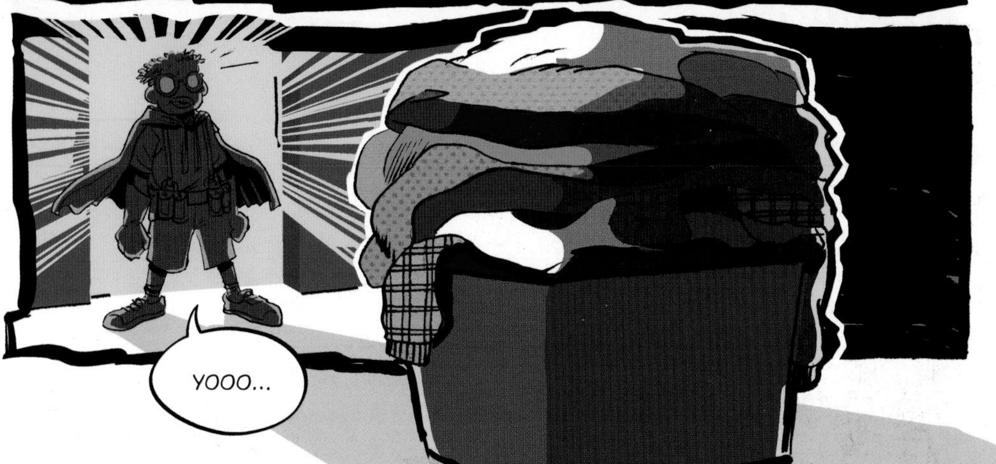
YOOO...

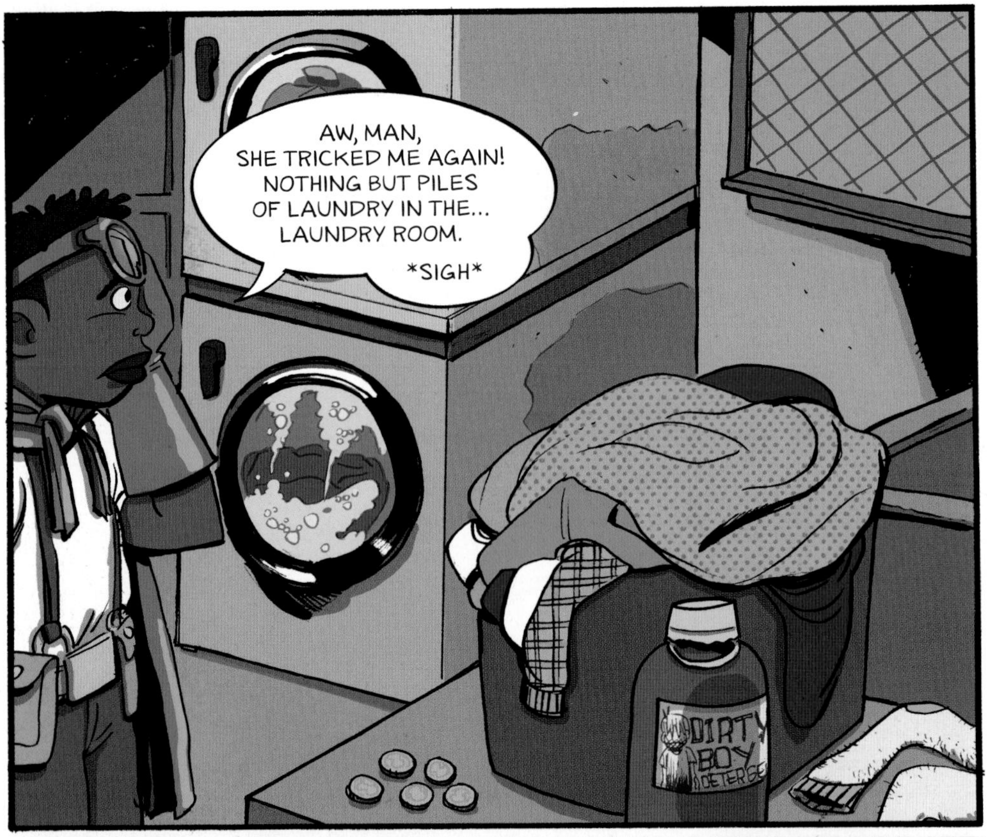
AW, MAN, SHE TRICKED ME AGAIN! NOTHING BUT PILES OF LAUNDRY IN THE... LAUNDRY ROOM.
SIGH
DIRTY BOY DETERGE

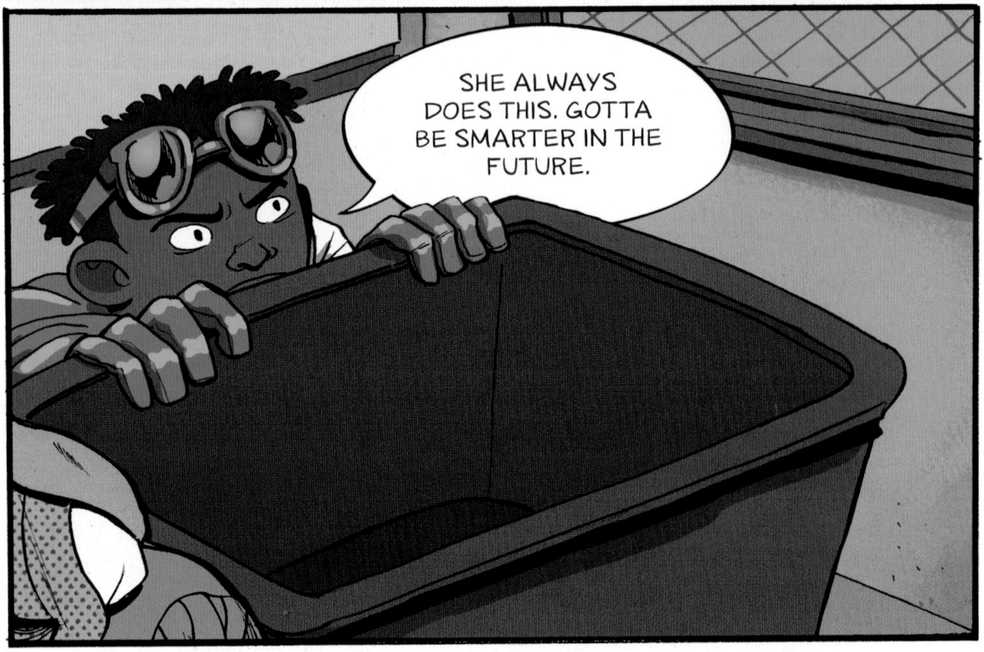
SHE ALWAYS DOES THIS. GOTTA BE SMARTER IN THE FUTURE.

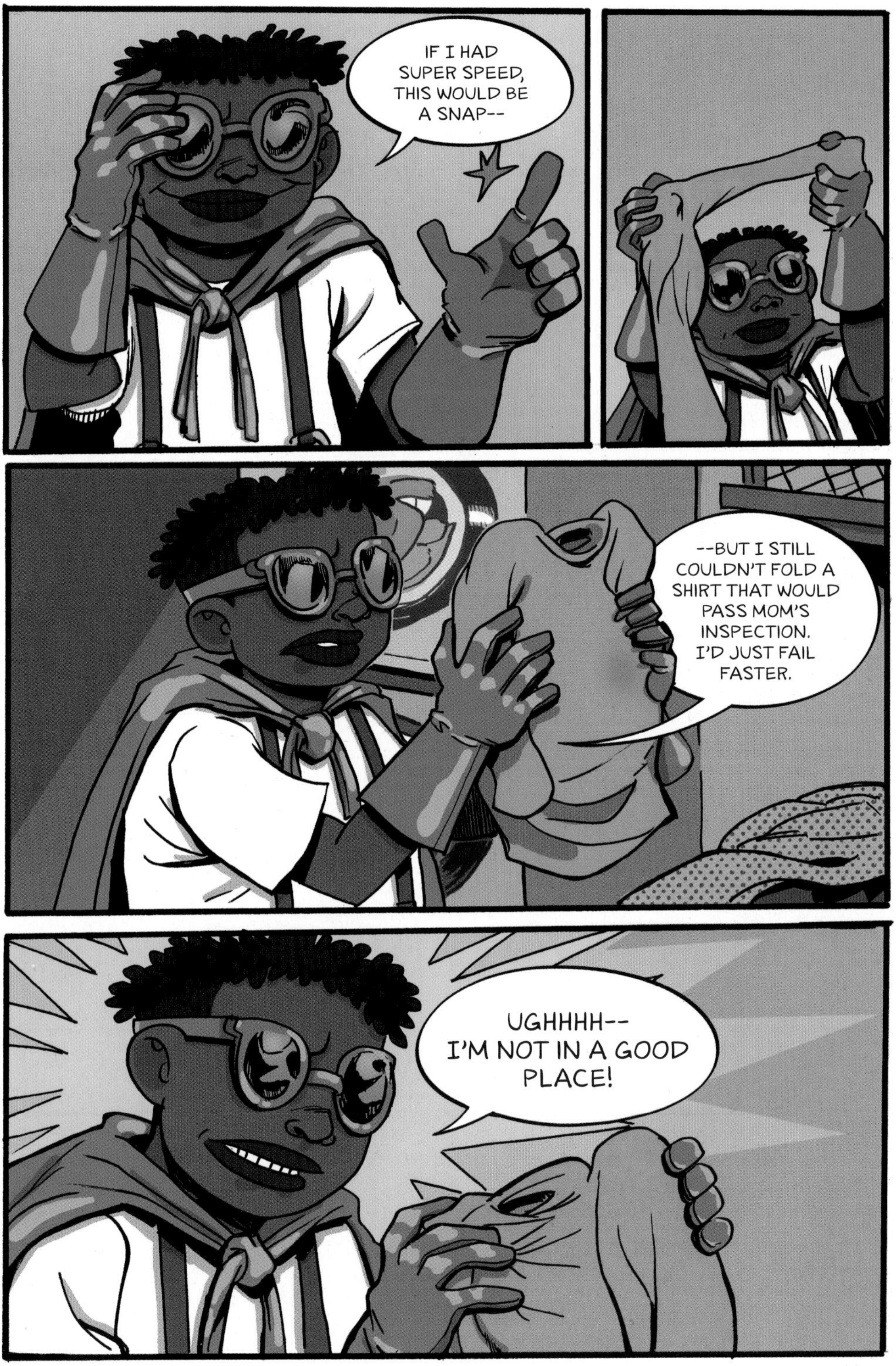
IF I HAD SUPER SPEED, THIS WOULD BE A SNAP--
--BUT I STILL COULDN'T FOLD A SHIRT THAT WOULD PASS MOM'S INSPECTION. I'D JUST FAIL FASTER.
UGHHHH-- I'M NOT IN A GOOD PLACE!

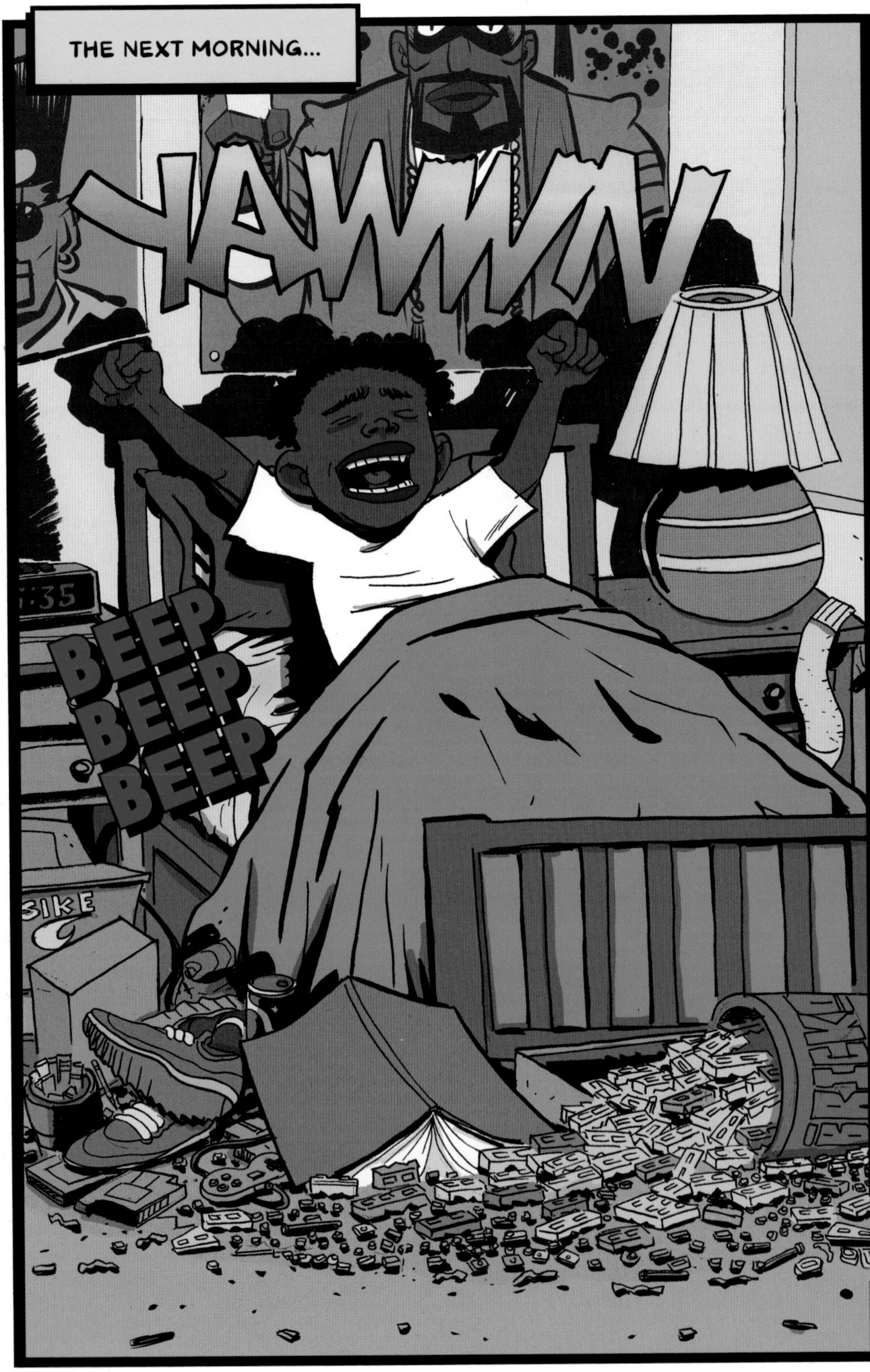
THE NEXT MORNING...
YAWWN
BEEP
BEEP
BEEP

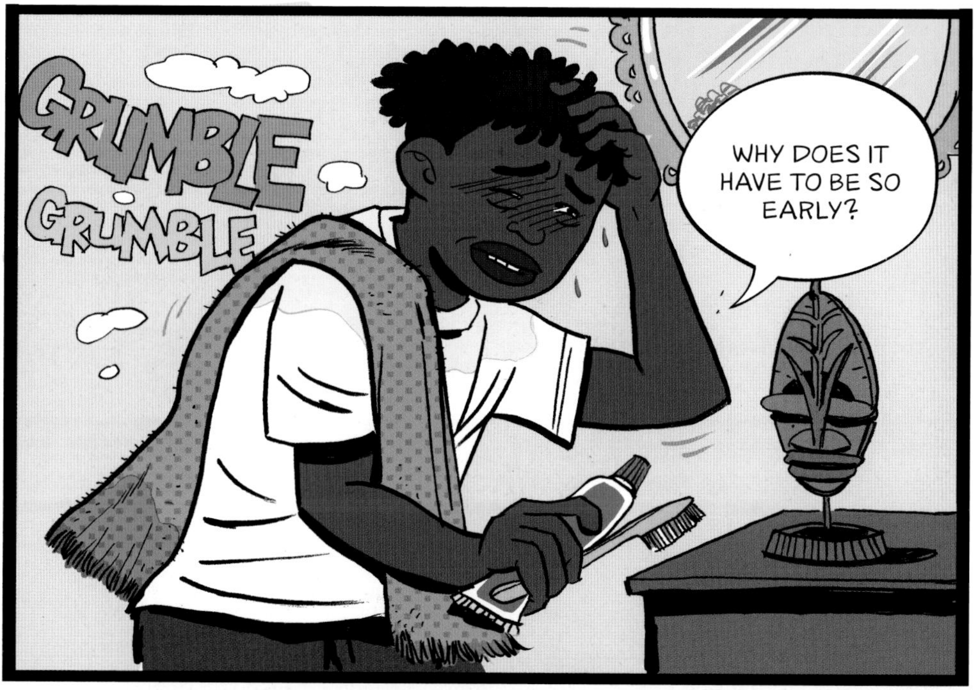
GRUMBLE
GRUMBLE
WHY DOES IT HAVE TO BE SO EARLY?

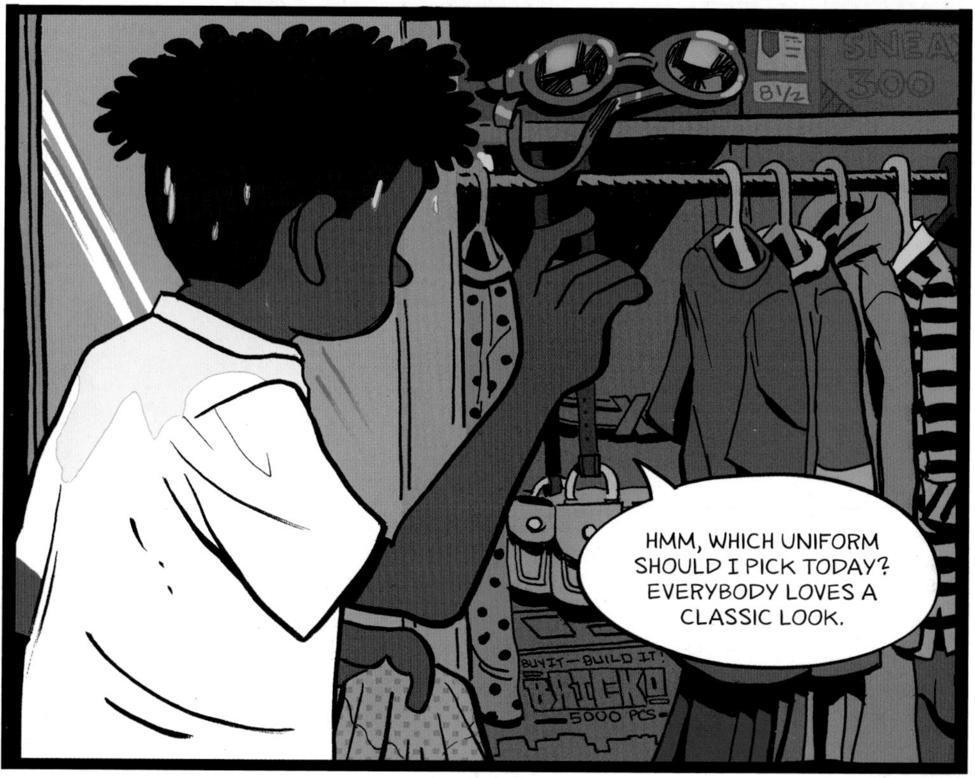
SNEA
300
8½
HMM, WHICH UNIFORM SHOULD I PICK TODAY? EVERYBODY LOVES A CLASSIC LOOK.
BUY IT—BUILD IT!
BRICKO
5000 PCS

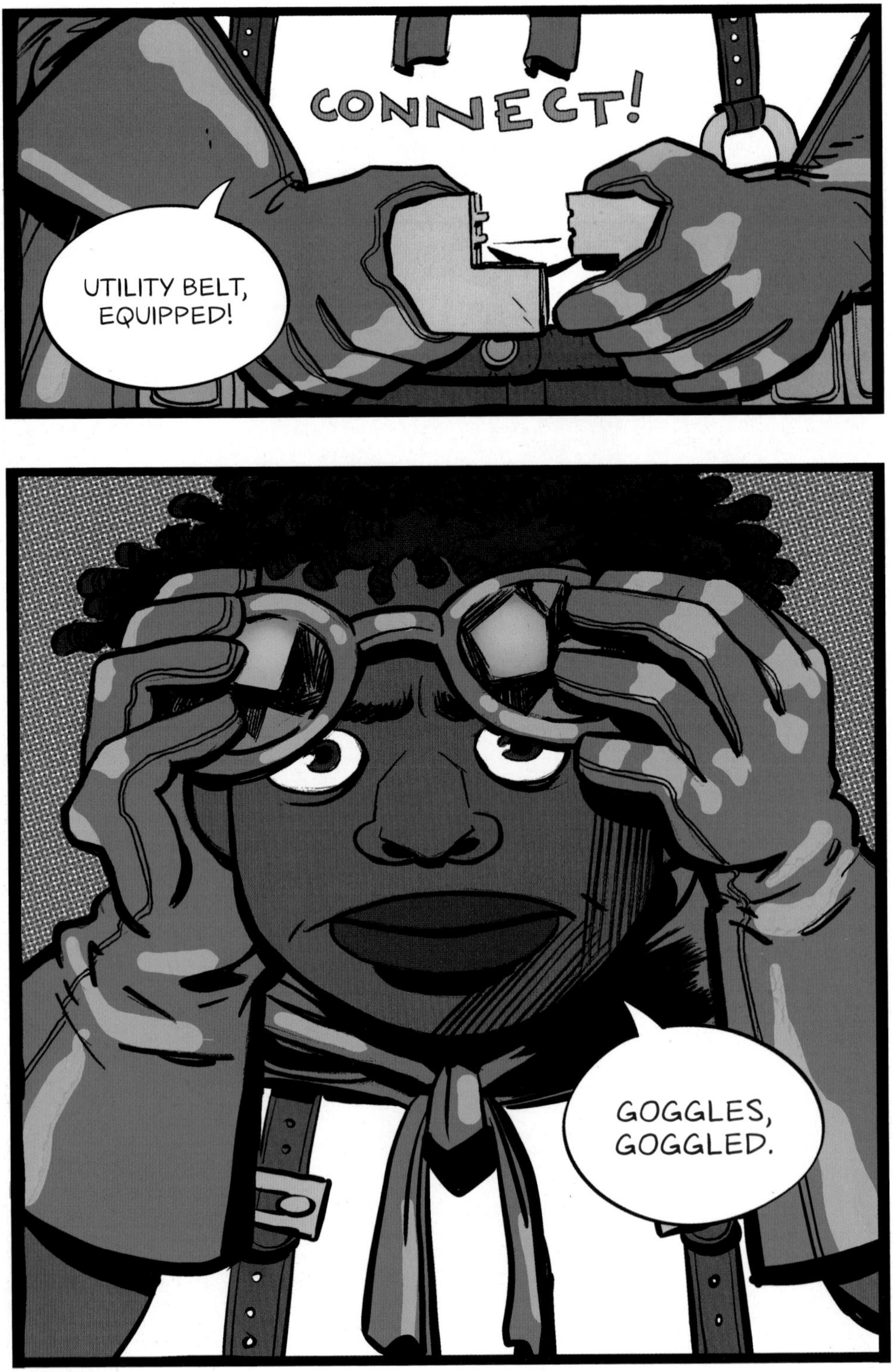
CONNECT!
UTILITY BELT, EQUIPPED!
GOGGLES, GOGGLED.

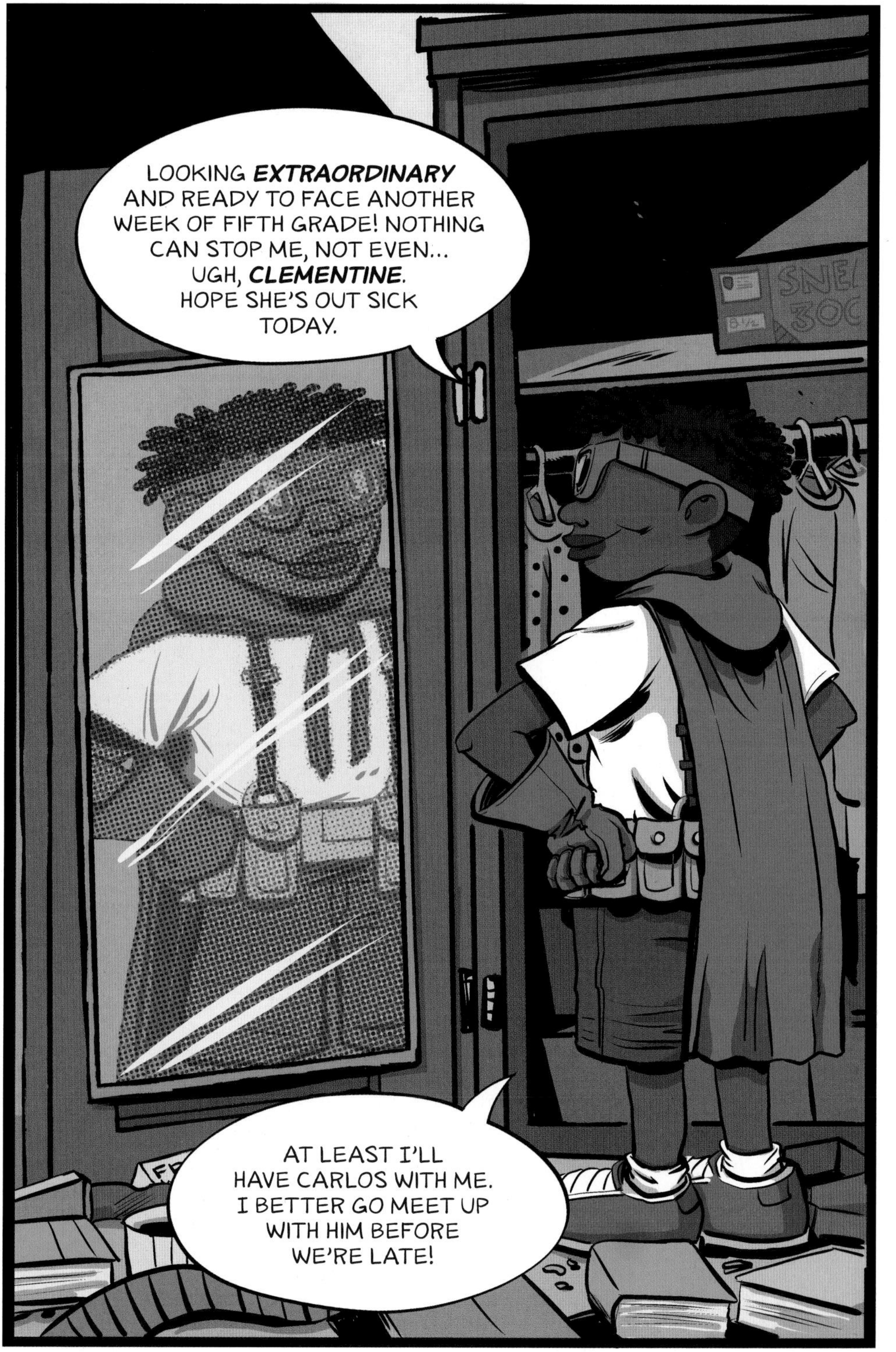
LOOKING **EXTRAORDINARY** AND READY TO FACE ANOTHER WEEK OF FIFTH GRADE! NOTHING CAN STOP ME, NOT EVEN... UGH, **CLEMENTINE**. HOPE SHE'S OUT SICK TODAY.
AT LEAST I'LL HAVE CARLOS WITH ME. I BETTER GO MEET UP WITH HIM BEFORE WE'RE LATE!

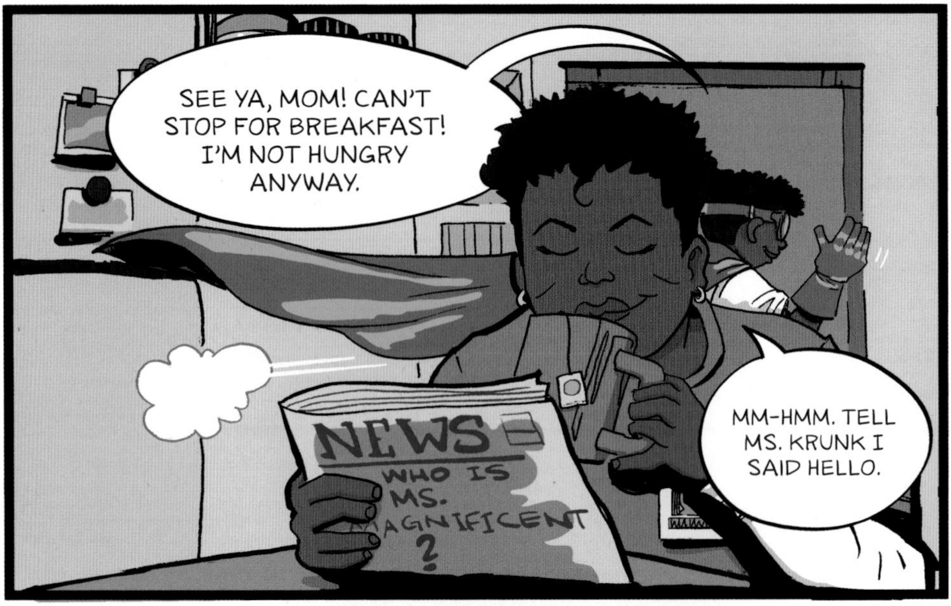
SEE YA, MOM! CAN'T STOP FOR BREAKFAST! I'M NOT HUNGRY ANYWAY.
NEWS
WHO IS MS. MAGNIFICENT ?
MM-HMM. TELL MS. KRUNK I SAID HELLO.

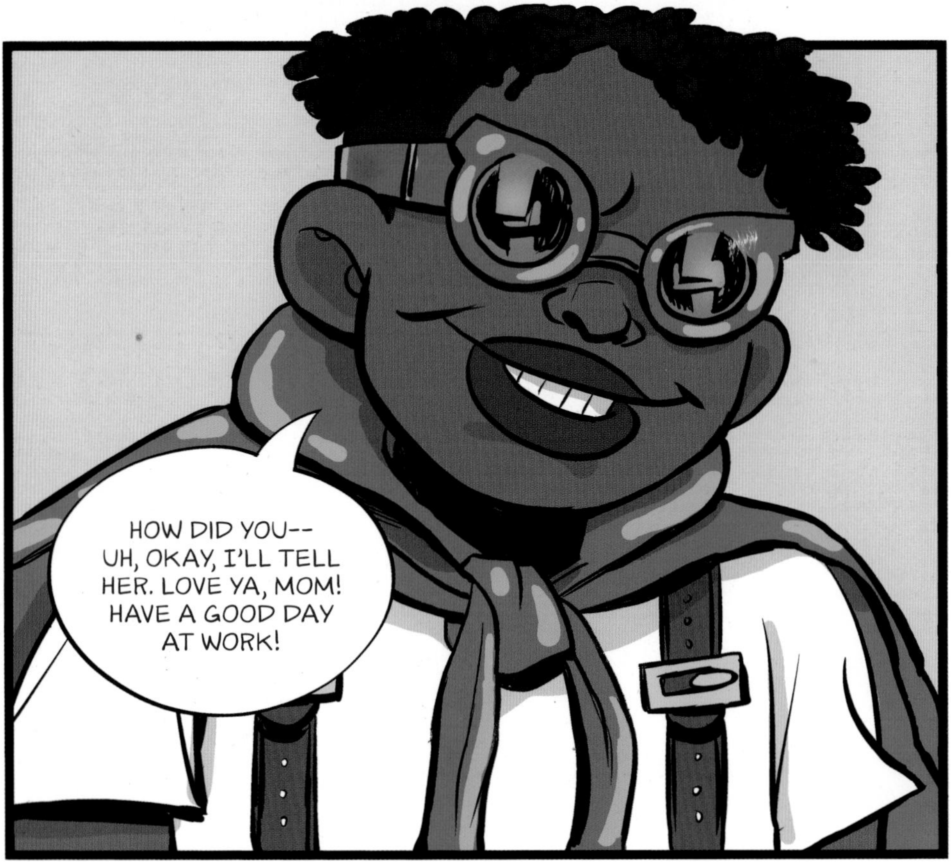
HOW DID YOU-- UH, OKAY, I'LL TELL HER. LOVE YA, MOM! HAVE A GOOD DAY AT WORK!

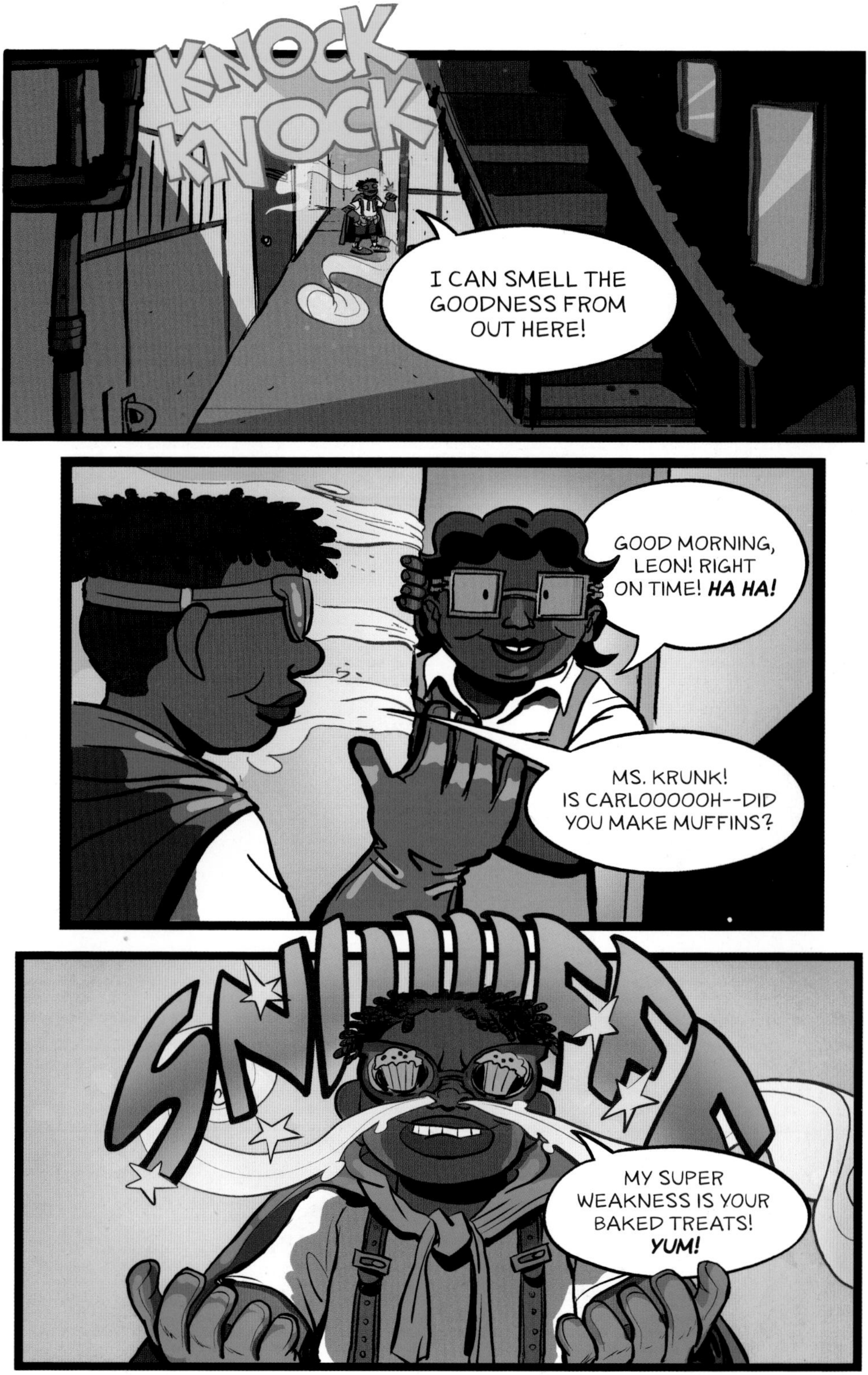
KNOCK KNOCK
I CAN SMELL THE GOODNESS FROM OUT HERE!
GOOD MORNING, LEON! RIGHT ON TIME! ***HA HA!***
MS. KRUNK! IS CARLOOOOOH--DID YOU MAKE MUFFINS?
MY SUPER WEAKNESS IS YOUR BAKED TREATS! ***YUM!***

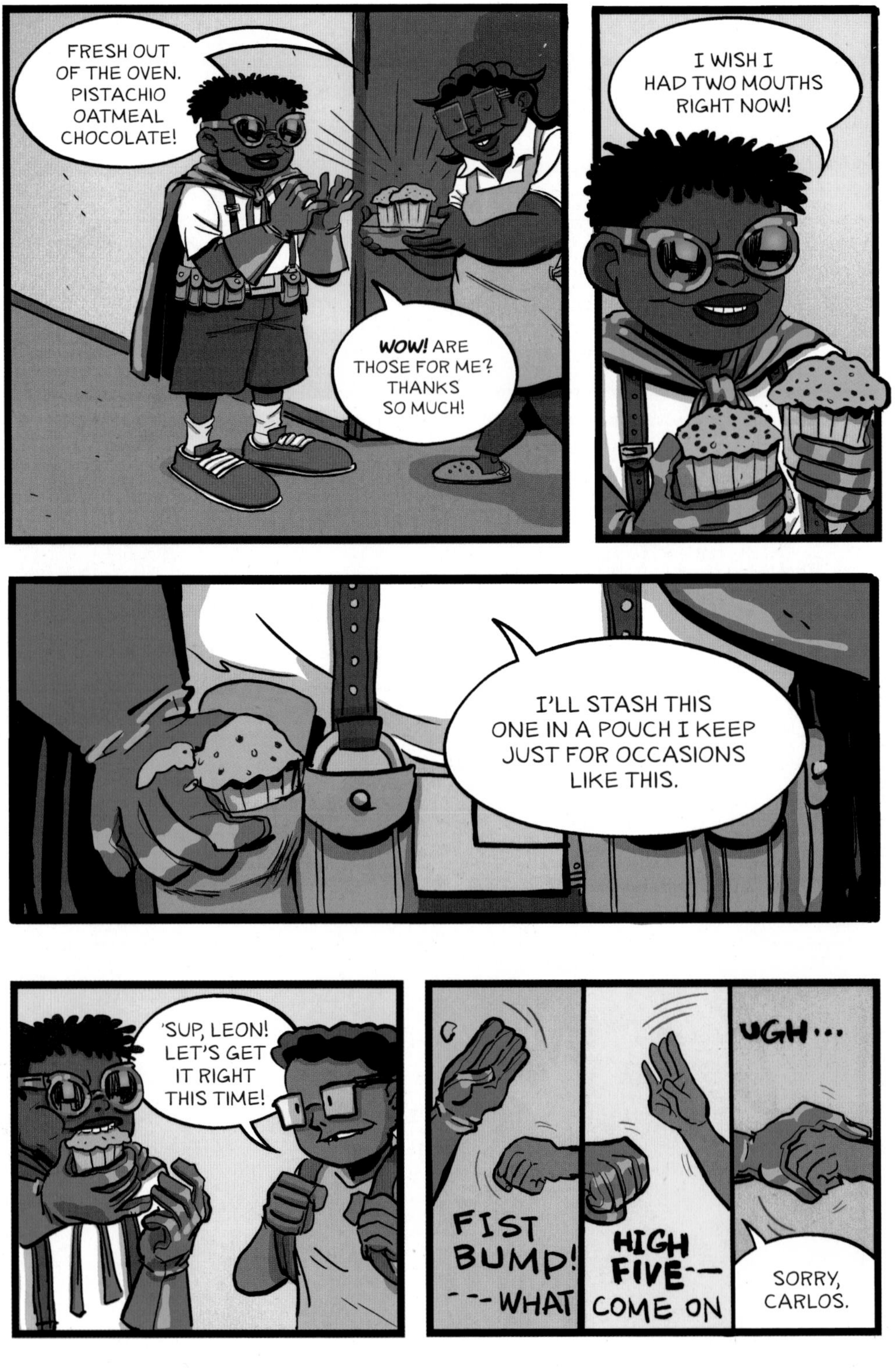
FRESH OUT OF THE OVEN. PISTACHIO OATMEAL CHOCOLATE!
WOW! ARE THOSE FOR ME? THANKS SO MUCH!
I WISH I HAD TWO MOUTHS RIGHT NOW!
I'LL STASH THIS ONE IN A POUCH I KEEP JUST FOR OCCASIONS LIKE THIS.
'SUP, LEON! LET'S GET IT RIGHT THIS TIME!
FIST BUMP!
---WHAT
HIGH FIVE--
COME ON
UGH...
SORRY, CARLOS.

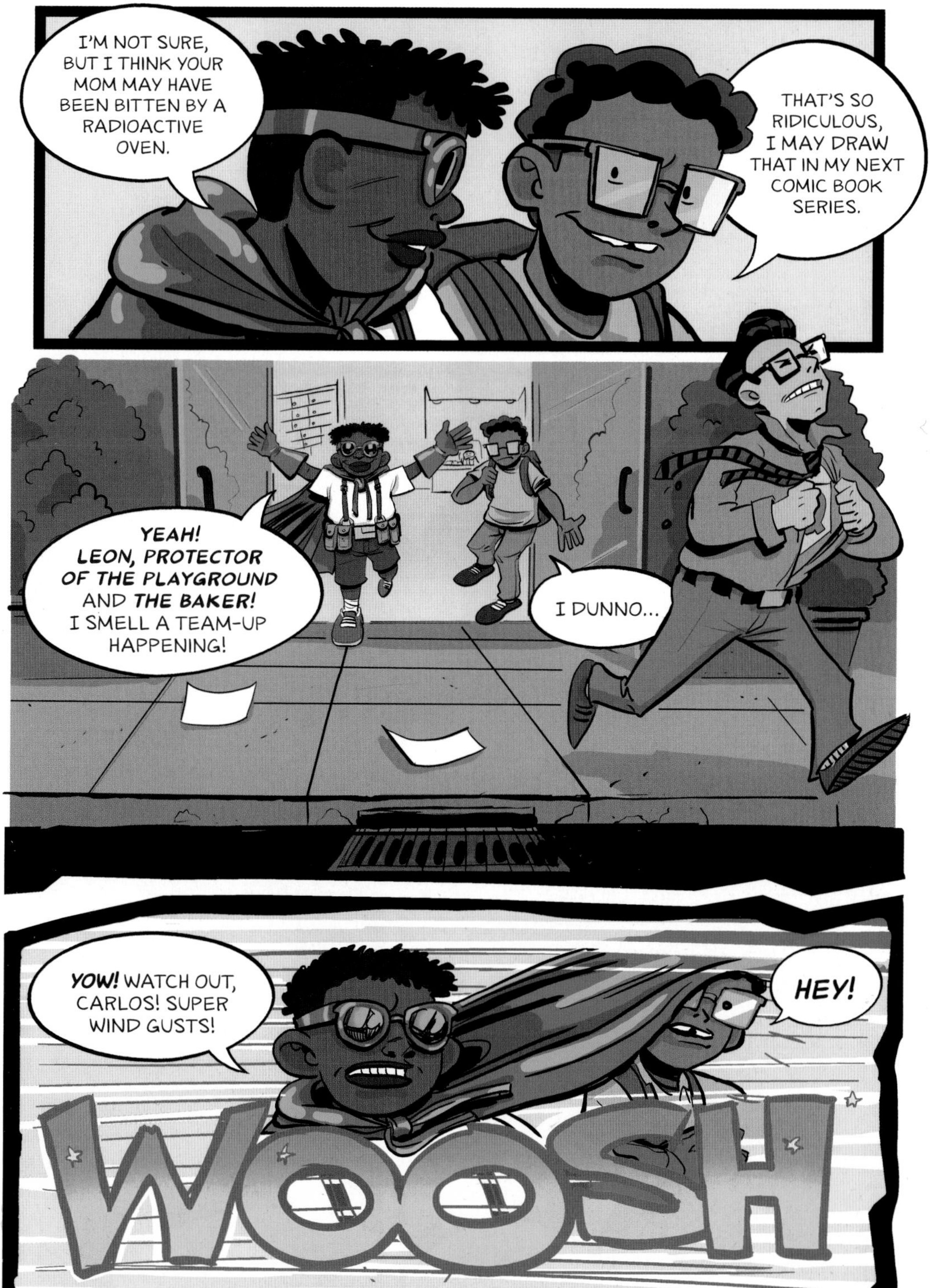
I'M NOT SURE, BUT I THINK YOUR MOM MAY HAVE BEEN BITTEN BY A RADIOACTIVE OVEN.
THAT'S SO RIDICULOUS, I MAY DRAW THAT IN MY NEXT COMIC BOOK SERIES.
YEAH! LEON, PROTECTOR OF THE PLAYGROUND AND THE BAKER! I SMELL A TEAM-UP HAPPENING!
I DUNNO...
YOW! WATCH OUT, CARLOS! SUPER WIND GUSTS!
HEY!
WOOSH

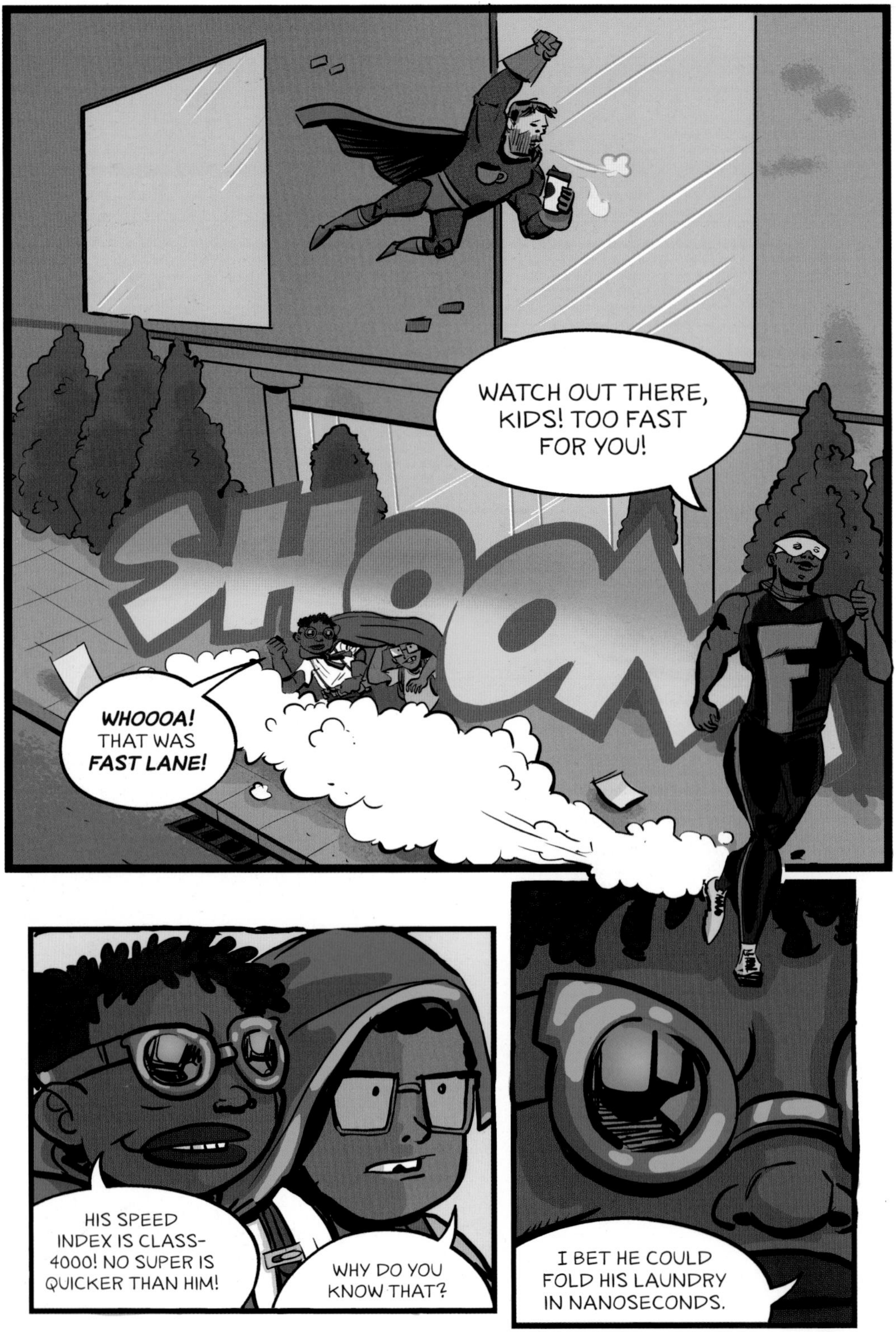
WATCH OUT THERE, KIDS! TOO FAST FOR YOU!
SHOOM
WHOOOA! THAT WAS **FAST LANE!**
HIS SPEED INDEX IS CLASS-4000! NO SUPER IS QUICKER THAN HIM!
WHY DO YOU KNOW THAT?
I BET HE COULD FOLD HIS LAUNDRY IN NANOSECONDS.

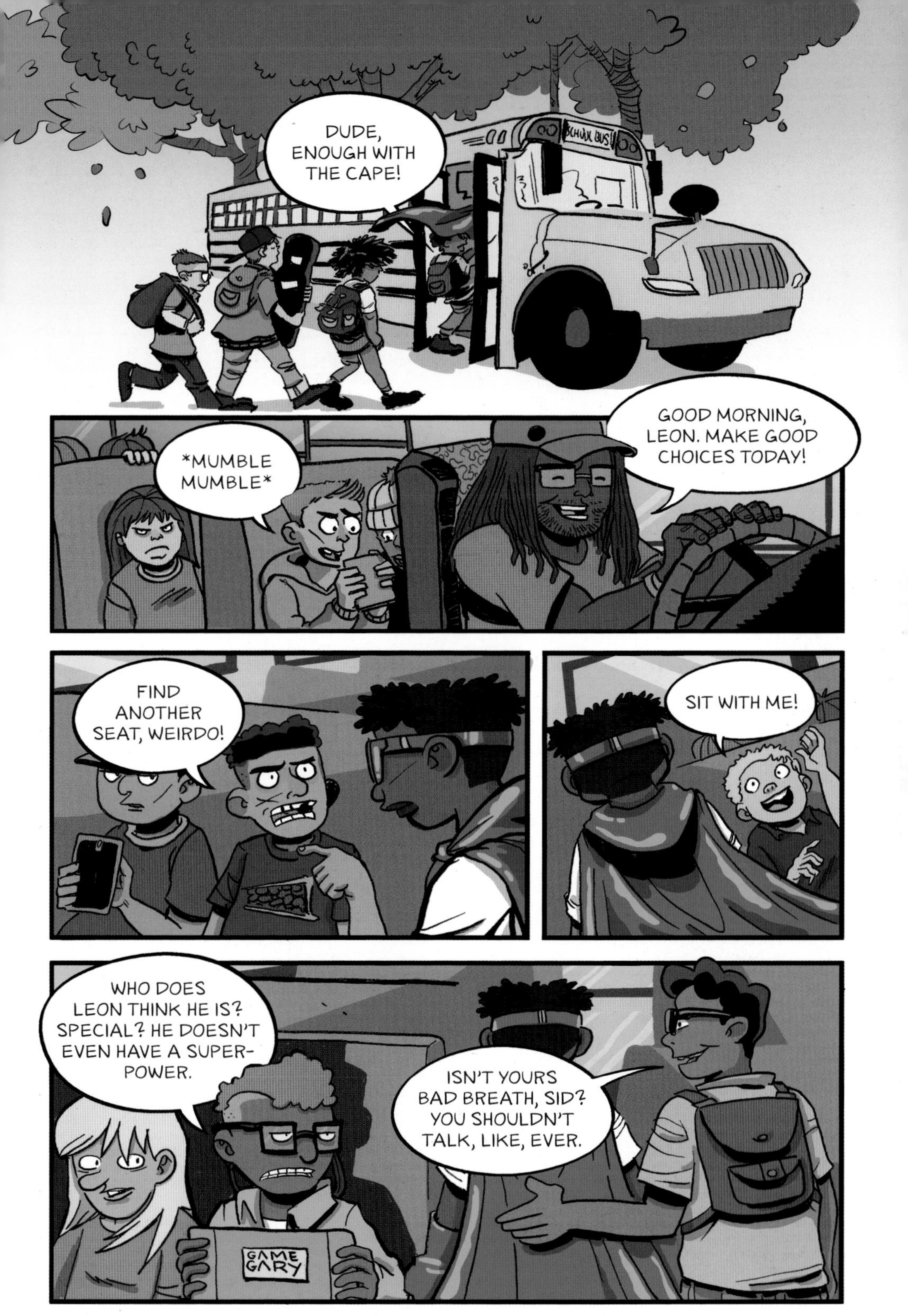
DUDE, ENOUGH WITH THE CAPE!
MUMBLE MUMBLE
GOOD MORNING, LEON. MAKE GOOD CHOICES TODAY!
FIND ANOTHER SEAT, WEIRDO!
SIT WITH ME!
WHO DOES LEON THINK HE IS? SPECIAL? HE DOESN'T EVEN HAVE A SUPER-POWER.
ISN'T YOURS BAD BREATH, SID? YOU SHOULDN'T TALK, LIKE, EVER.
GAME GARY

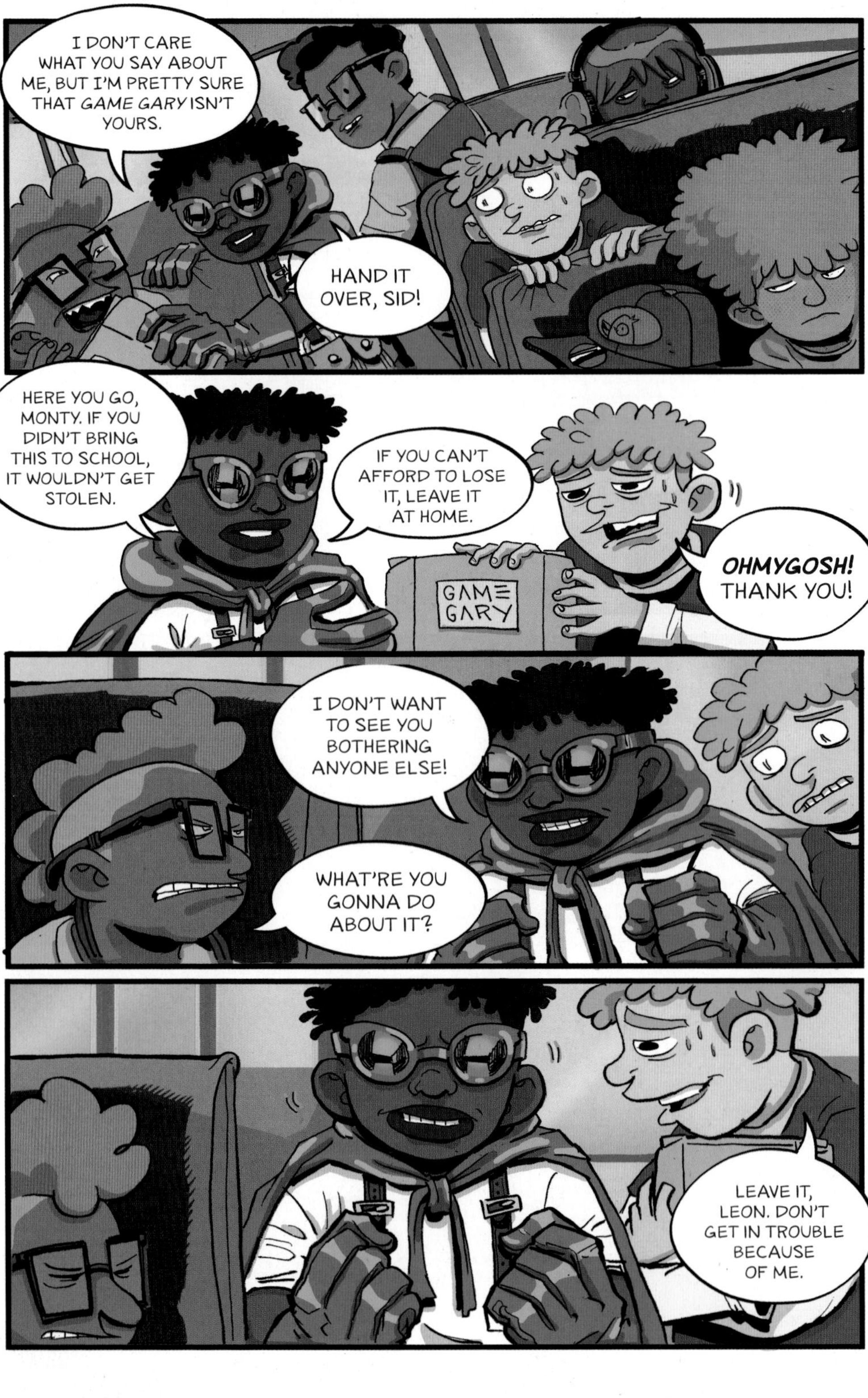
I DON'T CARE WHAT YOU SAY ABOUT ME, BUT I'M PRETTY SURE THAT *GAME GARY* ISN'T YOURS.
HAND IT OVER, SID!
HERE YOU GO, MONTY. IF YOU DIDN'T BRING THIS TO SCHOOL, IT WOULDN'T GET STOLEN.
IF YOU CAN'T AFFORD TO LOSE IT, LEAVE IT AT HOME.
GAME GARY
OHMYGOSH! THANK YOU!
I DON'T WANT TO SEE YOU BOTHERING ANYONE ELSE!
WHAT'RE YOU GONNA DO ABOUT IT?
LEAVE IT, LEON. DON'T GET IN TROUBLE BECAUSE OF ME.

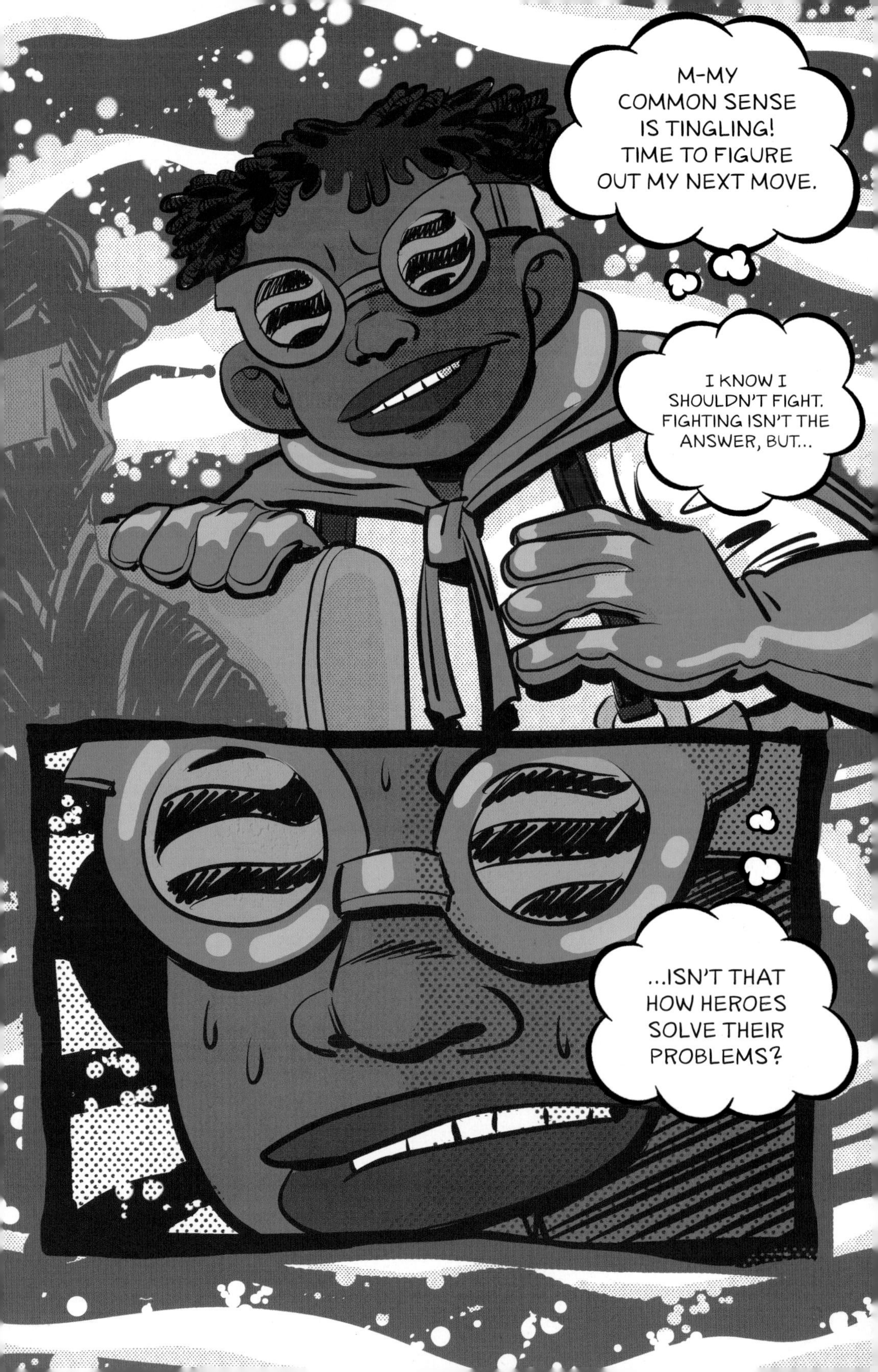
M-MY COMMON SENSE IS TINGLING! TIME TO FIGURE OUT MY NEXT MOVE.
I KNOW I SHOULDN'T FIGHT. FIGHTING ISN'T THE ANSWER, BUT...
...ISN'T THAT HOW HEROES SOLVE THEIR PROBLEMS?

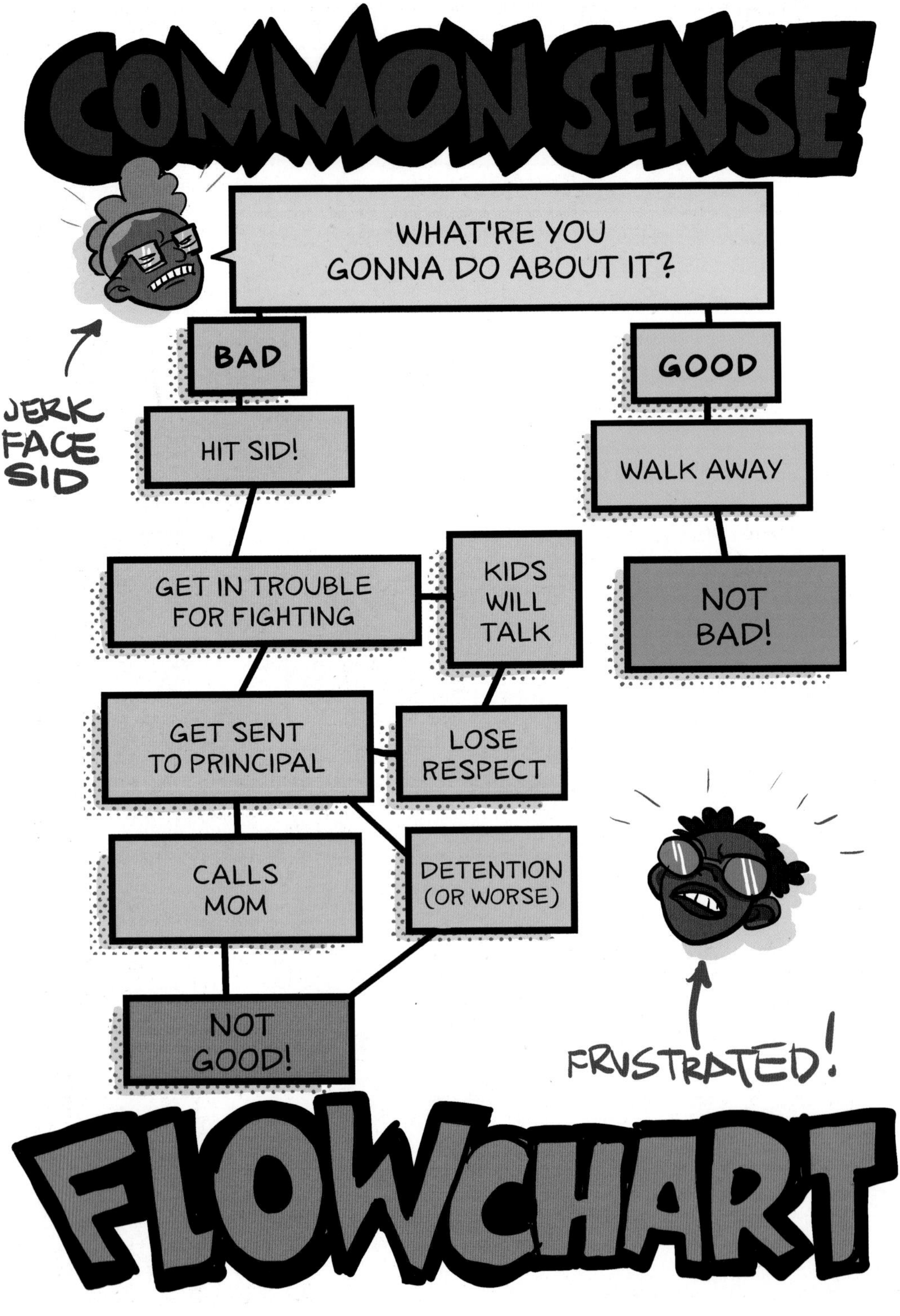
COMMON SENSE
WHAT'RE YOU GONNA DO ABOUT IT?
JERK FACE SID
BAD
GOOD
HIT SID!
WALK AWAY
GET IN TROUBLE FOR FIGHTING
KIDS WILL TALK
NOT BAD!
GET SENT TO PRINCIPAL
LOSE RESPECT
CALLS MOM
DETENTION (OR WORSE)
NOT GOOD!
FRUSTRATED!
FLOWCHART

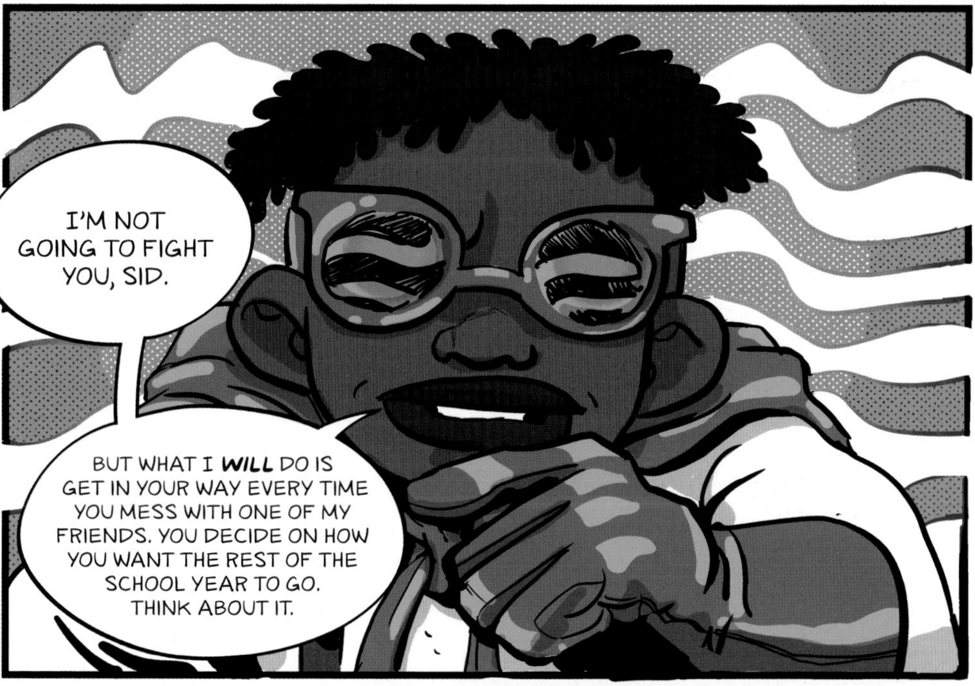
I'M NOT GOING TO FIGHT YOU, SID.
BUT WHAT I **WILL** DO IS GET IN YOUR WAY EVERY TIME YOU MESS WITH ONE OF MY FRIENDS. YOU DECIDE ON HOW YOU WANT THE REST OF THE SCHOOL YEAR TO GO. THINK ABOUT IT.

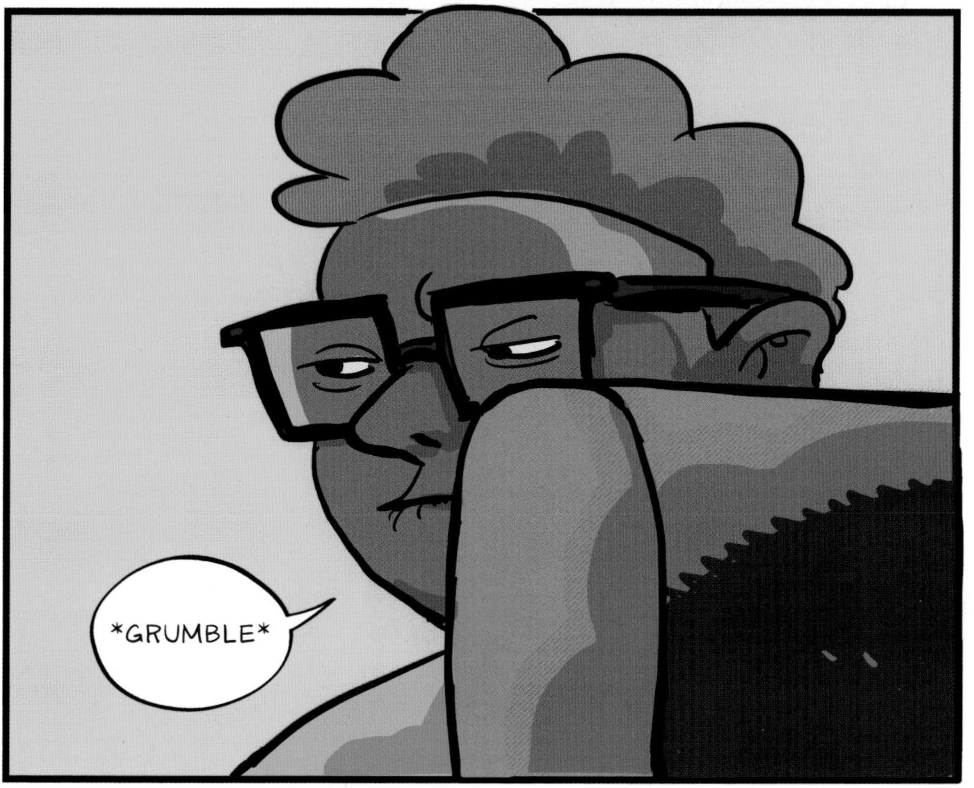
GRUMBLE

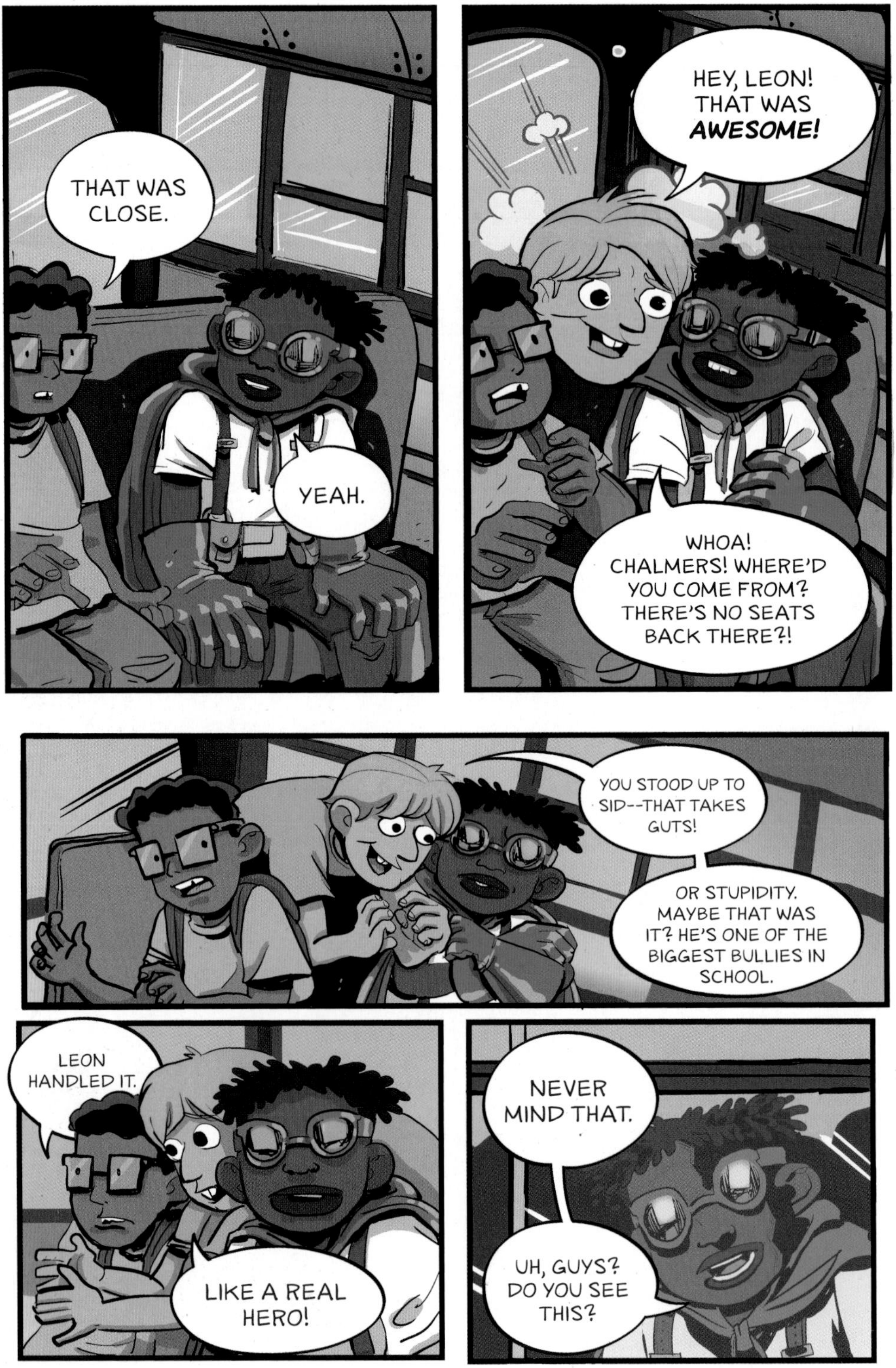
THAT WAS CLOSE.
YEAH.
HEY, LEON! THAT WAS **AWESOME!**
WHOA! CHALMERS! WHERE'D YOU COME FROM? THERE'S NO SEATS BACK THERE?!
YOU STOOD UP TO SID--THAT TAKES GUTS!
OR STUPIDITY. MAYBE THAT WAS IT? HE'S ONE OF THE BIGGEST BULLIES IN SCHOOL.
LEON HANDLED IT.
LIKE A REAL HERO!
NEVER MIND THAT.
UH, GUYS? DO YOU SEE THIS?

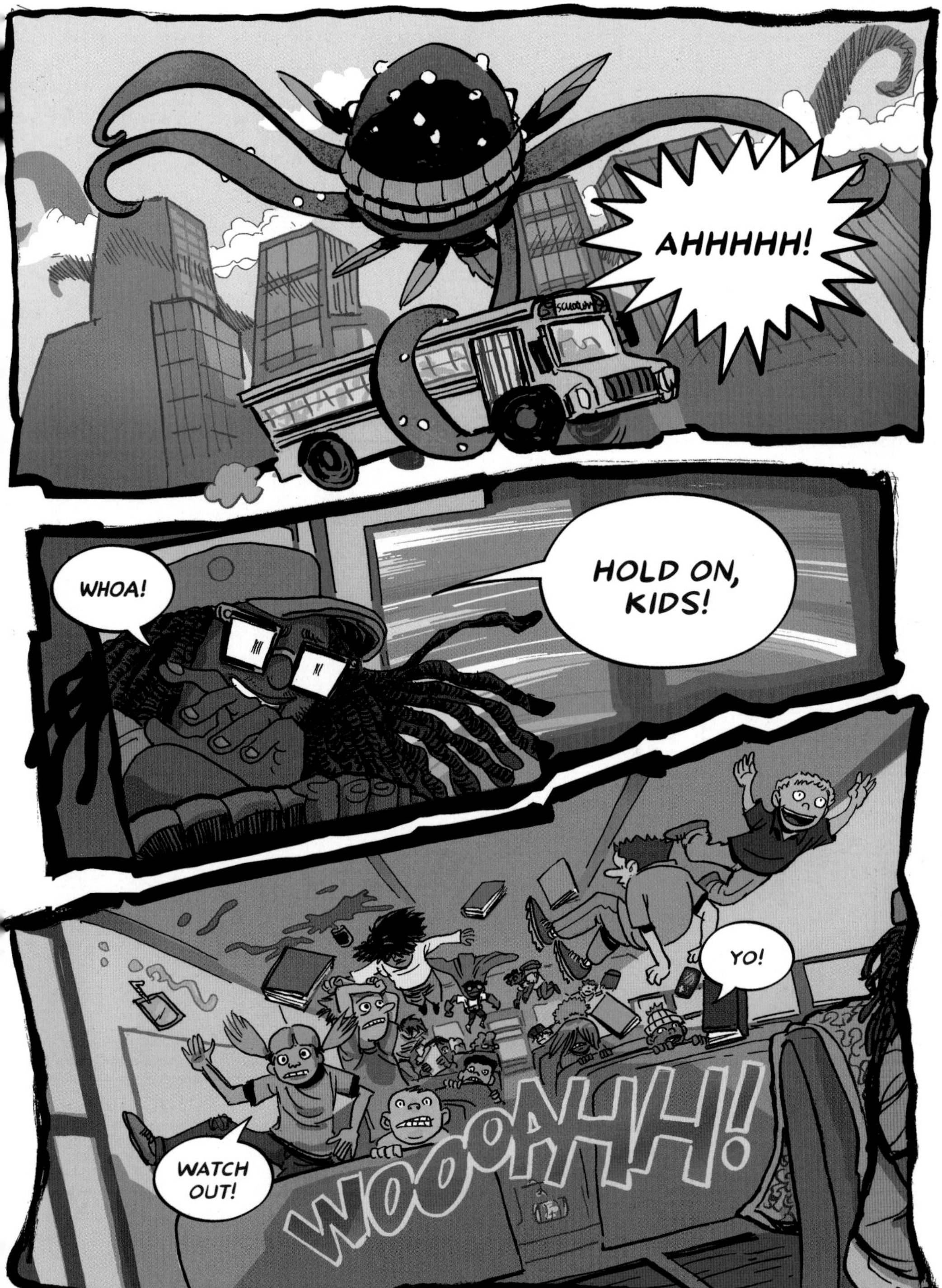
AHHHHH!
WHOA!
HOLD ON, KIDS!
YO!
WATCH OUT!
WOOOAHH!

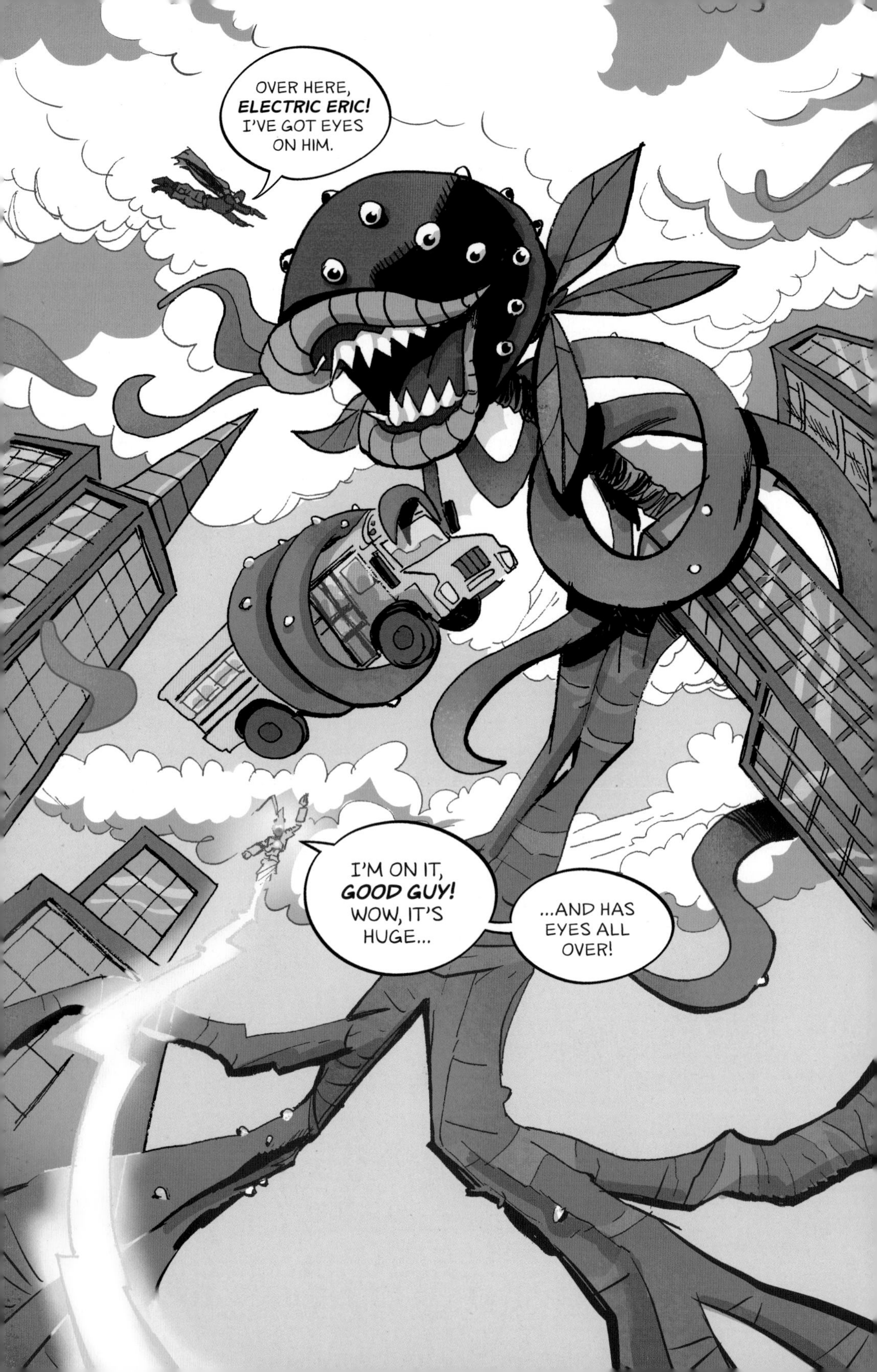
OVER HERE, ELECTRIC ERIC! I'VE GOT EYES ON HIM.
I'M ON IT, GOOD GUY! WOW, IT'S HUGE...
...AND HAS EYES ALL OVER!

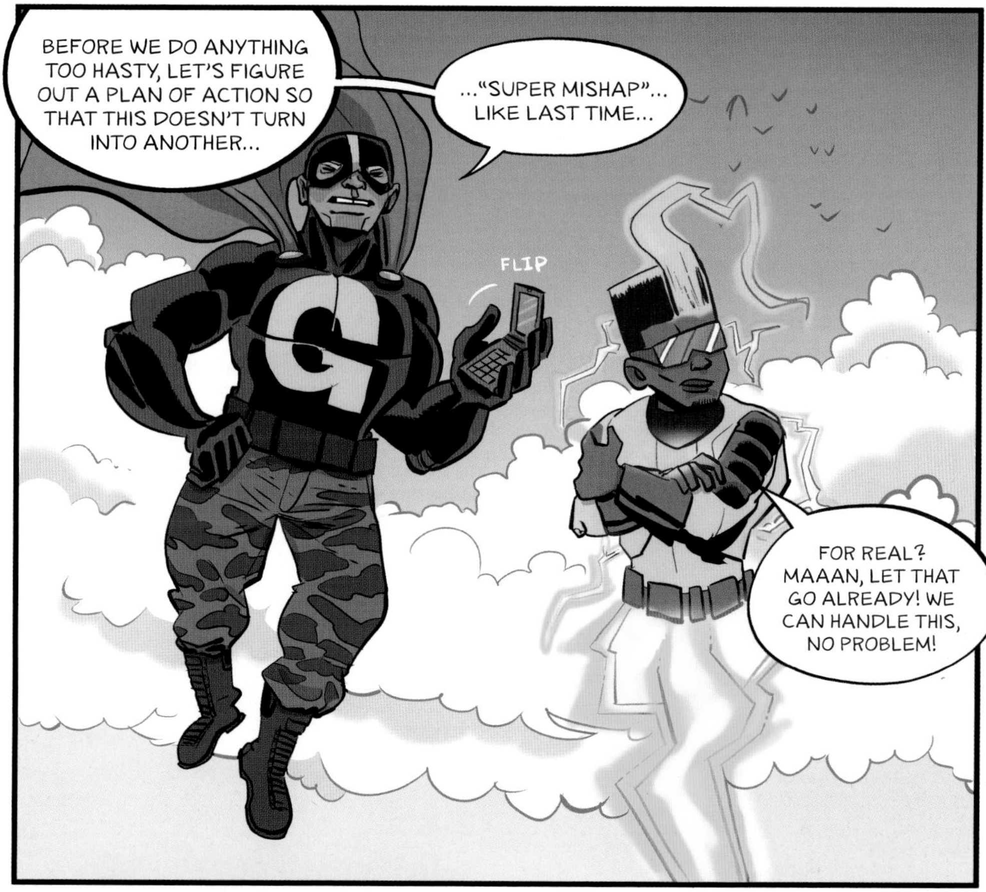
BEFORE WE DO ANYTHING TOO HASTY, LET'S FIGURE OUT A PLAN OF ACTION SO THAT THIS DOESN'T TURN INTO ANOTHER...
..."SUPER MISHAP"... LIKE LAST TIME...
FLIP
FOR REAL? MAAAN, LET THAT GO ALREADY! WE CAN HANDLE THIS, NO PROBLEM!

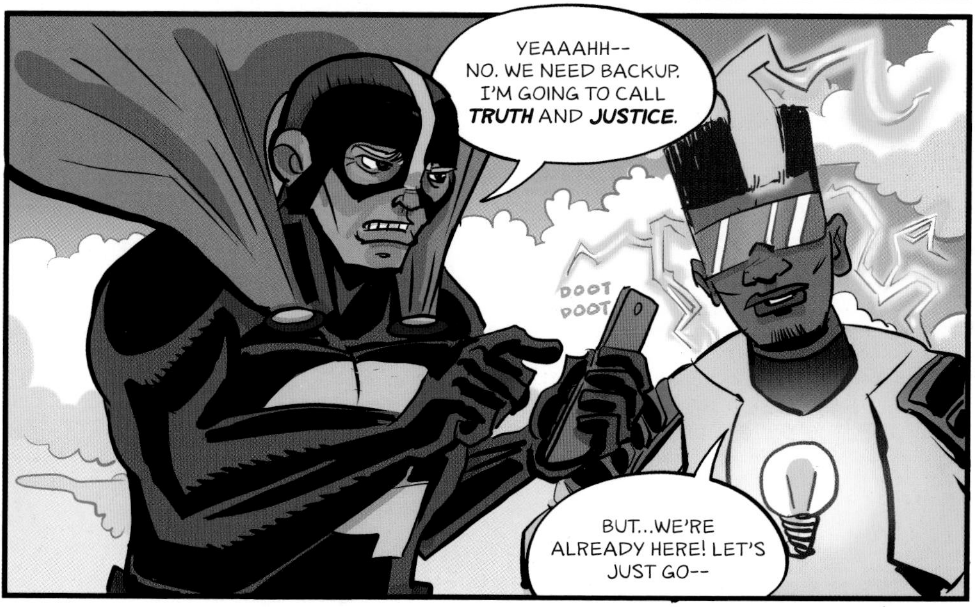
YEAAAHH-- NO. WE NEED BACKUP. I'M GOING TO CALL **TRUTH** AND **JUSTICE**.
DOOT DOOT
BUT...WE'RE ALREADY HERE! LET'S JUST GO--

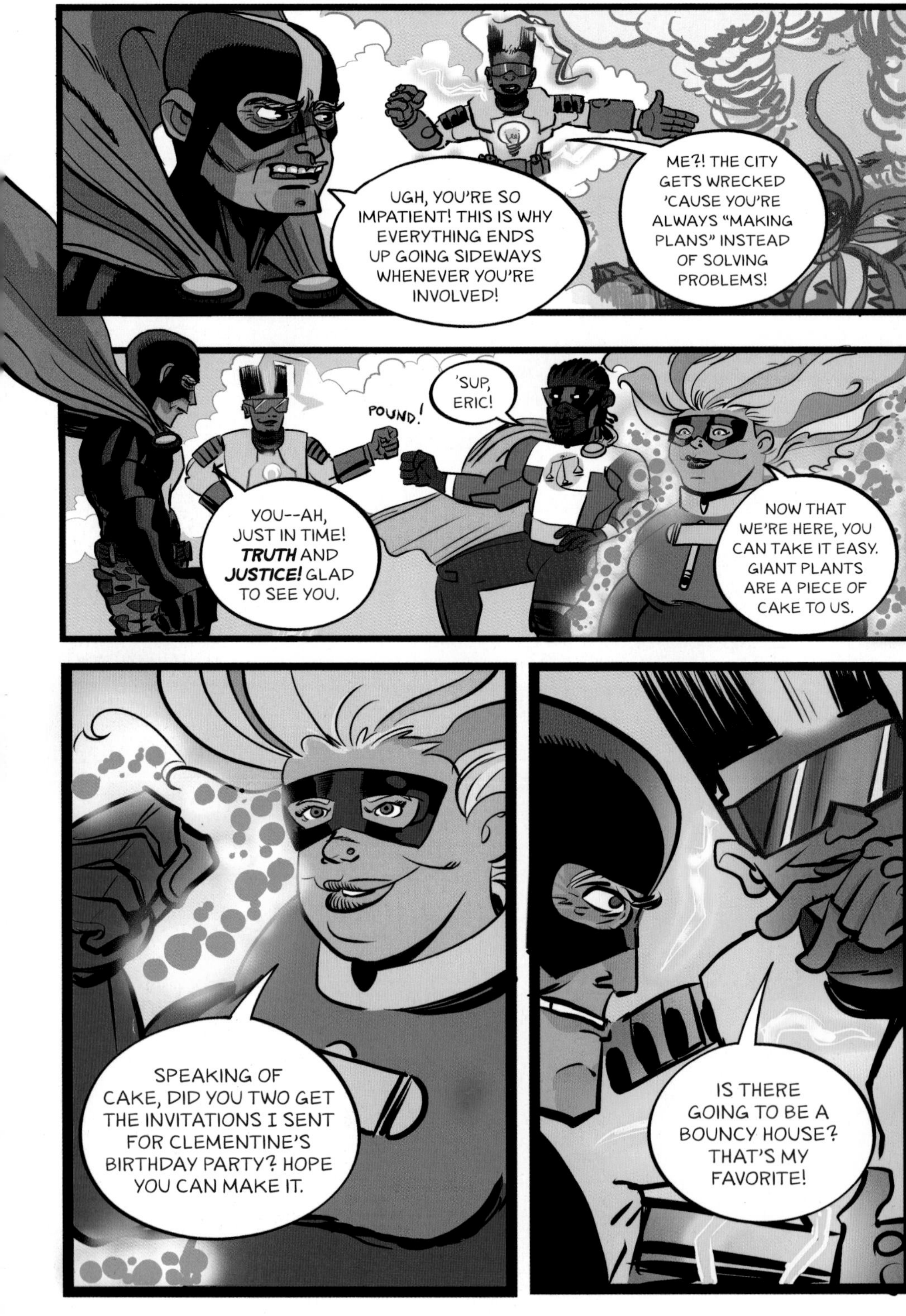
UGH, YOU'RE SO IMPATIENT! THIS IS WHY EVERYTHING ENDS UP GOING SIDEWAYS WHENEVER YOU'RE INVOLVED!
ME?! THE CITY GETS WRECKED 'CAUSE YOU'RE ALWAYS "MAKING PLANS" INSTEAD OF SOLVING PROBLEMS!
POUND!
'SUP, ERIC!
YOU--AH, JUST IN TIME! TRUTH AND JUSTICE! GLAD TO SEE YOU.
NOW THAT WE'RE HERE, YOU CAN TAKE IT EASY. GIANT PLANTS ARE A PIECE OF CAKE TO US.
SPEAKING OF CAKE, DID YOU TWO GET THE INVITATIONS I SENT FOR CLEMENTINE'S BIRTHDAY PARTY? HOPE YOU CAN MAKE IT.
IS THERE GOING TO BE A BOUNCY HOUSE? THAT'S MY FAVORITE!

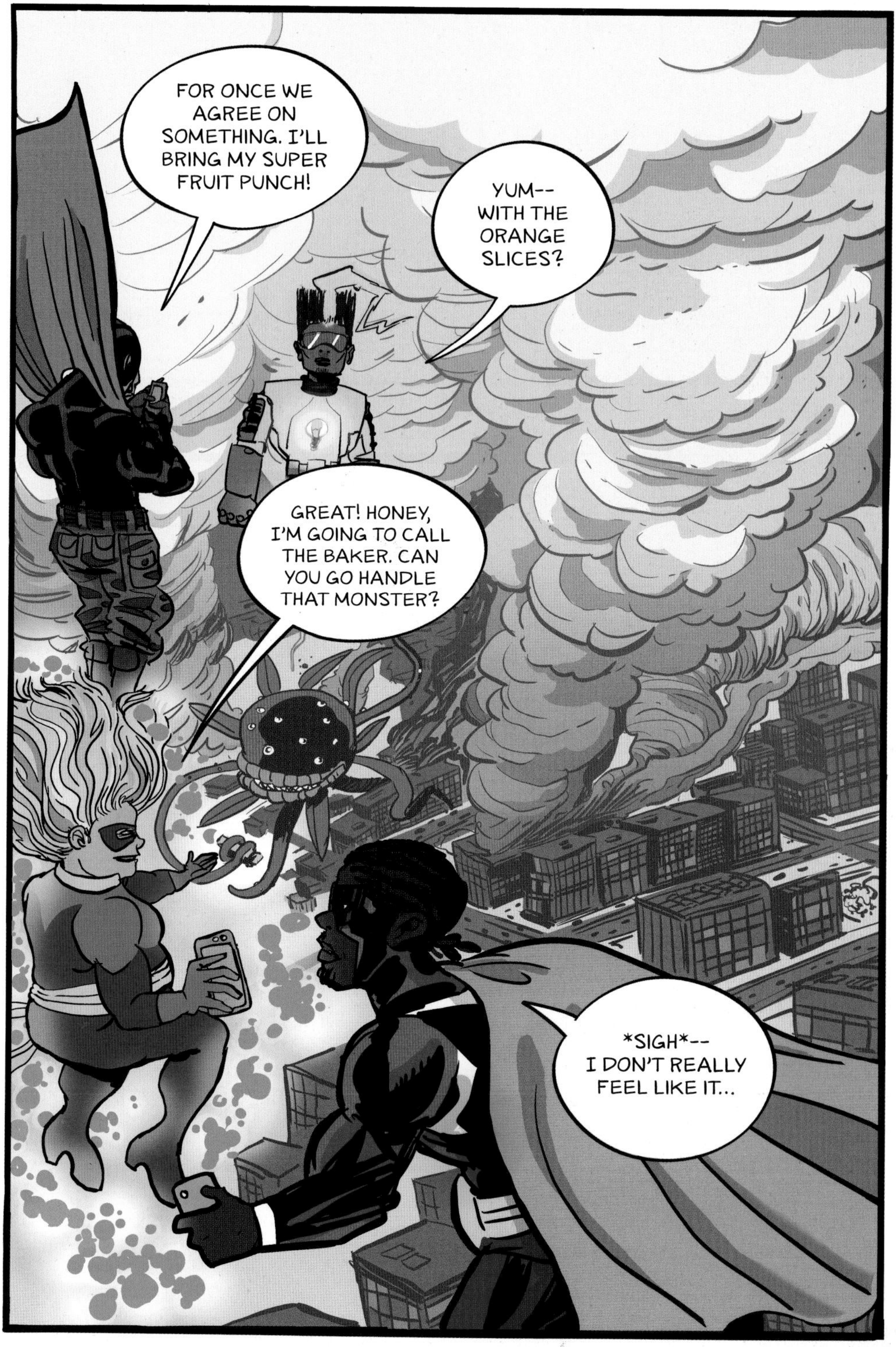
FOR ONCE WE AGREE ON SOMETHING. I'LL BRING MY SUPER FRUIT PUNCH!
YUM-- WITH THE ORANGE SLICES?
GREAT! HONEY, I'M GOING TO CALL THE BAKER. CAN YOU GO HANDLE THAT MONSTER?
SIGH-- I DON'T REALLY FEEL LIKE IT...

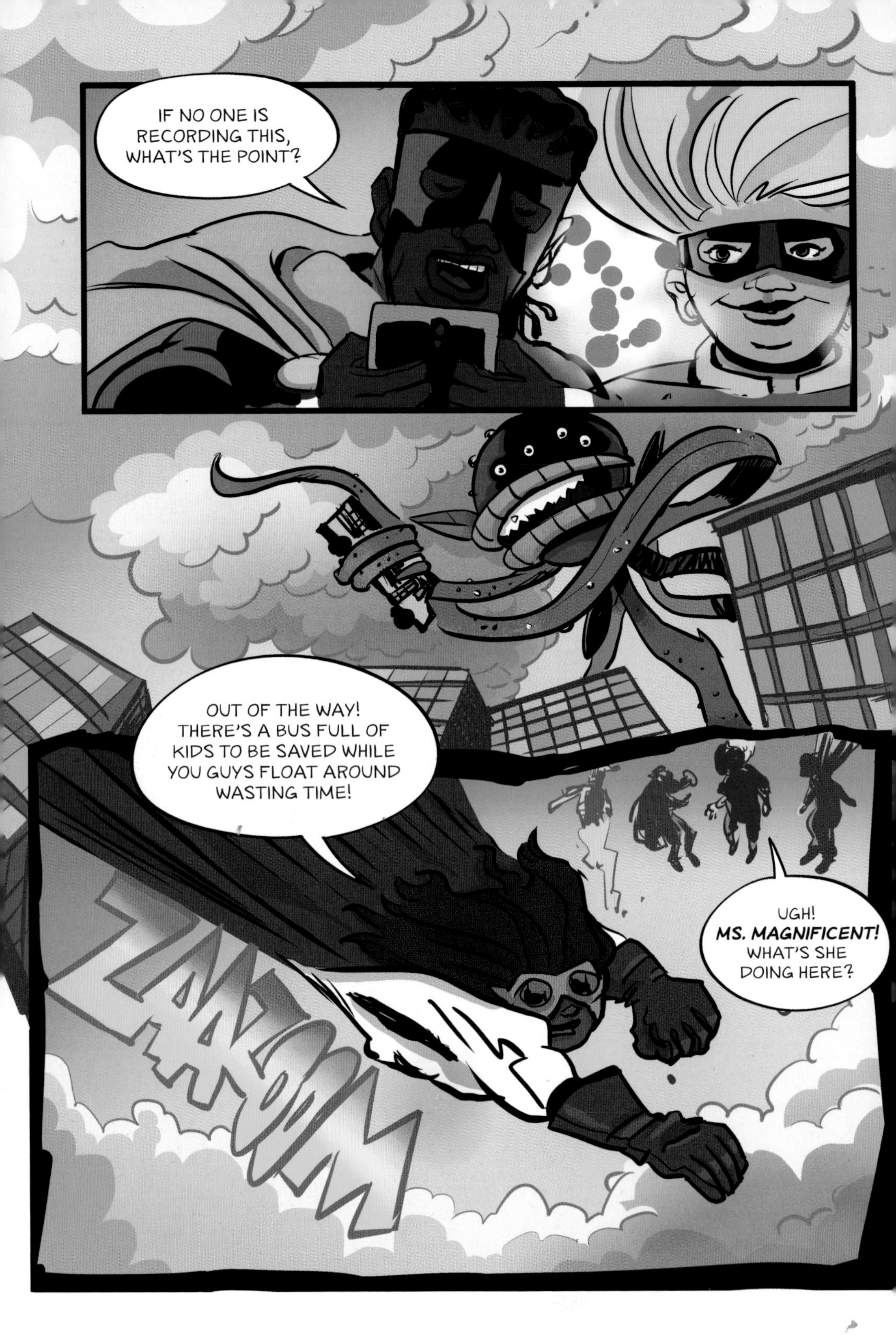
IF NO ONE IS RECORDING THIS, WHAT'S THE POINT?
OUT OF THE WAY! THERE'S A BUS FULL OF KIDS TO BE SAVED WHILE YOU GUYS FLOAT AROUND WASTING TIME!
UGH! **MS. MAGNIFICENT!** WHAT'S SHE DOING HERE?
ZWOOM

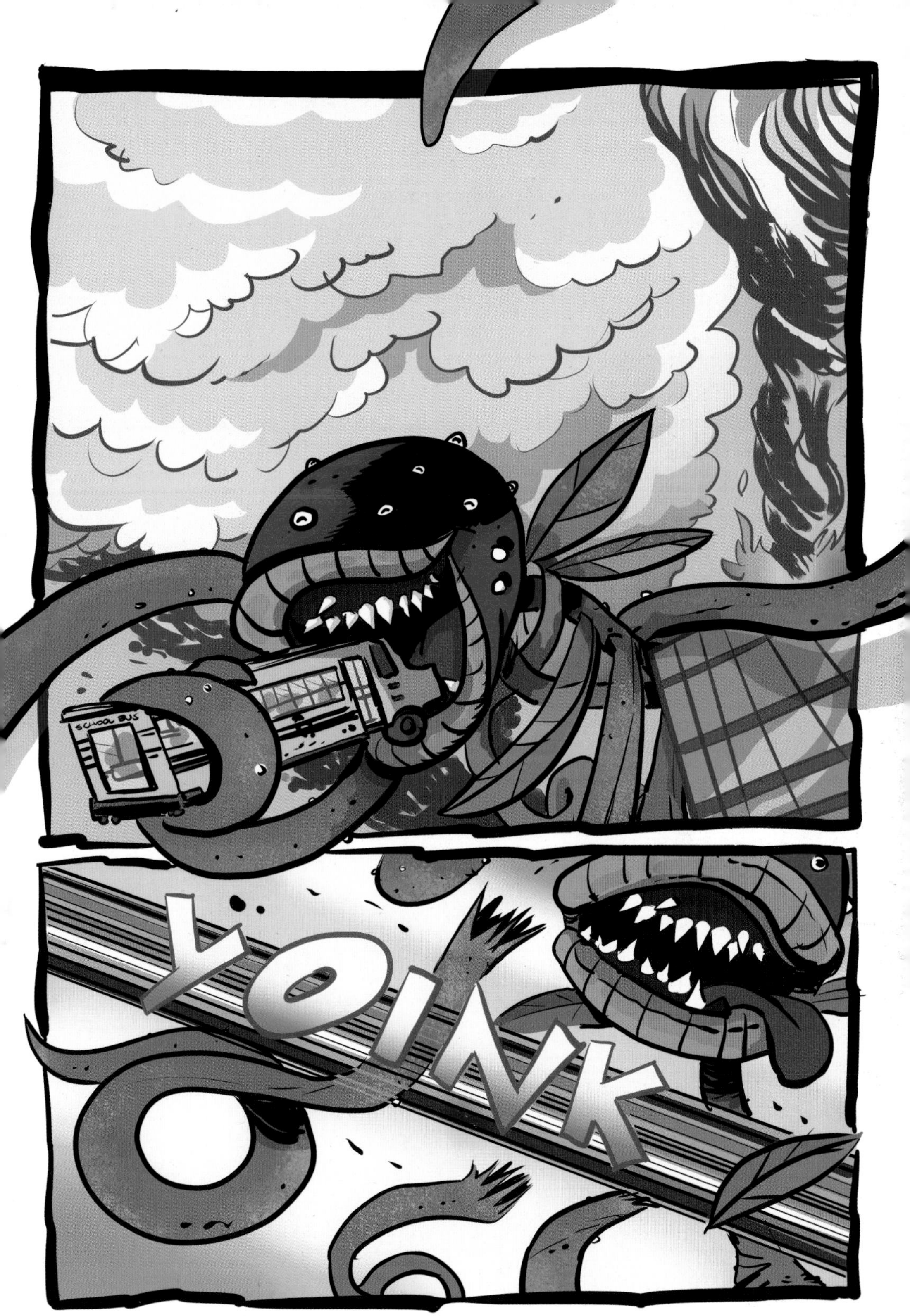
SCHOOL BUS
YOINK

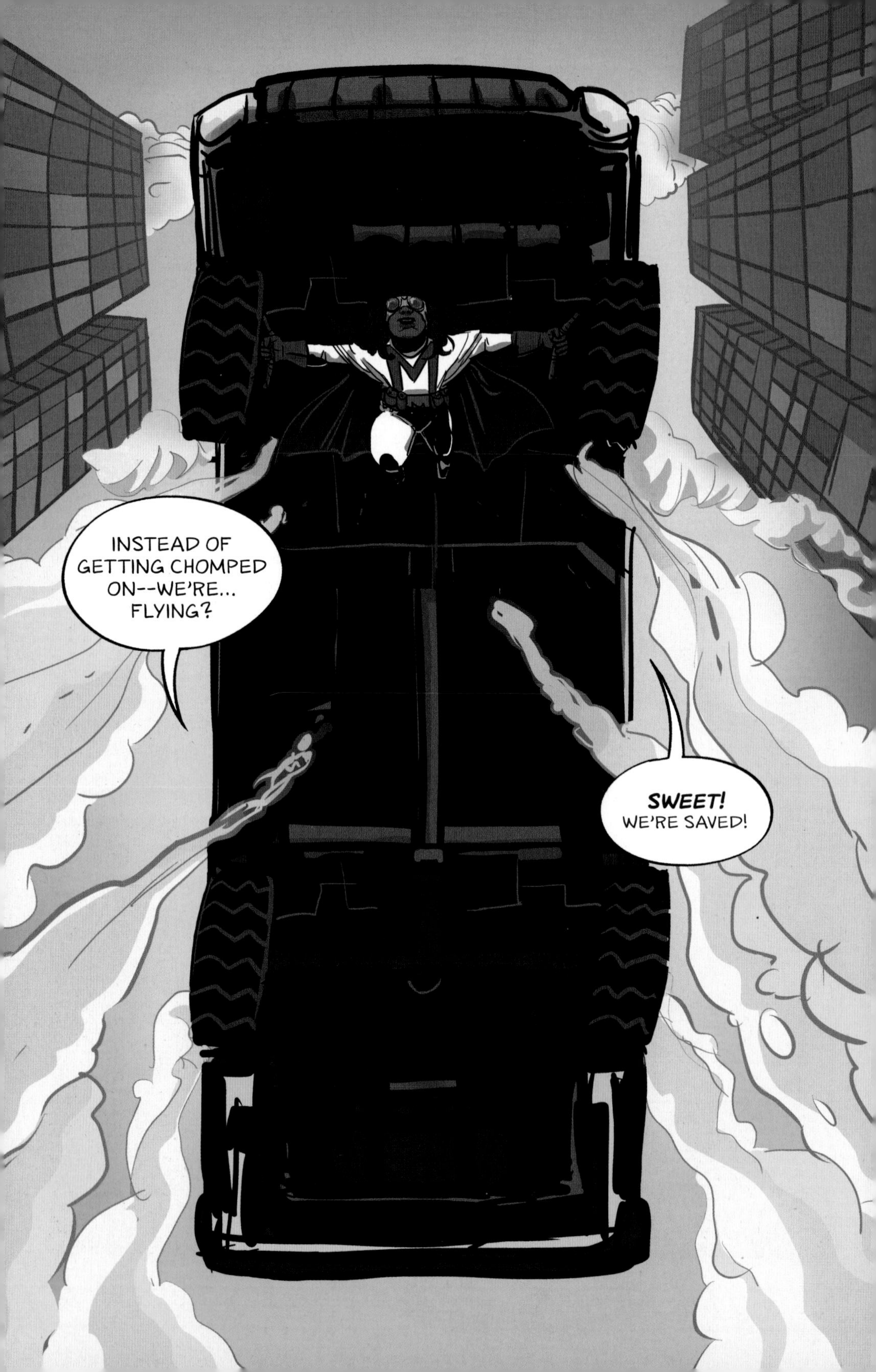
INSTEAD OF GETTING CHOMPED ON--WE'RE... FLYING?
SWEET! WE'RE SAVED!

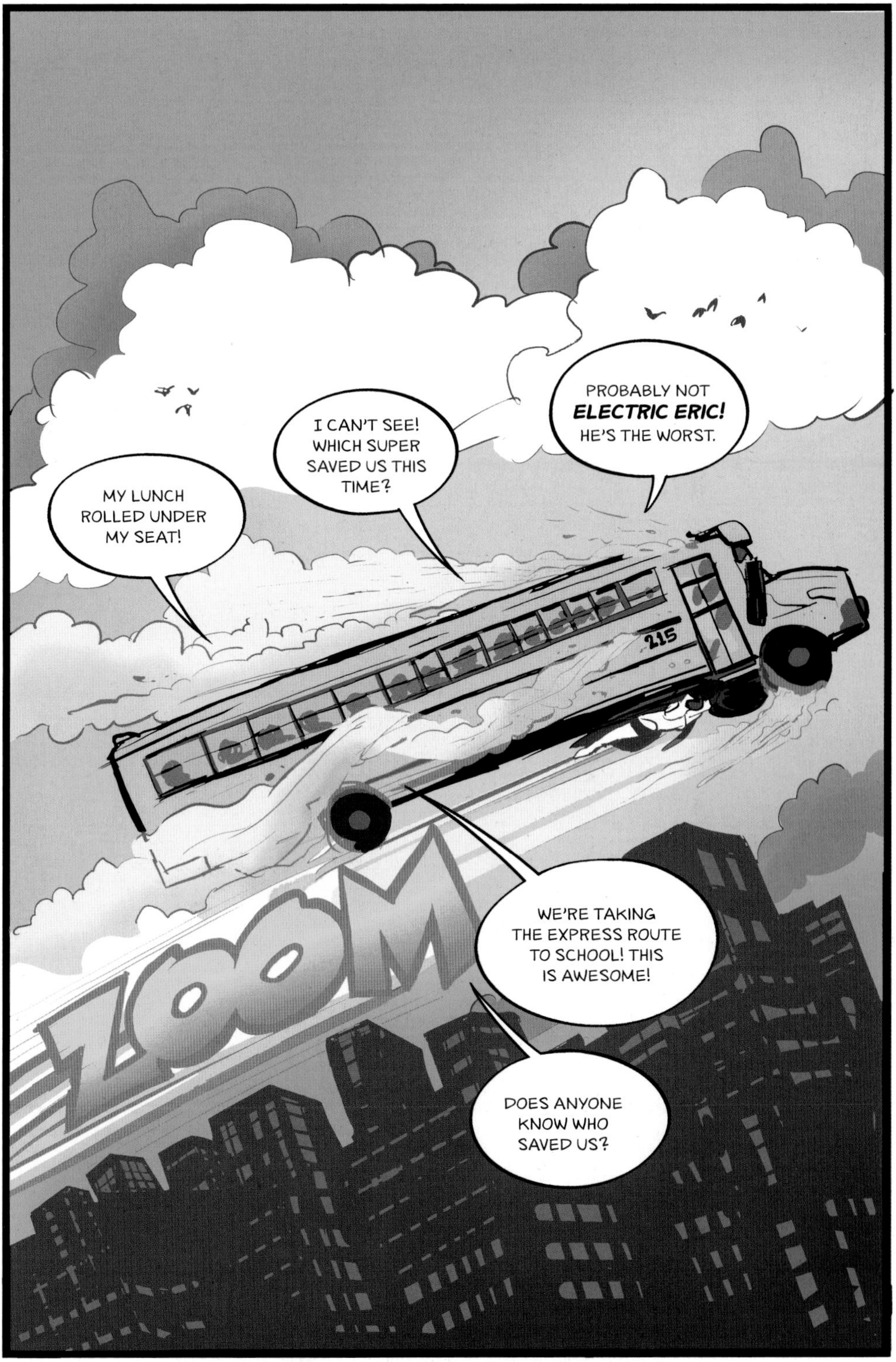
MY LUNCH ROLLED UNDER MY SEAT!
I CAN'T SEE! WHICH SUPER SAVED US THIS TIME?
PROBABLY NOT ELECTRIC ERIC! HE'S THE WORST.
215
ZOOM
WE'RE TAKING THE EXPRESS ROUTE TO SCHOOL! THIS IS AWESOME!
DOES ANYONE KNOW WHO SAVED US?

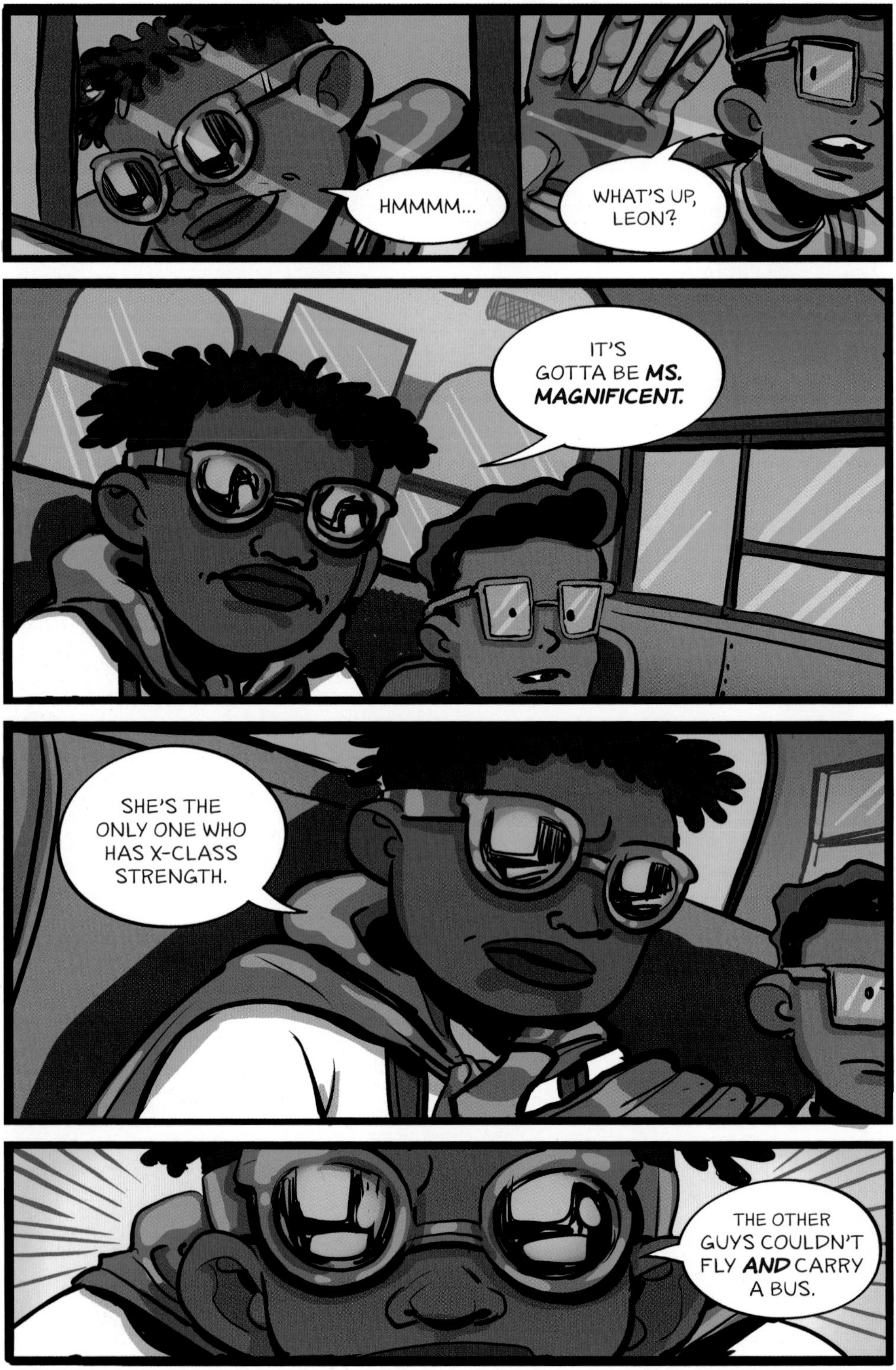
HMMMM...
WHAT'S UP, LEON?
IT'S GOTTA BE **MS. MAGNIFICENT.**
SHE'S THE ONLY ONE WHO HAS X-CLASS STRENGTH.
THE OTHER GUYS COULDN'T FLY **AND** CARRY A BUS.

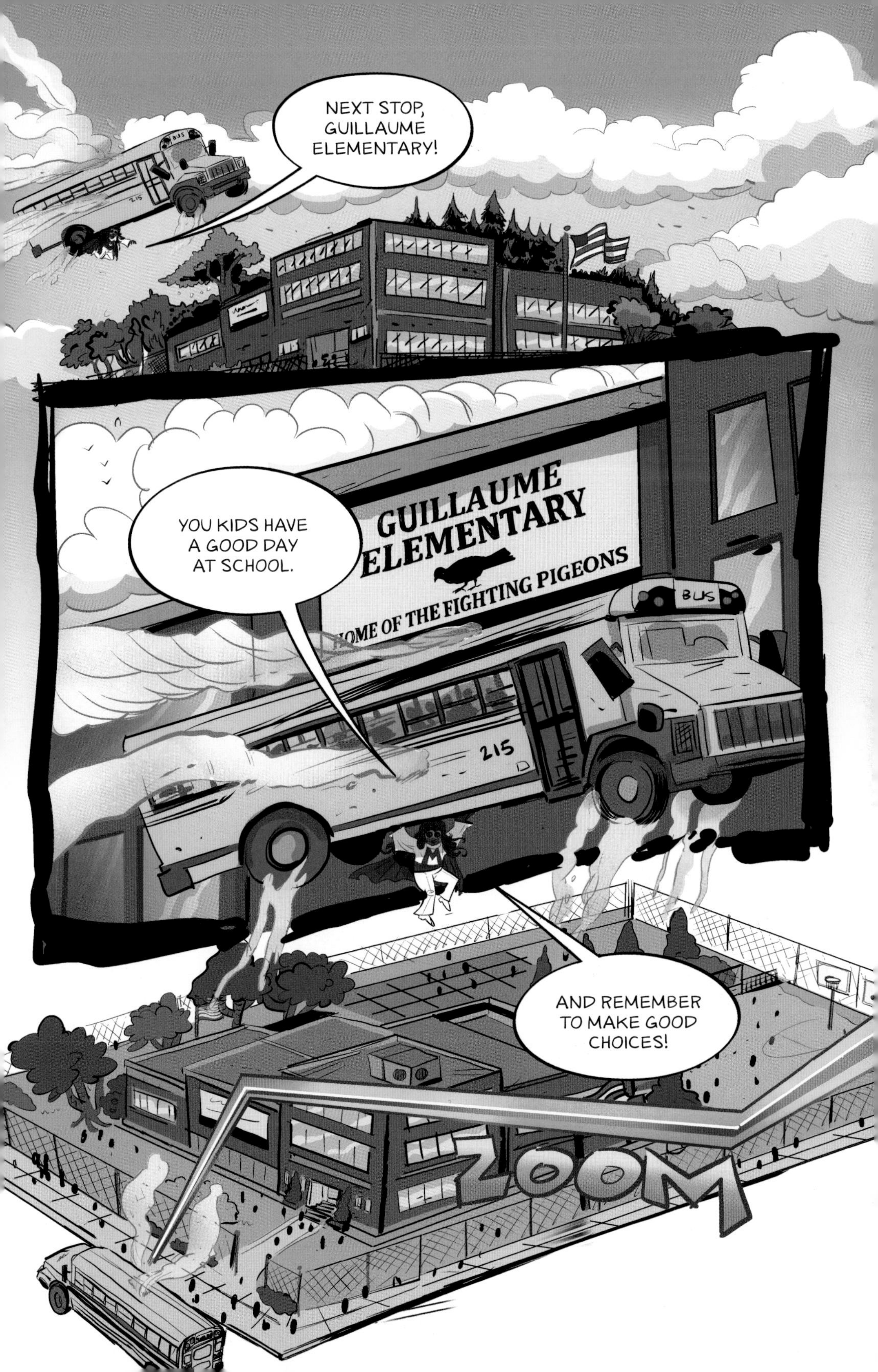

NEXT STOP, GUILLAUME ELEMENTARY!
BUS
215
GUILLAUME ELEMENTARY
HOME OF THE FIGHTING PIGEONS
YOU KIDS HAVE A GOOD DAY AT SCHOOL.
BUS
215
AND REMEMBER TO MAKE GOOD CHOICES!
ZOOM

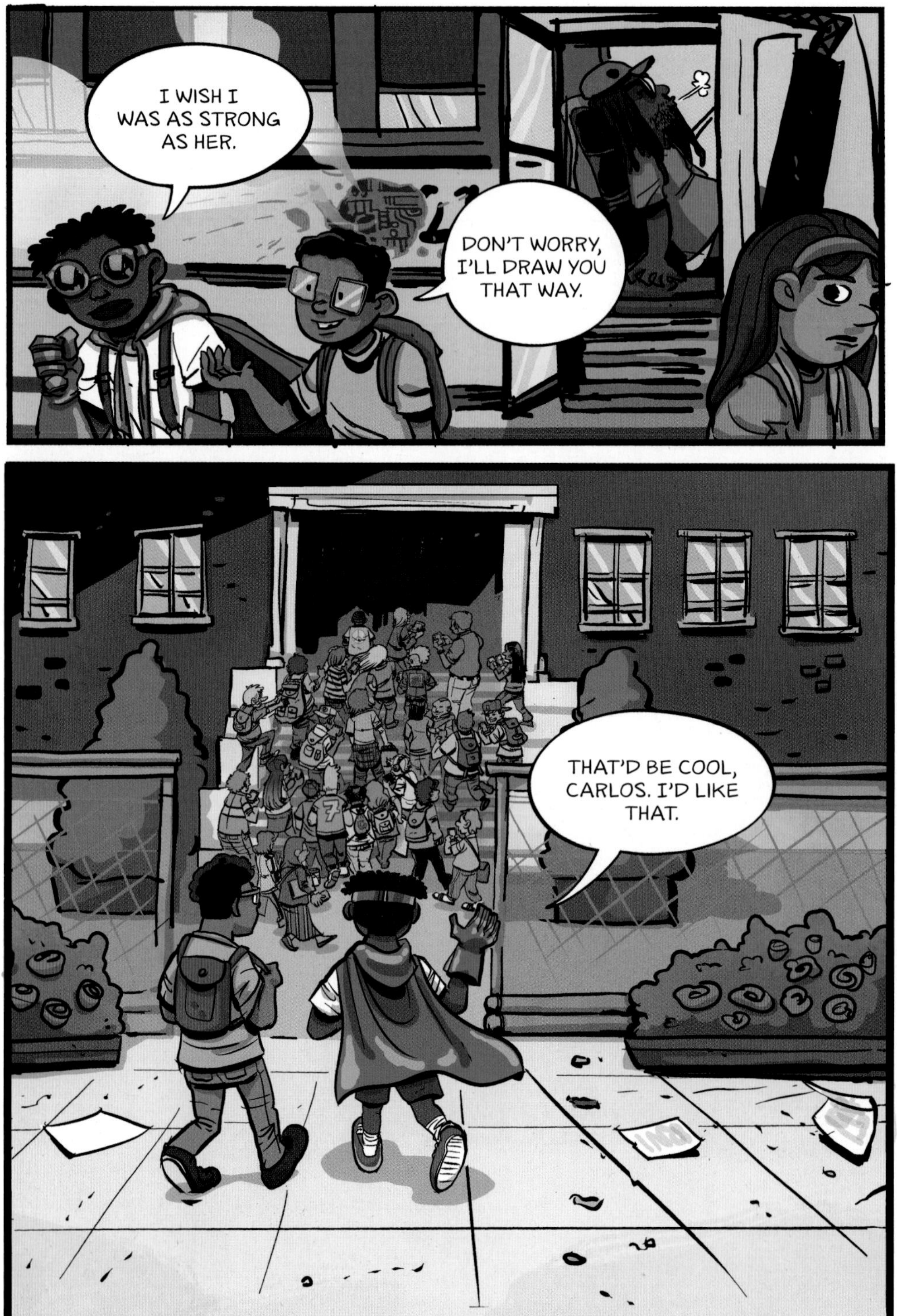
I WISH I
WAS AS STRONG
AS HER.
DON'T WORRY,
I'LL DRAW YOU
THAT WAY.
THAT'D BE COOL,
CARLOS. I'D LIKE
THAT.

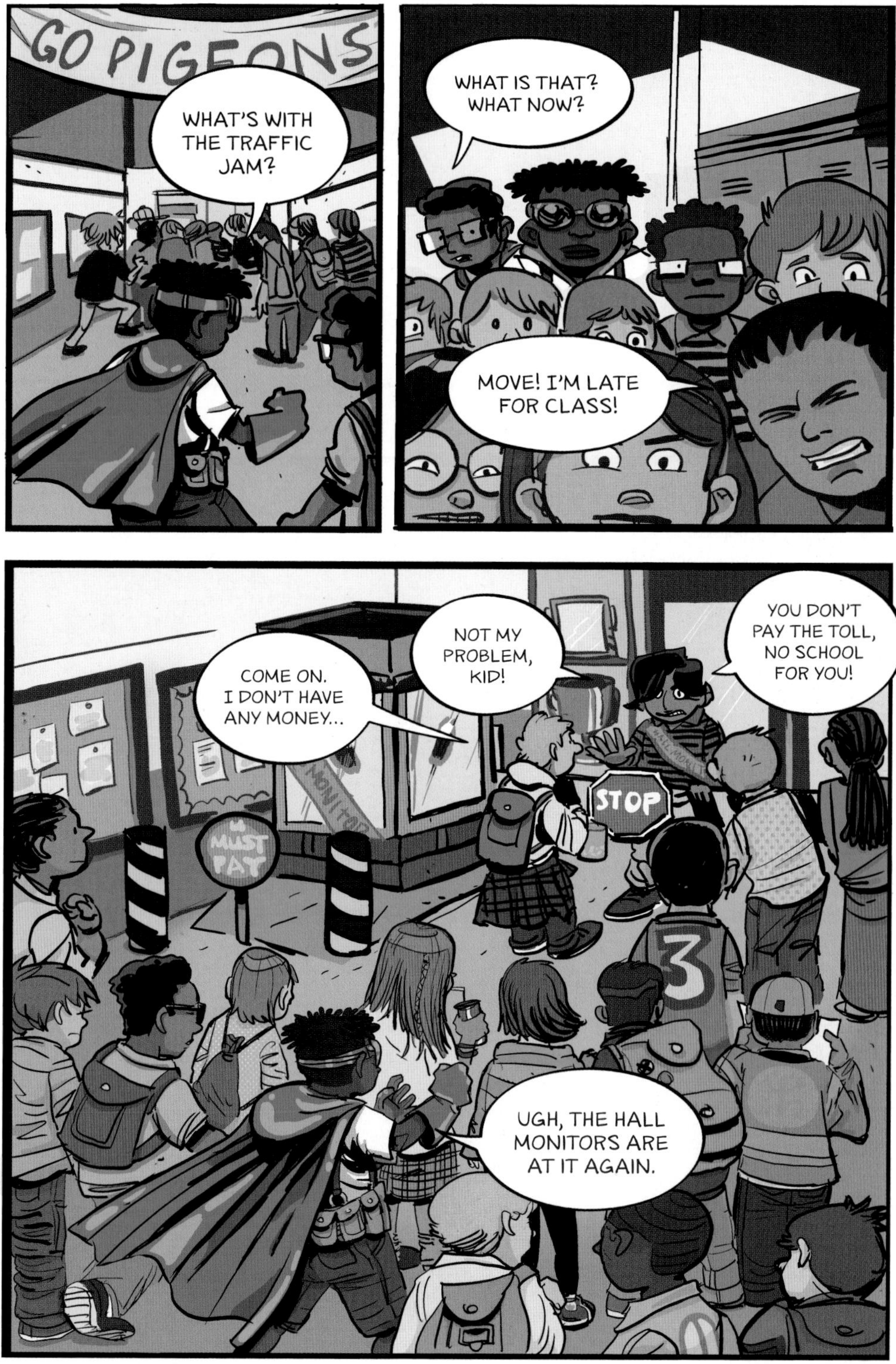
GO PIGEONS
WHAT'S WITH THE TRAFFIC JAM?
WHAT IS THAT? WHAT NOW?
MOVE! I'M LATE FOR CLASS!
COME ON. I DON'T HAVE ANY MONEY...
NOT MY PROBLEM, KID!
YOU DON'T PAY THE TOLL, NO SCHOOL FOR YOU!
MUST PAY
STOP
UGH, THE HALL MONITORS ARE AT IT AGAIN.

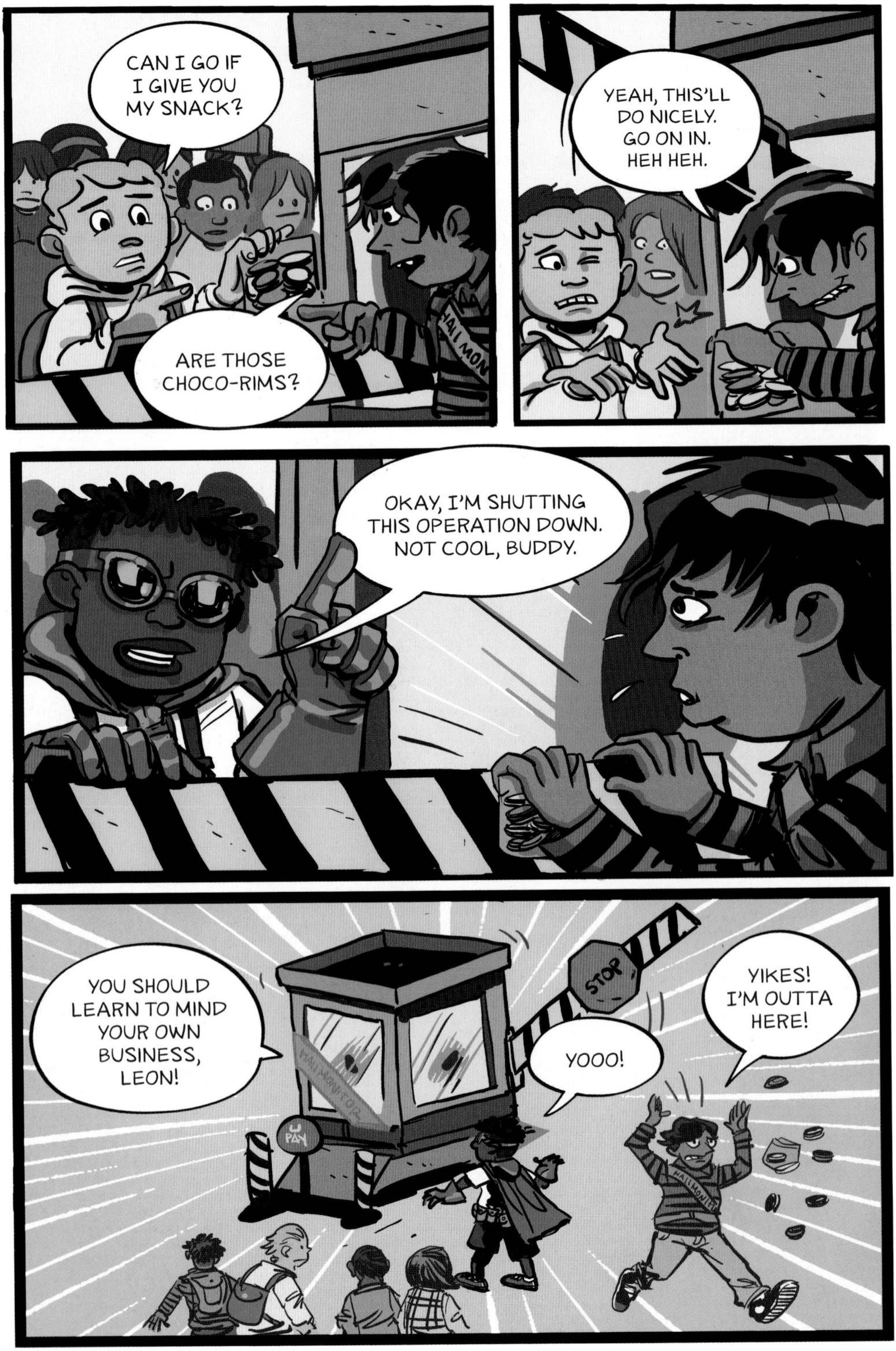
CAN I GO IF I GIVE YOU MY SNACK?
ARE THOSE CHOCO-RIMS?
YEAH, THIS'LL DO NICELY. GO ON IN. HEH HEH.
OKAY, I'M SHUTTING THIS OPERATION DOWN. NOT COOL, BUDDY.
YOU SHOULD LEARN TO MIND YOUR OWN BUSINESS, LEON!
STOP
YOOO!
YIKES! I'M OUTTA HERE!

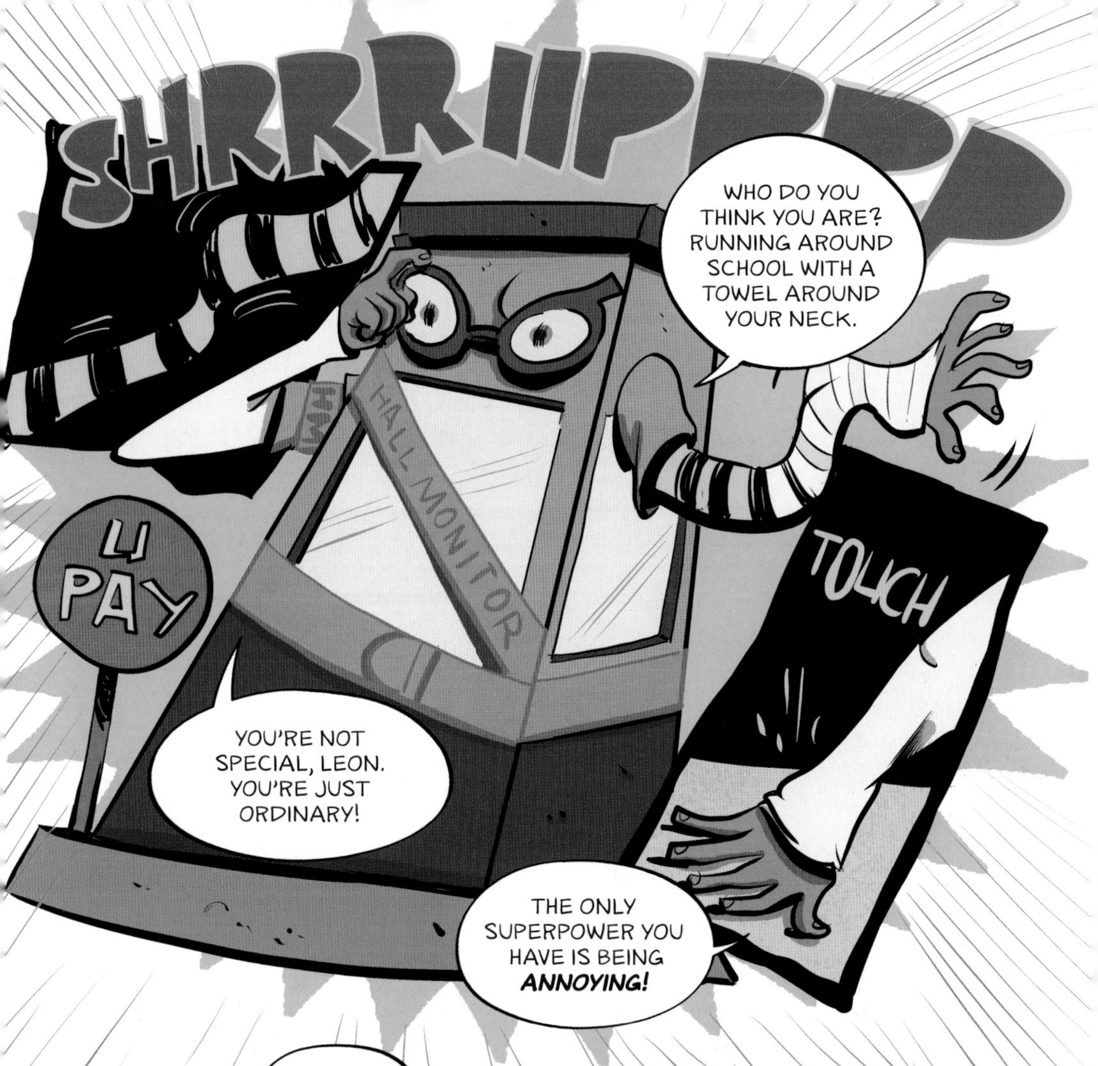
SHRRRIIPPPP
WHO DO YOU THINK YOU ARE? RUNNING AROUND SCHOOL WITH A TOWEL AROUND YOUR NECK.
HALL MONITOR
LI PAY
TOUCH
YOU'RE NOT SPECIAL, LEON. YOU'RE JUST ORDINARY!
THE ONLY SUPERPOWER YOU HAVE IS BEING ANNOYING!

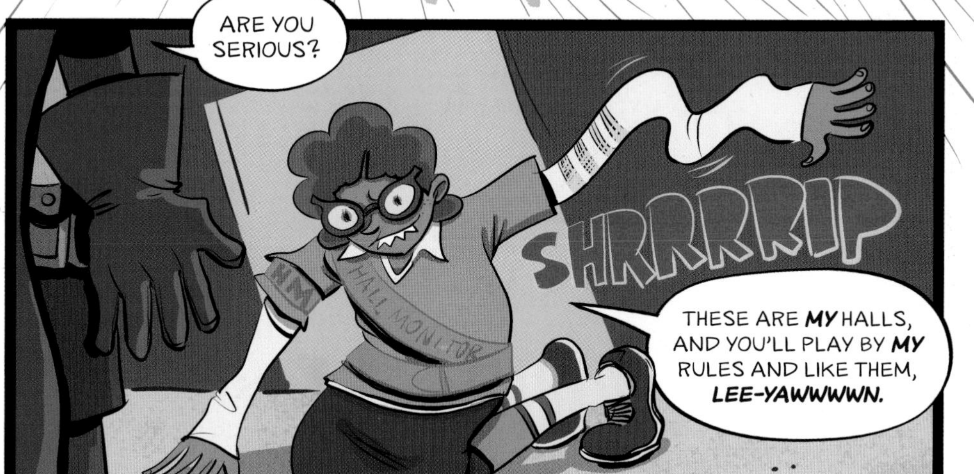
ARE YOU SERIOUS?
SHRRRRIP
HALL MONITOR
THESE ARE MY HALLS, AND YOU'LL PLAY BY MY RULES AND LIKE THEM, LEE-YAWWWWN.

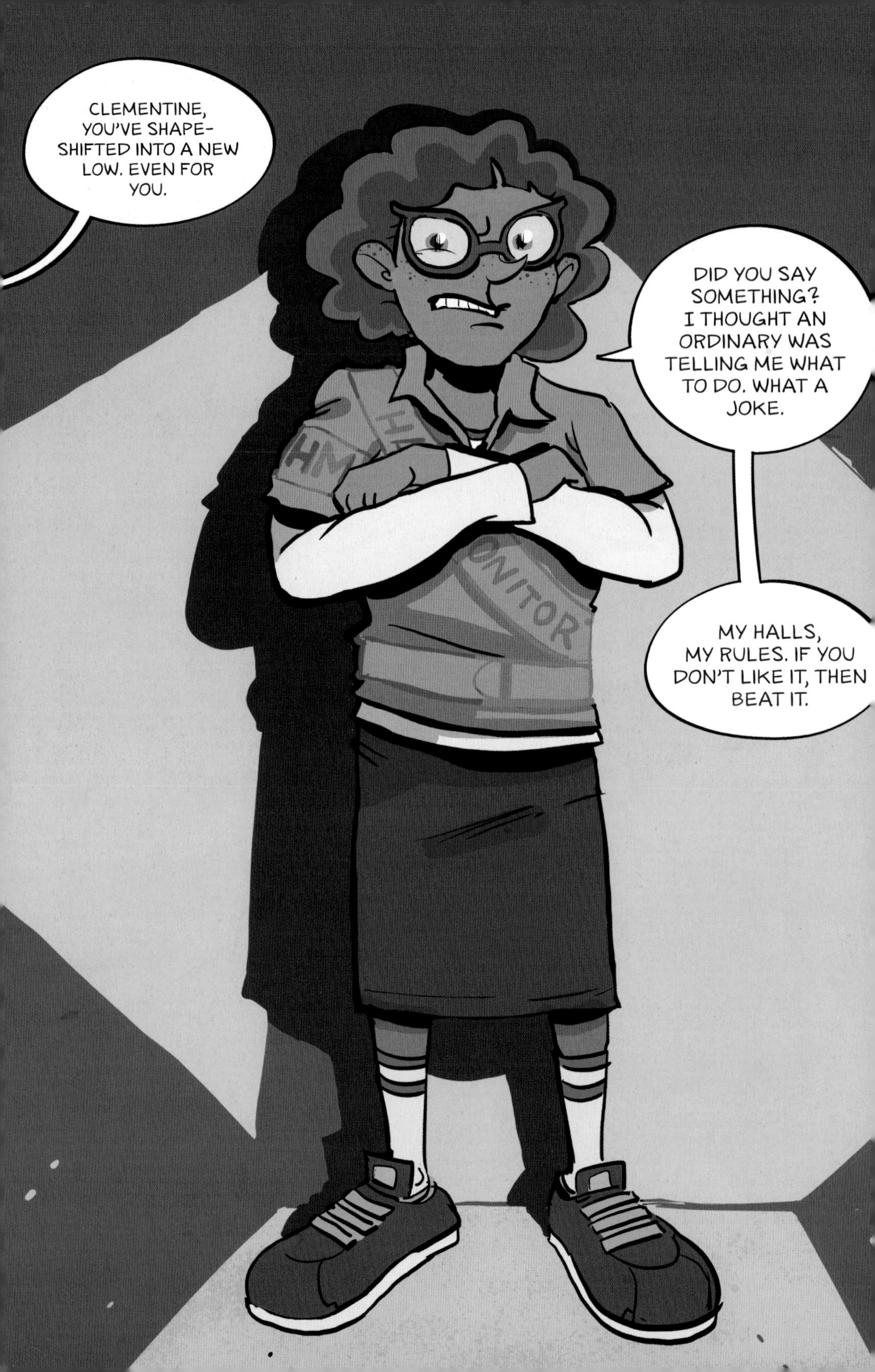
CLEMENTINE, YOU'VE SHAPE-SHIFTED INTO A NEW LOW. EVEN FOR YOU.
DID YOU SAY SOMETHING? I THOUGHT AN ORDINARY WAS TELLING ME WHAT TO DO. WHAT A JOKE.
MY HALLS, MY RULES. IF YOU DON'T LIKE IT, THEN BEAT IT.
HALL MONITOR
HM

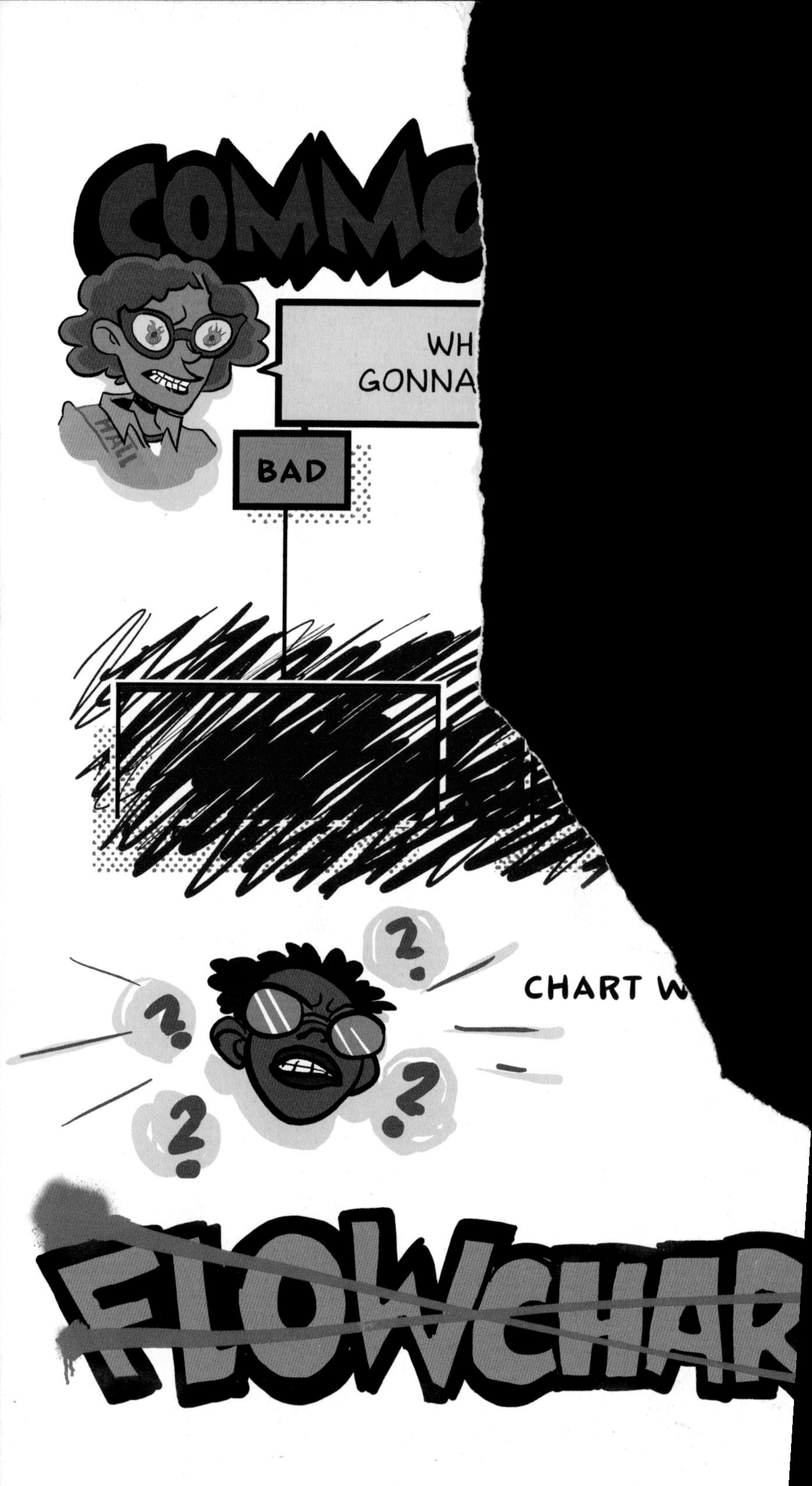
COMMO
WH
GONNA
MALL
BAD
CHART W
FLOWCHAR

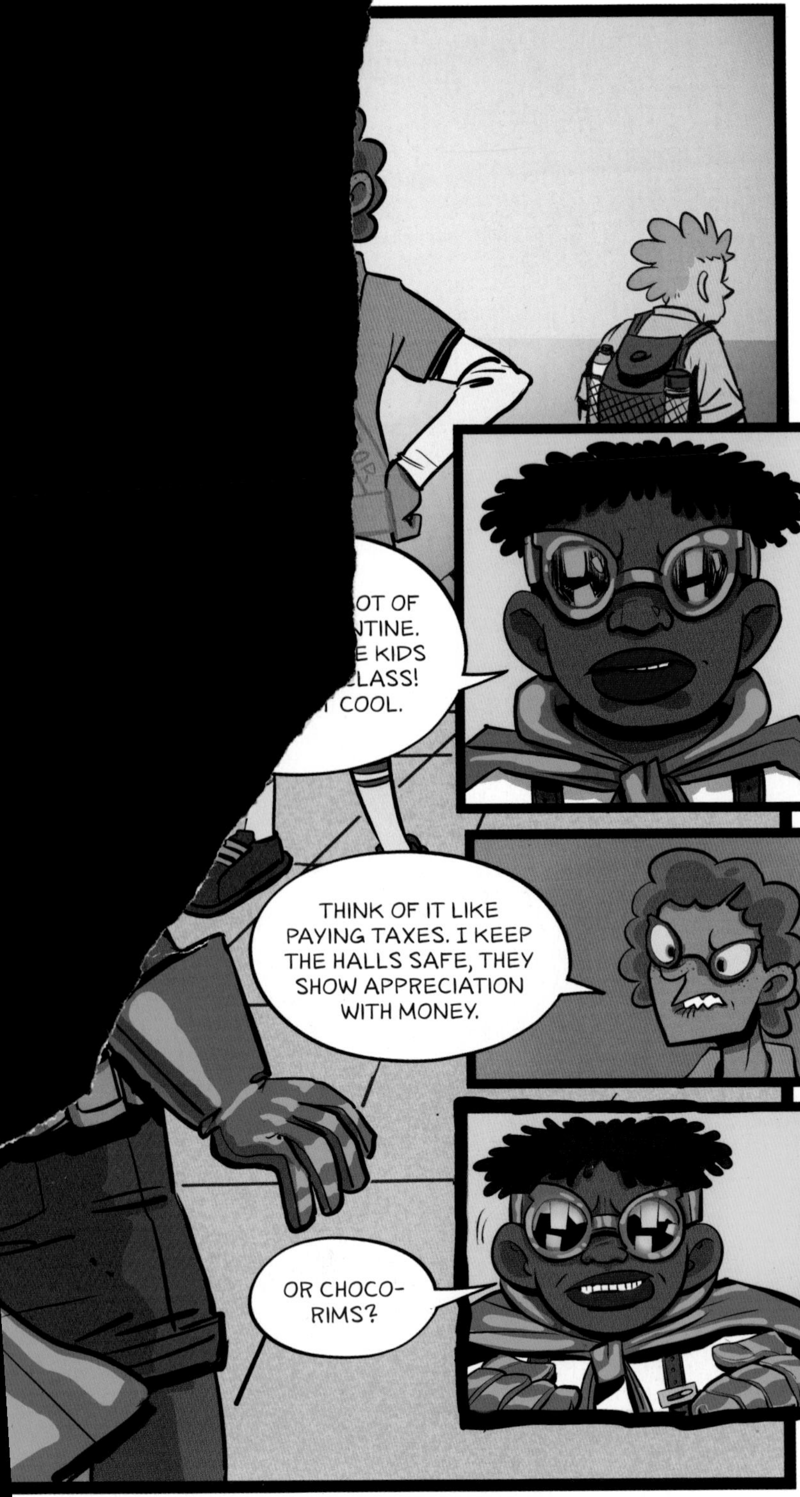
OT OF
NTINE.
E KIDS
CLASS!
T COOL.
THINK OF IT LIKE PAYING TAXES. I KEEP THE HALLS SAFE, THEY SHOW APPRECIATION WITH MONEY.
OR CHOCO-RIMS?

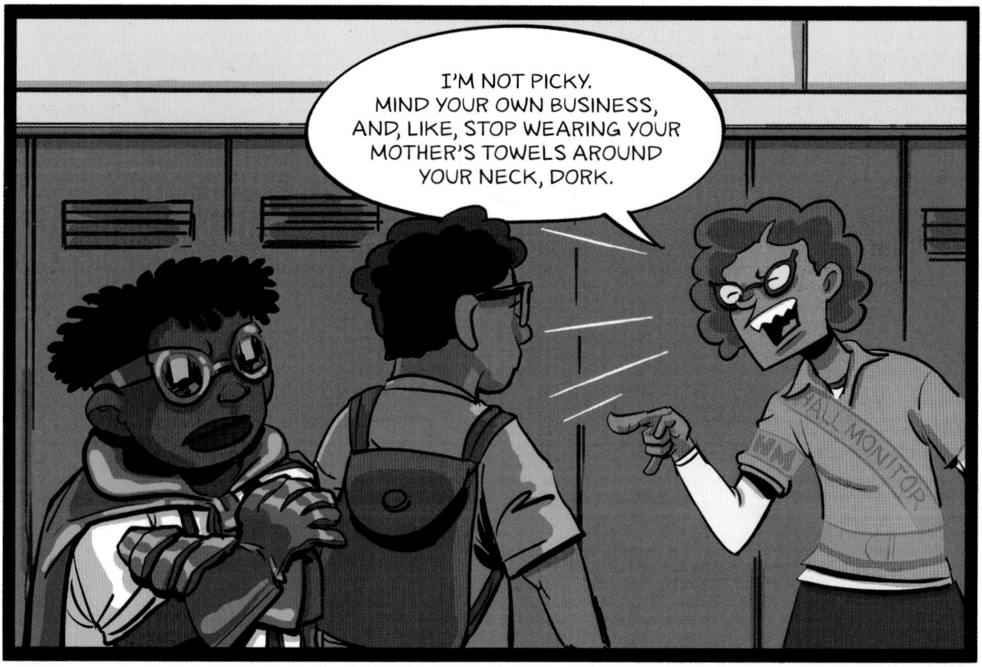
I'M NOT PICKY. MIND YOUR OWN BUSINESS, AND, LIKE, STOP WEARING YOUR MOTHER'S TOWELS AROUND YOUR NECK, DORK.
HALL MONITOR

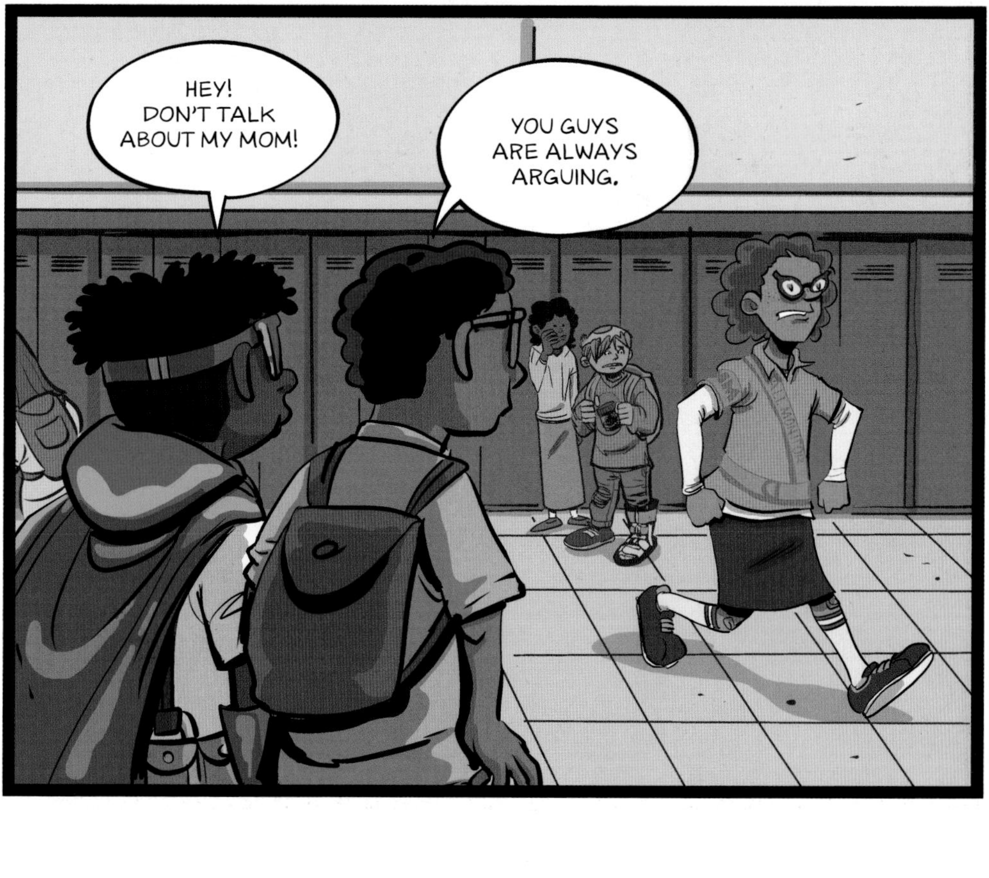
HEY! DON'T TALK ABOUT MY MOM!
YOU GUYS ARE ALWAYS ARGUING.

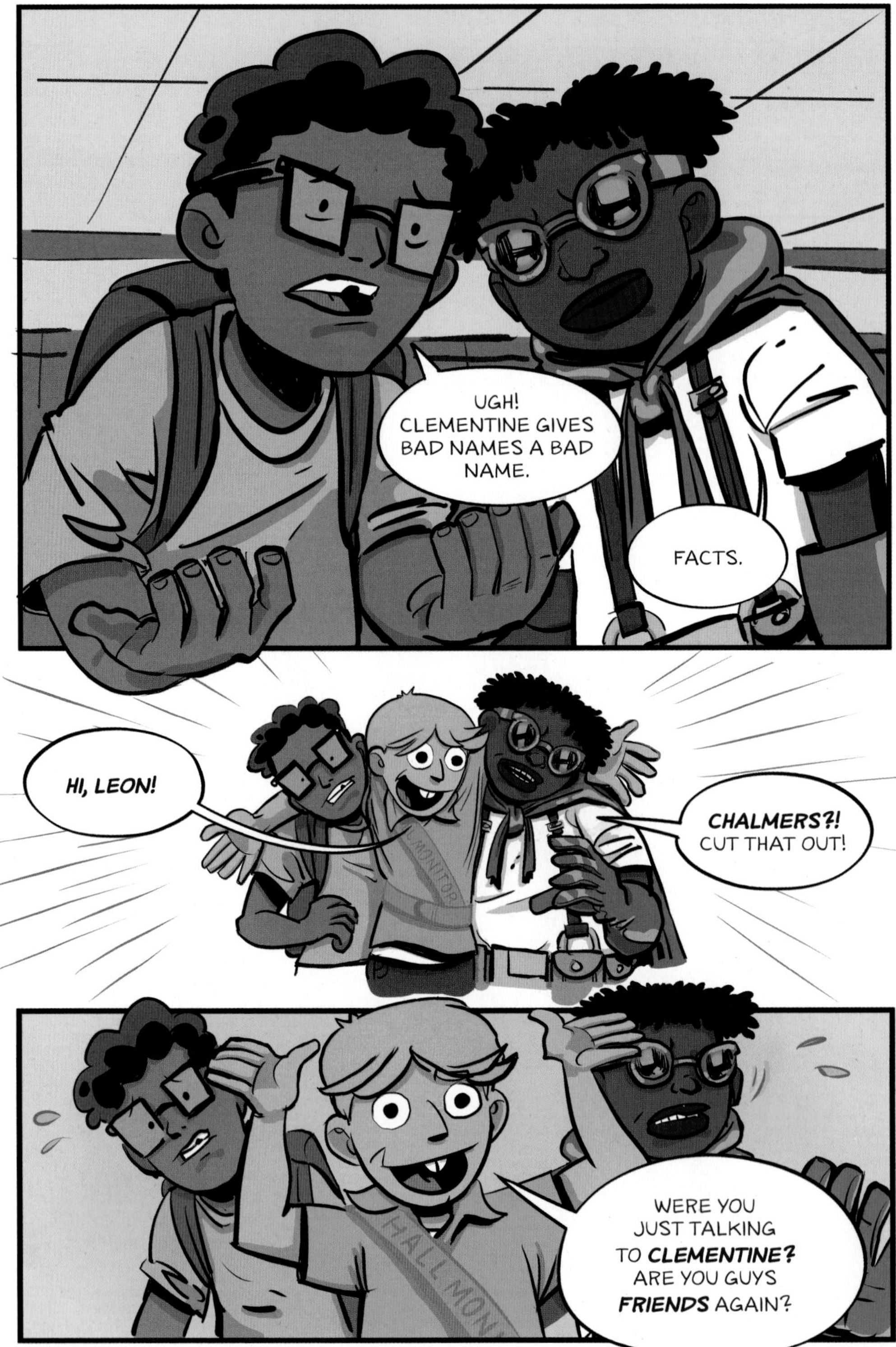
UGH! CLEMENTINE GIVES BAD NAMES A BAD NAME.
FACTS.
HI, LEON!
CHALMERS?! CUT THAT OUT!
HALL MONITOR
WERE YOU JUST TALKING TO **CLEMENTINE?** ARE YOU GUYS **FRIENDS** AGAIN?

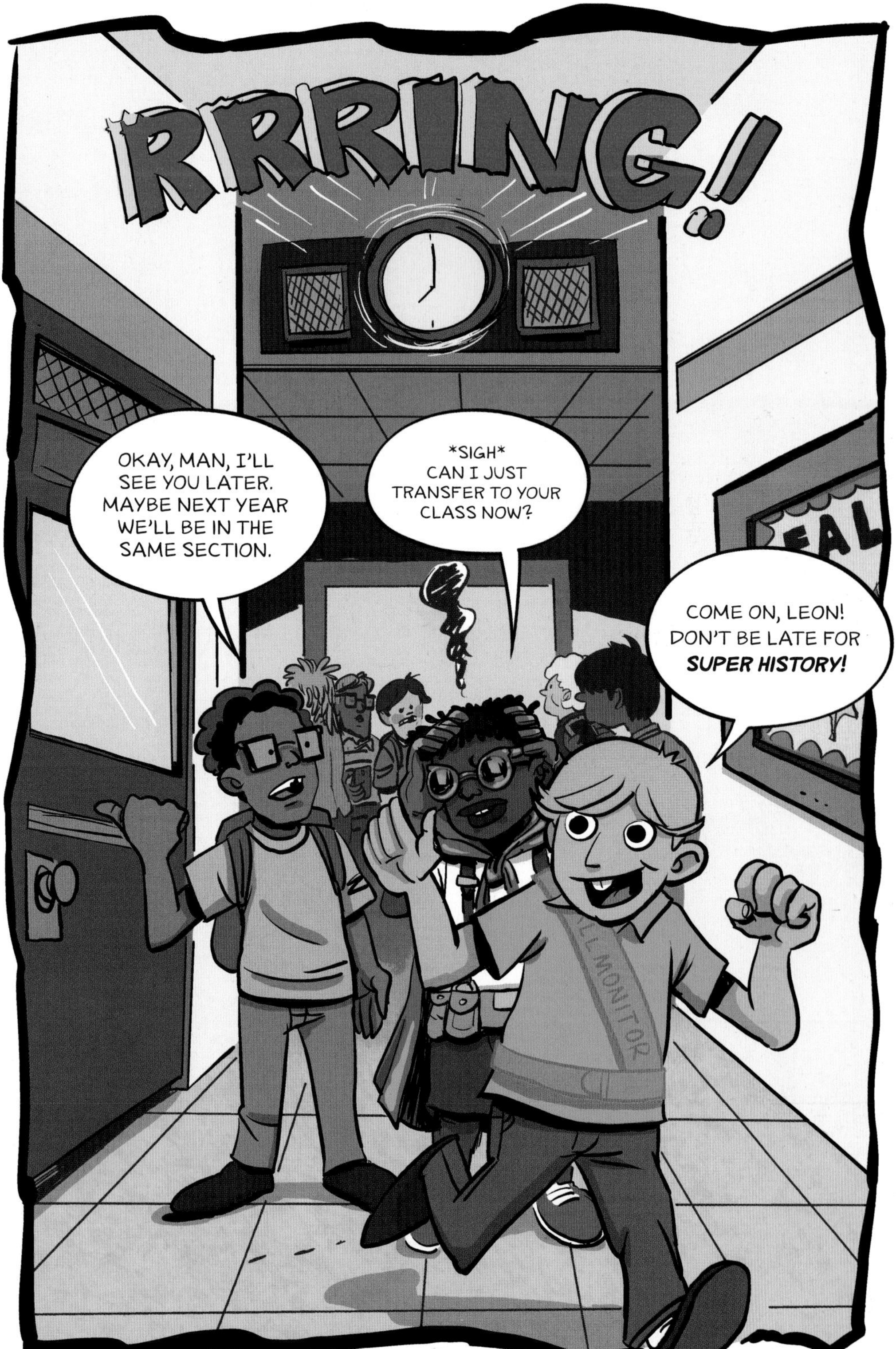
RRRIING!
OKAY, MAN, I'LL SEE YOU LATER. MAYBE NEXT YEAR WE'LL BE IN THE SAME SECTION.
SIGH CAN I JUST TRANSFER TO YOUR CLASS NOW?
COME ON, LEON! DON'T BE LATE FOR **SUPER HISTORY!**

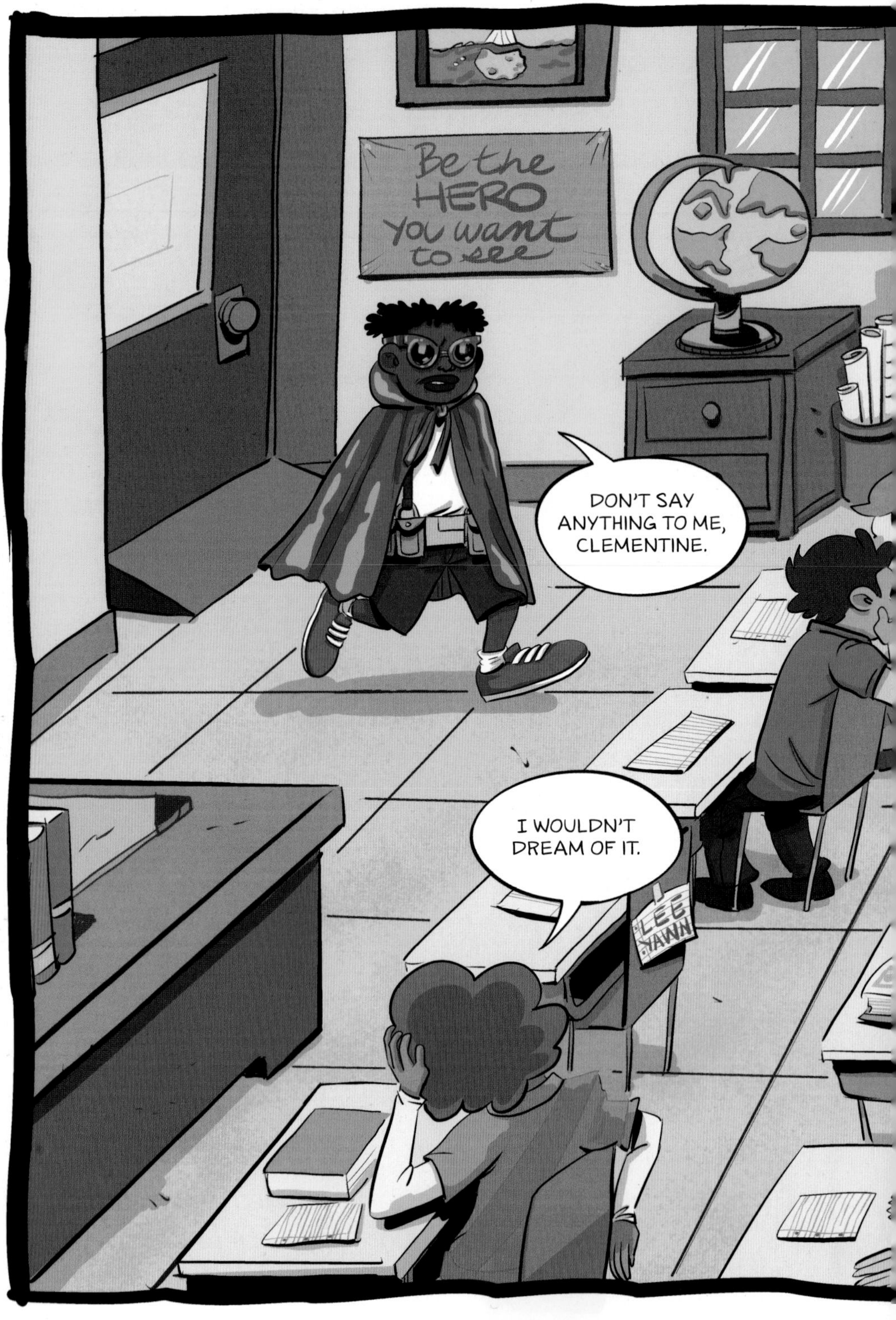
Be the HERO you want to see
DON'T SAY ANYTHING TO ME, CLEMENTINE.
I WOULDN'T DREAM OF IT.
LEE YAWN

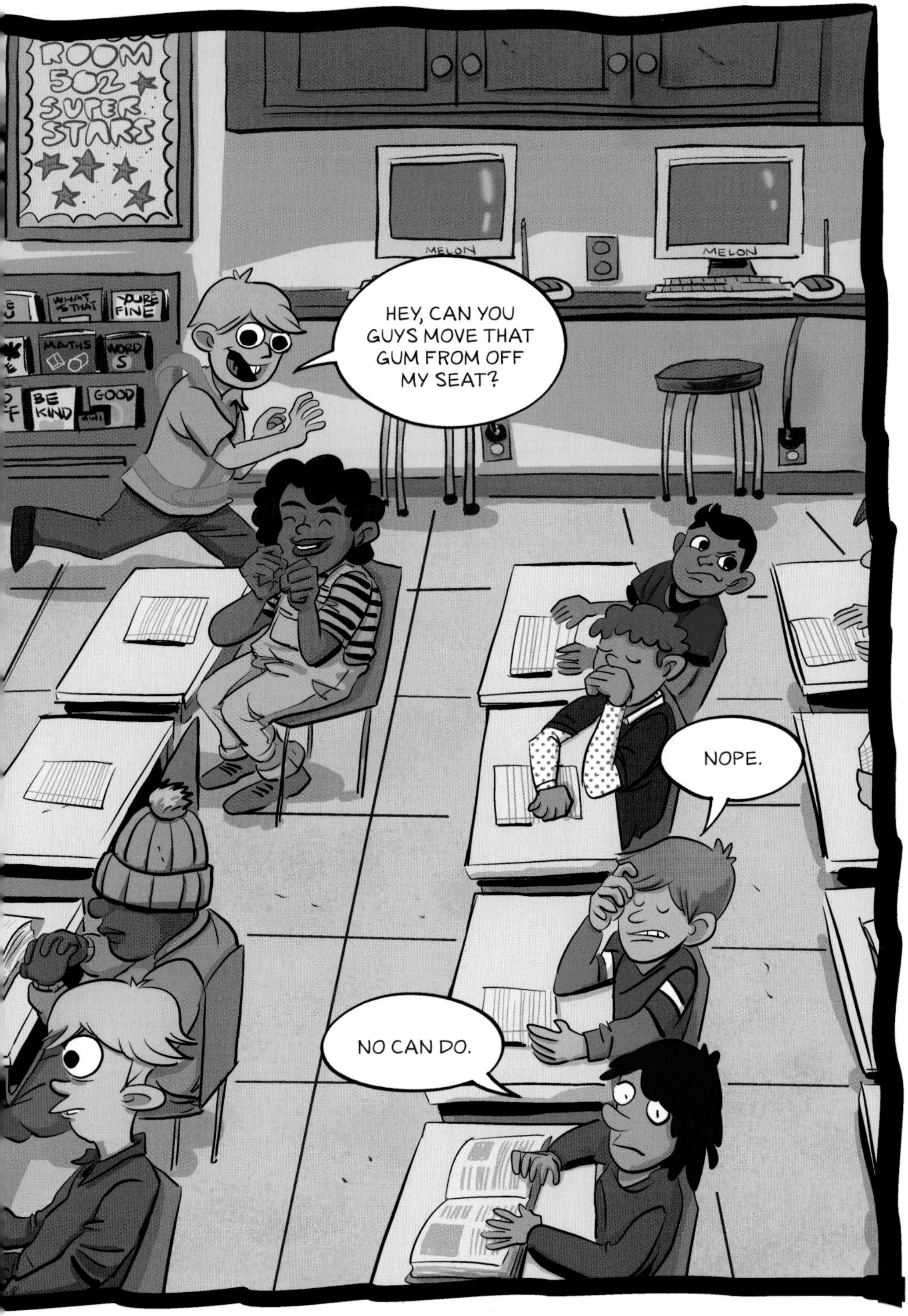
ROOM 502 SUPER STARS
WHAT IS THAT
YOU'RE FINE
MATHS
WORDS
BE KIND
GOOD
MELON
MELON
HEY, CAN YOU GUYS MOVE THAT GUM FROM OFF MY SEAT?
NOPE.
NO CAN DO.

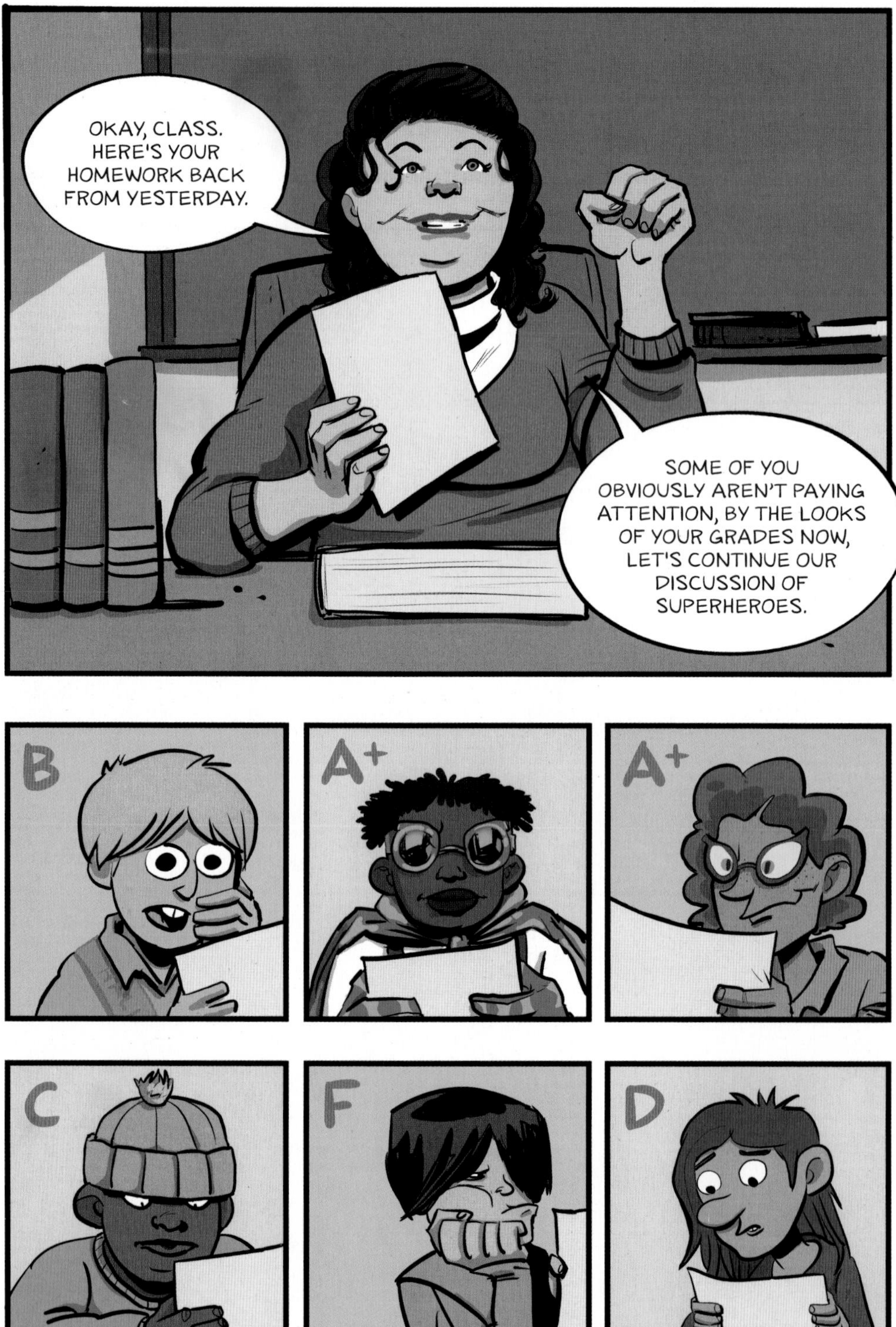
OKAY, CLASS. HERE'S YOUR HOMEWORK BACK FROM YESTERDAY.
SOME OF YOU OBVIOUSLY AREN'T PAYING ATTENTION, BY THE LOOKS OF YOUR GRADES NOW, LET'S CONTINUE OUR DISCUSSION OF SUPERHEROES.
B
A+
A+
C
F
D

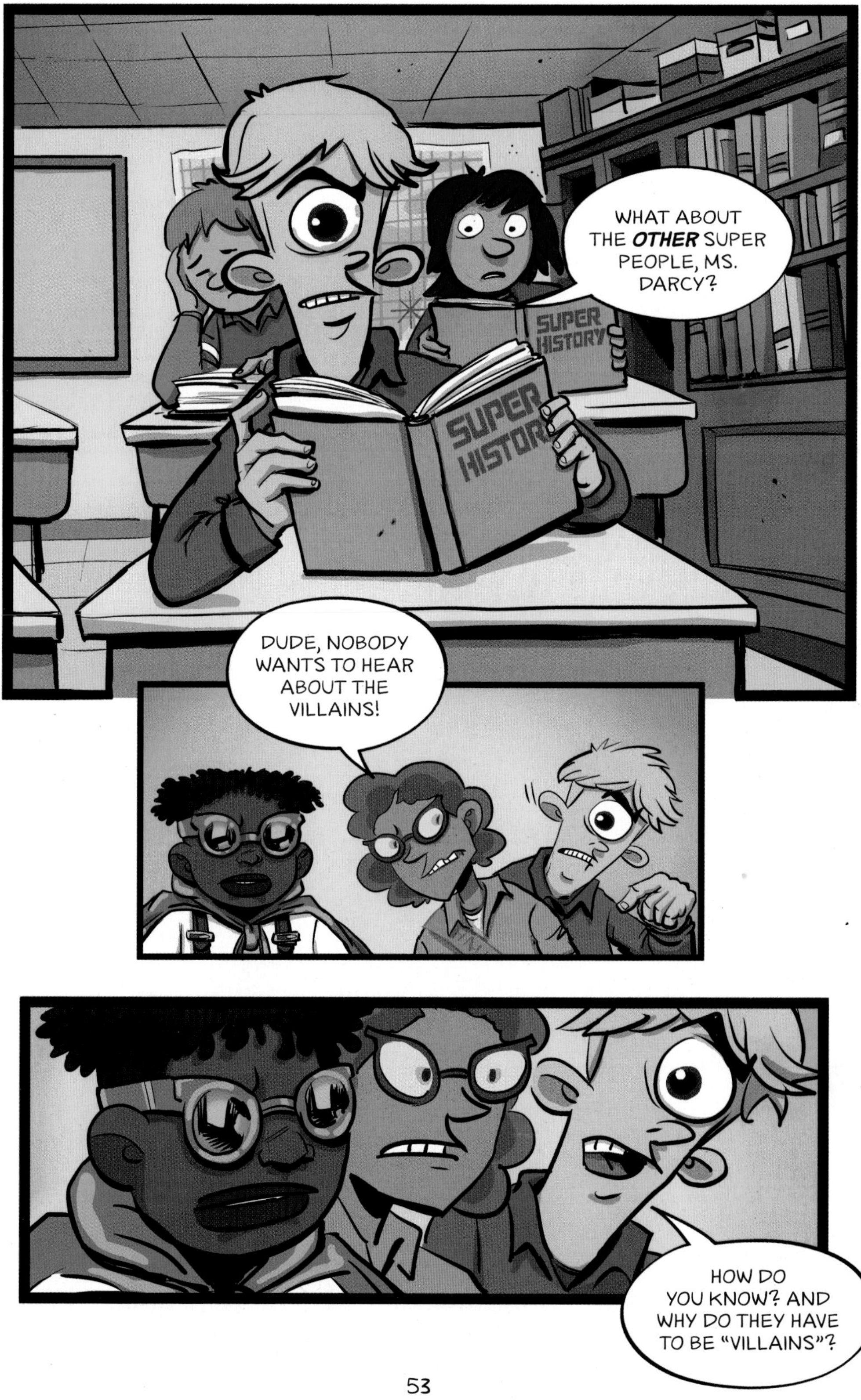
WHAT ABOUT THE *OTHER* SUPER PEOPLE, MS. DARCY?
SUPER HISTORY
SUPER HISTORY
DUDE, NOBODY WANTS TO HEAR ABOUT THE VILLAINS!
HOW DO YOU KNOW? AND WHY DO THEY HAVE TO BE "VILLAINS"?

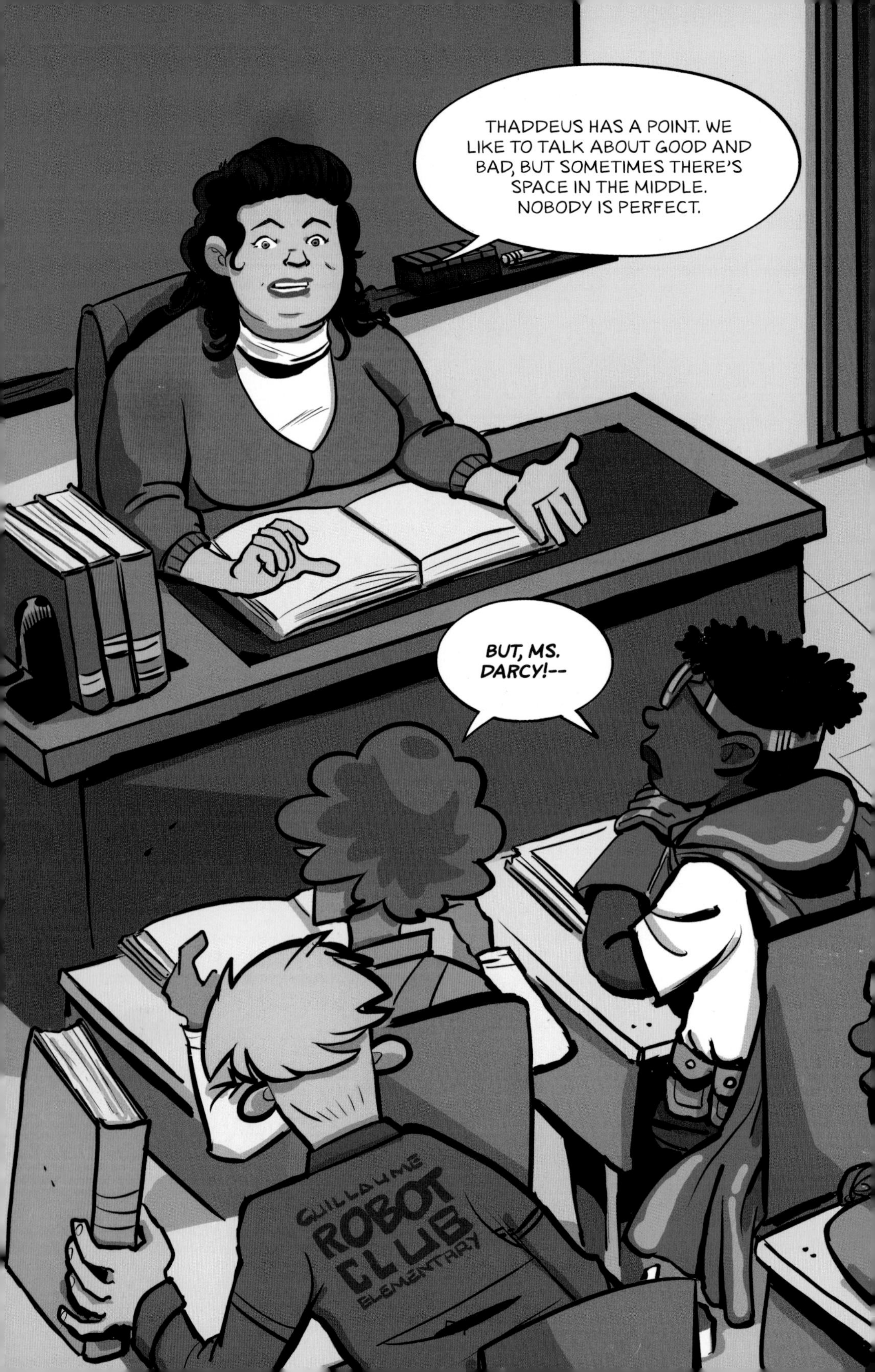
THADDEUS HAS A POINT. WE LIKE TO TALK ABOUT GOOD AND BAD, BUT SOMETIMES THERE'S SPACE IN THE MIDDLE. NOBODY IS PERFECT.
BUT, MS. DARCY!--
GUILLAUME ROBOT CLUB ELEMENTARY

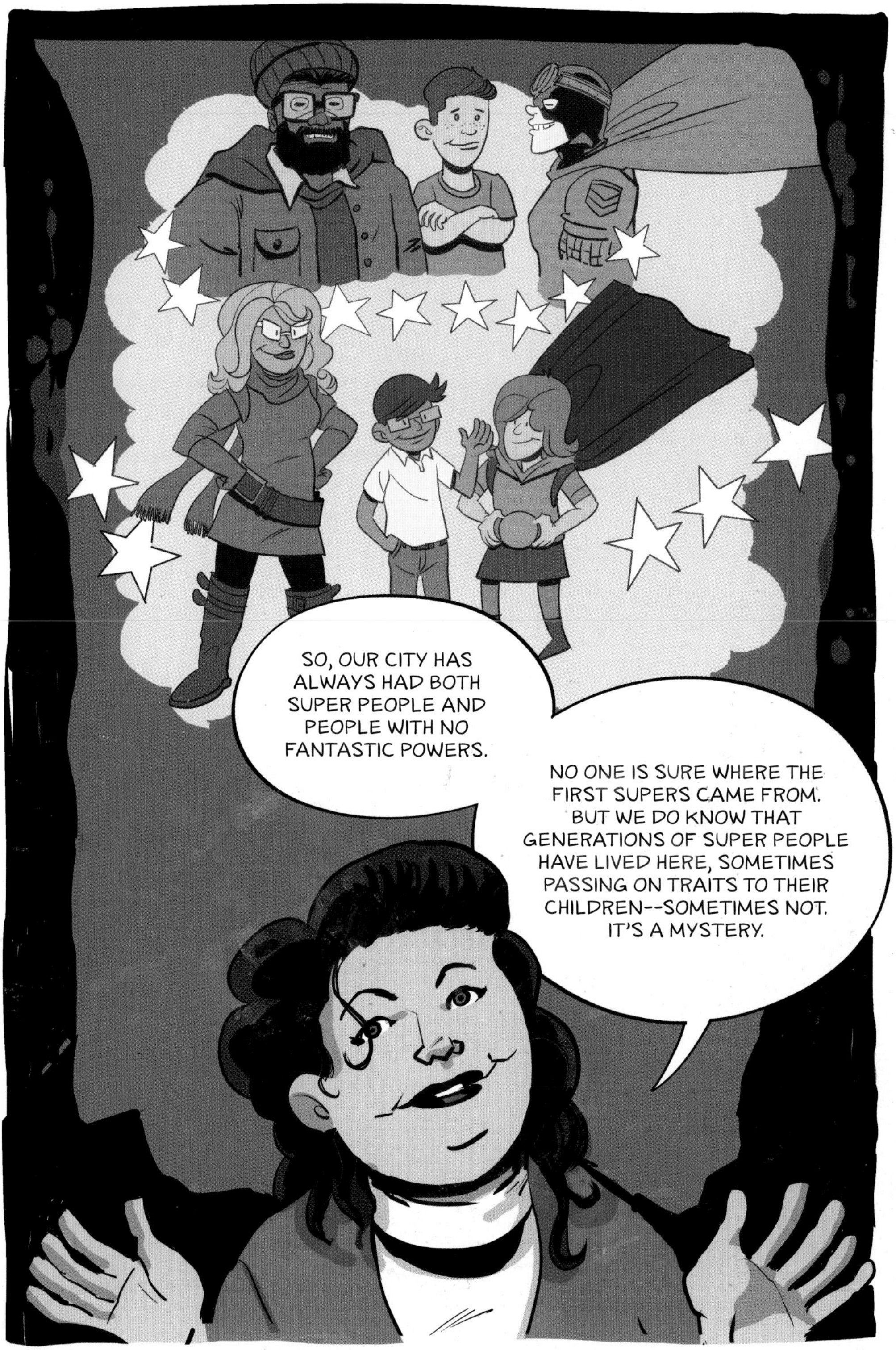
SO, OUR CITY HAS ALWAYS HAD BOTH SUPER PEOPLE AND PEOPLE WITH NO FANTASTIC POWERS.
NO ONE IS SURE WHERE THE FIRST SUPERS CAME FROM. BUT WE DO KNOW THAT GENERATIONS OF SUPER PEOPLE HAVE LIVED HERE, SOMETIMES PASSING ON TRAITS TO THEIR CHILDREN--SOMETIMES NOT. IT'S A MYSTERY.

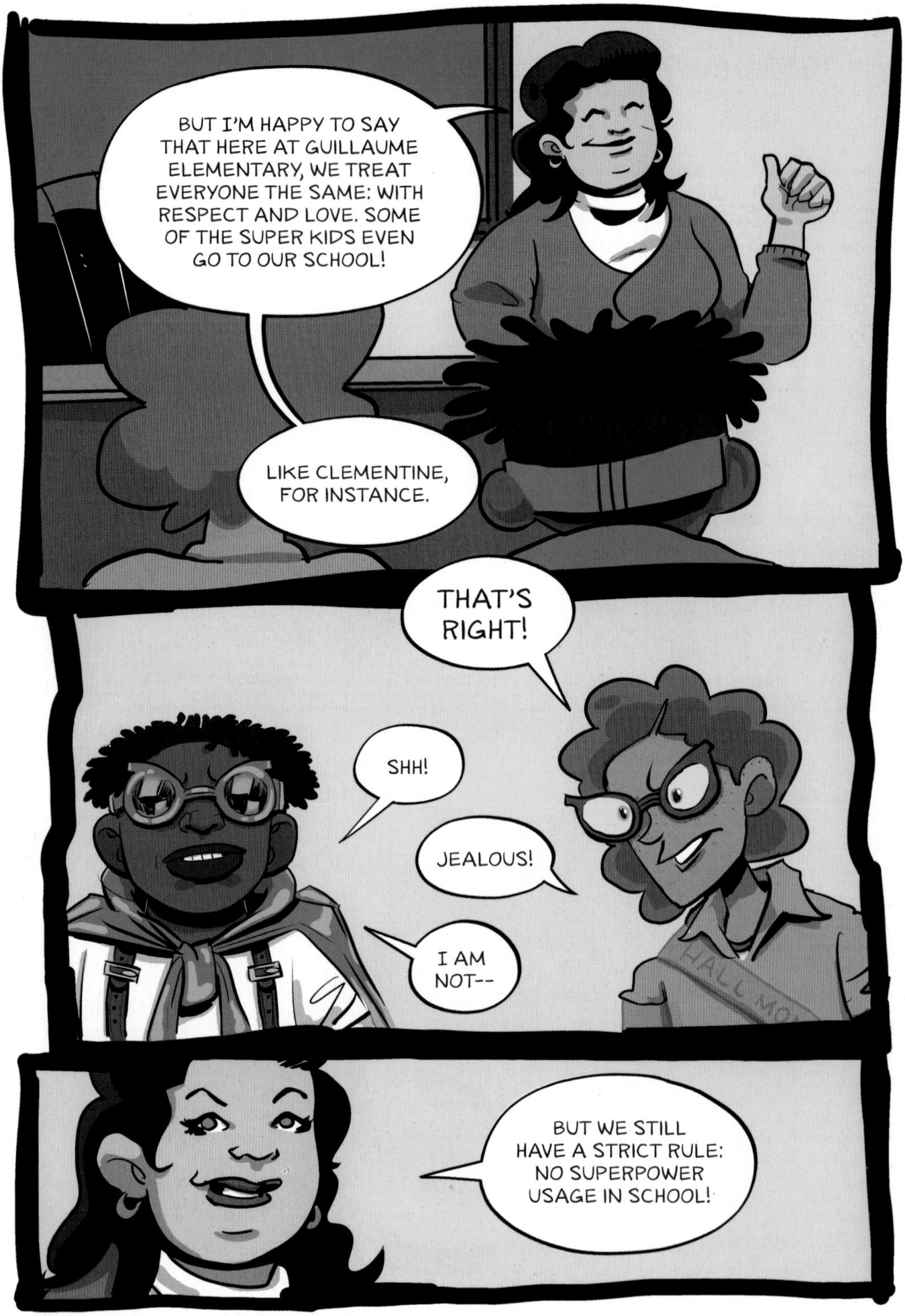
BUT I'M HAPPY TO SAY THAT HERE AT GUILLAUME ELEMENTARY, WE TREAT EVERYONE THE SAME: WITH RESPECT AND LOVE. SOME OF THE SUPER KIDS EVEN GO TO OUR SCHOOL!
LIKE CLEMENTINE, FOR INSTANCE.
THAT'S RIGHT!
SHH!
JEALOUS!
I AM NOT--
BUT WE STILL HAVE A STRICT RULE: NO SUPERPOWER USAGE IN SCHOOL!

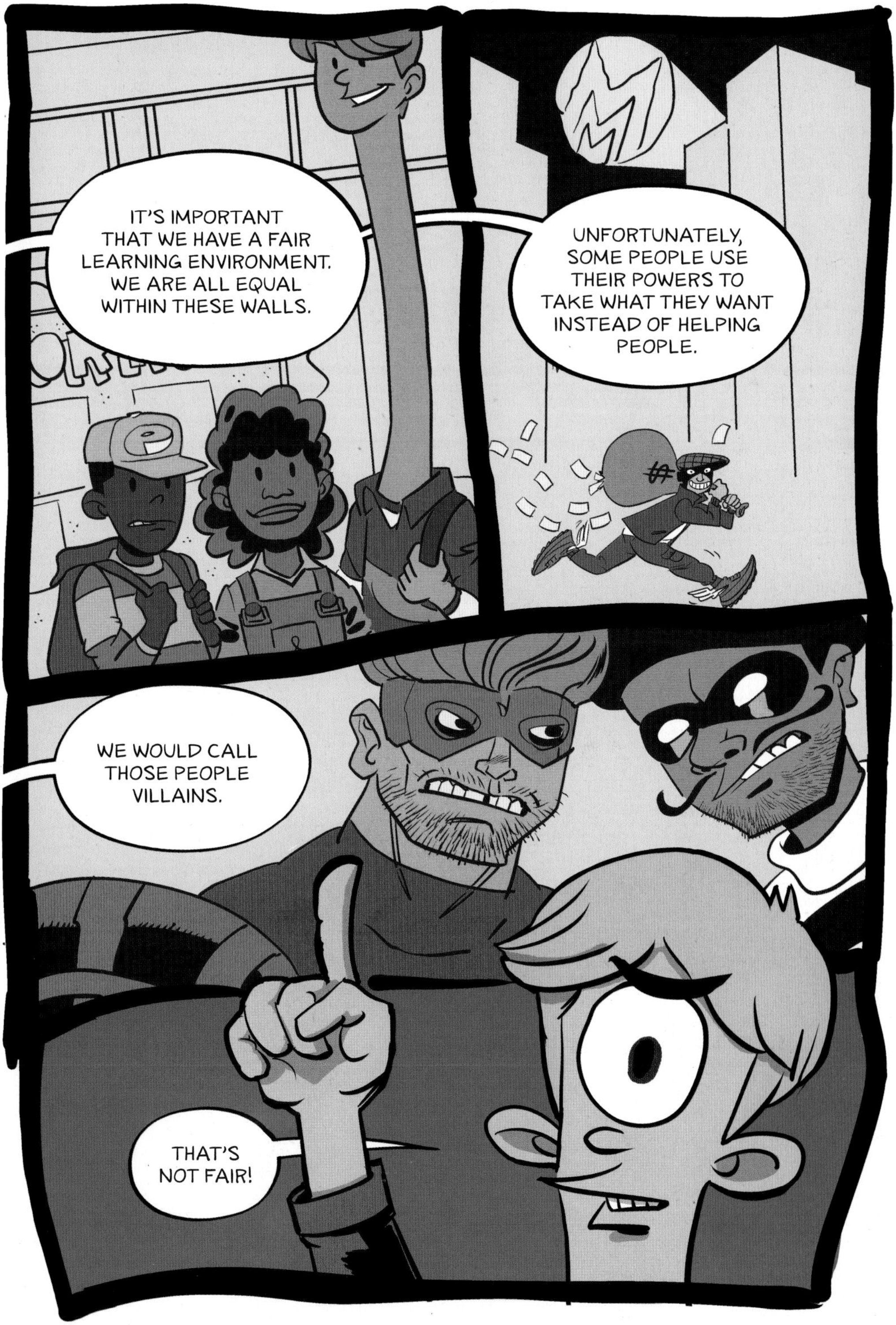

IT'S IMPORTANT THAT WE HAVE A FAIR LEARNING ENVIRONMENT. WE ARE ALL EQUAL WITHIN THESE WALLS.
UNFORTUNATELY, SOME PEOPLE USE THEIR POWERS TO TAKE WHAT THEY WANT INSTEAD OF HELPING PEOPLE.
WE WOULD CALL THOSE PEOPLE VILLAINS.
THAT'S NOT FAIR!

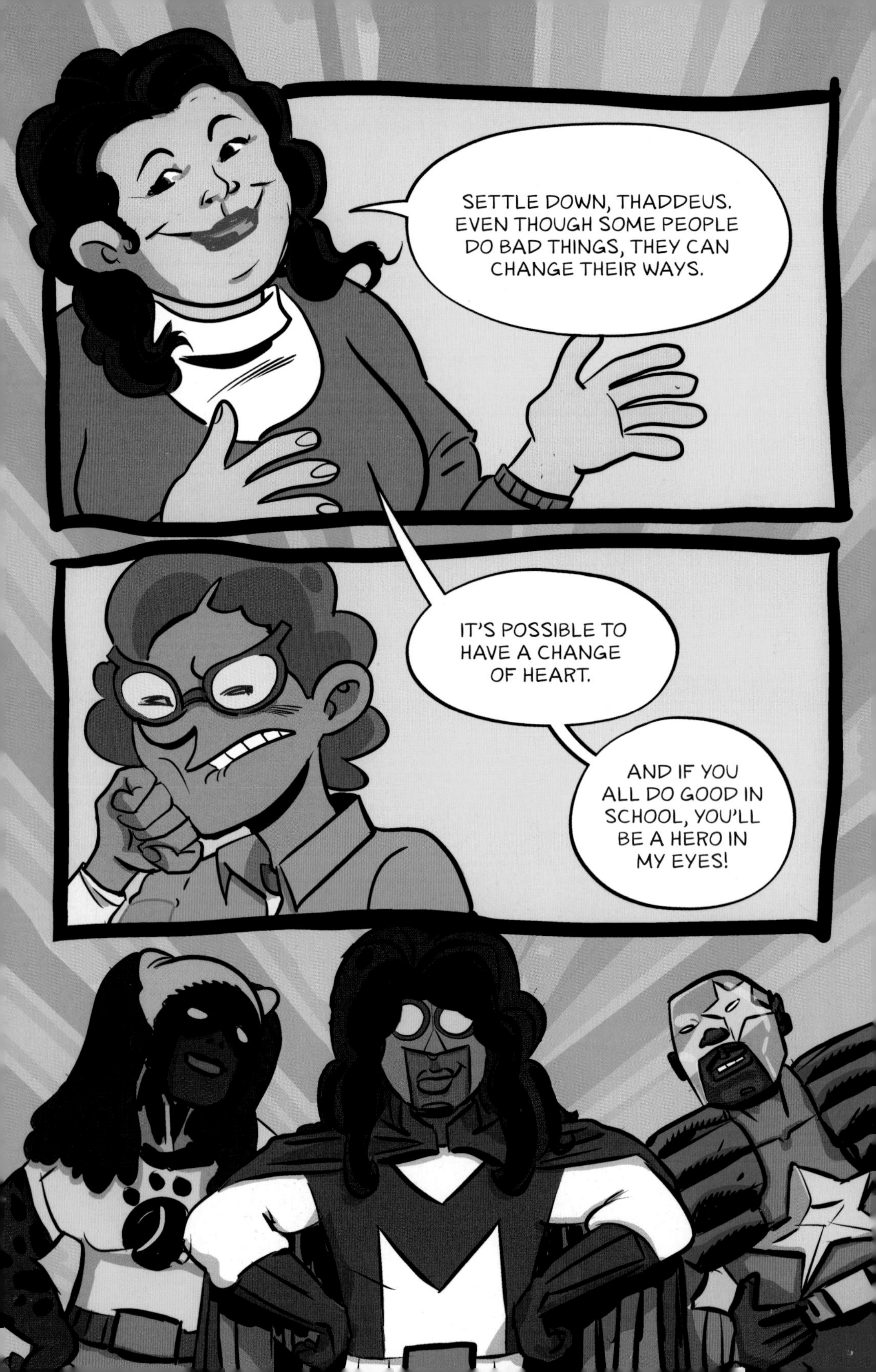
SETTLE DOWN, THADDEUS. EVEN THOUGH SOME PEOPLE DO BAD THINGS, THEY CAN CHANGE THEIR WAYS.
IT'S POSSIBLE TO HAVE A CHANGE OF HEART.
AND IF YOU ALL DO GOOD IN SCHOOL, YOU'LL BE A HERO IN MY EYES!

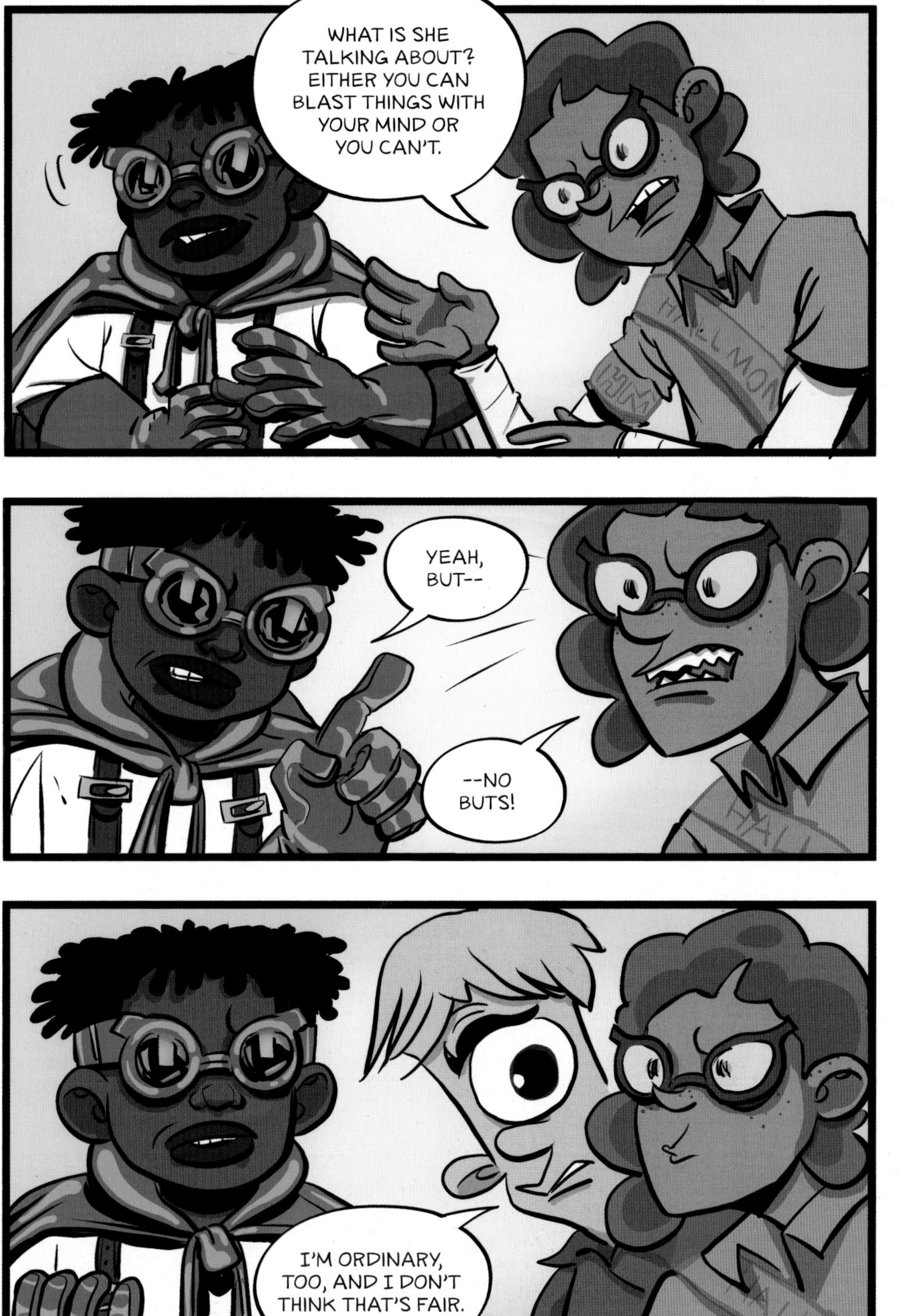
WHAT IS SHE TALKING ABOUT? EITHER YOU CAN BLAST THINGS WITH YOUR MIND OR YOU CAN'T.
HALL MON
YEAH, BUT--
--NO BUTS!
I'M ORDINARY, TOO, AND I DON'T THINK THAT'S FAIR.

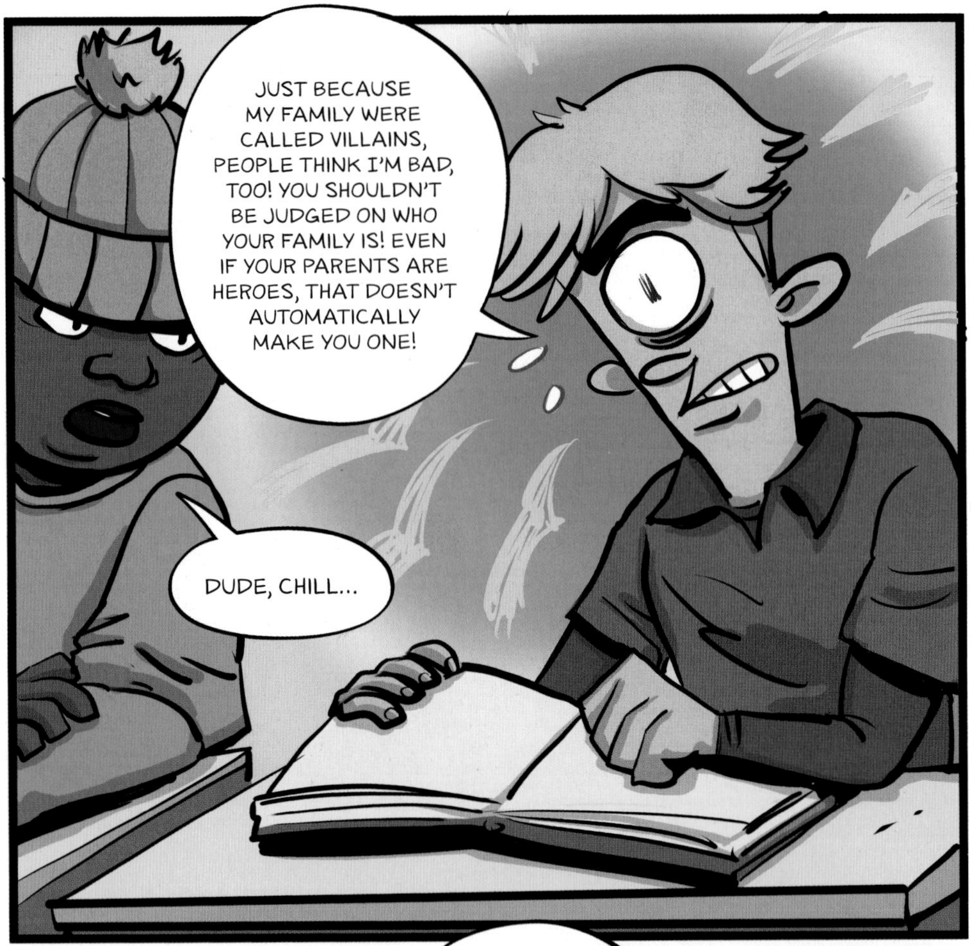
JUST BECAUSE MY FAMILY WERE CALLED VILLAINS, PEOPLE THINK I'M BAD, TOO! YOU SHOULDN'T BE JUDGED ON WHO YOUR FAMILY IS! EVEN IF YOUR PARENTS ARE HEROES, THAT DOESN'T AUTOMATICALLY MAKE YOU ONE!
DUDE, CHILL...

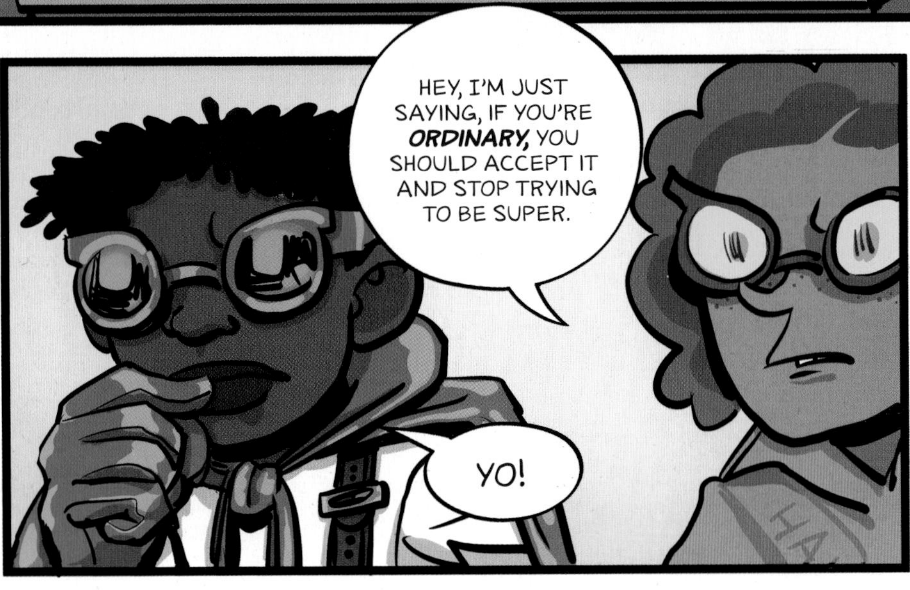
HEY, I'M JUST SAYING, IF YOU'RE **ORDINARY,** YOU SHOULD ACCEPT IT AND STOP TRYING TO BE SUPER.
YO!

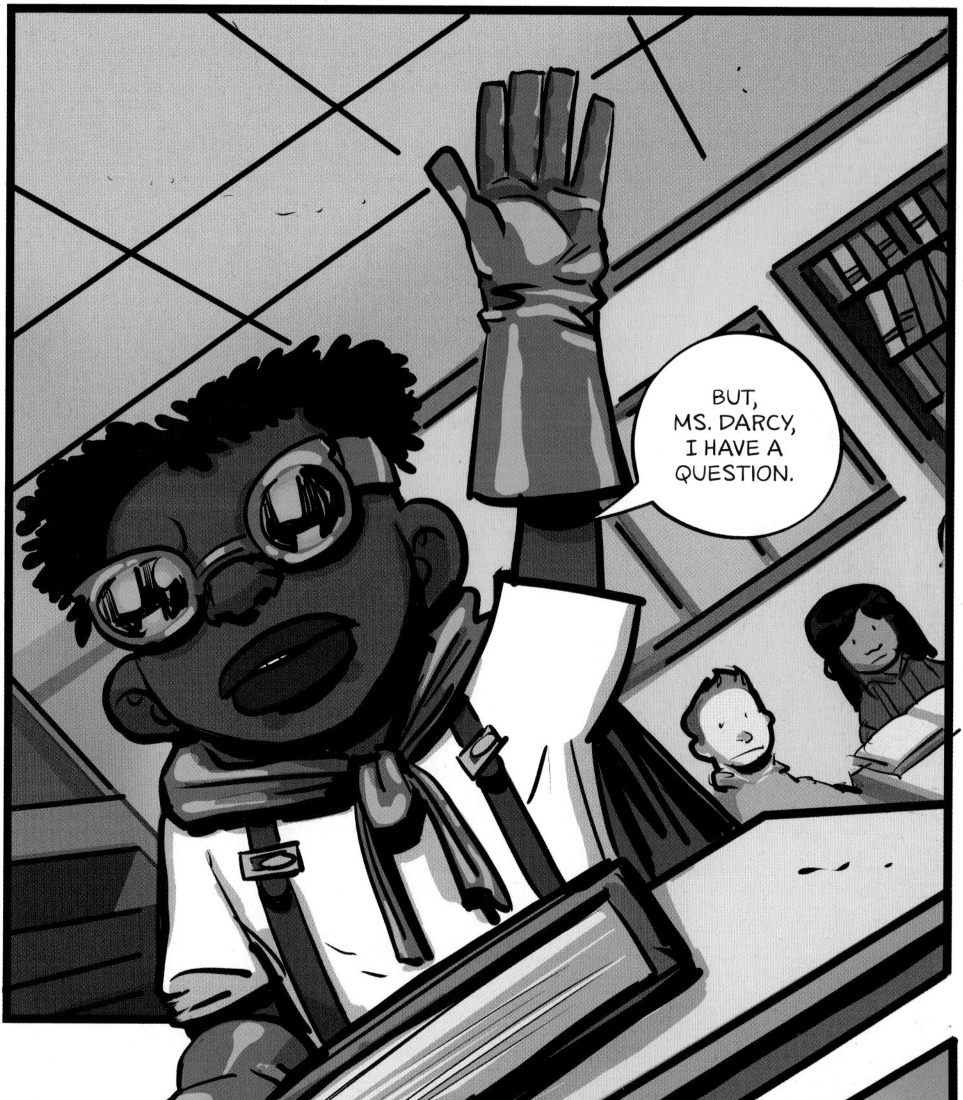
BUT, MS. DARCY, I HAVE A QUESTION.

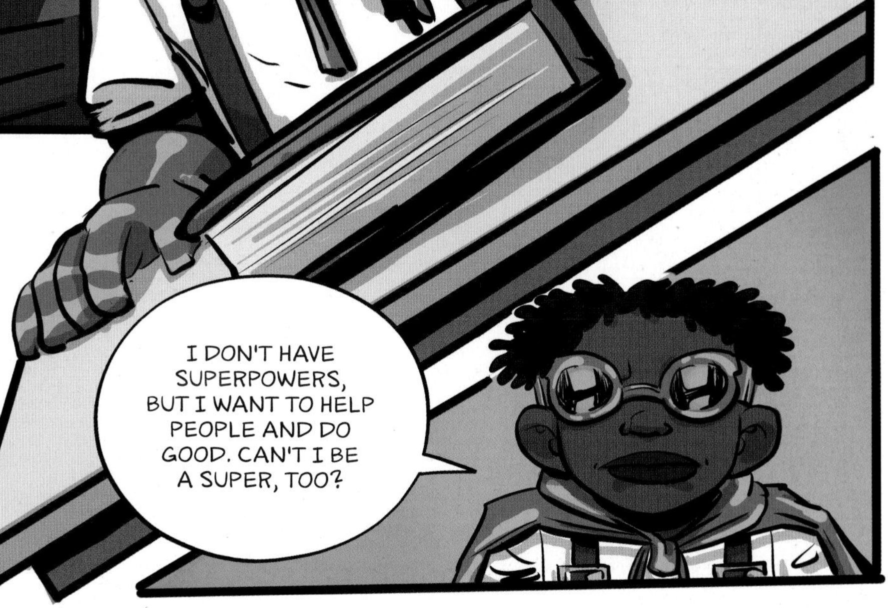
I DON'T HAVE SUPERPOWERS, BUT I WANT TO HELP PEOPLE AND DO GOOD. CAN'T I BE A SUPER, TOO?

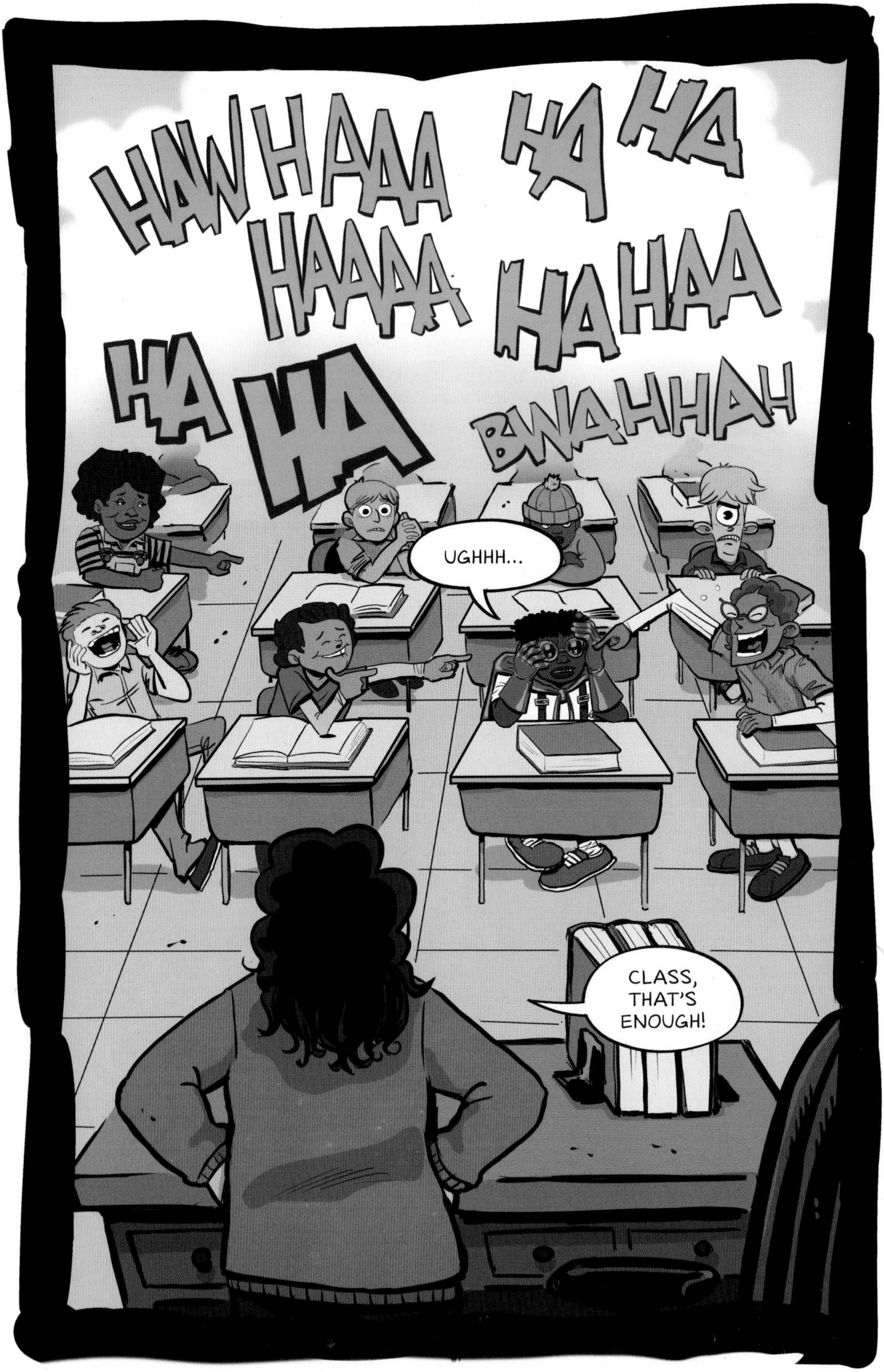
HAW HAAA
HA HA
HAAAA
HAHAA
HA
HA
BWAHHAH
UGHHH...
CLASS, THAT'S ENOUGH!

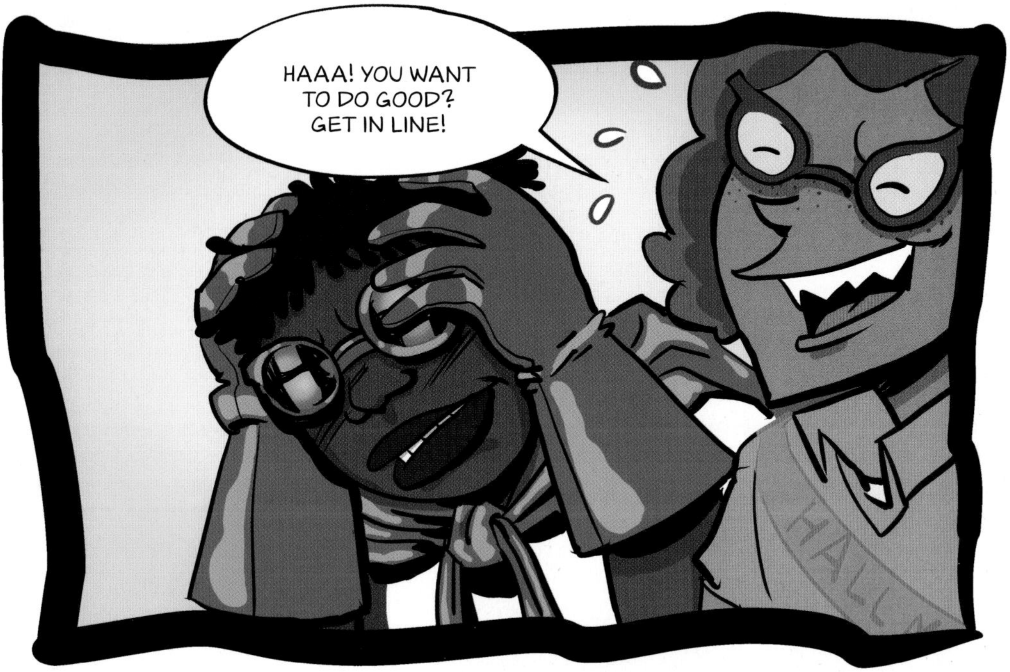
HAAA! YOU WANT TO DO GOOD? GET IN LINE!

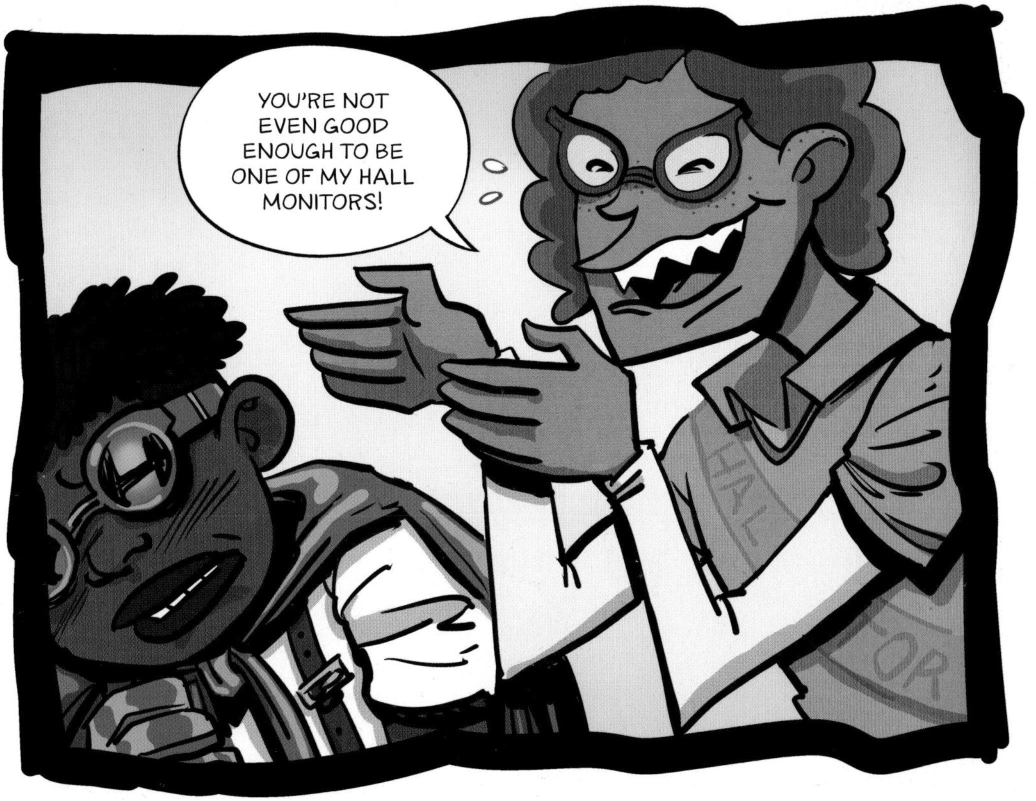
YOU'RE NOT EVEN GOOD ENOUGH TO BE ONE OF MY HALL MONITORS!

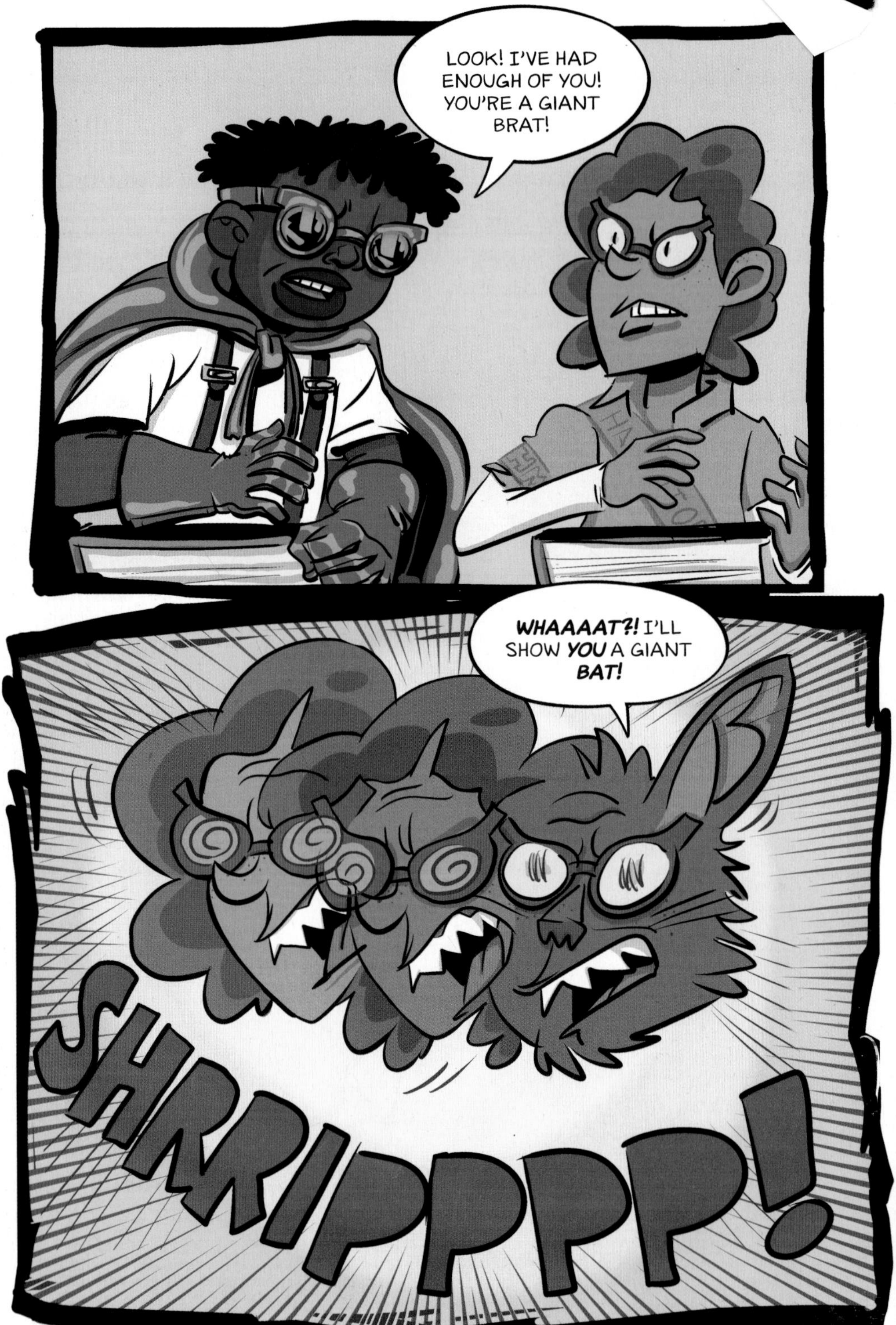
LOOK! I'VE HAD ENOUGH OF YOU! YOU'RE A GIANT BRAT!
WHAAAAT?! I'LL SHOW YOU A GIANT BAT!
SHRRIPPPP!

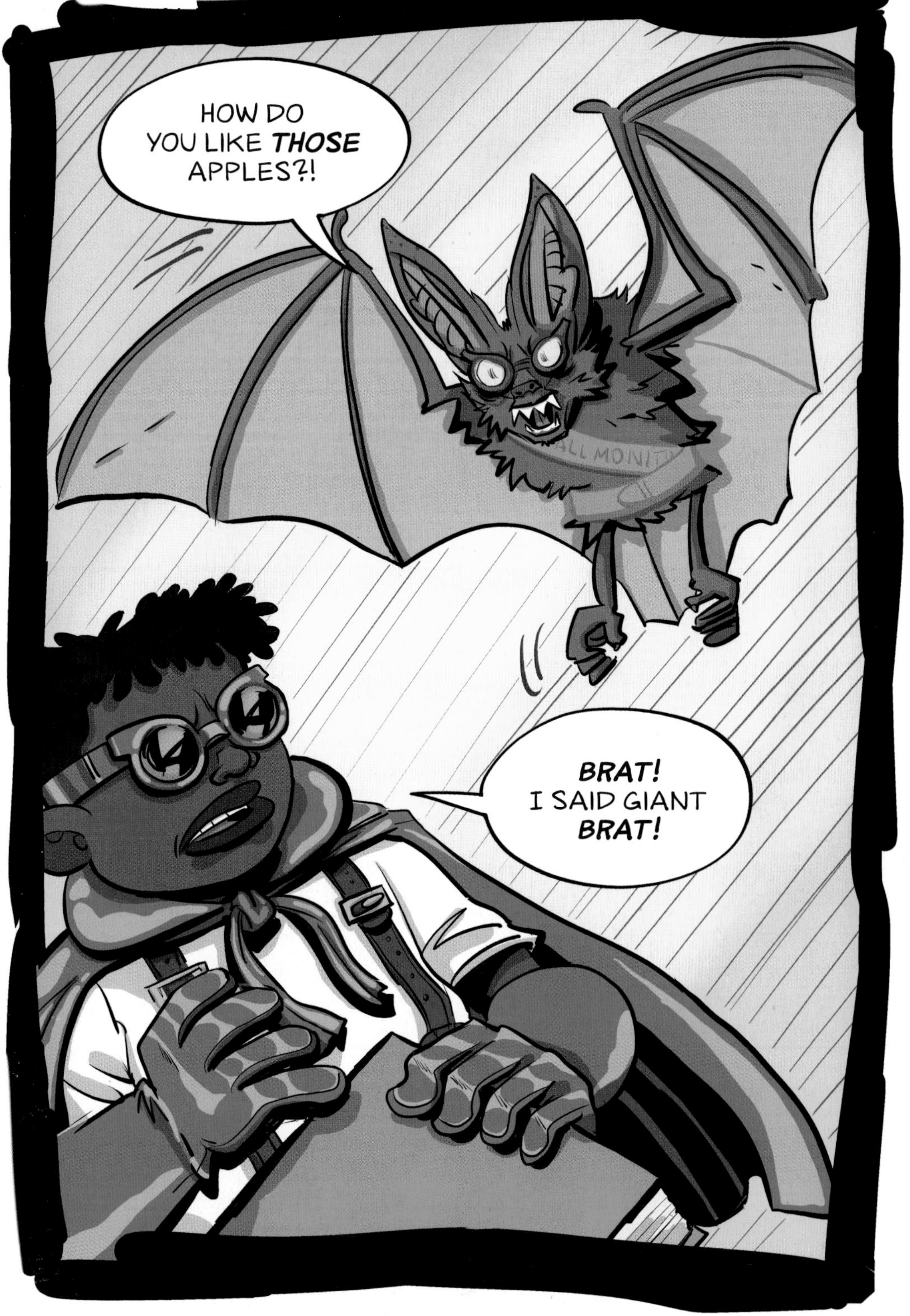
HOW DO YOU LIKE ***THOSE*** APPLES?!
BRAT! I SAID GIANT ***BRAT!***

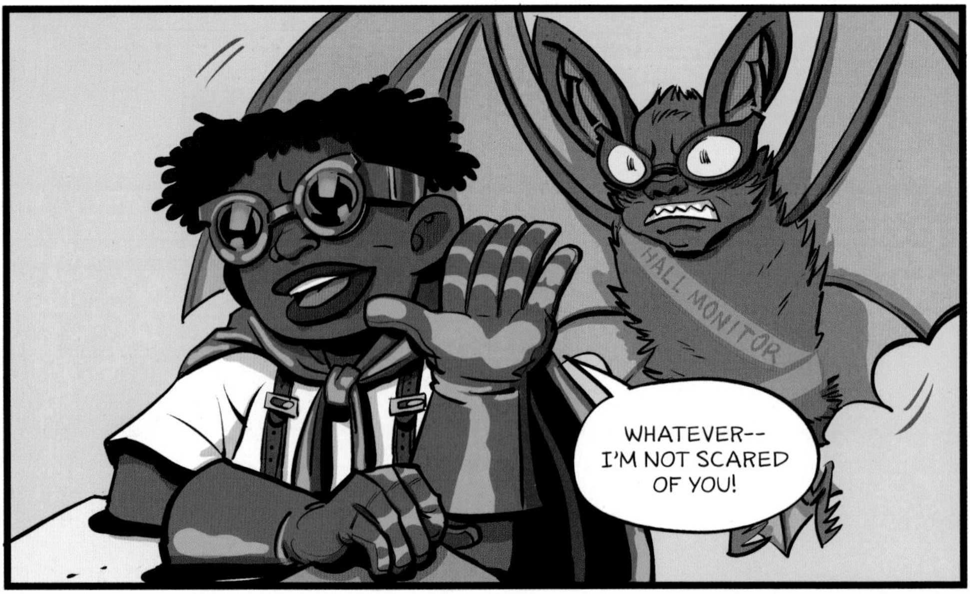
HALL MONITOR
WHATEVER-- I'M NOT SCARED OF YOU!

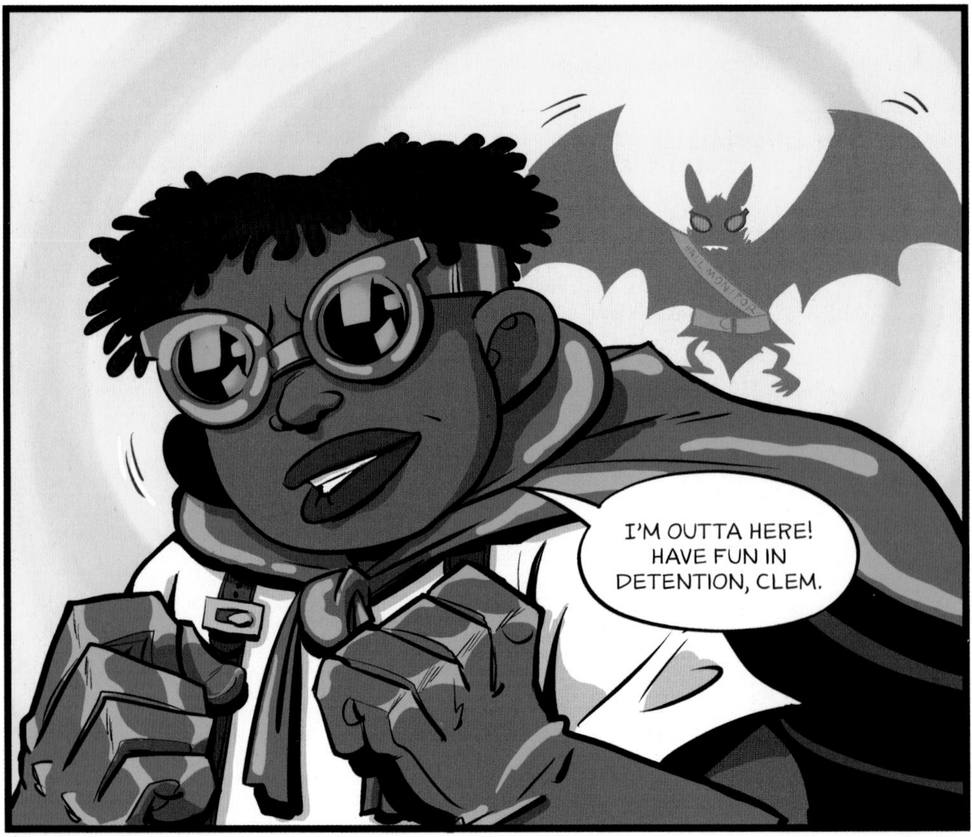
HALL MONITOR
I'M OUTTA HERE! HAVE FUN IN DETENTION, CLEM.

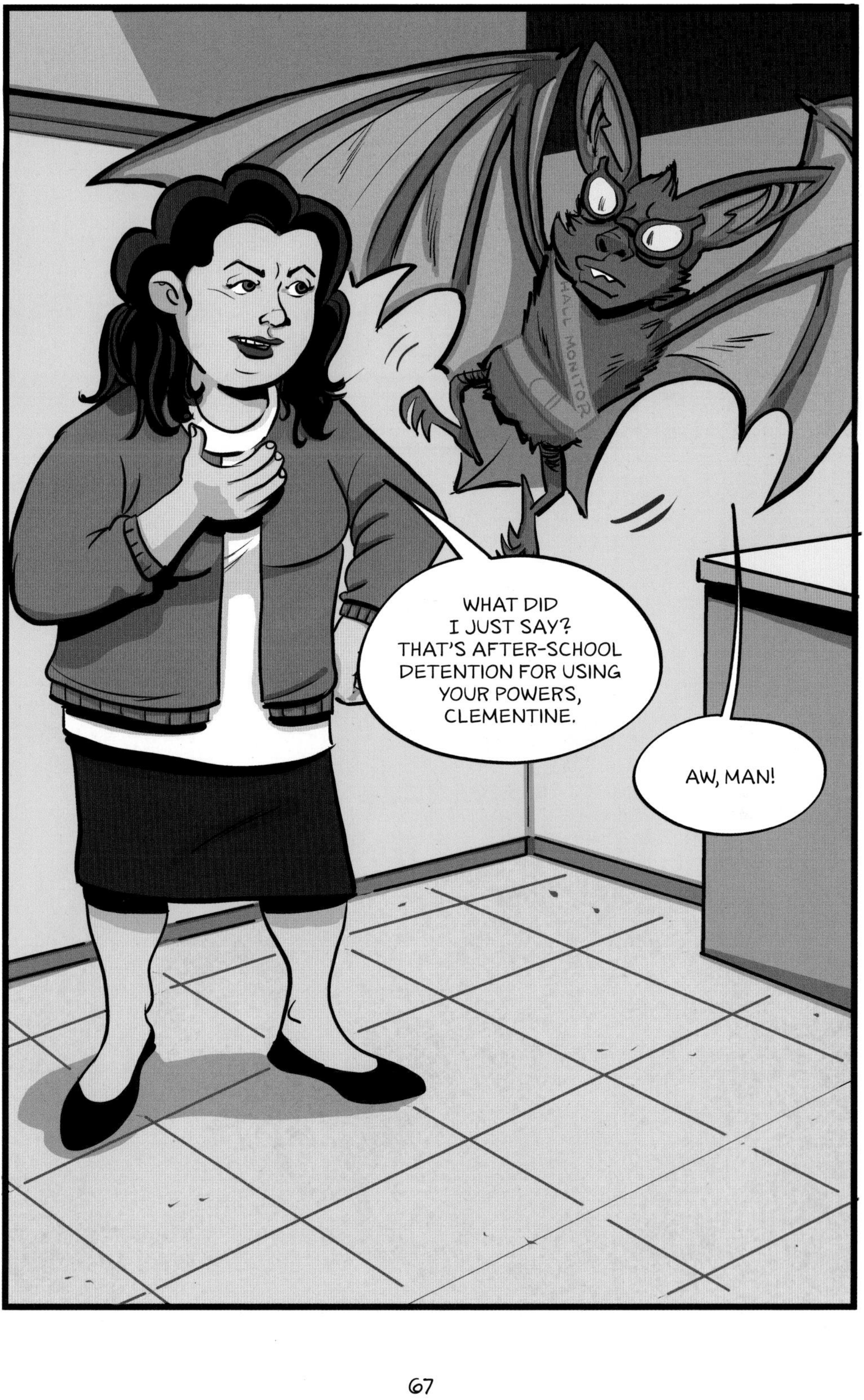
HALL MONITOR
WHAT DID I JUST SAY? THAT'S AFTER-SCHOOL DETENTION FOR USING YOUR POWERS, CLEMENTINE.
AW, MAN!

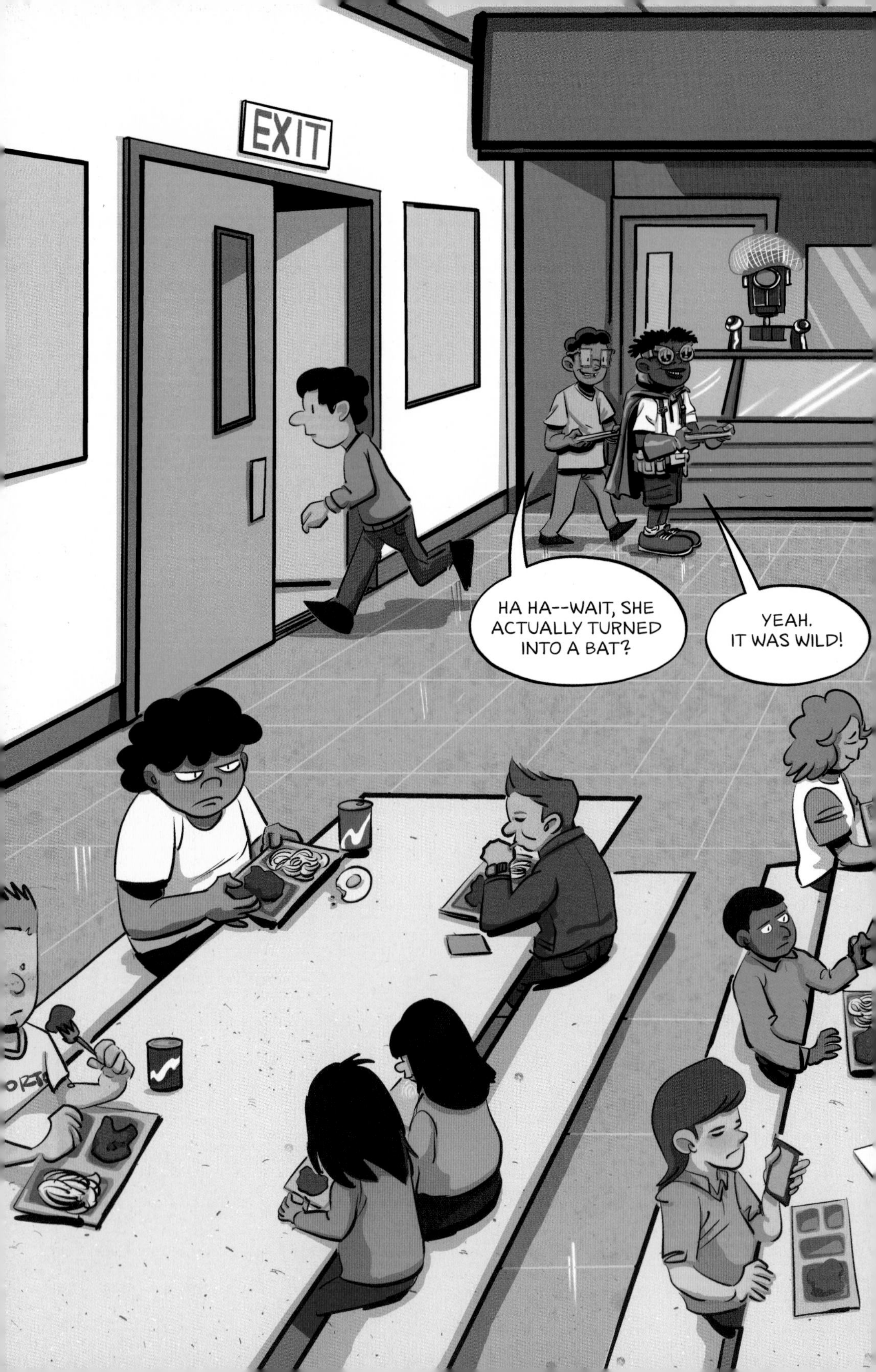
EXIT
HA HA--WAIT, SHE ACTUALLY TURNED INTO A BAT?
YEAH. IT WAS WILD!

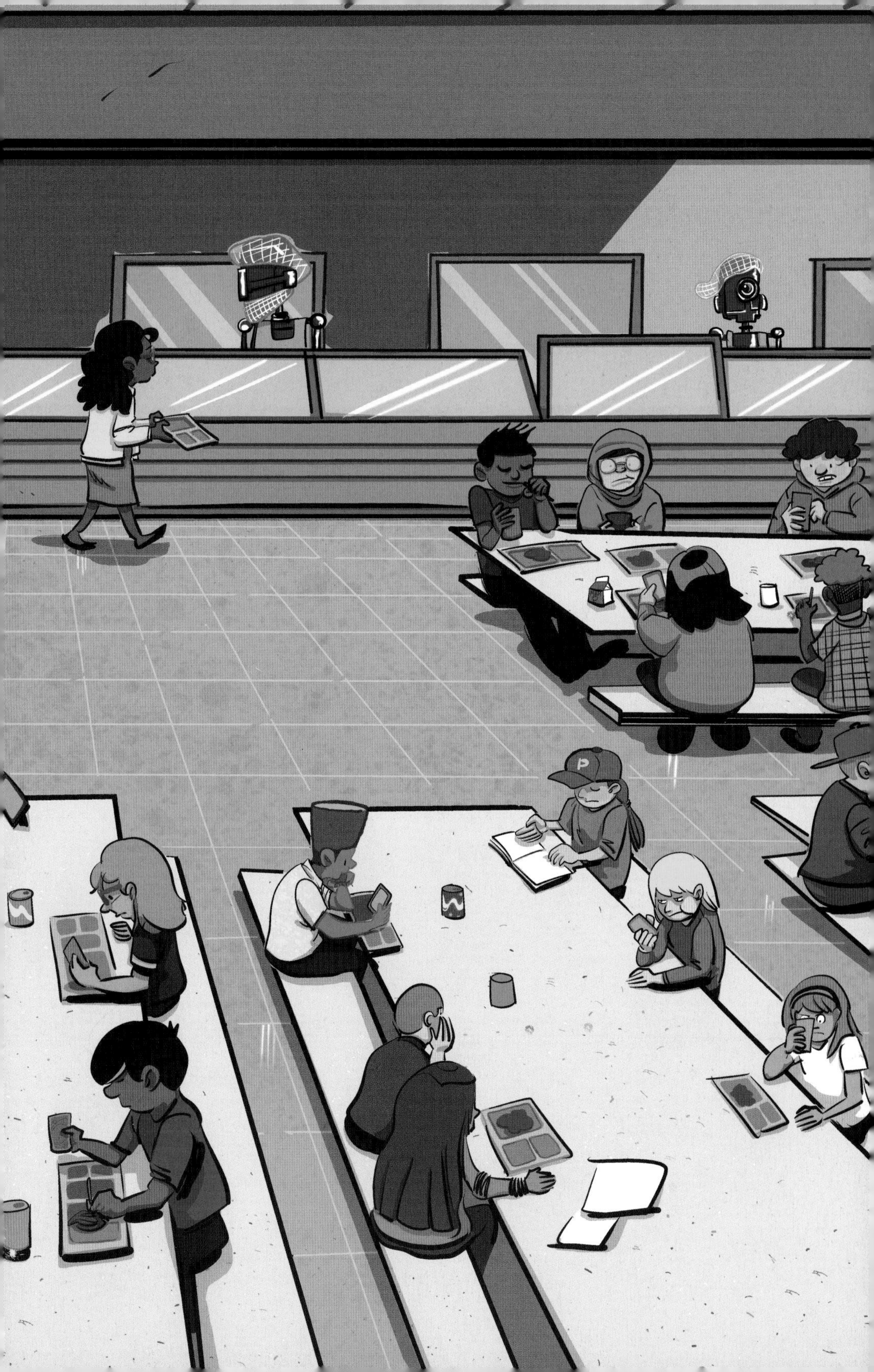

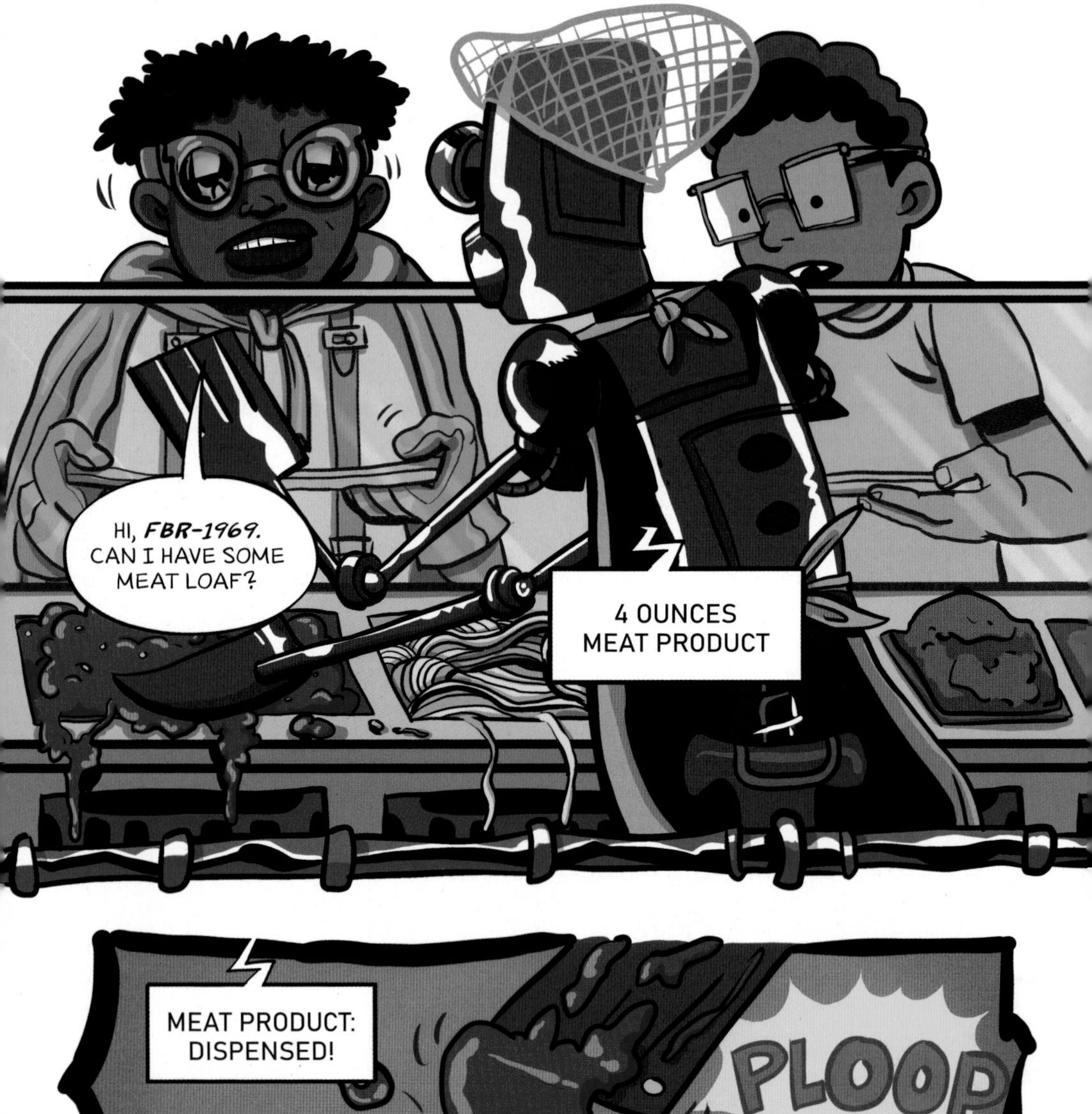
HI, ***FBR-1969.*** CAN I HAVE SOME MEAT LOAF?
4 OUNCES MEAT PRODUCT

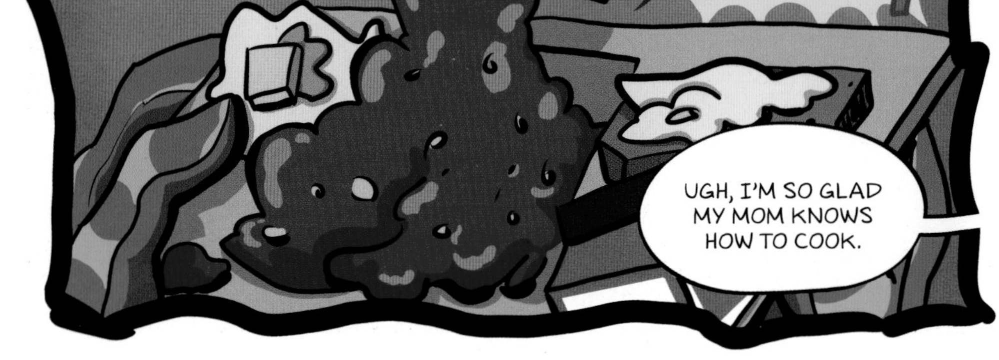
MEAT PRODUCT: DISPENSED!
PLOOP
UGH, I'M SO GLAD MY MOM KNOWS HOW TO COOK.

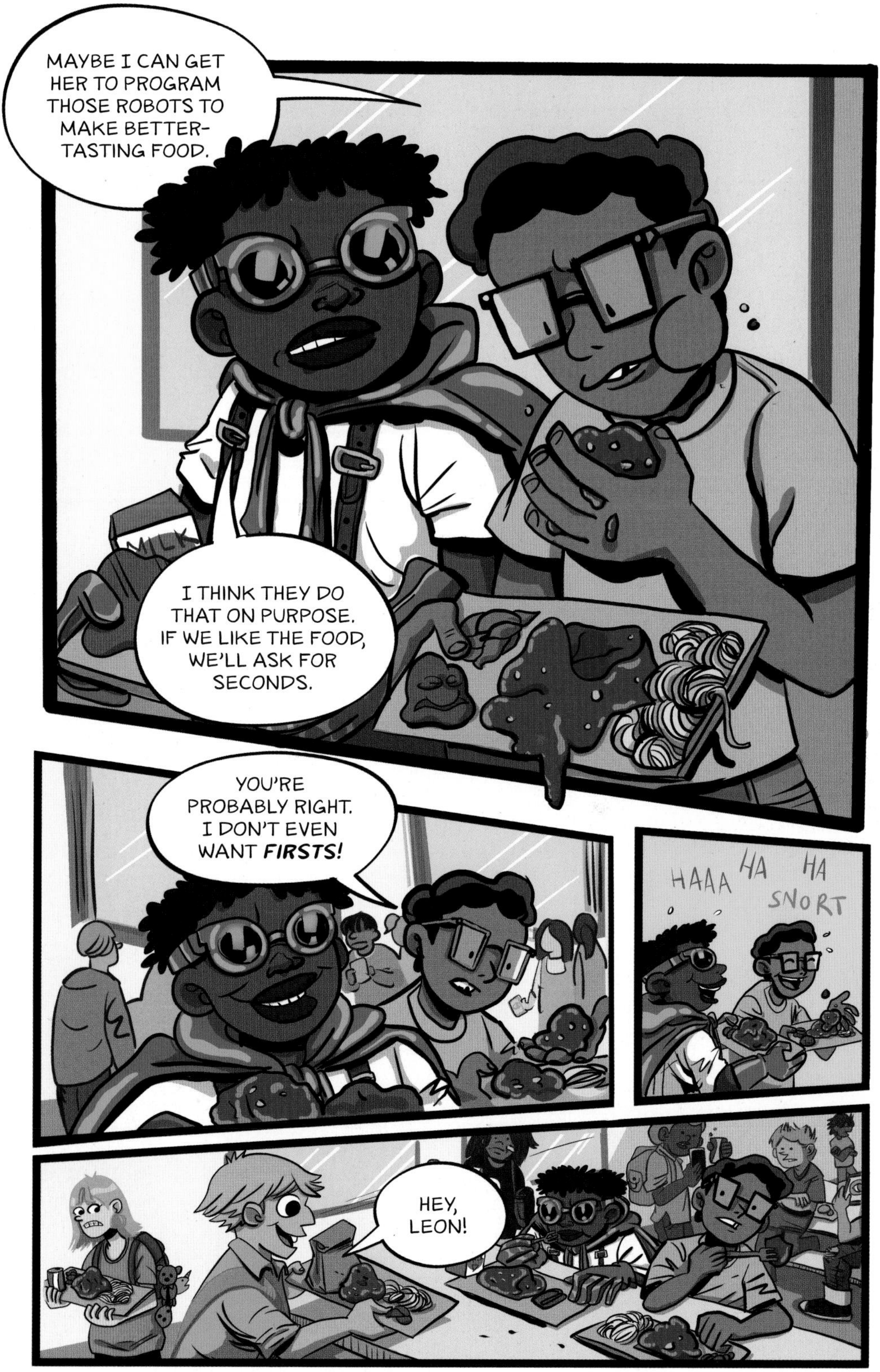
MAYBE I CAN GET HER TO PROGRAM THOSE ROBOTS TO MAKE BETTER-TASTING FOOD.
MILK
I THINK THEY DO THAT ON PURPOSE. IF WE LIKE THE FOOD, WE'LL ASK FOR SECONDS.
YOU'RE PROBABLY RIGHT. I DON'T EVEN WANT ***FIRSTS!***
HAAA HA HA SNORT
HEY, LEON!

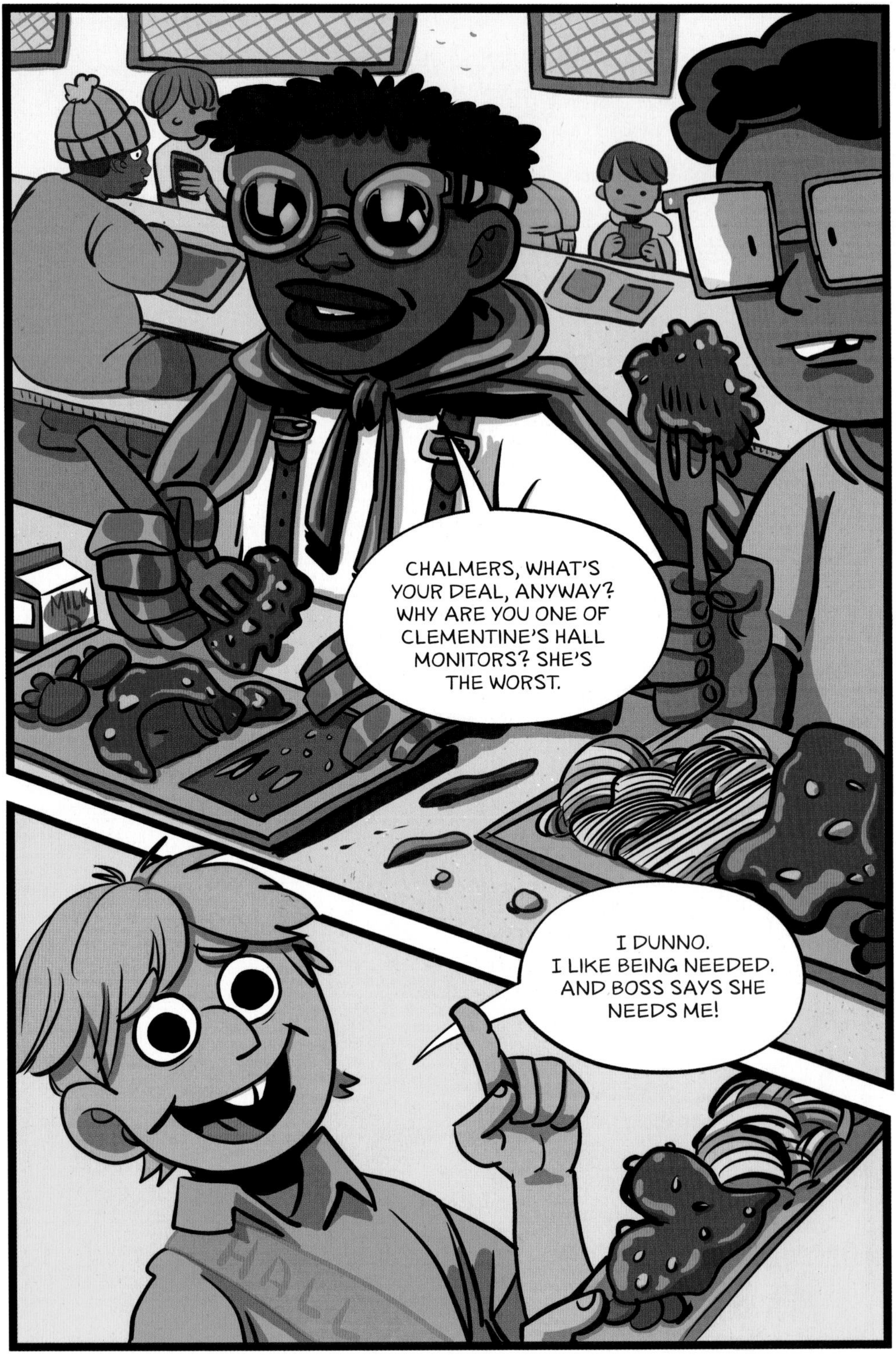
CHALMERS, WHAT'S YOUR DEAL, ANYWAY? WHY ARE YOU ONE OF CLEMENTINE'S HALL MONITORS? SHE'S THE WORST.
I DUNNO. I LIKE BEING NEEDED. AND BOSS SAYS SHE NEEDS ME!
HALL

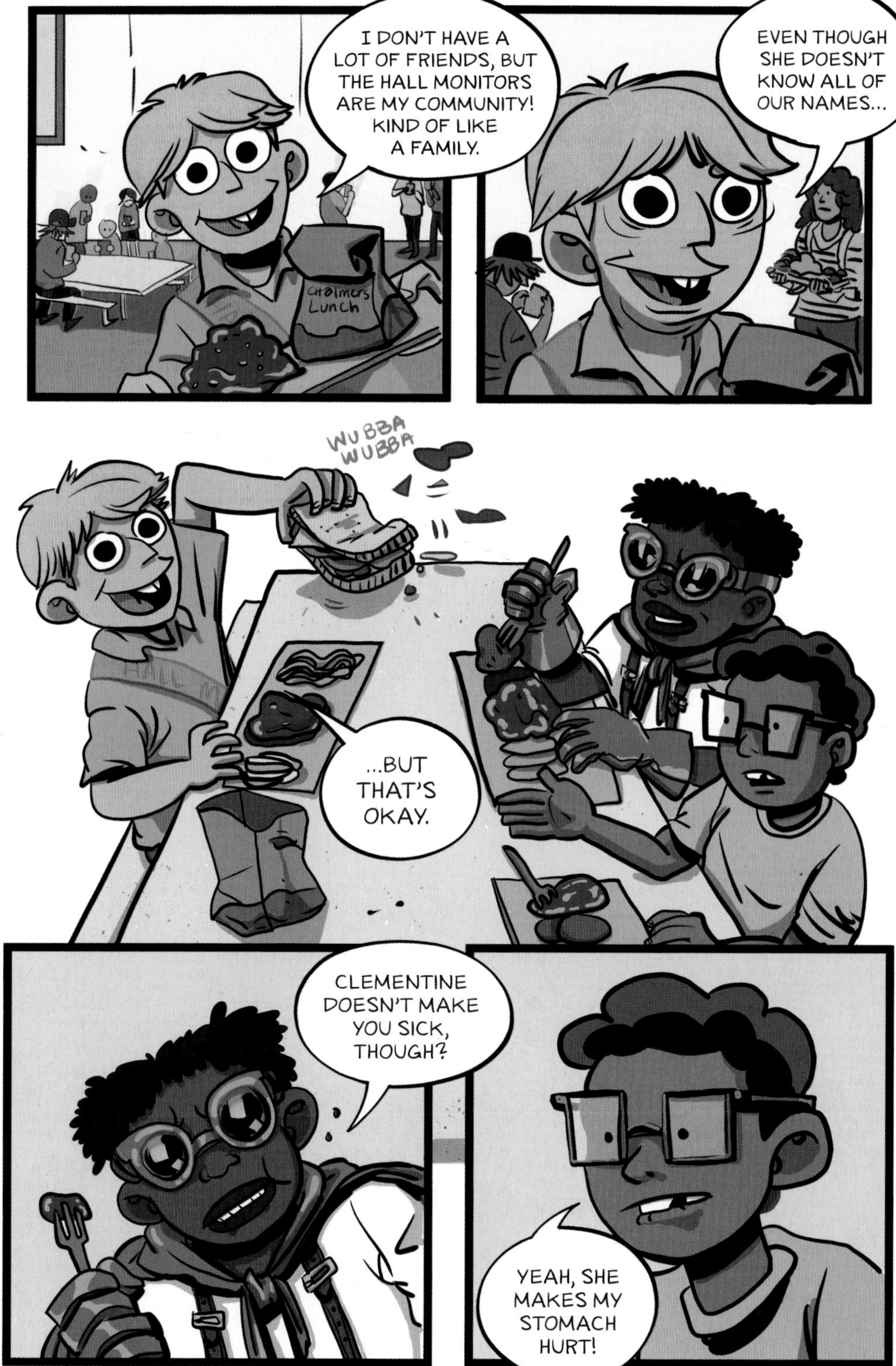

I DON'T HAVE A LOT OF FRIENDS, BUT THE HALL MONITORS ARE MY COMMUNITY! KIND OF LIKE A FAMILY.
Chalmers Lunch
EVEN THOUGH SHE DOESN'T KNOW ALL OF OUR NAMES...
WUBBA WUBBA
...BUT THAT'S OKAY.
CLEMENTINE DOESN'T MAKE YOU SICK, THOUGH?
YEAH, SHE MAKES MY STOMACH HURT!

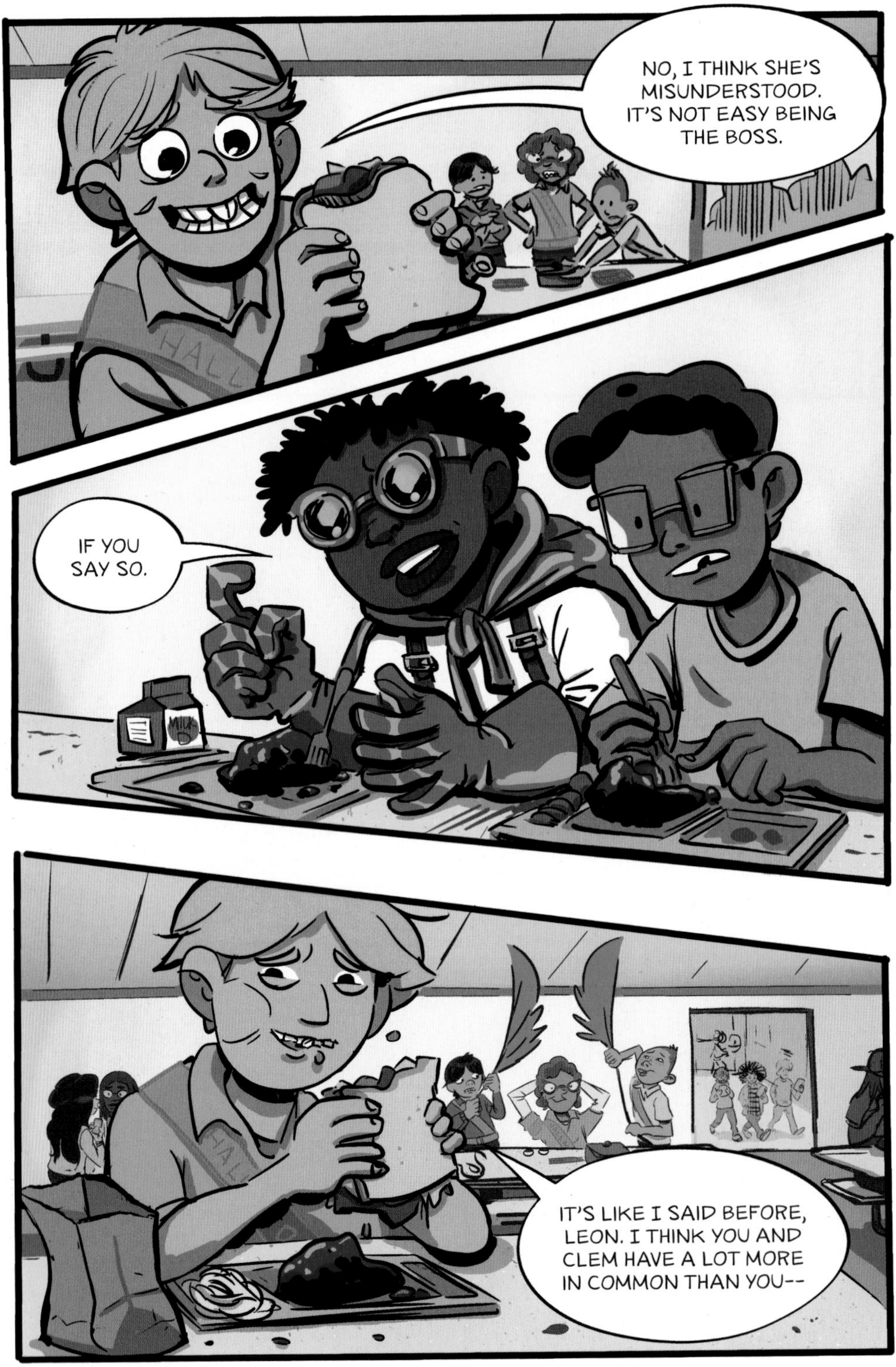
NO, I THINK SHE'S MISUNDERSTOOD. IT'S NOT EASY BEING THE BOSS.
HALL
IF YOU SAY SO.
IT'S LIKE I SAID BEFORE, LEON. I THINK YOU AND CLEM HAVE A LOT MORE IN COMMON THAN YOU--

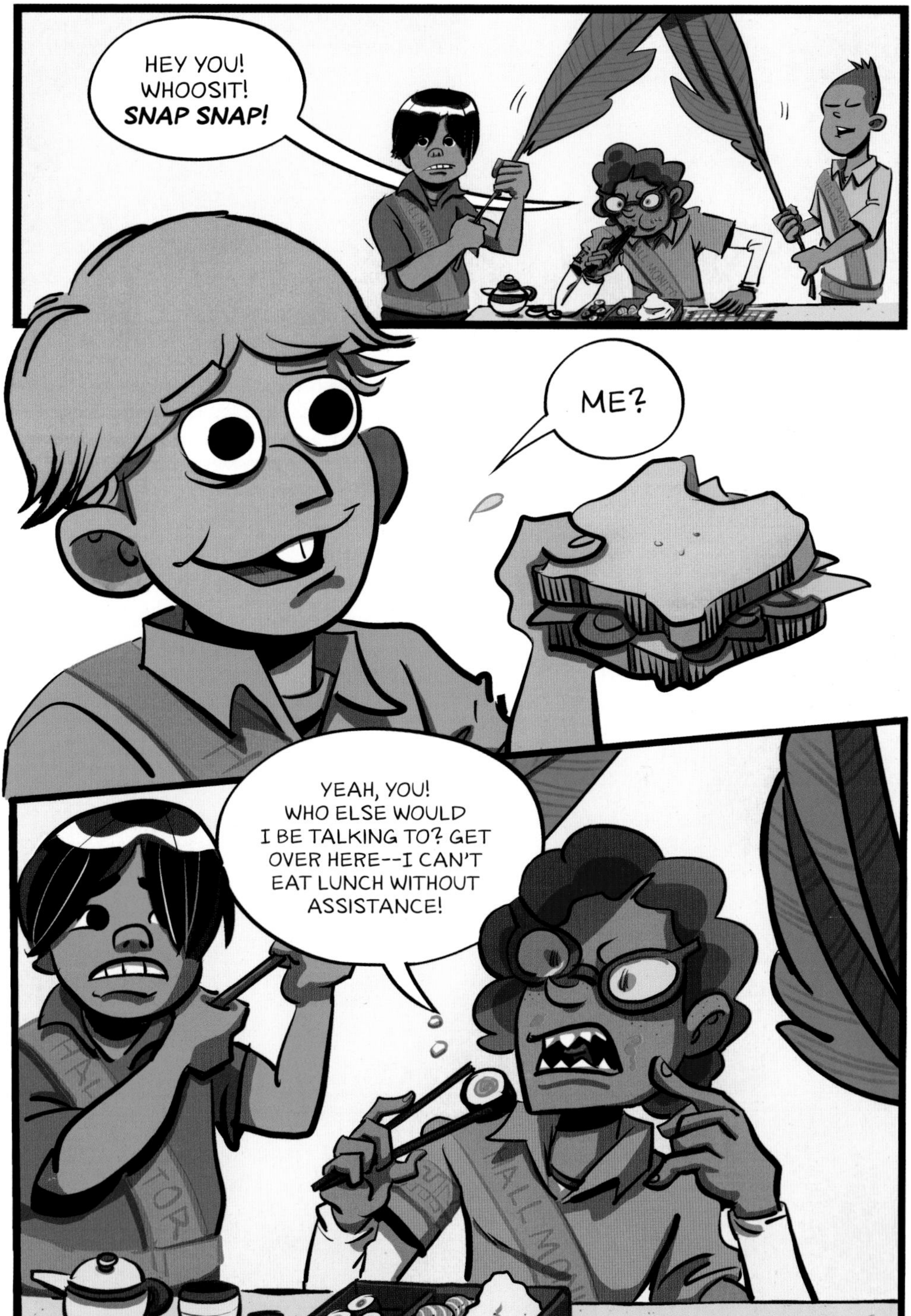
HEY YOU!
WHOOSIT!
SNAP SNAP!
ME?
YEAH, YOU! WHO ELSE WOULD I BE TALKING TO? GET OVER HERE--I CAN'T EAT LUNCH WITHOUT ASSISTANCE!

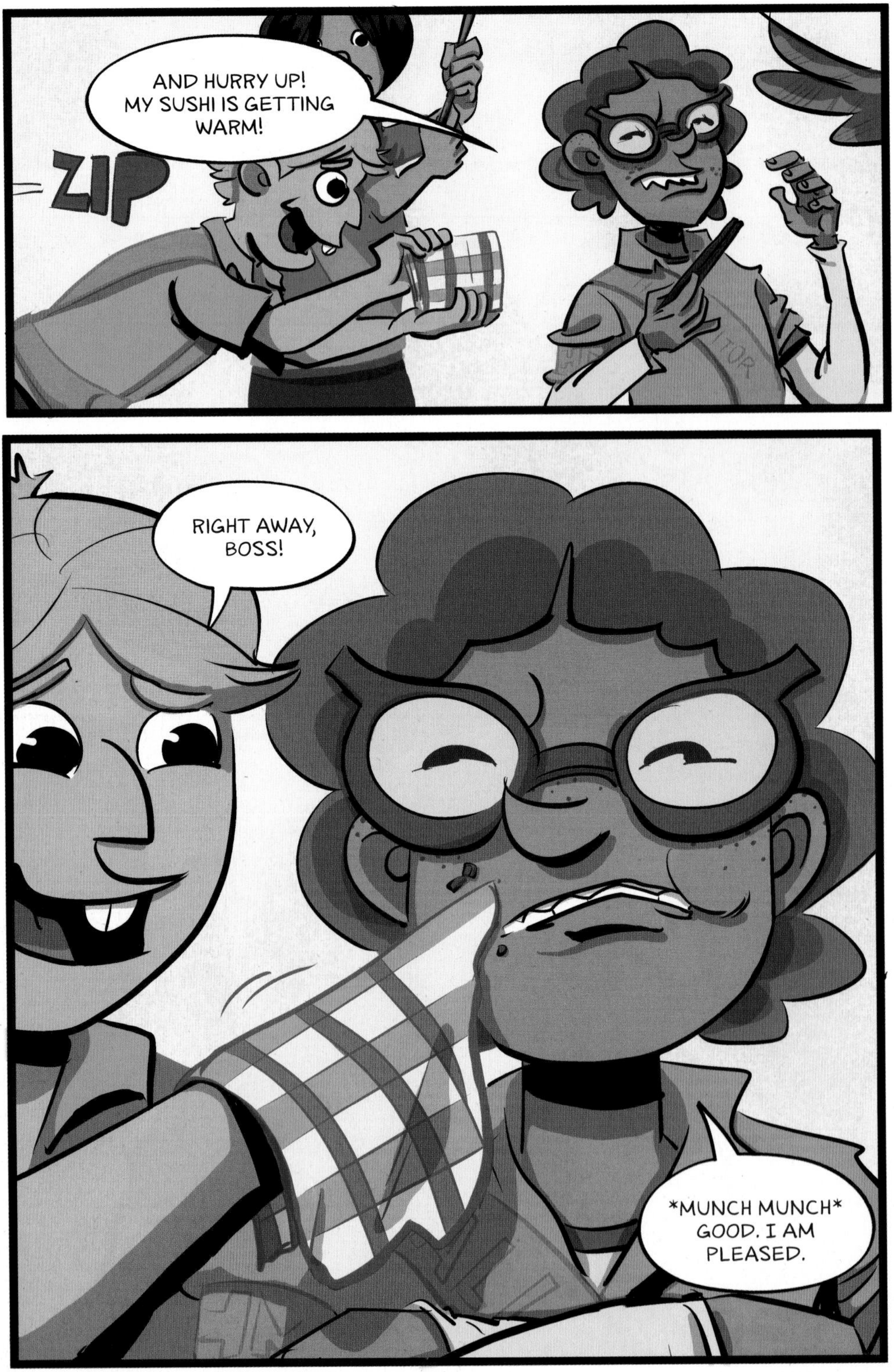
AND HURRY UP! MY SUSHI IS GETTING WARM!
ZIP
RIGHT AWAY, BOSS!
MUNCH MUNCH GOOD. I AM PLEASED.

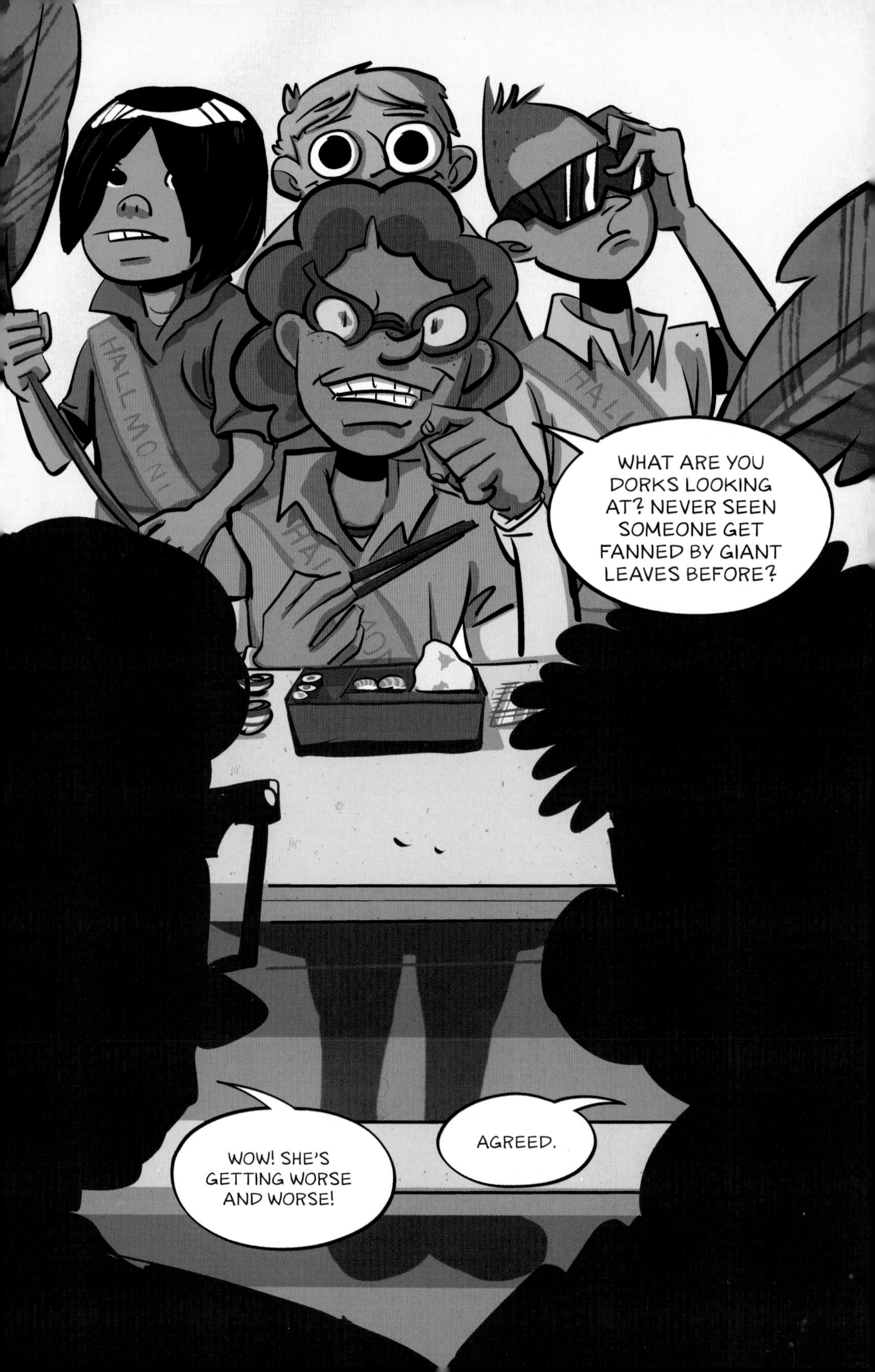
HALLMONI
HALLMONI
HALL
HAL
WHAT ARE YOU DORKS LOOKING AT? NEVER SEEN SOMEONE GET FANNED BY GIANT LEAVES BEFORE?
WOW! SHE'S GETTING WORSE AND WORSE!
AGREED.

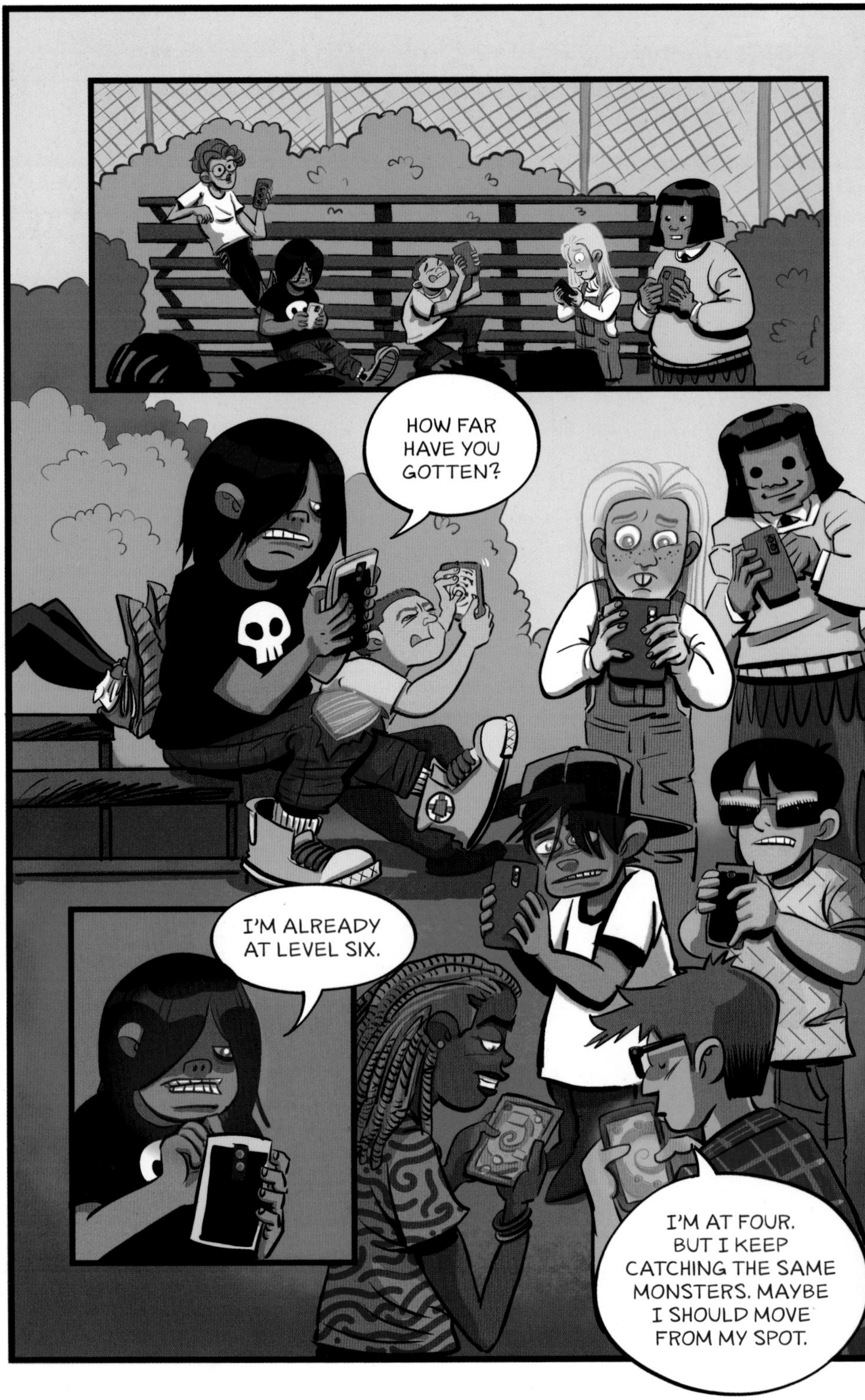
HOW FAR HAVE YOU GOTTEN?
I'M ALREADY AT LEVEL SIX.
I'M AT FOUR. BUT I KEEP CATCHING THE SAME MONSTERS. MAYBE I SHOULD MOVE FROM MY SPOT.

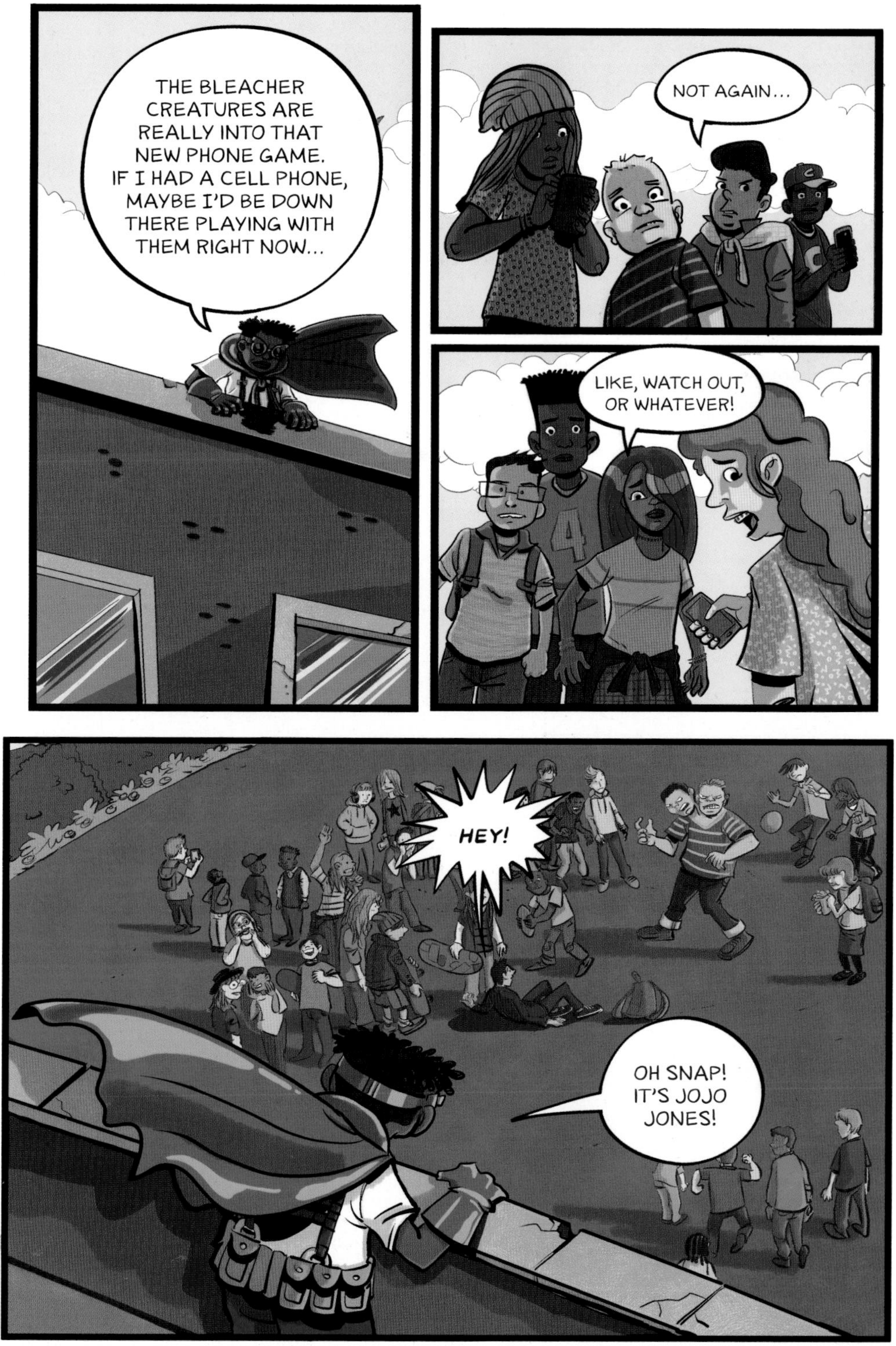
THE BLEACHER CREATURES ARE REALLY INTO THAT NEW PHONE GAME. IF I HAD A CELL PHONE, MAYBE I'D BE DOWN THERE PLAYING WITH THEM RIGHT NOW...
NOT AGAIN...
LIKE, WATCH OUT, OR WHATEVER!
HEY!
OH SNAP! IT'S JOJO JONES!

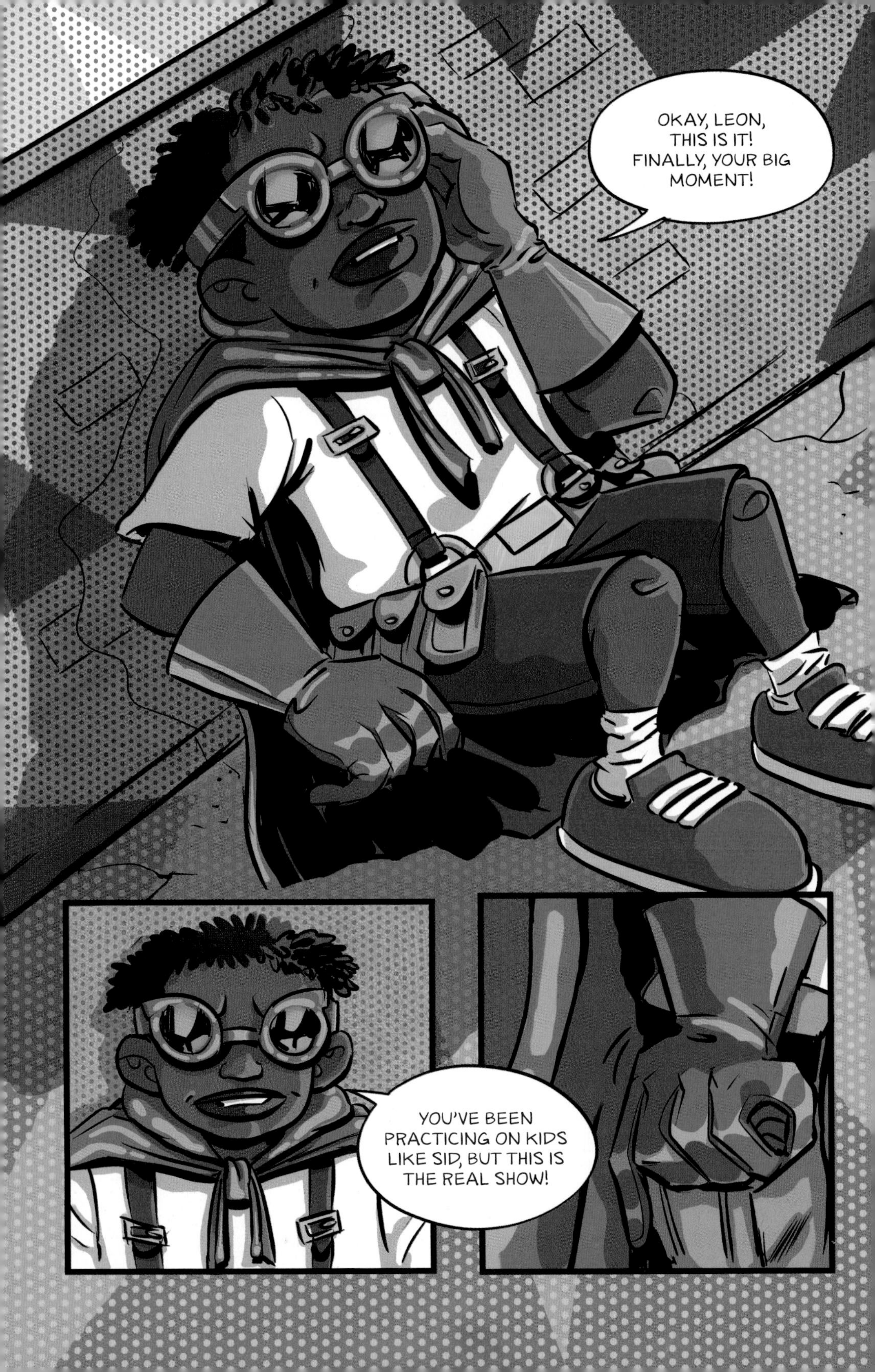
OKAY, LEON, THIS IS IT! FINALLY, YOUR BIG MOMENT!
YOU'VE BEEN PRACTICING ON KIDS LIKE SID, BUT THIS IS THE REAL SHOW!

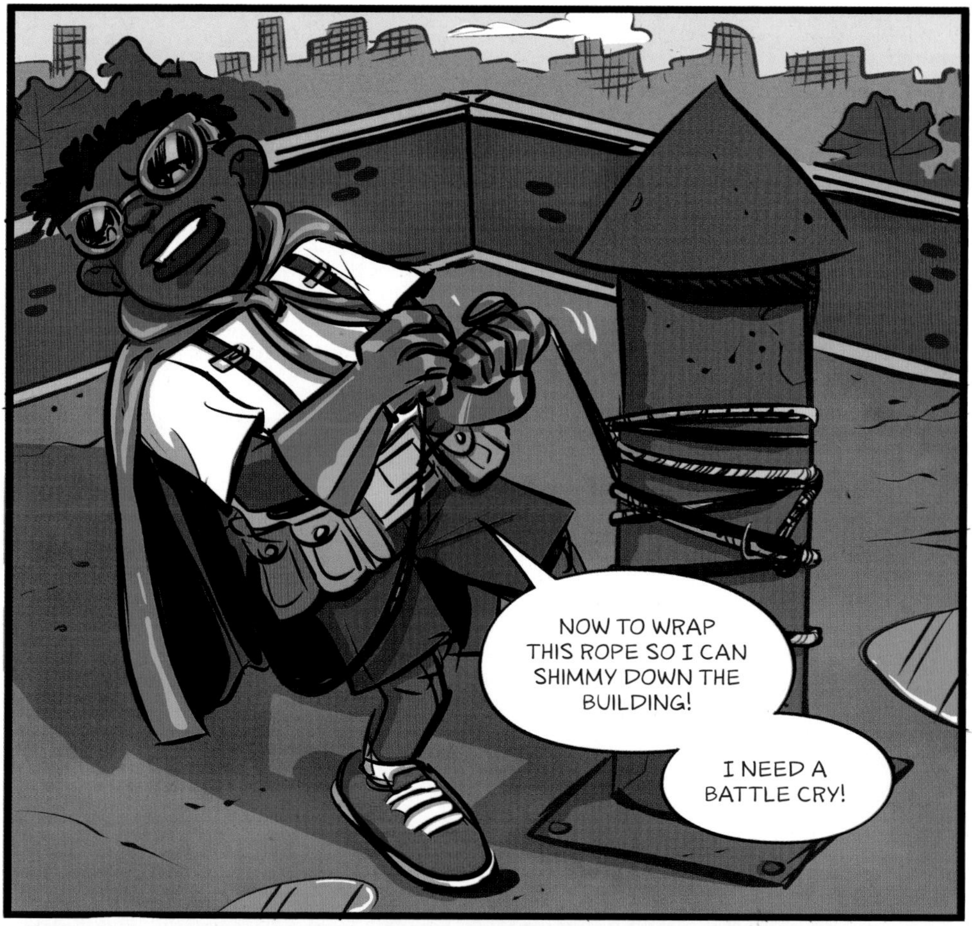
NOW TO WRAP THIS ROPE SO I CAN SHIMMY DOWN THE BUILDING!
I NEED A BATTLE CRY!

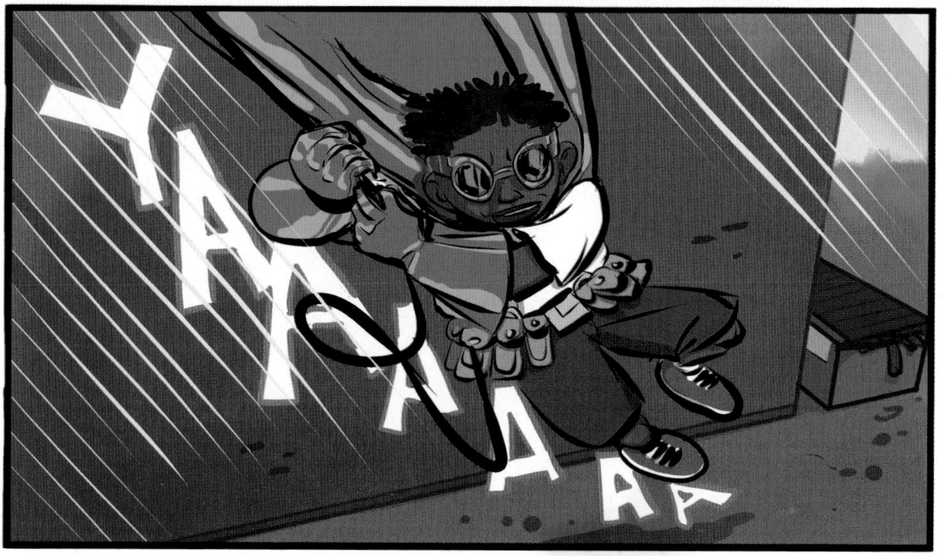
YAAAAAAA

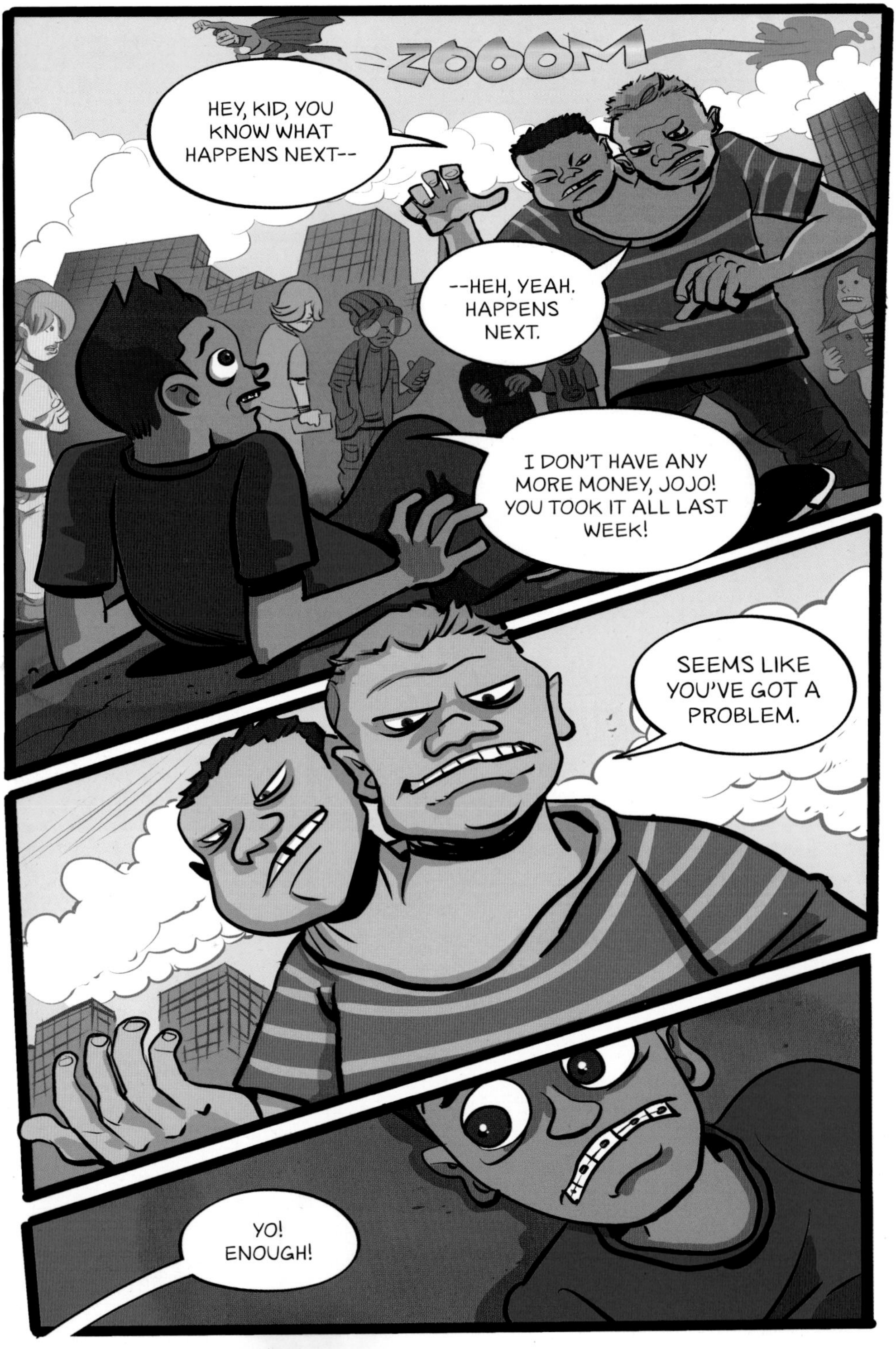
ZOOOM
HEY, KID, YOU KNOW WHAT HAPPENS NEXT--
--HEH, YEAH. HAPPENS NEXT.
I DON'T HAVE ANY MORE MONEY, JOJO! YOU TOOK IT ALL LAST WEEK!
SEEMS LIKE YOU'VE GOT A PROBLEM.
YO! ENOUGH!

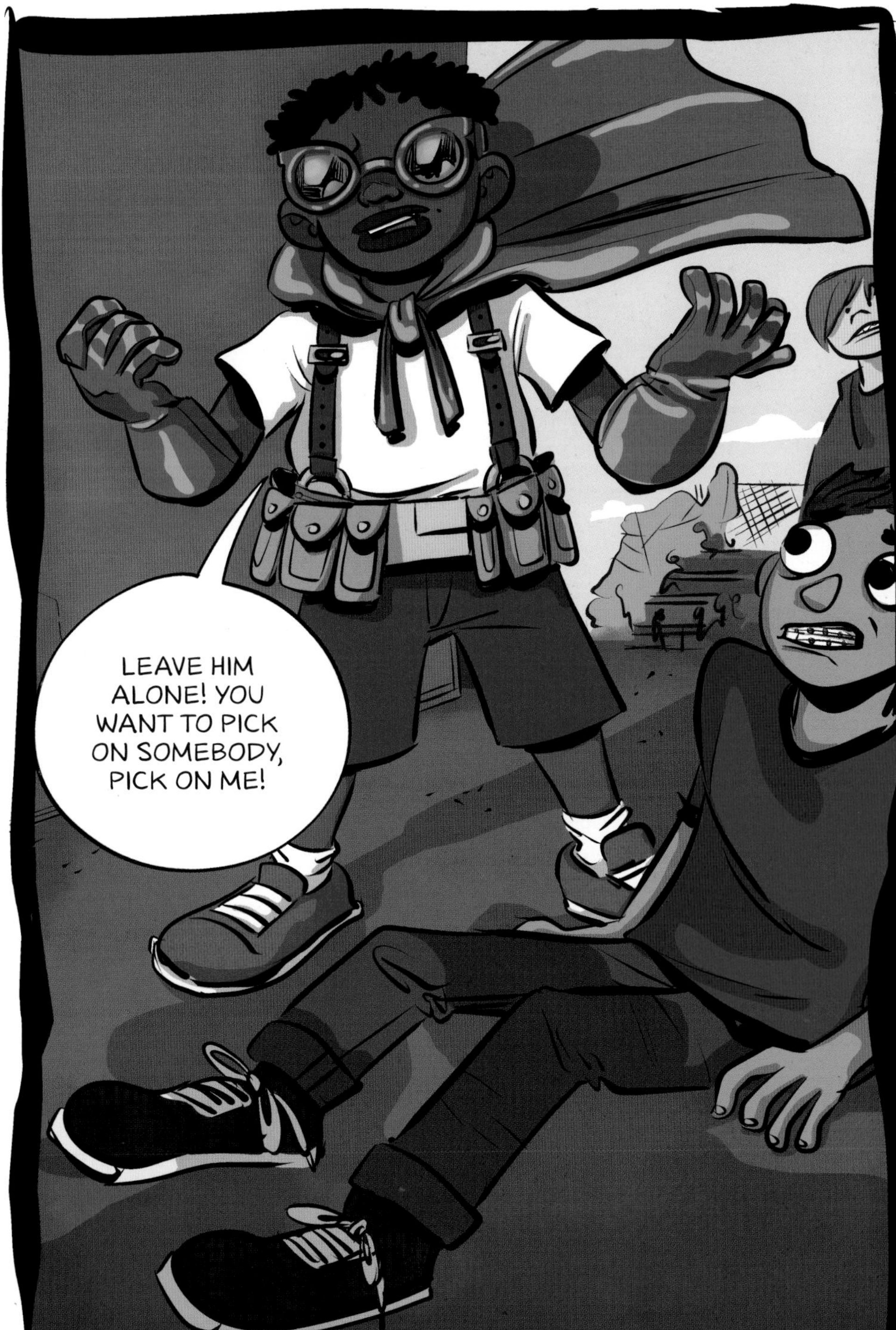
LEAVE HIM ALONE! YOU WANT TO PICK ON SOMEBODY, PICK ON ME!

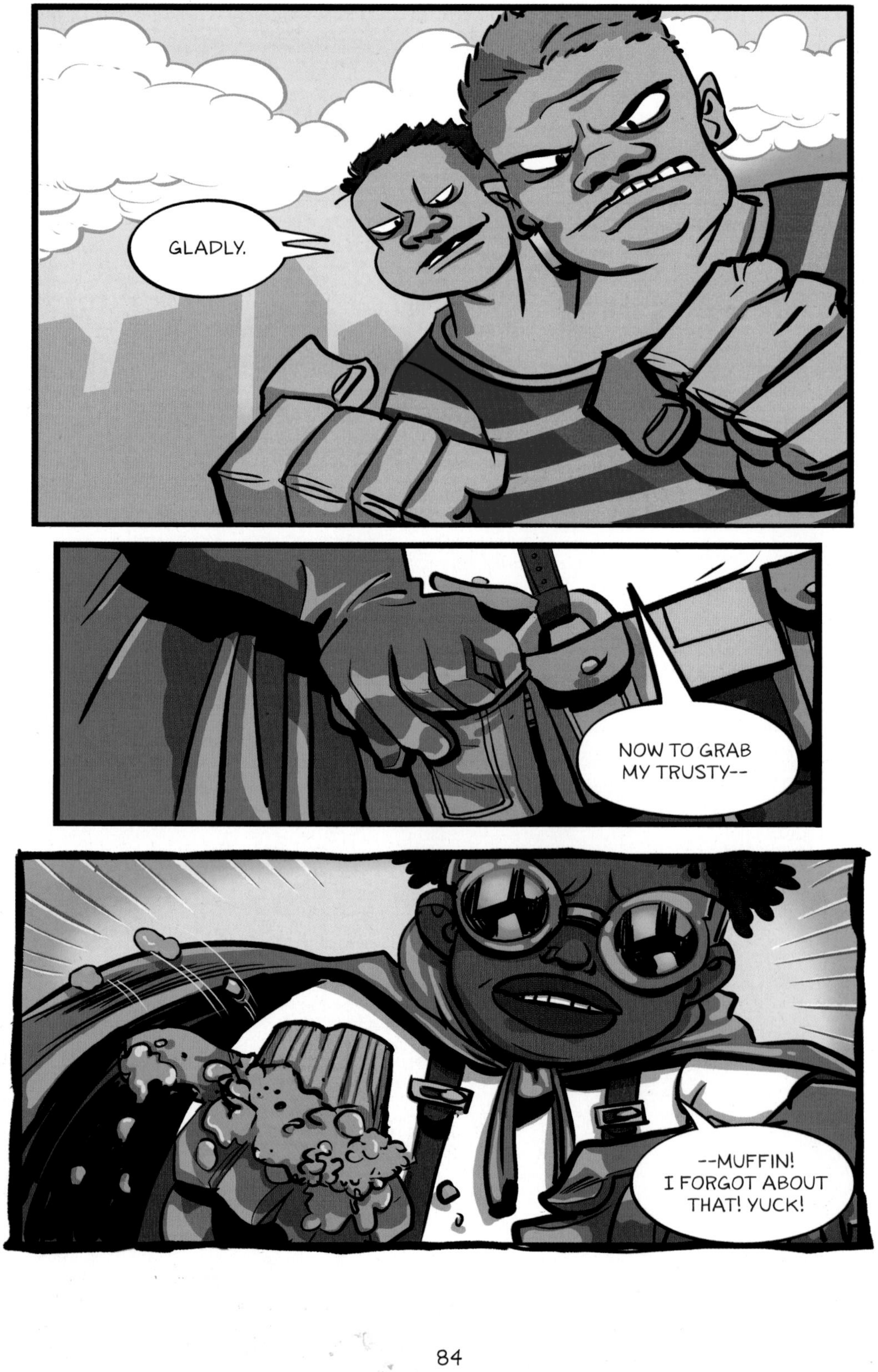
GLADLY.
NOW TO GRAB MY TRUSTY--
--MUFFIN! I FORGOT ABOUT THAT! YUCK!

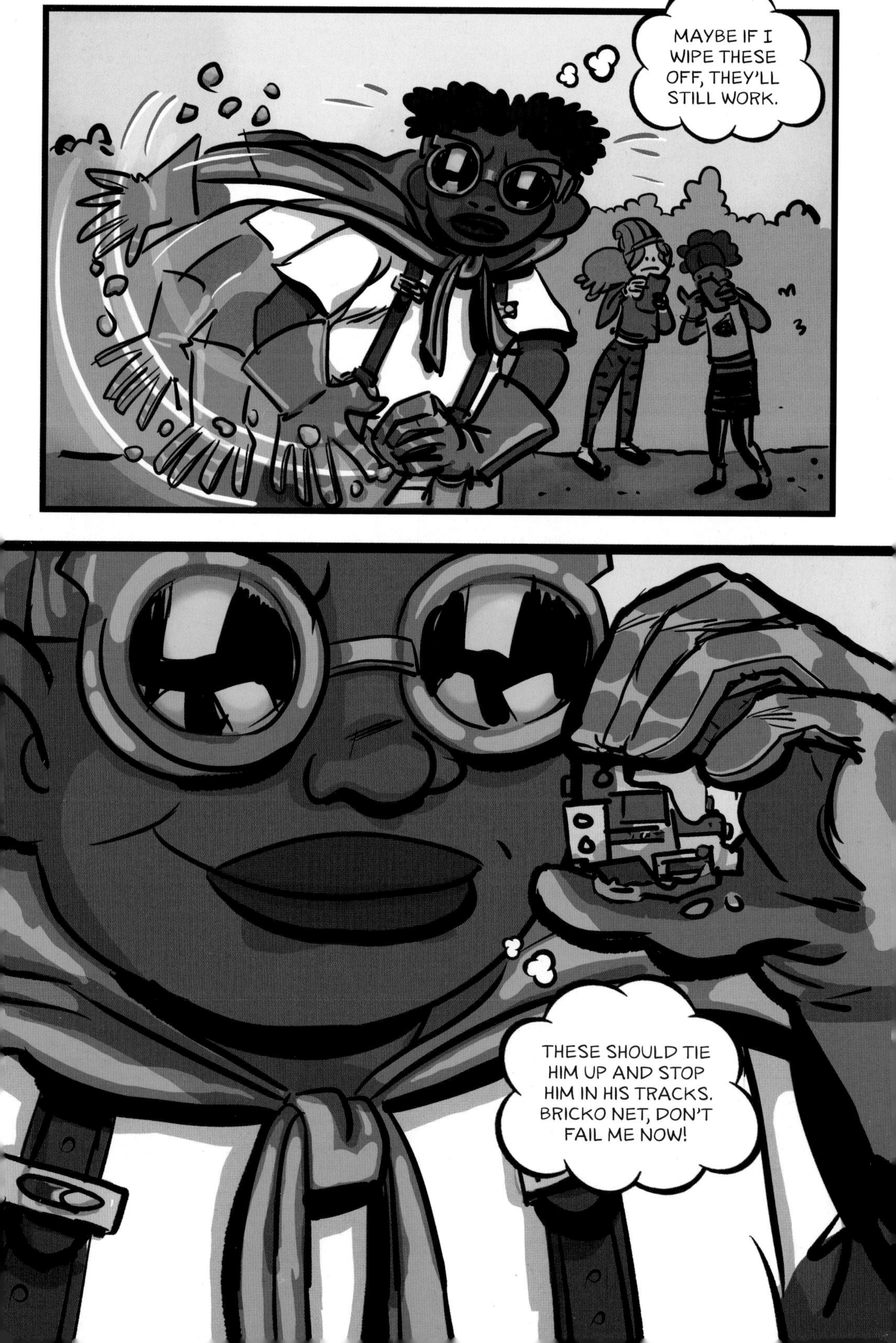
MAYBE IF I WIPE THESE OFF, THEY'LL STILL WORK.
THESE SHOULD TIE HIM UP AND STOP HIM IN HIS TRACKS. BRICKO NET, DON'T FAIL ME NOW!

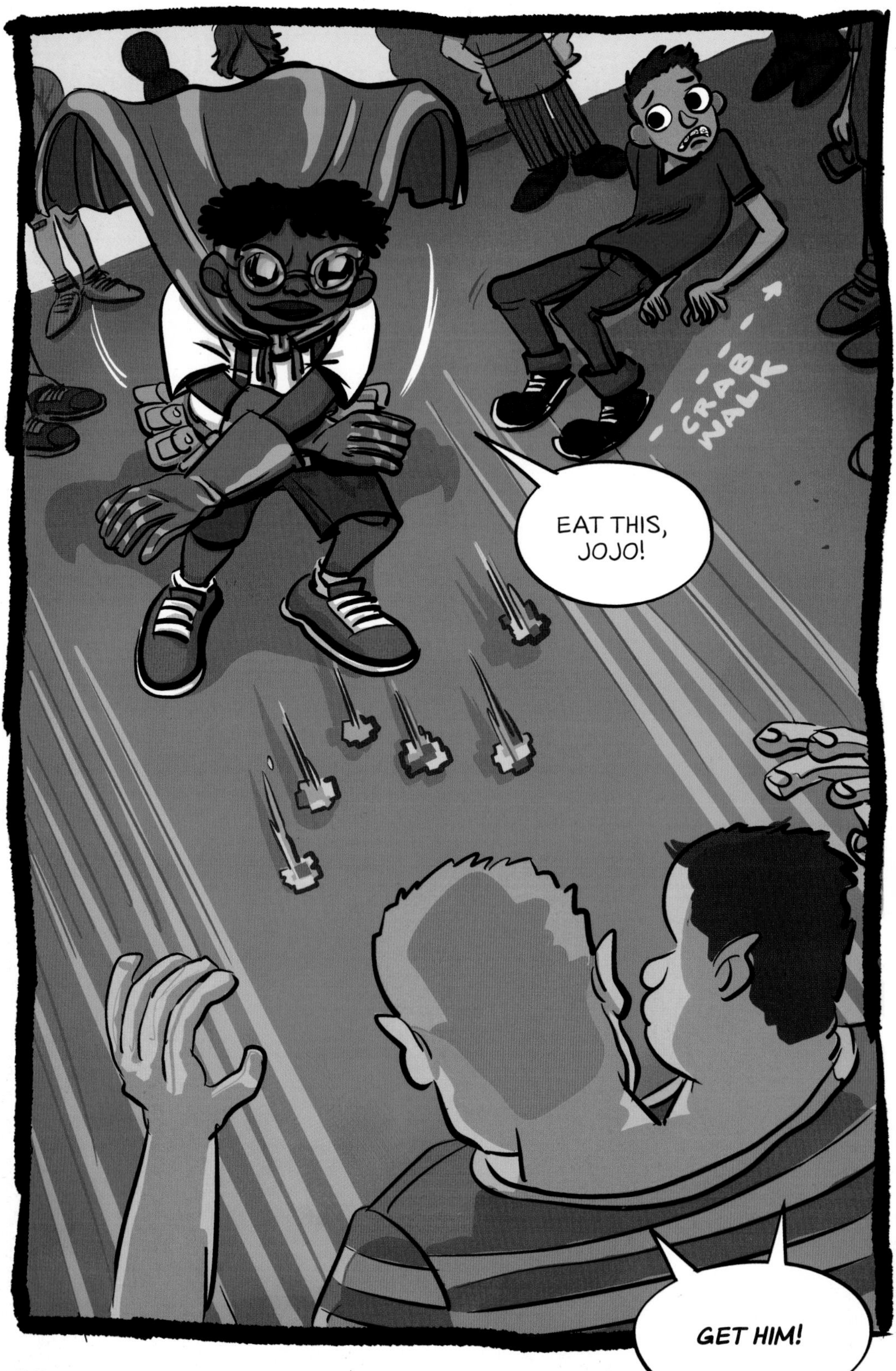
CRAB WALK
EAT THIS, JOJO!
GET HIM!

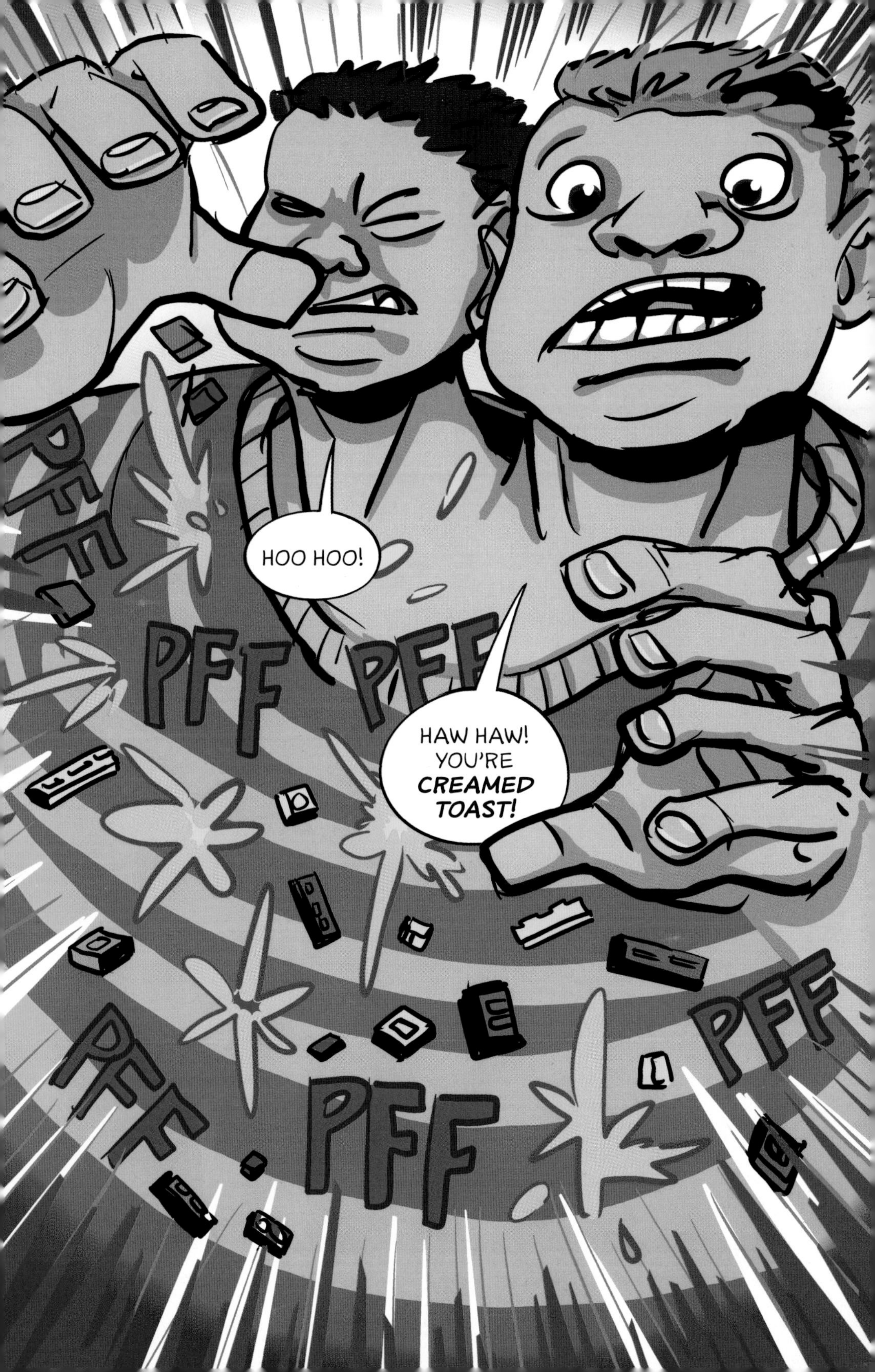
PFF
PFF
PFF
HOO HOO!
PFF
HAW HAW! YOU'RE CREAMED TOAST!
PFF
PFF
PFF

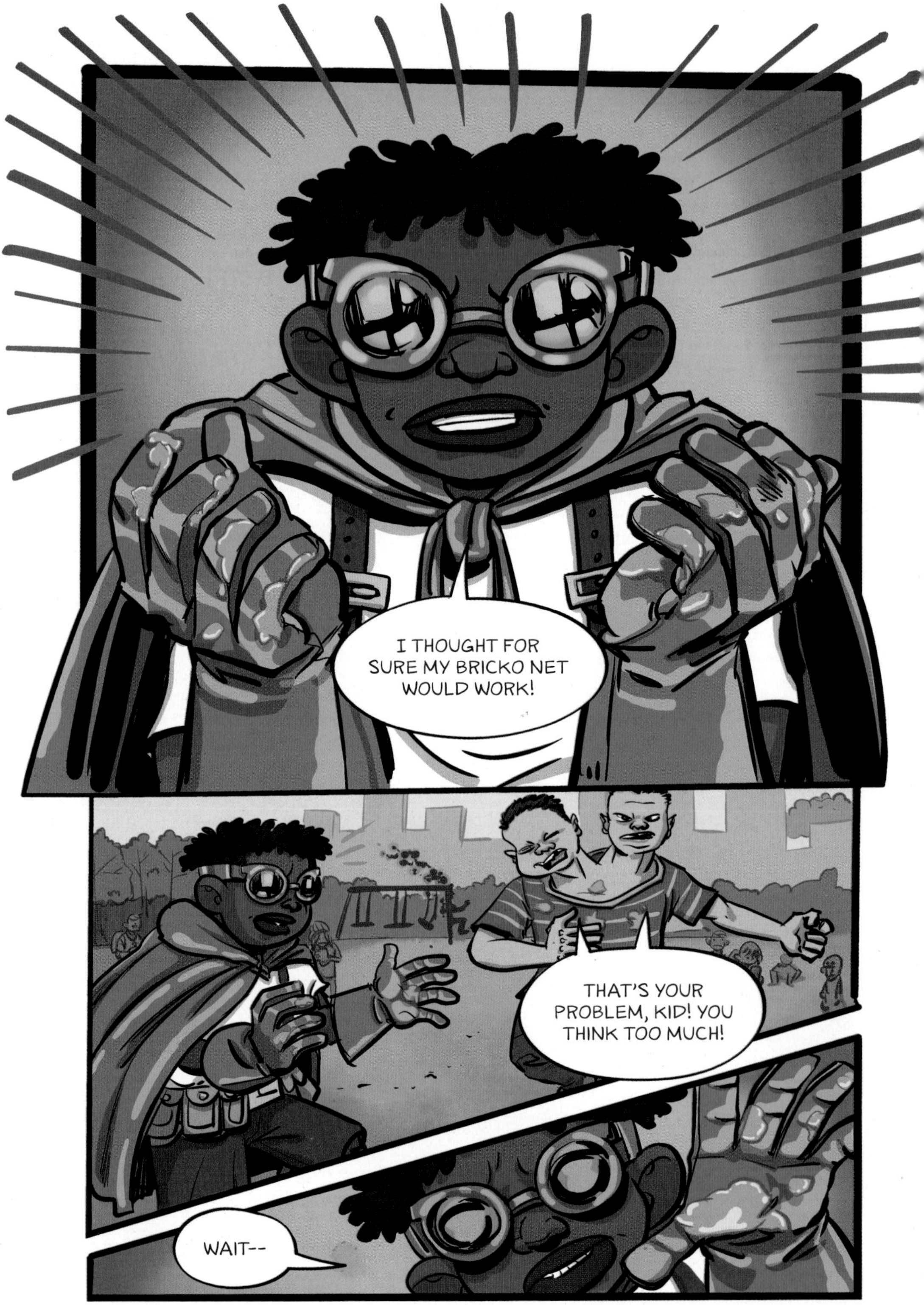
I THOUGHT FOR SURE MY BRICKO NET WOULD WORK!
THAT'S YOUR PROBLEM, KID! YOU THINK TOO MUCH!
WAIT--

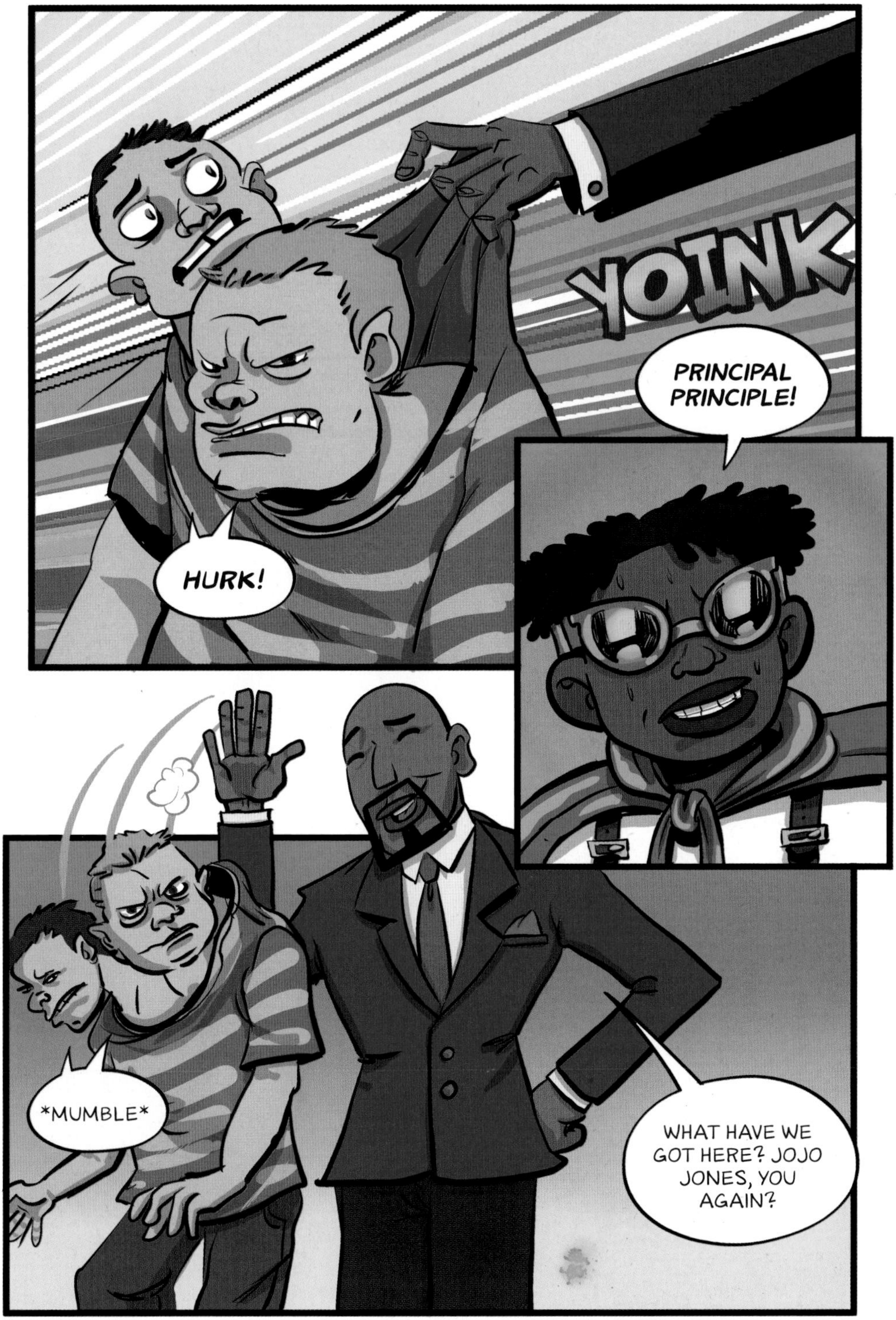
YOINK
HURK!
PRINCIPAL PRINCIPLE!
MUMBLE
WHAT HAVE WE GOT HERE? JOJO JONES, YOU AGAIN?

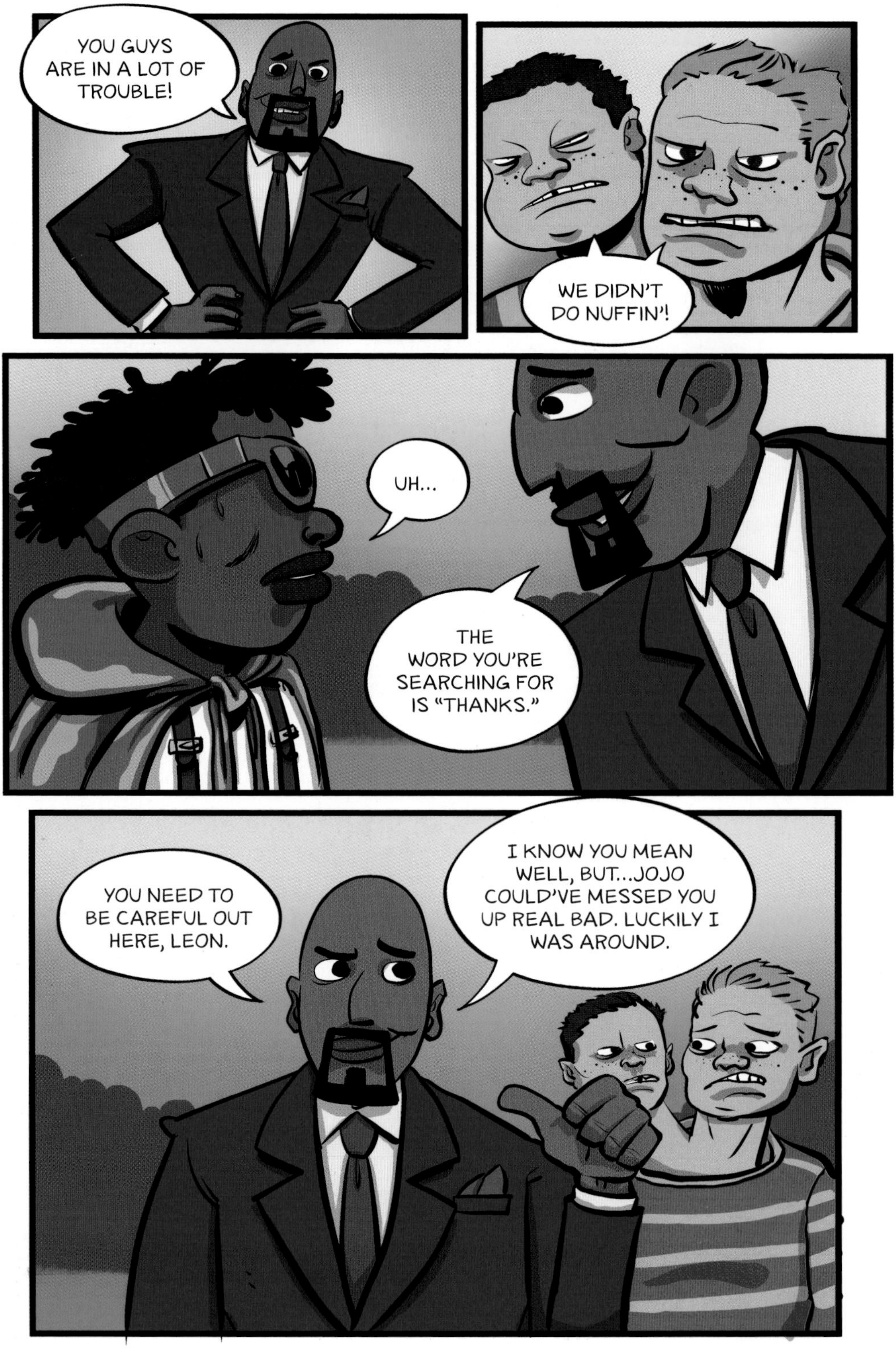
YOU GUYS ARE IN A LOT OF TROUBLE!
WE DIDN'T DO NUFFIN'!
UH...
THE WORD YOU'RE SEARCHING FOR IS "THANKS."
YOU NEED TO BE CAREFUL OUT HERE, LEON.
I KNOW YOU MEAN WELL, BUT...JOJO COULD'VE MESSED YOU UP REAL BAD. LUCKILY I WAS AROUND.

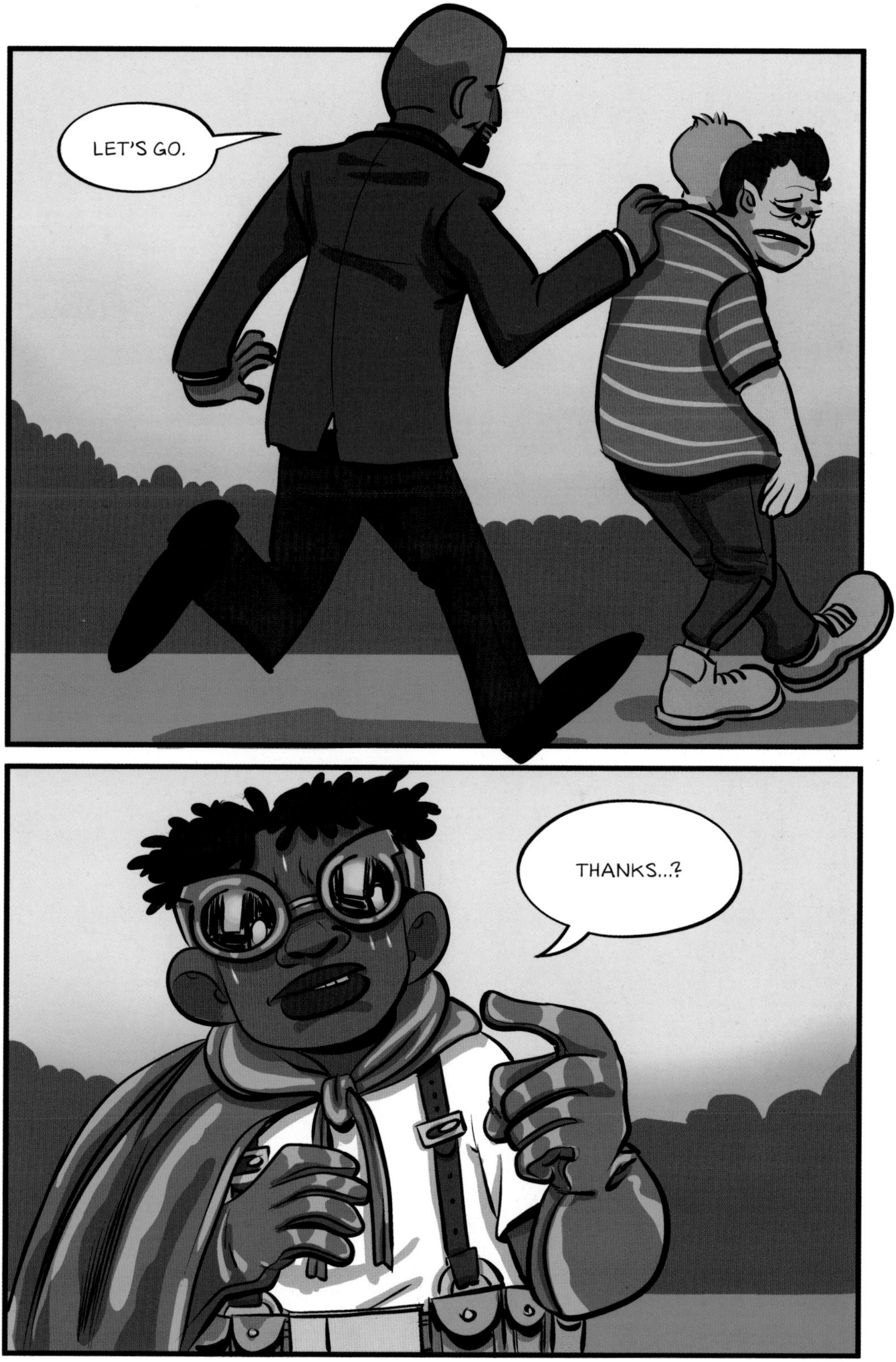
LET'S GO.
THANKS...?

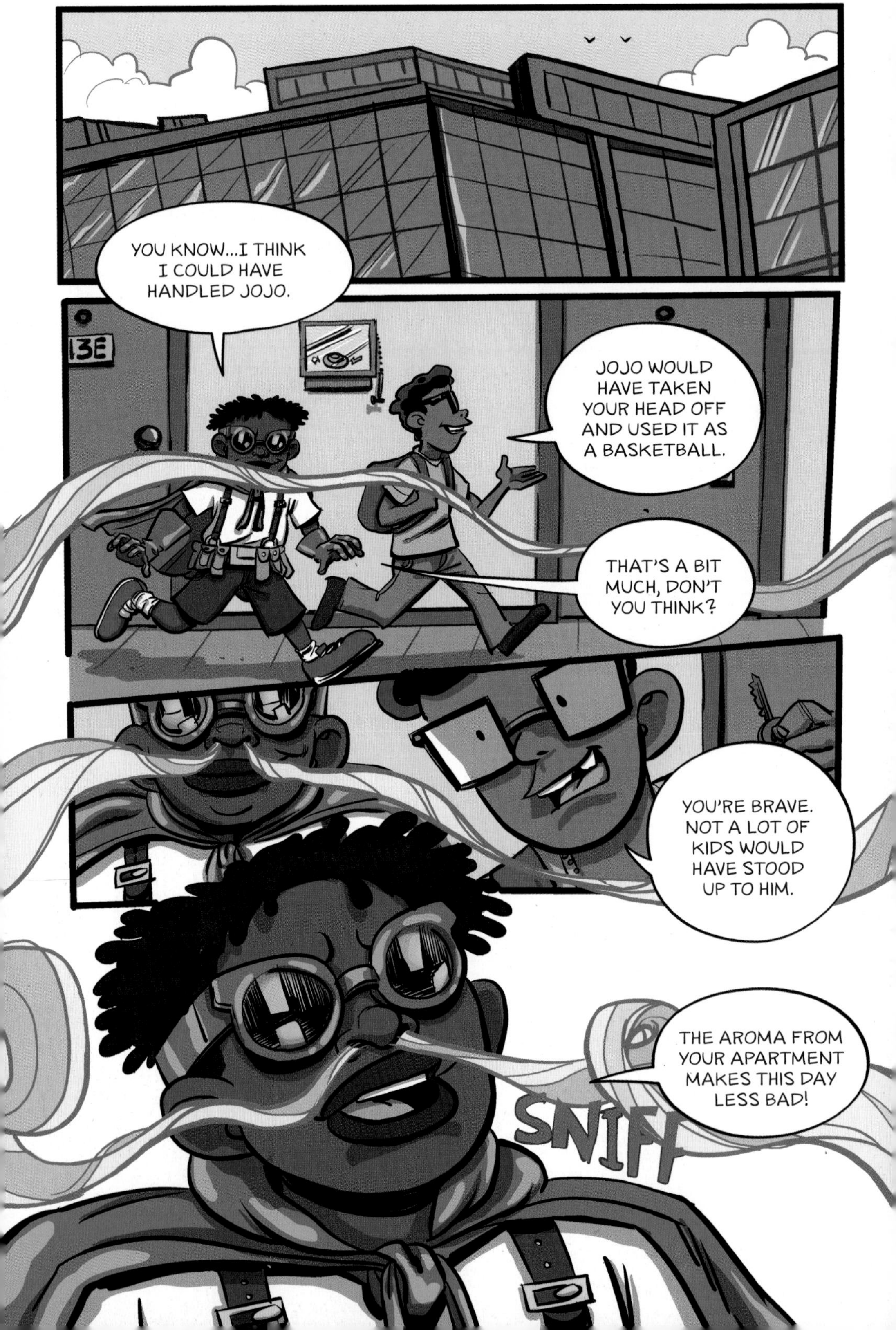
YOU KNOW...I THINK I COULD HAVE HANDLED JOJO.
13E
JOJO WOULD HAVE TAKEN YOUR HEAD OFF AND USED IT AS A BASKETBALL.
THAT'S A BIT MUCH, DON'T YOU THINK?
YOU'RE BRAVE. NOT A LOT OF KIDS WOULD HAVE STOOD UP TO HIM.
THE AROMA FROM YOUR APARTMENT MAKES THIS DAY LESS BAD!
SNIFF

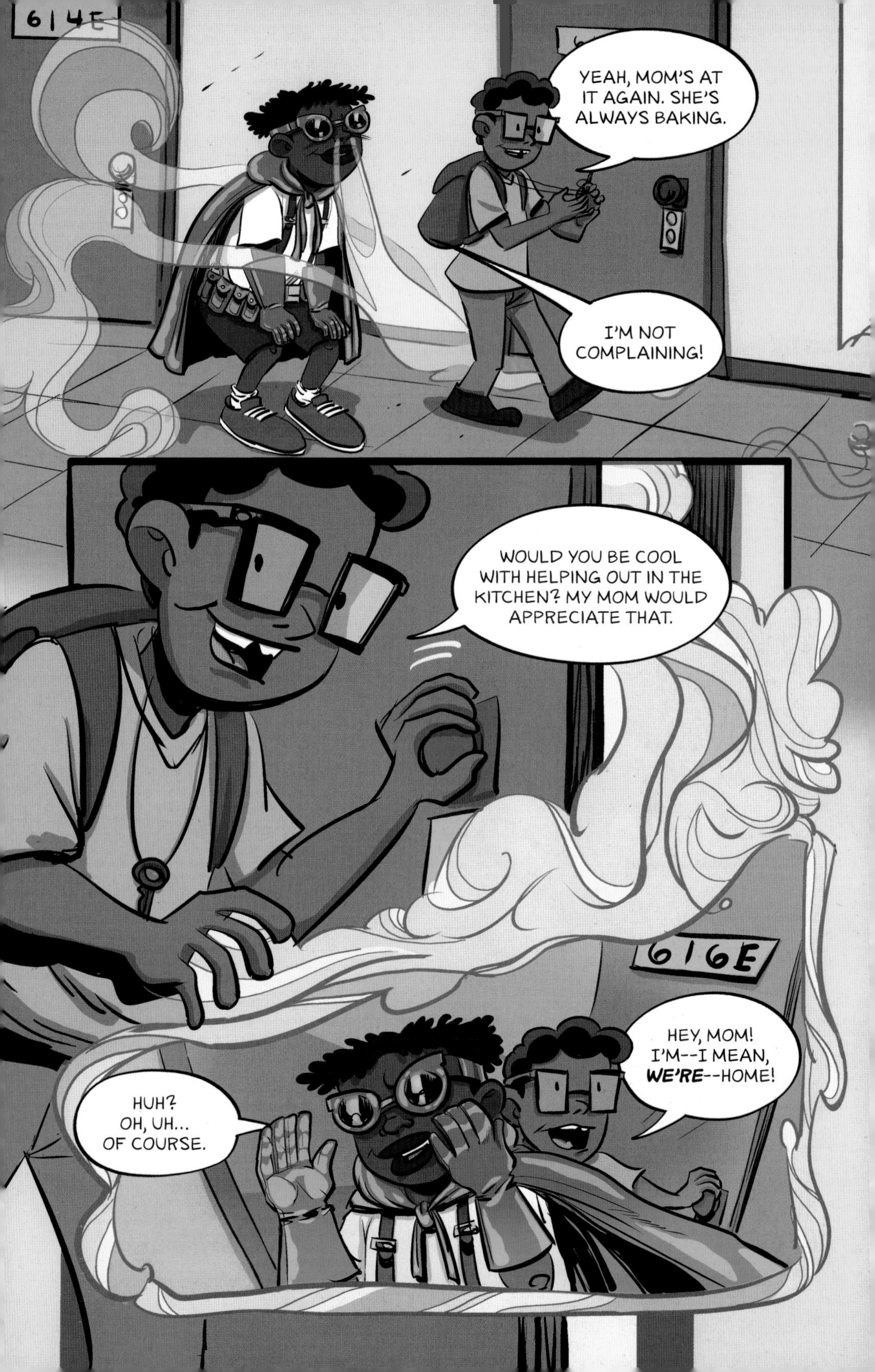
614E
YEAH, MOM'S AT IT AGAIN. SHE'S ALWAYS BAKING.
I'M NOT COMPLAINING!
WOULD YOU BE COOL WITH HELPING OUT IN THE KITCHEN? MY MOM WOULD APPRECIATE THAT.
616E
HUH? OH, UH... OF COURSE.
HEY, MOM! I'M--I MEAN, **WE'RE**--HOME!

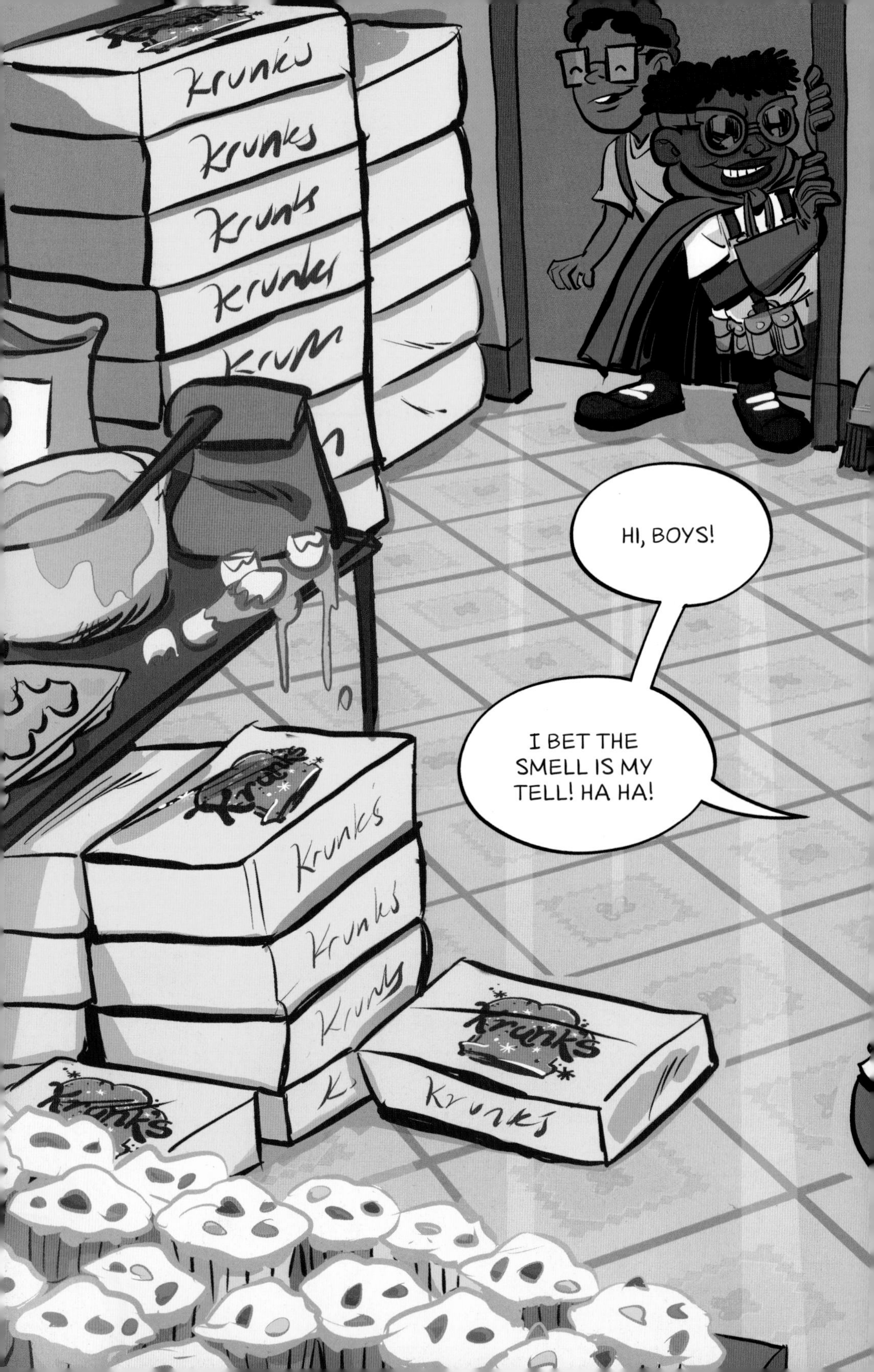
HI, BOYS!
I BET THE SMELL IS MY TELL! HA HA!

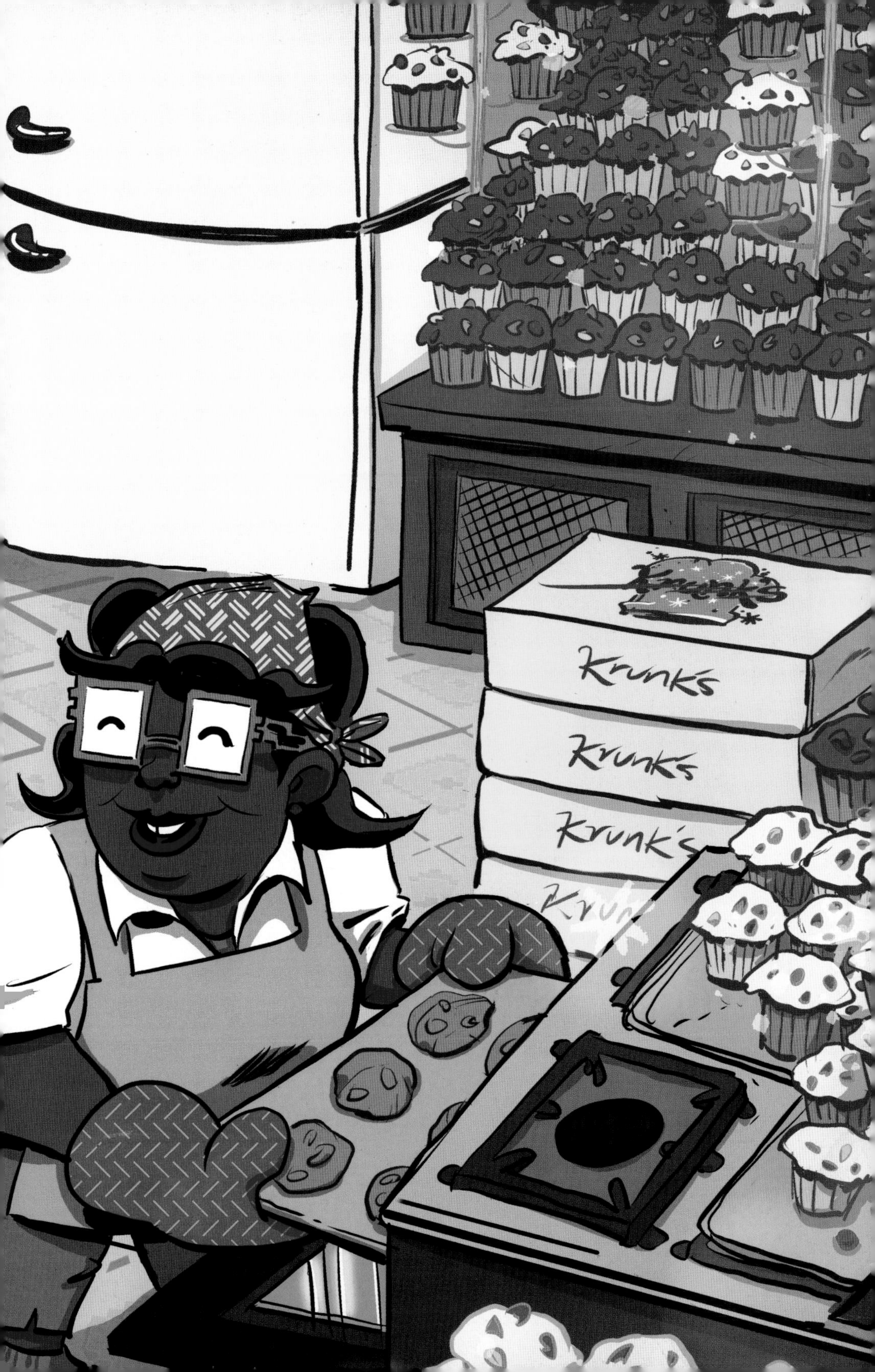
Krunk's
Krunk's
Krunk's

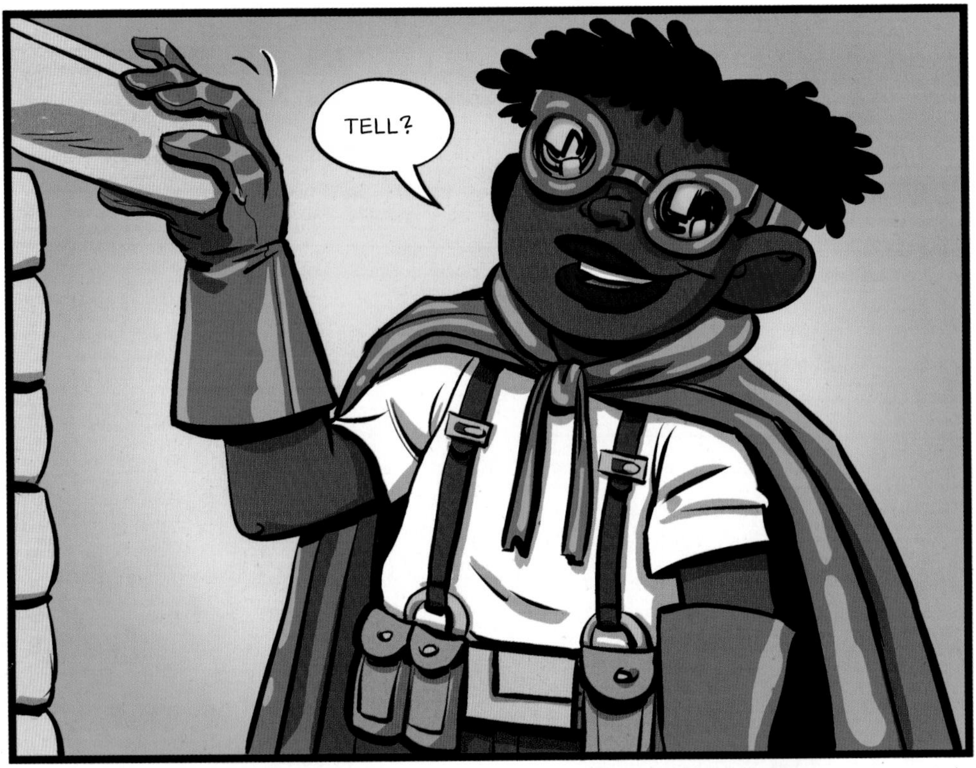
TELL?

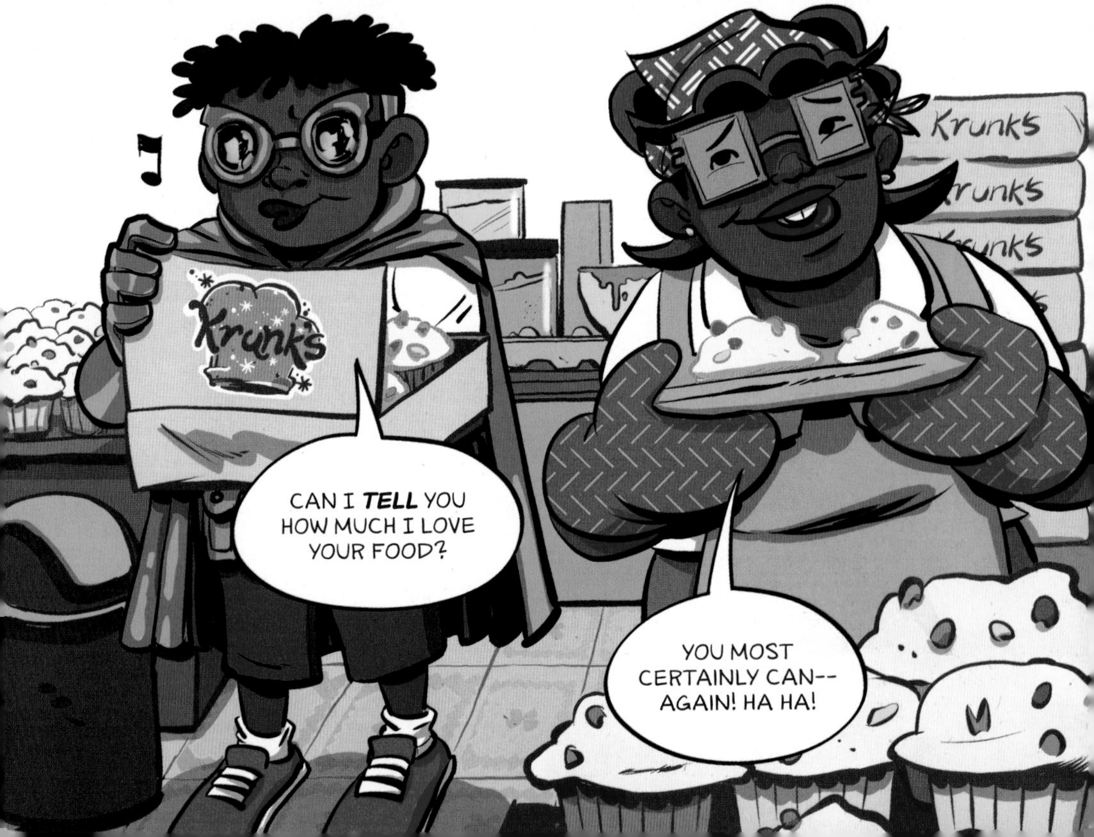
Krunk's
CAN I **TELL** YOU HOW MUCH I LOVE YOUR FOOD?
YOU MOST CERTAINLY CAN-- AGAIN! HA HA!

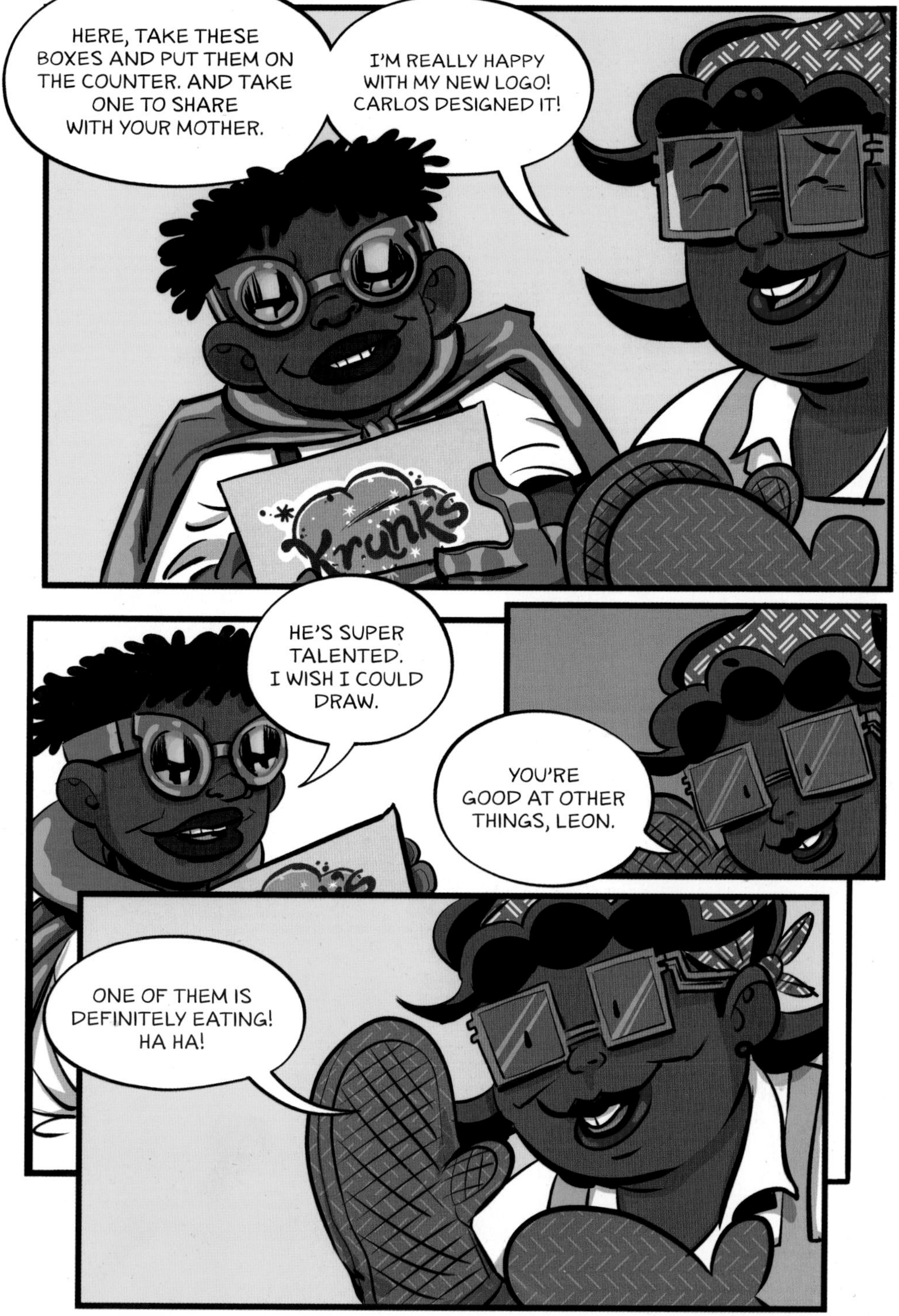
HERE, TAKE THESE BOXES AND PUT THEM ON THE COUNTER. AND TAKE ONE TO SHARE WITH YOUR MOTHER.
I'M REALLY HAPPY WITH MY NEW LOGO! CARLOS DESIGNED IT!
Krunks
HE'S SUPER TALENTED. I WISH I COULD DRAW.
YOU'RE GOOD AT OTHER THINGS, LEON.
ONE OF THEM IS DEFINITELY EATING! HA HA!

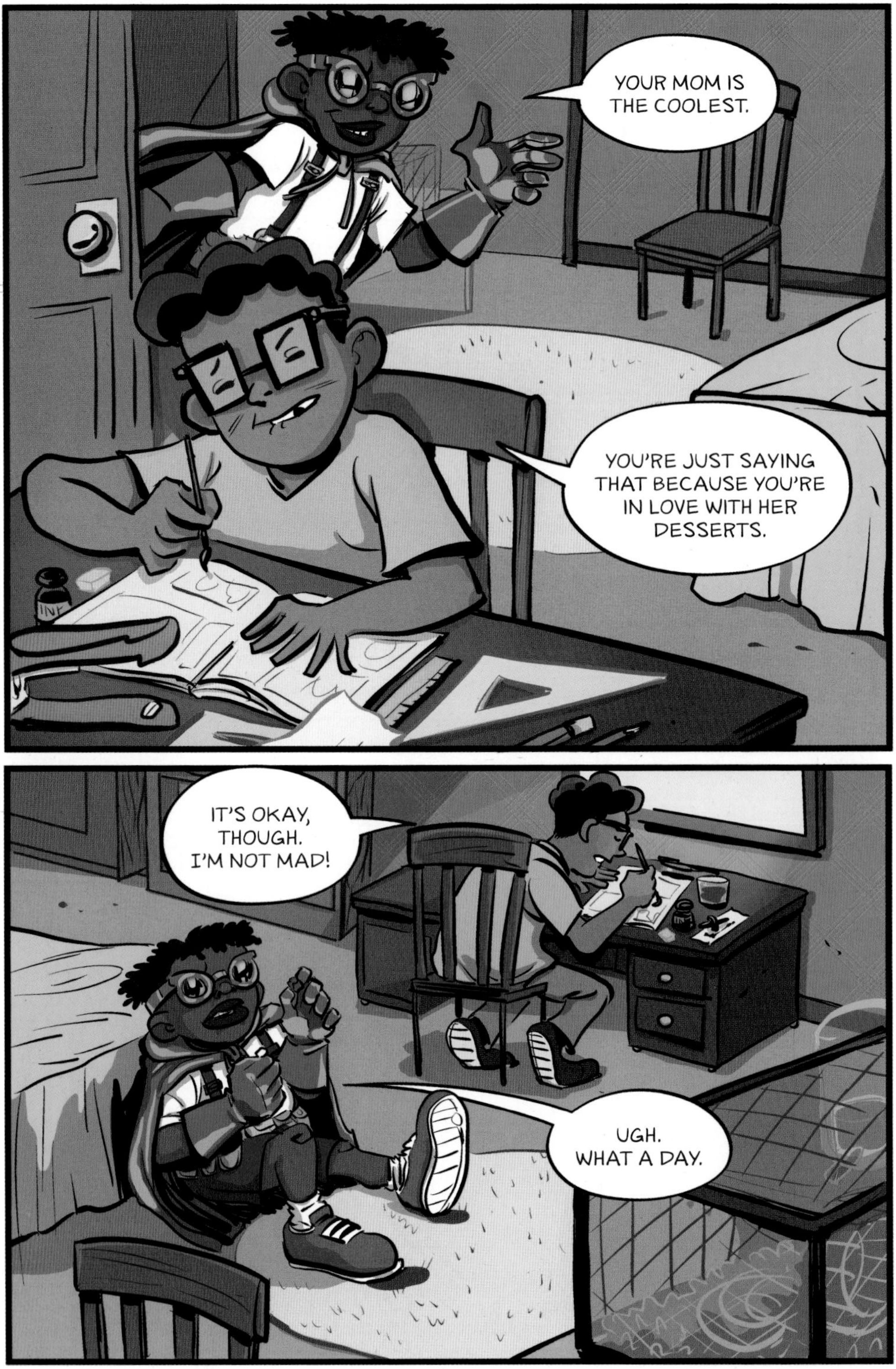
YOUR MOM IS THE COOLEST.
YOU'RE JUST SAYING THAT BECAUSE YOU'RE IN LOVE WITH HER DESSERTS.
INK
IT'S OKAY, THOUGH. I'M NOT MAD!
UGH. WHAT A DAY.

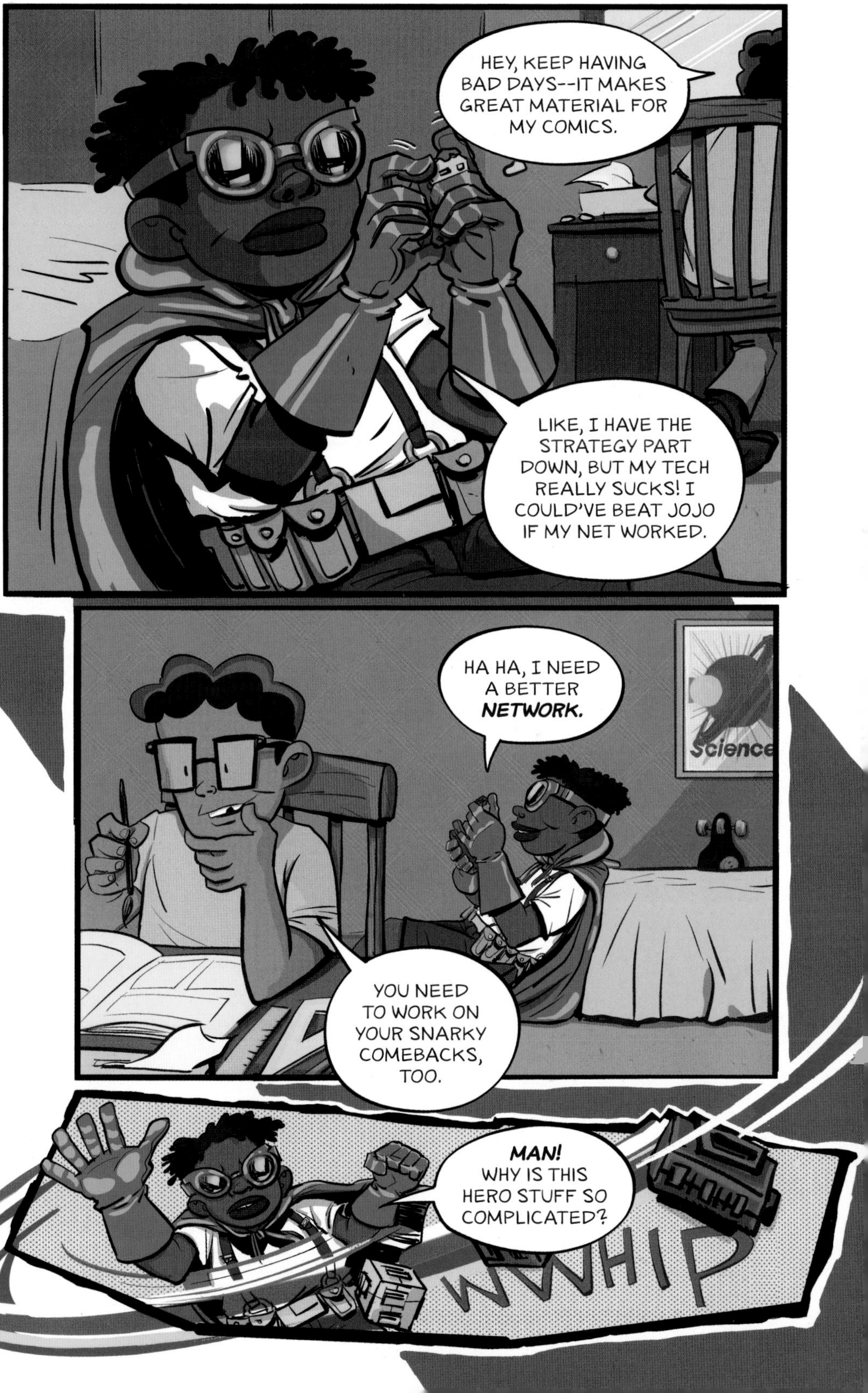
HEY, KEEP HAVING BAD DAYS--IT MAKES GREAT MATERIAL FOR MY COMICS.
LIKE, I HAVE THE STRATEGY PART DOWN, BUT MY TECH REALLY SUCKS! I COULD'VE BEAT JOJO IF MY NET WORKED.
HA HA, I NEED A BETTER ***NETWORK.***
Science
YOU NEED TO WORK ON YOUR SNARKY COMEBACKS, TOO.
MAN! WHY IS THIS HERO STUFF SO COMPLICATED?
WWHIP

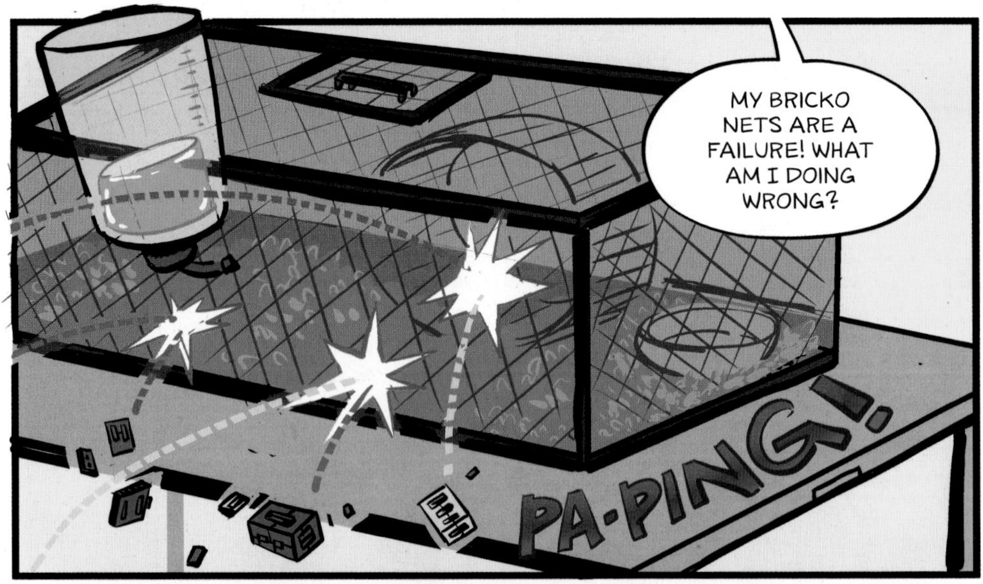
MY BRICKO NETS ARE A FAILURE! WHAT AM I DOING WRONG?
PA-PING!

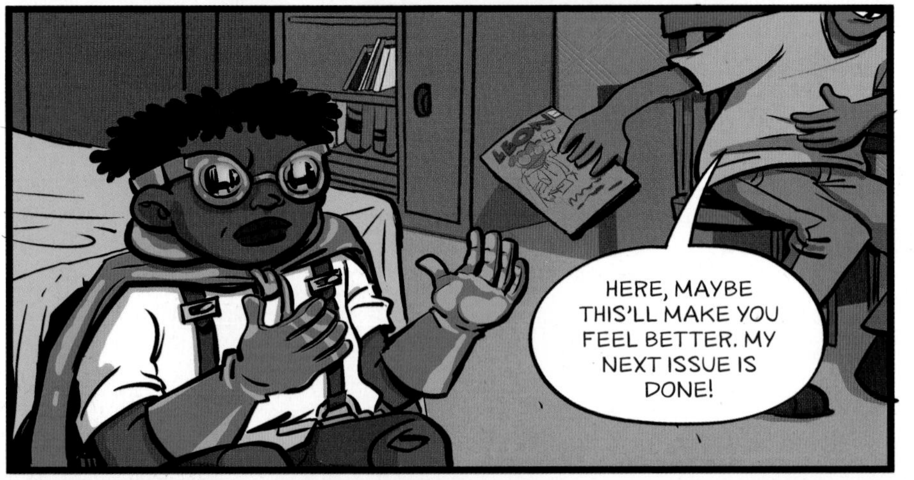
LEON
HERE, MAYBE THIS'LL MAKE YOU FEEL BETTER. MY NEXT ISSUE IS DONE!

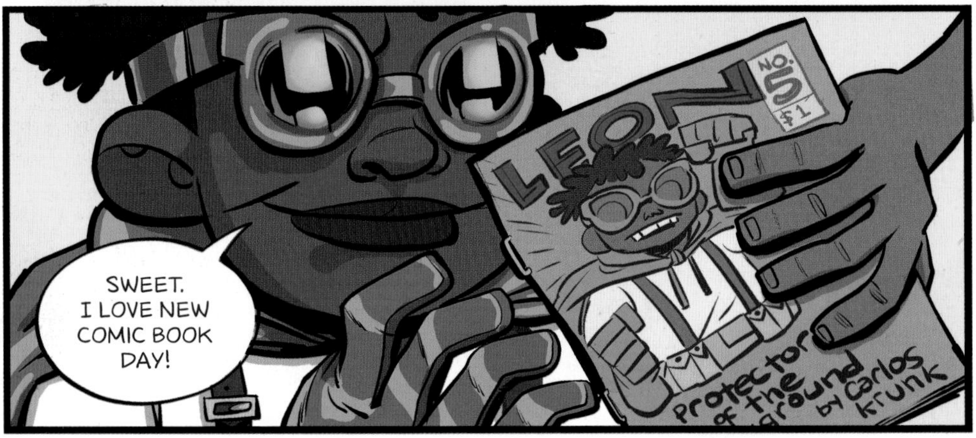
SWEET. I LOVE NEW COMIC BOOK DAY!
LEON
NO. 5
$1
protector of the ground
by Carlos Krunk

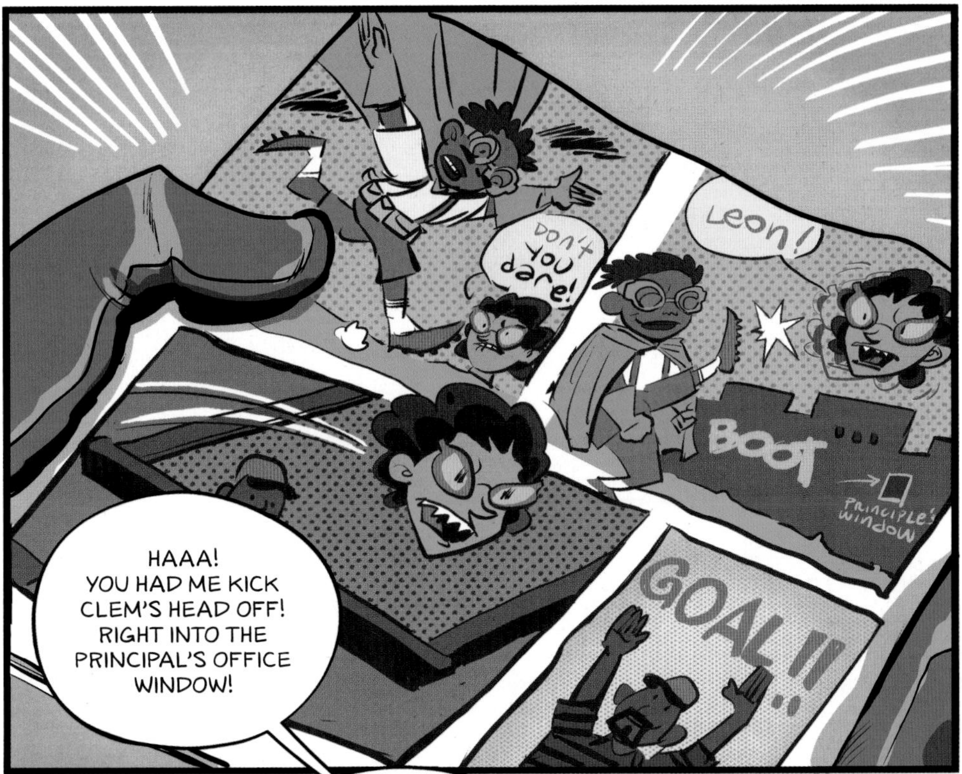
Don't you dare!
Leon!
BOOT
PRINCIPLE'S WINDOW
GOAL!!
HAAA! YOU HAD ME KICK CLEM'S HEAD OFF! RIGHT INTO THE PRINCIPAL'S OFFICE WINDOW!

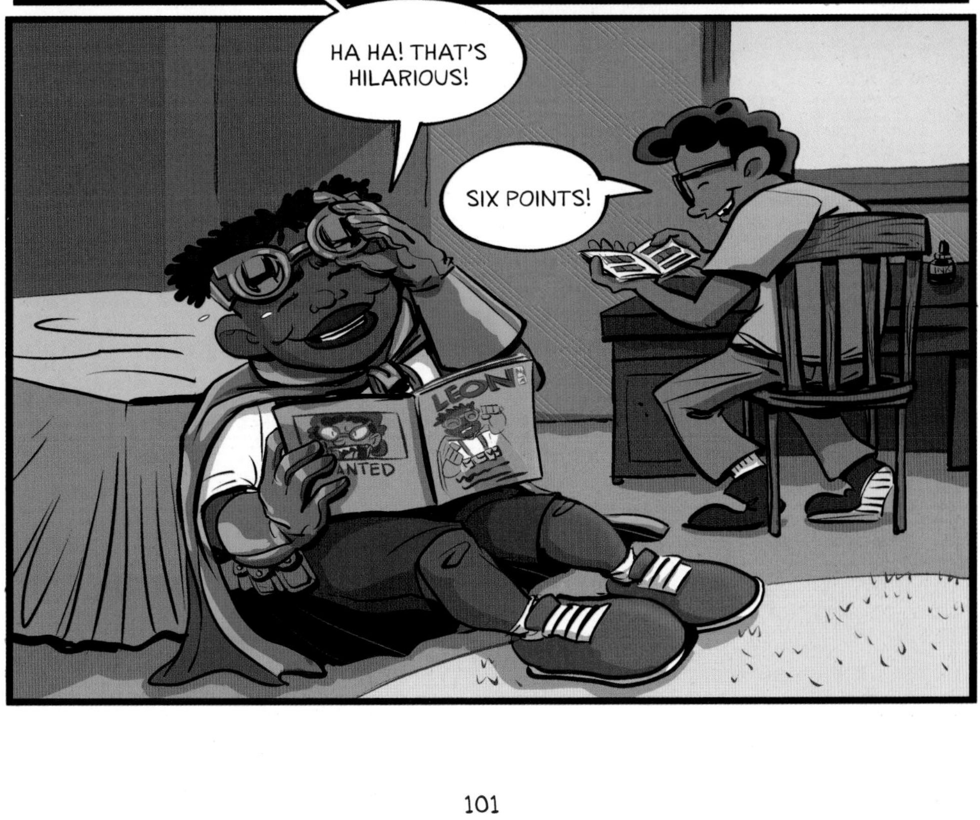
HA HA! THAT'S HILARIOUS!
SIX POINTS!
LEON
WANTED

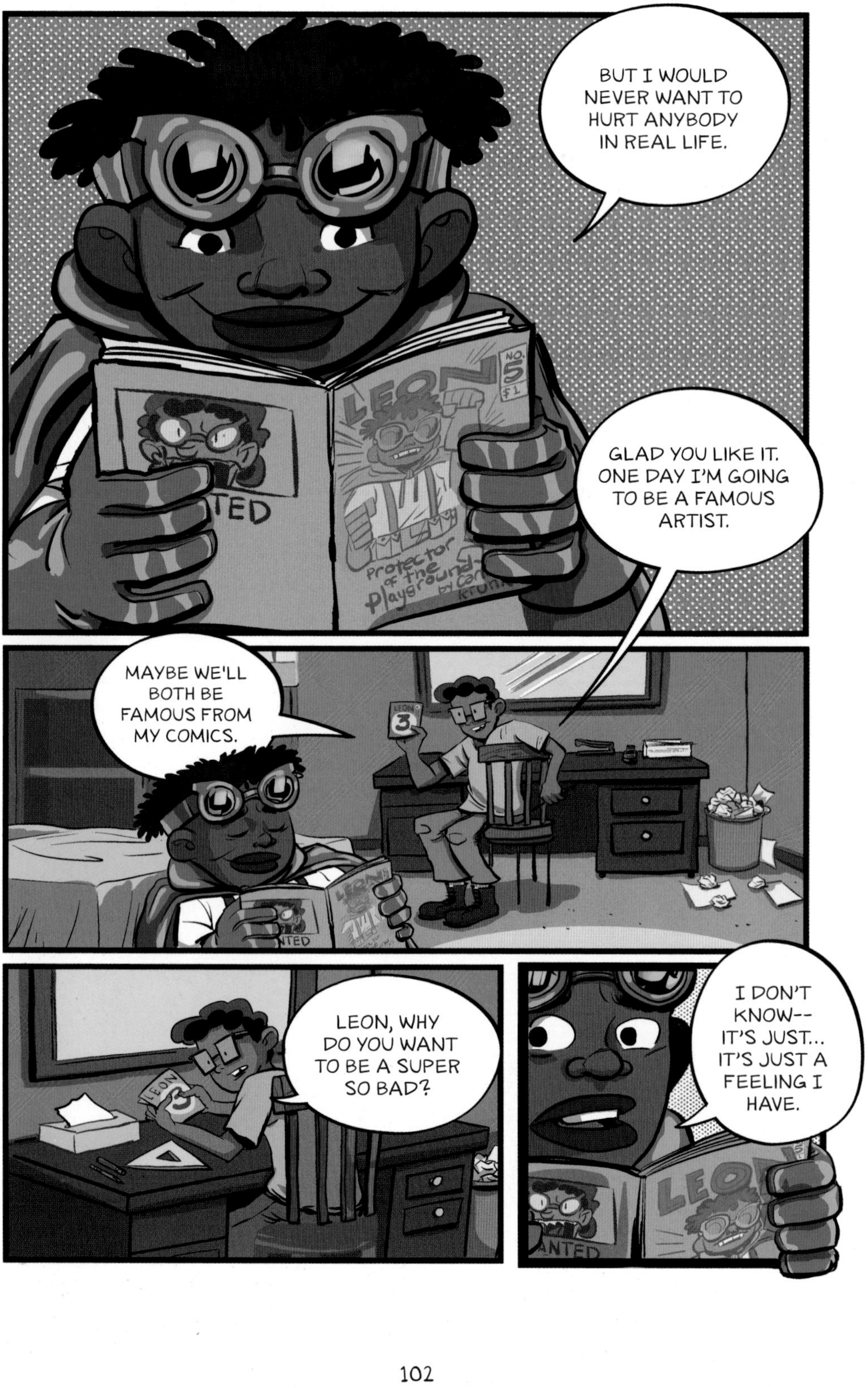
BUT I WOULD NEVER WANT TO HURT ANYBODY IN REAL LIFE.
LEON
NO. 5
$1
TED
Protector of the Playground
GLAD YOU LIKE IT. ONE DAY I'M GOING TO BE A FAMOUS ARTIST.
MAYBE WE'LL BOTH BE FAMOUS FROM MY COMICS.
LEON
3
LEON, WHY DO YOU WANT TO BE A SUPER SO BAD?
I DON'T KNOW-- IT'S JUST... IT'S JUST A FEELING I HAVE.

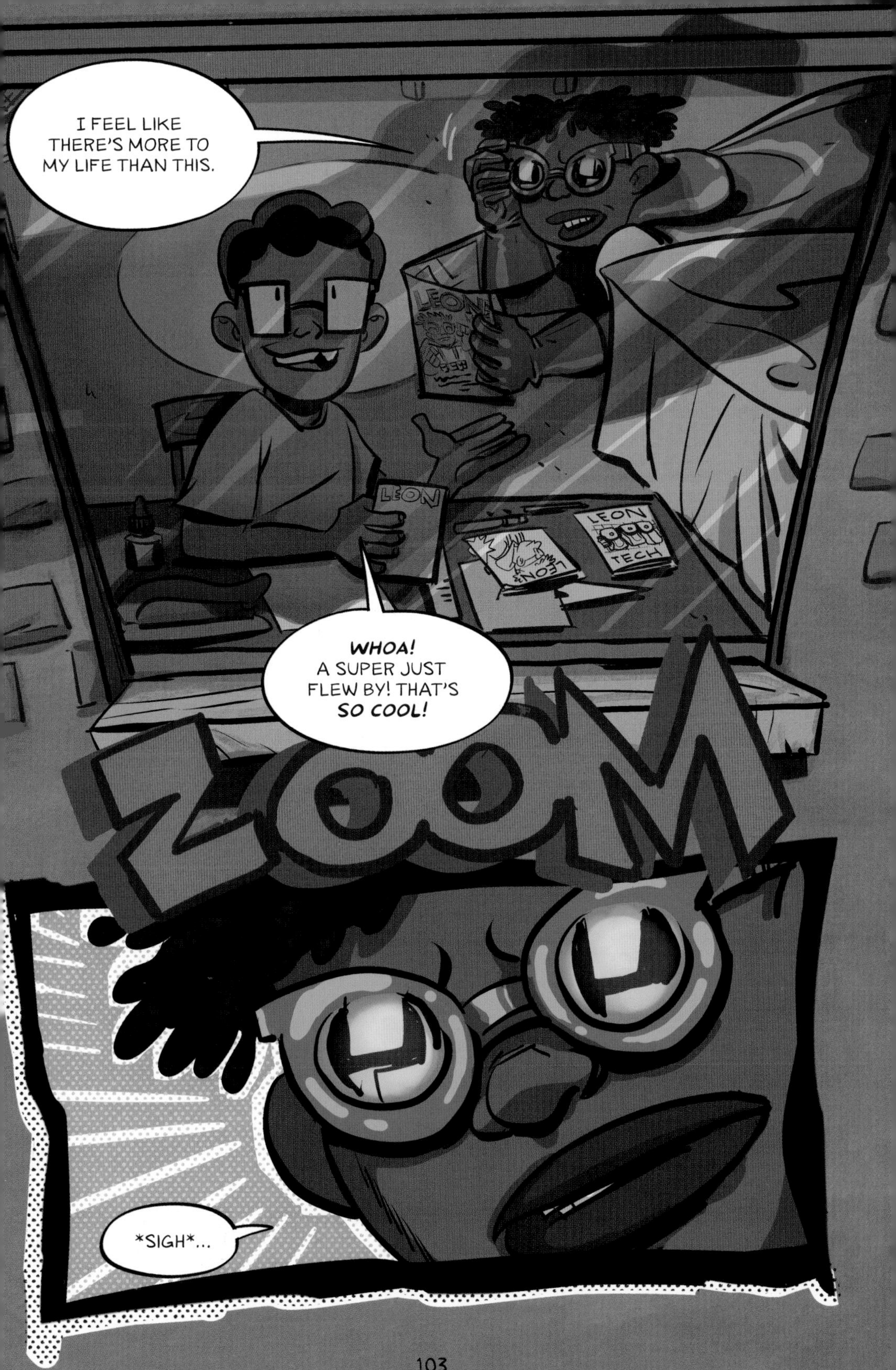
I FEEL LIKE THERE'S MORE TO MY LIFE THAN THIS.
LEON
LEON
LEON
LEON TECH
WHOA! A SUPER JUST FLEW BY! THAT'S SO COOL!
ZOOM
SIGH...

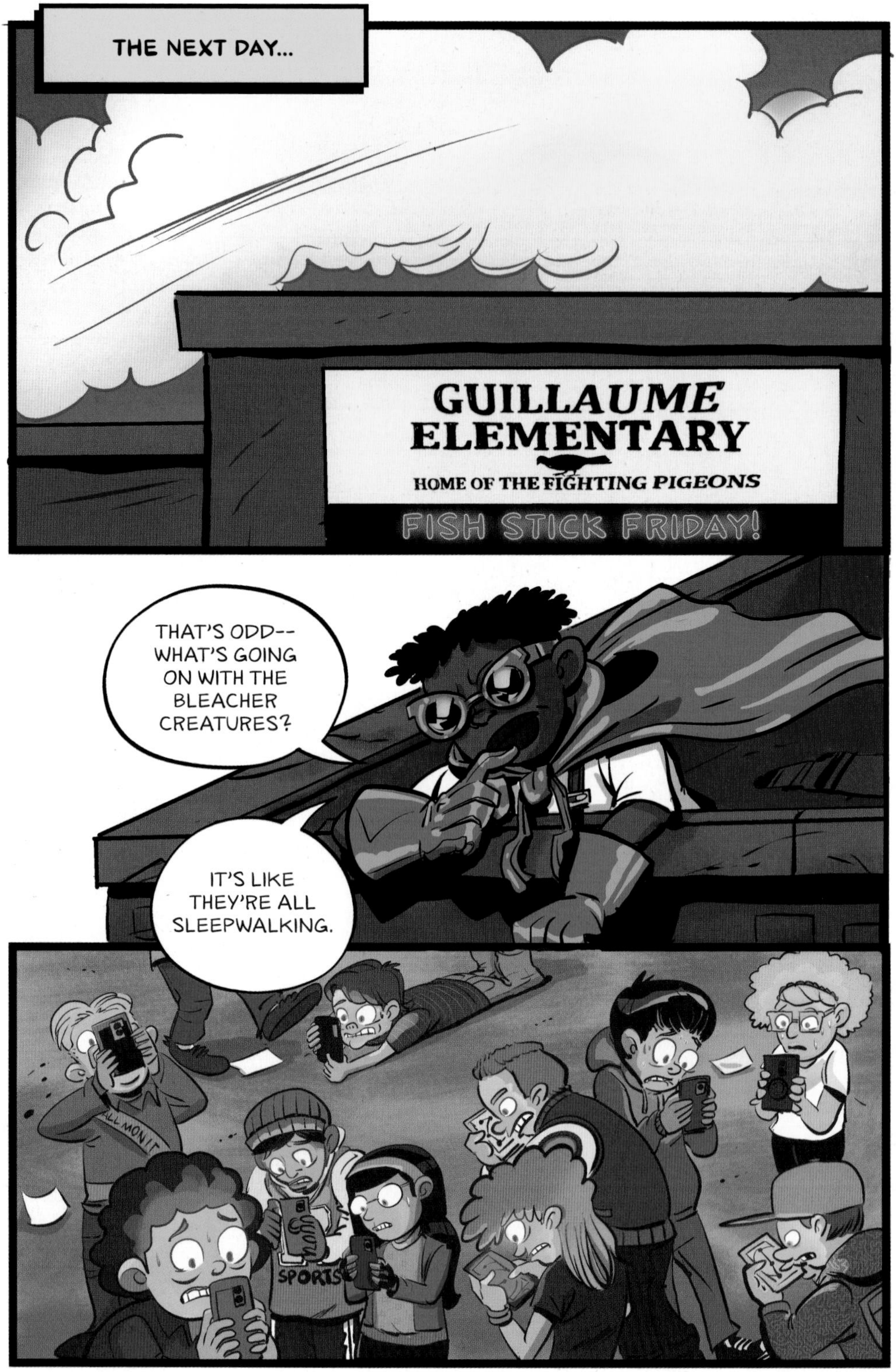
THE NEXT DAY...
GUILLAUME ELEMENTARY
HOME OF THE FIGHTING PIGEONS
FISH STICK FRIDAY!
THAT'S ODD--WHAT'S GOING ON WITH THE BLEACHER CREATURES?
IT'S LIKE THEY'RE ALL SLEEPWALKING.
SPORTS

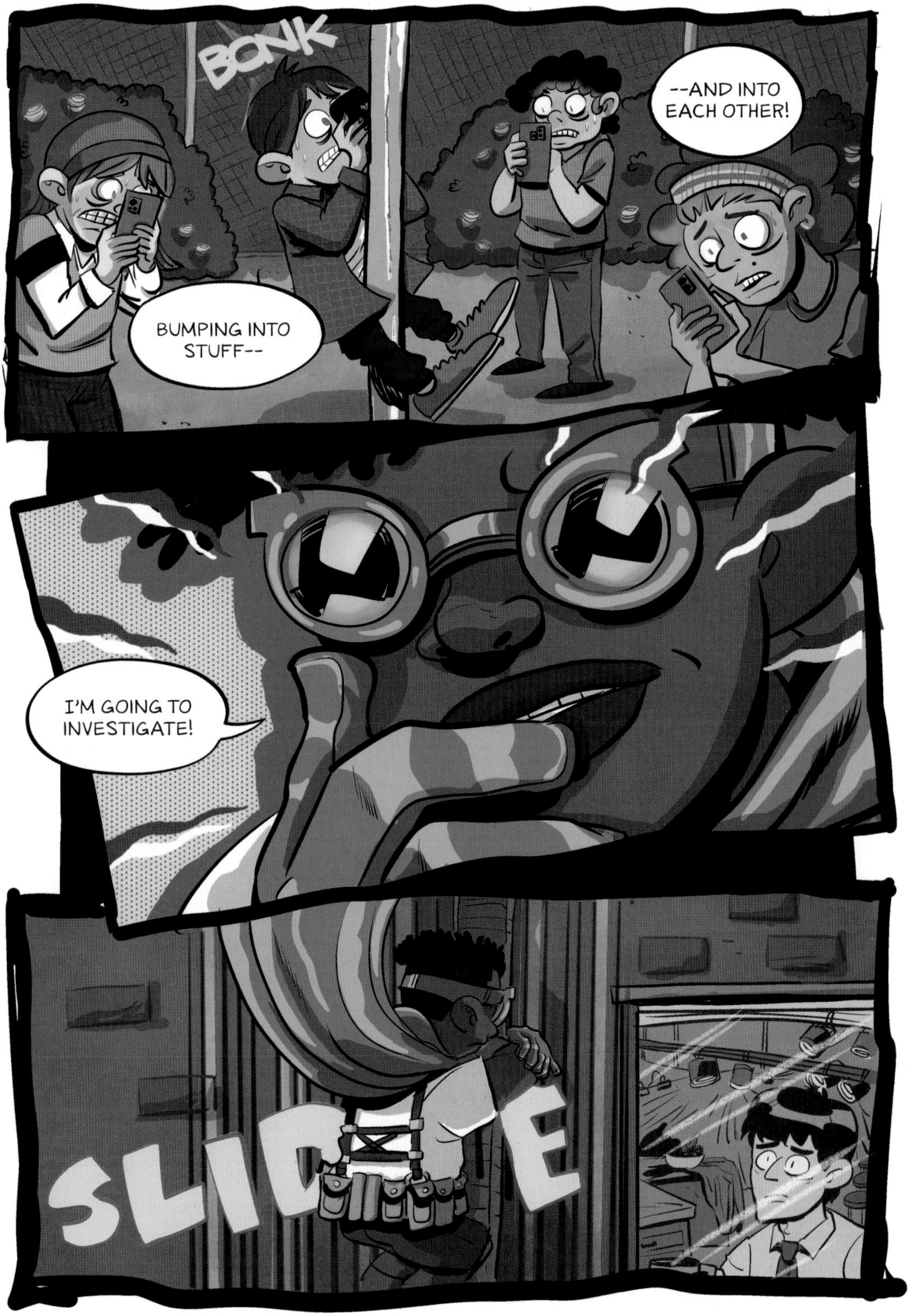
BONK
BUMPING INTO STUFF--
--AND INTO EACH OTHER!
I'M GOING TO INVESTIGATE!
SLIDE

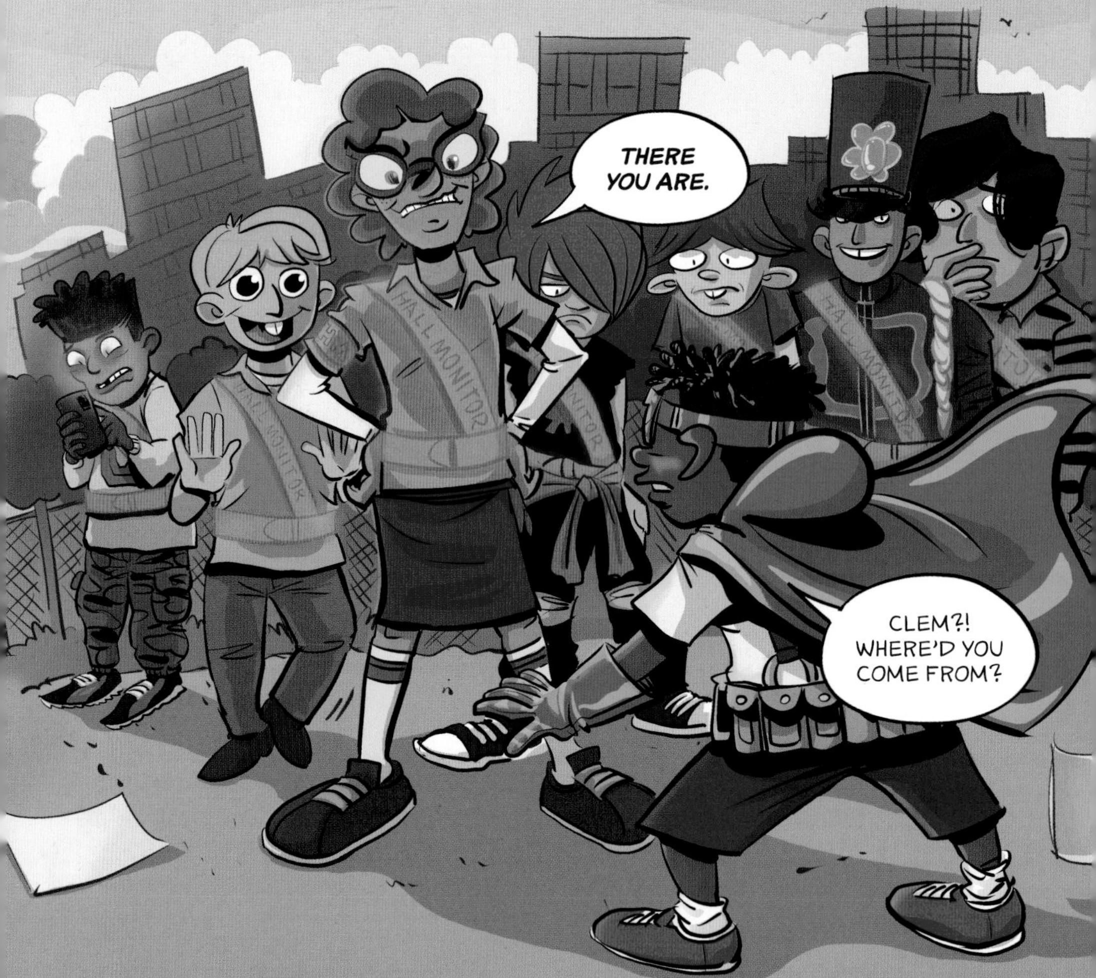
THERE YOU ARE.
CLEM?! WHERE'D YOU COME FROM?

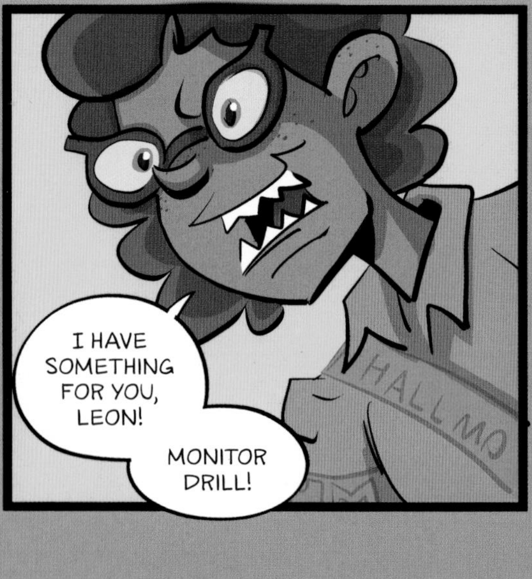
I HAVE SOMETHING FOR YOU, LEON!
MONITOR DRILL!

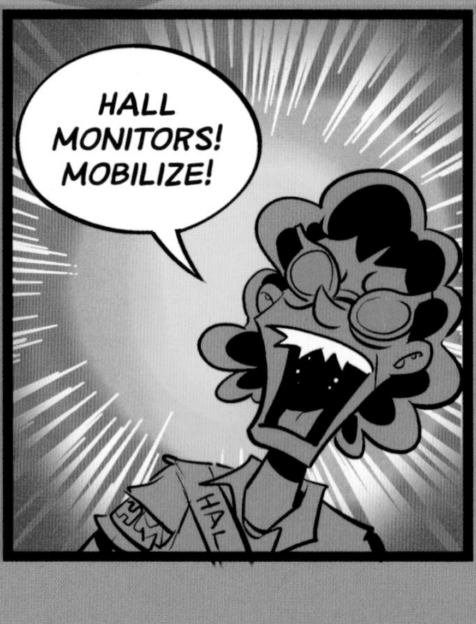
HALL MONITORS! MOBILIZE!

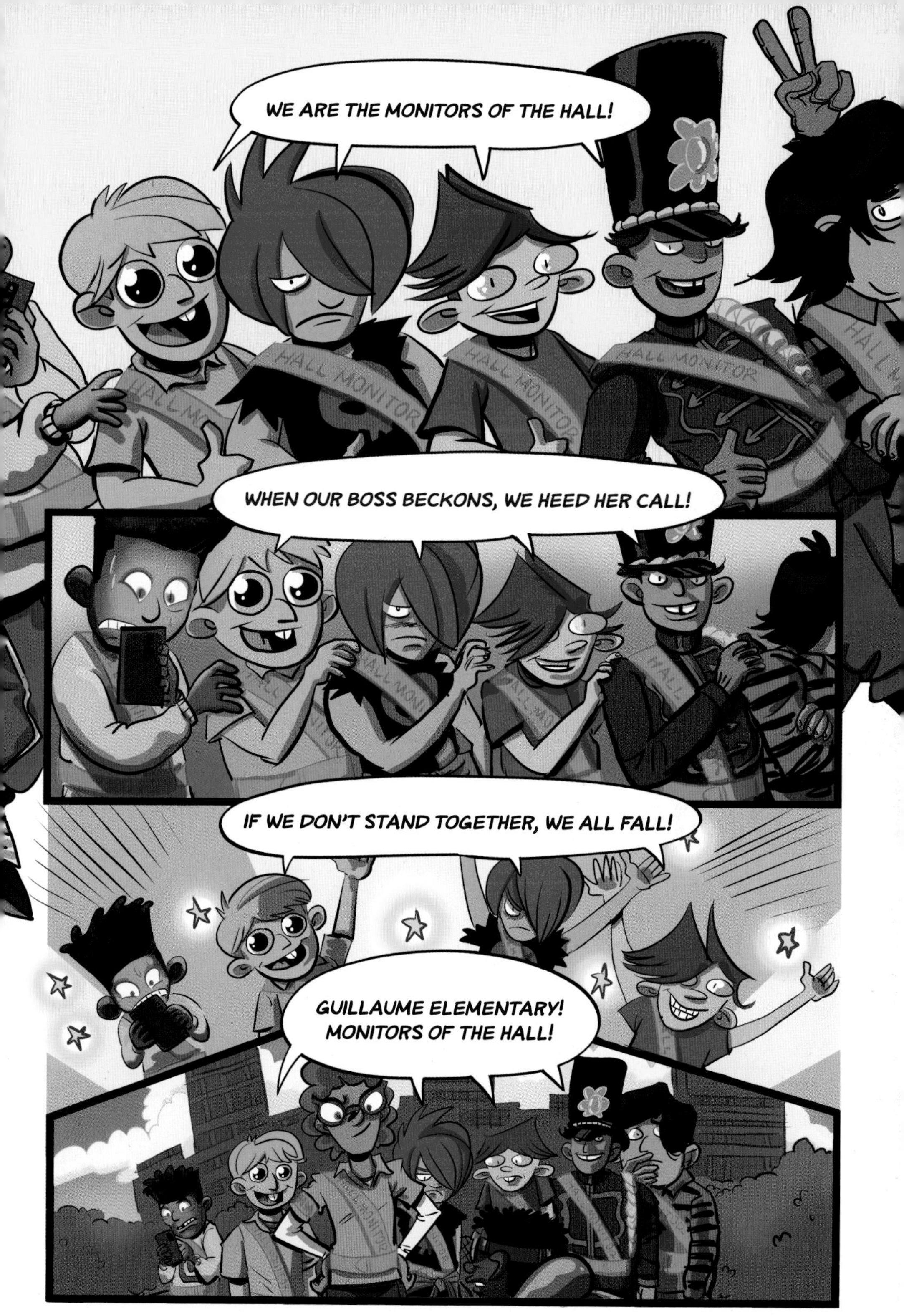
WE ARE THE MONITORS OF THE HALL!
HALL MONITOR
HALL MONITOR
HALL MONITOR
HALL MONITOR
WHEN OUR BOSS BECKONS, WE HEED HER CALL!
IF WE DON'T STAND TOGETHER, WE ALL FALL!
GUILLAUME ELEMENTARY!
MONITORS OF THE HALL!

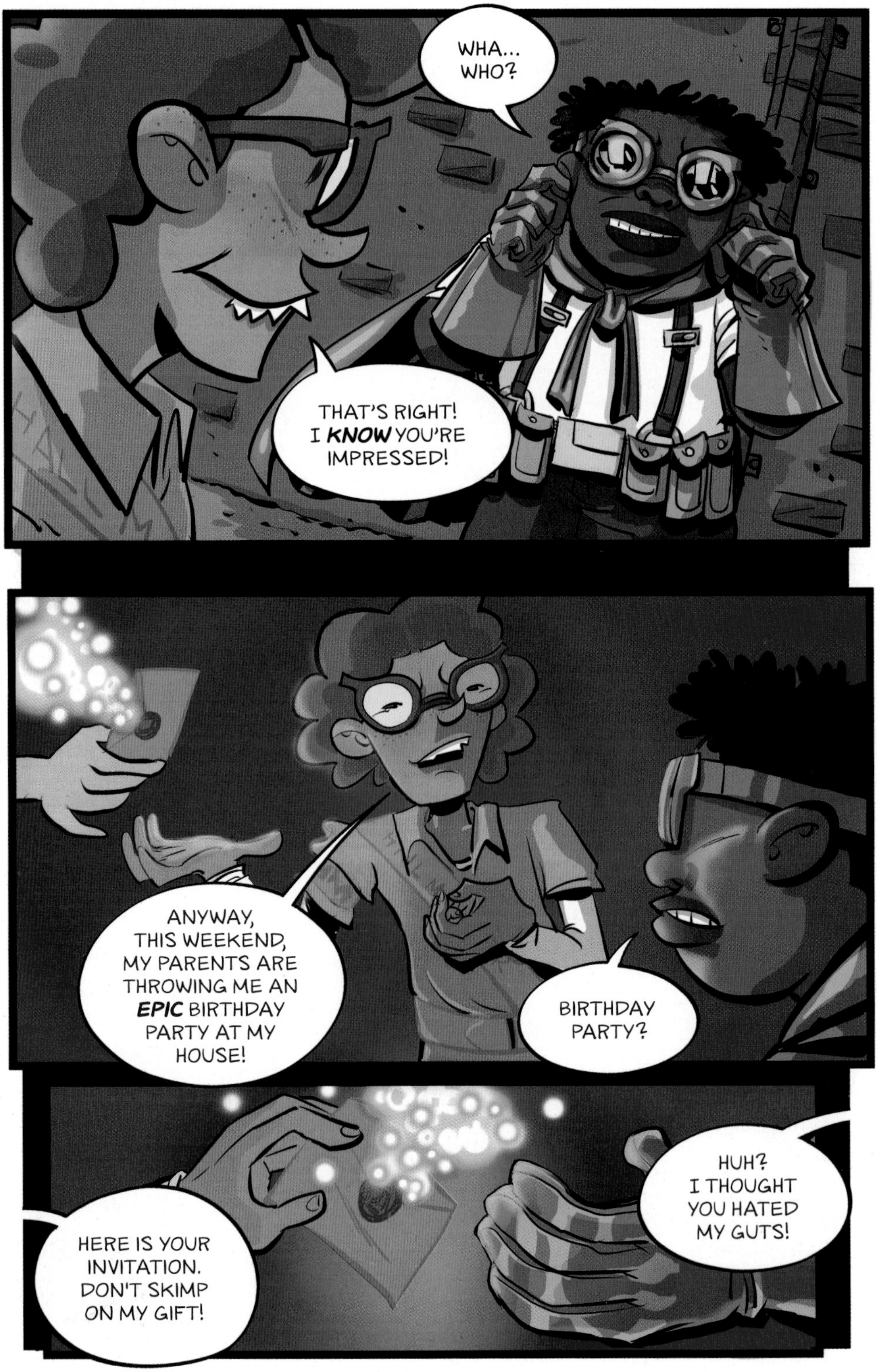
WHA... WHO?
THAT'S RIGHT! I **KNOW** YOU'RE IMPRESSED!
ANYWAY, THIS WEEKEND, MY PARENTS ARE THROWING ME AN **EPIC** BIRTHDAY PARTY AT MY HOUSE!
BIRTHDAY PARTY?
HERE IS YOUR INVITATION. DON'T SKIMP ON MY GIFT!
HUH? I THOUGHT YOU HATED MY GUTS!

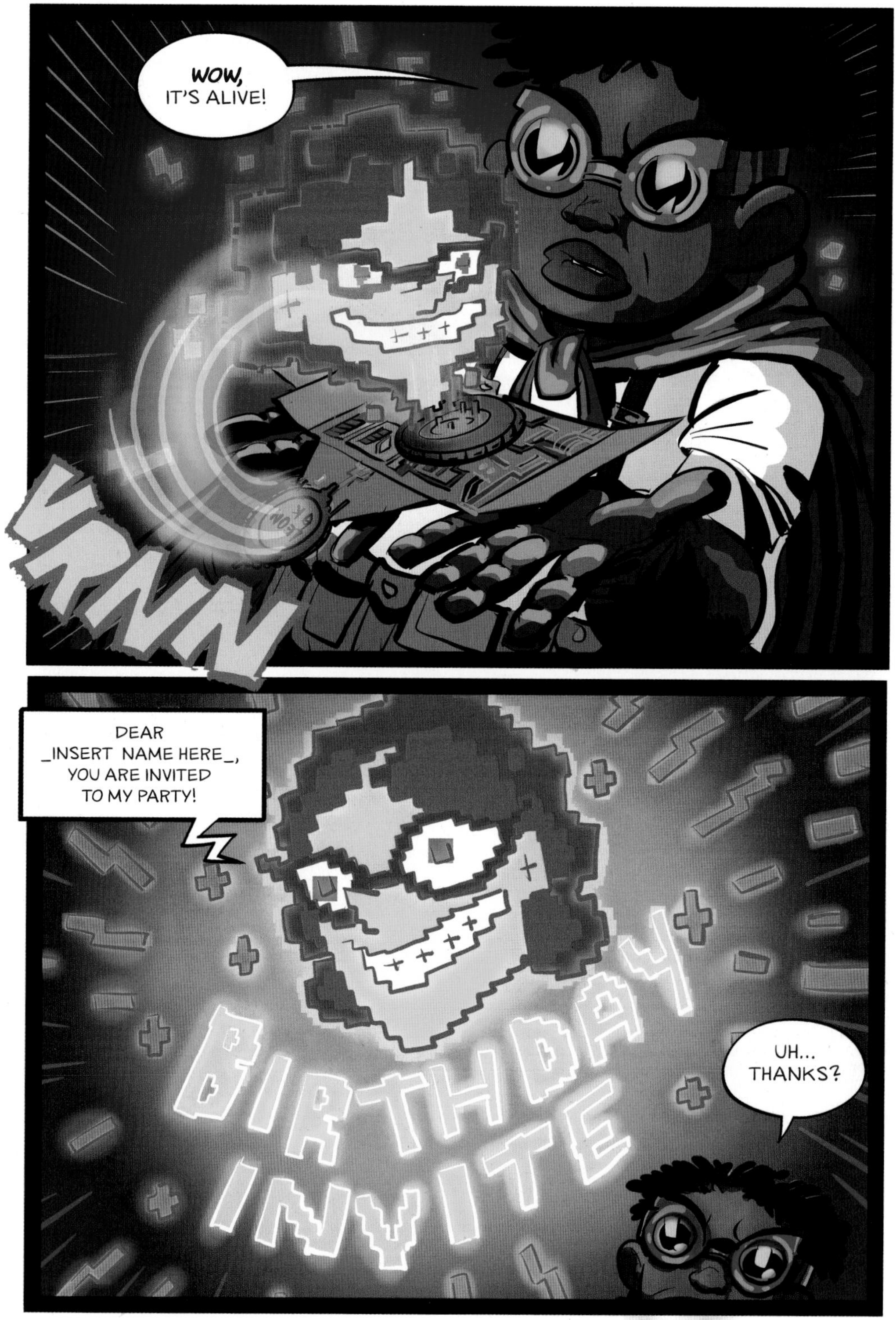
WOW, IT'S ALIVE!
VRNN
DEAR _INSERT NAME HERE_, YOU ARE INVITED TO MY PARTY!
BIRTHDAY INVITE
UH... THANKS?

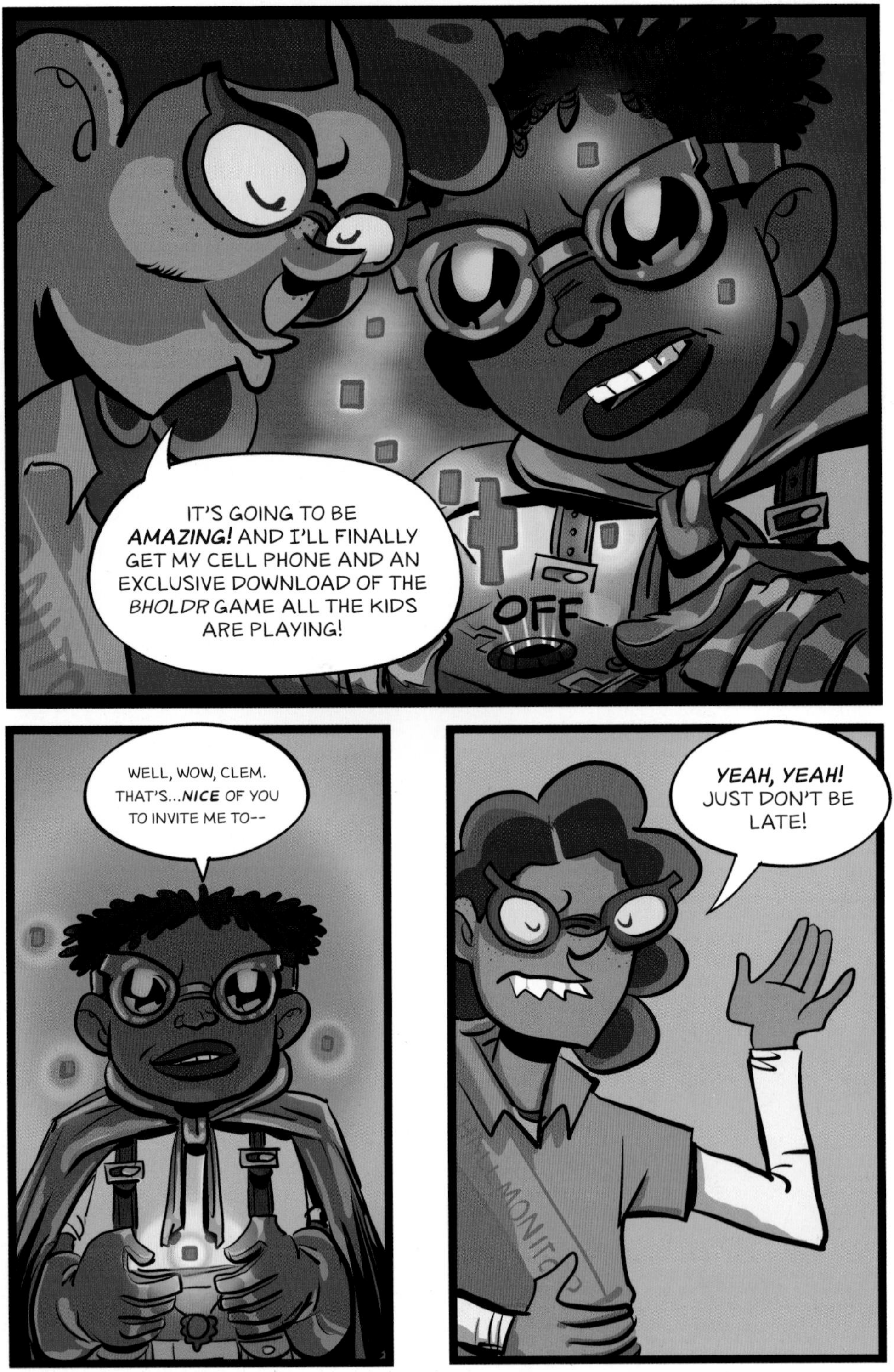
IT'S GOING TO BE **AMAZING!** AND I'LL FINALLY GET MY CELL PHONE AND AN EXCLUSIVE DOWNLOAD OF THE *BHOLDR* GAME ALL THE KIDS ARE PLAYING!
OFF
WELL, WOW, CLEM. THAT'S...***NICE*** OF YOU TO INVITE ME TO--
YEAH, YEAH! JUST DON'T BE LATE!

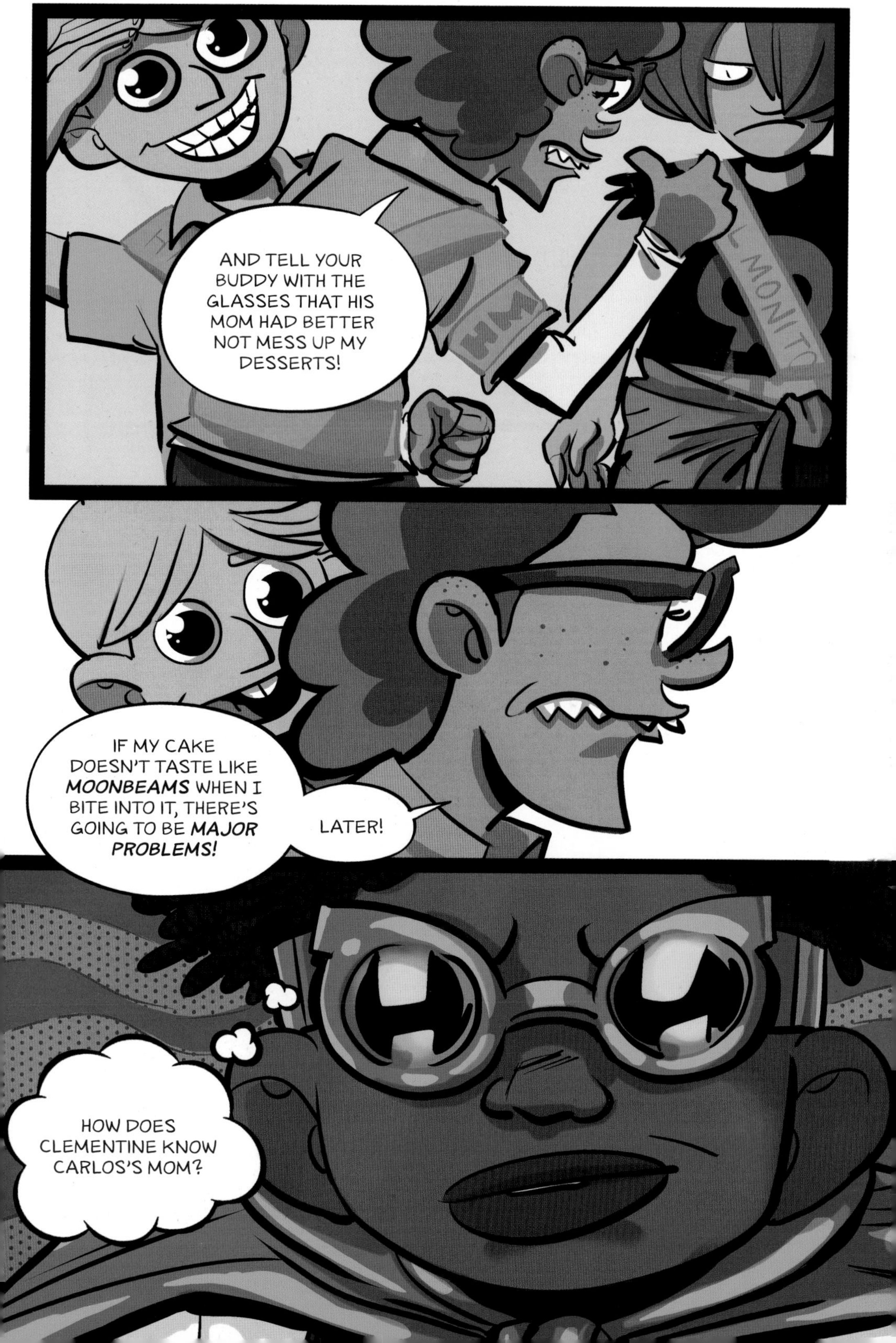
AND TELL YOUR BUDDY WITH THE GLASSES THAT HIS MOM HAD BETTER NOT MESS UP MY DESSERTS!
IF MY CAKE DOESN'T TASTE LIKE *MOONBEAMS* WHEN I BITE INTO IT, THERE'S GOING TO BE *MAJOR PROBLEMS!*
LATER!
HOW DOES CLEMENTINE KNOW CARLOS'S MOM?

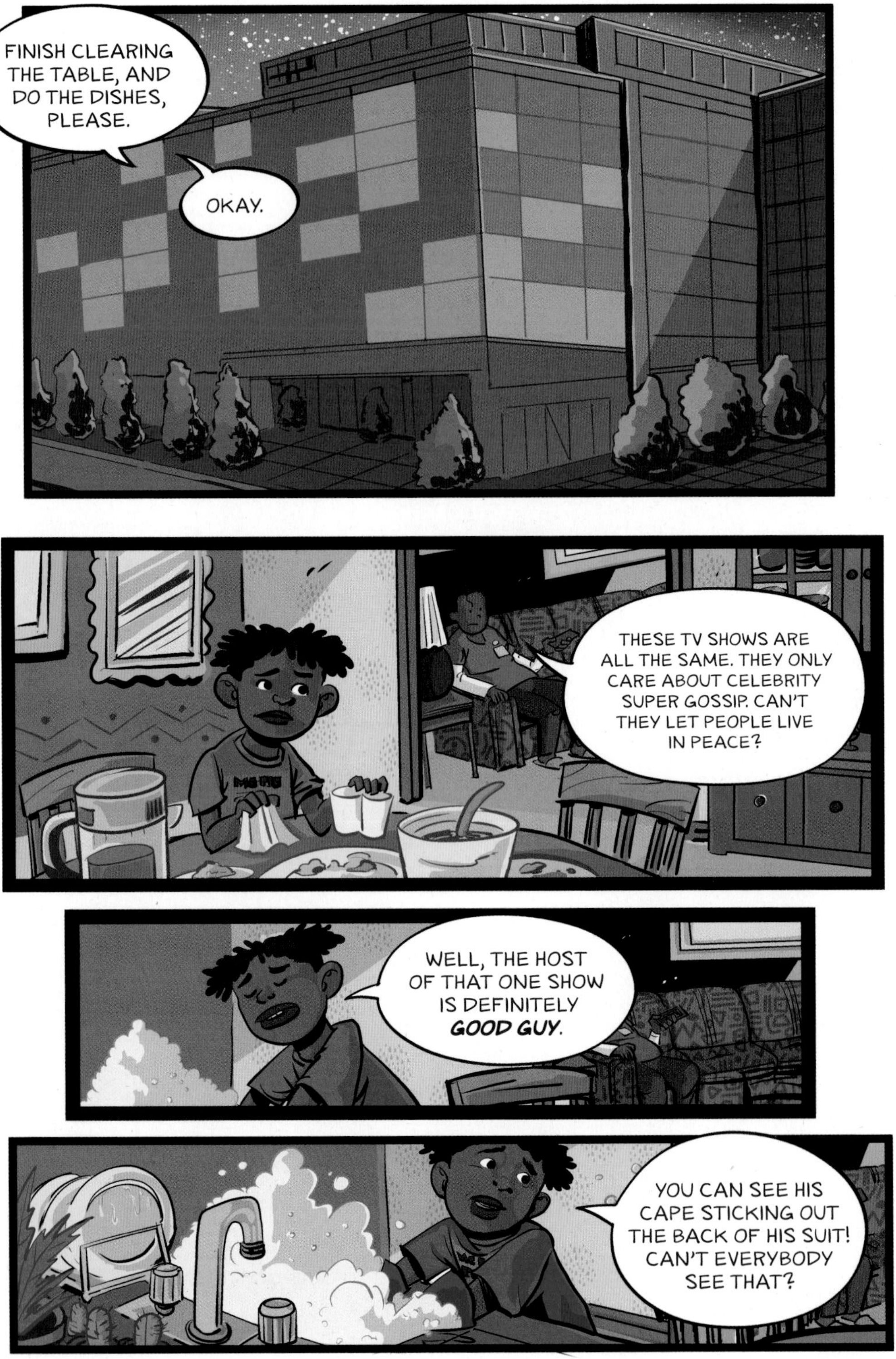
FINISH CLEARING THE TABLE, AND DO THE DISHES, PLEASE.
OKAY.
THESE TV SHOWS ARE ALL THE SAME. THEY ONLY CARE ABOUT CELEBRITY SUPER GOSSIP. CAN'T THEY LET PEOPLE LIVE IN PEACE?
WELL, THE HOST OF THAT ONE SHOW IS DEFINITELY ***GOOD GUY***.
YOU CAN SEE HIS CAPE STICKING OUT THE BACK OF HIS SUIT! CAN'T EVERYBODY SEE THAT?

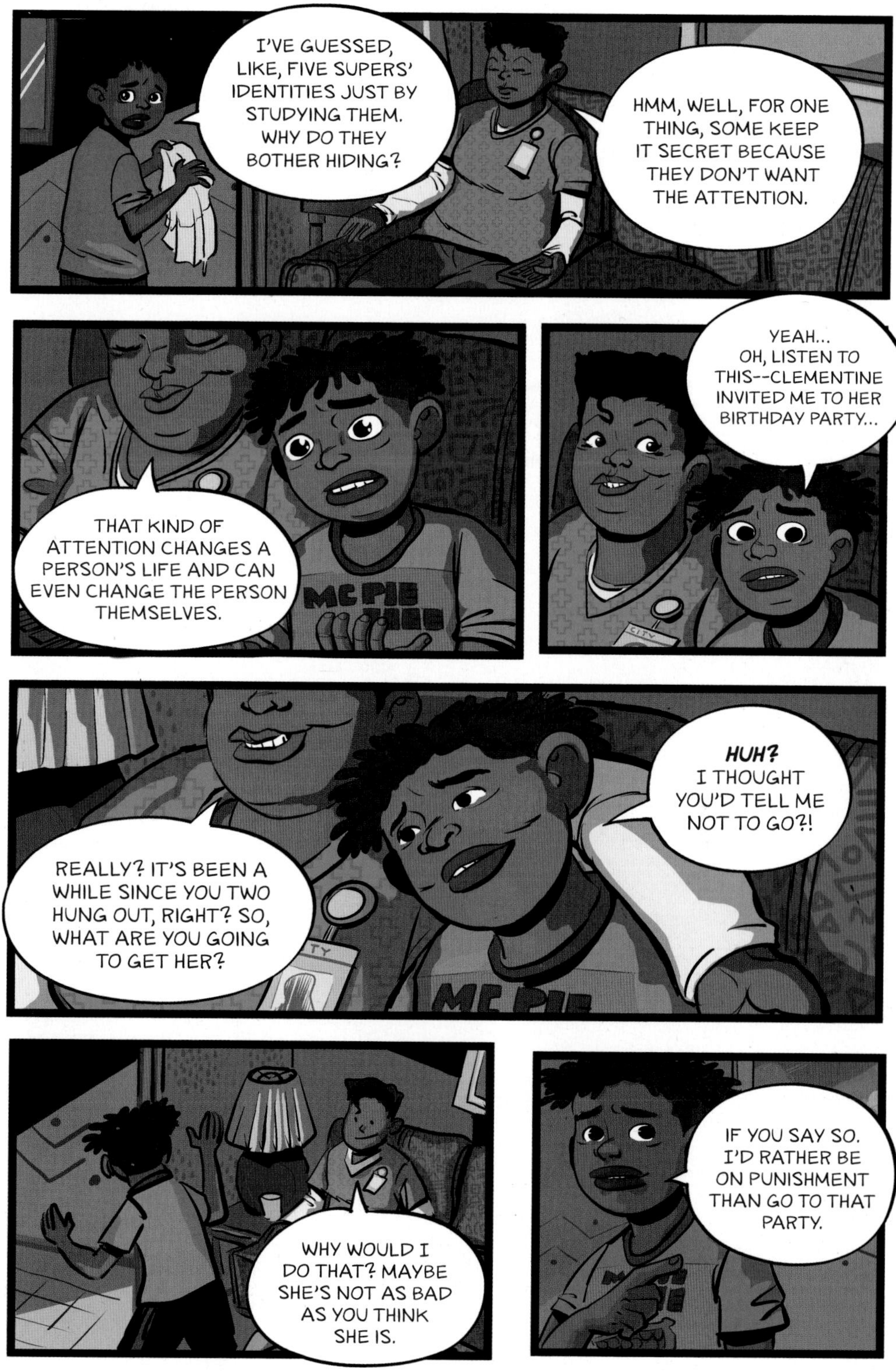
I'VE GUESSED, LIKE, FIVE SUPERS' IDENTITIES JUST BY STUDYING THEM. WHY DO THEY BOTHER HIDING?
HMM, WELL, FOR ONE THING, SOME KEEP IT SECRET BECAUSE THEY DON'T WANT THE ATTENTION.
THAT KIND OF ATTENTION CHANGES A PERSON'S LIFE AND CAN EVEN CHANGE THE PERSON THEMSELVES.
YEAH... OH, LISTEN TO THIS--CLEMENTINE INVITED ME TO HER BIRTHDAY PARTY...
REALLY? IT'S BEEN A WHILE SINCE YOU TWO HUNG OUT, RIGHT? SO, WHAT ARE YOU GOING TO GET HER?
HUH? I THOUGHT YOU'D TELL ME NOT TO GO?!
WHY WOULD I DO THAT? MAYBE SHE'S NOT AS BAD AS YOU THINK SHE IS.
IF YOU SAY SO. I'D RATHER BE ON PUNISHMENT THAN GO TO THAT PARTY.

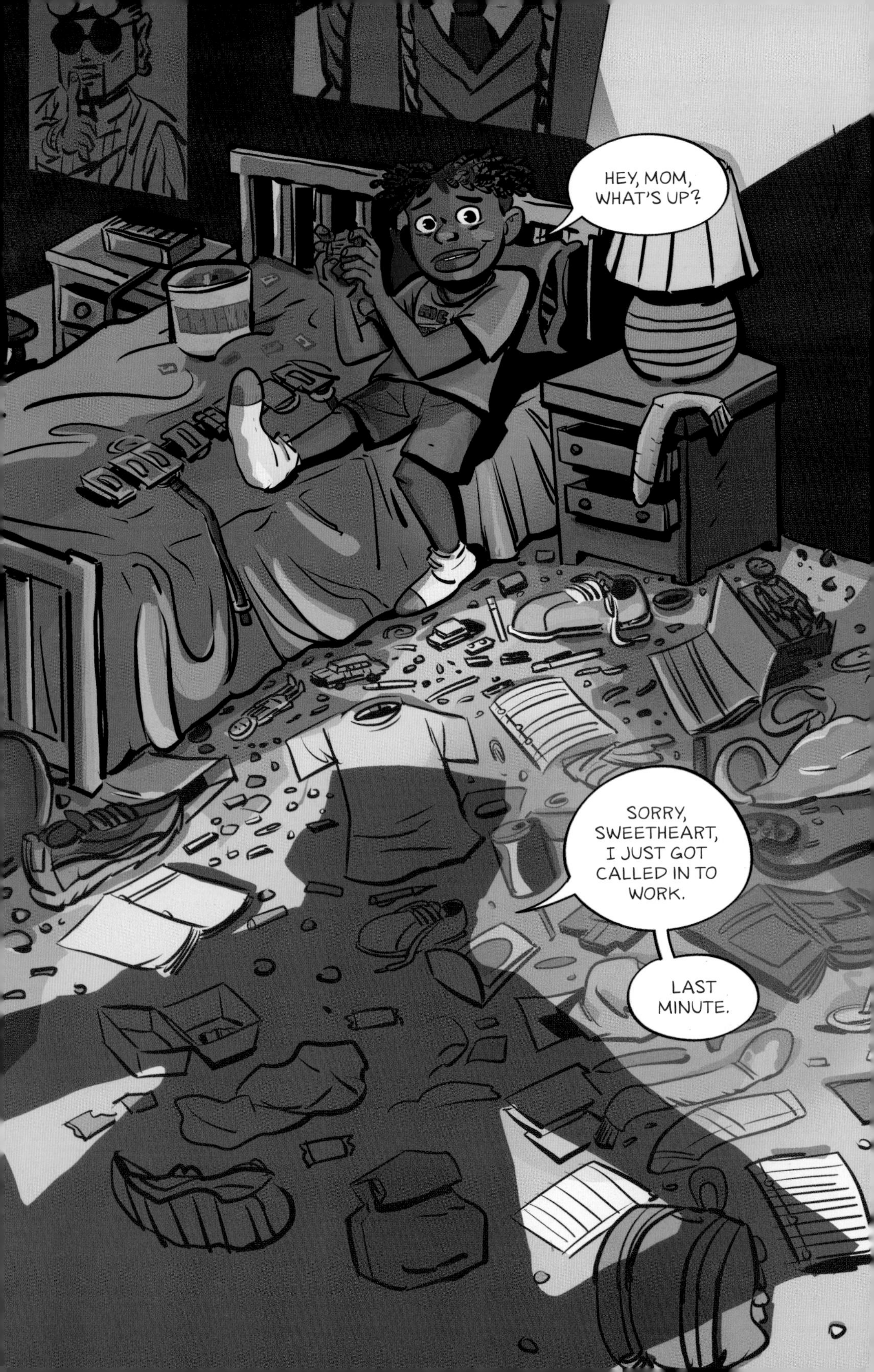
HEY, MOM, WHAT'S UP?
SORRY, SWEETHEART, I JUST GOT CALLED IN TO WORK.
LAST MINUTE.

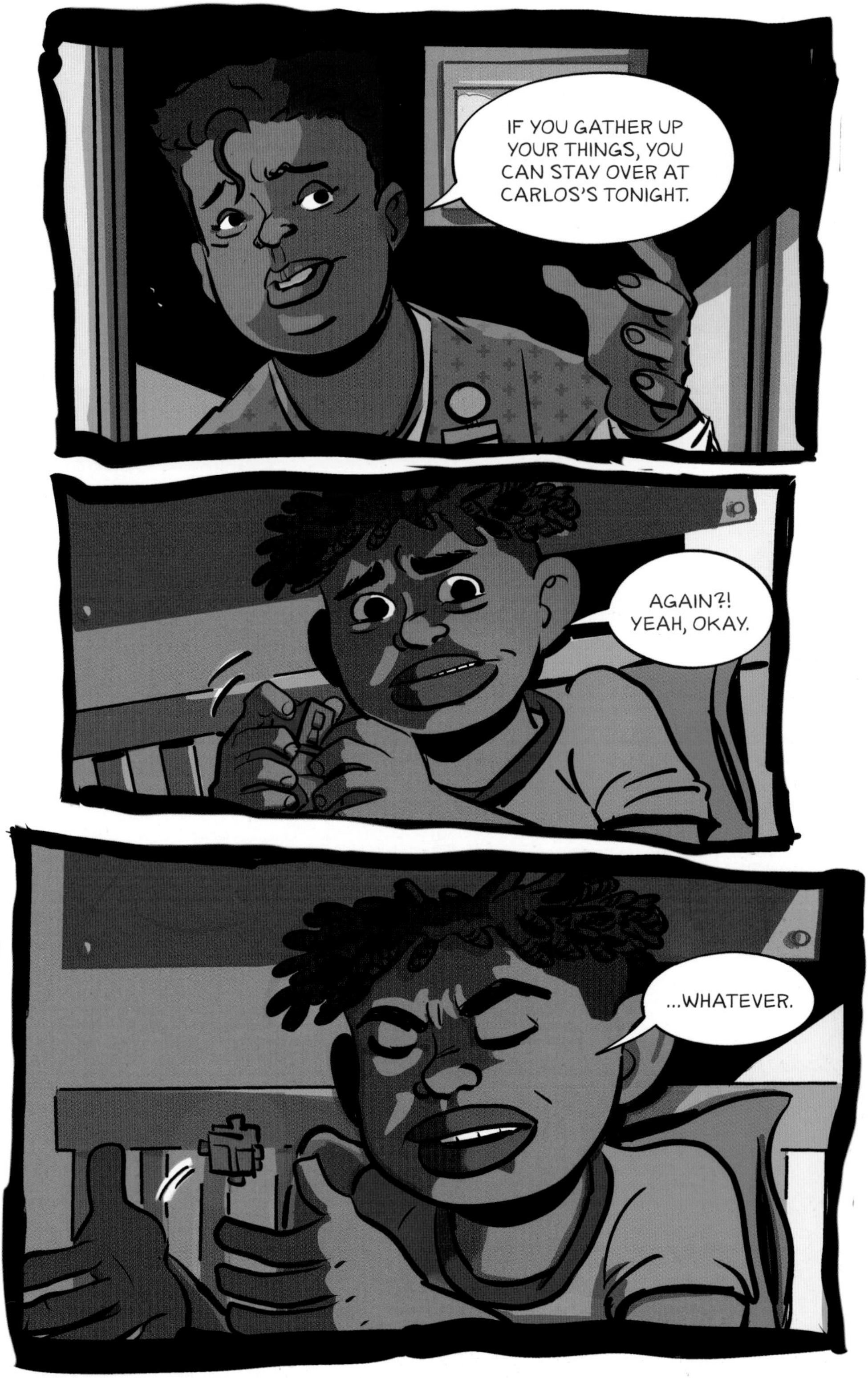
IF YOU GATHER UP YOUR THINGS, YOU CAN STAY OVER AT CARLOS'S TONIGHT.
AGAIN?! YEAH, OKAY.
...WHATEVER.

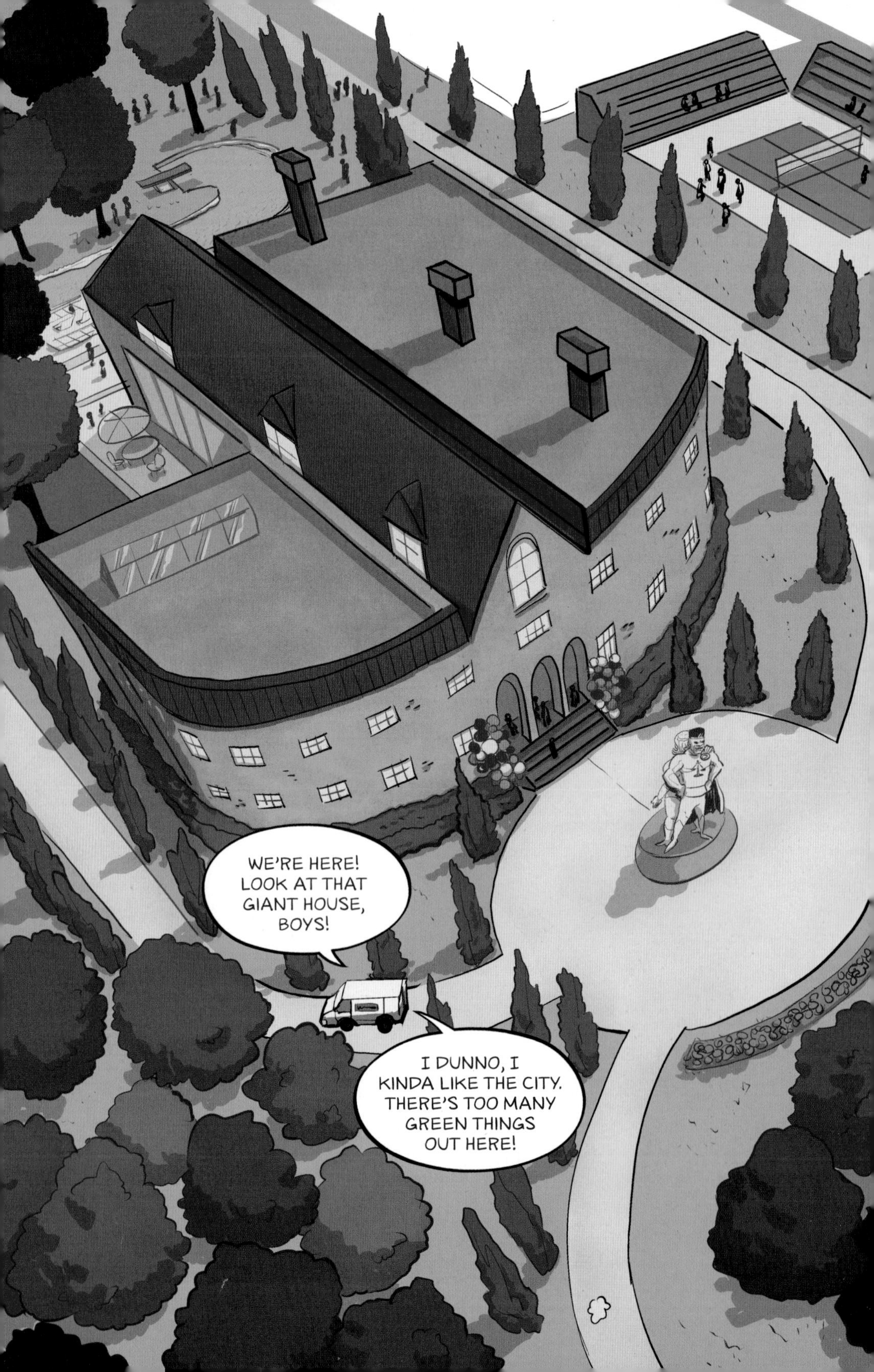
WE'RE HERE! LOOK AT THAT GIANT HOUSE, BOYS!
I DUNNO, I KINDA LIKE THE CITY. THERE'S TOO MANY GREEN THINGS OUT HERE!

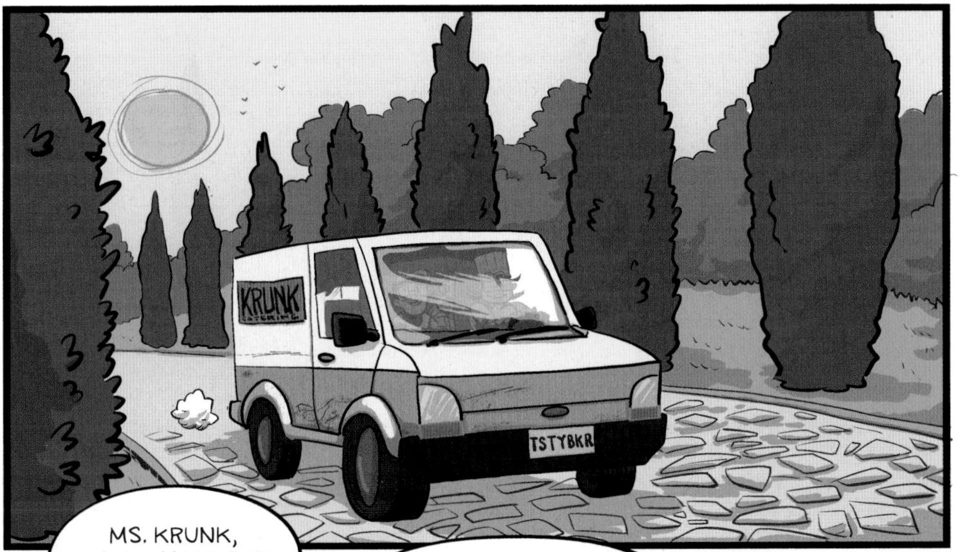
KRUNK
TSTYBKR

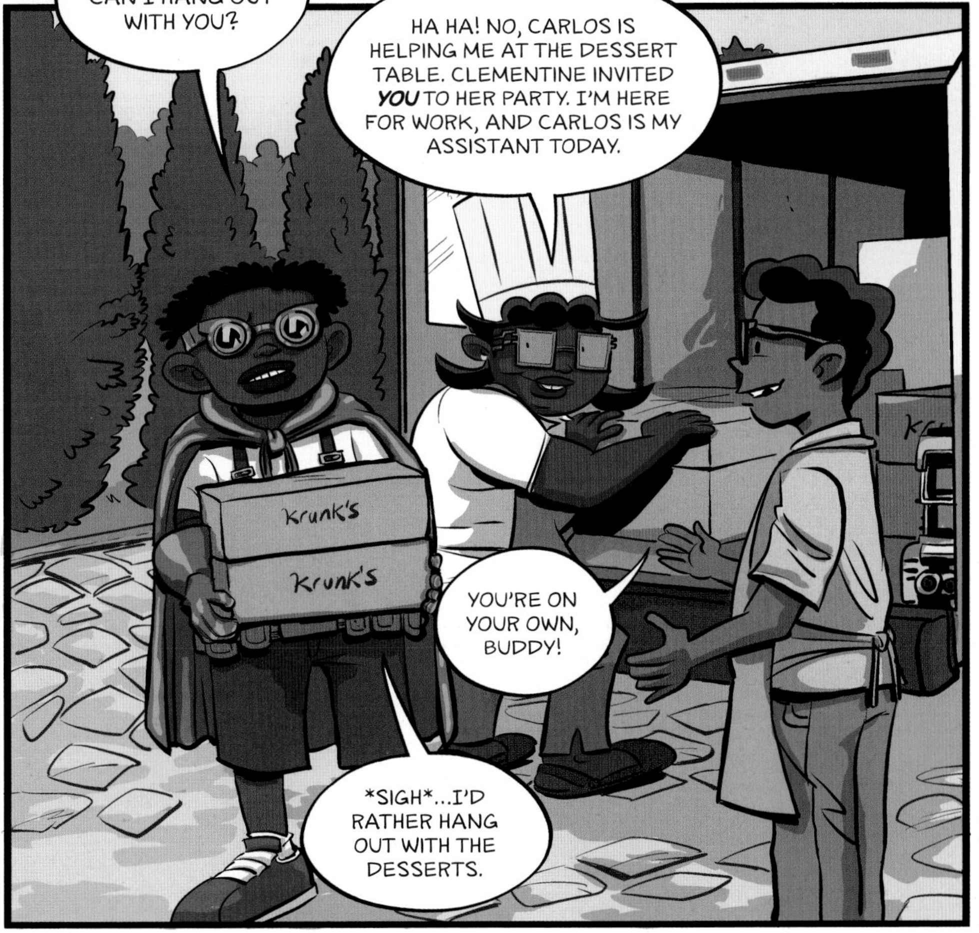
MS. KRUNK, CAN I HANG OUT WITH YOU?
HA HA! NO, CARLOS IS HELPING ME AT THE DESSERT TABLE. CLEMENTINE INVITED **YOU** TO HER PARTY. I'M HERE FOR WORK, AND CARLOS IS MY ASSISTANT TODAY.
Krunk's
Krunk's
YOU'RE ON YOUR OWN, BUDDY!
SIGH...I'D RATHER HANG OUT WITH THE DESSERTS.

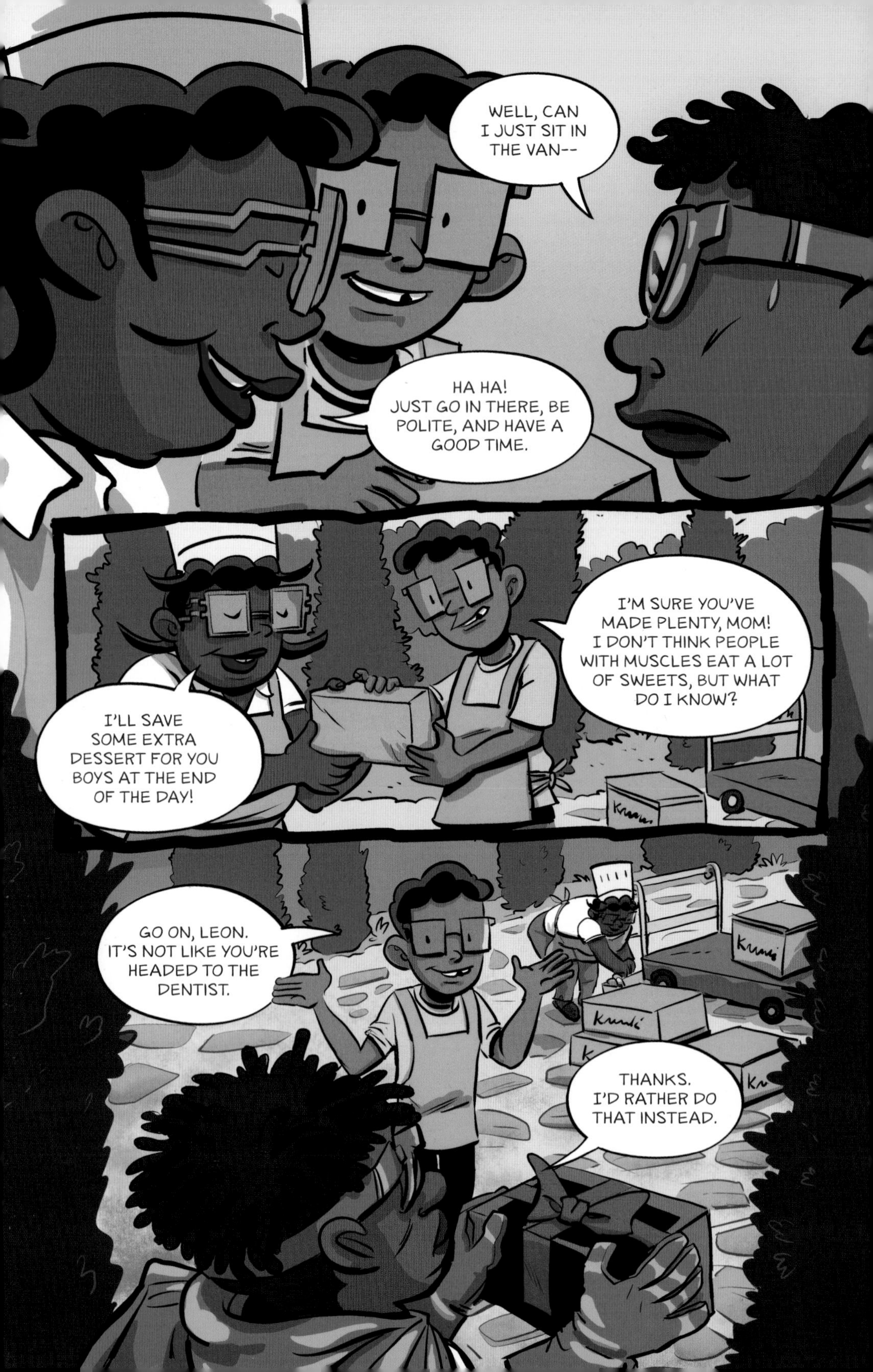
WELL, CAN I JUST SIT IN THE VAN--
HA HA! JUST GO IN THERE, BE POLITE, AND HAVE A GOOD TIME.
I'M SURE YOU'VE MADE PLENTY, MOM! I DON'T THINK PEOPLE WITH MUSCLES EAT A LOT OF SWEETS, BUT WHAT DO I KNOW?
I'LL SAVE SOME EXTRA DESSERT FOR YOU BOYS AT THE END OF THE DAY!
GO ON, LEON. IT'S NOT LIKE YOU'RE HEADED TO THE DENTIST.
THANKS. I'D RATHER DO THAT INSTEAD.

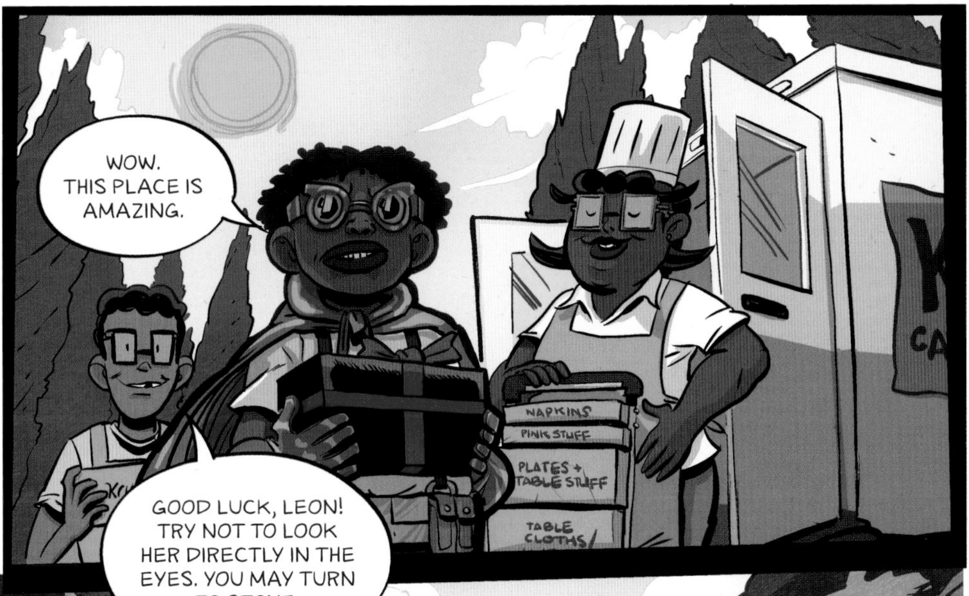
WOW. THIS PLACE IS AMAZING.
NAPKINS
PINK STUFF
PLATES + TABLE STUFF
TABLE CLOTHS
GOOD LUCK, LEON! TRY NOT TO LOOK HER DIRECTLY IN THE EYES. YOU MAY TURN TO STONE.

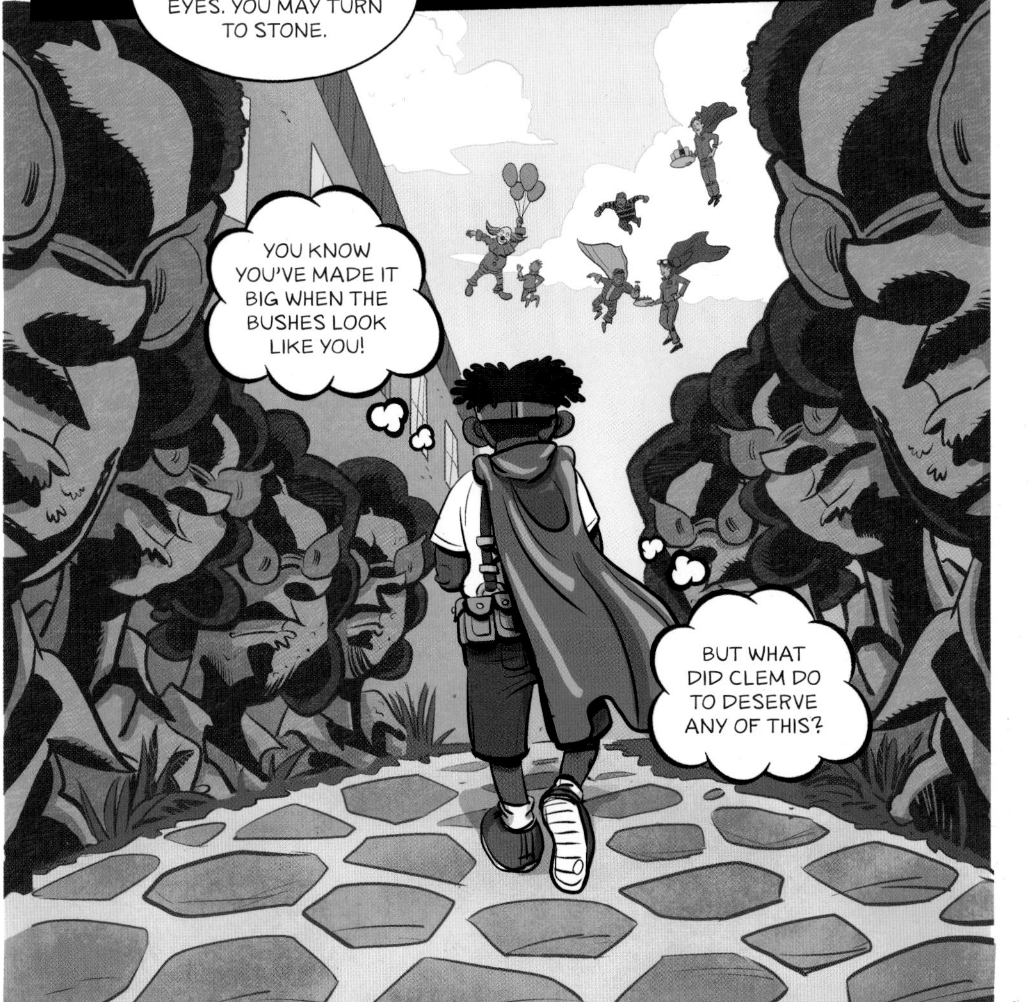
YOU KNOW YOU'VE MADE IT BIG WHEN THE BUSHES LOOK LIKE YOU!
BUT WHAT DID CLEM DO TO DESERVE ANY OF THIS?

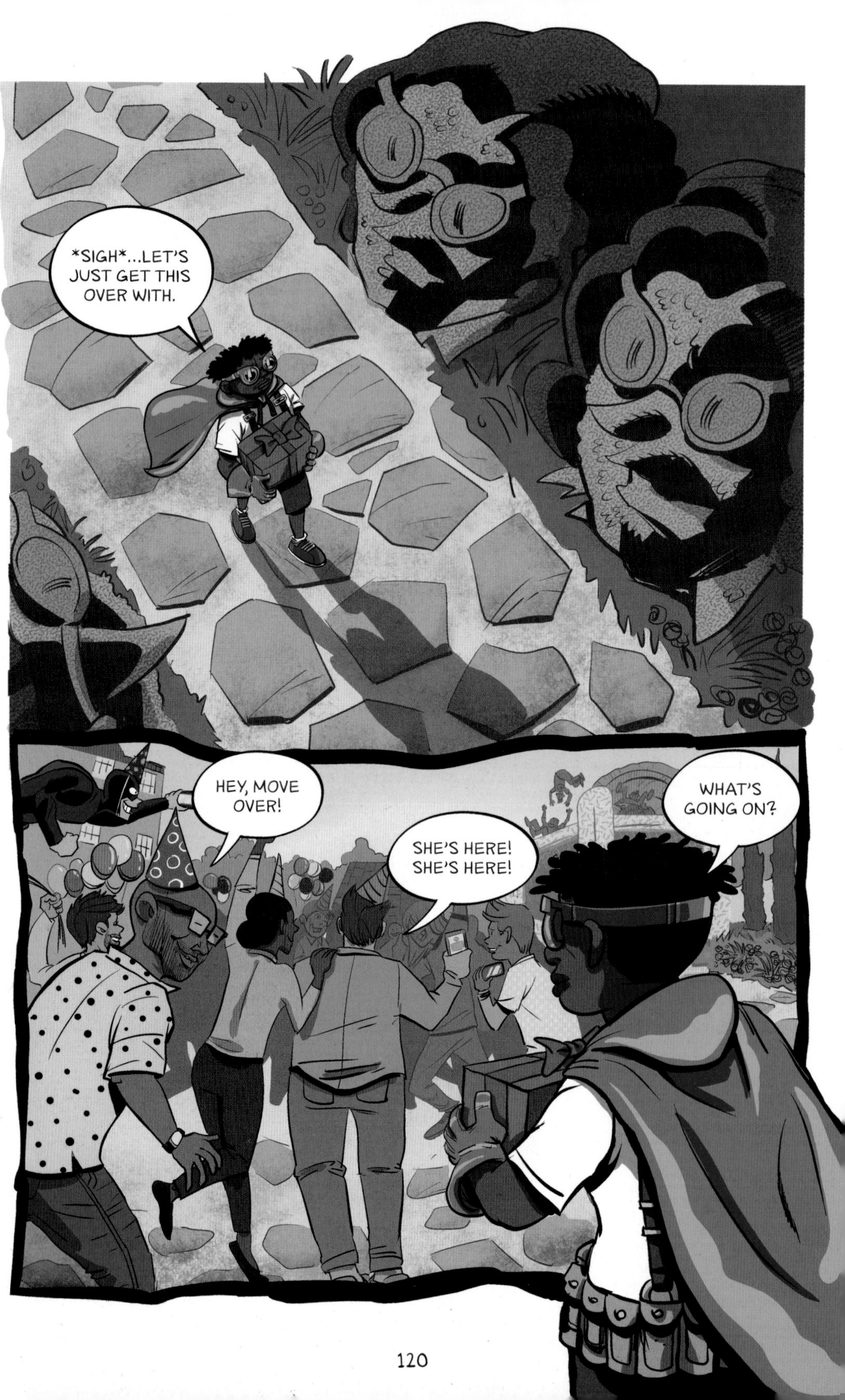
SIGH...LET'S JUST GET THIS OVER WITH.
HEY, MOVE OVER!
SHE'S HERE! SHE'S HERE!
WHAT'S GOING ON?

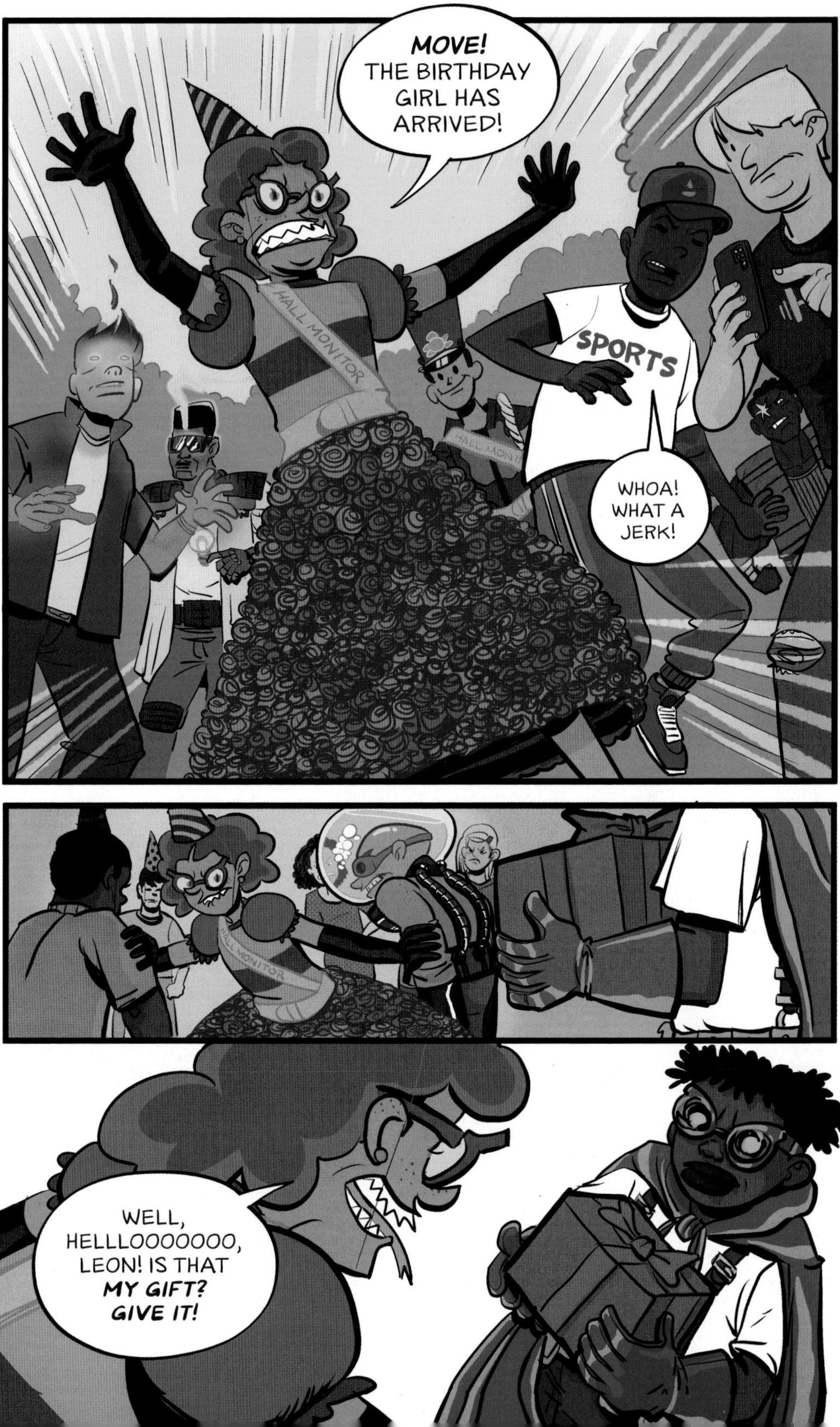
MOVE! THE BIRTHDAY GIRL HAS ARRIVED!
HALL MONITOR
HALL MONITOR
SPORTS
WHOA! WHAT A JERK!
HALL MONITOR
WELL, HELLLOOOOOOO, LEON! IS THAT MY GIFT? GIVE IT!

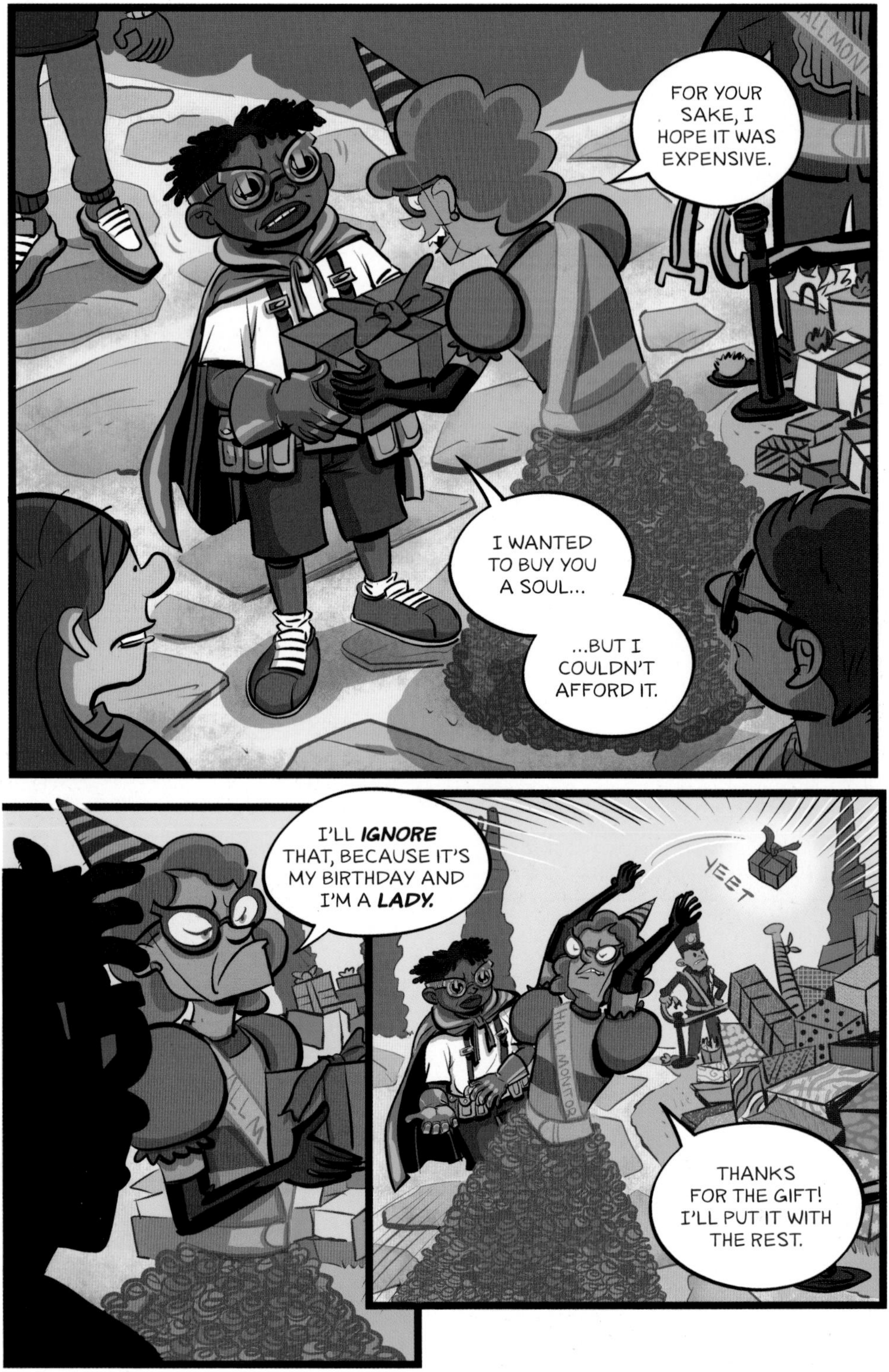
FOR YOUR SAKE, I HOPE IT WAS EXPENSIVE.
I WANTED TO BUY YOU A SOUL...
...BUT I COULDN'T AFFORD IT.
I'LL **IGNORE** THAT, BECAUSE IT'S MY BIRTHDAY AND I'M A **LADY.**
YEET
HALL MONITOR
THANKS FOR THE GIFT! I'LL PUT IT WITH THE REST.

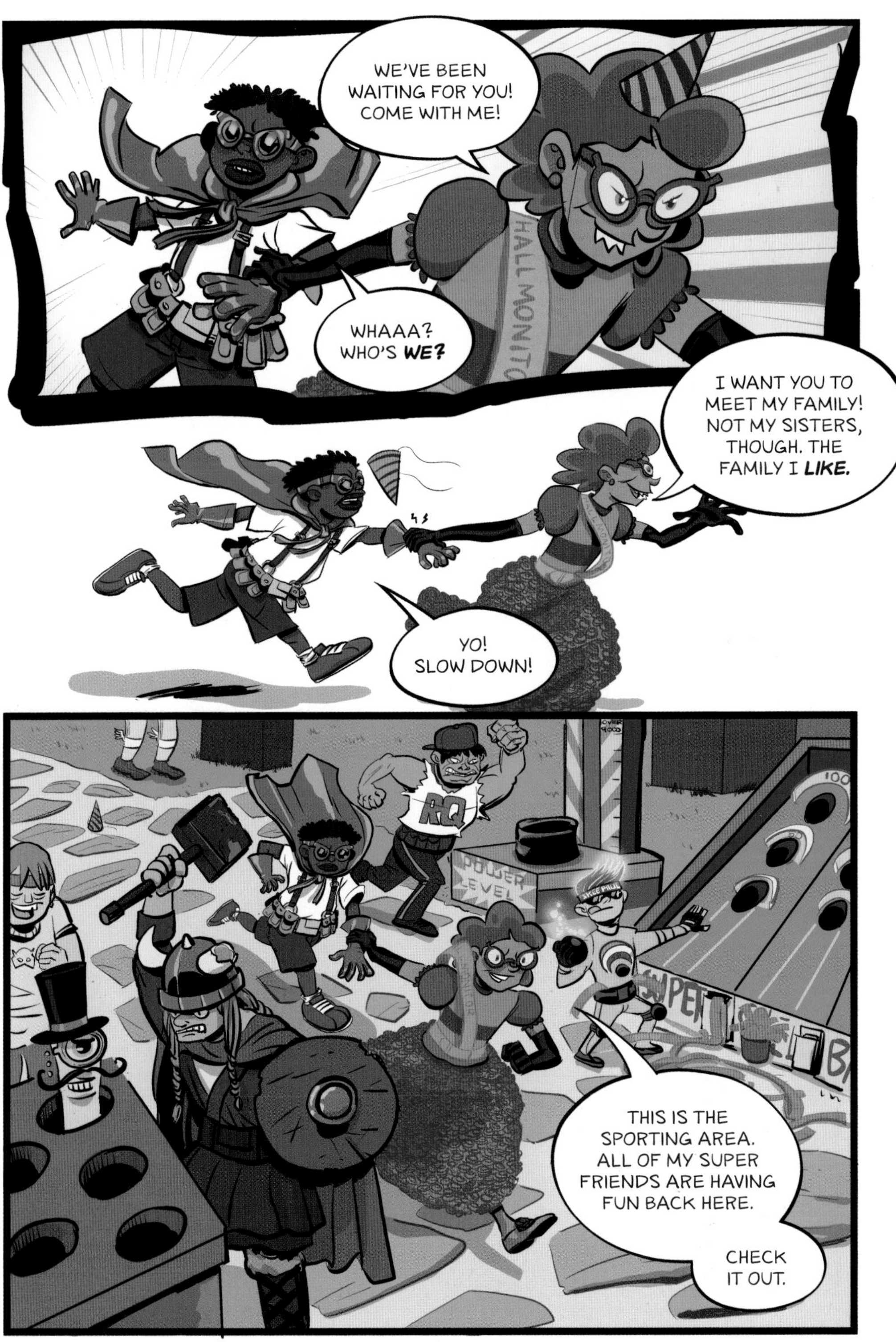
WE'VE BEEN WAITING FOR YOU! COME WITH ME!
WHAAA? WHO'S **WE?**
I WANT YOU TO MEET MY FAMILY! NOT MY SISTERS, THOUGH. THE FAMILY I **LIKE.**
YO! SLOW DOWN!
POWER LEVEL
THIS IS THE SPORTING AREA. ALL OF MY SUPER FRIENDS ARE HAVING FUN BACK HERE.
CHECK IT OUT.

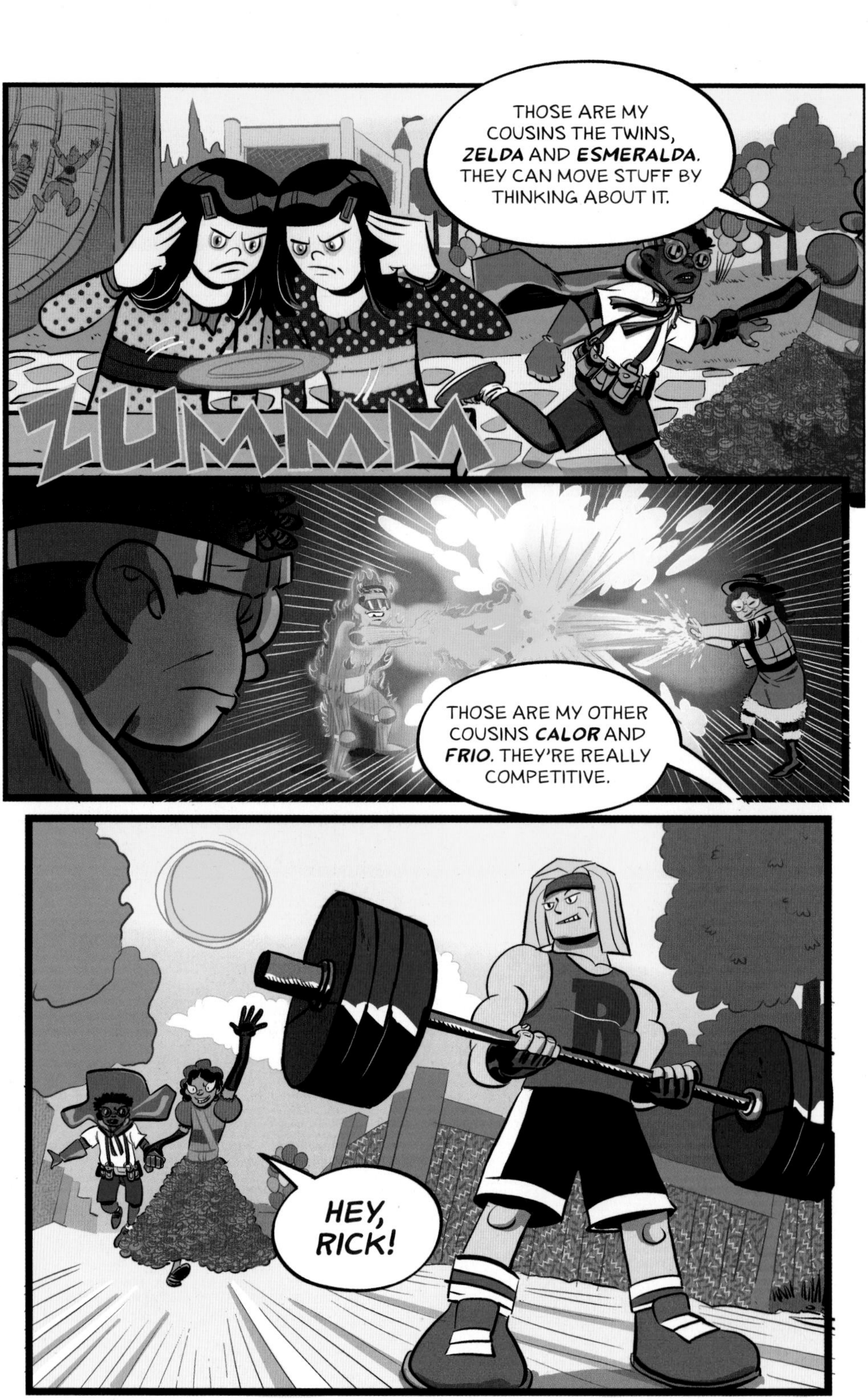
THOSE ARE MY COUSINS THE TWINS, **ZELDA** AND **ESMERALDA**. THEY CAN MOVE STUFF BY THINKING ABOUT IT.
ZUMMM
THOSE ARE MY OTHER COUSINS **CALOR** AND **FRIO**. THEY'RE REALLY COMPETITIVE.
HEY, RICK!

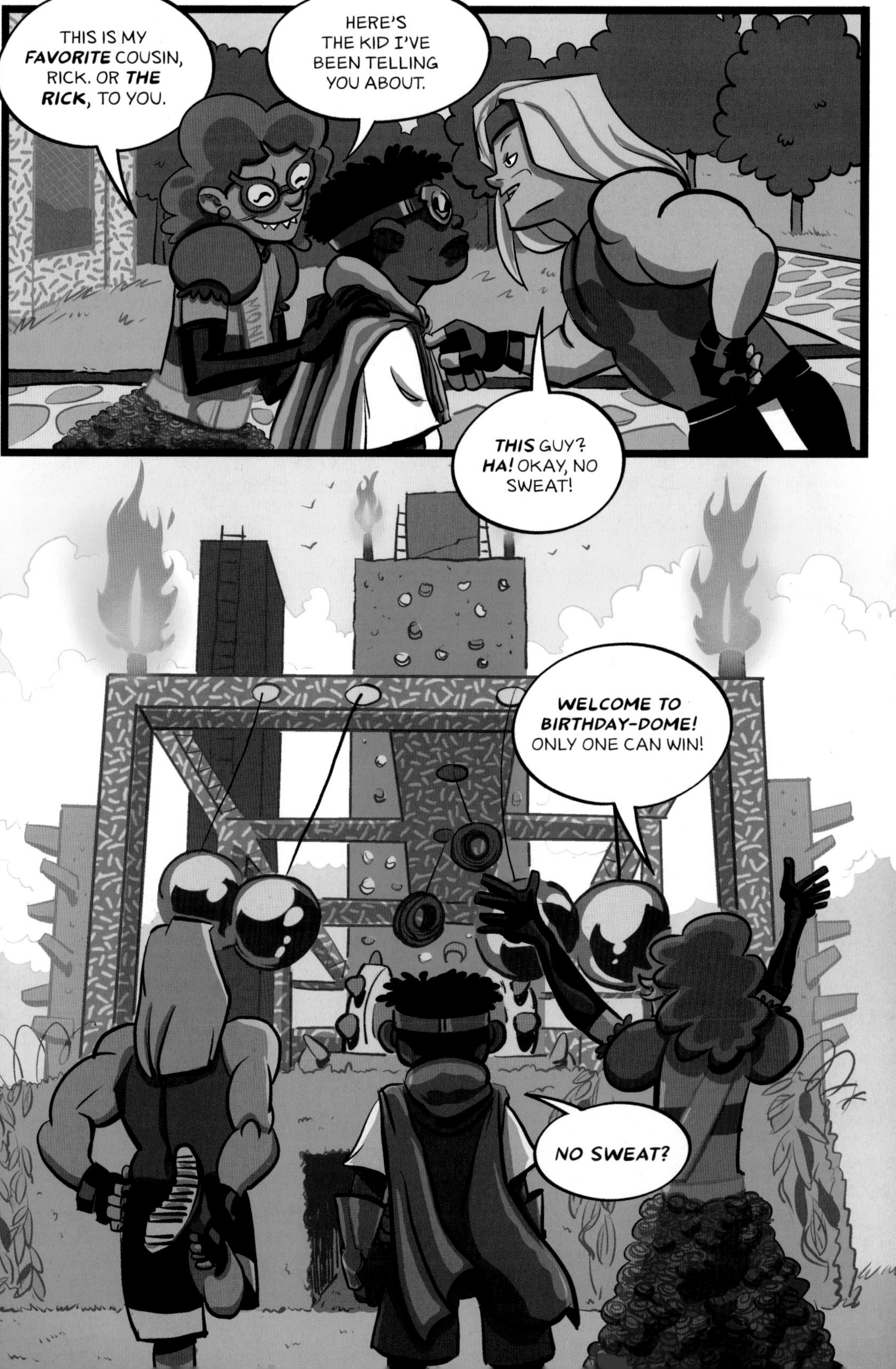
THIS IS MY FAVORITE COUSIN, RICK. OR THE RICK, TO YOU.
HERE'S THE KID I'VE BEEN TELLING YOU ABOUT.
THIS GUY? HA! OKAY, NO SWEAT!
WELCOME TO BIRTHDAY-DOME! ONLY ONE CAN WIN!
NO SWEAT?

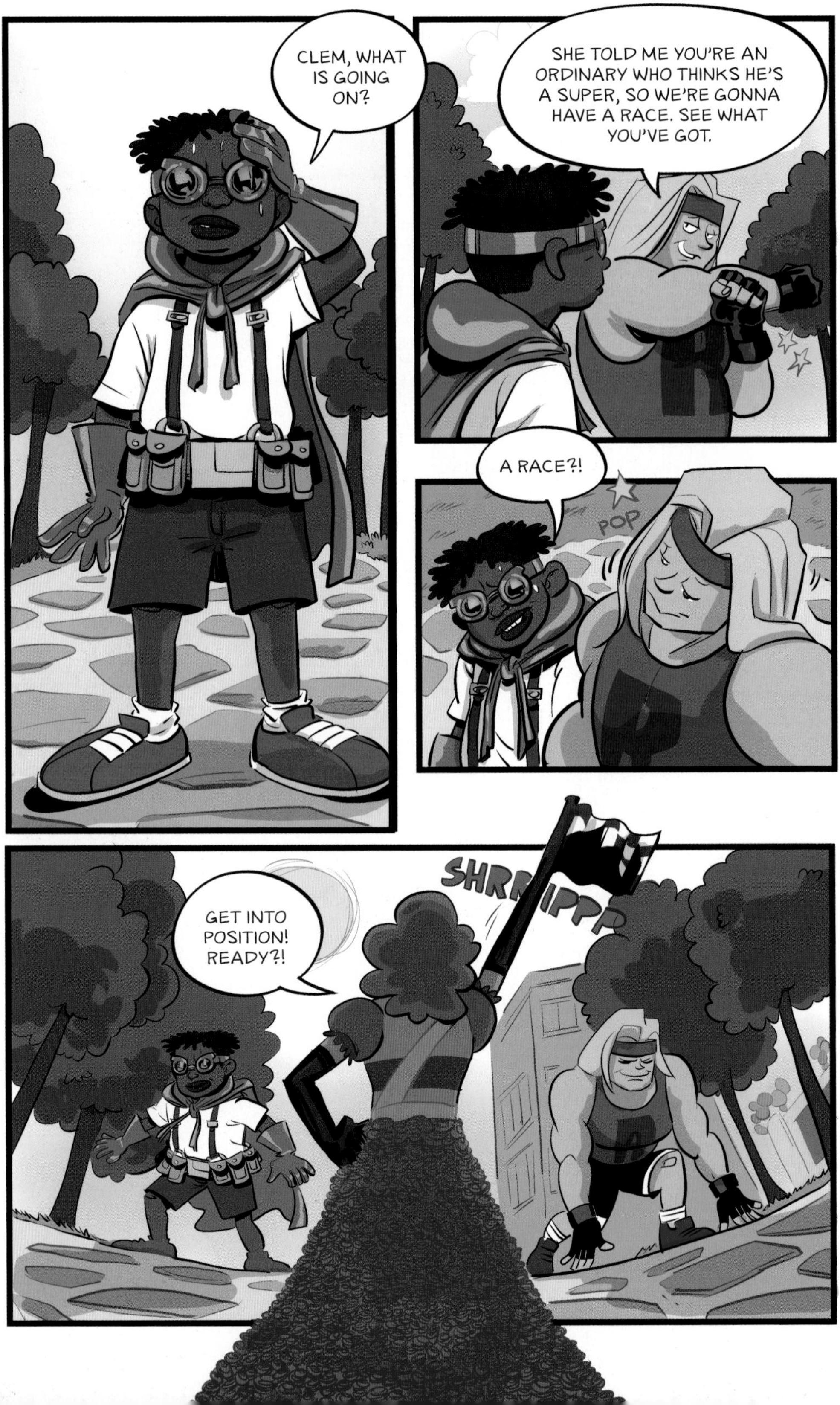
CLEM, WHAT IS GOING ON?
SHE TOLD ME YOU'RE AN ORDINARY WHO THINKS HE'S A SUPER, SO WE'RE GONNA HAVE A RACE. SEE WHAT YOU'VE GOT.
A RACE?!
POP
GET INTO POSITION! READY?!

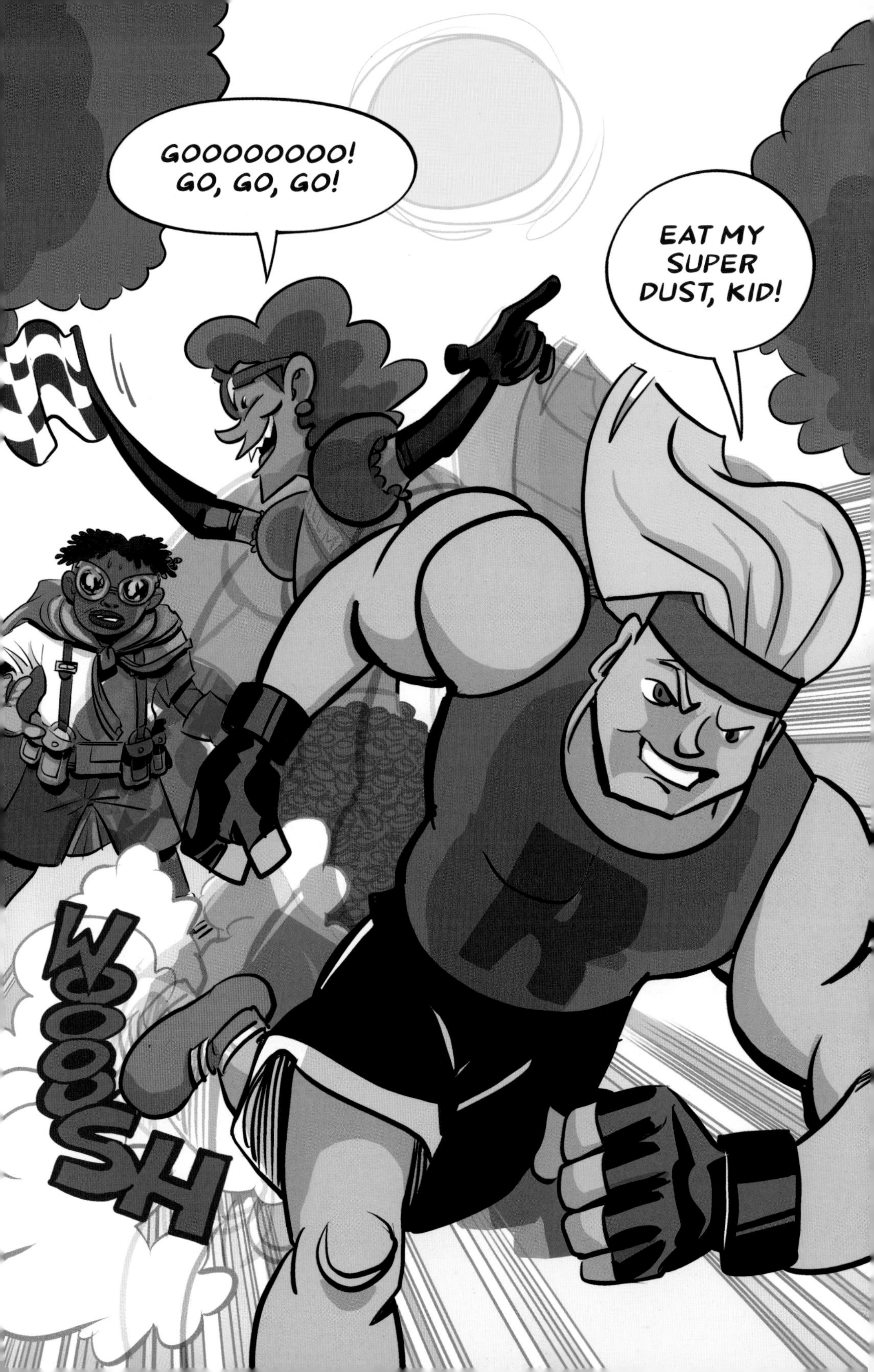
GOOOOOOOO! GO, GO, GO!
EAT MY SUPER DUST, KID!
WOOOOSH

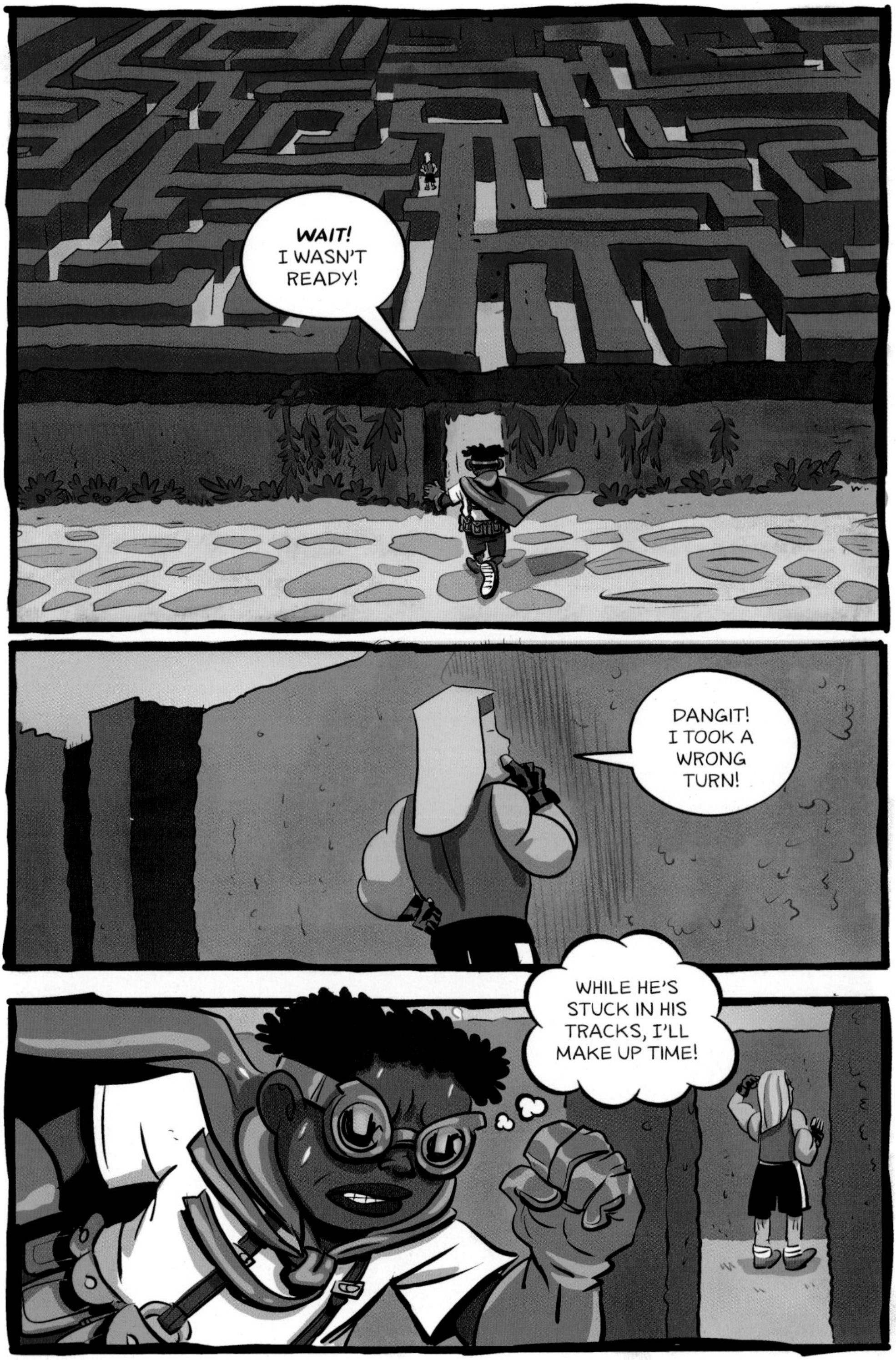
WAIT! I WASN'T READY!
DANGIT! I TOOK A WRONG TURN!
WHILE HE'S STUCK IN HIS TRACKS, I'LL MAKE UP TIME!

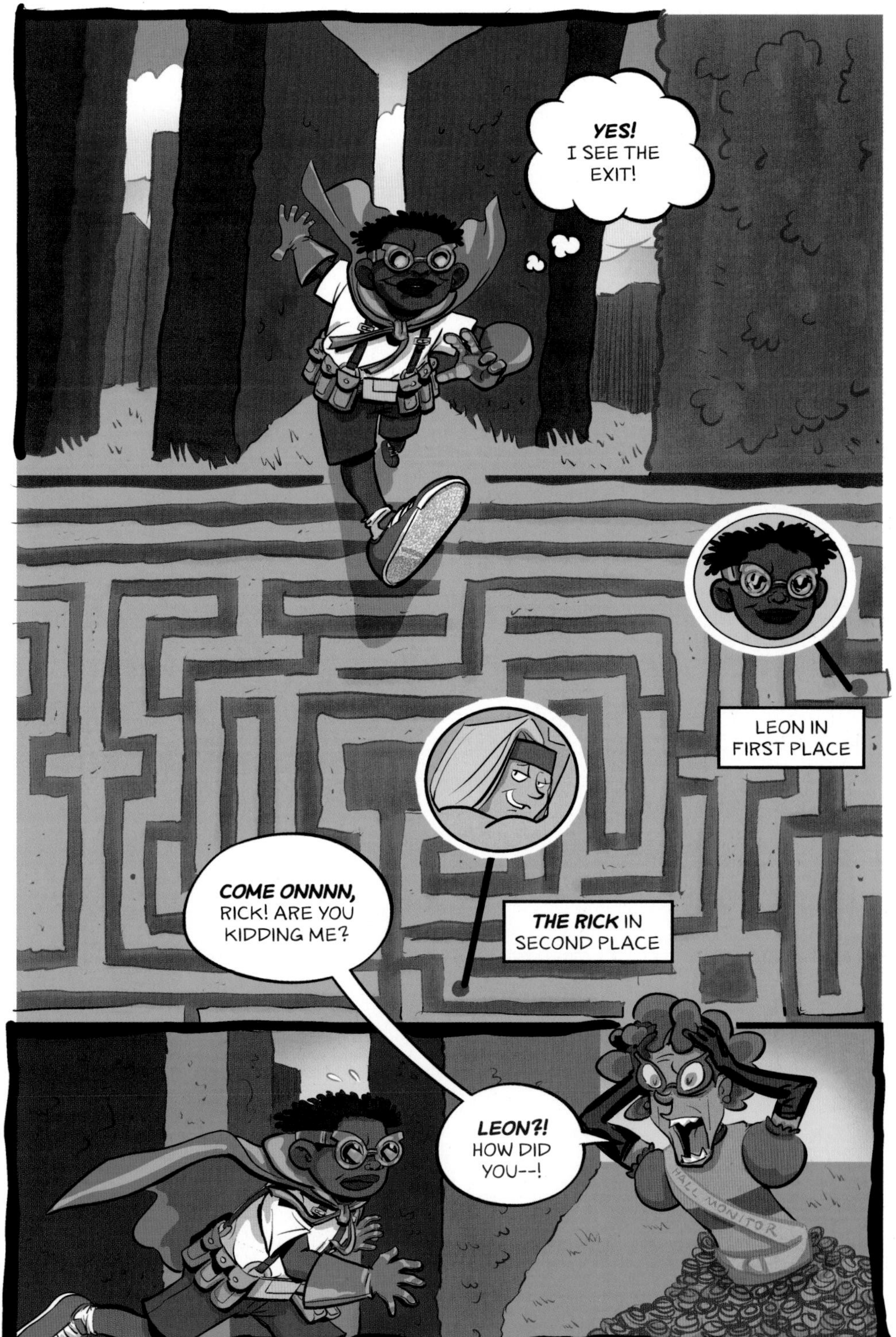
YES! I SEE THE EXIT!
LEON IN FIRST PLACE
THE RICK IN SECOND PLACE
COME ONNNN, RICK! ARE YOU KIDDING ME?
LEON?! HOW DID YOU--!
HALL MONITOR

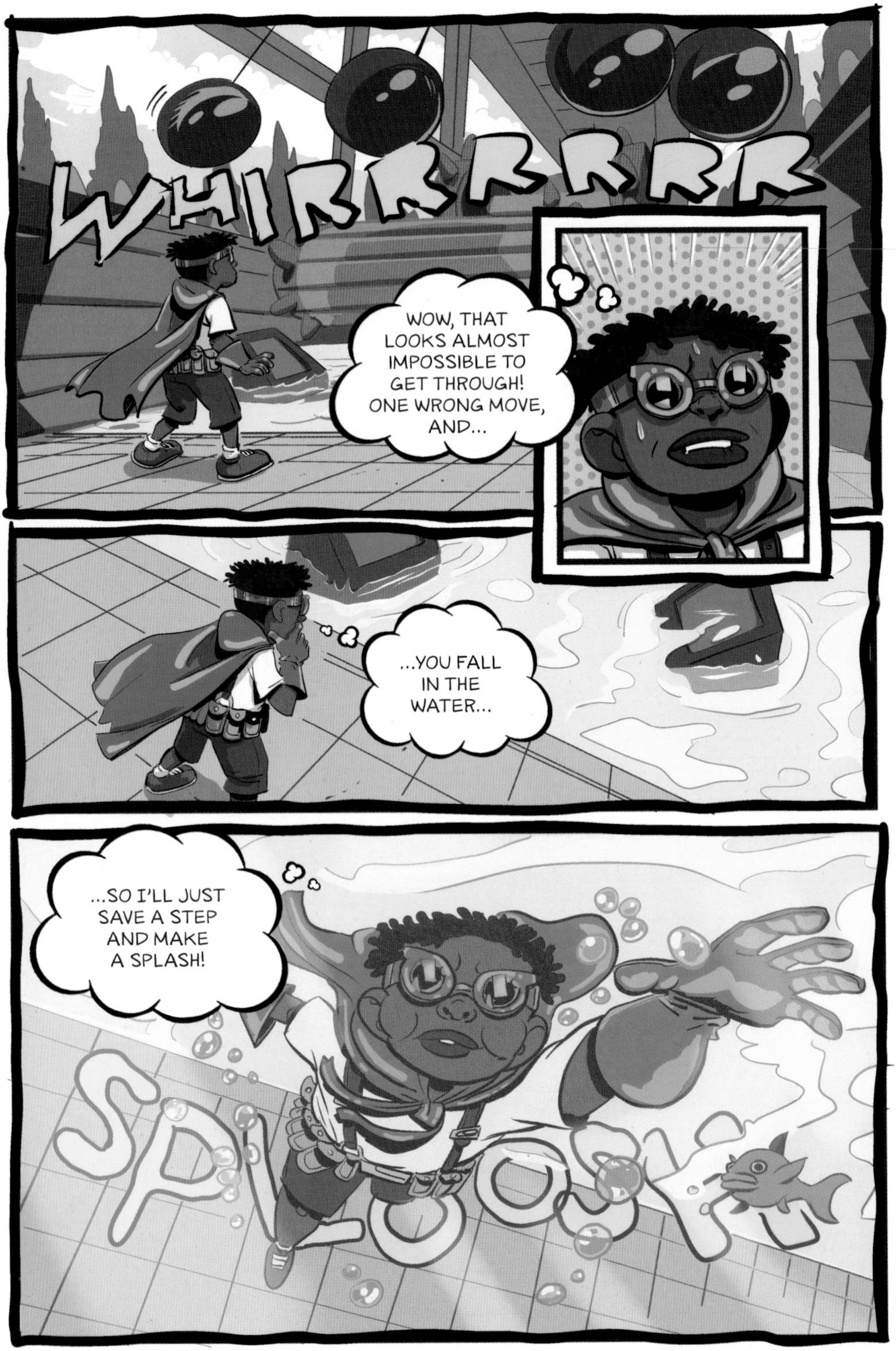
WHIRRRRRR
WOW, THAT LOOKS ALMOST IMPOSSIBLE TO GET THROUGH! ONE WRONG MOVE, AND...
...YOU FALL IN THE WATER...
...SO I'LL JUST SAVE A STEP AND MAKE A SPLASH!
SPLOOSH

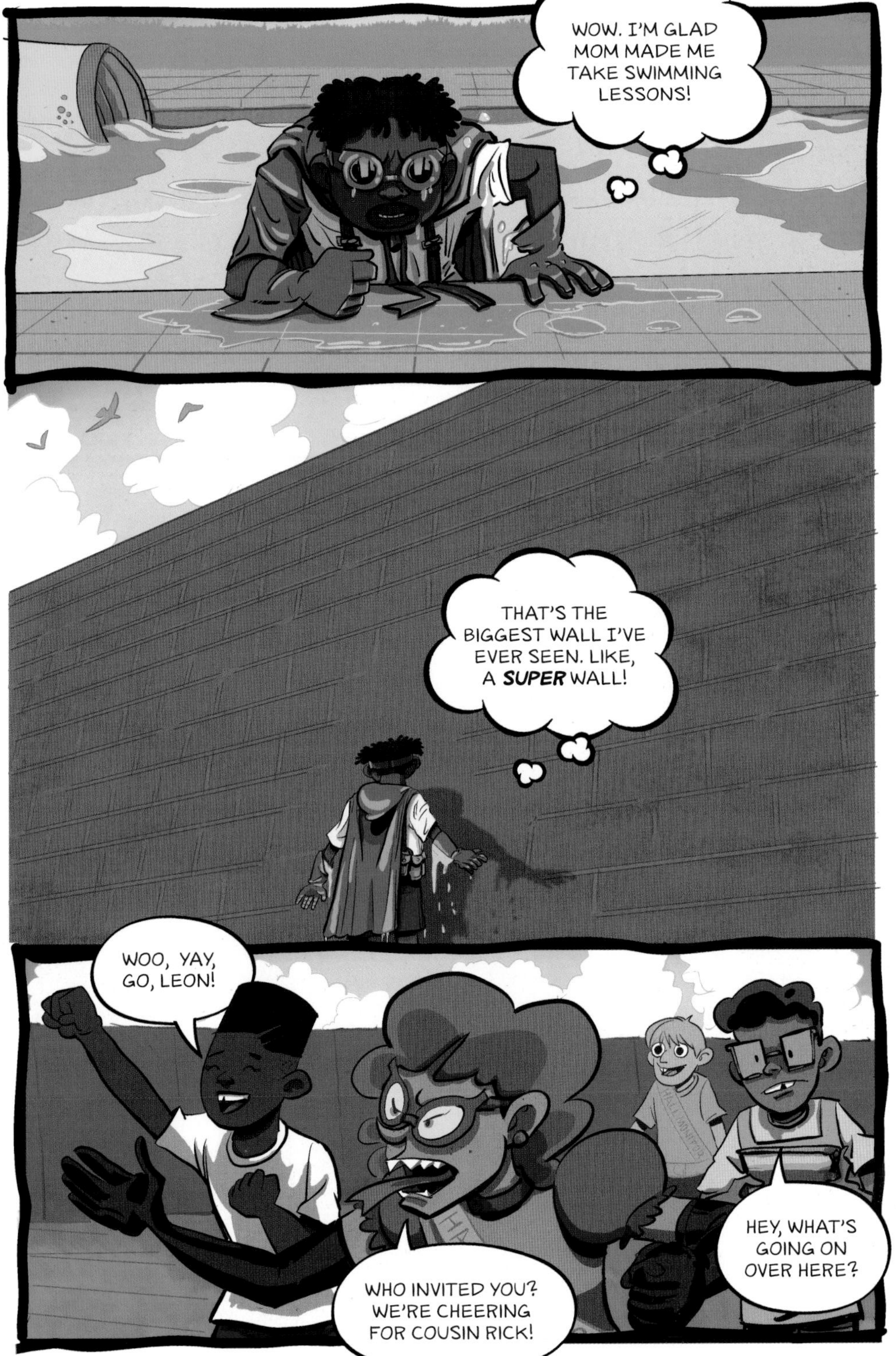
WOW. I'M GLAD MOM MADE ME TAKE SWIMMING LESSONS!
THAT'S THE BIGGEST WALL I'VE EVER SEEN. LIKE, A ***SUPER*** WALL!
WOO, YAY, GO, LEON!
WHO INVITED YOU? WE'RE CHEERING FOR COUSIN RICK!
HEY, WHAT'S GOING ON OVER HERE?

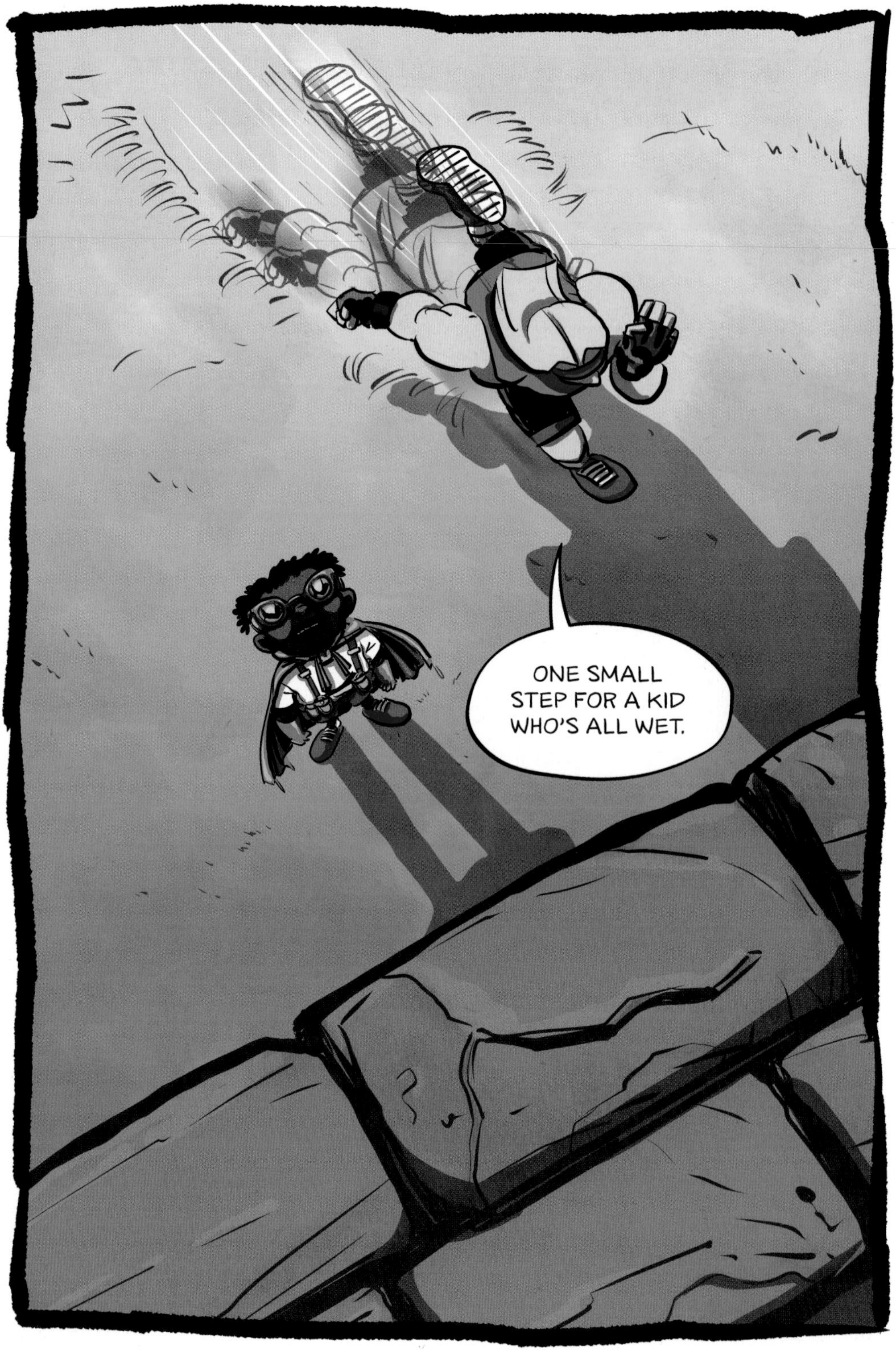
ONE SMALL STEP FOR A KID WHO'S ALL WET.

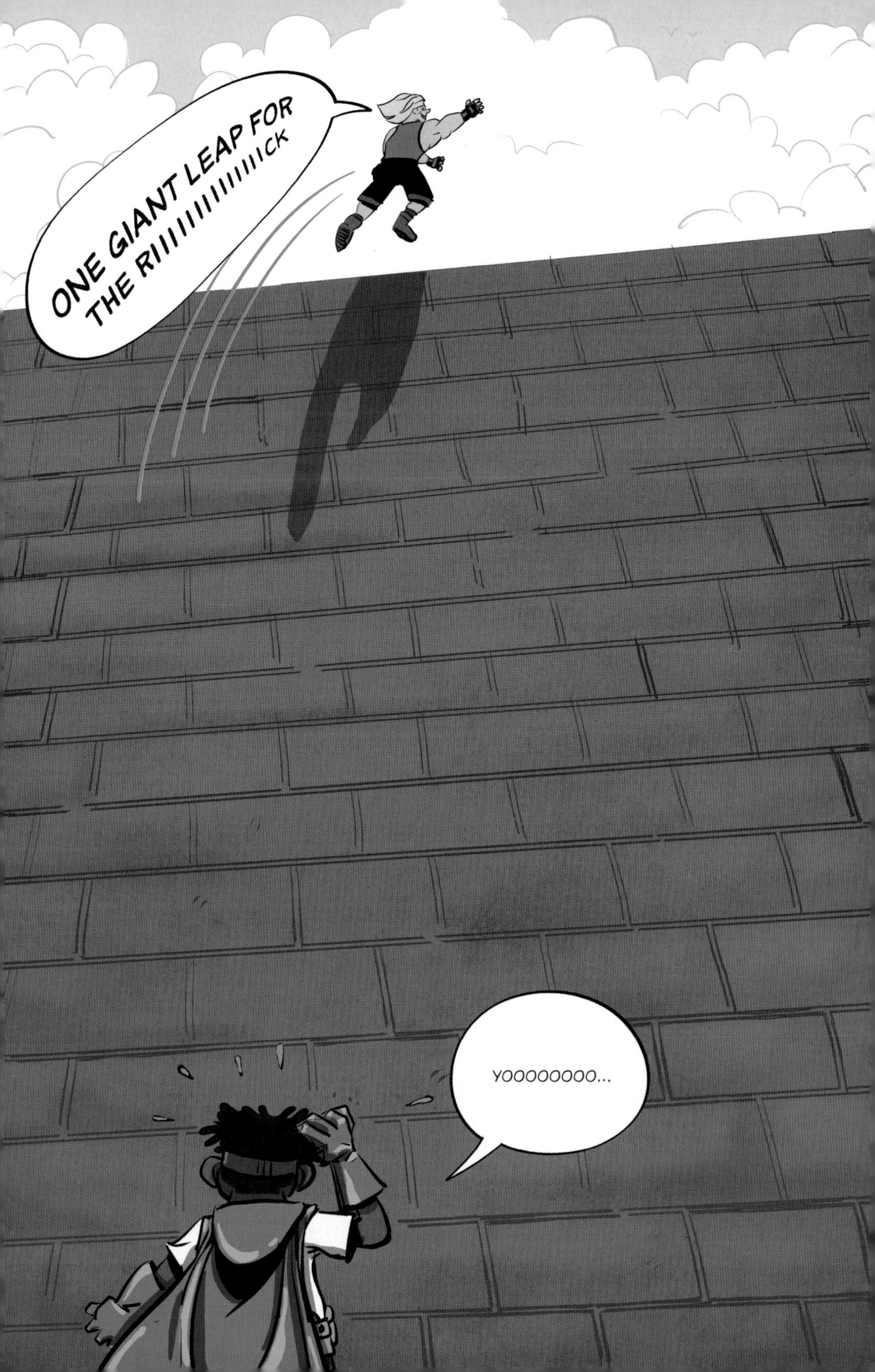
ONE GIANT LEAP FOR THE RIIIIIIIIIIIIICK
YOOOOOOOO...

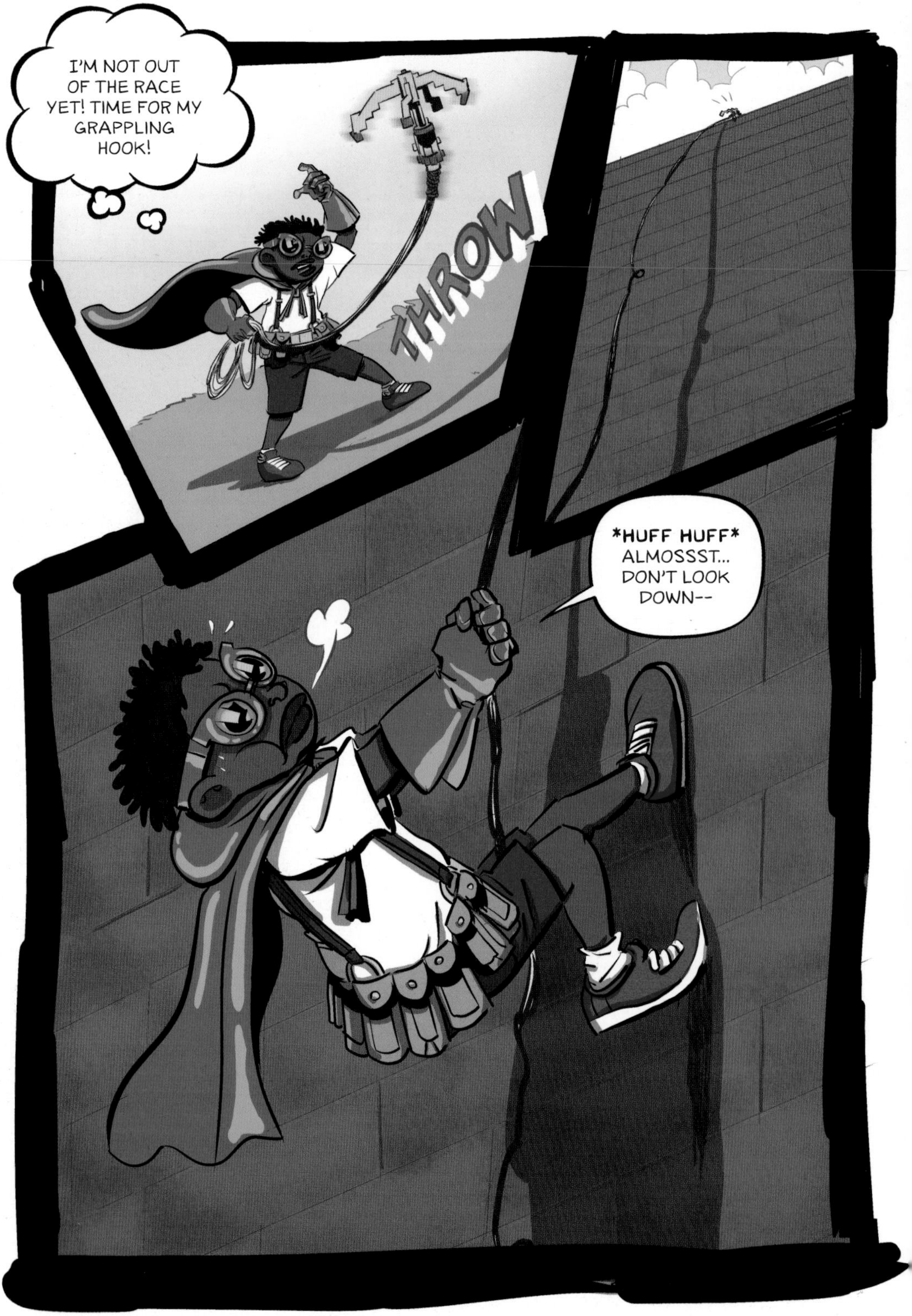
I'M NOT OUT OF THE RACE YET! TIME FOR MY GRAPPLING HOOK!
THROW
HUFF HUFF ALMOSSST... DON'T LOOK DOWN--

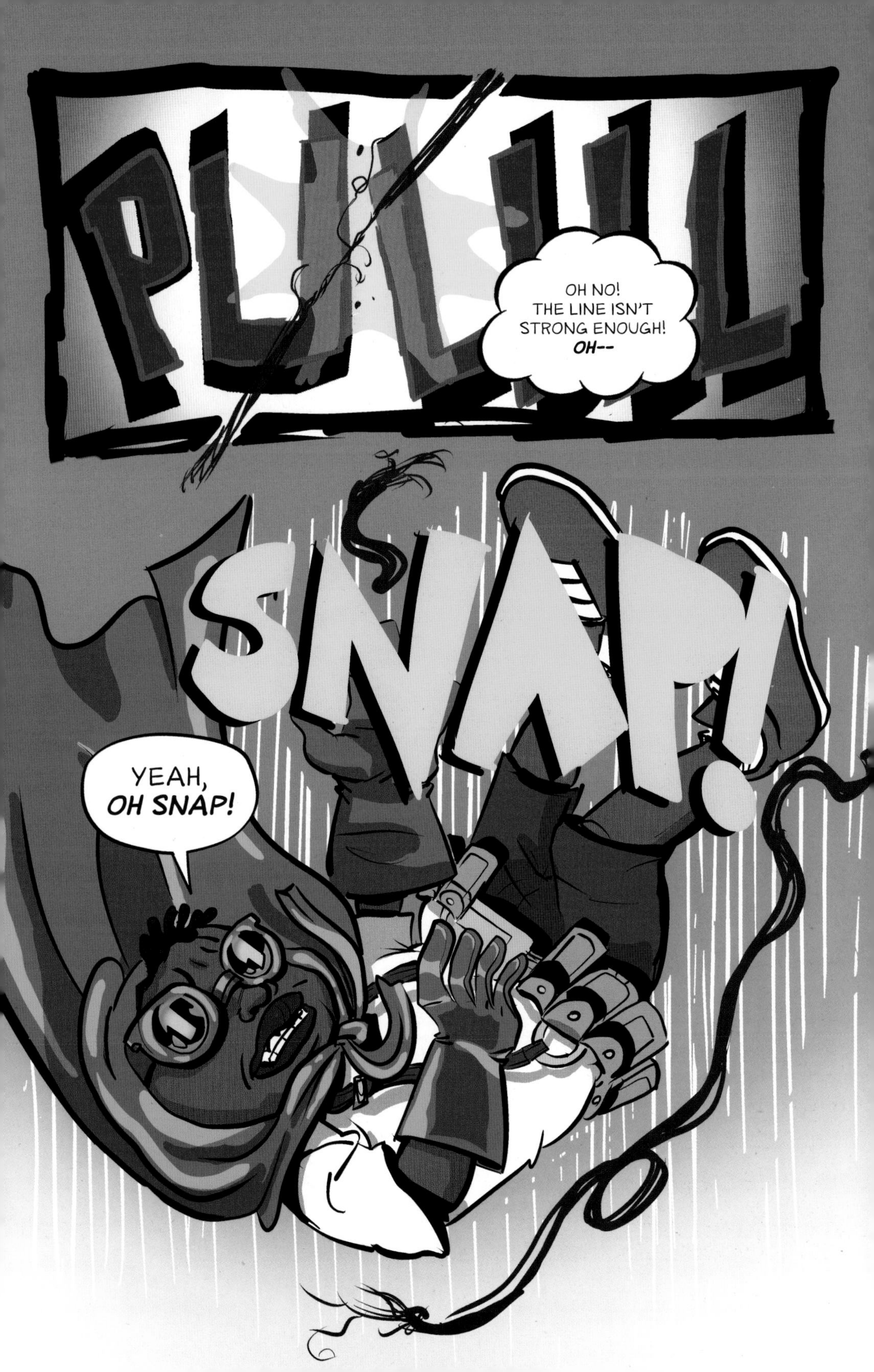
PLLLLLL
OH NO! THE LINE ISN'T STRONG ENOUGH! OH--
SNAP!
YEAH, OH SNAP!

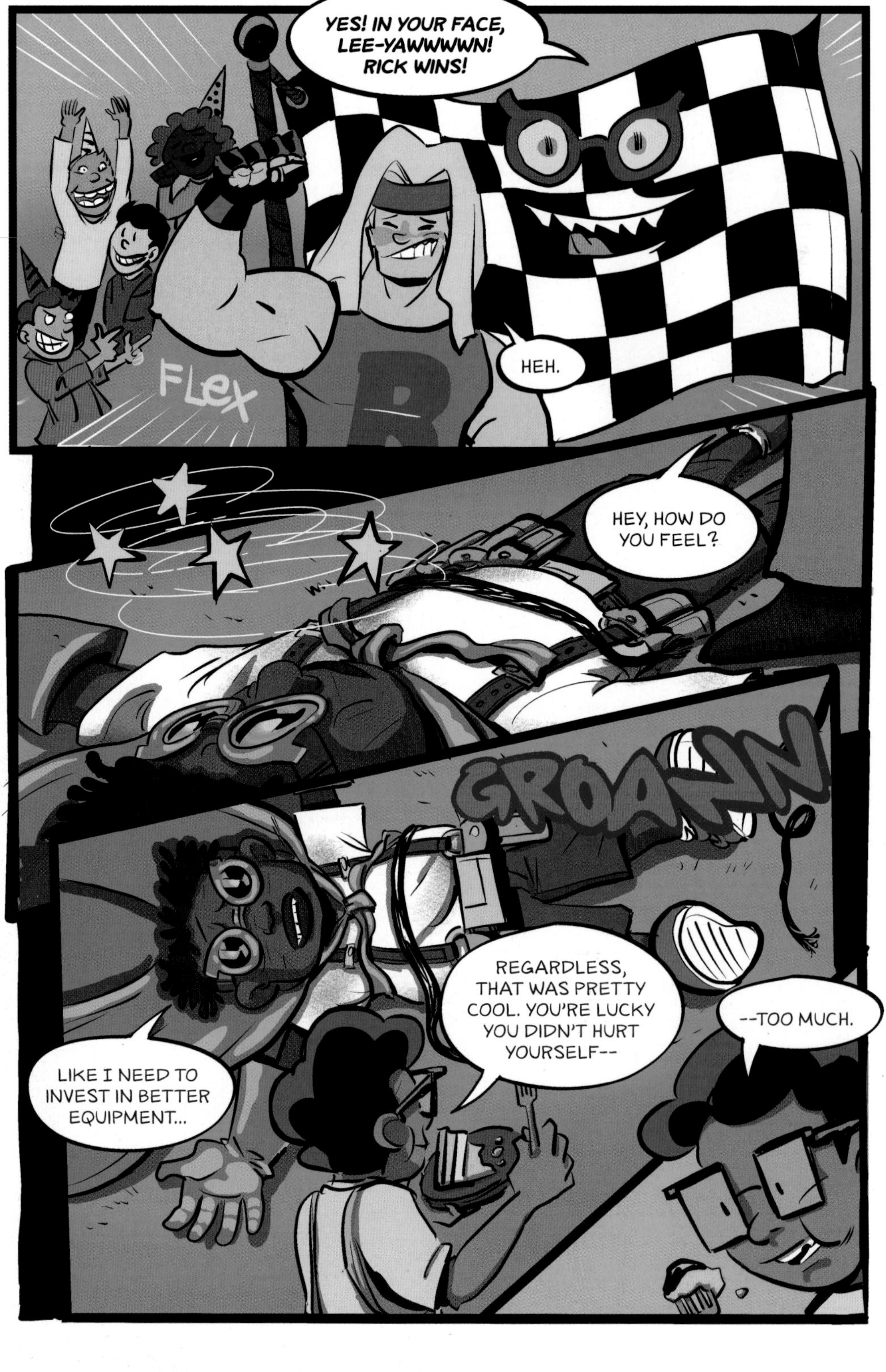

YES! IN YOUR FACE, LEE-YAWWWWN! RICK WINS!
FLEX
HEH.
HEY, HOW DO YOU FEEL?
GROANN
LIKE I NEED TO INVEST IN BETTER EQUIPMENT...
REGARDLESS, THAT WAS PRETTY COOL. YOU'RE LUCKY YOU DIDN'T HURT YOURSELF--
--TOO MUCH.

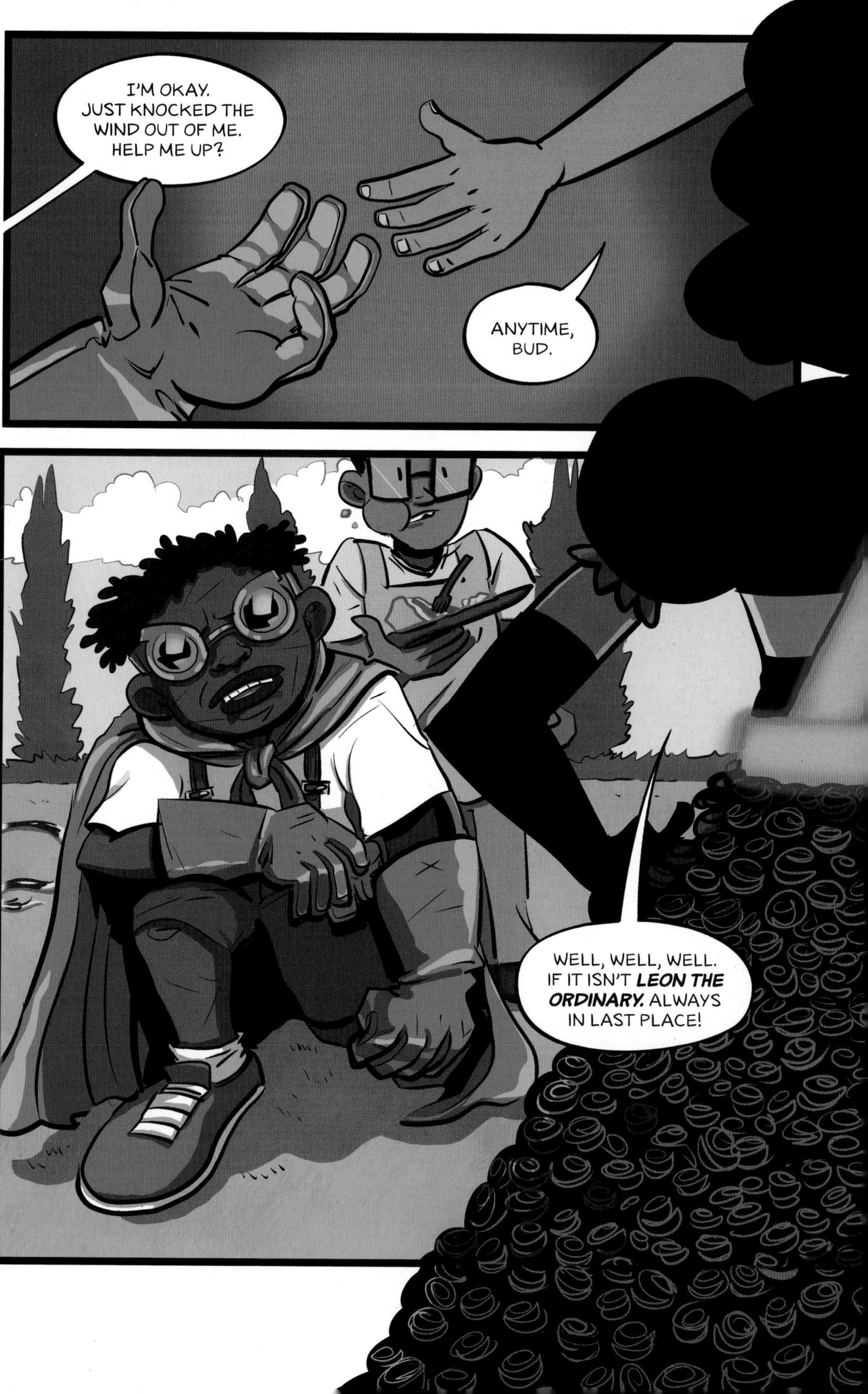
I'M OKAY. JUST KNOCKED THE WIND OUT OF ME. HELP ME UP?
ANYTIME, BUD.
WELL, WELL, WELL. IF IT ISN'T **LEON THE ORDINARY.** ALWAYS IN LAST PLACE!

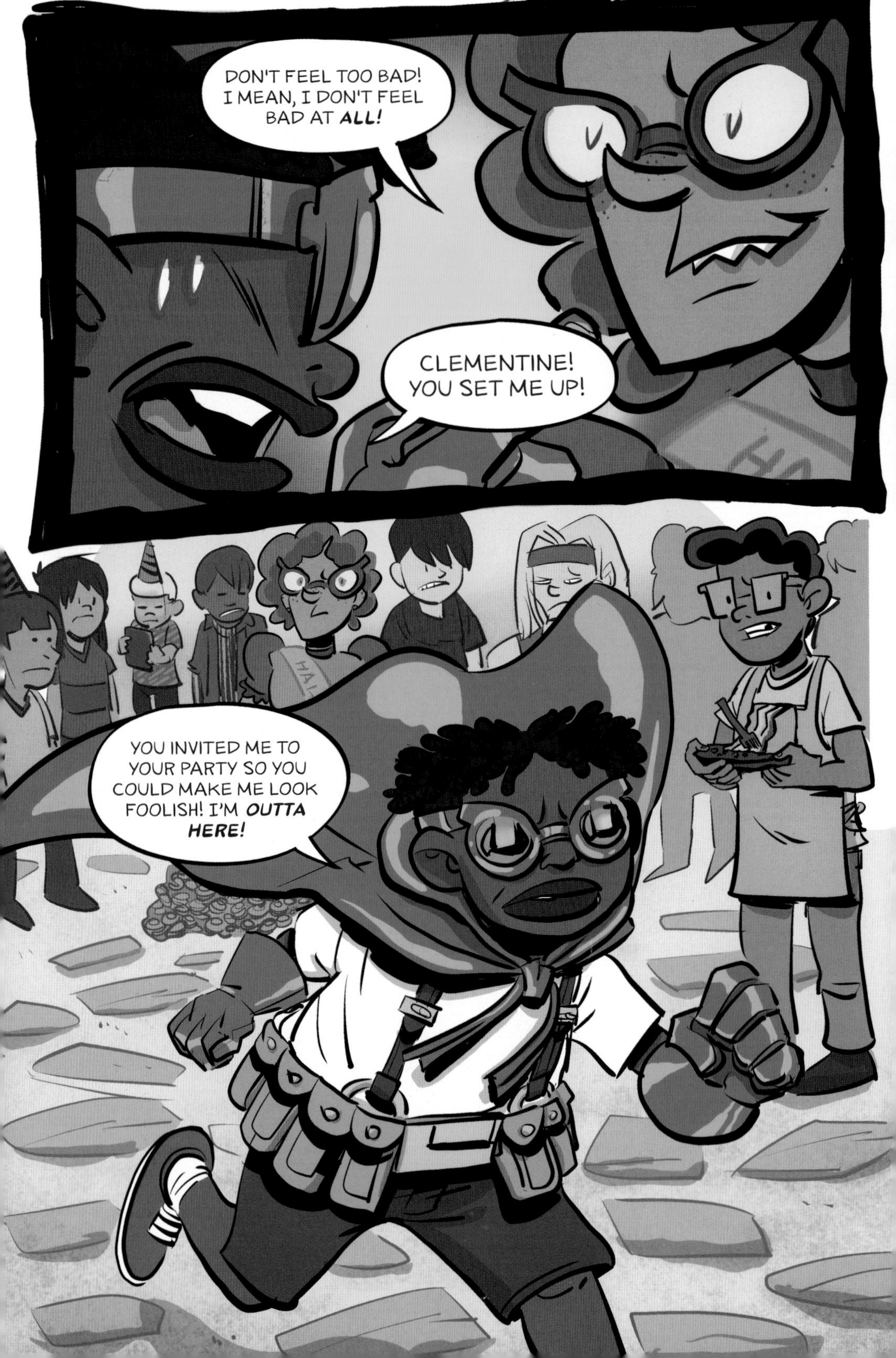
DON'T FEEL TOO BAD! I MEAN, I DON'T FEEL BAD AT ALL!
CLEMENTINE! YOU SET ME UP!
YOU INVITED ME TO YOUR PARTY SO YOU COULD MAKE ME LOOK FOOLISH! I'M OUTTA HERE!

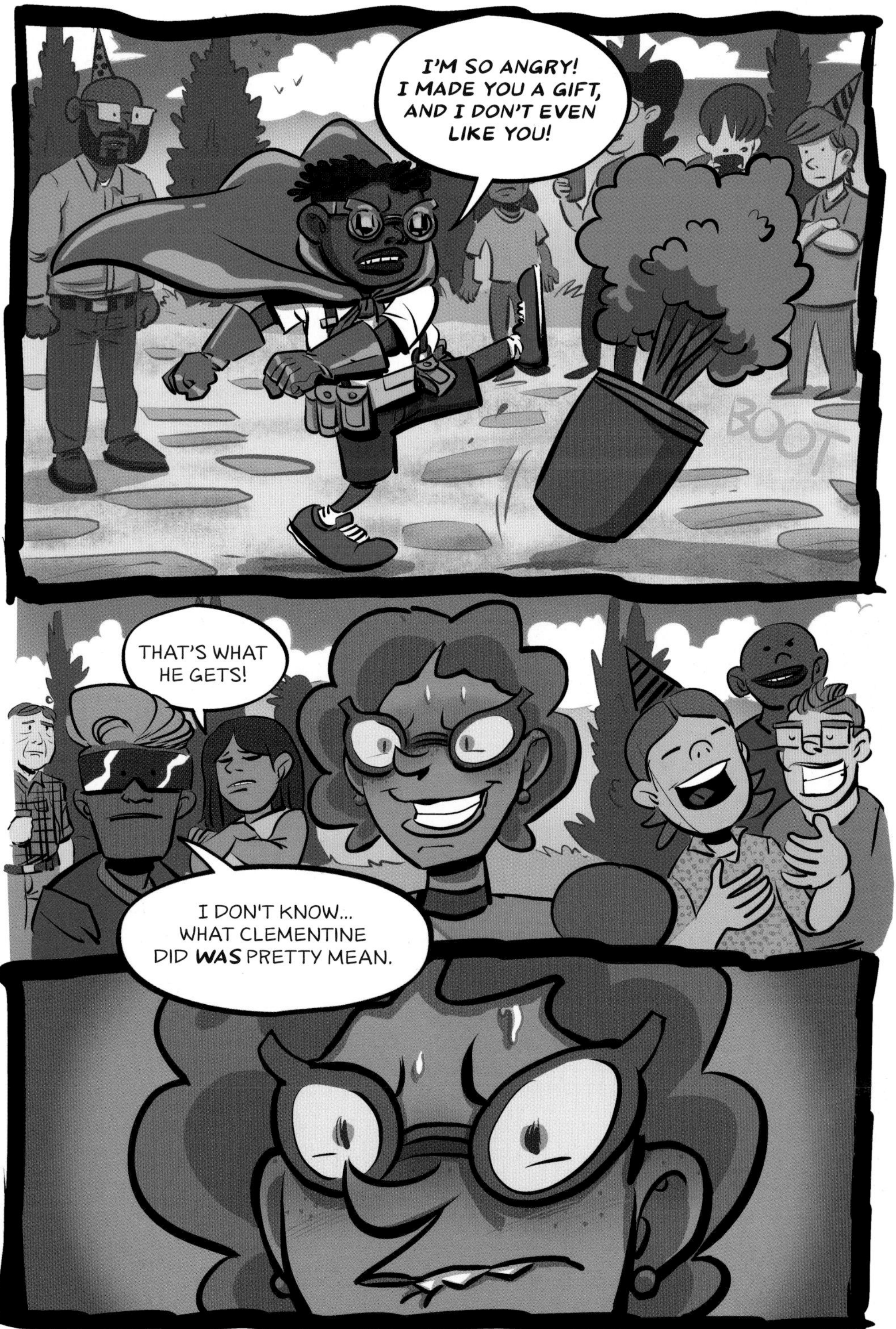
I'M SO ANGRY! I MADE YOU A GIFT, AND I DON'T EVEN LIKE YOU!
BOOT
THAT'S WHAT HE GETS!
I DON'T KNOW... WHAT CLEMENTINE DID WAS PRETTY MEAN.

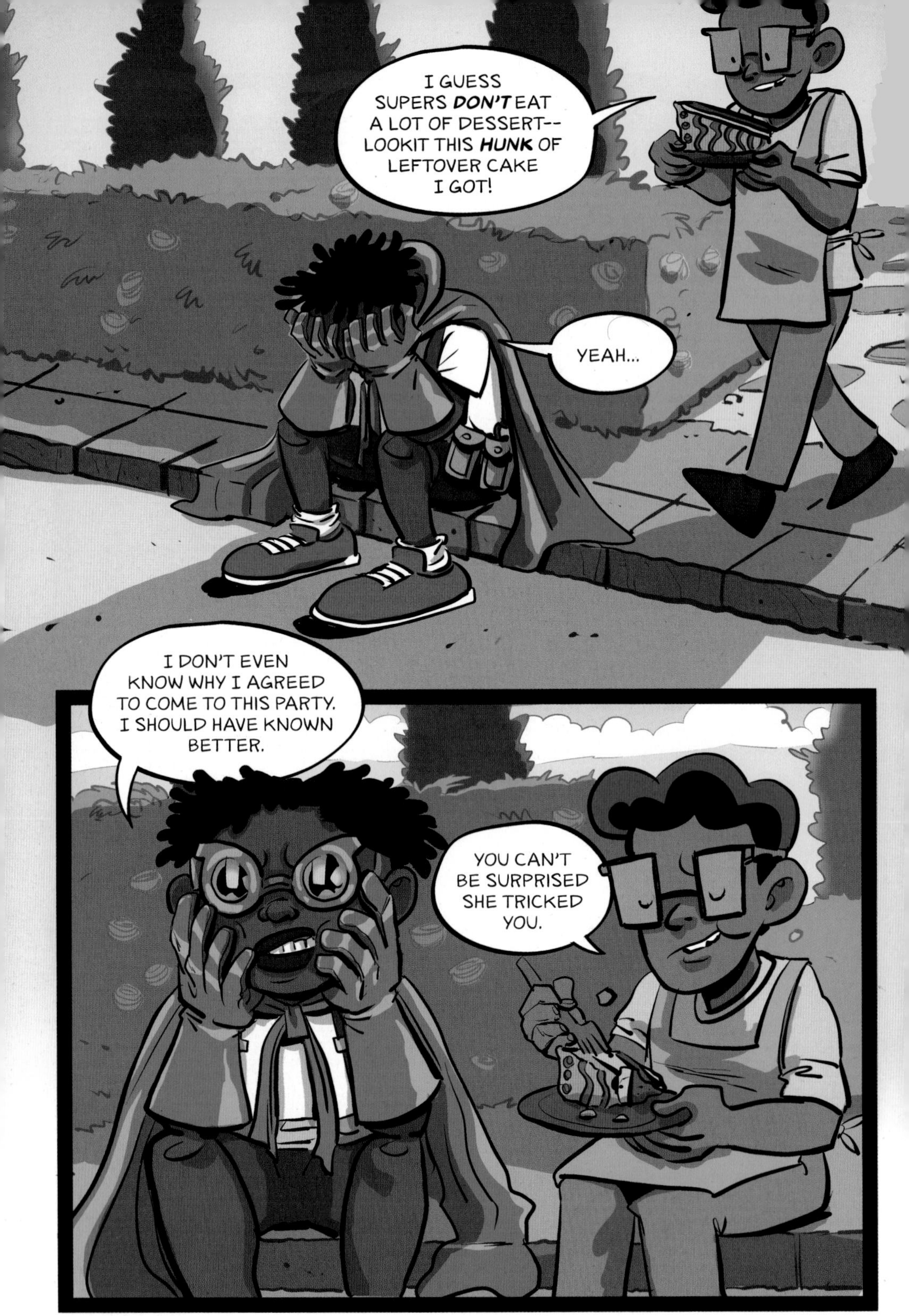
I GUESS SUPERS DON'T EAT A LOT OF DESSERT--LOOKIT THIS HUNK OF LEFTOVER CAKE I GOT!
YEAH...
I DON'T EVEN KNOW WHY I AGREED TO COME TO THIS PARTY. I SHOULD HAVE KNOWN BETTER.
YOU CAN'T BE SURPRISED SHE TRICKED YOU.

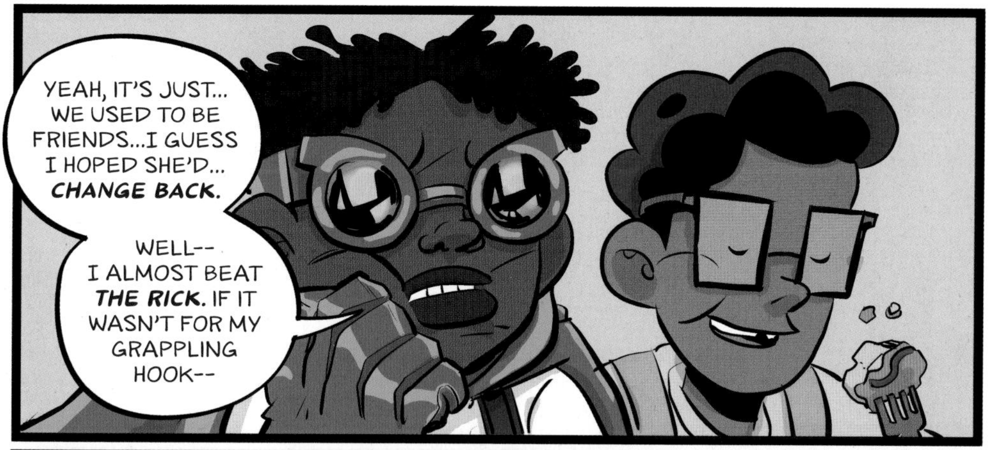
YEAH, IT'S JUST... WE USED TO BE FRIENDS...I GUESS I HOPED SHE'D... ***CHANGE BACK.***
WELL-- I ALMOST BEAT ***THE RICK.*** IF IT WASN'T FOR MY GRAPPLING HOOK--

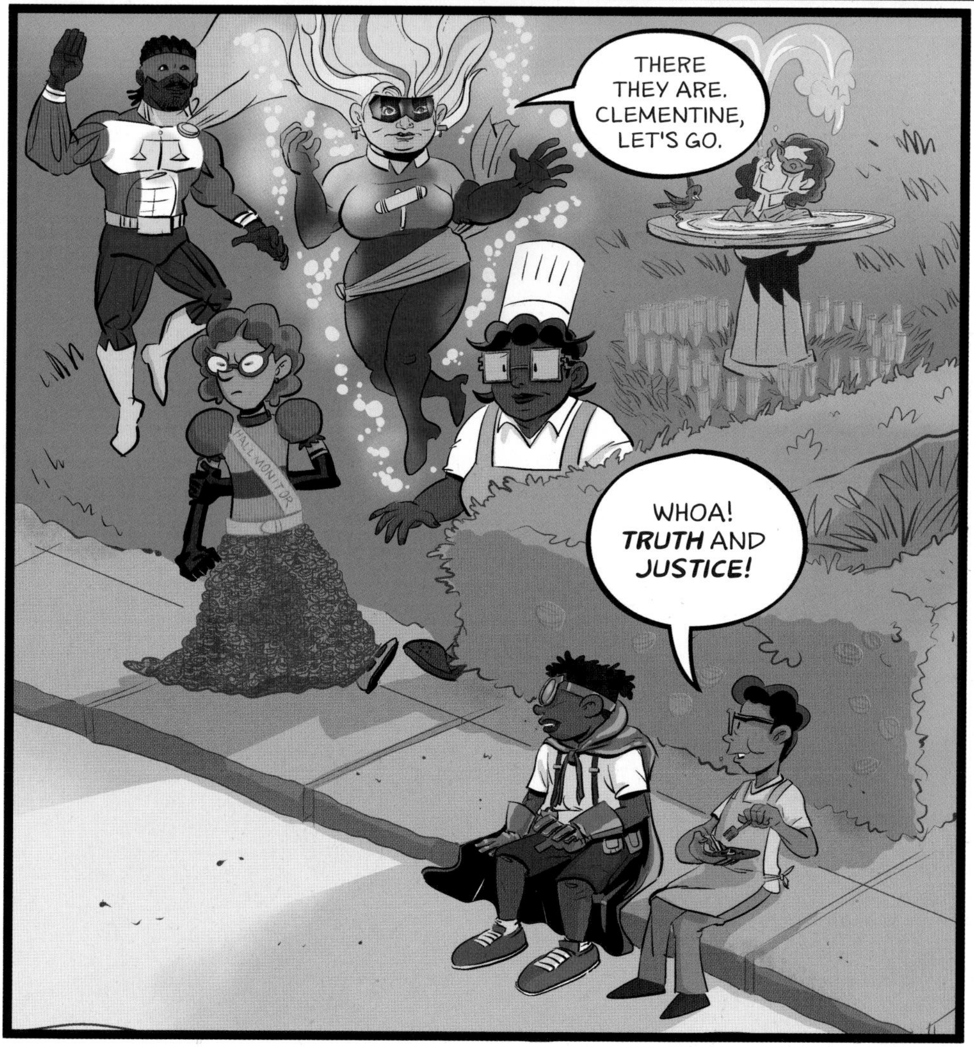
THERE THEY ARE. CLEMENTINE, LET'S GO.
HALL MONITOR
WHOA! ***TRUTH*** AND ***JUSTICE!***

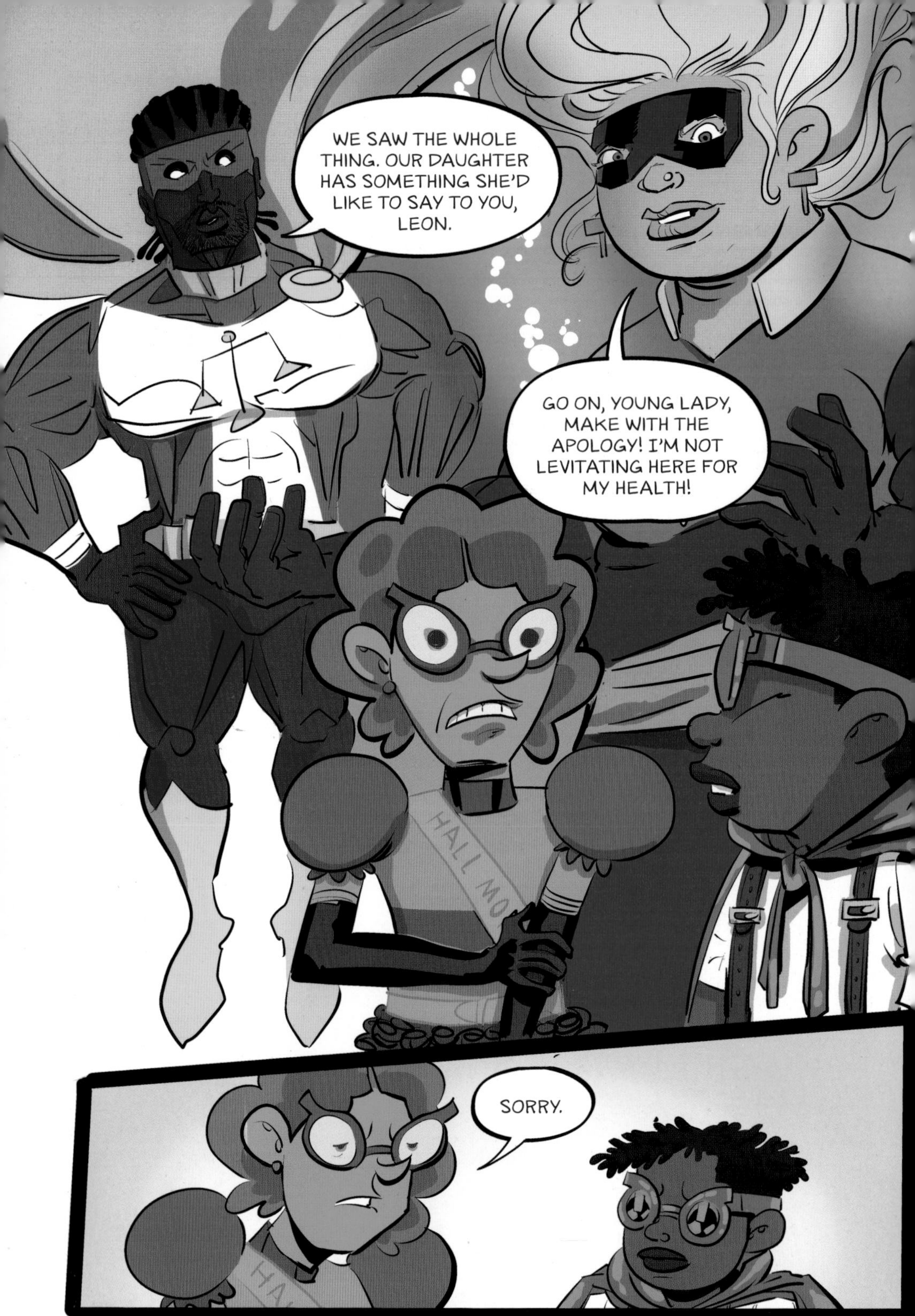
WE SAW THE WHOLE THING. OUR DAUGHTER HAS SOMETHING SHE'D LIKE TO SAY TO YOU, LEON.
GO ON, YOUNG LADY, MAKE WITH THE APOLOGY! I'M NOT LEVITATING HERE FOR MY HEALTH!
SORRY.

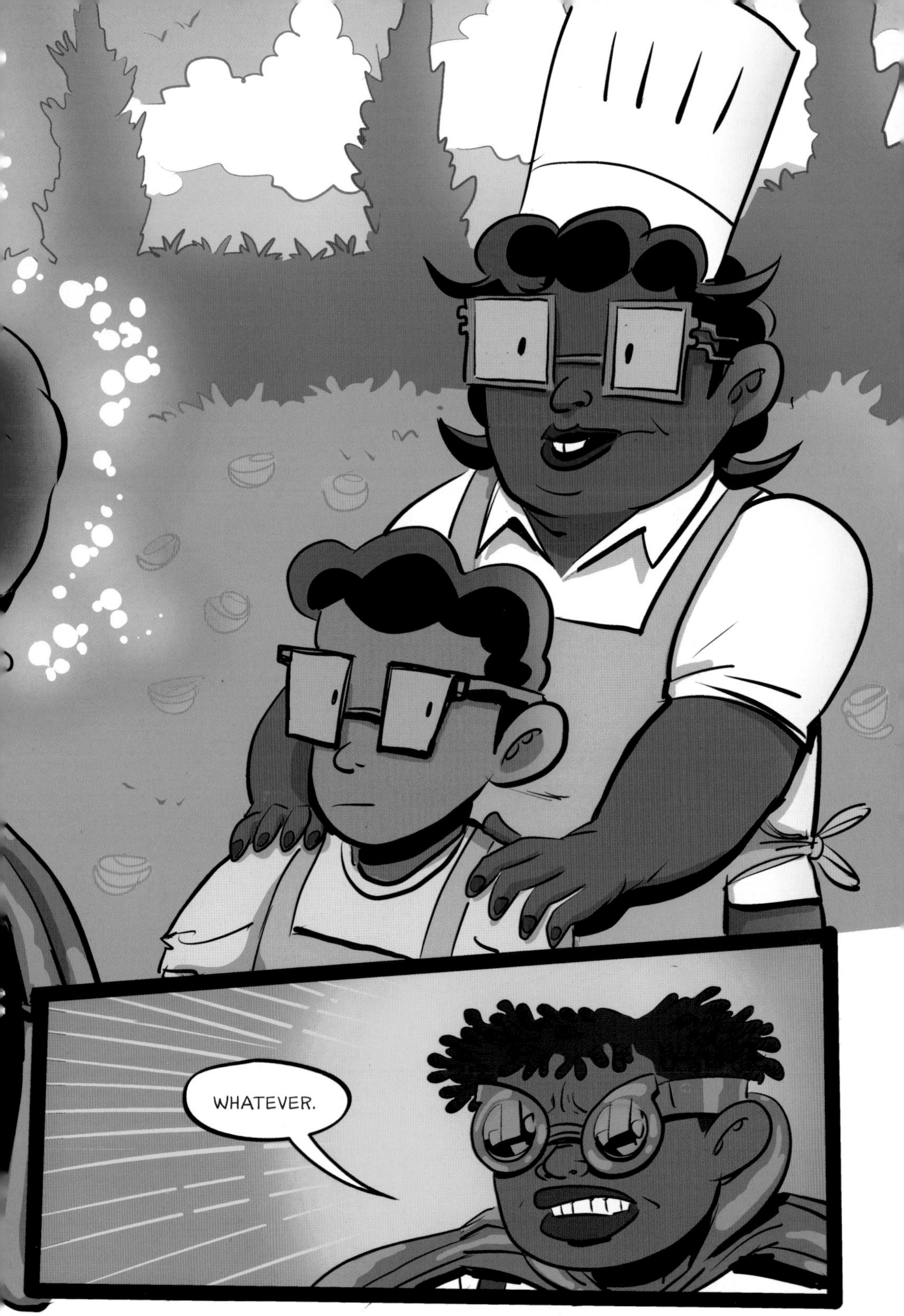
WHATEVER.

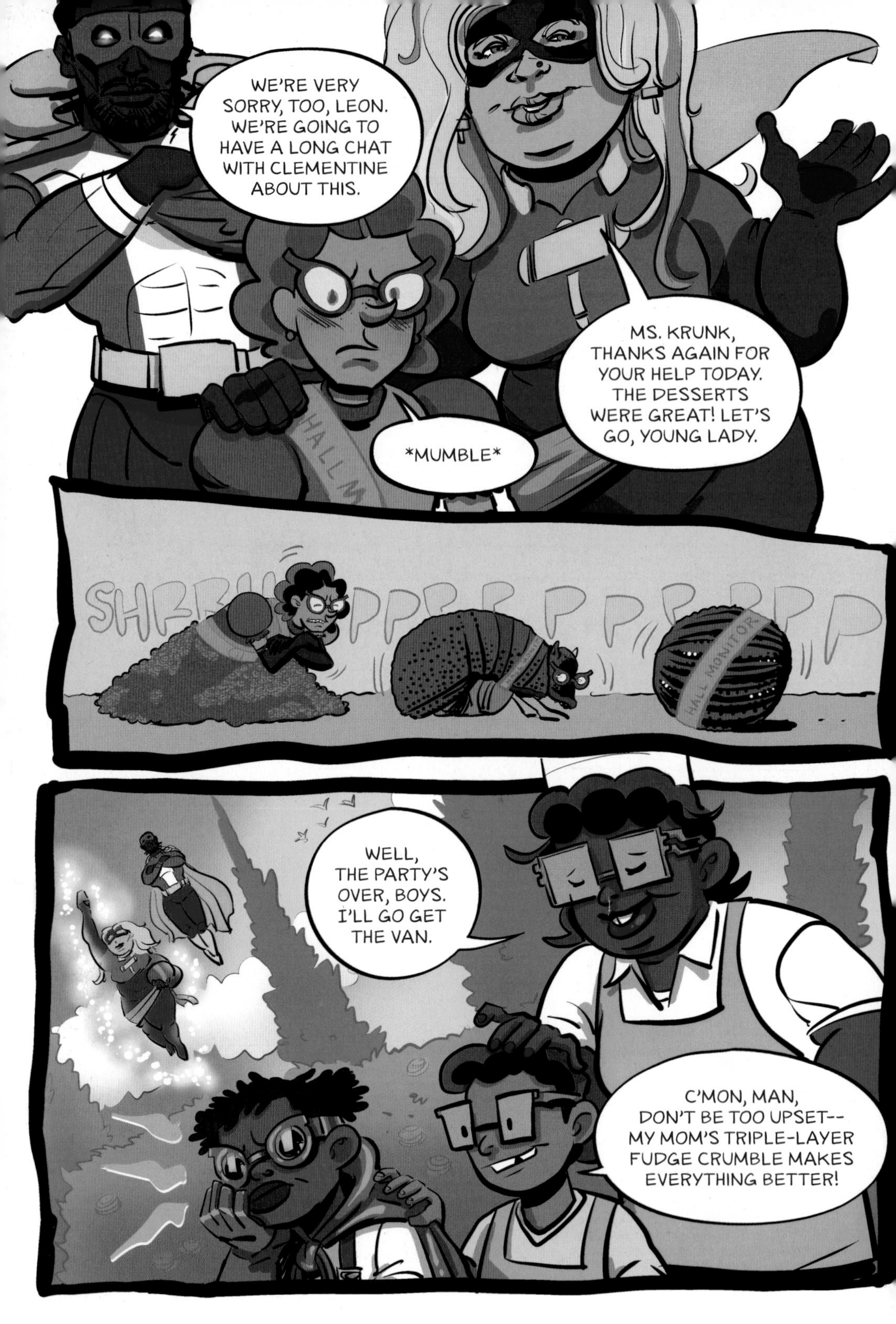
WE'RE VERY SORRY, TOO, LEON. WE'RE GOING TO HAVE A LONG CHAT WITH CLEMENTINE ABOUT THIS.
MS. KRUNK, THANKS AGAIN FOR YOUR HELP TODAY. THE DESSERTS WERE GREAT! LET'S GO, YOUNG LADY.
MUMBLE
HALL M
SHRRR PPPPPPPPPP
HALL MONITOR
WELL, THE PARTY'S OVER, BOYS. I'LL GO GET THE VAN.
C'MON, MAN, DON'T BE TOO UPSET-- MY MOM'S TRIPLE-LAYER FUDGE CRUMBLE MAKES EVERYTHING BETTER!

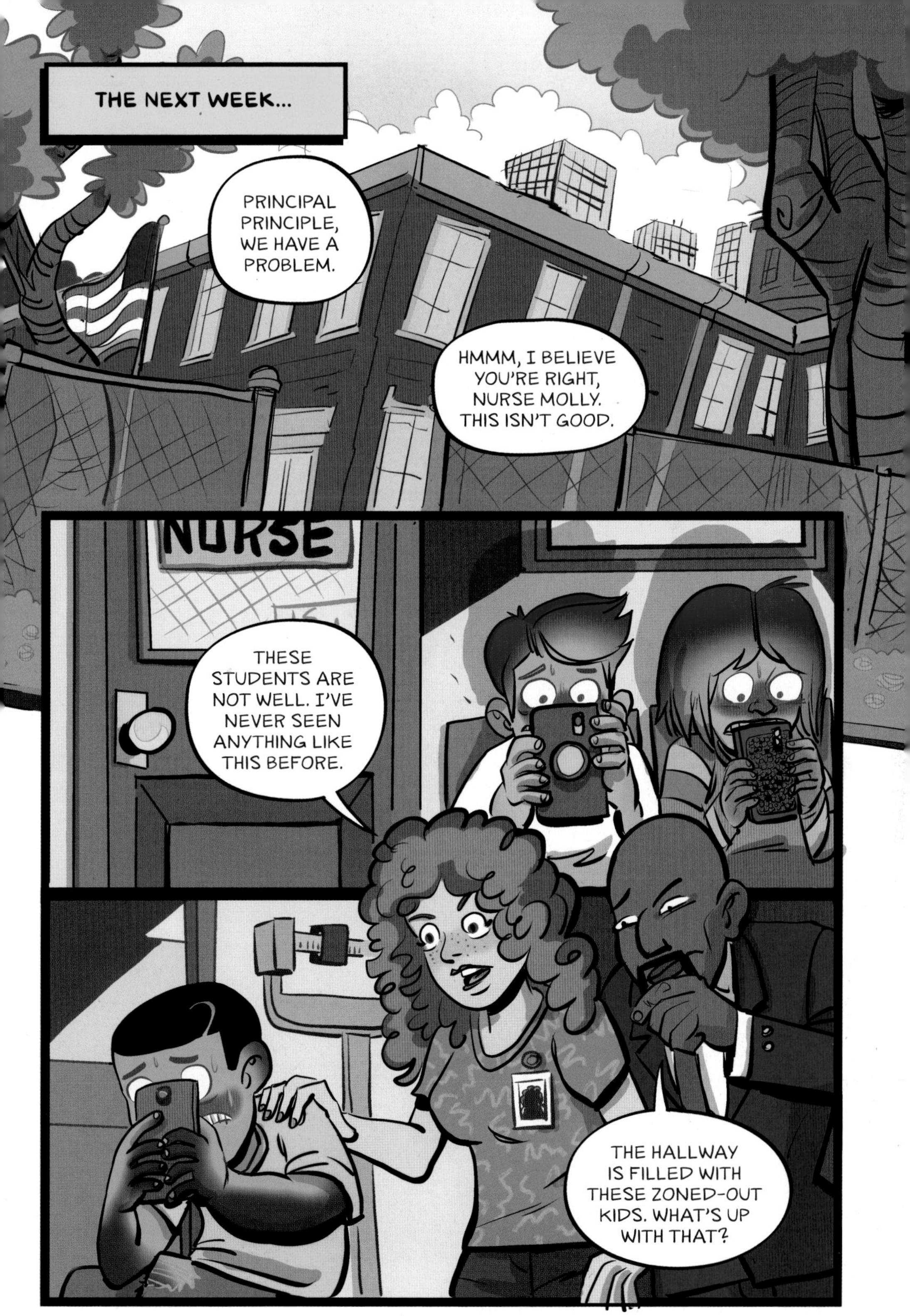
THE NEXT WEEK...
PRINCIPAL PRINCIPLE, WE HAVE A PROBLEM.
HMMM, I BELIEVE YOU'RE RIGHT, NURSE MOLLY. THIS ISN'T GOOD.
NURSE
THESE STUDENTS ARE NOT WELL. I'VE NEVER SEEN ANYTHING LIKE THIS BEFORE.
THE HALLWAY IS FILLED WITH THESE ZONED-OUT KIDS. WHAT'S UP WITH THAT?

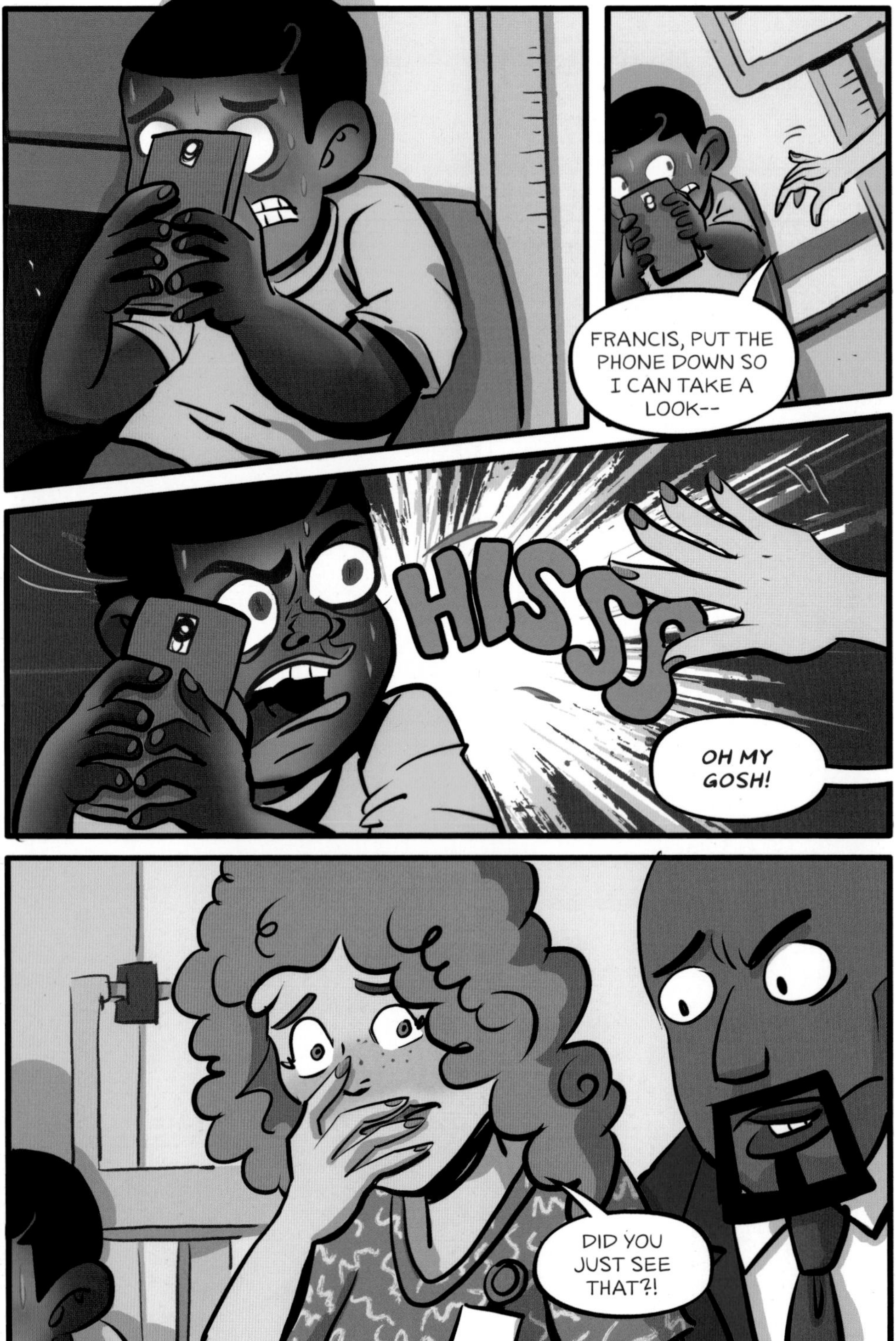
FRANCIS, PUT THE PHONE DOWN SO I CAN TAKE A LOOK--
HISSS
OH MY GOSH!
DID YOU JUST SEE THAT?!

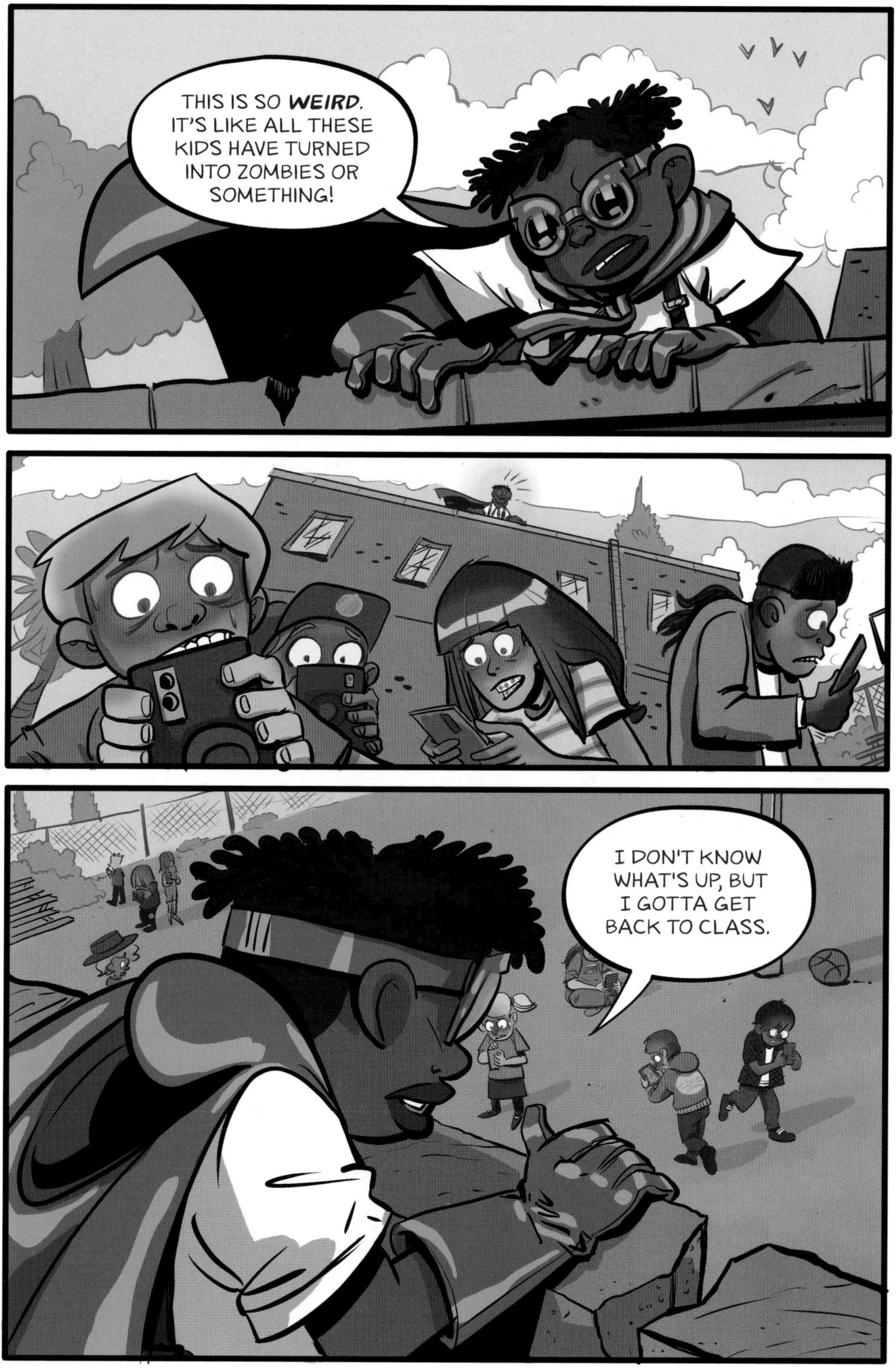
THIS IS SO **WEIRD**. IT'S LIKE ALL THESE KIDS HAVE TURNED INTO ZOMBIES OR SOMETHING!
I DON'T KNOW WHAT'S UP, BUT I GOTTA GET BACK TO CLASS.

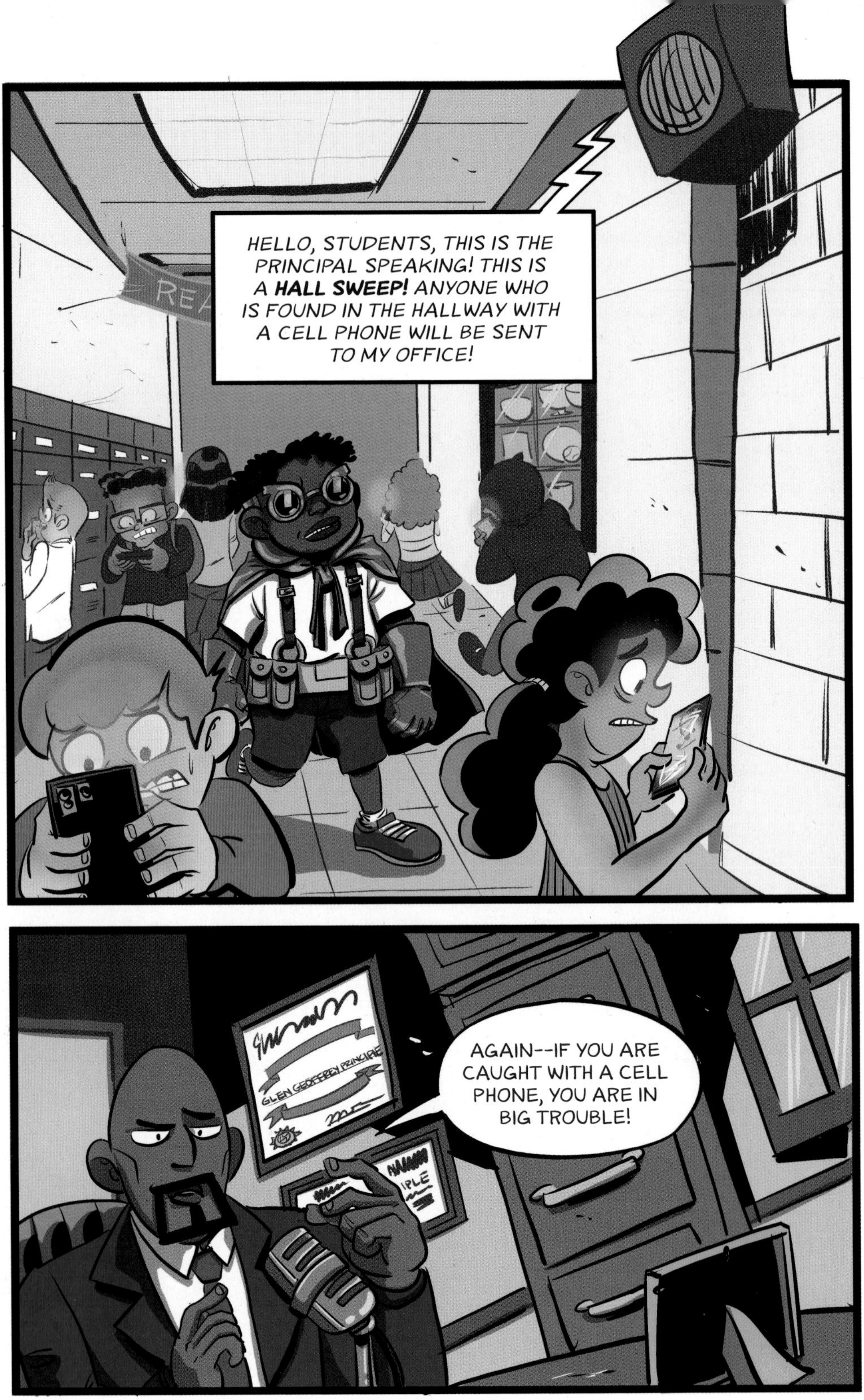
HELLO, STUDENTS, THIS IS THE PRINCIPAL SPEAKING! THIS IS A **HALL SWEEP!** ANYONE WHO IS FOUND IN THE HALLWAY WITH A CELL PHONE WILL BE SENT TO MY OFFICE!
GLEN GEOFFREY PRINCIPLE
AGAIN--IF YOU ARE CAUGHT WITH A CELL PHONE, YOU ARE IN BIG TROUBLE!

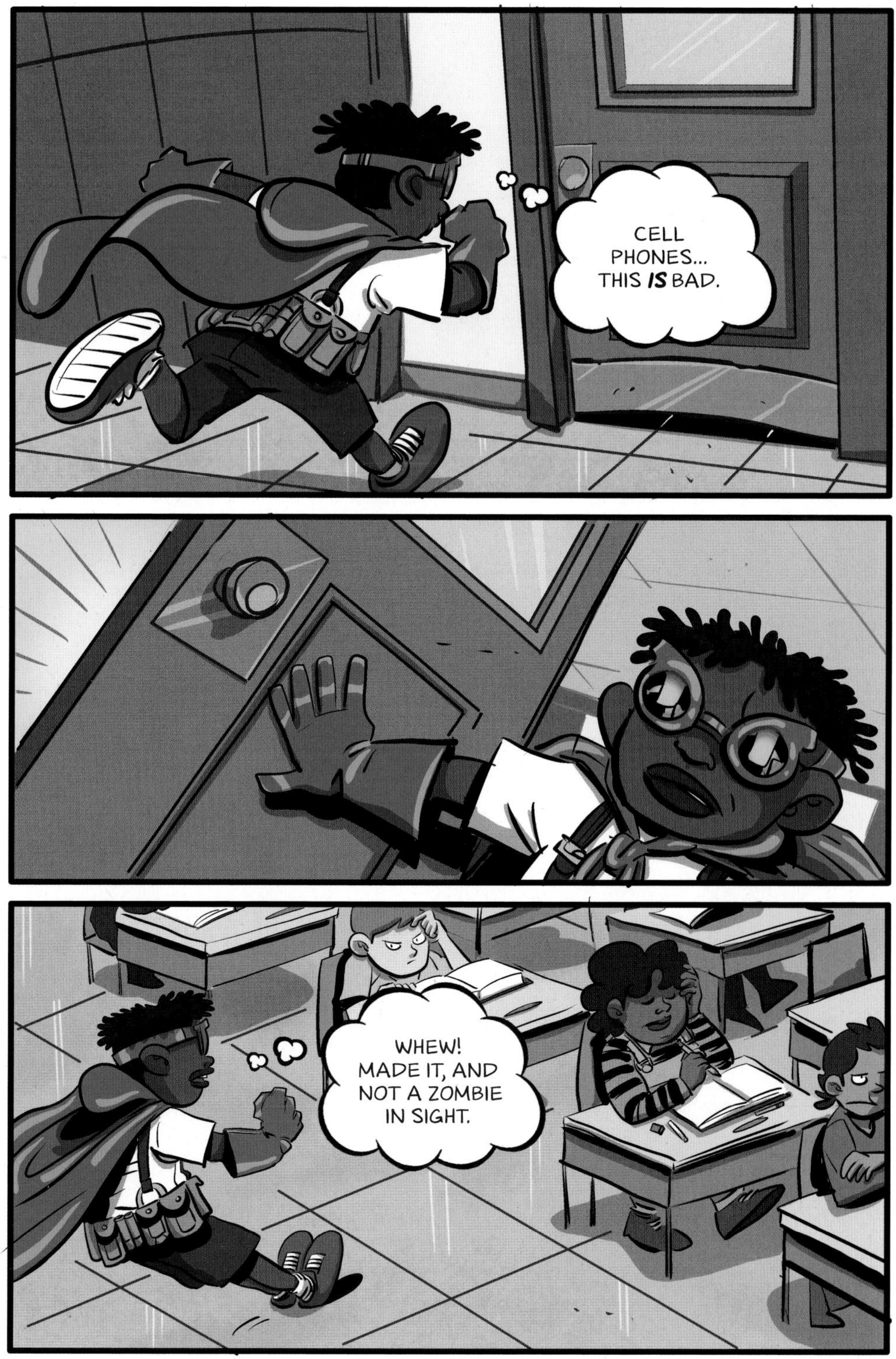
CELL PHONES... THIS *IS* BAD.
WHEW! MADE IT, AND NOT A ZOMBIE IN SIGHT.

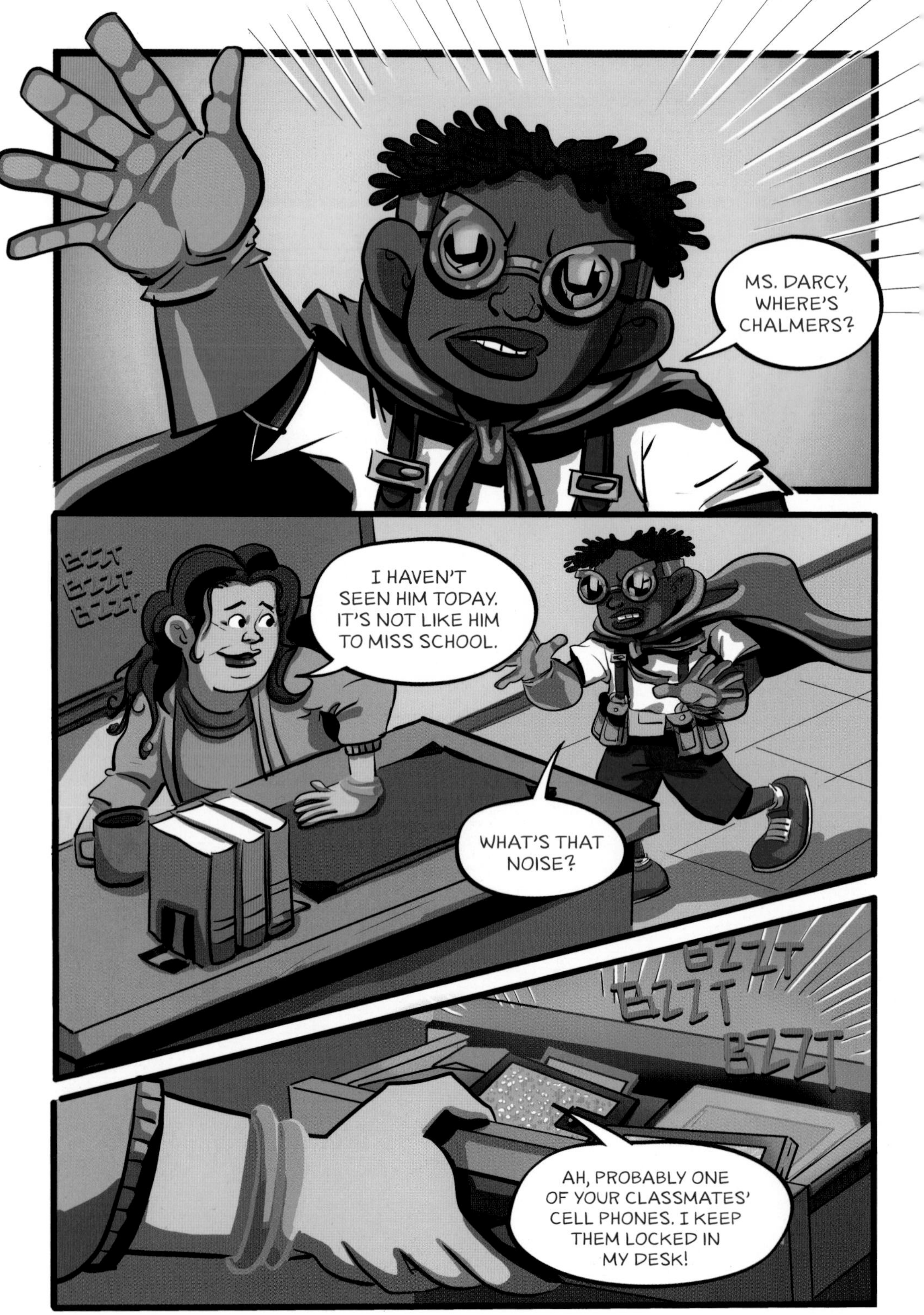
MS. DARCY, WHERE'S CHALMERS?
BZZT BZZT BZZT
I HAVEN'T SEEN HIM TODAY. IT'S NOT LIKE HIM TO MISS SCHOOL.
WHAT'S THAT NOISE?
BZZT BZZT BZZT
AH, PROBABLY ONE OF YOUR CLASSMATES' CELL PHONES. I KEEP THEM LOCKED IN MY DESK!

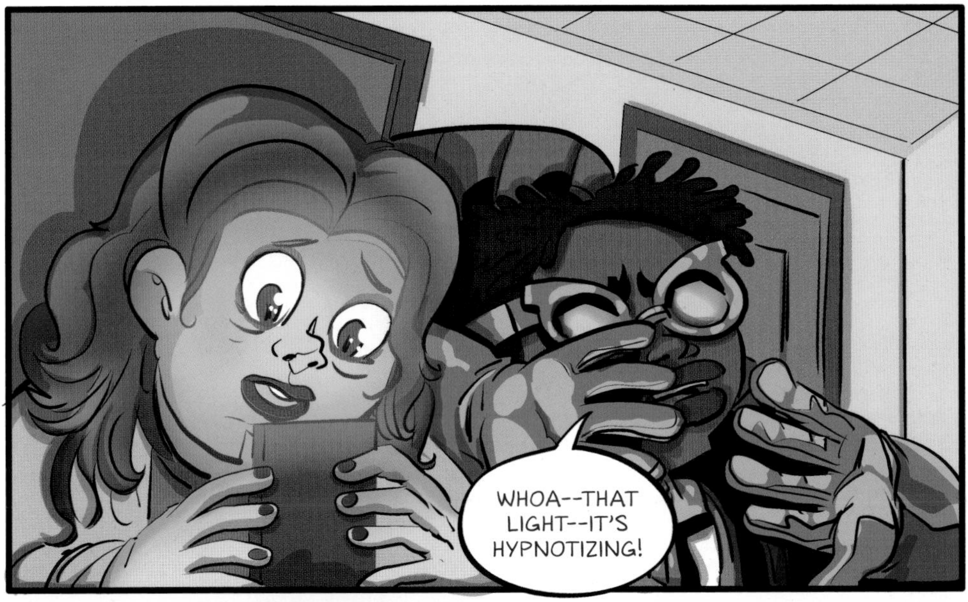
WHOA--THAT LIGHT--IT'S HYPNOTIZING!

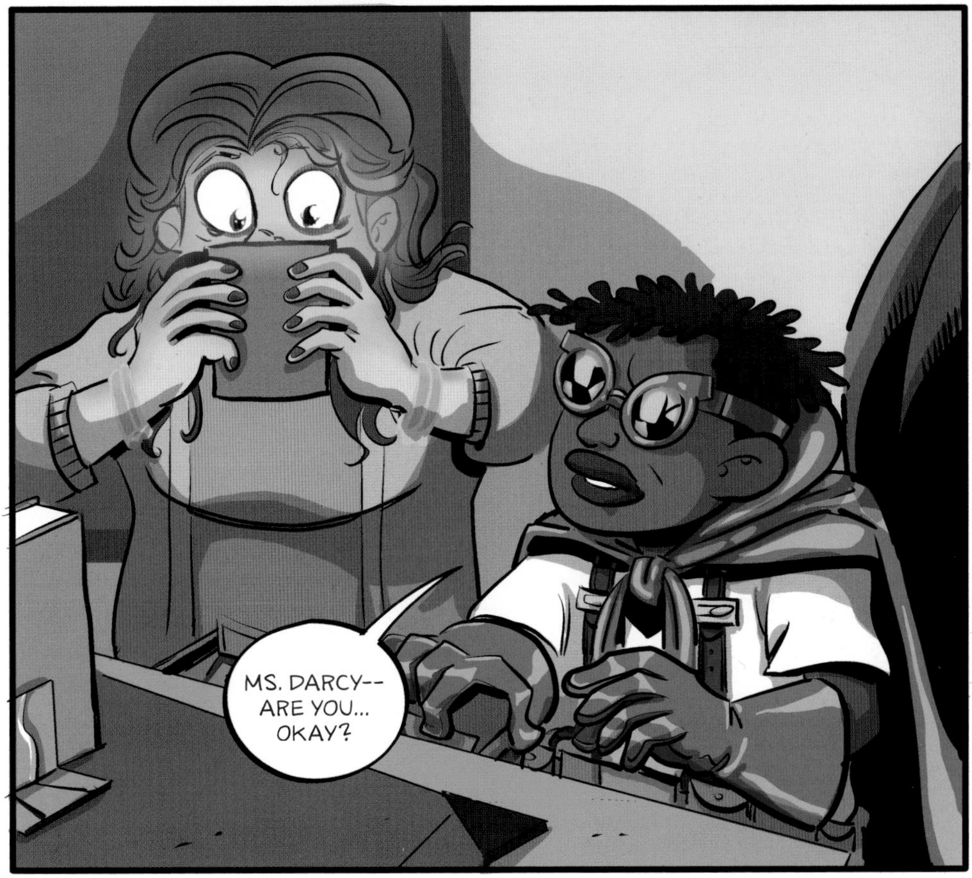
MS. DARCY--ARE YOU... OKAY?

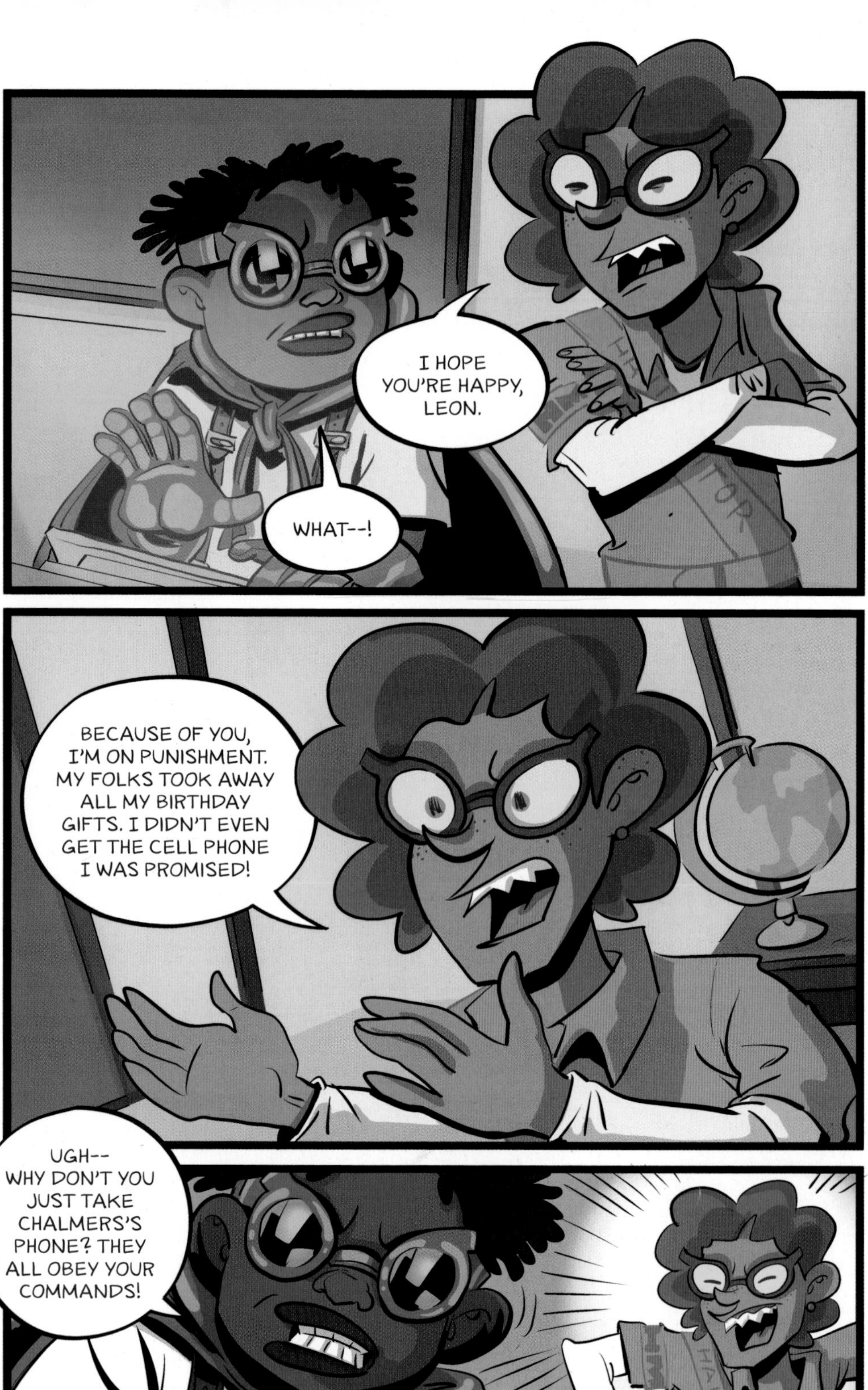
I HOPE YOU'RE HAPPY, LEON.
WHAT--!
BECAUSE OF YOU, I'M ON PUNISHMENT. MY FOLKS TOOK AWAY ALL MY BIRTHDAY GIFTS. I DIDN'T EVEN GET THE CELL PHONE I WAS PROMISED!
UGH-- WHY DON'T YOU JUST TAKE CHALMERS'S PHONE? THEY ALL OBEY YOUR COMMANDS!

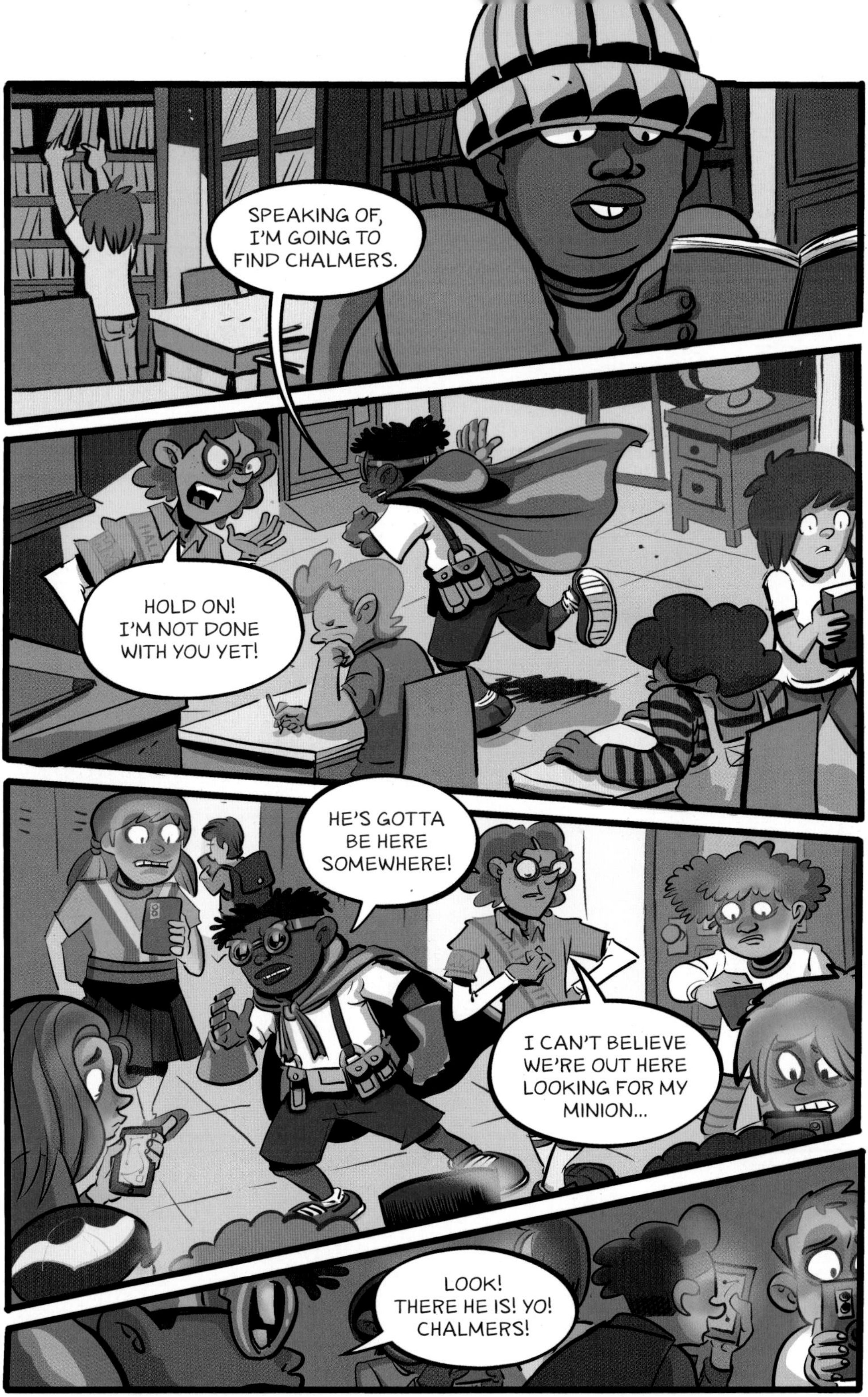
SPEAKING OF, I'M GOING TO FIND CHALMERS.
HOLD ON! I'M NOT DONE WITH YOU YET!
HE'S GOTTA BE HERE SOMEWHERE!
I CAN'T BELIEVE WE'RE OUT HERE LOOKING FOR MY MINION...
LOOK! THERE HE IS! YO! CHALMERS!

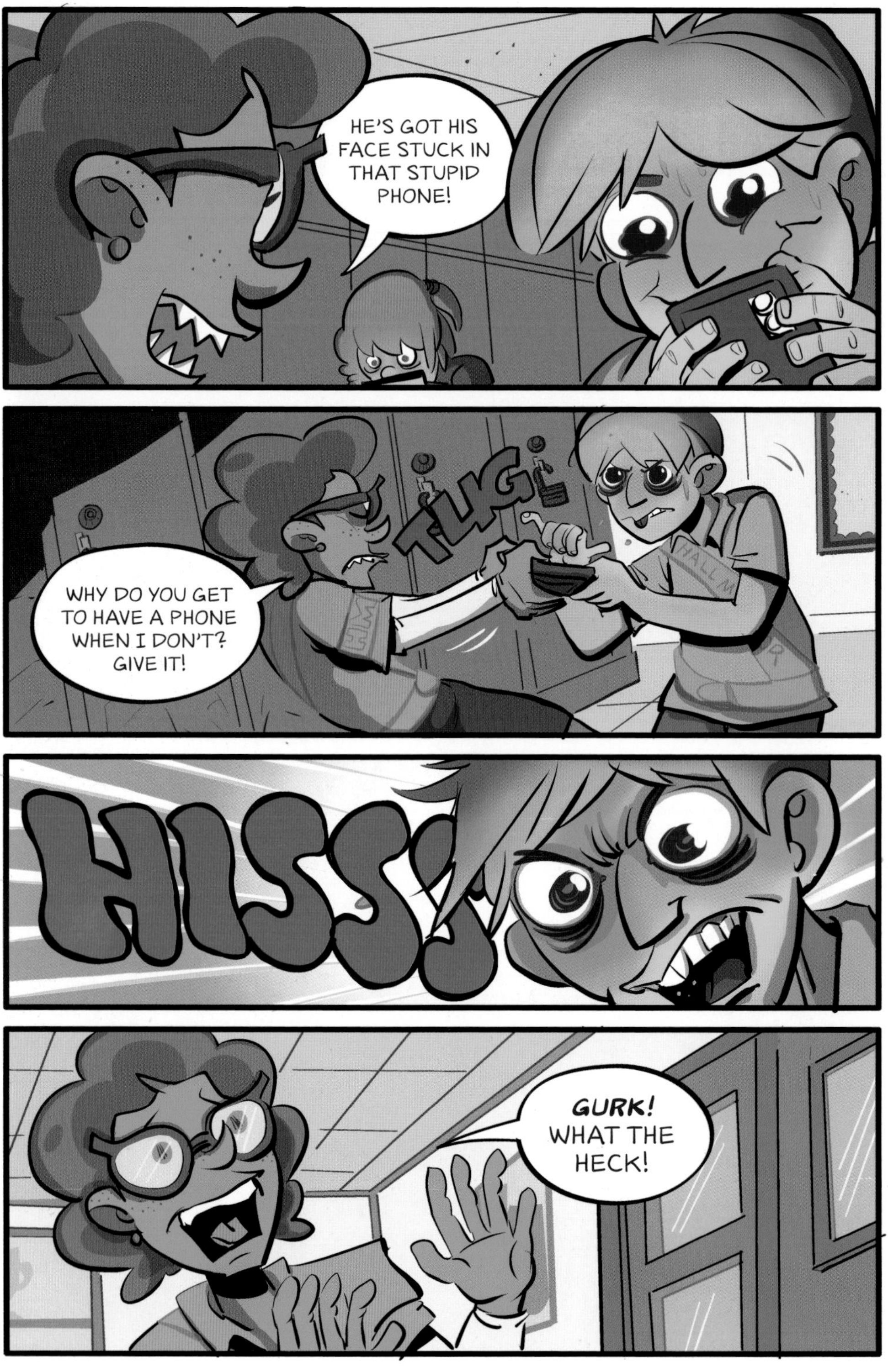
HE'S GOT HIS FACE STUCK IN THAT STUPID PHONE!
TUG
WHY DO YOU GET TO HAVE A PHONE WHEN I DON'T? GIVE IT!
HISS!
GURK! WHAT THE HECK!

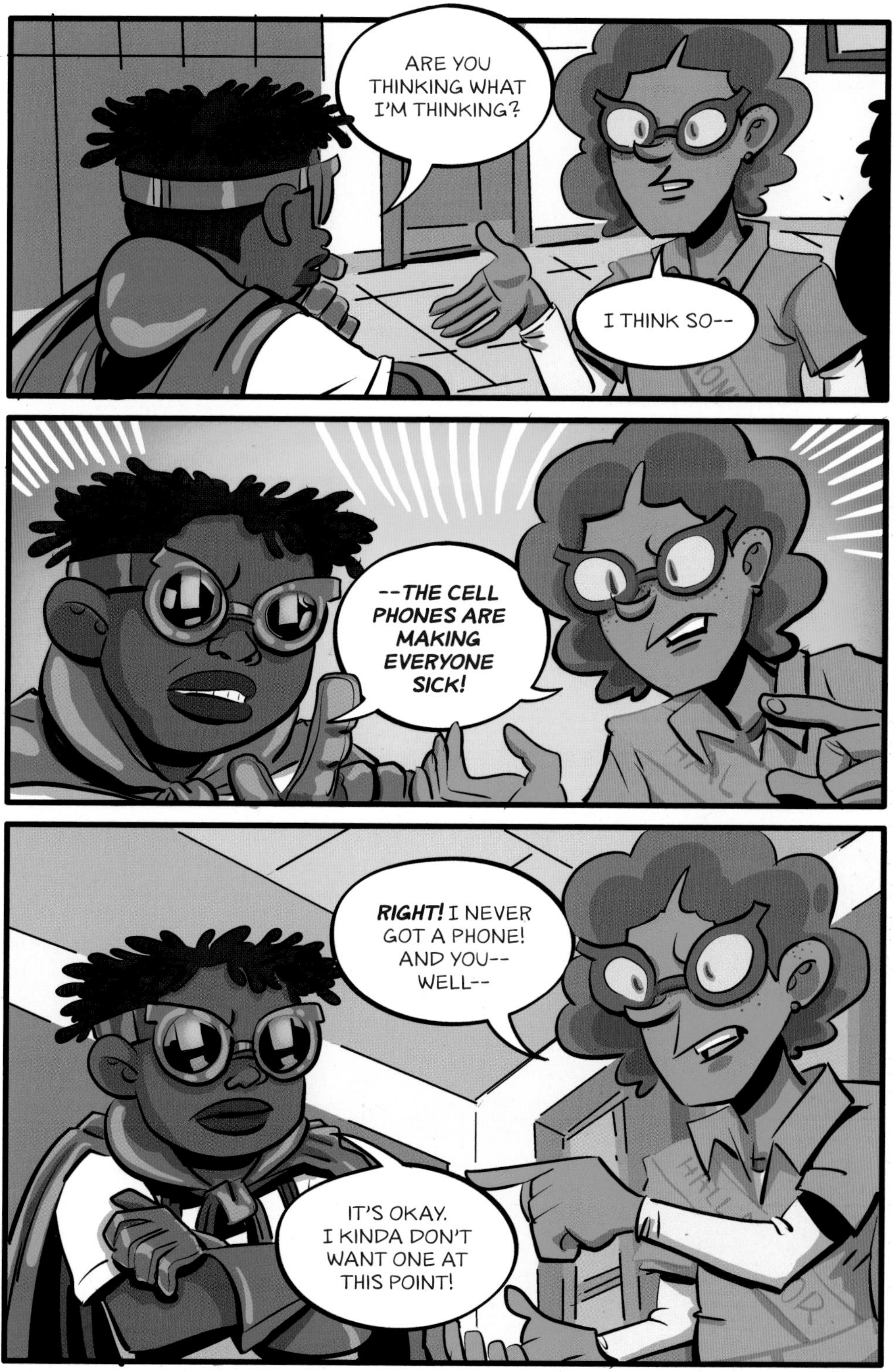
ARE YOU THINKING WHAT I'M THINKING?
I THINK SO--
--THE CELL PHONES ARE MAKING EVERYONE SICK!
RIGHT! I NEVER GOT A PHONE! AND YOU-- WELL--
IT'S OKAY. I KINDA DON'T WANT ONE AT THIS POINT!

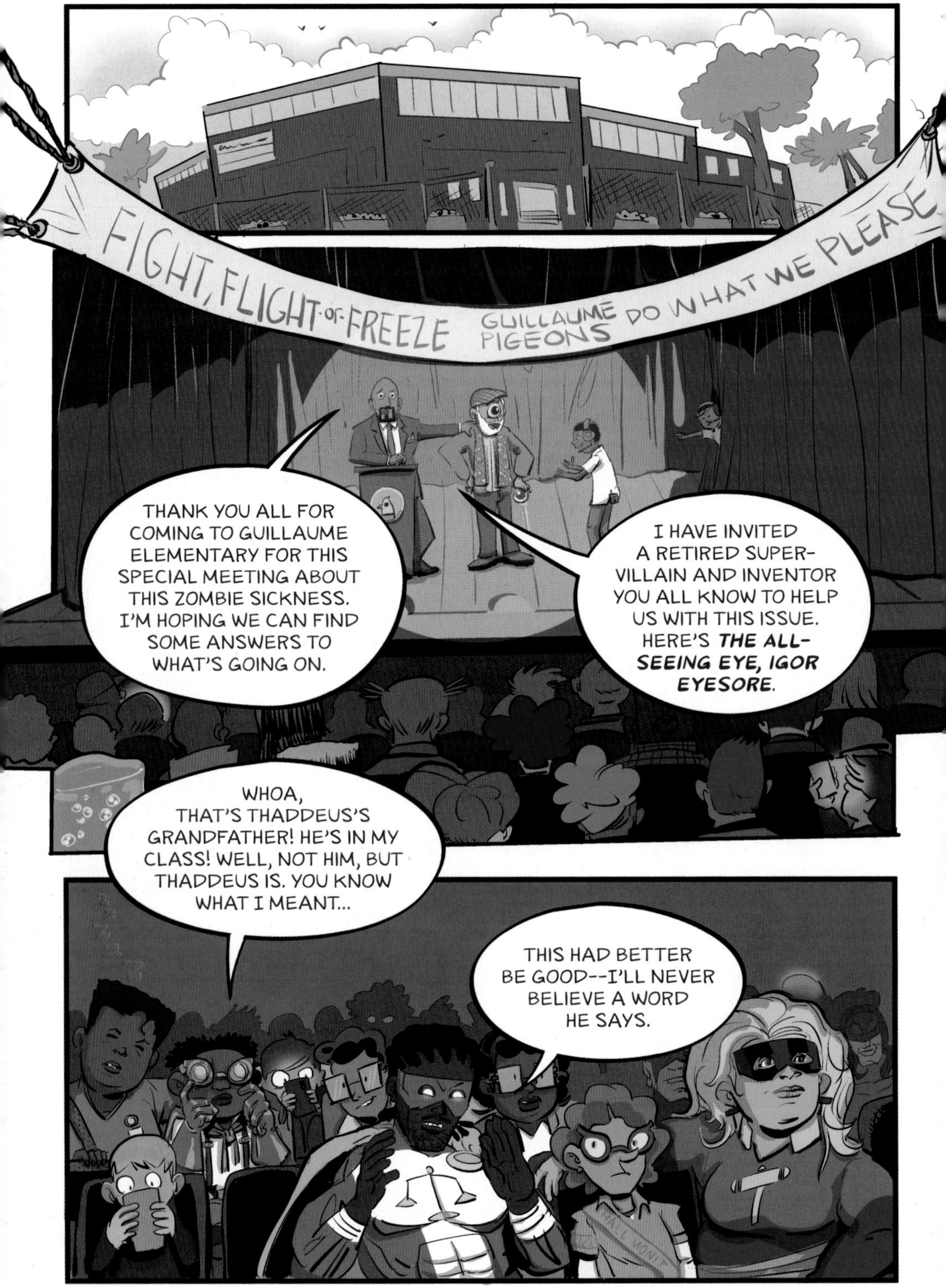
FIGHT, FLIGHT-OF-FREEZE
GUILLAUME PIGEONS
DO WHAT WE PLEASE
THANK YOU ALL FOR COMING TO GUILLAUME ELEMENTARY FOR THIS SPECIAL MEETING ABOUT THIS ZOMBIE SICKNESS. I'M HOPING WE CAN FIND SOME ANSWERS TO WHAT'S GOING ON.
I HAVE INVITED A RETIRED SUPER-VILLAIN AND INVENTOR YOU ALL KNOW TO HELP US WITH THIS ISSUE. HERE'S **THE ALL-SEEING EYE, IGOR EYESORE**.
WHOA, THAT'S THADDEUS'S GRANDFATHER! HE'S IN MY CLASS! WELL, NOT HIM, BUT THADDEUS IS. YOU KNOW WHAT I MEANT...
THIS HAD BETTER BE GOOD--I'LL NEVER BELIEVE A WORD HE SAYS.

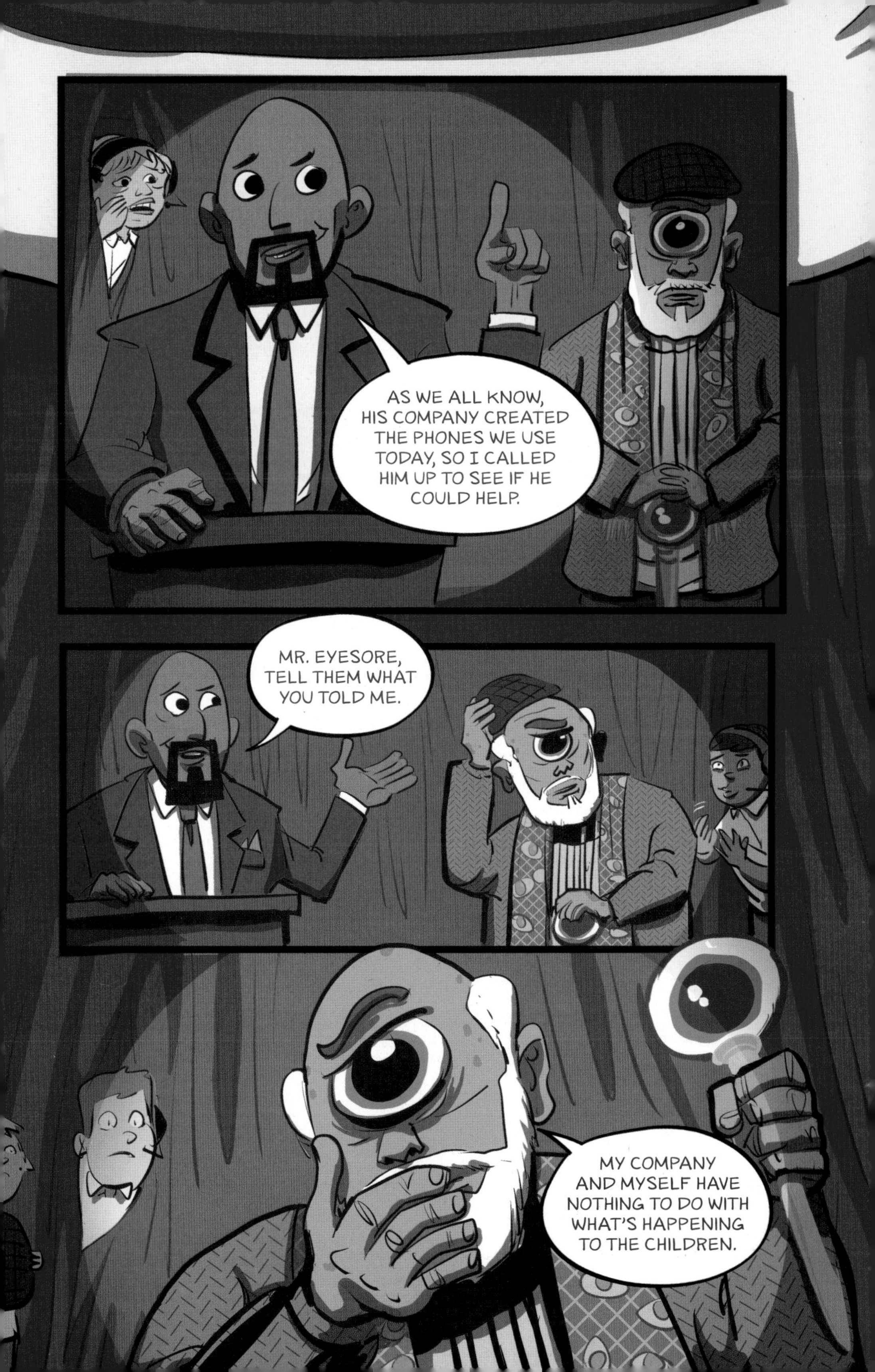
AS WE ALL KNOW, HIS COMPANY CREATED THE PHONES WE USE TODAY, SO I CALLED HIM UP TO SEE IF HE COULD HELP.
MR. EYESORE, TELL THEM WHAT YOU TOLD ME.
MY COMPANY AND MYSELF HAVE NOTHING TO DO WITH WHAT'S HAPPENING TO THE CHILDREN.

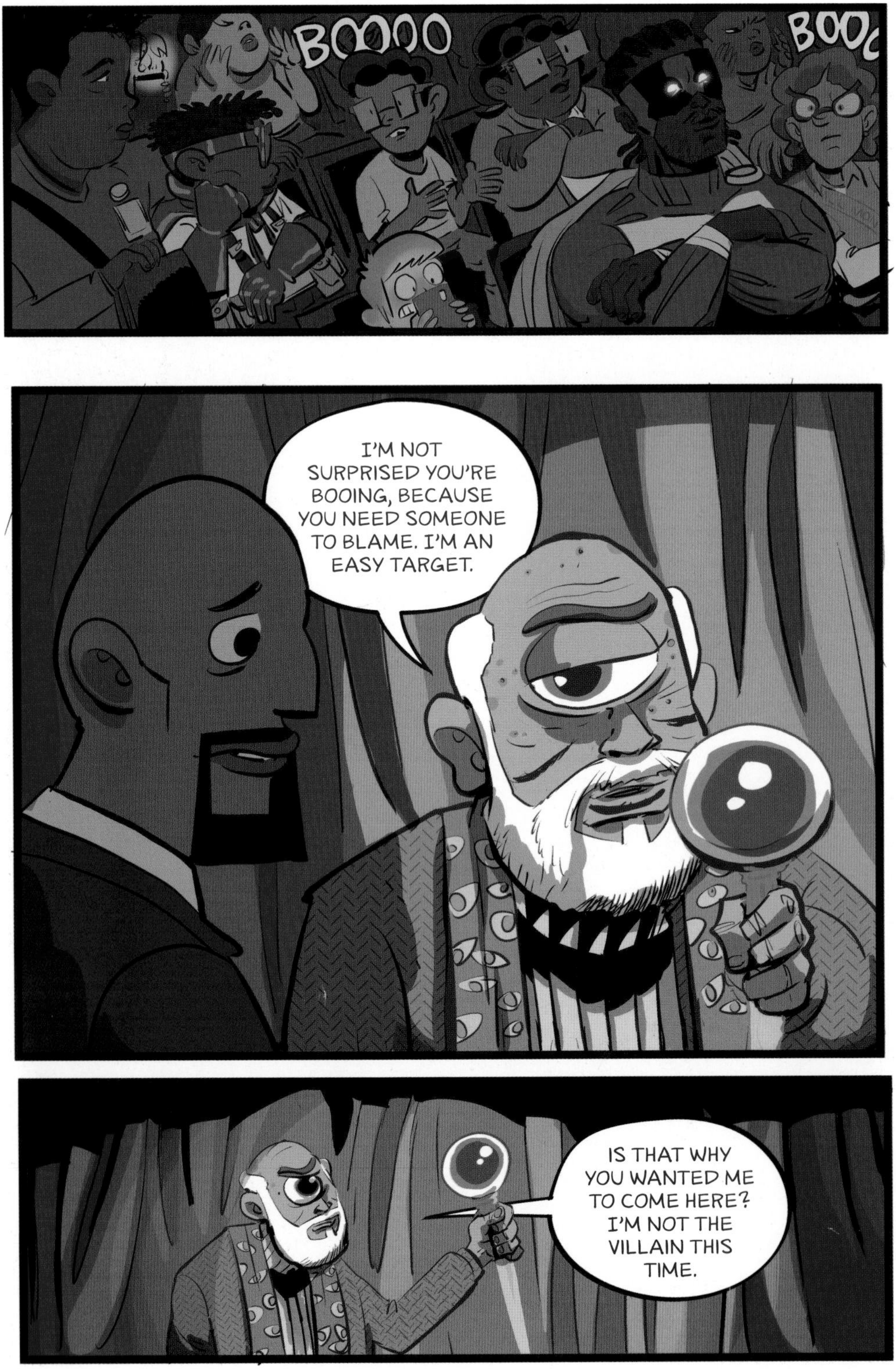
BOOOO
BOOO
I'M NOT SURPRISED YOU'RE BOOING, BECAUSE YOU NEED SOMEONE TO BLAME. I'M AN EASY TARGET.
IS THAT WHY YOU WANTED ME TO COME HERE? I'M NOT THE VILLAIN THIS TIME.

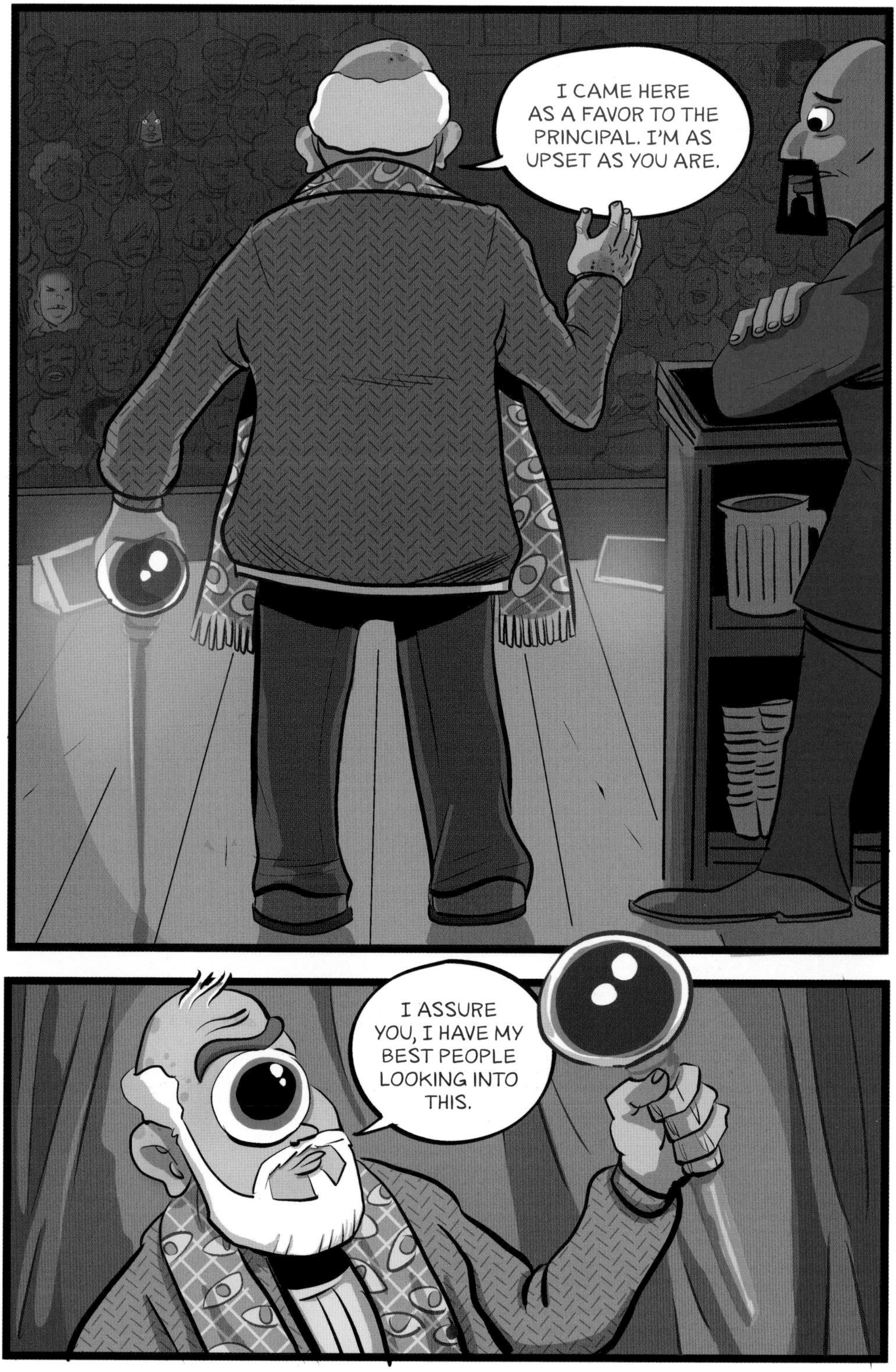
I CAME HERE AS A FAVOR TO THE PRINCIPAL. I'M AS UPSET AS YOU ARE.
I ASSURE YOU, I HAVE MY BEST PEOPLE LOOKING INTO THIS.

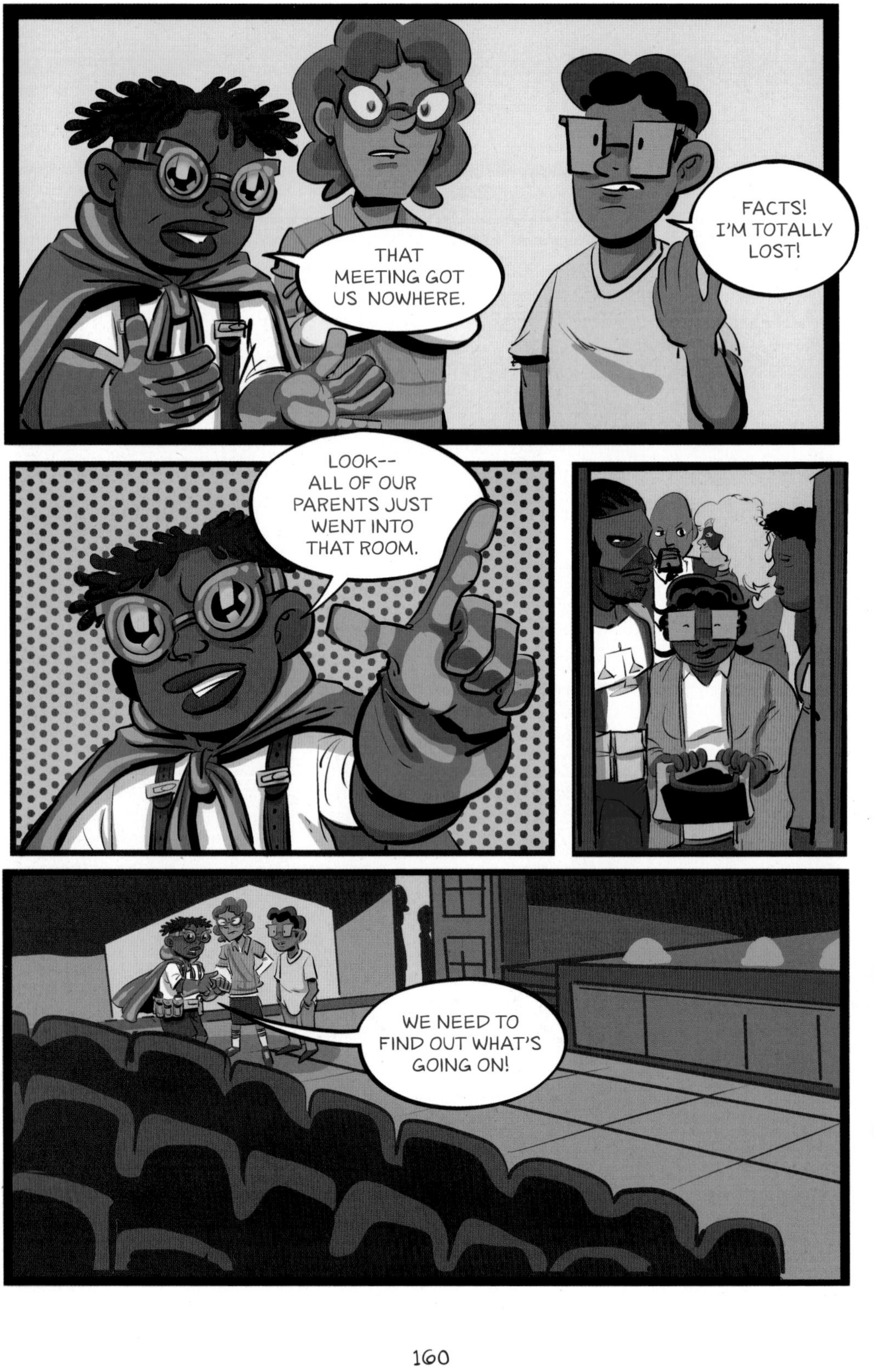

THAT MEETING GOT US NOWHERE.
FACTS! I'M TOTALLY LOST!
LOOK-- ALL OF OUR PARENTS JUST WENT INTO THAT ROOM.
WE NEED TO FIND OUT WHAT'S GOING ON!

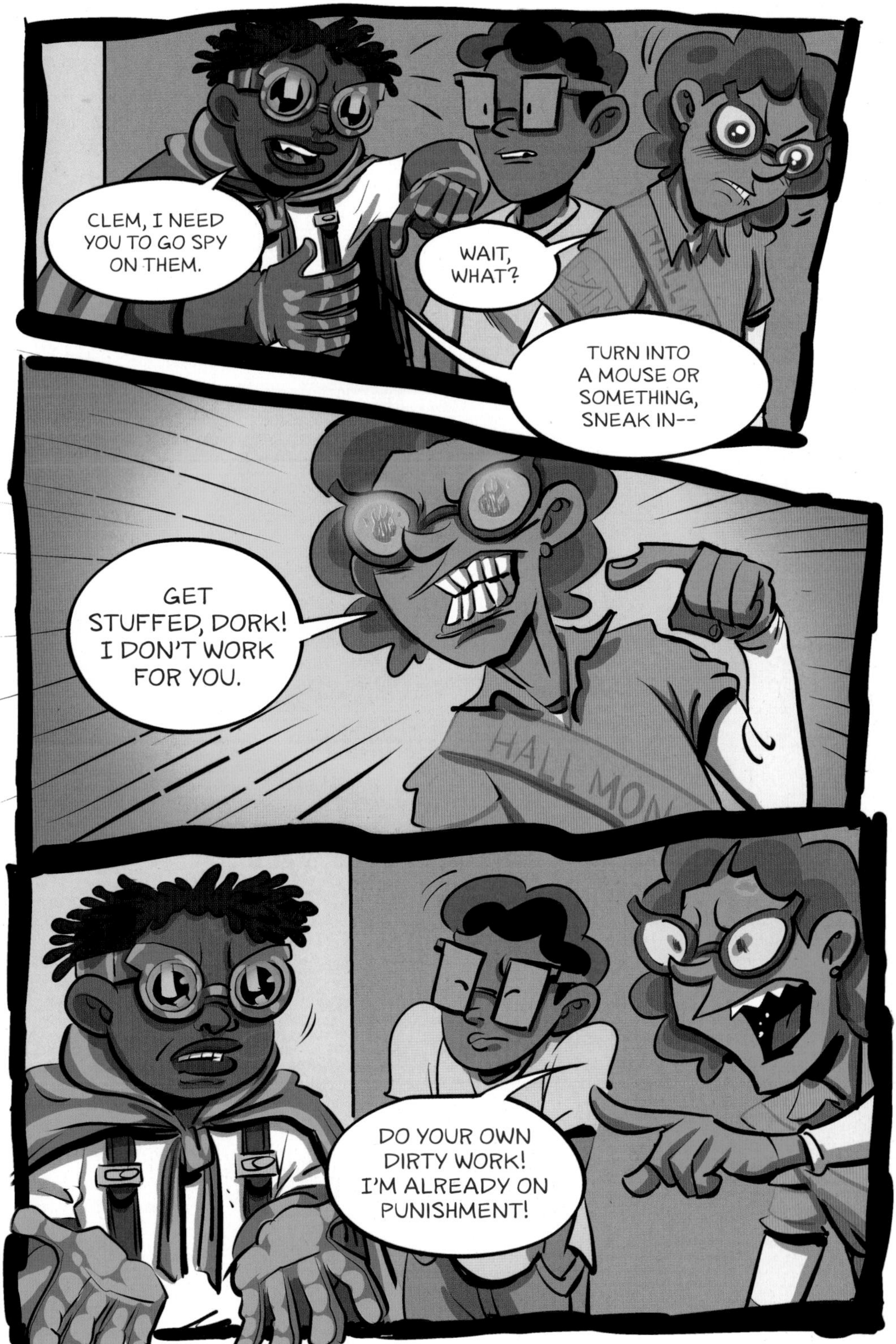
CLEM, I NEED YOU TO GO SPY ON THEM.
WAIT, WHAT?
TURN INTO A MOUSE OR SOMETHING, SNEAK IN--
GET STUFFED, DORK! I DON'T WORK FOR YOU.
HALL MON
DO YOUR OWN DIRTY WORK! I'M ALREADY ON PUNISHMENT!

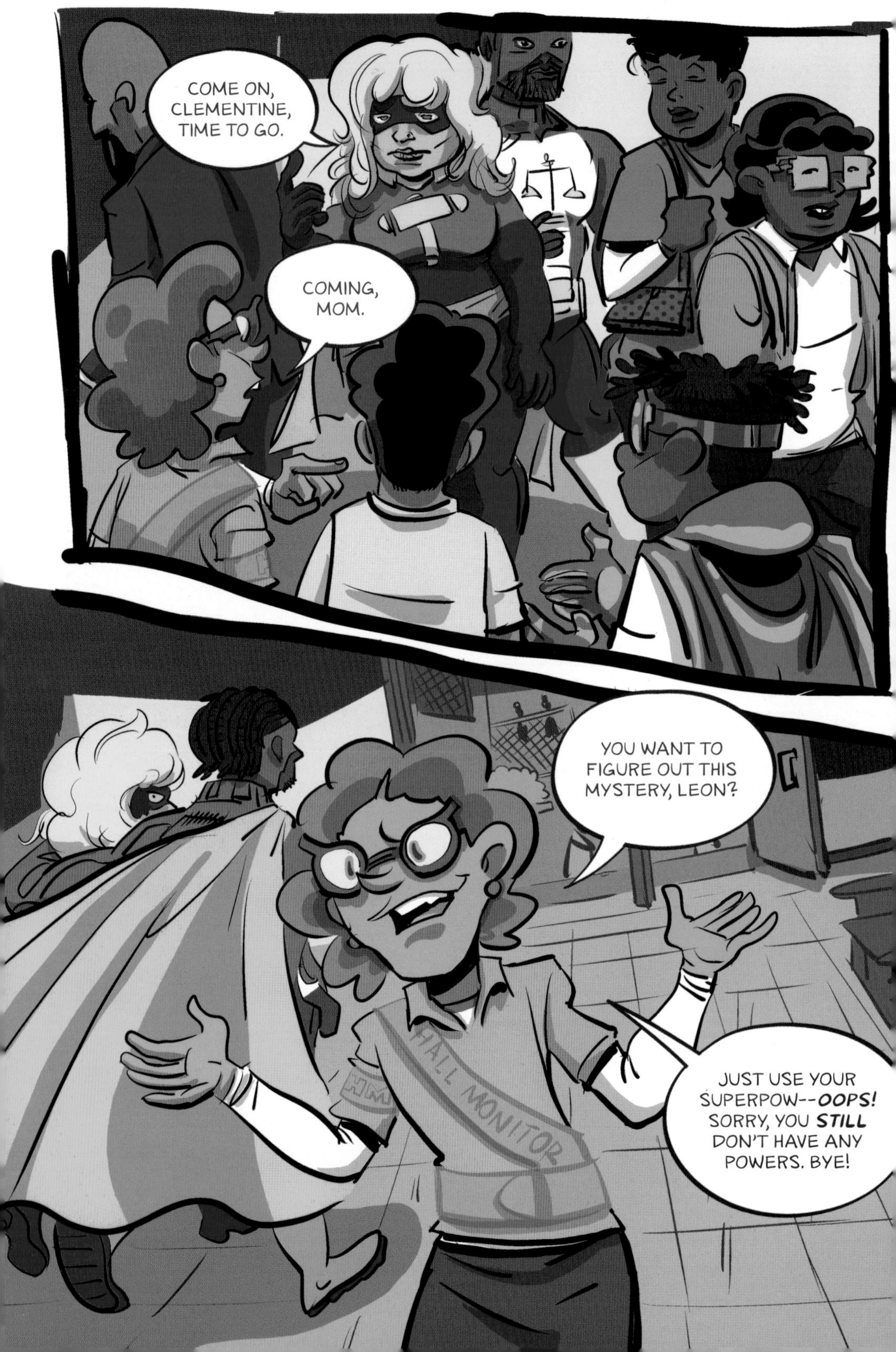
COME ON, CLEMENTINE, TIME TO GO.
COMING, MOM.
HALL MONITOR
YOU WANT TO FIGURE OUT THIS MYSTERY, LEON?
JUST USE YOUR SUPERPOW--**OOPS!** SORRY, YOU **STILL** DON'T HAVE ANY POWERS. BYE!

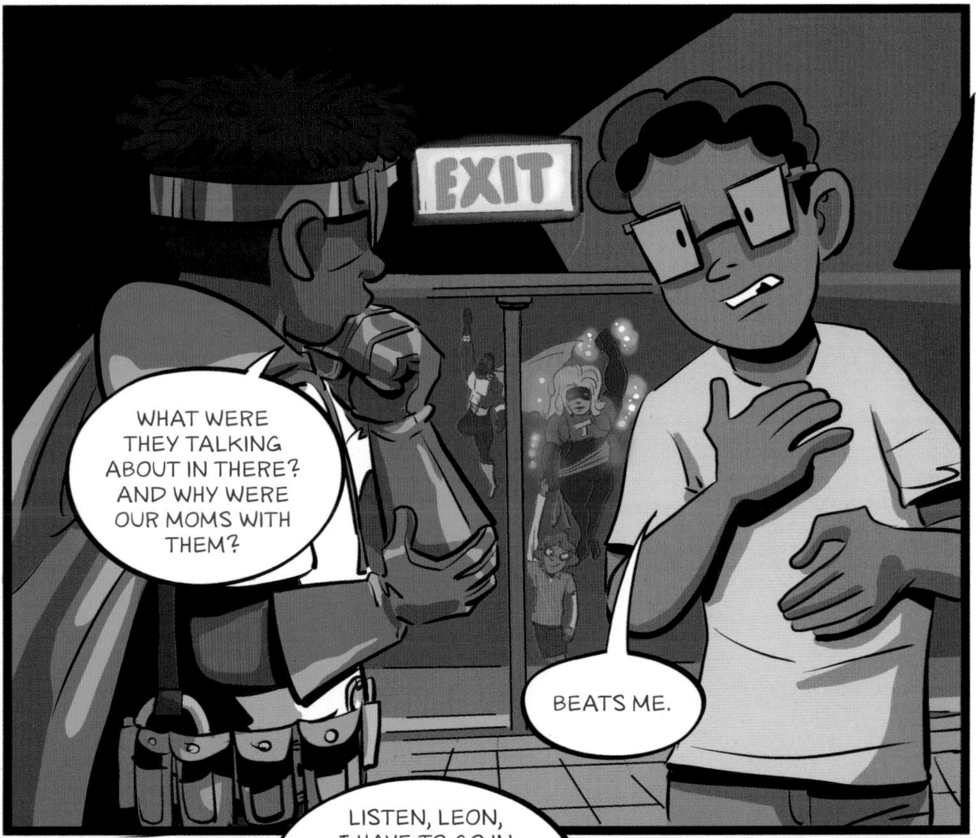
EXIT
WHAT WERE THEY TALKING ABOUT IN THERE? AND WHY WERE OUR MOMS WITH THEM?
BEATS ME.

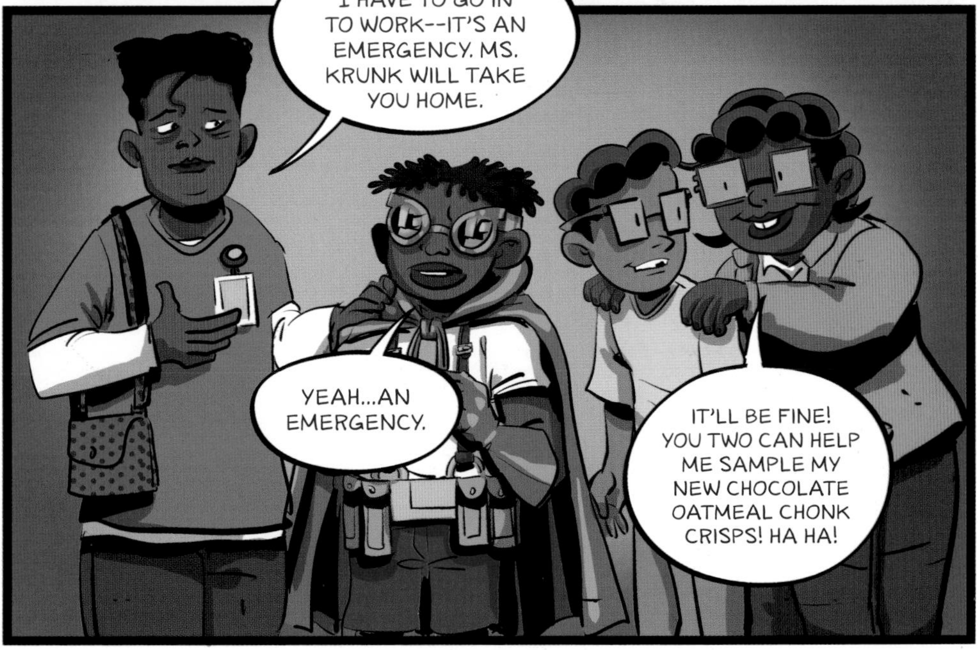
LISTEN, LEON, I HAVE TO GO IN TO WORK--IT'S AN EMERGENCY. MS. KRUNK WILL TAKE YOU HOME.
YEAH...AN EMERGENCY.
IT'LL BE FINE! YOU TWO CAN HELP ME SAMPLE MY NEW CHOCOLATE OATMEAL CHONK CRISPS! HA HA!

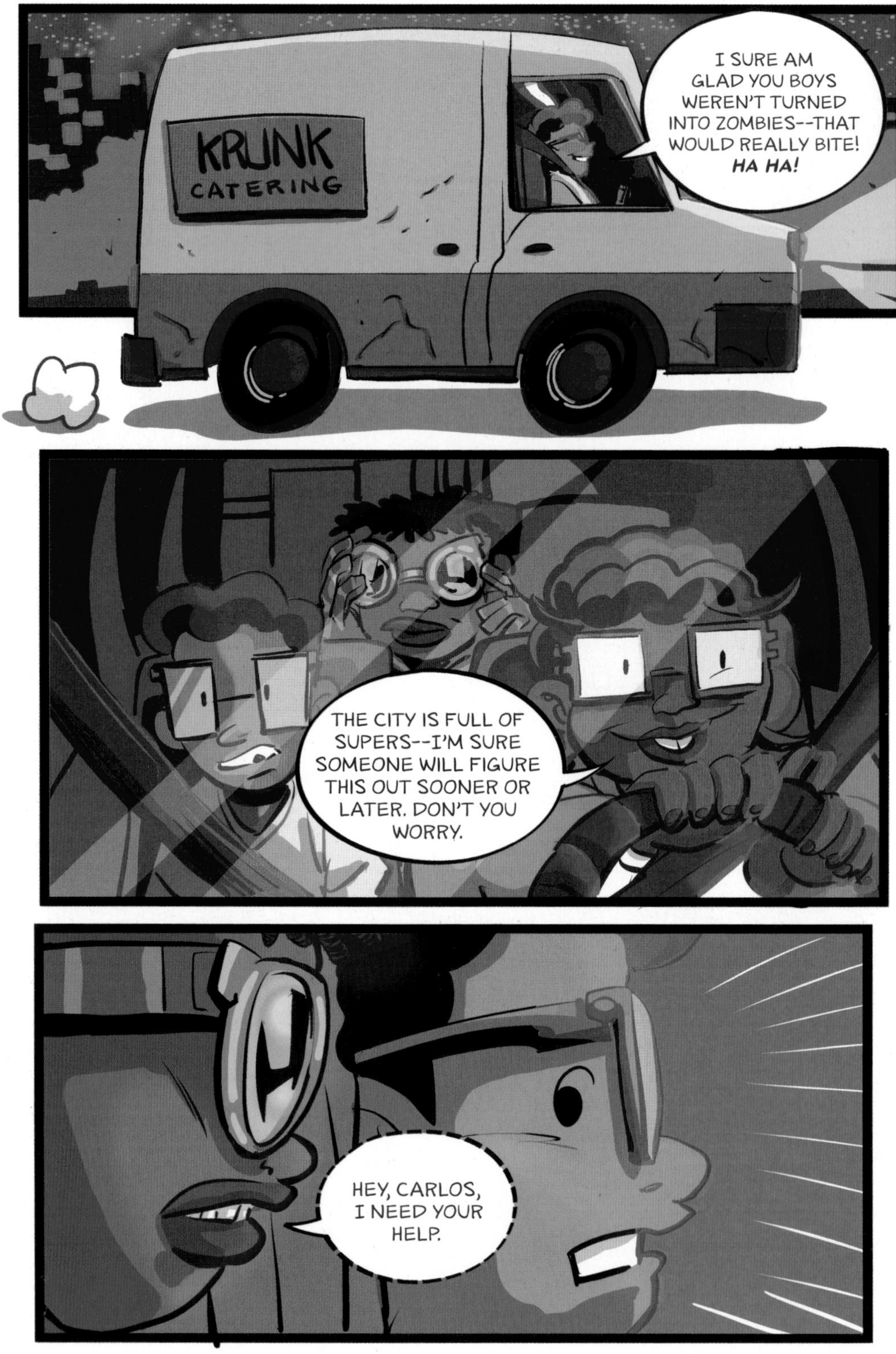
KRUNK CATERING
I SURE AM GLAD YOU BOYS WEREN'T TURNED INTO ZOMBIES--THAT WOULD REALLY BITE! **HA HA!**
THE CITY IS FULL OF SUPERS--I'M SURE SOMEONE WILL FIGURE THIS OUT SOONER OR LATER. DON'T YOU WORRY.
HEY, CARLOS, I NEED YOUR HELP.

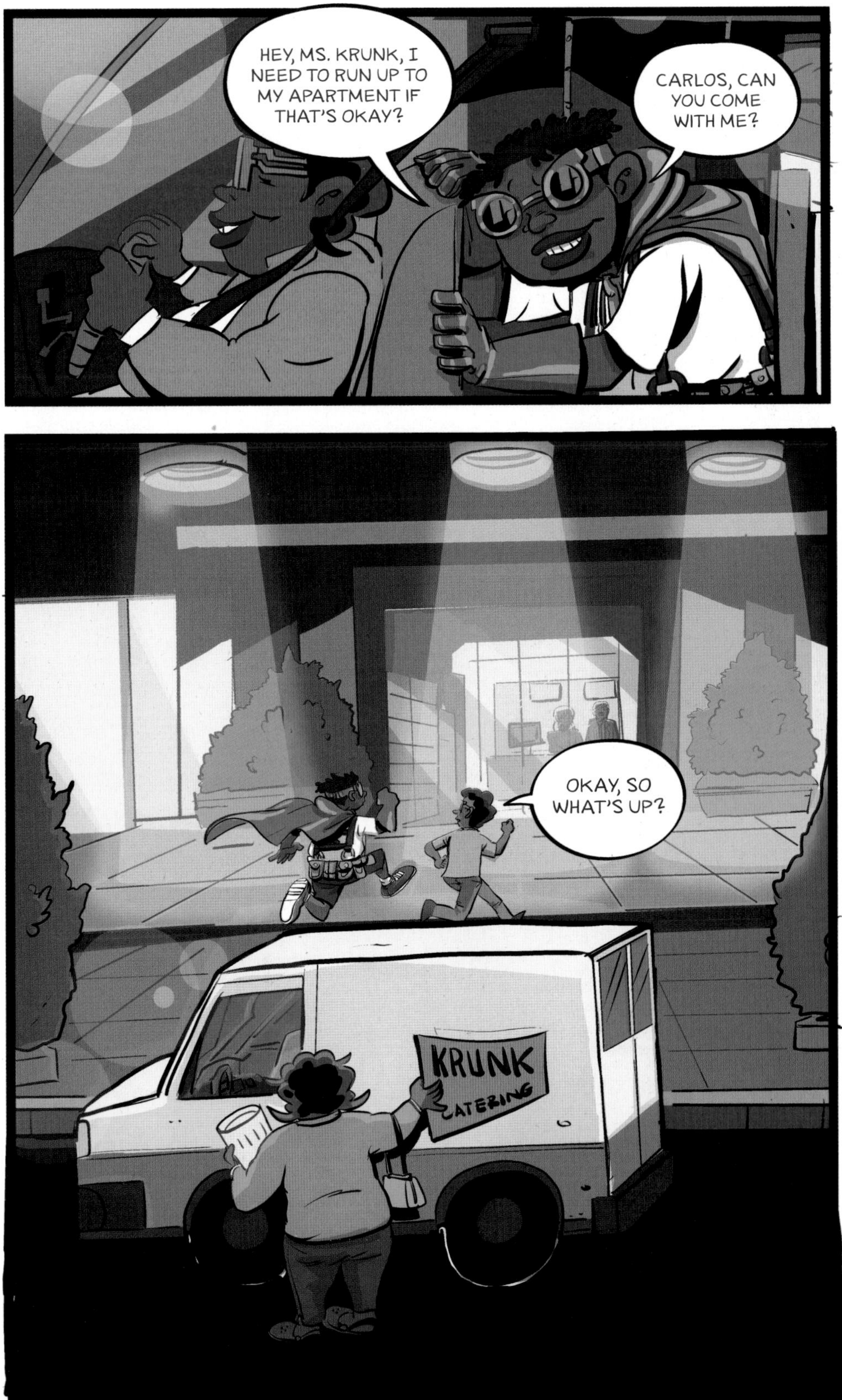
HEY, MS. KRUNK, I NEED TO RUN UP TO MY APARTMENT IF THAT'S OKAY?
CARLOS, CAN YOU COME WITH ME?
OKAY, SO WHAT'S UP?
KRUNK CATERING

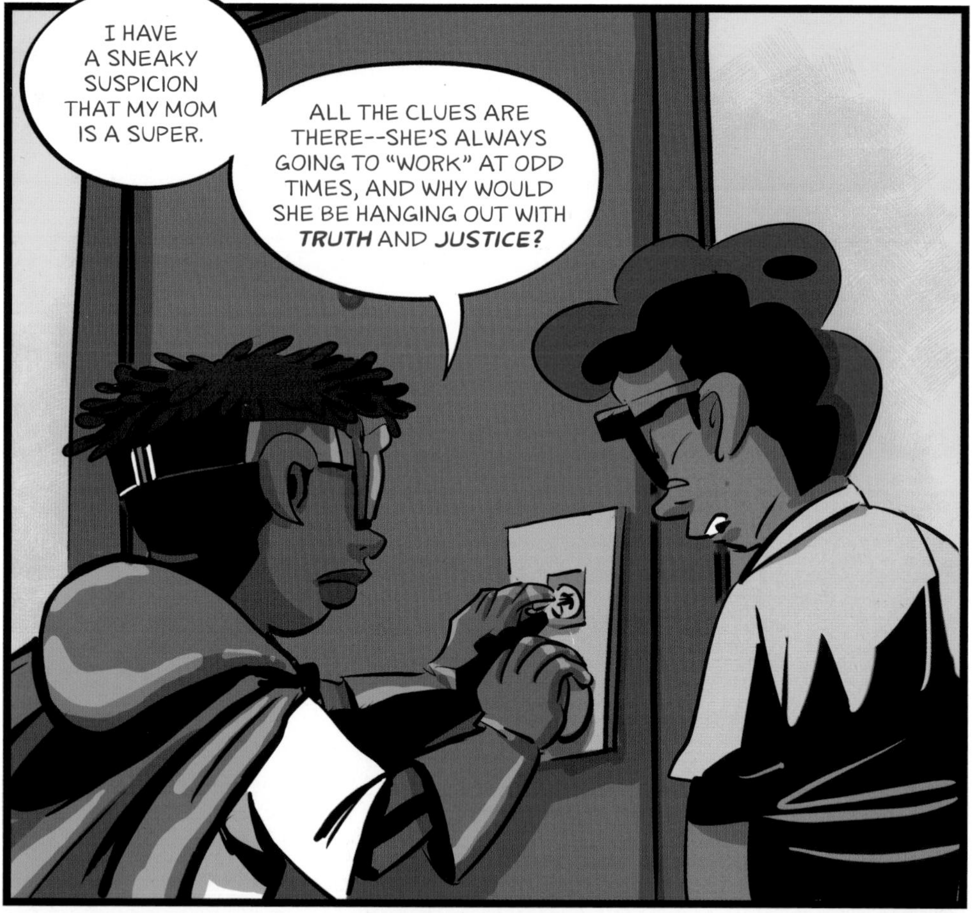
I HAVE A SNEAKY SUSPICION THAT MY MOM IS A SUPER.
ALL THE CLUES ARE THERE--SHE'S ALWAYS GOING TO "WORK" AT ODD TIMES, AND WHY WOULD SHE BE HANGING OUT WITH ***TRUTH*** AND ***JUSTICE?***

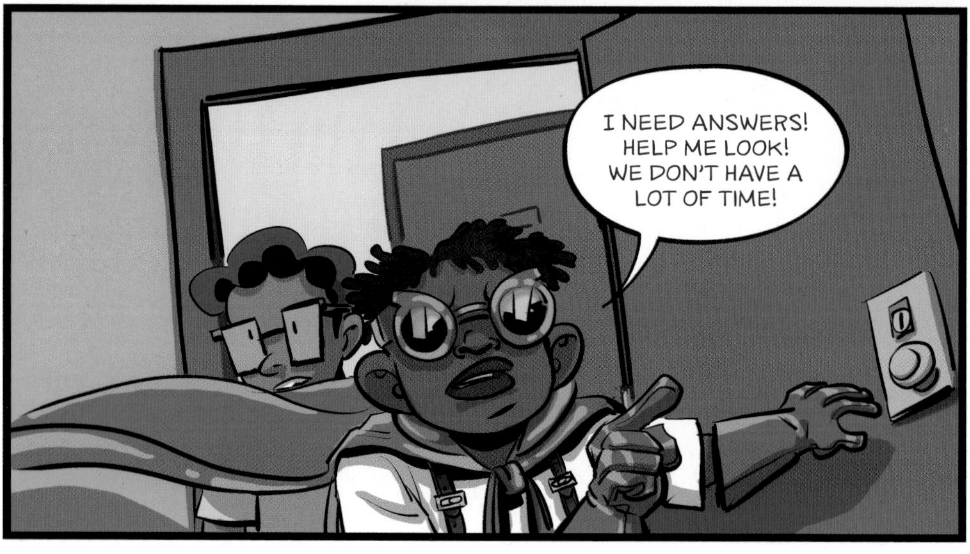
I NEED ANSWERS! HELP ME LOOK! WE DON'T HAVE A LOT OF TIME!

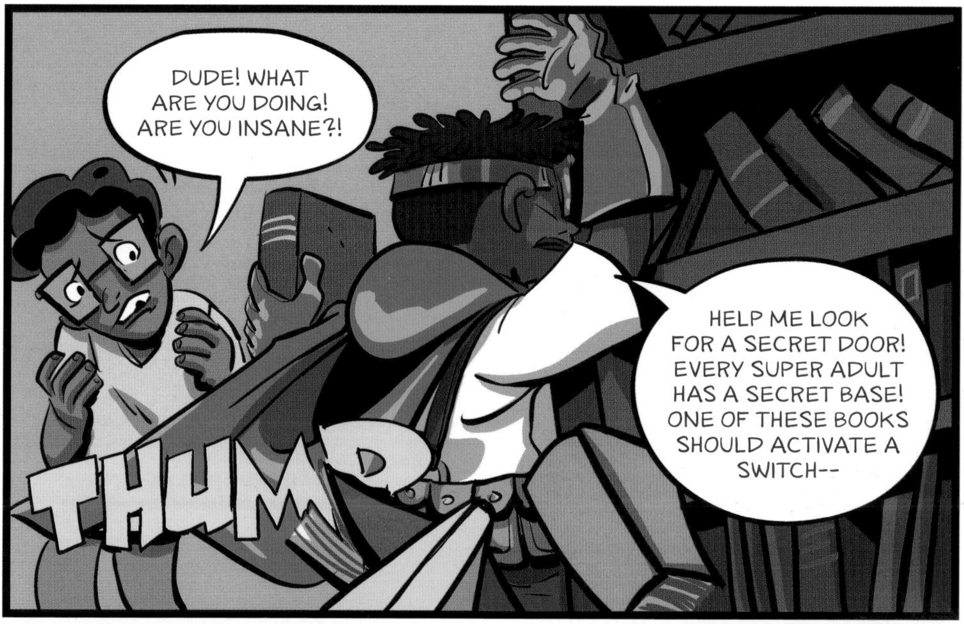
DUDE! WHAT ARE YOU DOING! ARE YOU INSANE?!
HELP ME LOOK FOR A SECRET DOOR! EVERY SUPER ADULT HAS A SECRET BASE! ONE OF THESE BOOKS SHOULD ACTIVATE A SWITCH--
THUMP

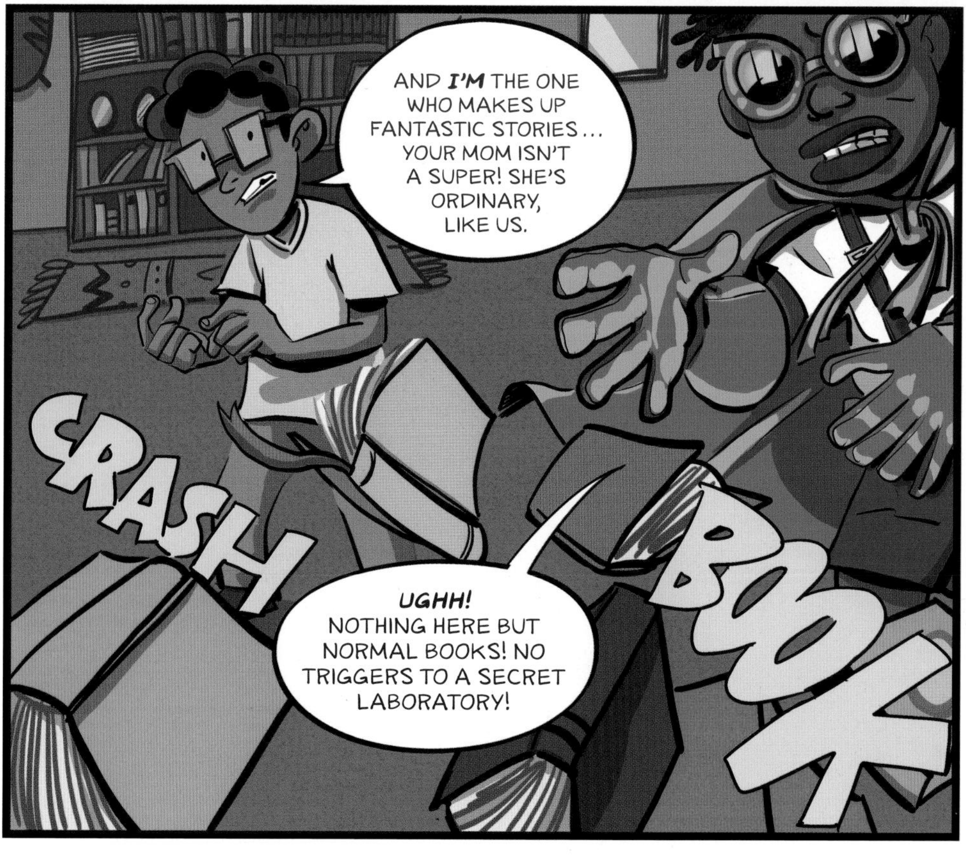
AND *I'M* THE ONE WHO MAKES UP FANTASTIC STORIES... YOUR MOM ISN'T A SUPER! SHE'S ORDINARY, LIKE US.
CRASH
BOOK
UGHH! NOTHING HERE BUT NORMAL BOOKS! NO TRIGGERS TO A SECRET LABORATORY!

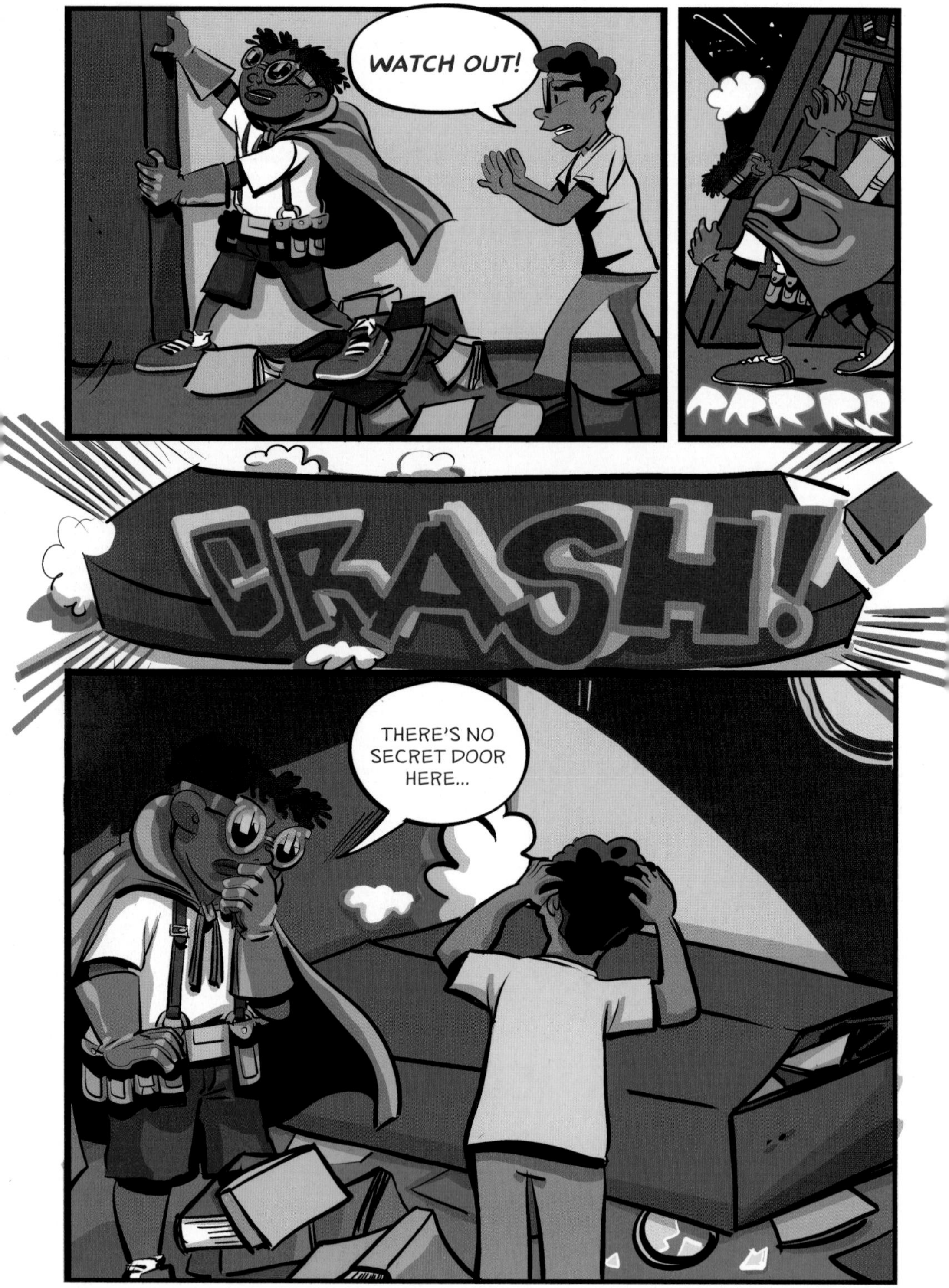
WATCH OUT!
RRRRRR
CRASH!
THERE'S NO SECRET DOOR HERE...

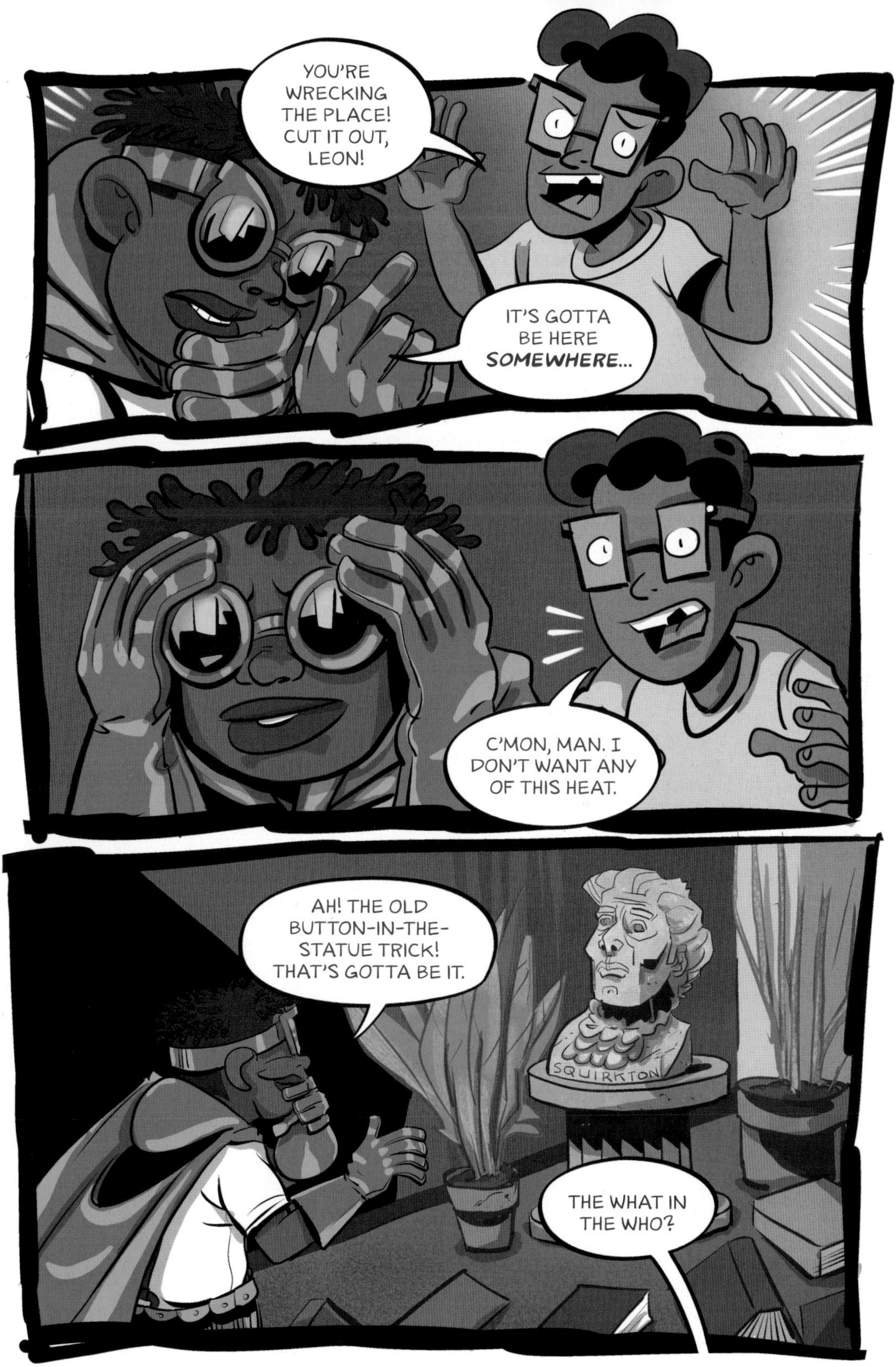
YOU'RE WRECKING THE PLACE! CUT IT OUT, LEON!
IT'S GOTTA BE HERE **SOMEWHERE...**
C'MON, MAN. I DON'T WANT ANY OF THIS HEAT.
AH! THE OLD BUTTON-IN-THE-STATUE TRICK! THAT'S GOTTA BE IT.
SQUIRKTON
THE WHAT IN THE WHO?

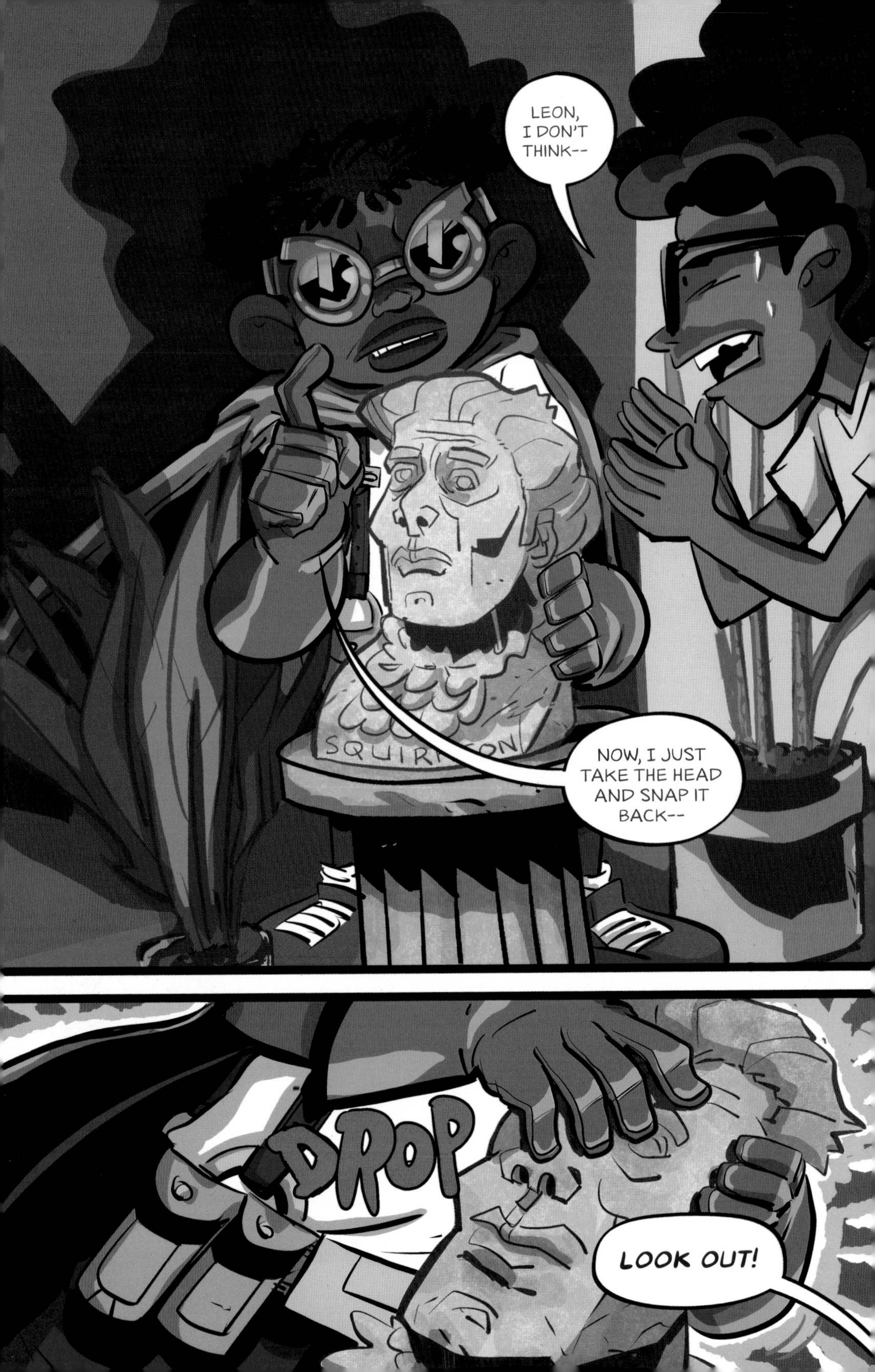
LEON, I DON'T THINK--
NOW, I JUST TAKE THE HEAD AND SNAP IT BACK--
SQUIRR
DROP
LOOK OUT!

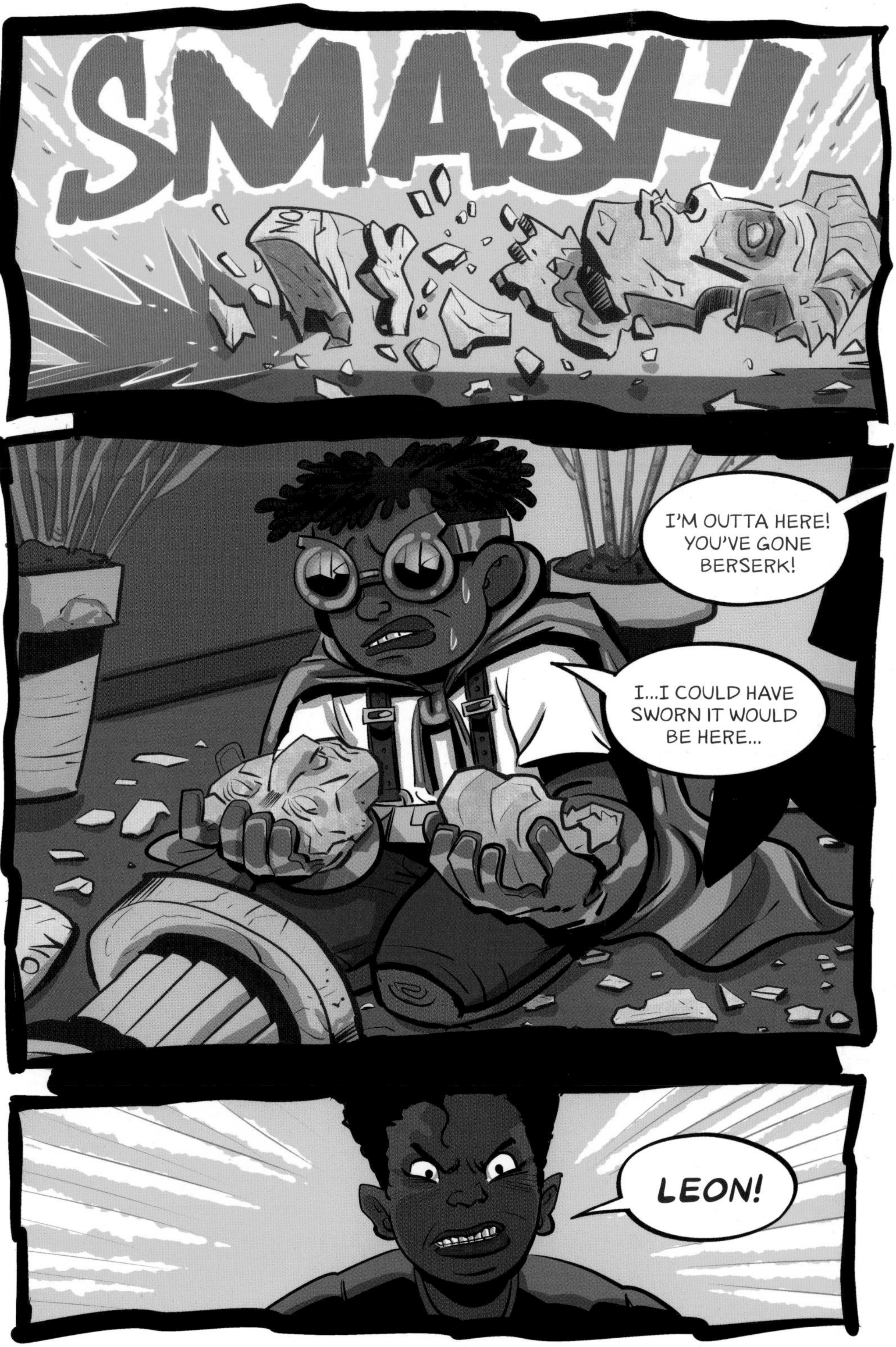
SMASH
I'M OUTTA HERE! YOU'VE GONE BERSERK!
I...I COULD HAVE SWORN IT WOULD BE HERE...
LEON!

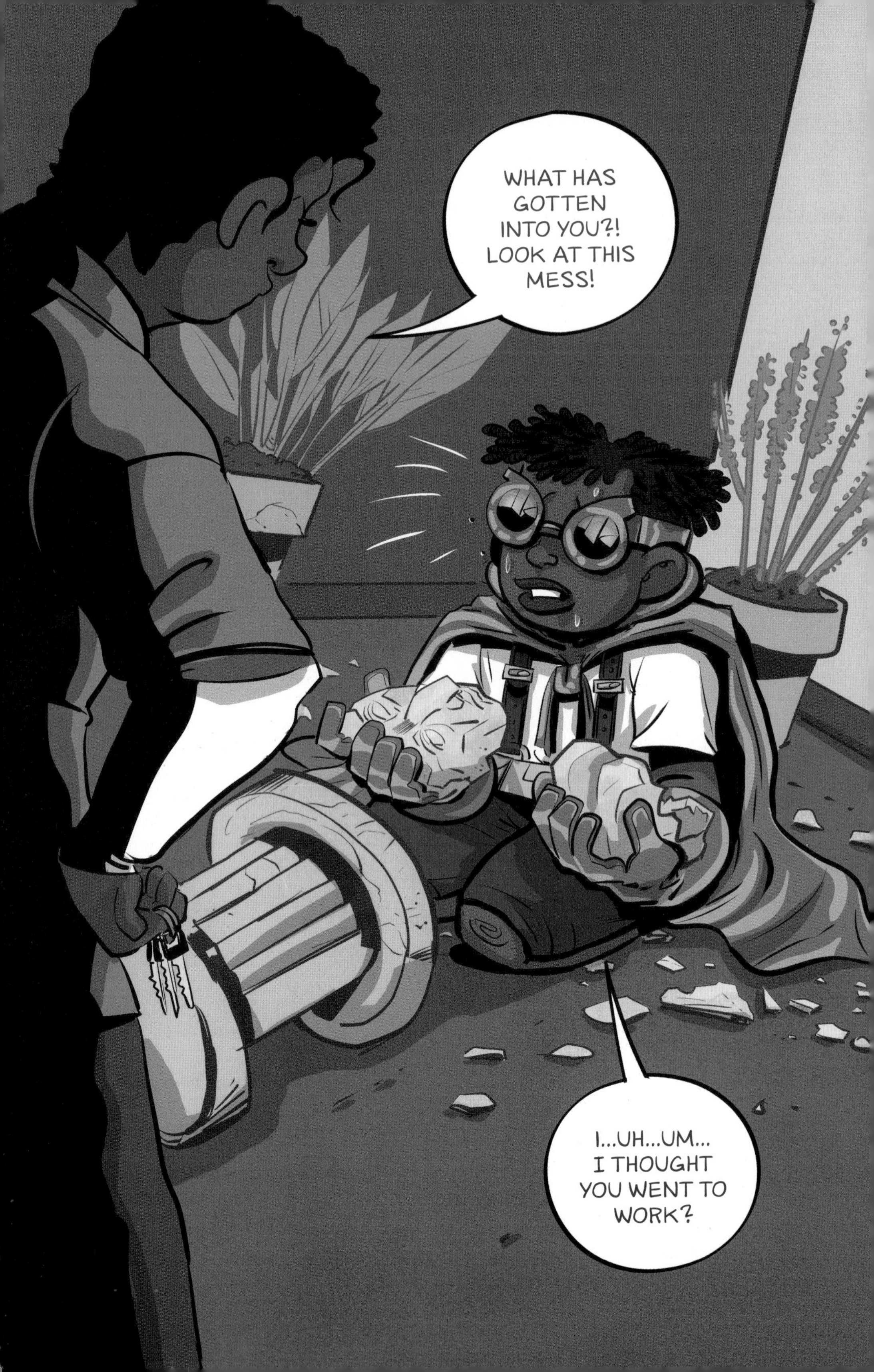
WHAT HAS GOTTEN INTO YOU?! LOOK AT THIS MESS!
I...UH...UM... I THOUGHT YOU WENT TO WORK?

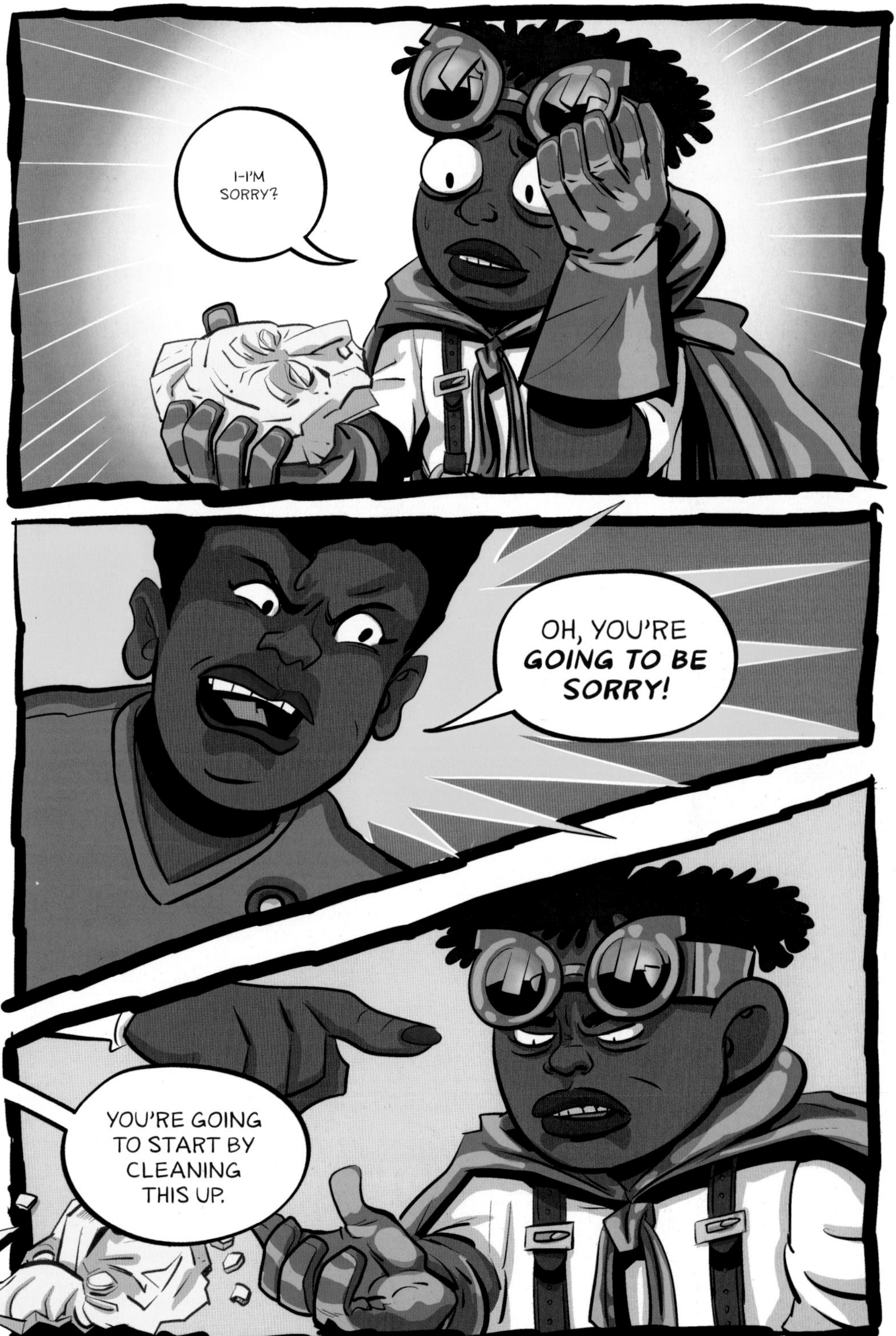
I-I'M SORRY?
OH, YOU'RE GOING TO BE SORRY!
YOU'RE GOING TO START BY CLEANING THIS UP.

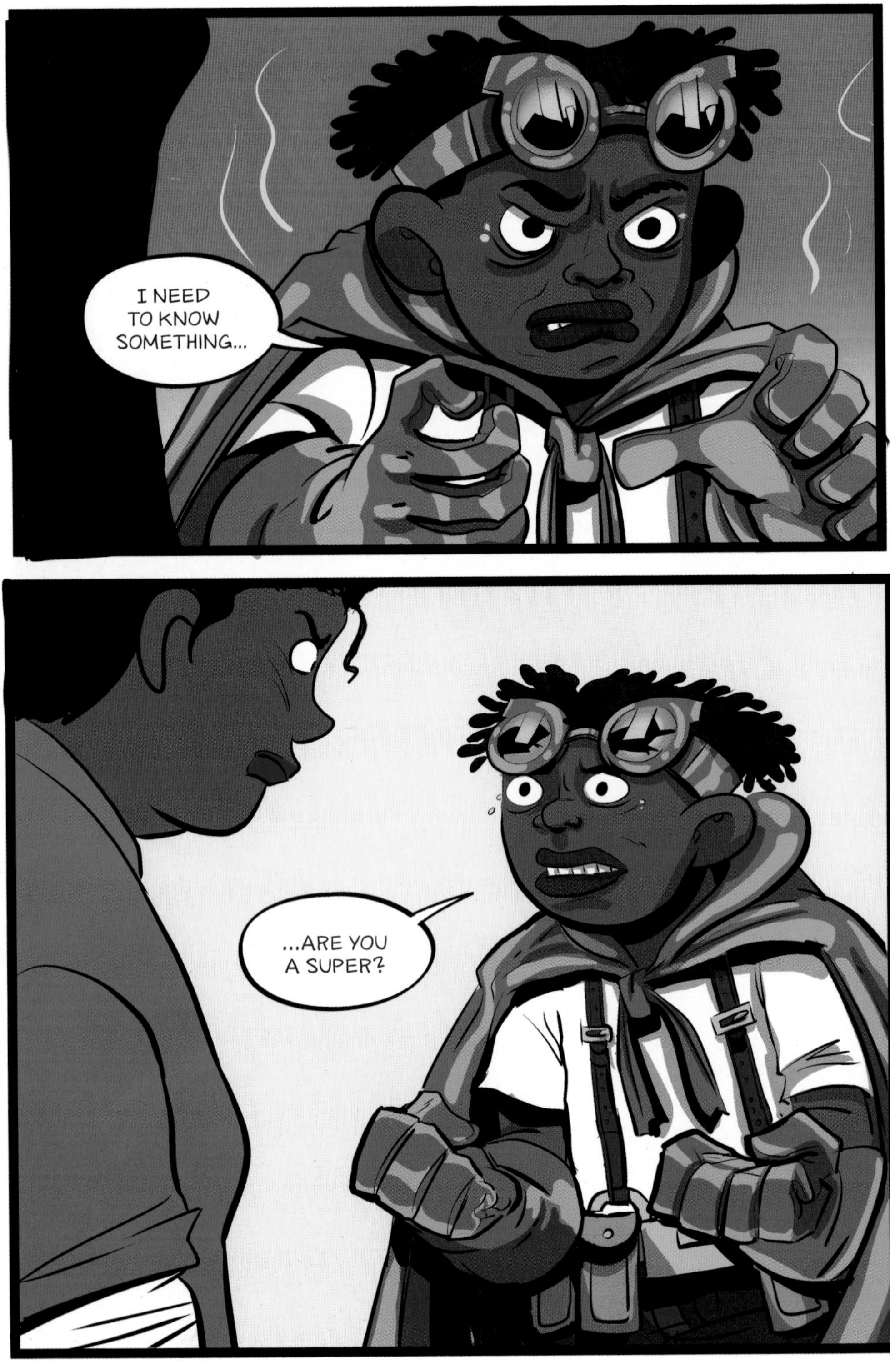
I NEED TO KNOW SOMETHING...
...ARE YOU A SUPER?

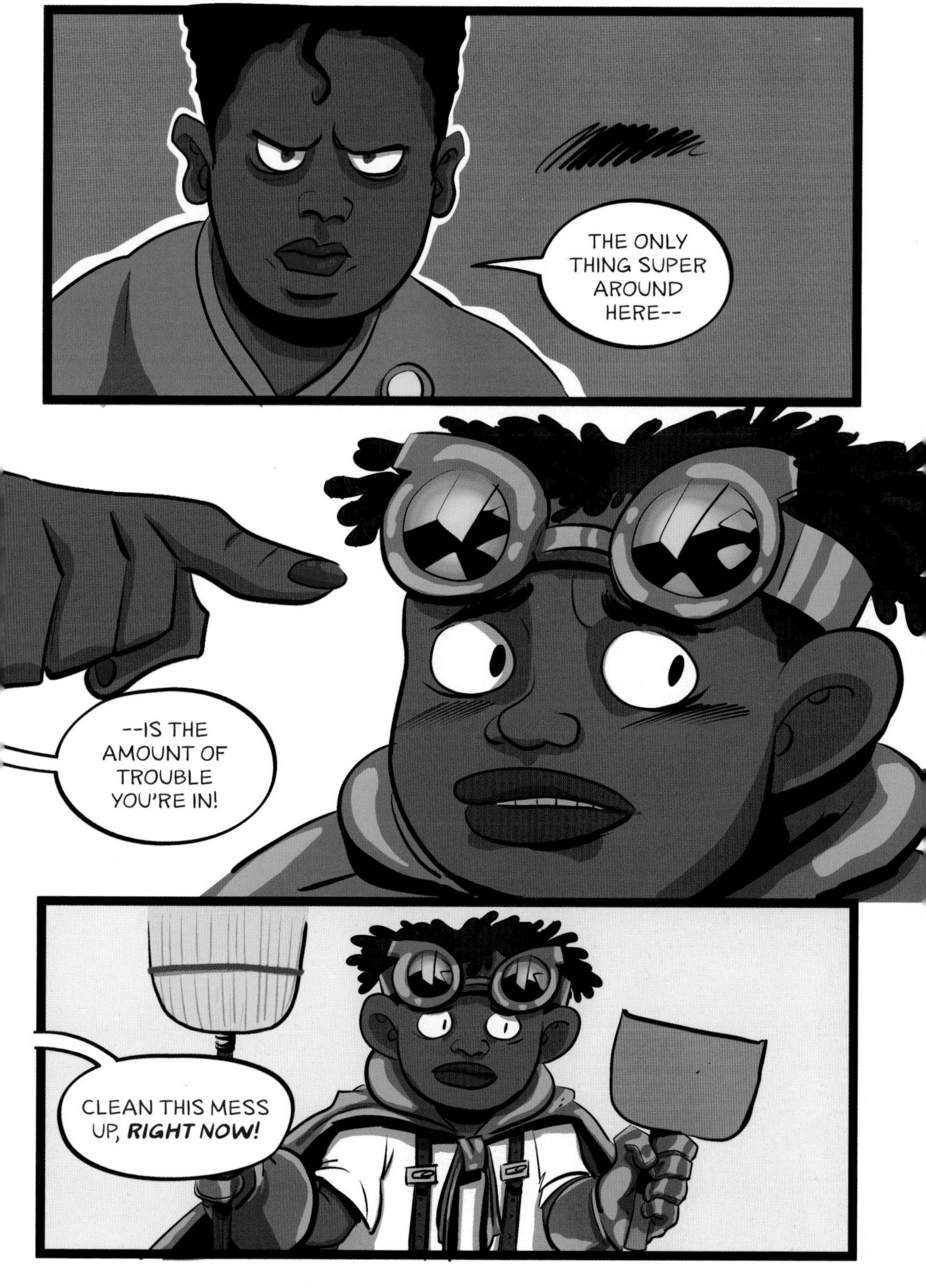
THE ONLY THING SUPER AROUND HERE--
--IS THE AMOUNT OF TROUBLE YOU'RE IN!
CLEAN THIS MESS UP, **RIGHT NOW!**

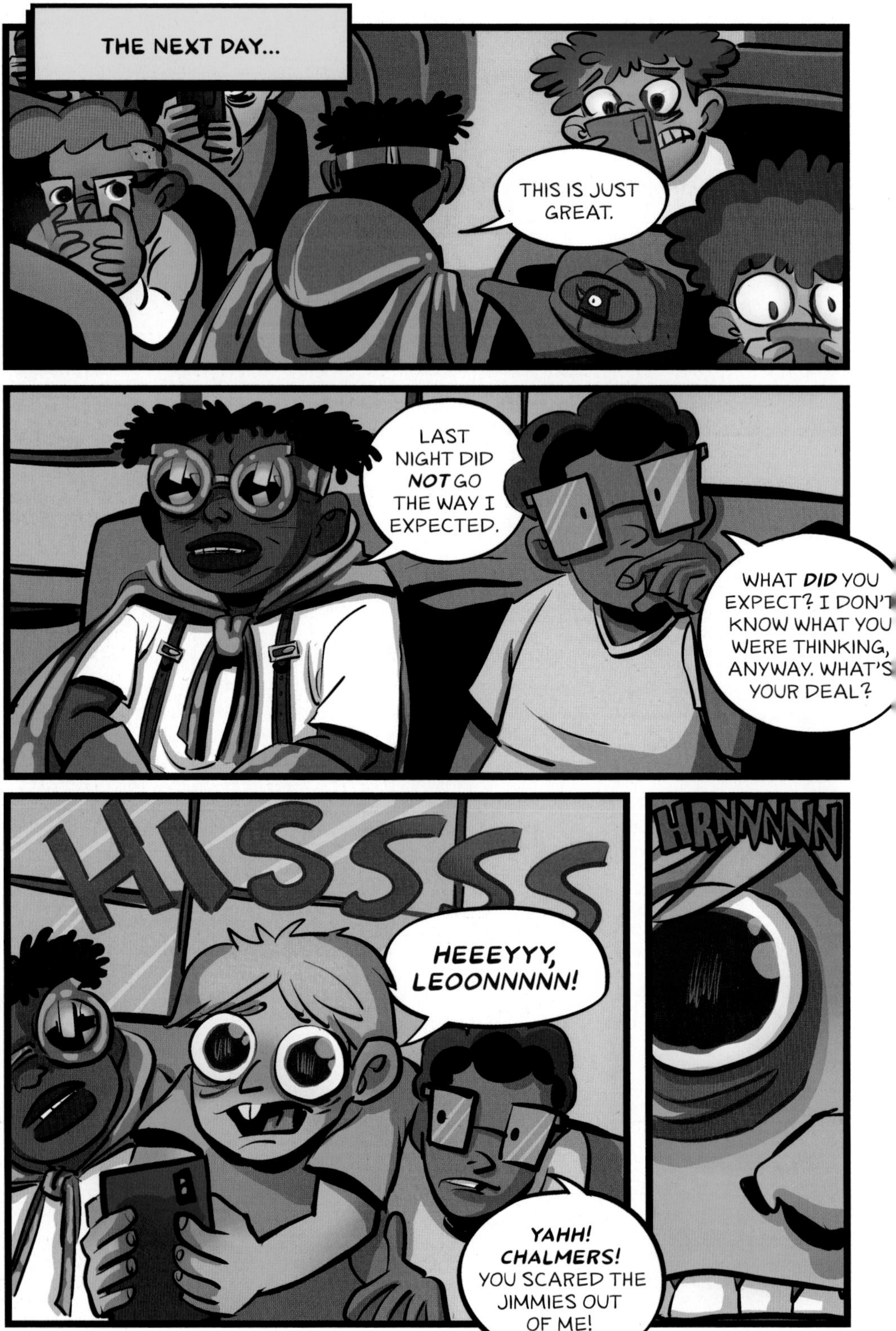
THE NEXT DAY...
THIS IS JUST GREAT.
LAST NIGHT DID NOT GO THE WAY I EXPECTED.
WHAT DID YOU EXPECT? I DON'T KNOW WHAT YOU WERE THINKING, ANYWAY. WHAT'S YOUR DEAL?
HISSSS
HEEEYYY, LEOONNNNN!
HRNNNNN
YAHH! CHALMERS! YOU SCARED THE JIMMIES OUT OF ME!

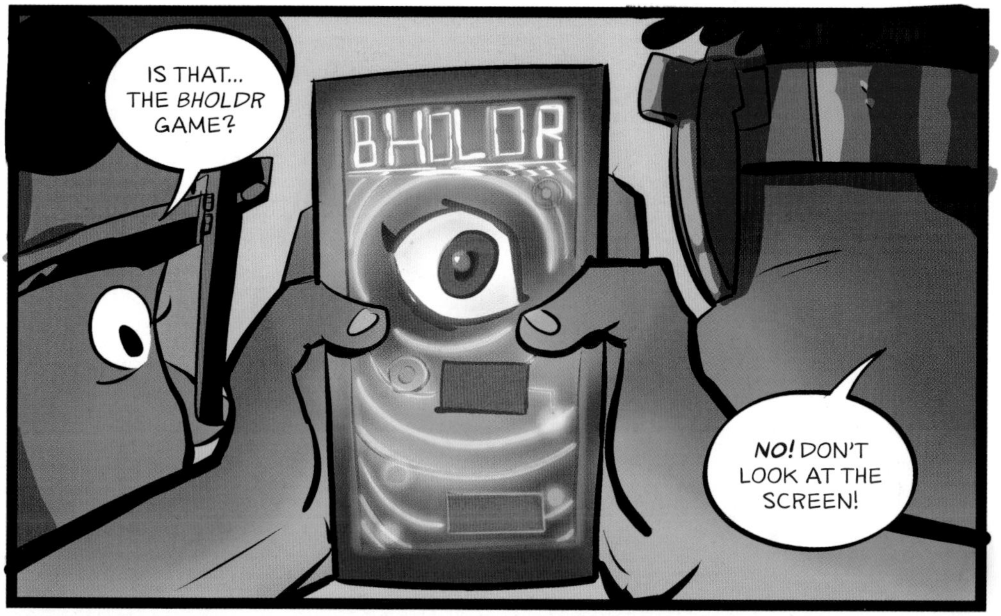
IS THAT... THE *BHOLDR* GAME?
BHOLDR
NO! DON'T LOOK AT THE SCREEN!

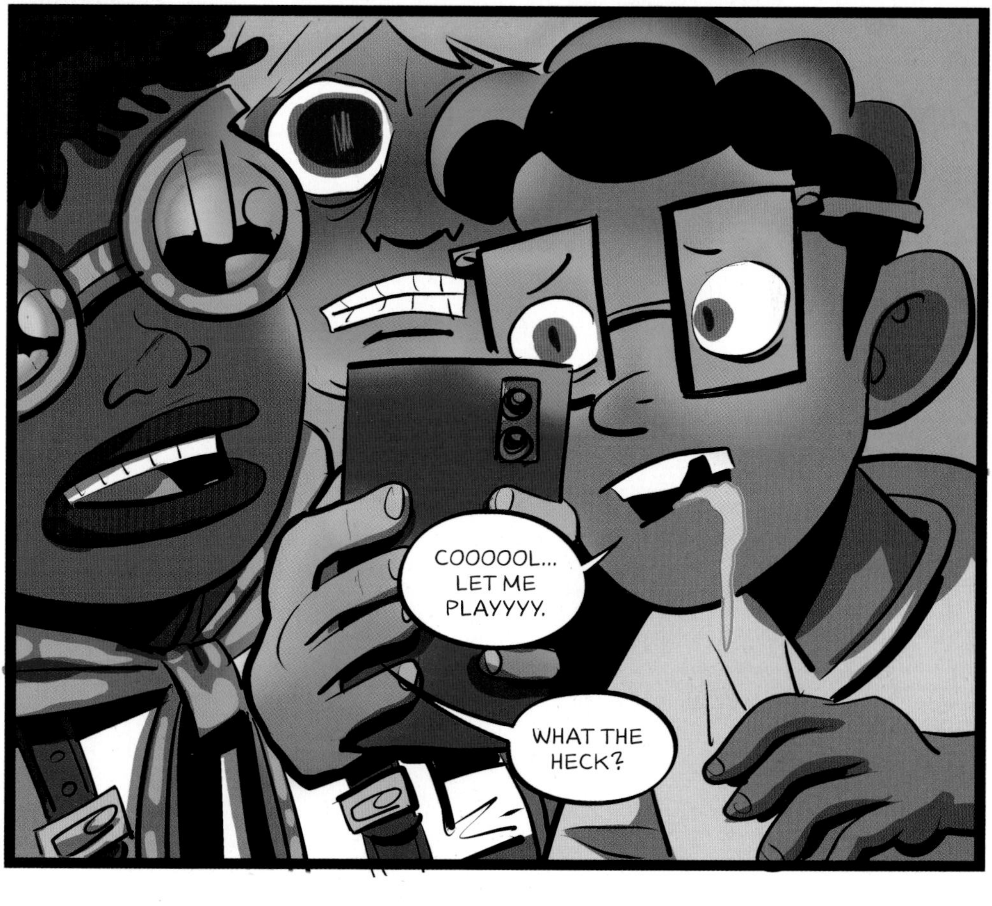
COOOOOL... LET ME PLAYYYY.
WHAT THE HECK?

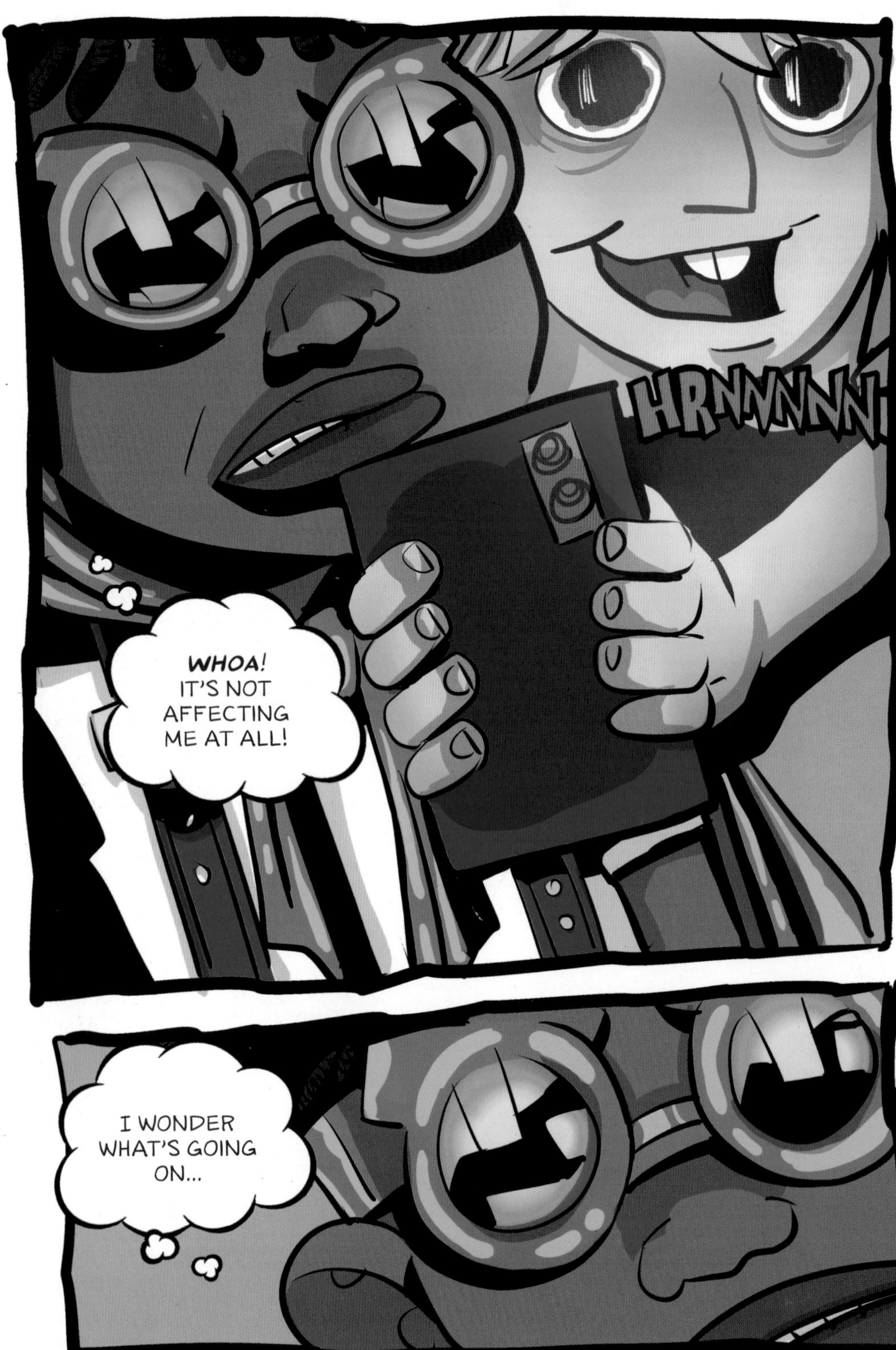
HRNNNNN
WHOA! IT'S NOT AFFECTING ME AT ALL!
I WONDER WHAT'S GOING ON...

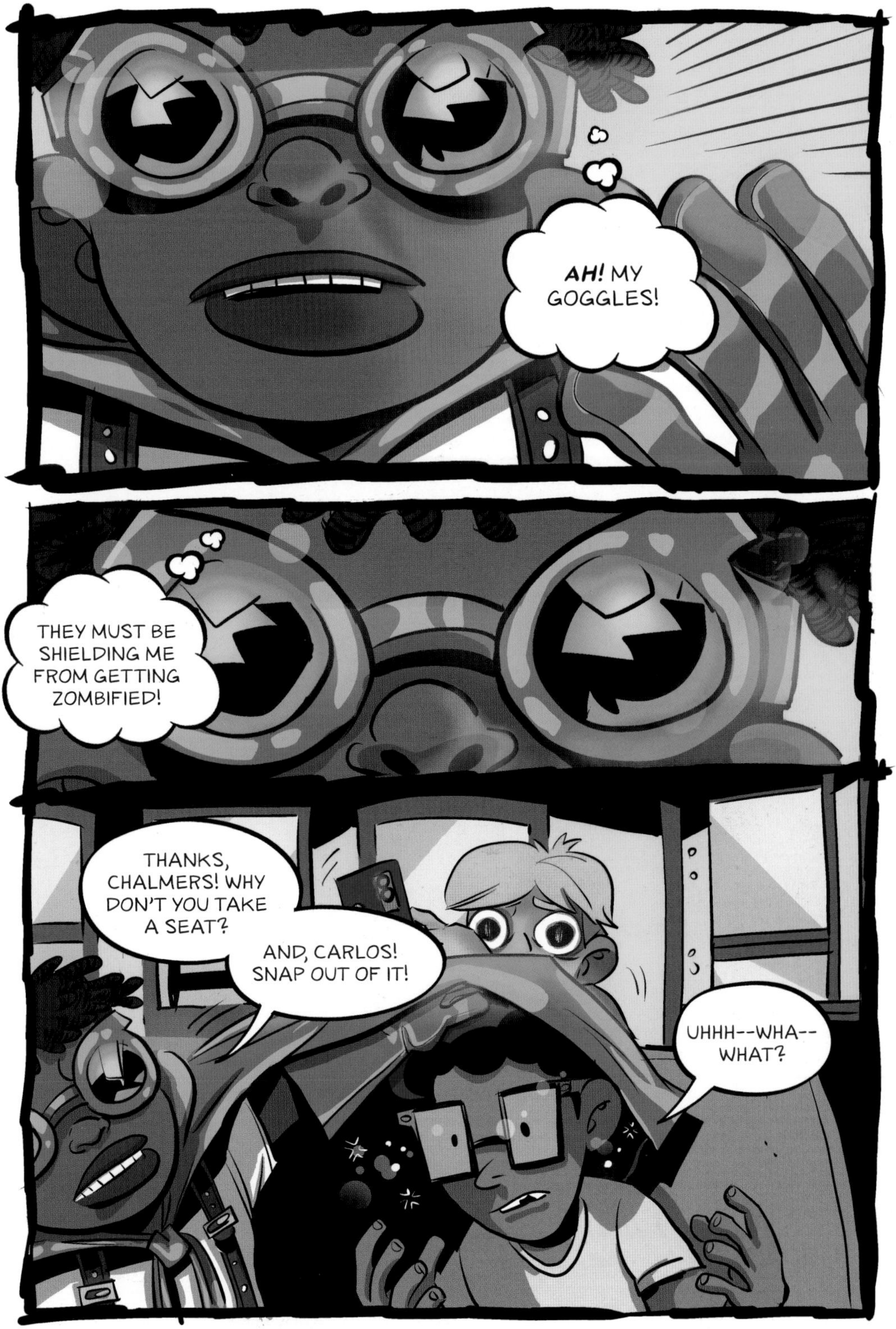
AH! MY GOGGLES!
THEY MUST BE SHIELDING ME FROM GETTING ZOMBIFIED!
THANKS, CHALMERS! WHY DON'T YOU TAKE A SEAT?
AND, CARLOS! SNAP OUT OF IT!
UHHH--WHA--WHAT?

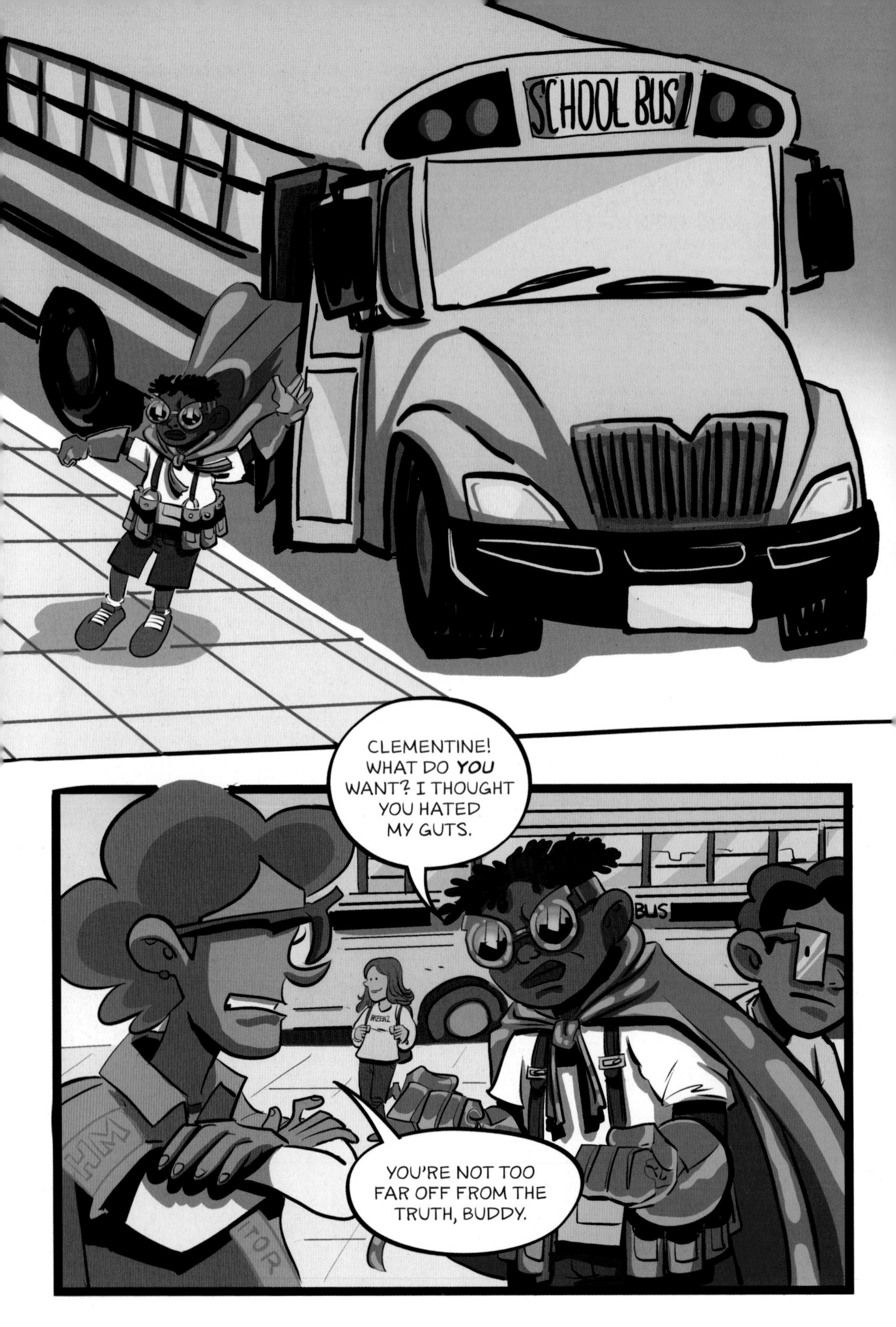
SCHOOL BUS
CLEMENTINE! WHAT DO ***YOU*** WANT? I THOUGHT YOU HATED MY GUTS.
BUS
YOU'RE NOT TOO FAR OFF FROM THE TRUTH, BUDDY.

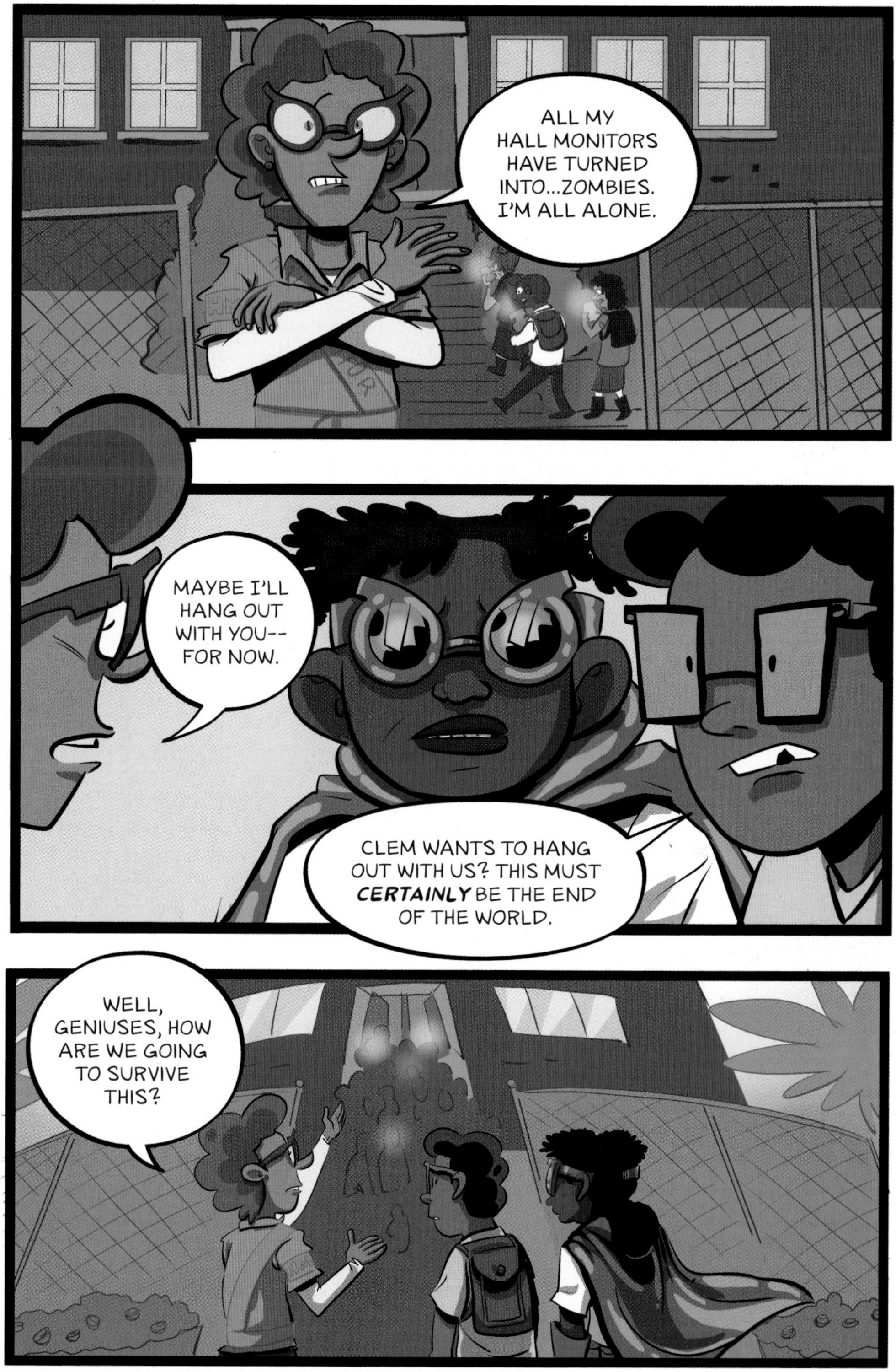
ALL MY HALL MONITORS HAVE TURNED INTO...ZOMBIES. I'M ALL ALONE.
MAYBE I'LL HANG OUT WITH YOU-- FOR NOW.
CLEM WANTS TO HANG OUT WITH US? THIS MUST **CERTAINLY** BE THE END OF THE WORLD.
WELL, GENIUSES, HOW ARE WE GOING TO SURVIVE THIS?

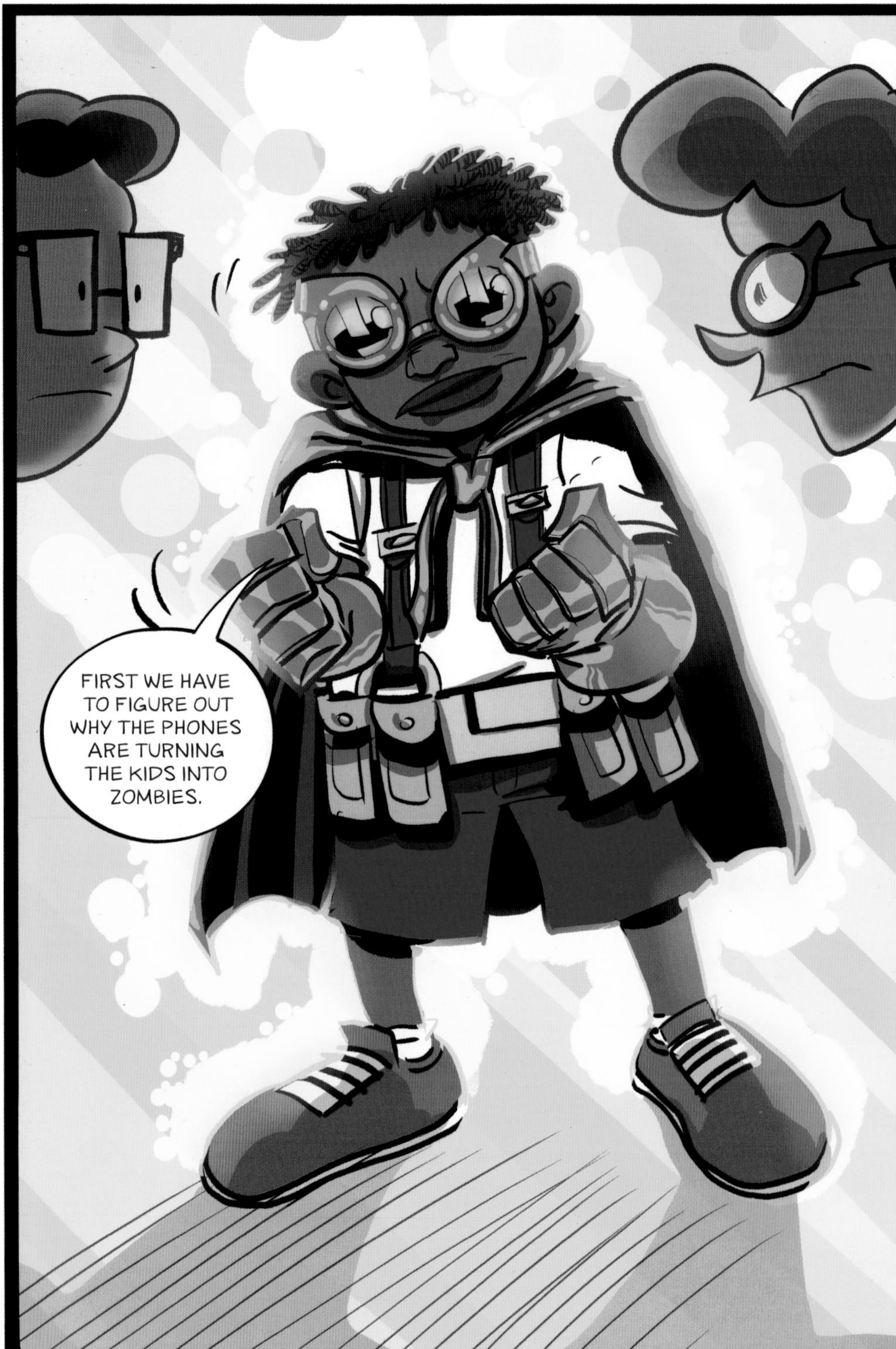
FIRST WE HAVE TO FIGURE OUT WHY THE PHONES ARE TURNING THE KIDS INTO ZOMBIES.

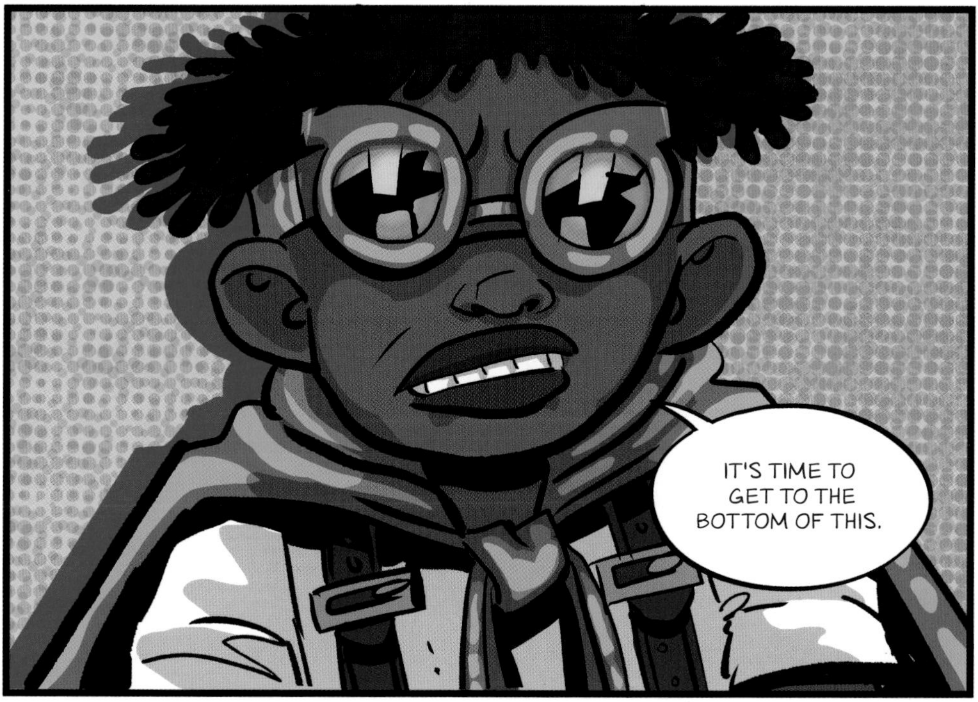
IT'S TIME TO GET TO THE BOTTOM OF THIS.

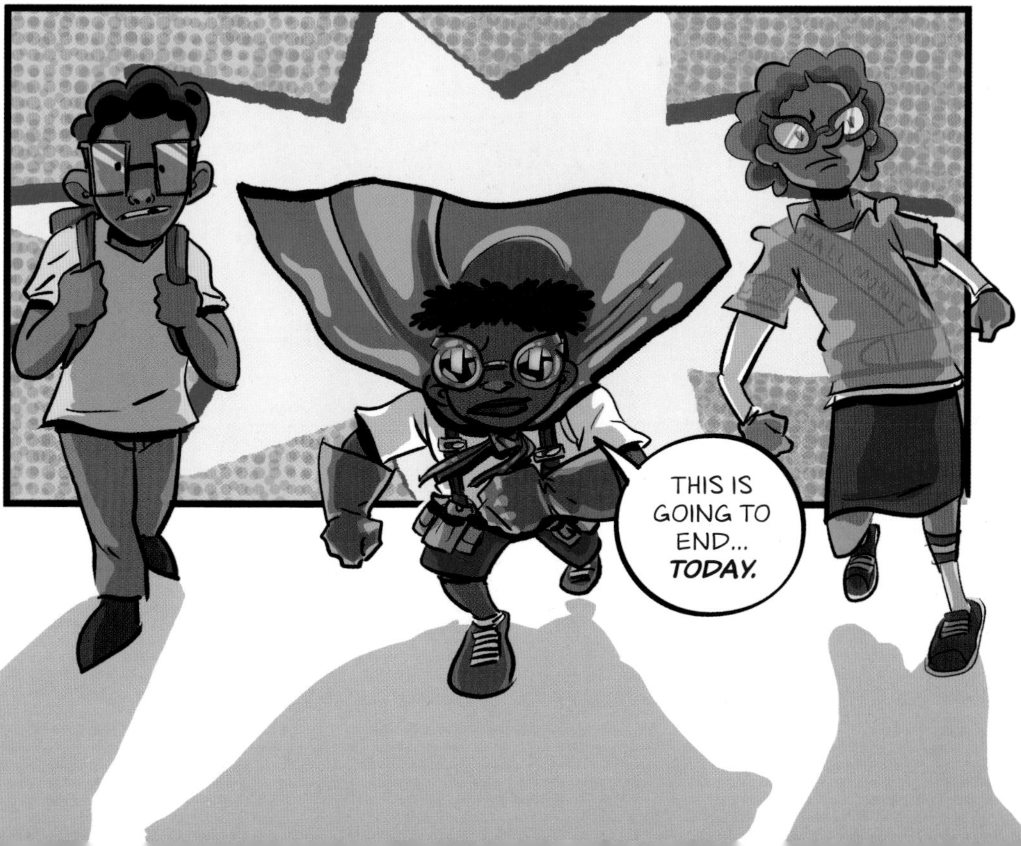
THIS IS GOING TO END... ***TODAY.***

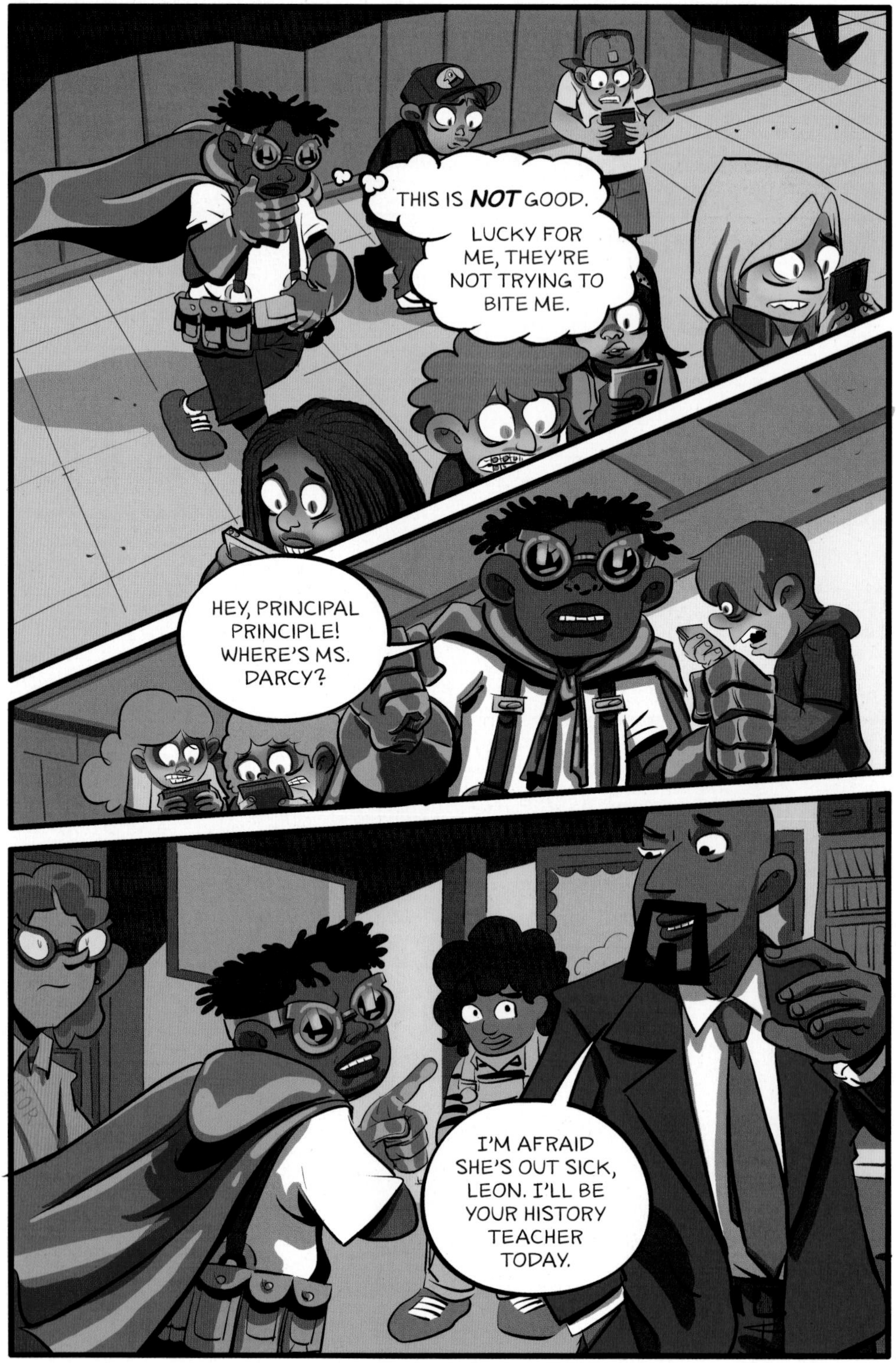
THIS IS NOT GOOD.
LUCKY FOR ME, THEY'RE NOT TRYING TO BITE ME.
HEY, PRINCIPAL PRINCIPLE! WHERE'S MS. DARCY?
I'M AFRAID SHE'S OUT SICK, LEON. I'LL BE YOUR HISTORY TEACHER TODAY.

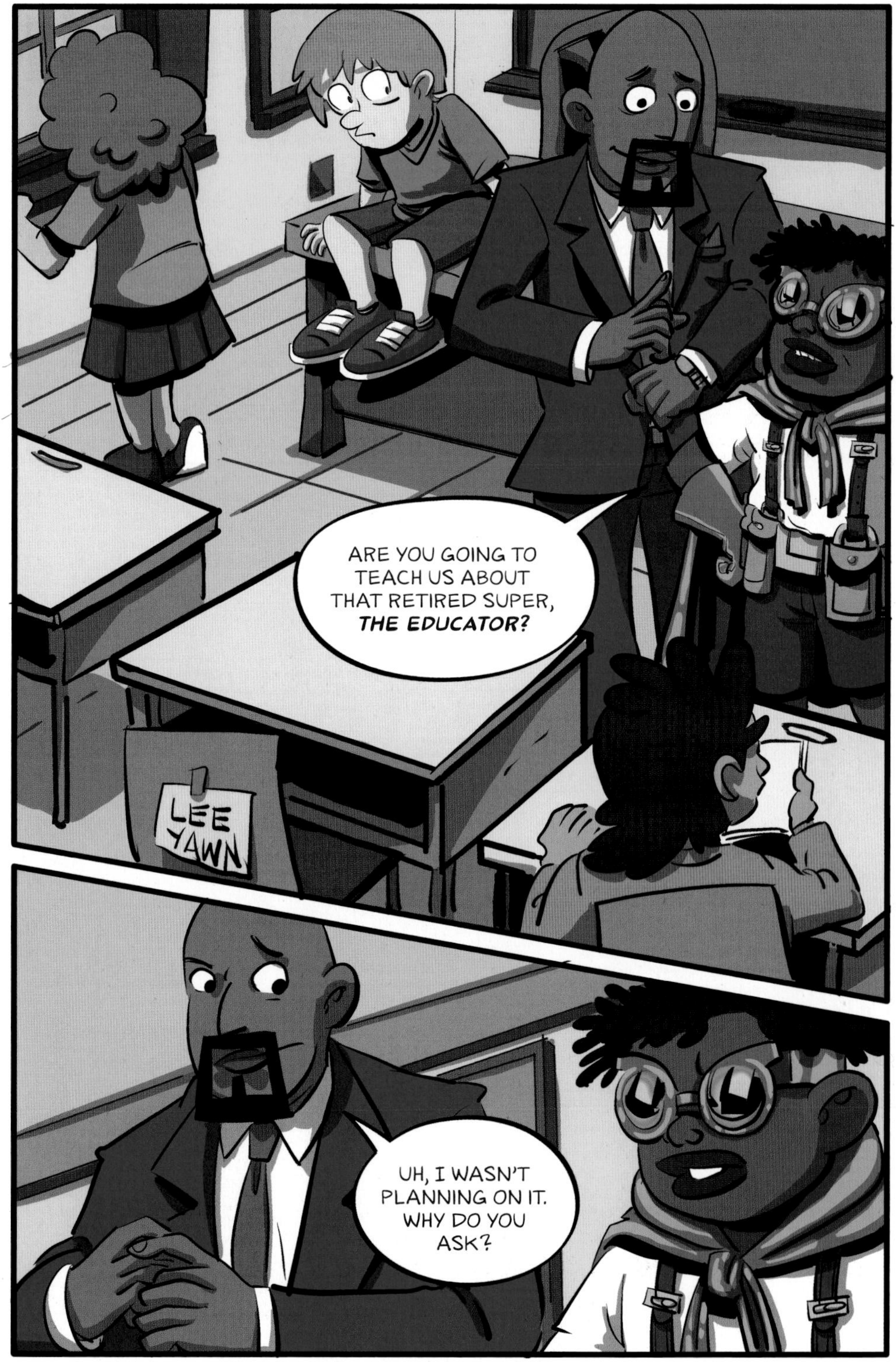
ARE YOU GOING TO TEACH US ABOUT THAT RETIRED SUPER, ***THE EDUCATOR?***
LEE YAWN
UH, I WASN'T PLANNING ON IT. WHY DO YOU ASK?

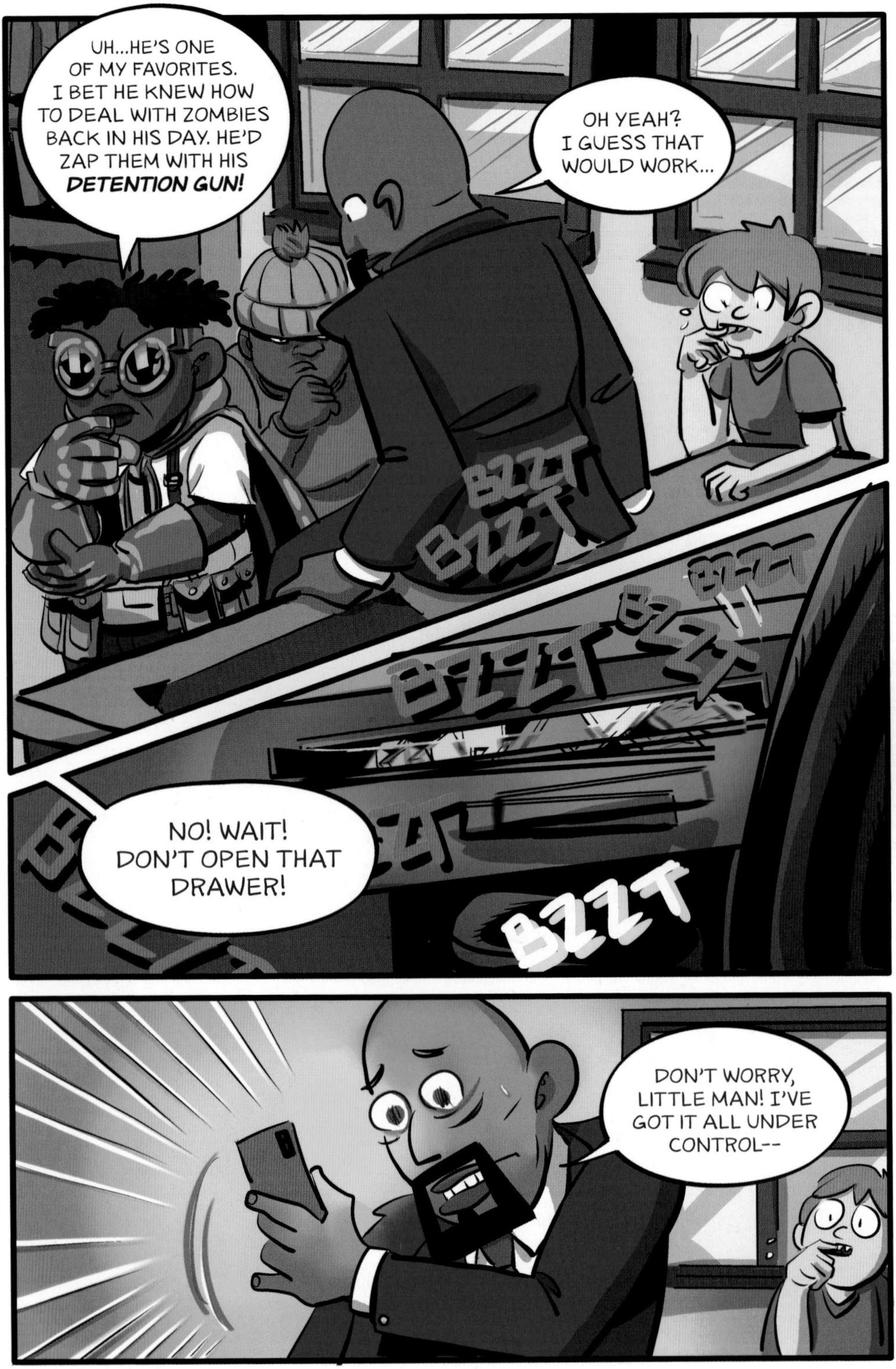
UH...HE'S ONE OF MY FAVORITES. I BET HE KNEW HOW TO DEAL WITH ZOMBIES BACK IN HIS DAY. HE'D ZAP THEM WITH HIS ***DETENTION GUN!***
OH YEAH? I GUESS THAT WOULD WORK...
BZZT
BZZT
BZZT
BZZT
NO! WAIT! DON'T OPEN THAT DRAWER!
BZZT
DON'T WORRY, LITTLE MAN! I'VE GOT IT ALL UNDER CONTROL--

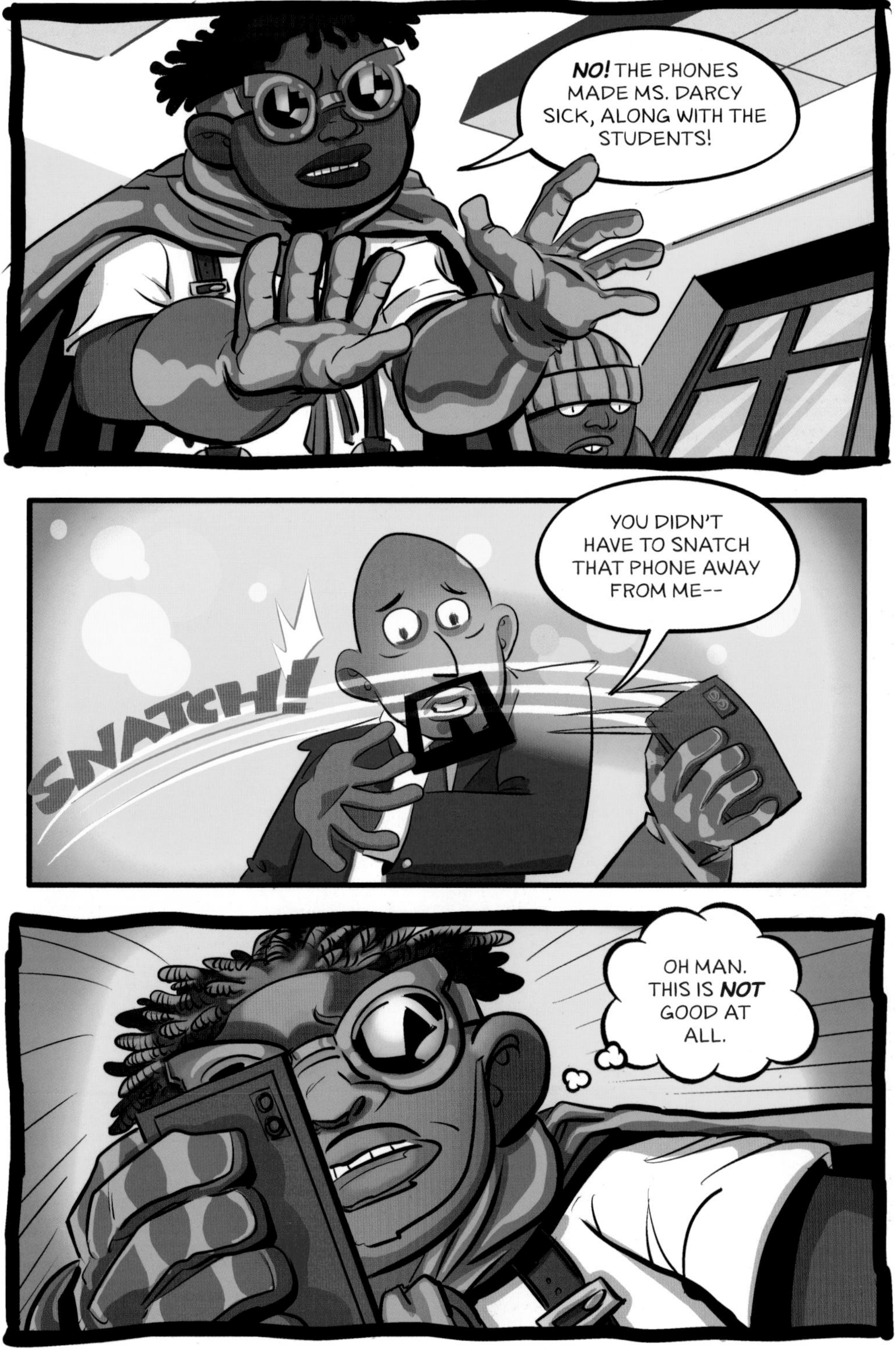
NO! THE PHONES MADE MS. DARCY SICK, ALONG WITH THE STUDENTS!
YOU DIDN'T HAVE TO SNATCH THAT PHONE AWAY FROM ME--
SNATCH!
OH MAN. THIS IS **NOT** GOOD AT ALL.

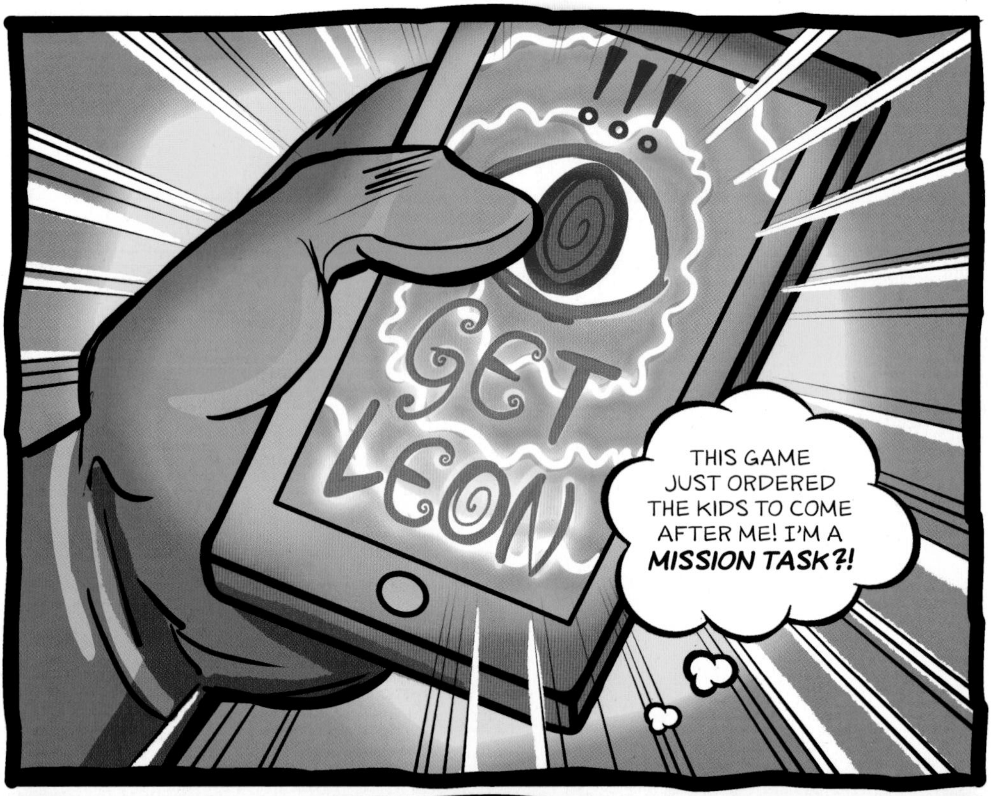
!!!
GET LEON
THIS GAME JUST ORDERED THE KIDS TO COME AFTER ME! I'M A **MISSION TASK?!**

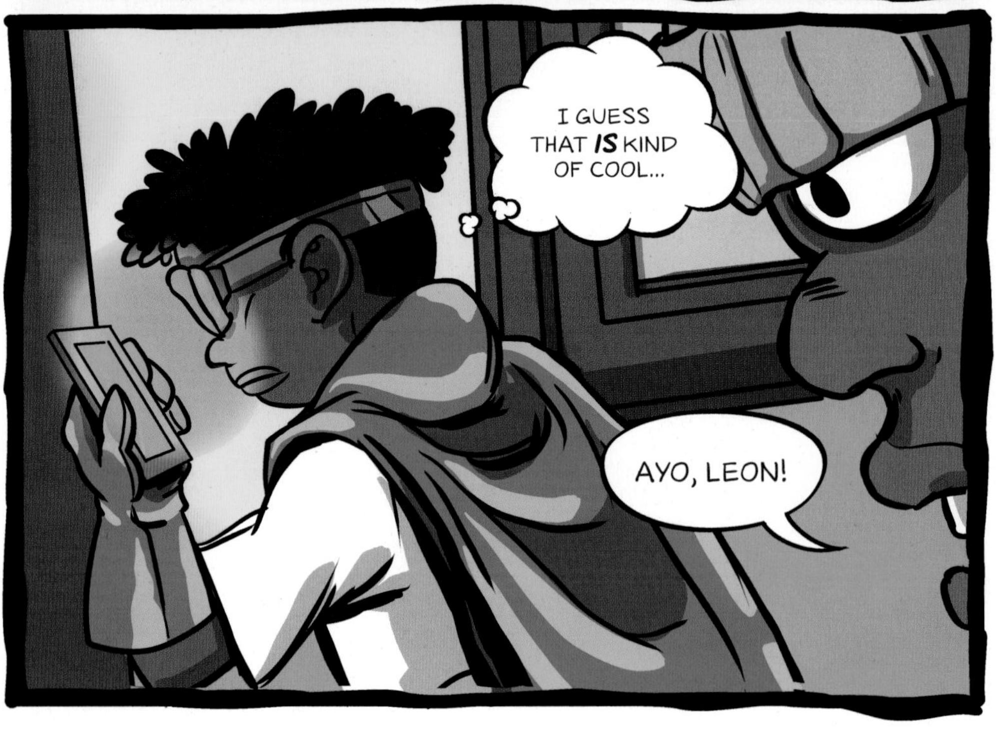
I GUESS THAT **IS** KIND OF COOL...
AYO, LEON!

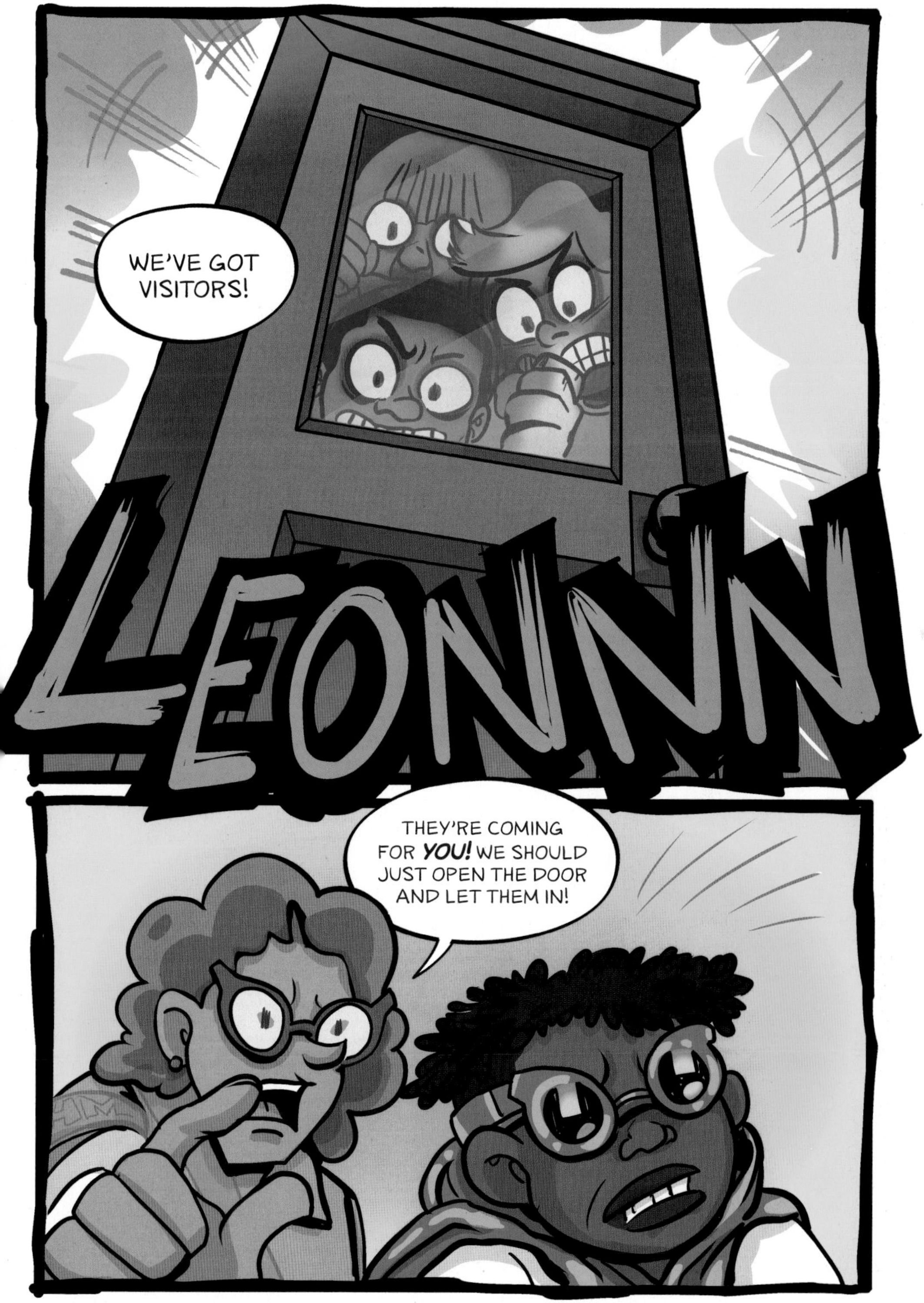
WE'VE GOT VISITORS!
LEONNN
THEY'RE COMING FOR ***YOU!*** WE SHOULD JUST OPEN THE DOOR AND LET THEM IN!

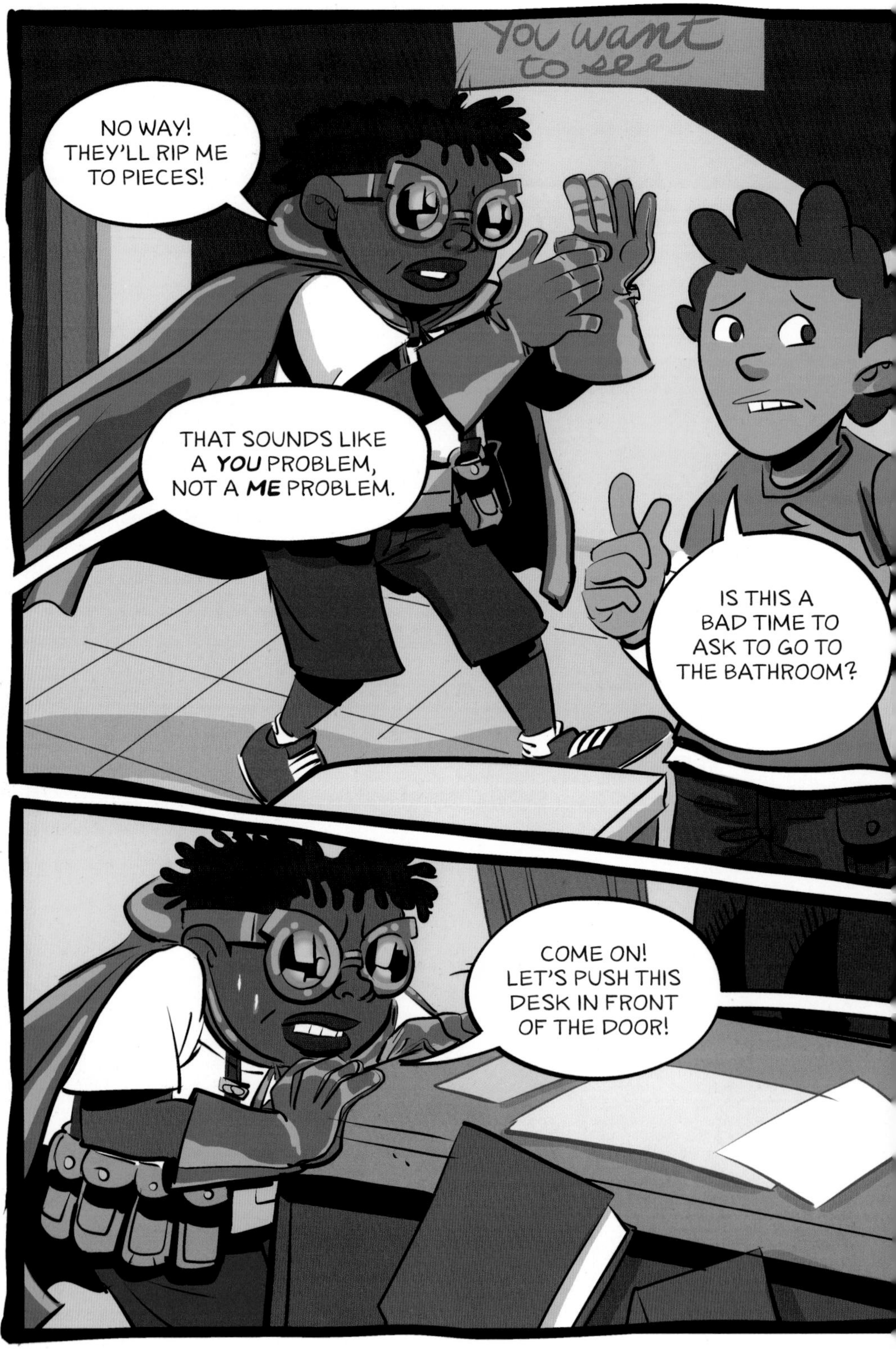
You want to see
NO WAY! THEY'LL RIP ME TO PIECES!
THAT SOUNDS LIKE A ***YOU*** PROBLEM, NOT A ***ME*** PROBLEM.
IS THIS A BAD TIME TO ASK TO GO TO THE BATHROOM?
COME ON! LET'S PUSH THIS DESK IN FRONT OF THE DOOR!

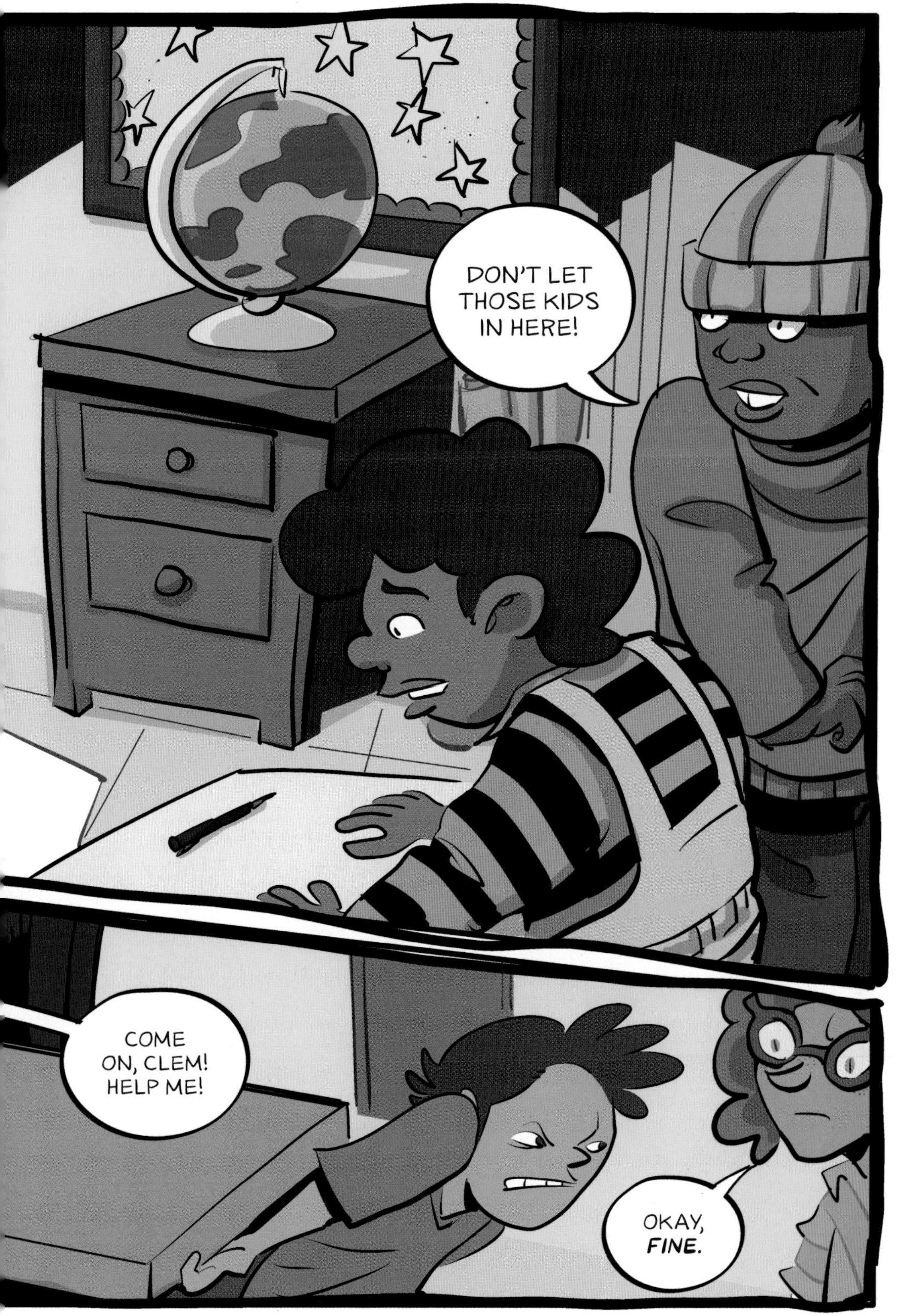
DON'T LET THOSE KIDS IN HERE!
COME ON, CLEM! HELP ME!
OKAY, *FINE.*

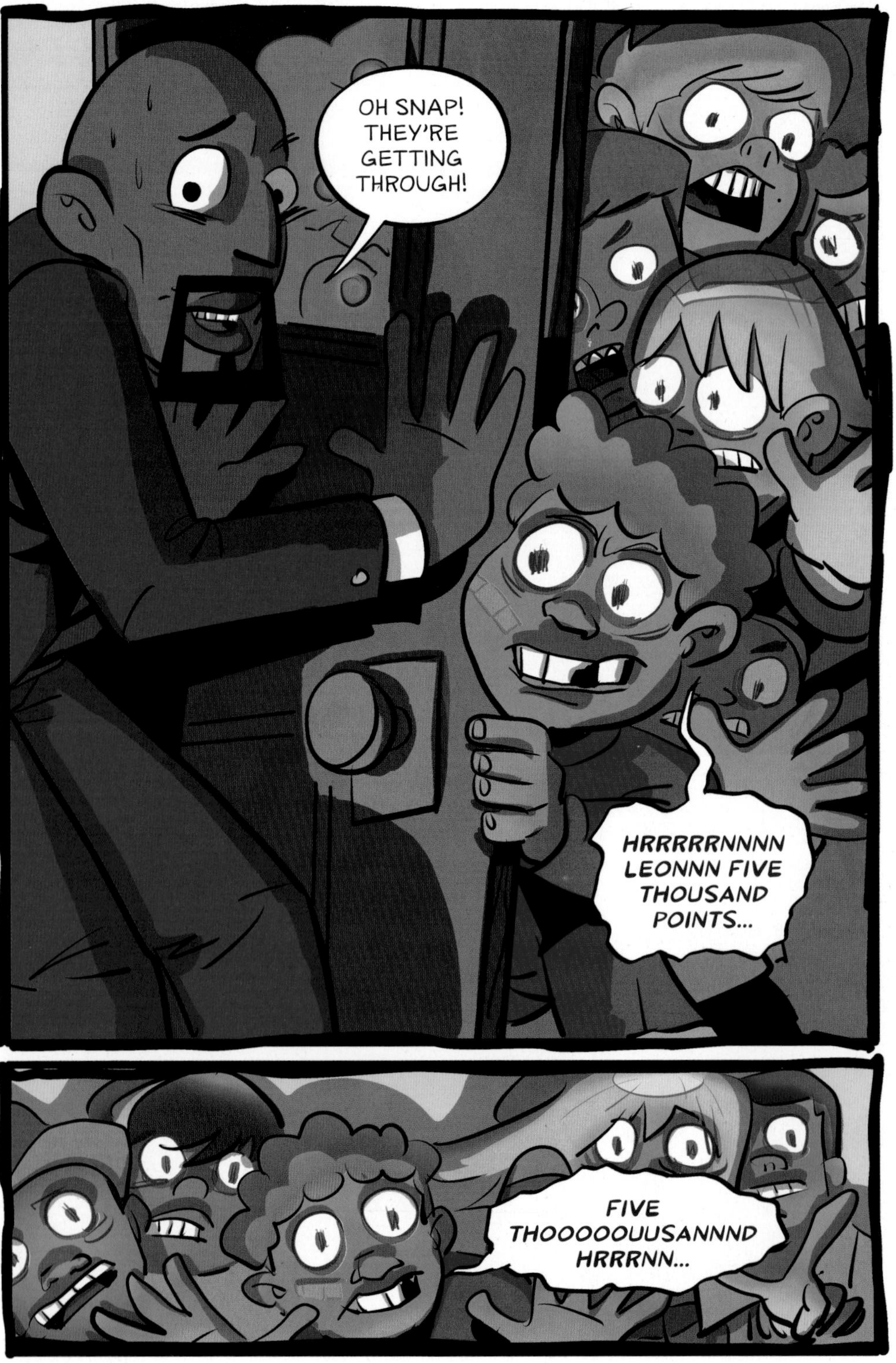
OH SNAP! THEY'RE GETTING THROUGH!
HRRRRRNNNN LEONNN FIVE THOUSAND POINTS...
FIVE THOOOOOUUSANNND HRRRNN...

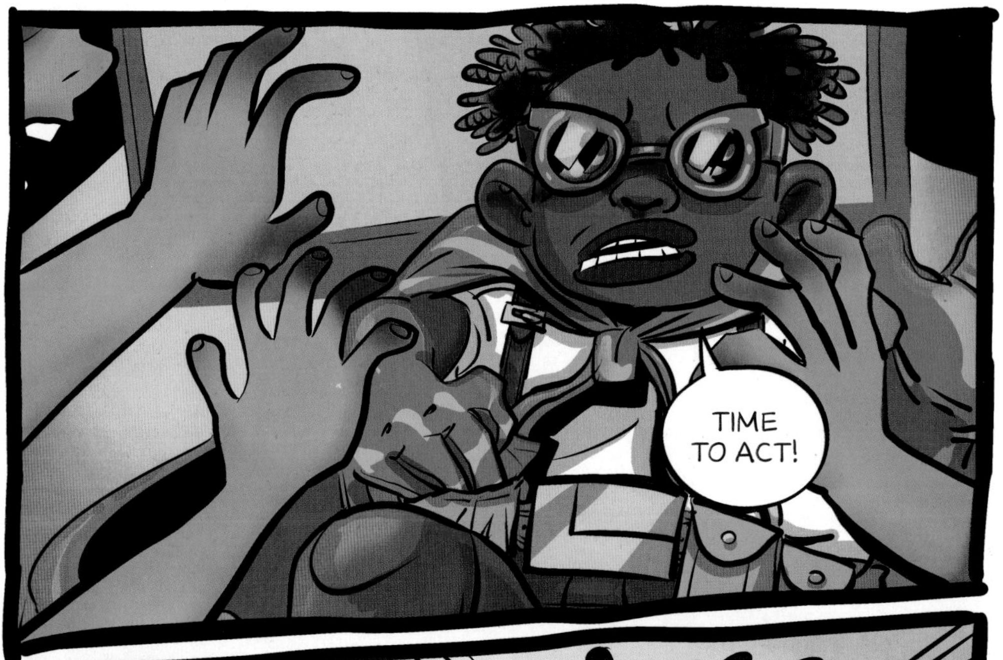
TIME TO ACT!

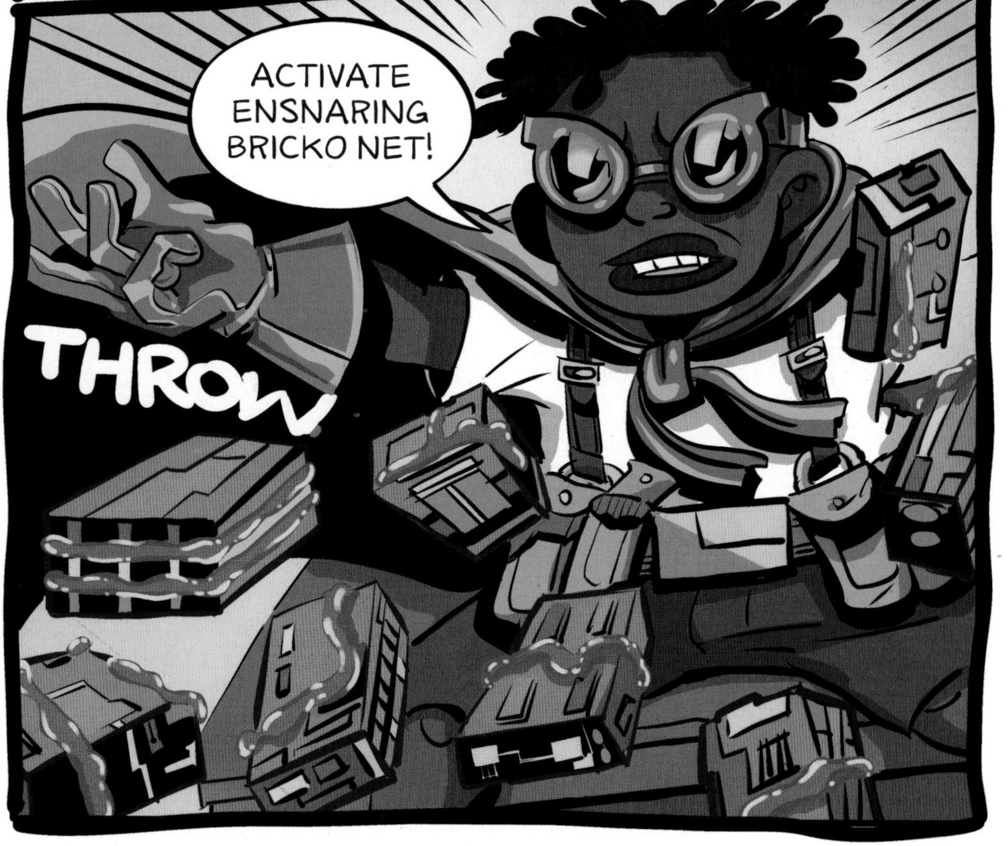
ACTIVATE ENSNARING BRICKO NET!
THROW

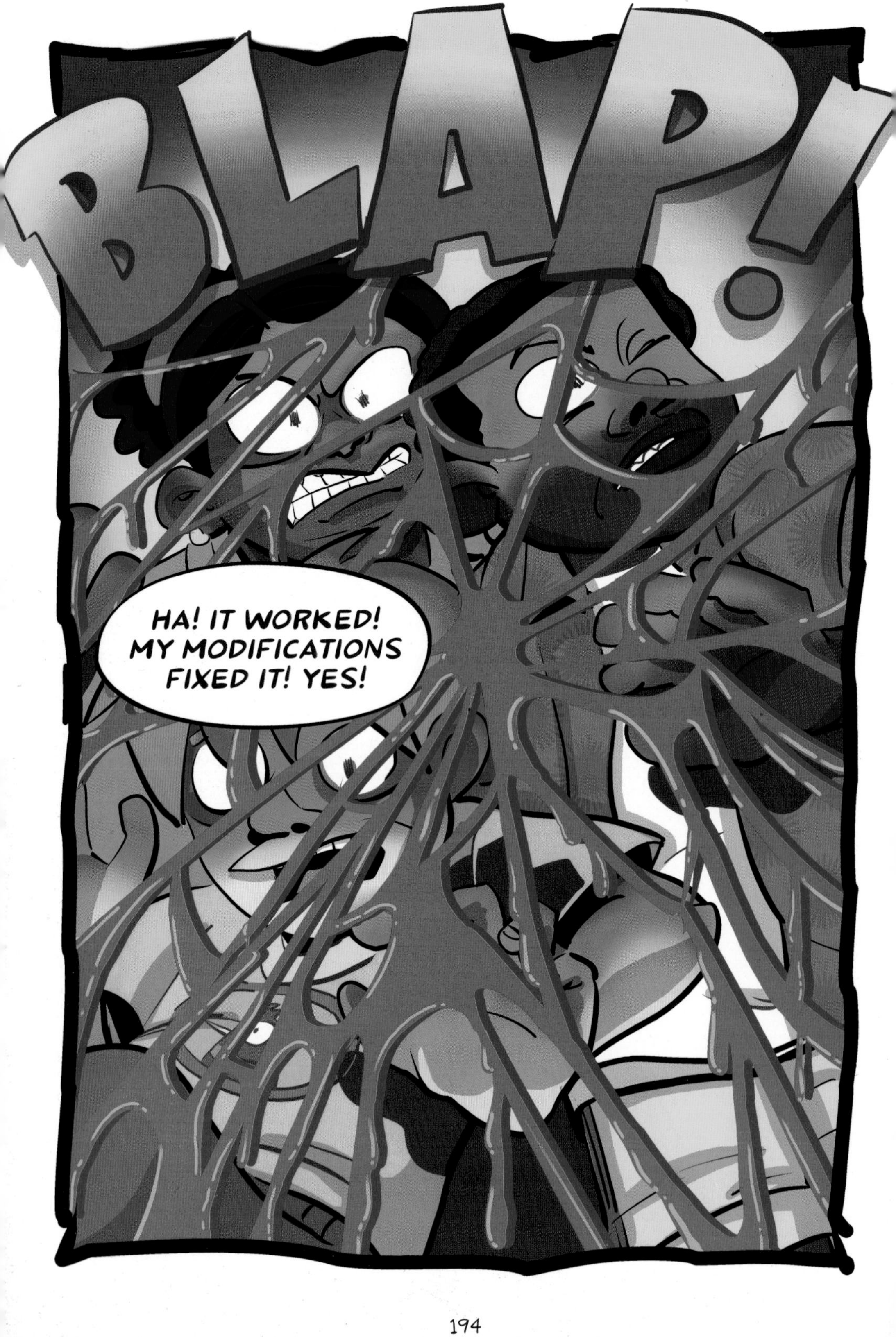
BLAP!
HA! IT WORKED! MY MODIFICATIONS FIXED IT! YES!

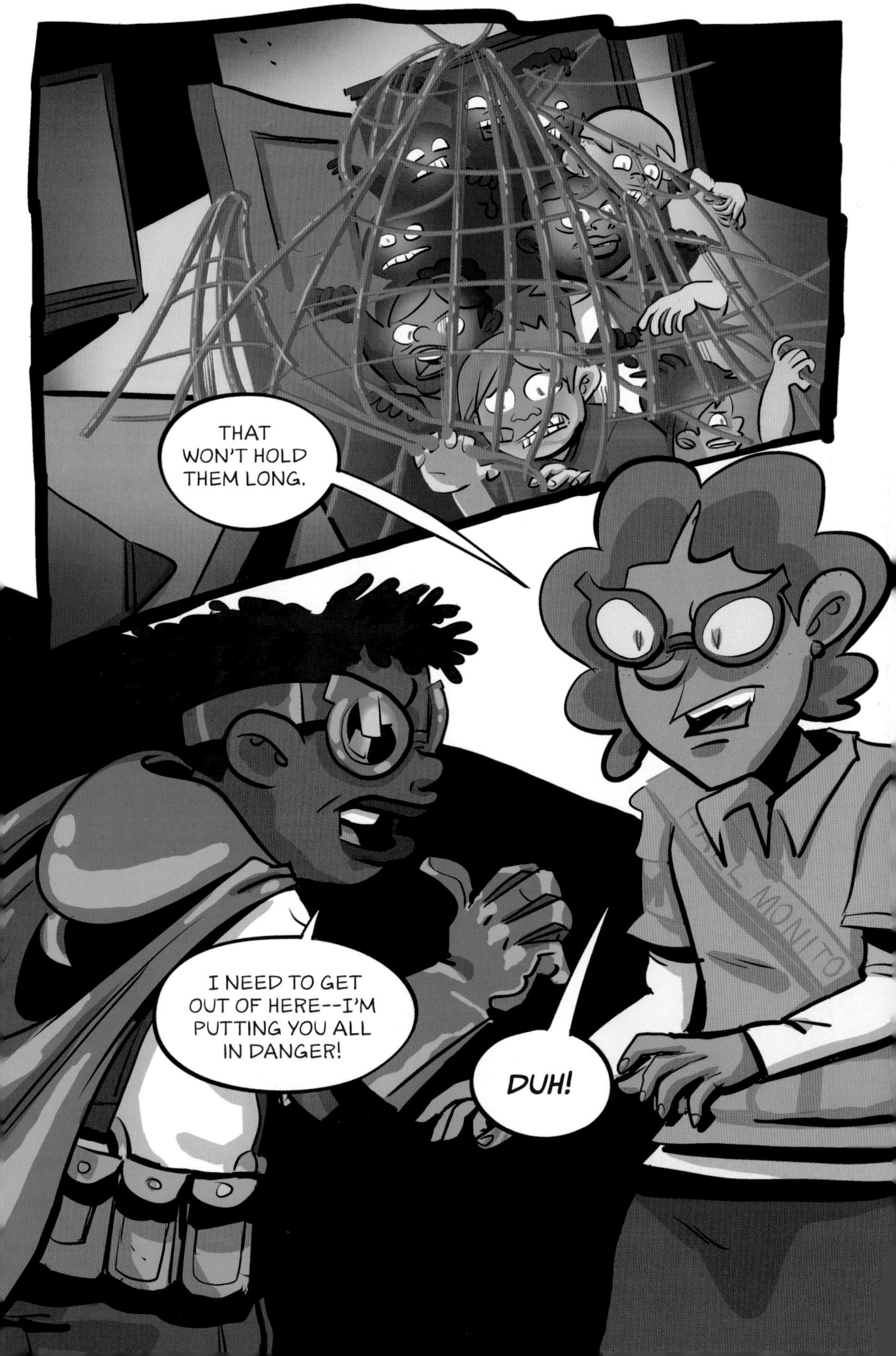
THAT WON'T HOLD THEM LONG.
I NEED TO GET OUT OF HERE--I'M PUTTING YOU ALL IN DANGER!
DUH!

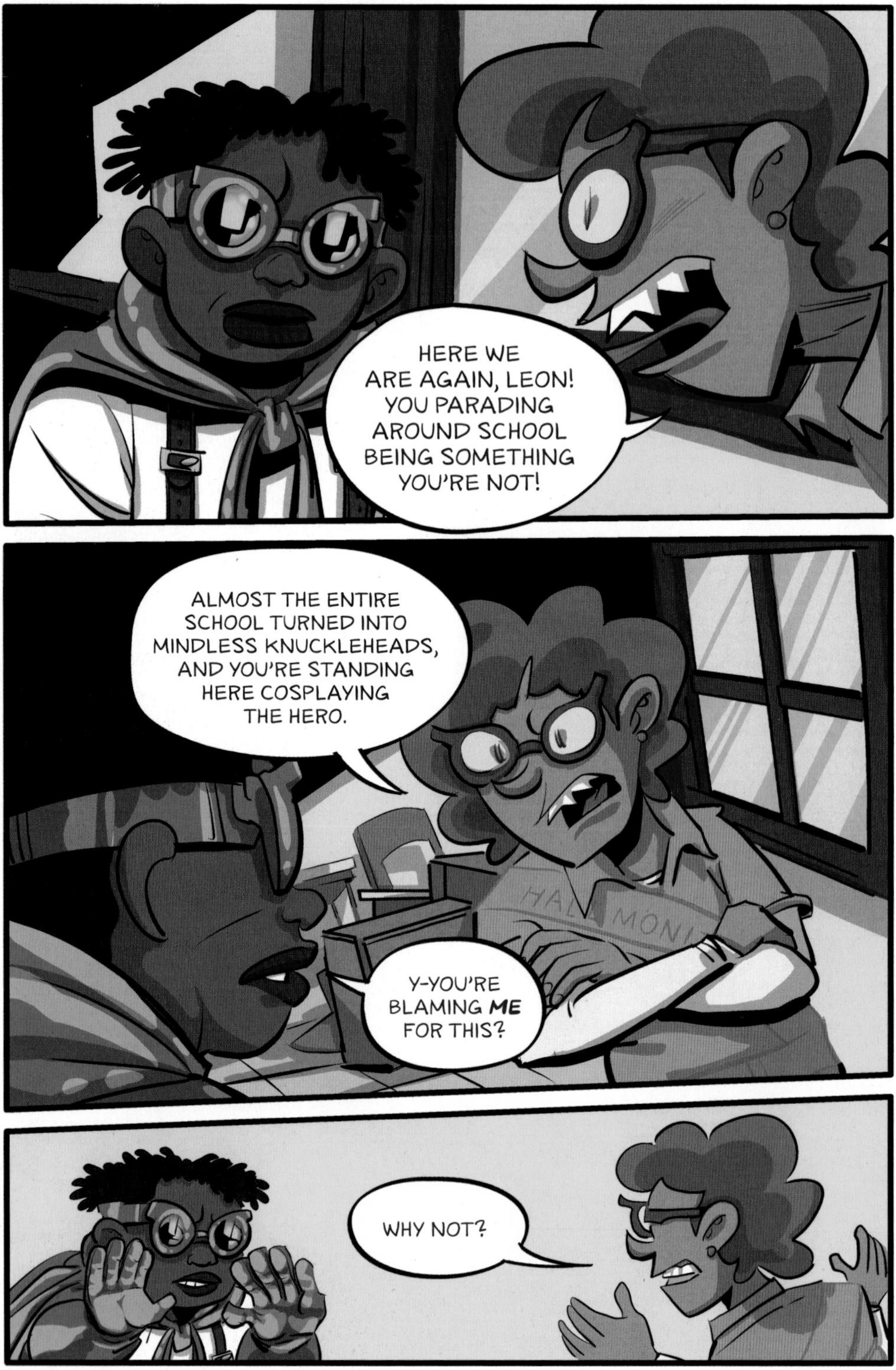
HERE WE ARE AGAIN, LEON! YOU PARADING AROUND SCHOOL BEING SOMETHING YOU'RE NOT!
ALMOST THE ENTIRE SCHOOL TURNED INTO MINDLESS KNUCKLEHEADS, AND YOU'RE STANDING HERE COSPLAYING THE HERO.
Y-YOU'RE BLAMING ME FOR THIS?
WHY NOT?

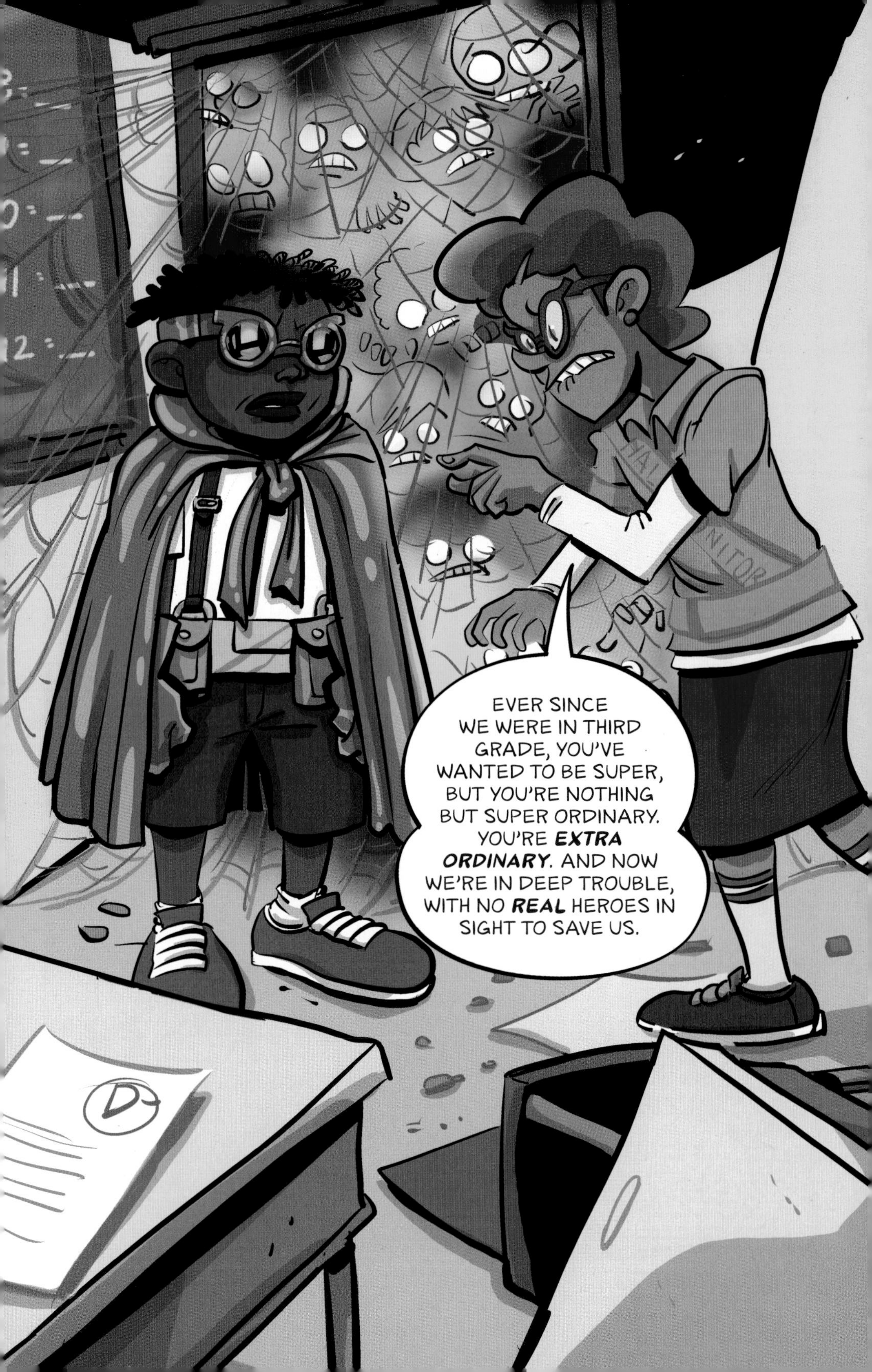
EVER SINCE WE WERE IN THIRD GRADE, YOU'VE WANTED TO BE SUPER, BUT YOU'RE NOTHING BUT SUPER ORDINARY. YOU'RE **EXTRA ORDINARY**. AND NOW WE'RE IN DEEP TROUBLE, WITH NO **REAL** HEROES IN SIGHT TO SAVE US.

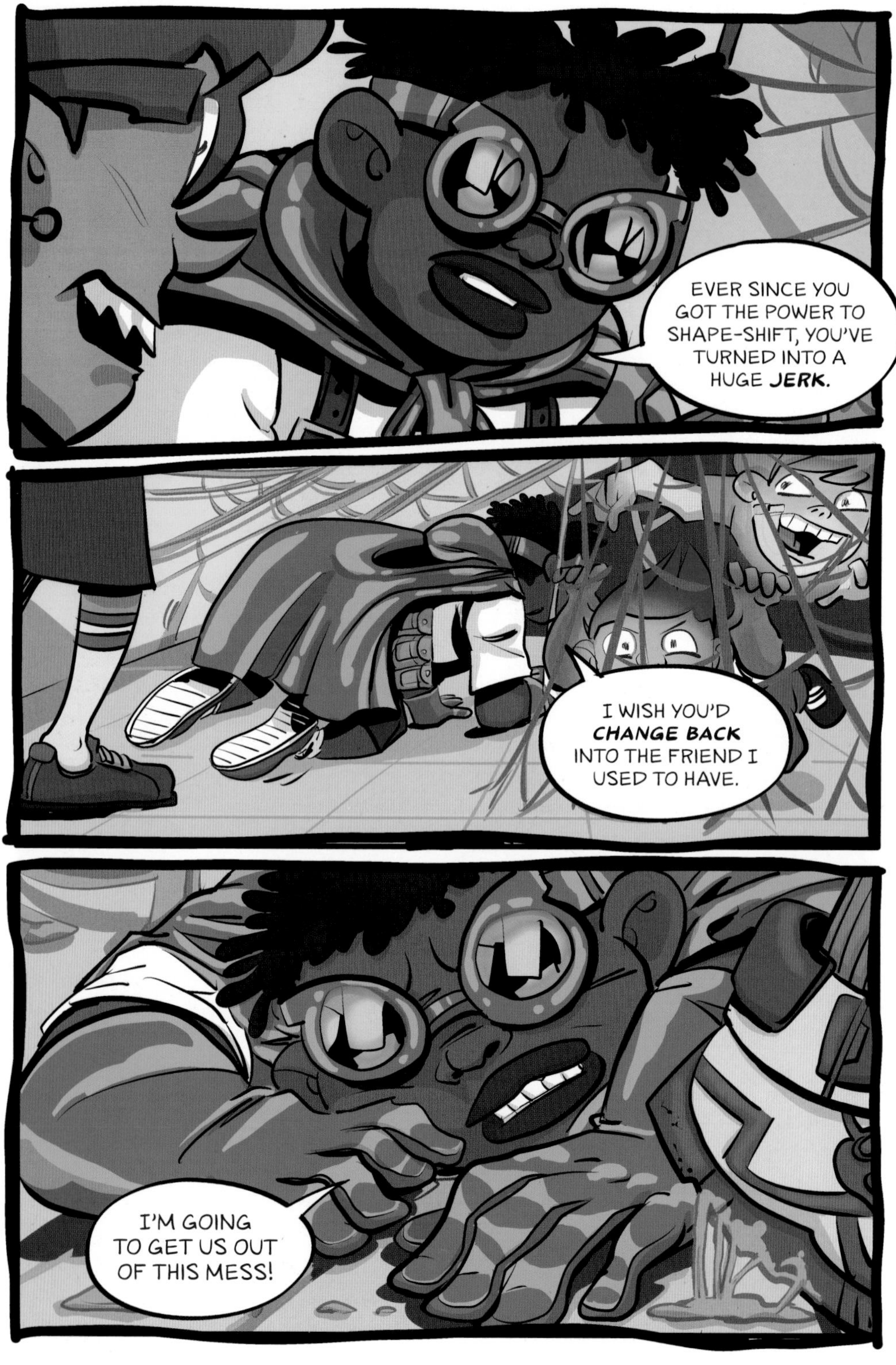
EVER SINCE YOU GOT THE POWER TO SHAPE-SHIFT, YOU'VE TURNED INTO A HUGE **JERK.**
I WISH YOU'D **CHANGE BACK** INTO THE FRIEND I USED TO HAVE.
I'M GOING TO GET US OUT OF THIS MESS!

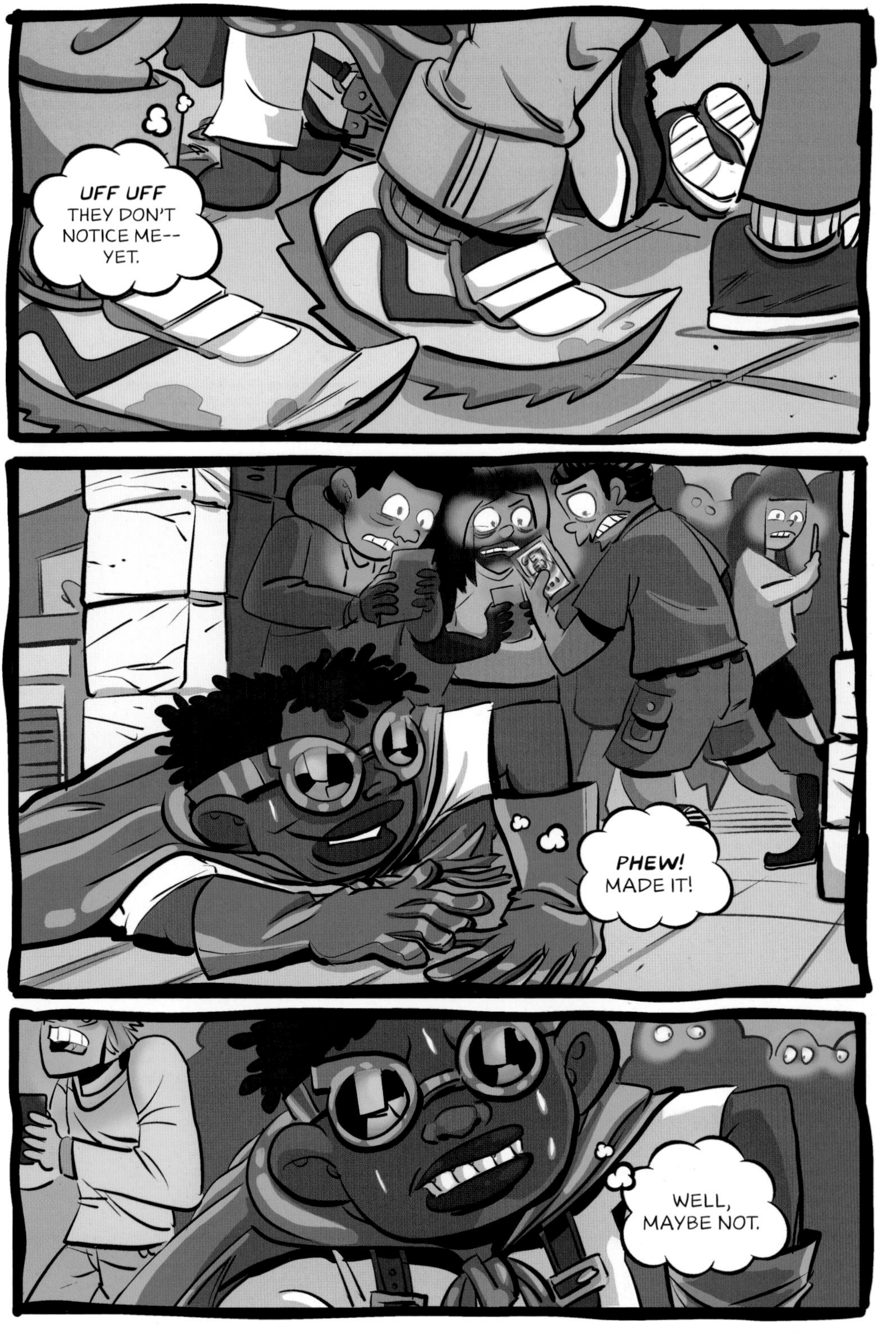
UFF UFF
THEY DON'T NOTICE ME-- YET.
PHEW! MADE IT!
WELL, MAYBE NOT.

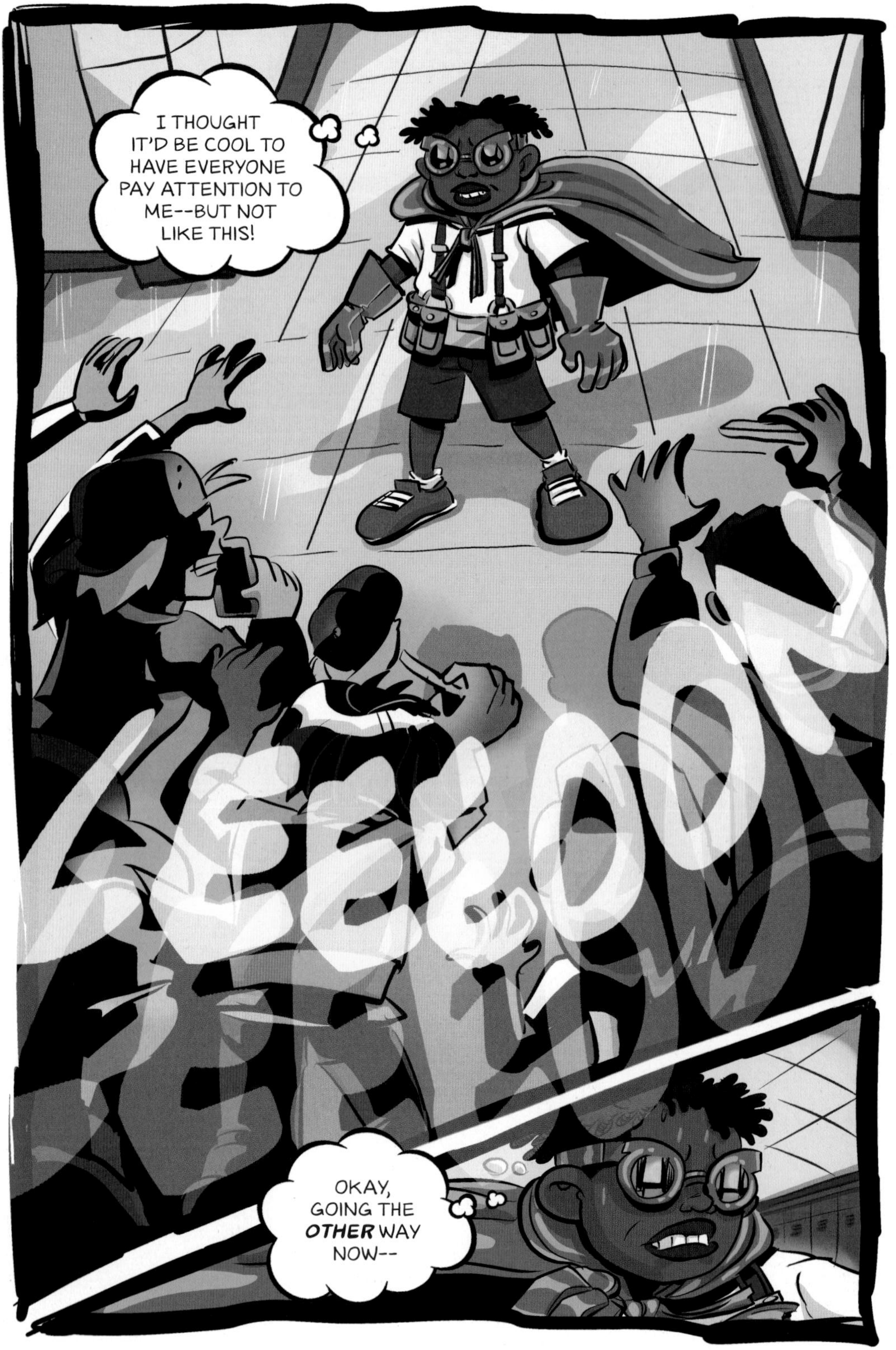
I THOUGHT IT'D BE COOL TO HAVE EVERYONE PAY ATTENTION TO ME--BUT NOT LIKE THIS!
OKAY, GOING THE ***OTHER*** WAY NOW--

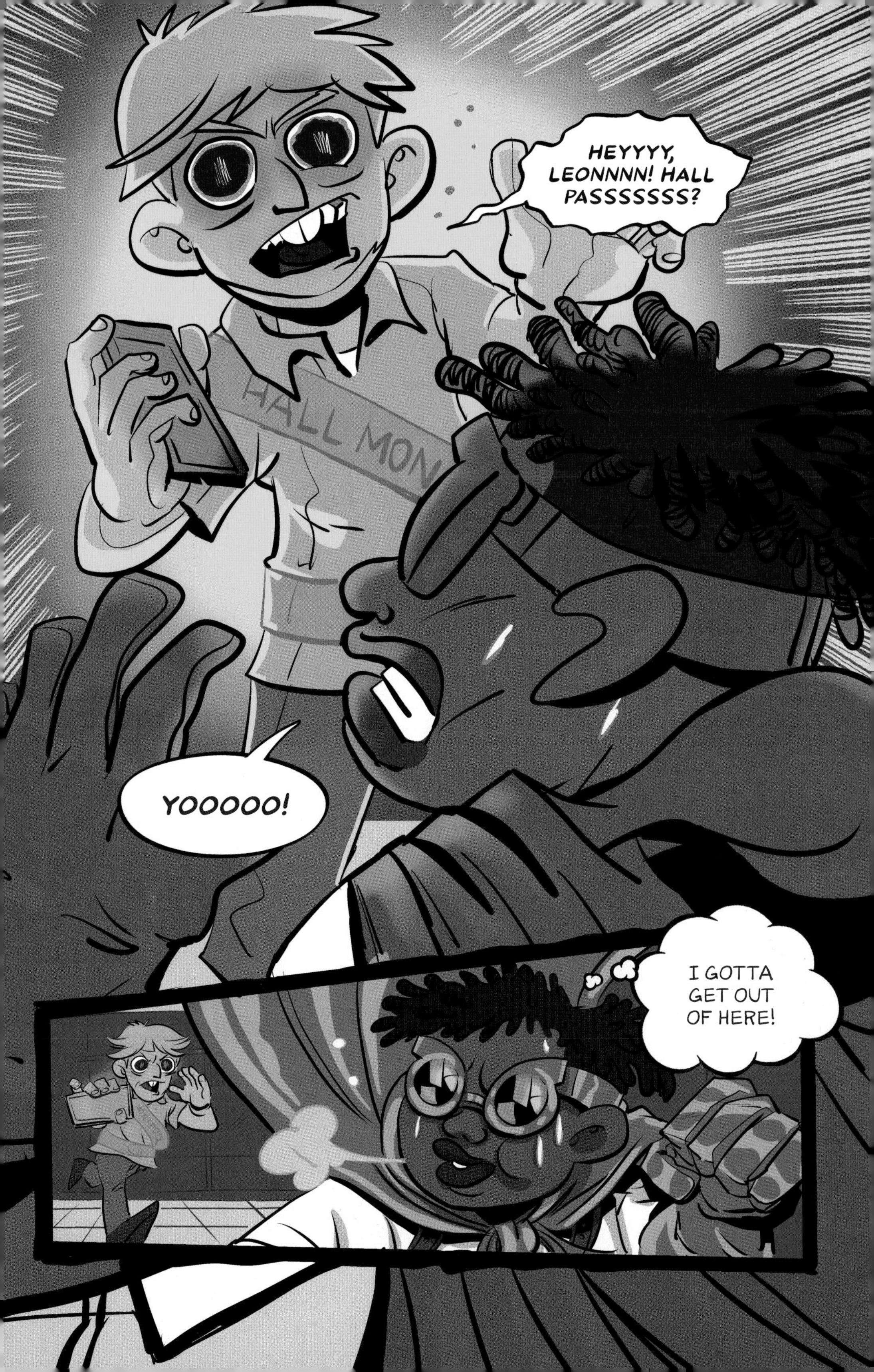
HEYYYY, LEONNNN! HALL PASSSSSSS?
HALL MON
YOOOOO!
I GOTTA GET OUT OF HERE!

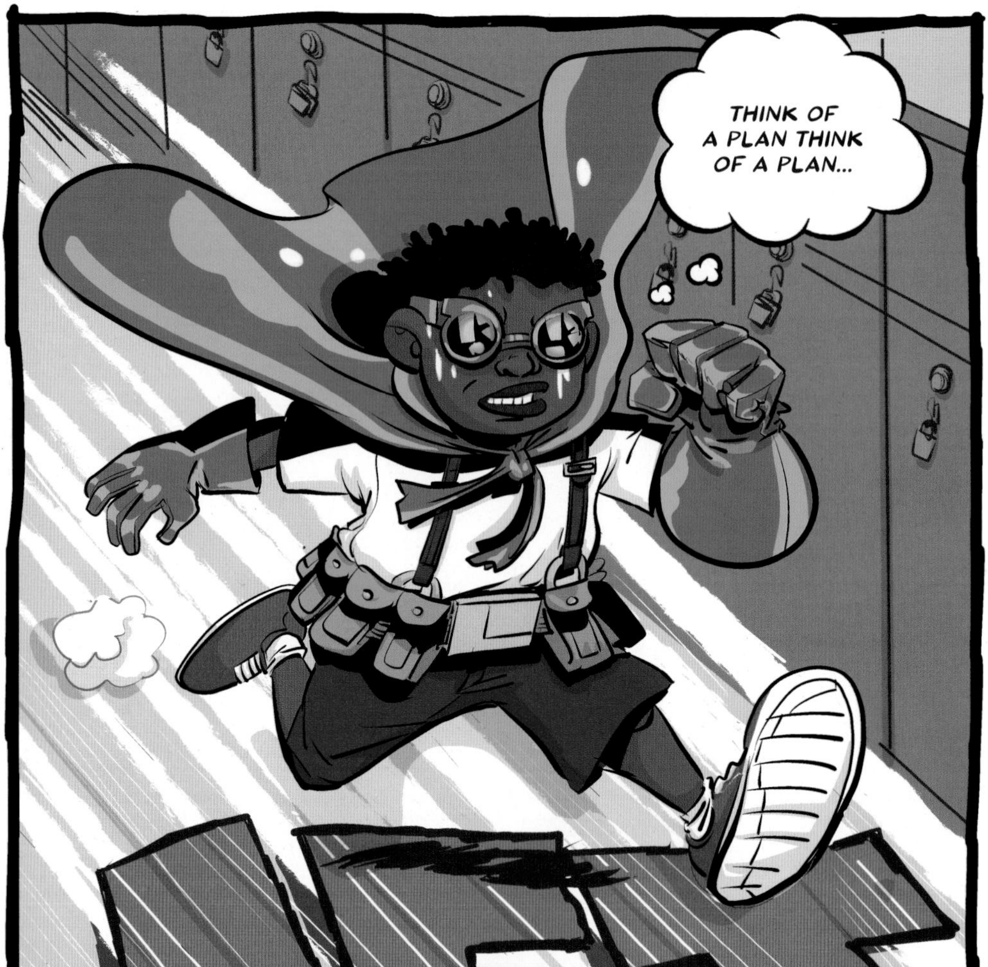
THINK OF A PLAN THINK OF A PLAN...

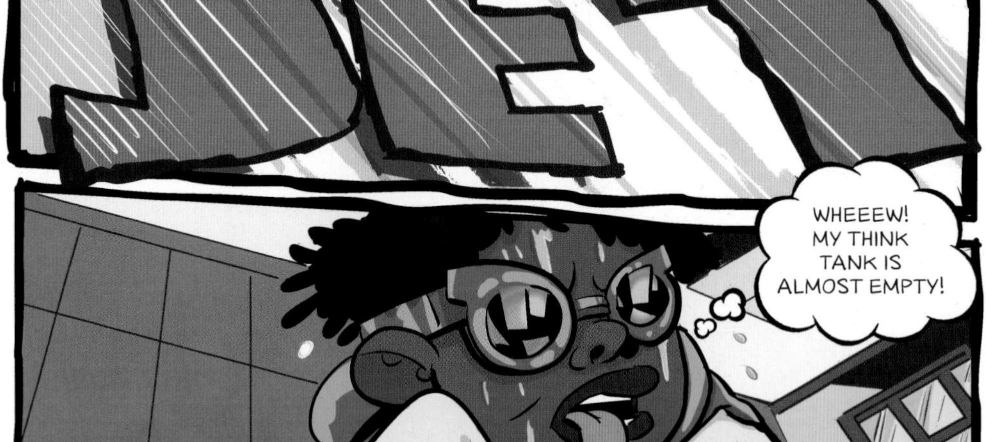
WHEEEW! MY THINK TANK IS ALMOST EMPTY!

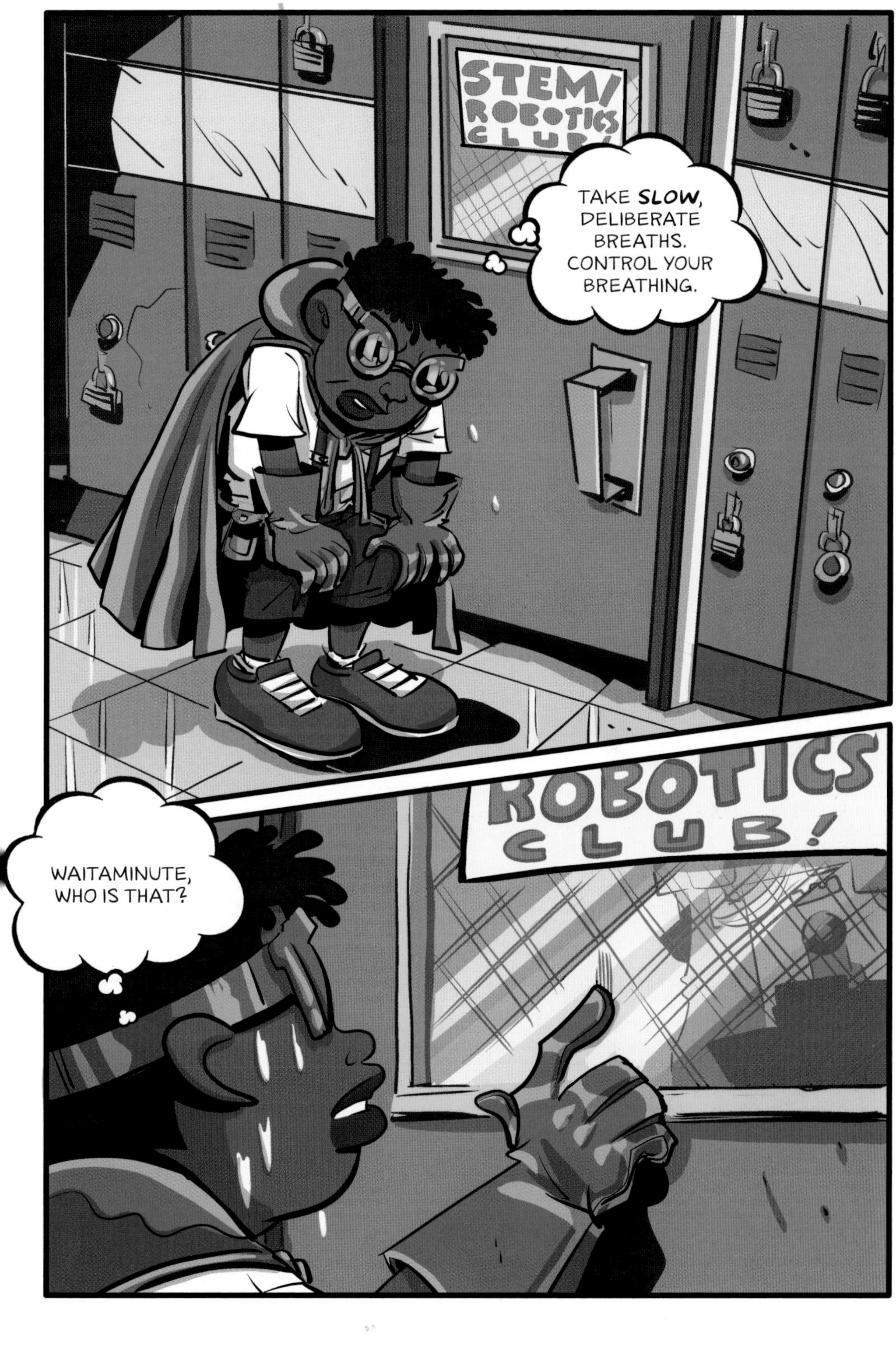
STEM/ ROBOTICS CLUB!
TAKE SLOW, DELIBERATE BREATHS. CONTROL YOUR BREATHING.
ROBOTICS CLUB!
WAITAMINUTE, WHO IS THAT?

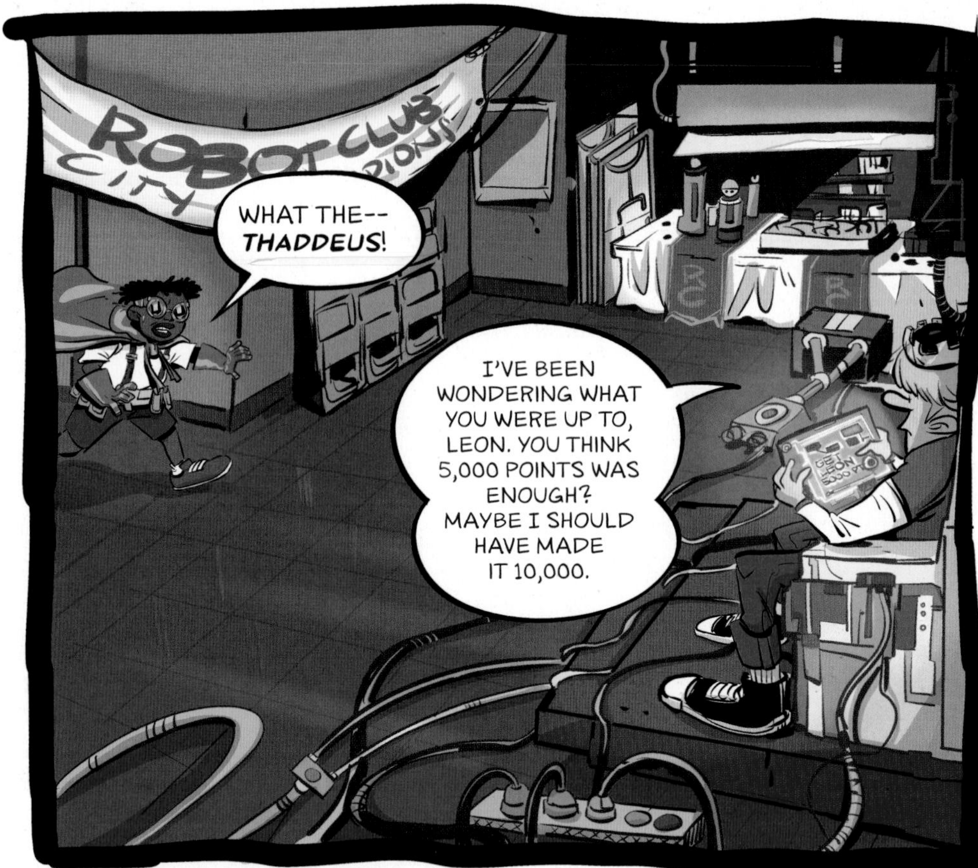
ROBOT CLUB
CITY
WHAT THE--
THADDEUS!
I'VE BEEN WONDERING WHAT YOU WERE UP TO, LEON. YOU THINK 5,000 POINTS WAS ENOUGH? MAYBE I SHOULD HAVE MADE IT 10,000.
GET LEON

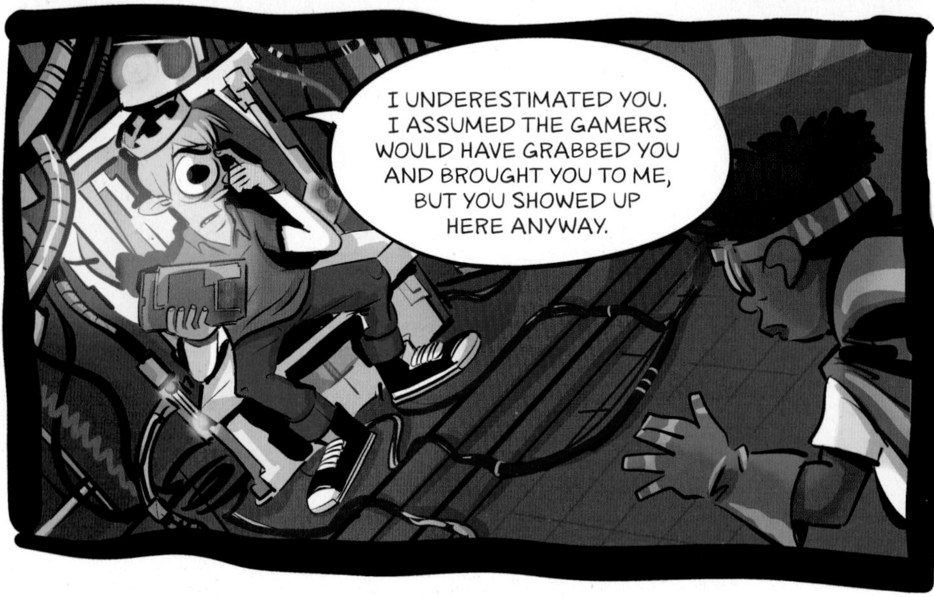
I UNDERESTIMATED YOU. I ASSUMED THE GAMERS WOULD HAVE GRABBED YOU AND BROUGHT YOU TO ME, BUT YOU SHOWED UP HERE ANYWAY.

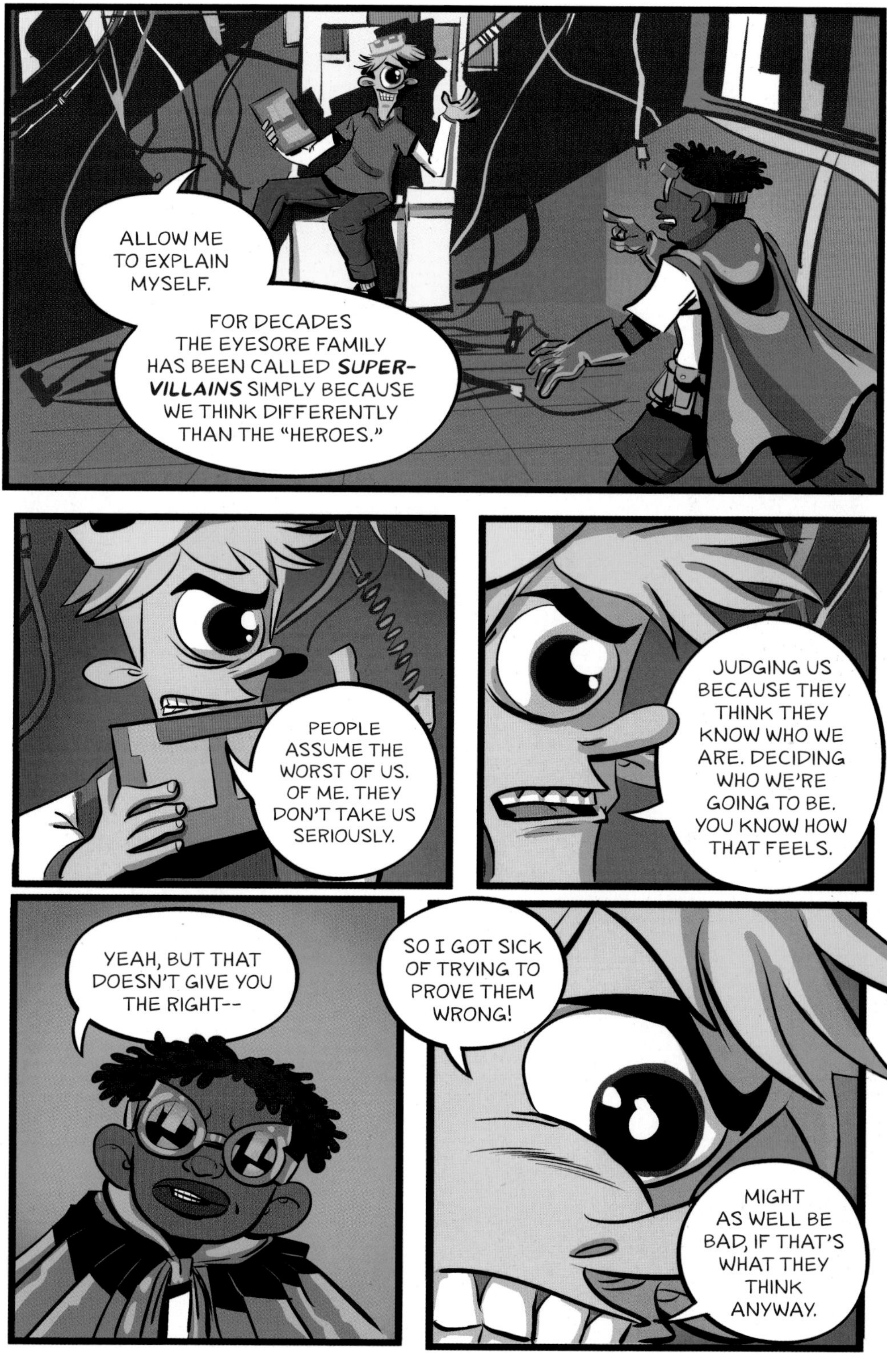
ALLOW ME TO EXPLAIN MYSELF.
FOR DECADES THE EYESORE FAMILY HAS BEEN CALLED **SUPER-VILLAINS** SIMPLY BECAUSE WE THINK DIFFERENTLY THAN THE "HEROES."
PEOPLE ASSUME THE WORST OF US. OF ME. THEY DON'T TAKE US SERIOUSLY.
JUDGING US BECAUSE THEY THINK THEY KNOW WHO WE ARE. DECIDING WHO WE'RE GOING TO BE. YOU KNOW HOW THAT FEELS.
YEAH, BUT THAT DOESN'T GIVE YOU THE RIGHT--
SO I GOT SICK OF TRYING TO PROVE THEM WRONG!
MIGHT AS WELL BE BAD, IF THAT'S WHAT THEY THINK ANYWAY.

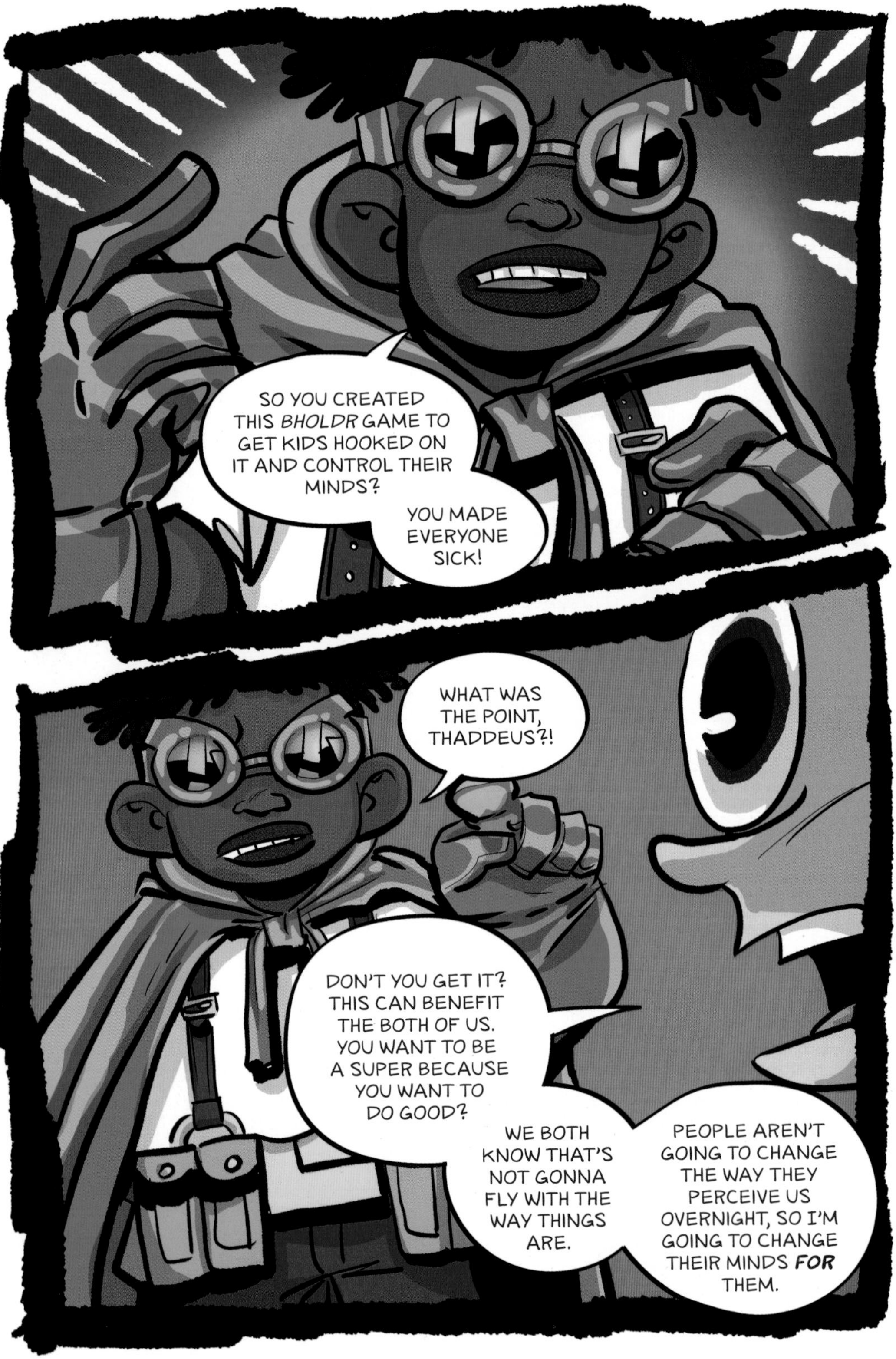
SO YOU CREATED THIS *BHOLDR* GAME TO GET KIDS HOOKED ON IT AND CONTROL THEIR MINDS?
YOU MADE EVERYONE SICK!
WHAT WAS THE POINT, THADDEUS?!
DON'T YOU GET IT? THIS CAN BENEFIT THE BOTH OF US. YOU WANT TO BE A SUPER BECAUSE YOU WANT TO DO GOOD?
WE BOTH KNOW THAT'S NOT GONNA FLY WITH THE WAY THINGS ARE.
PEOPLE AREN'T GOING TO CHANGE THE WAY THEY PERCEIVE US OVERNIGHT, SO I'M GOING TO CHANGE THEIR MINDS **FOR** THEM.

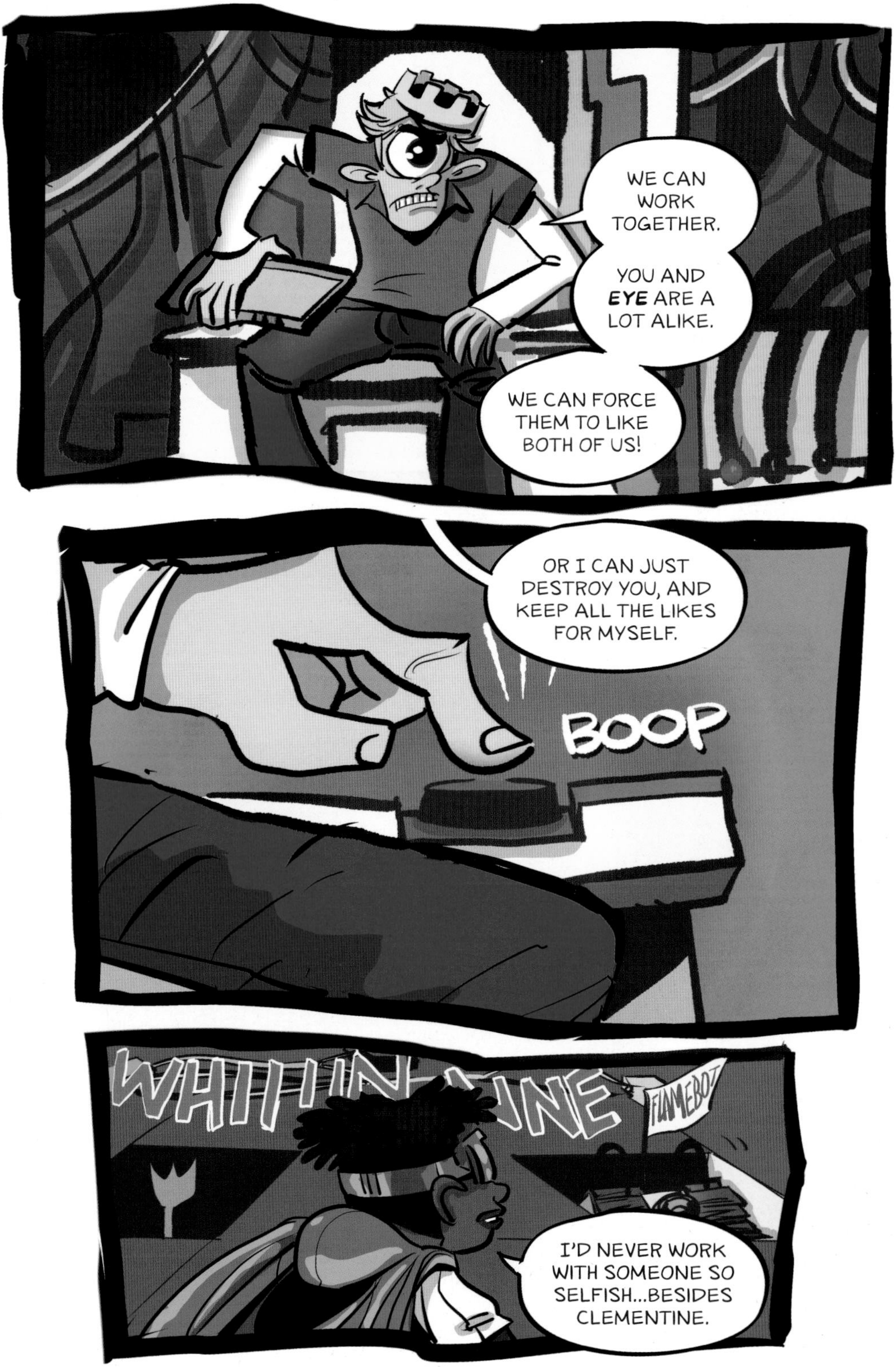
WE CAN WORK TOGETHER.
YOU AND **EYE** ARE A LOT ALIKE.
WE CAN FORCE THEM TO LIKE BOTH OF US!
OR I CAN JUST DESTROY YOU, AND KEEP ALL THE LIKES FOR MYSELF.
BOOP
FLAMEBOT
I'D NEVER WORK WITH SOMEONE SO SELFISH...BESIDES CLEMENTINE.

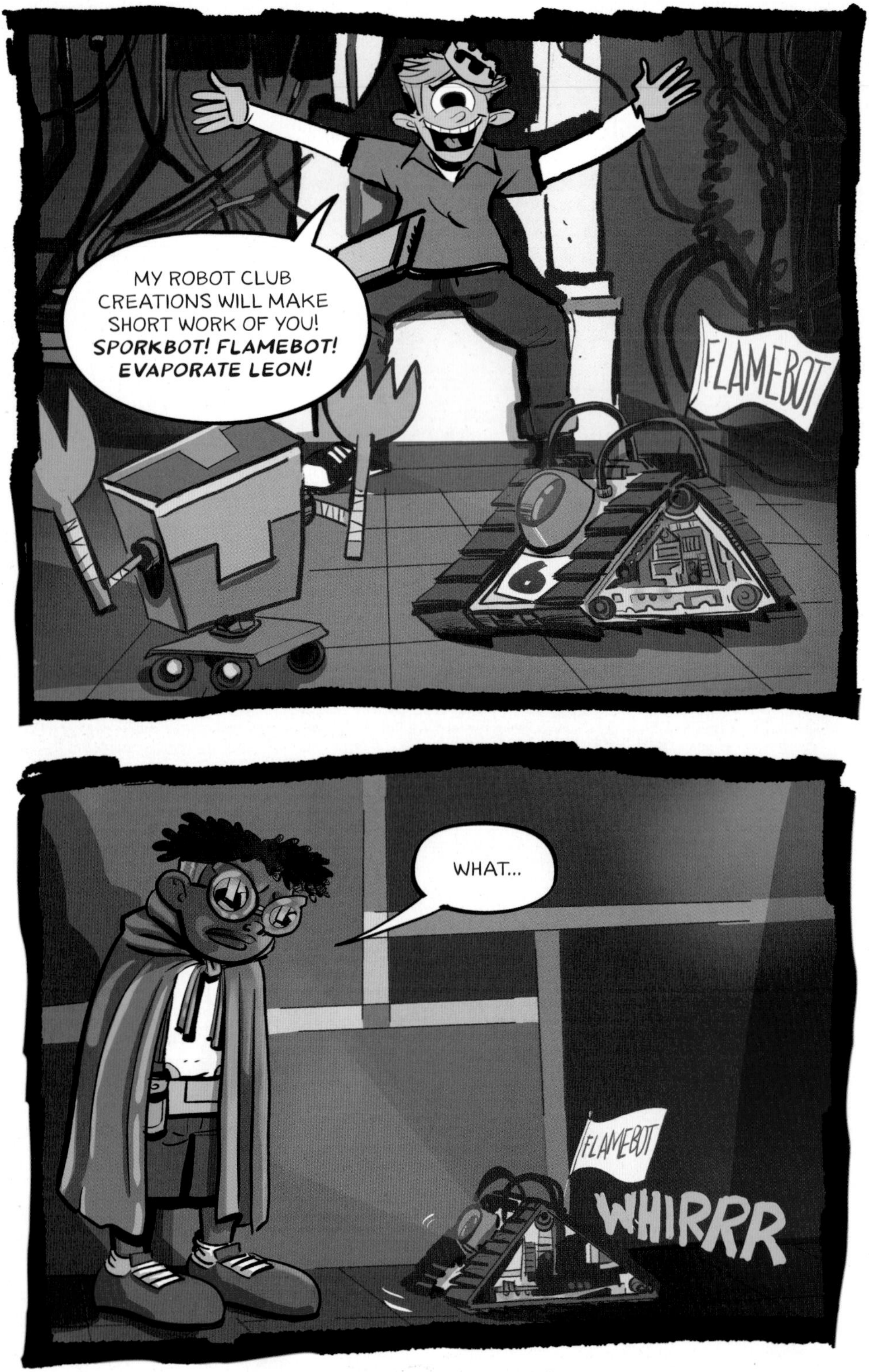
MY ROBOT CLUB CREATIONS WILL MAKE SHORT WORK OF YOU! **SPORKBOT! FLAMEBOT! EVAPORATE LEON!**
FLAMEBOT
6
WHAT...
FLAMEBOT
WHIRRR

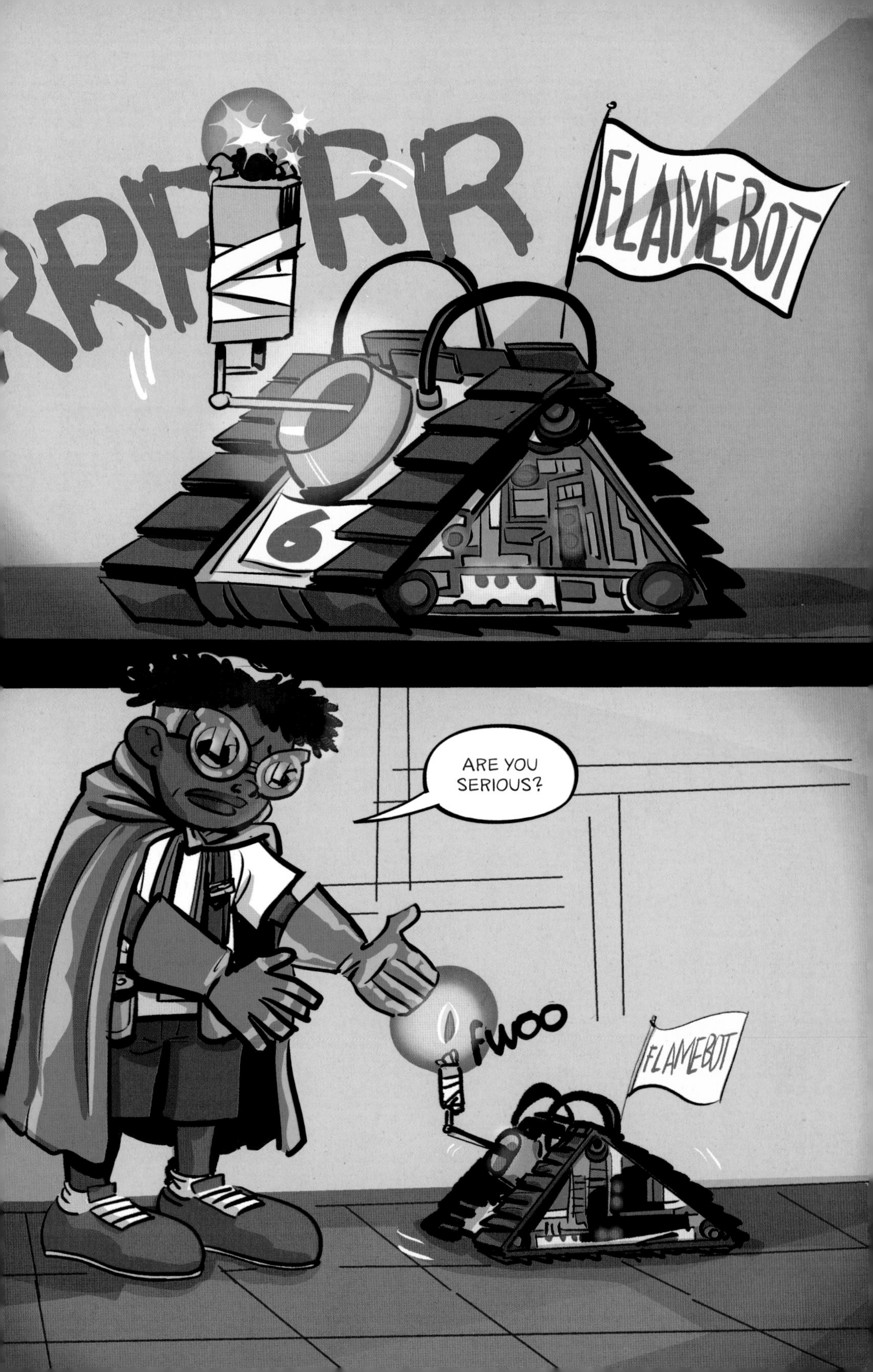
RRRRRR
FLAMEBOT
6
ARE YOU SERIOUS?
FWOO
FLAMEBOT

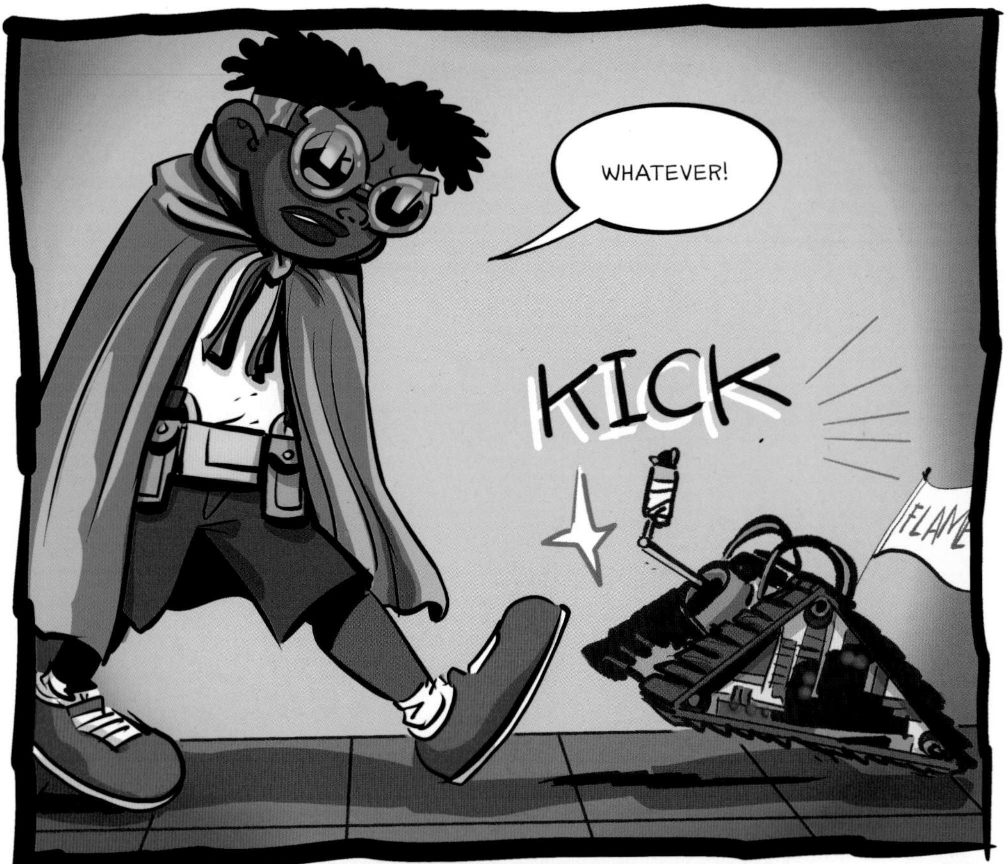
WHATEVER!
KICK
FLAME

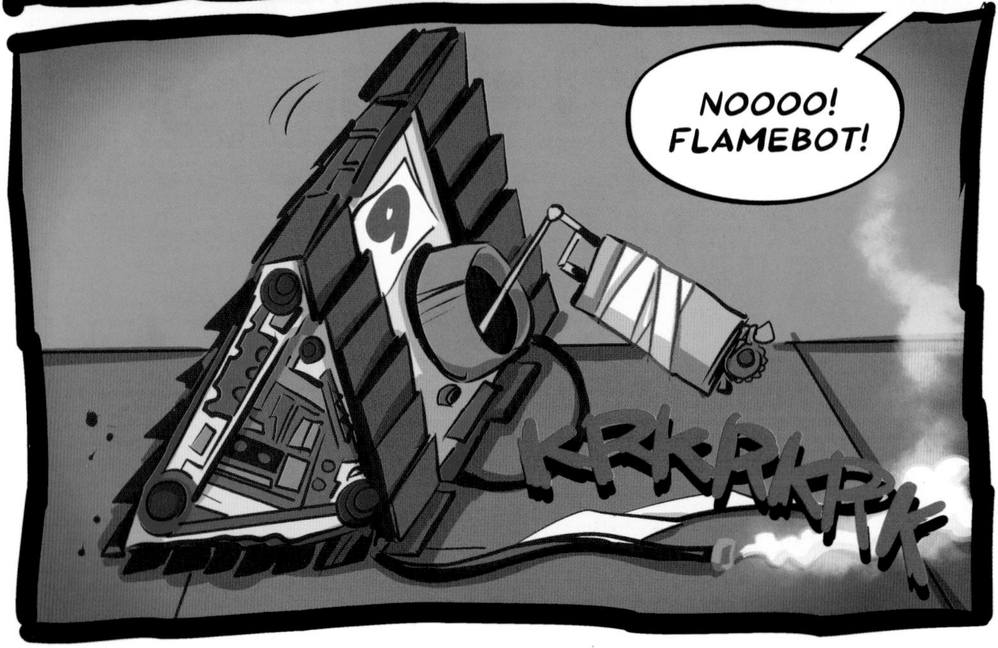
NOOOO! FLAMEBOT!
9
KRKRKRKRK

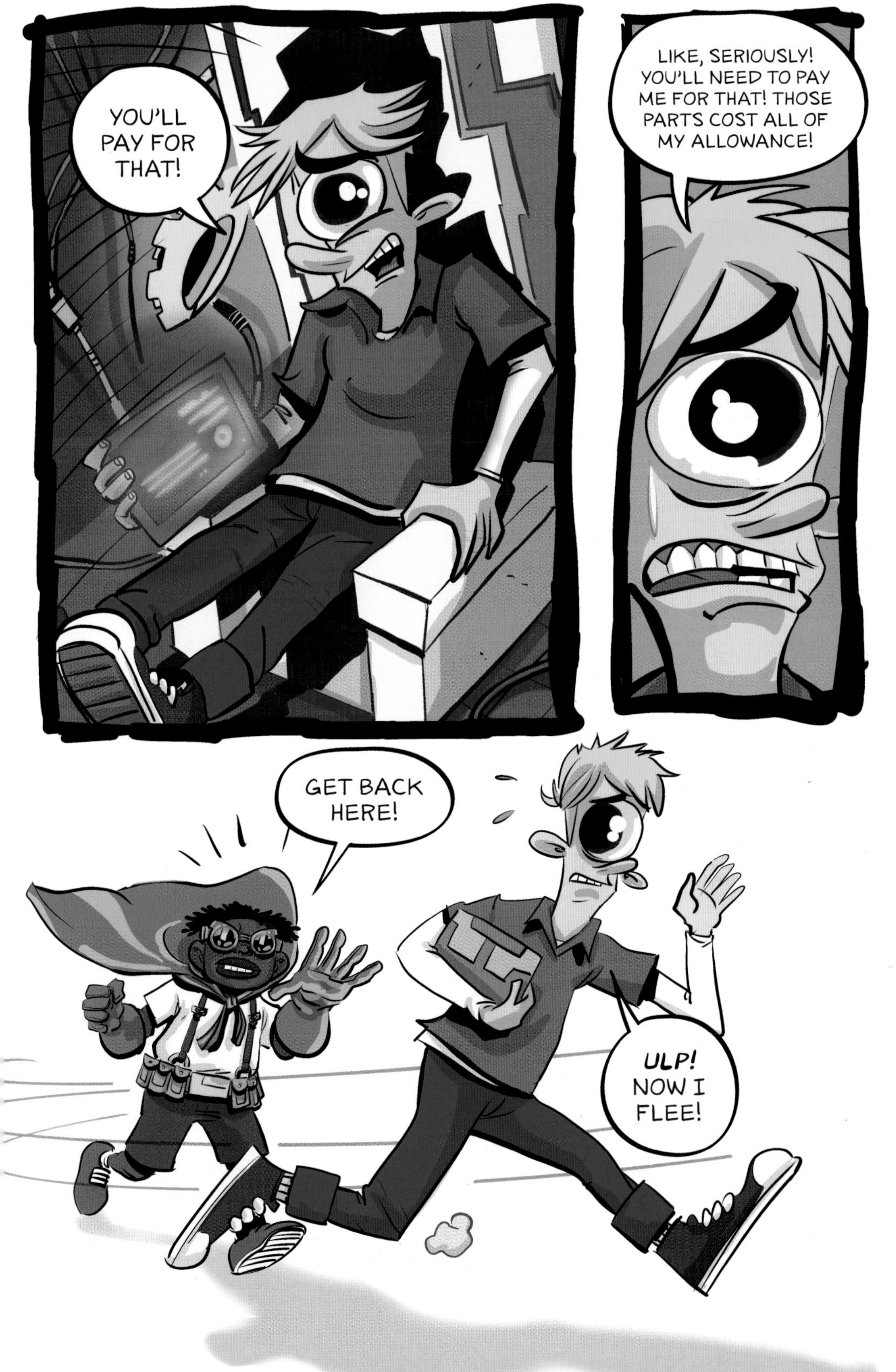
YOU'LL PAY FOR THAT!
LIKE, SERIOUSLY! YOU'LL NEED TO PAY ME FOR THAT! THOSE PARTS COST ALL OF MY ALLOWANCE!
GET BACK HERE!
ULP! NOW I FLEE!

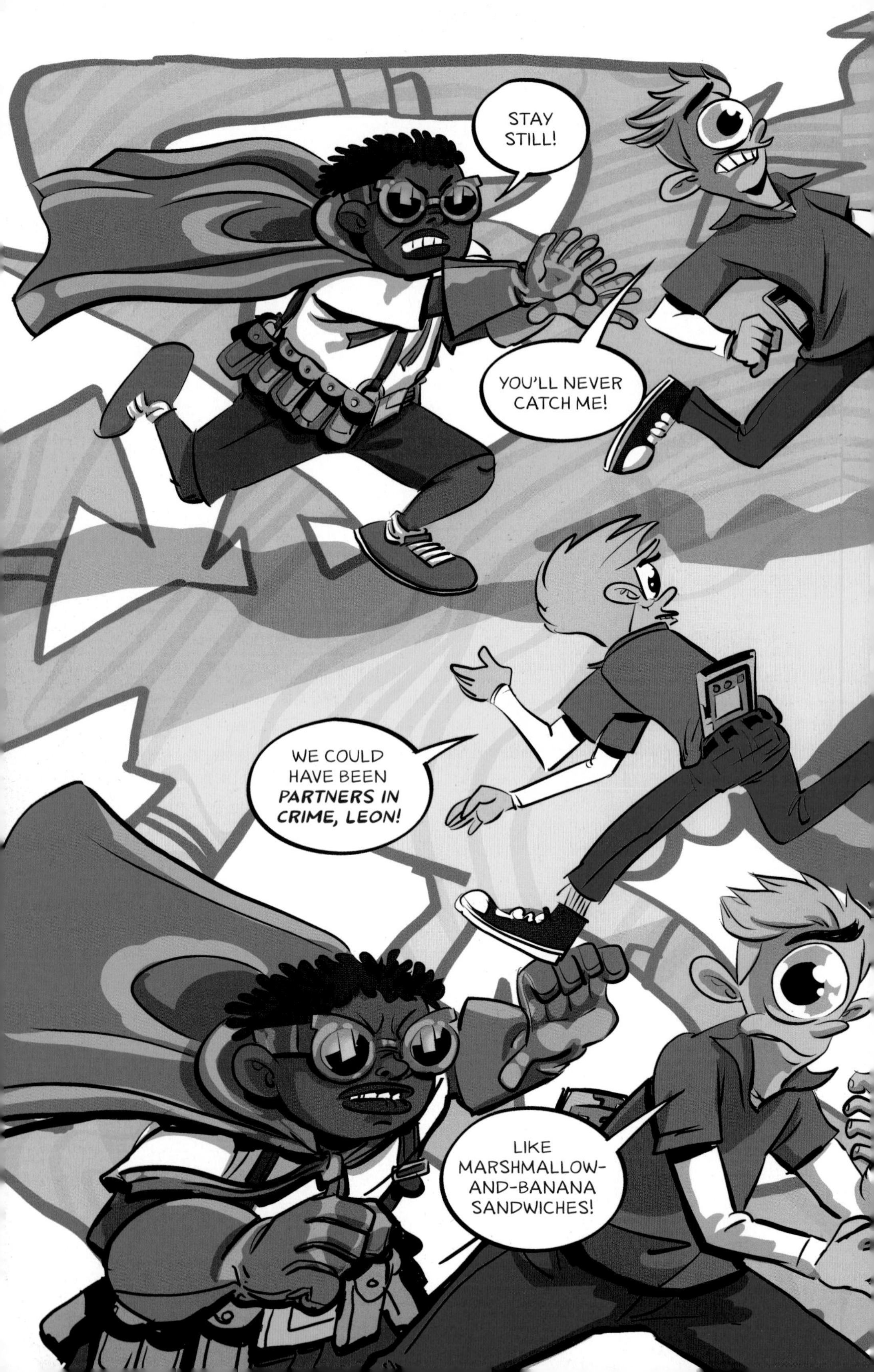
STAY STILL!
YOU'LL NEVER CATCH ME!
WE COULD HAVE BEEN **PARTNERS IN CRIME, LEON!**
LIKE MARSHMALLOW-AND-BANANA SANDWICHES!

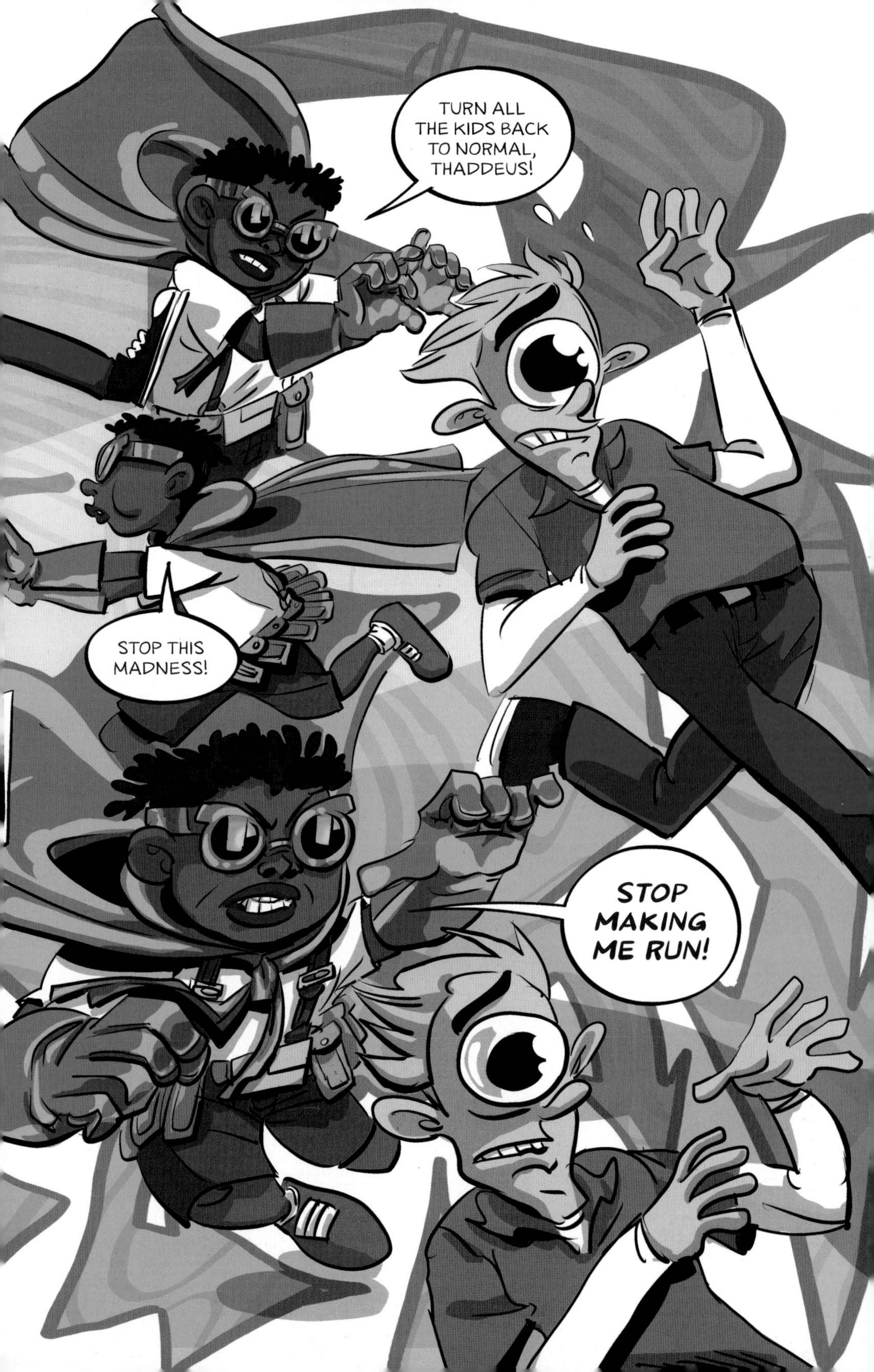
TURN ALL THE KIDS BACK TO NORMAL, THADDEUS!
STOP THIS MADNESS!
STOP MAKING ME RUN!

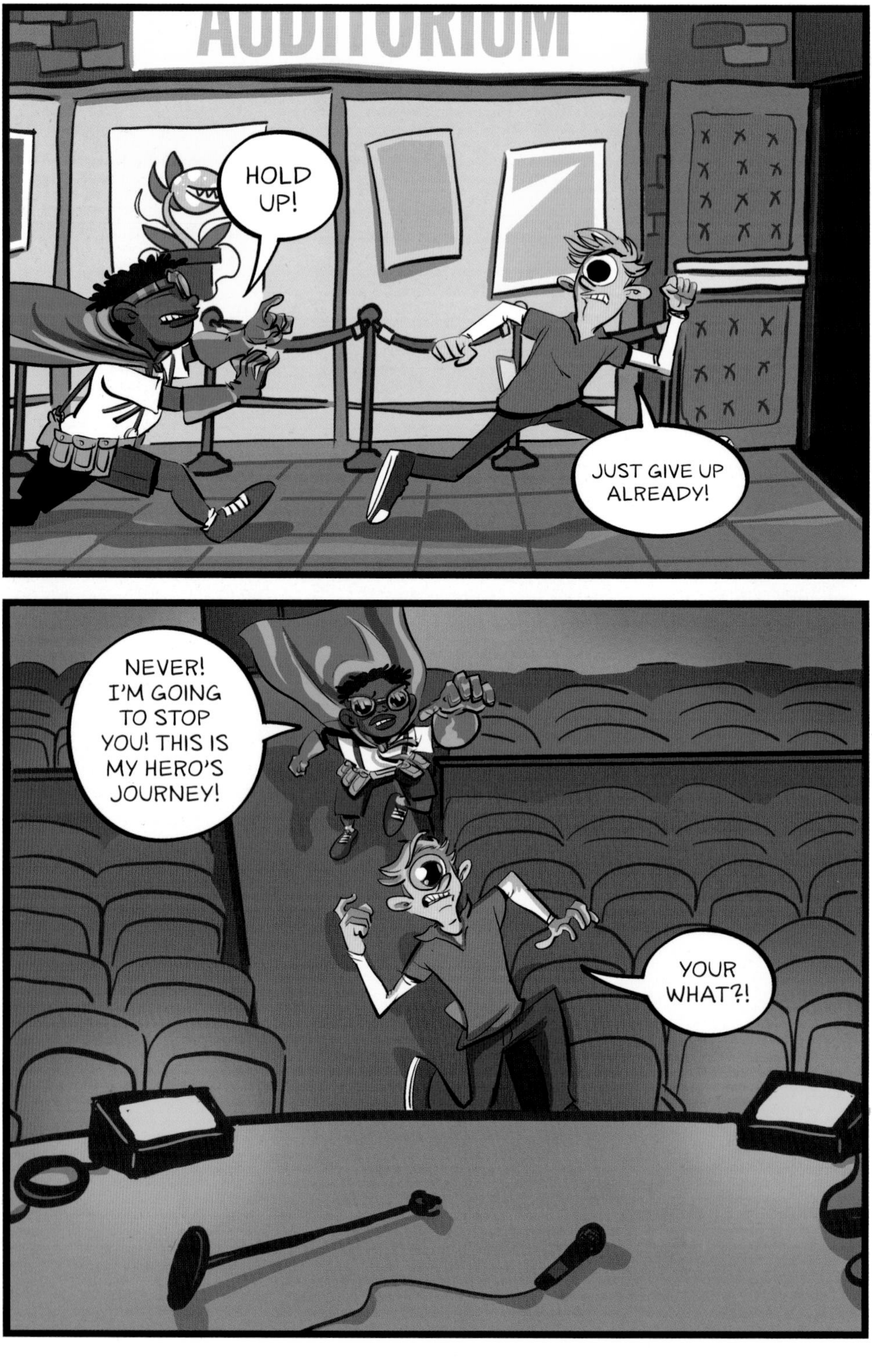
AUDITORIUM
HOLD UP!
JUST GIVE UP ALREADY!
NEVER! I'M GOING TO STOP YOU! THIS IS MY HERO'S JOURNEY!
YOUR WHAT?!

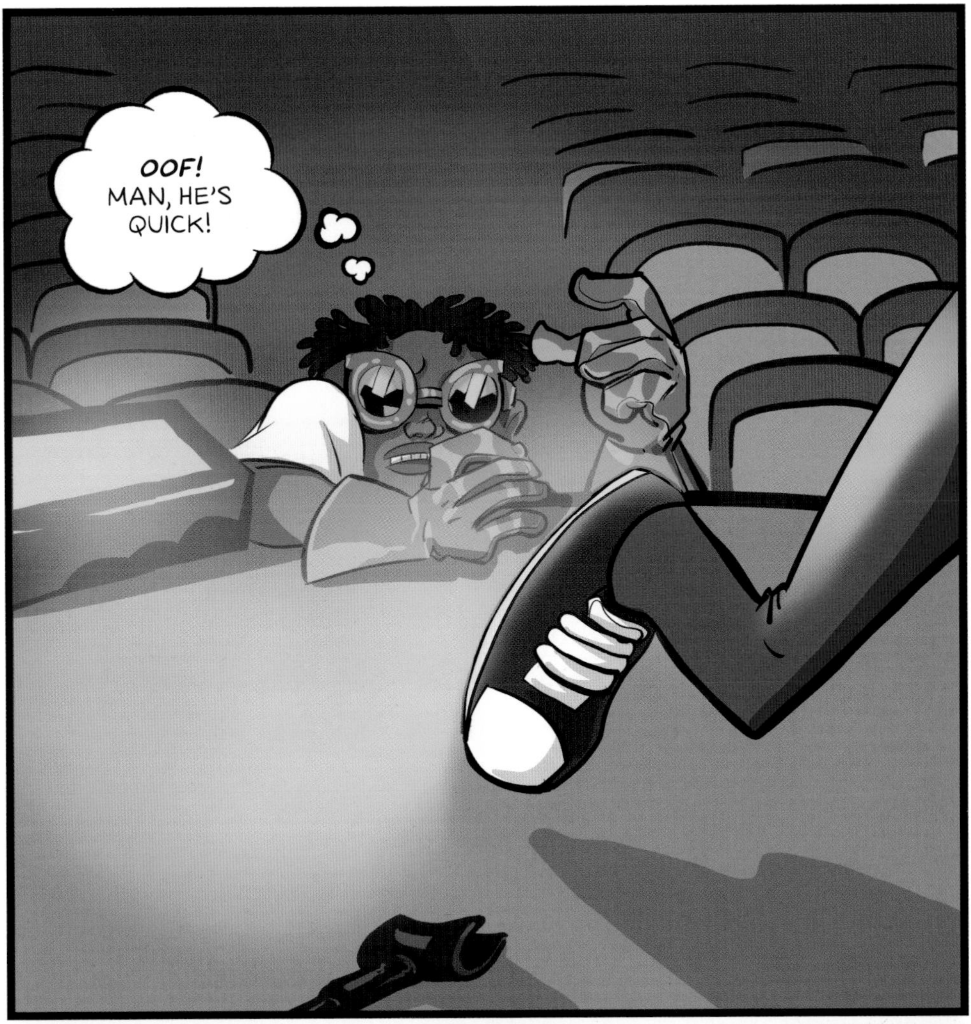
OOF!
MAN, HE'S
QUICK!

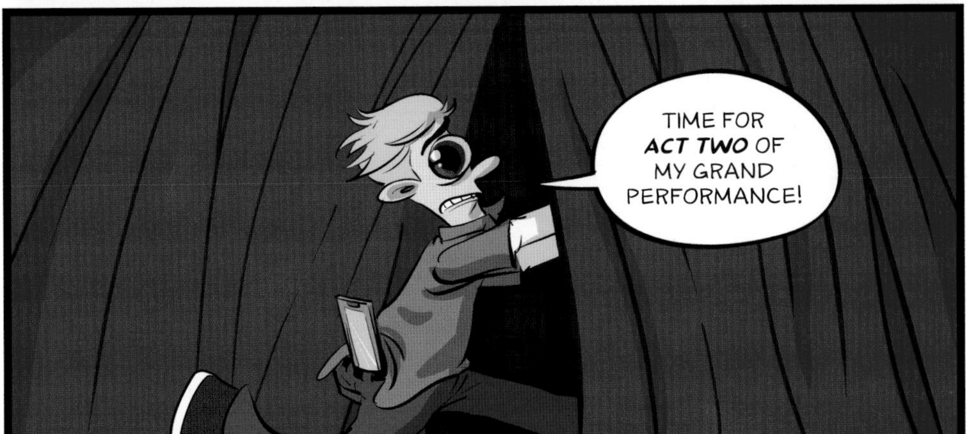
TIME FOR
ACT TWO OF
MY GRAND
PERFORMANCE!

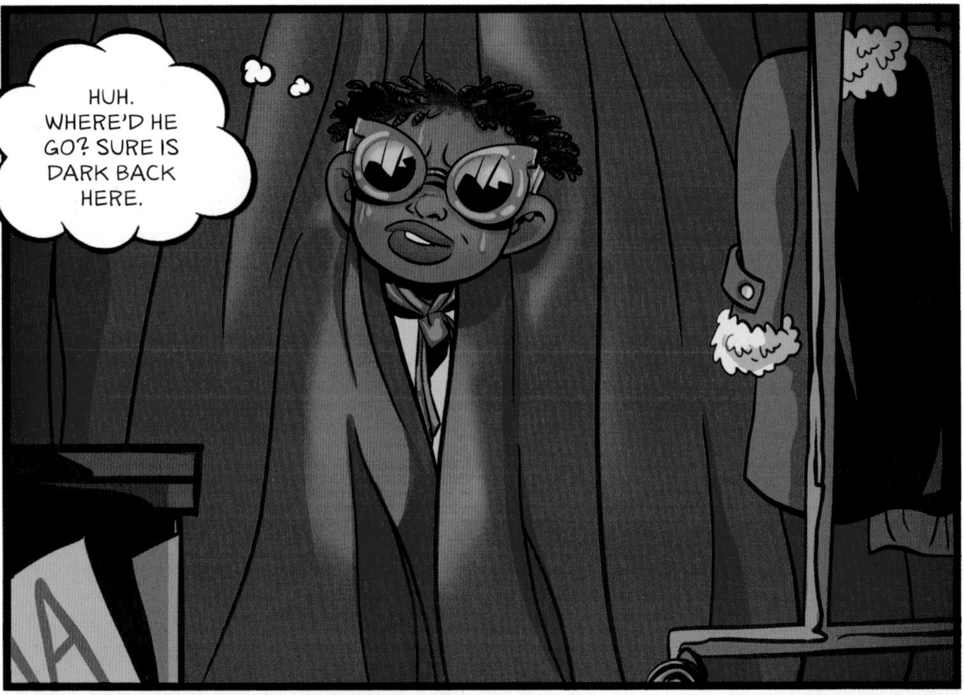
HUH. WHERE'D HE GO? SURE IS DARK BACK HERE.

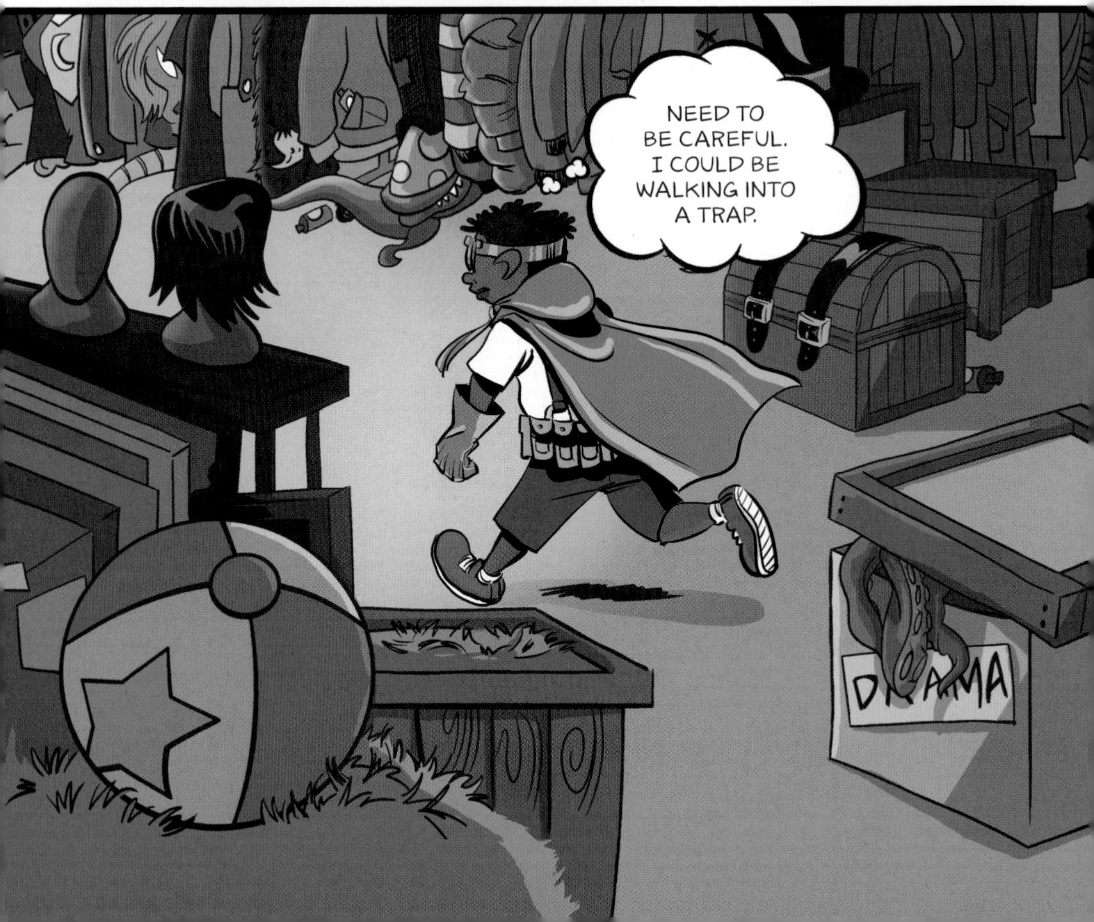
NEED TO BE CAREFUL. I COULD BE WALKING INTO A TRAP.
DRAMA

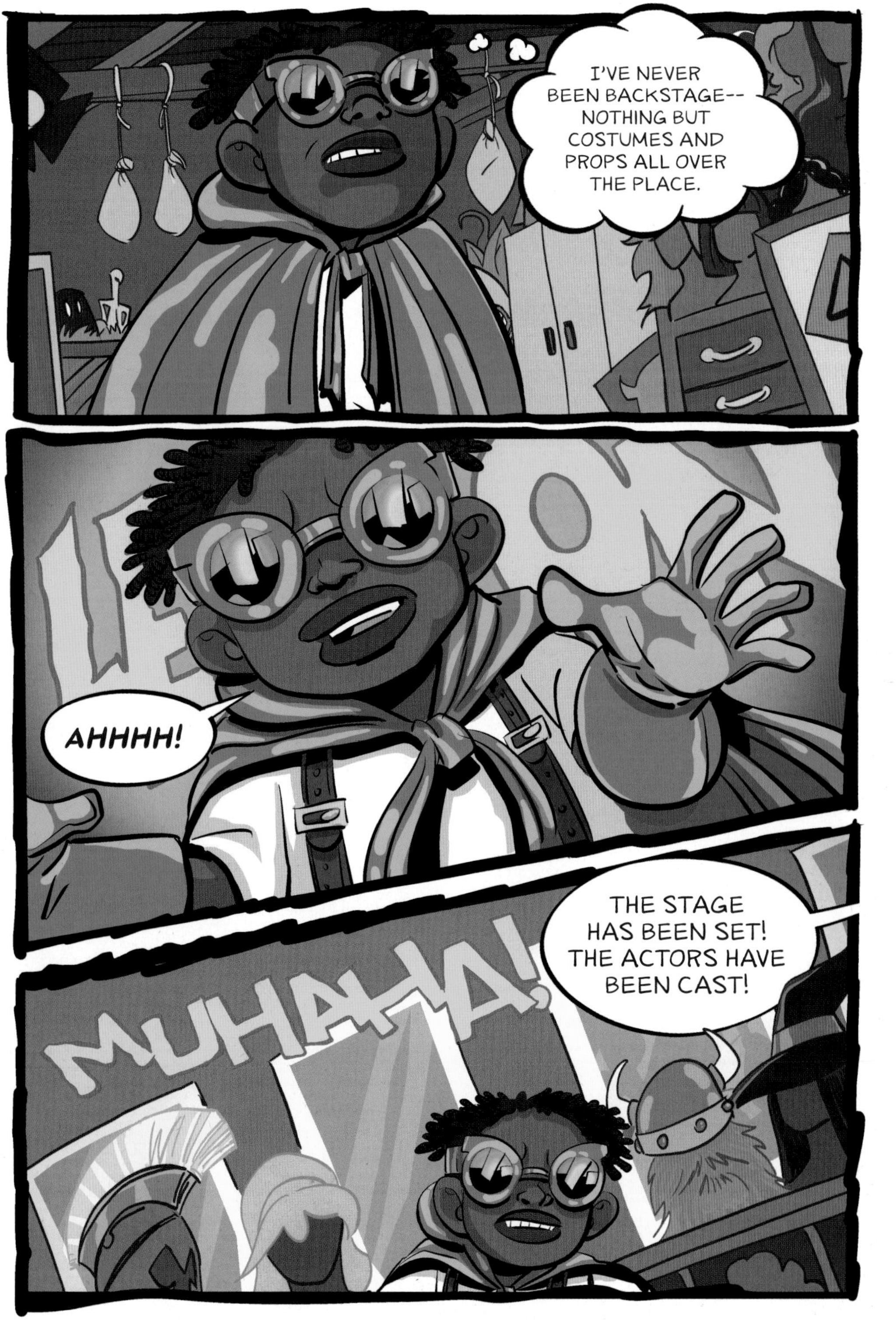
I'VE NEVER BEEN BACKSTAGE-- NOTHING BUT COSTUMES AND PROPS ALL OVER THE PLACE.
AHHHH!
THE STAGE HAS BEEN SET! THE ACTORS HAVE BEEN CAST!
MUHAHA!

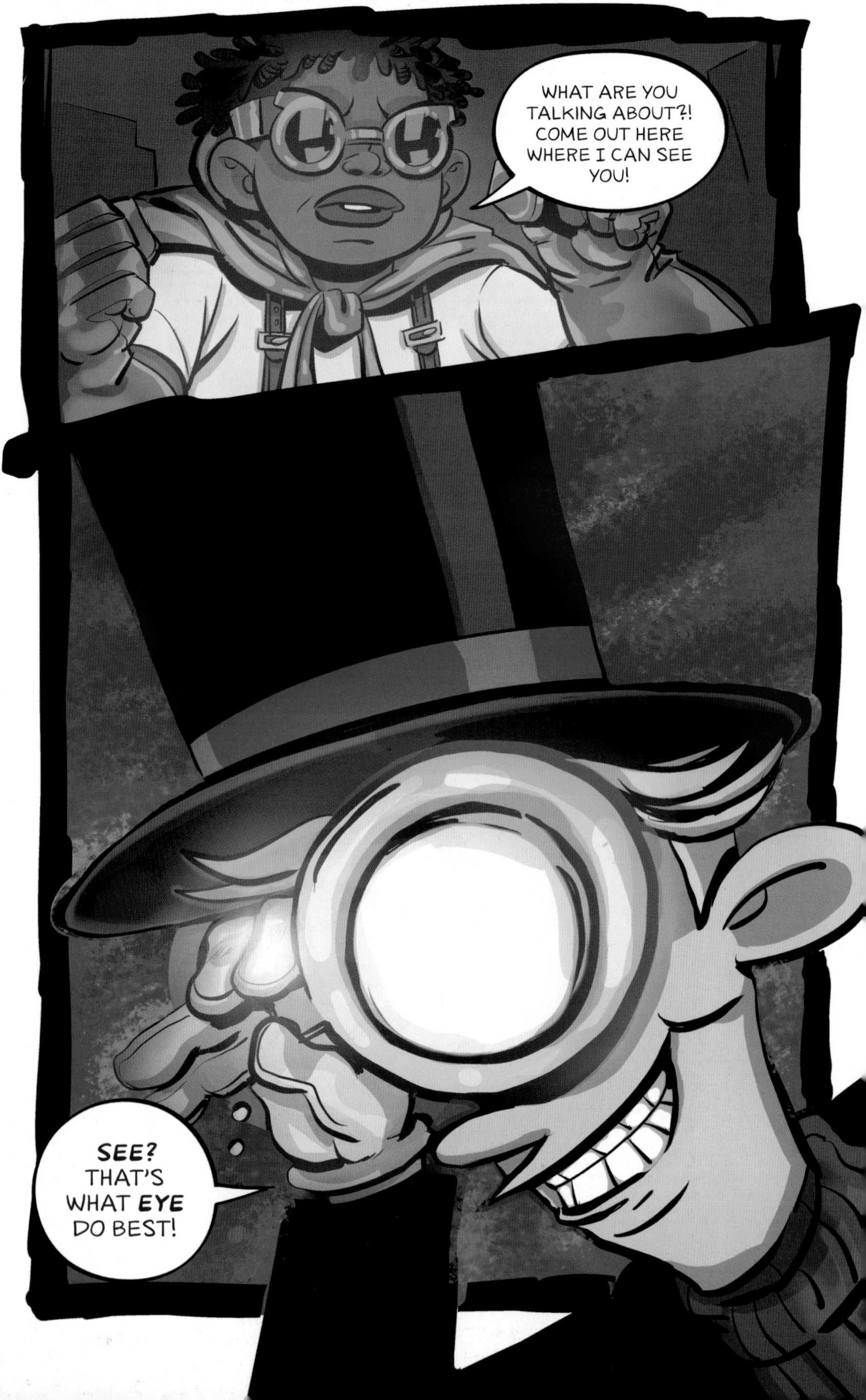
WHAT ARE YOU TALKING ABOUT?! COME OUT HERE WHERE I CAN SEE YOU!
SEE? THAT'S WHAT EYE DO BEST!

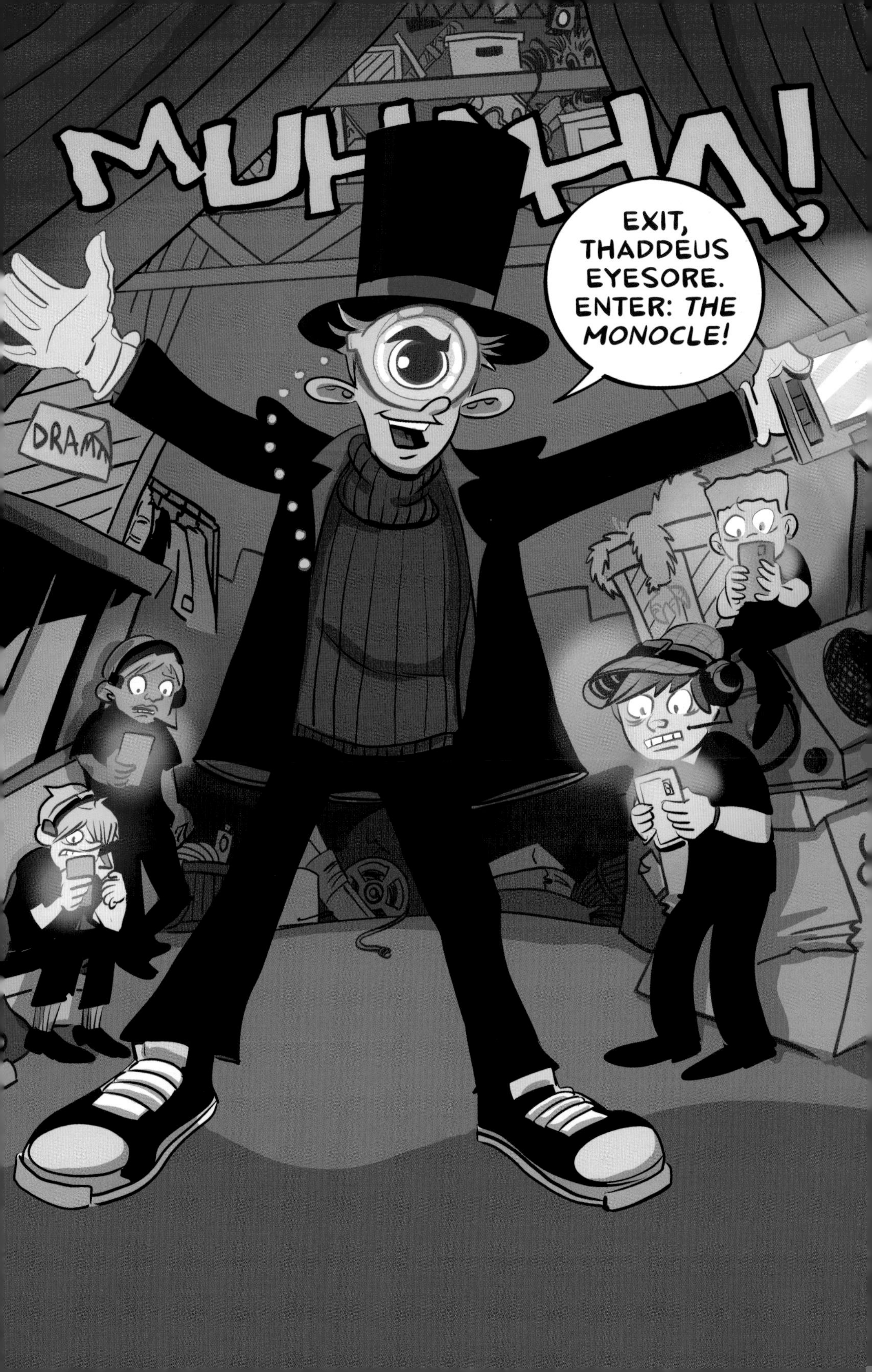
MUHAHA!
EXIT, THADDEUS EYESORE. ENTER: *THE MONOCLE!*
DRAMA

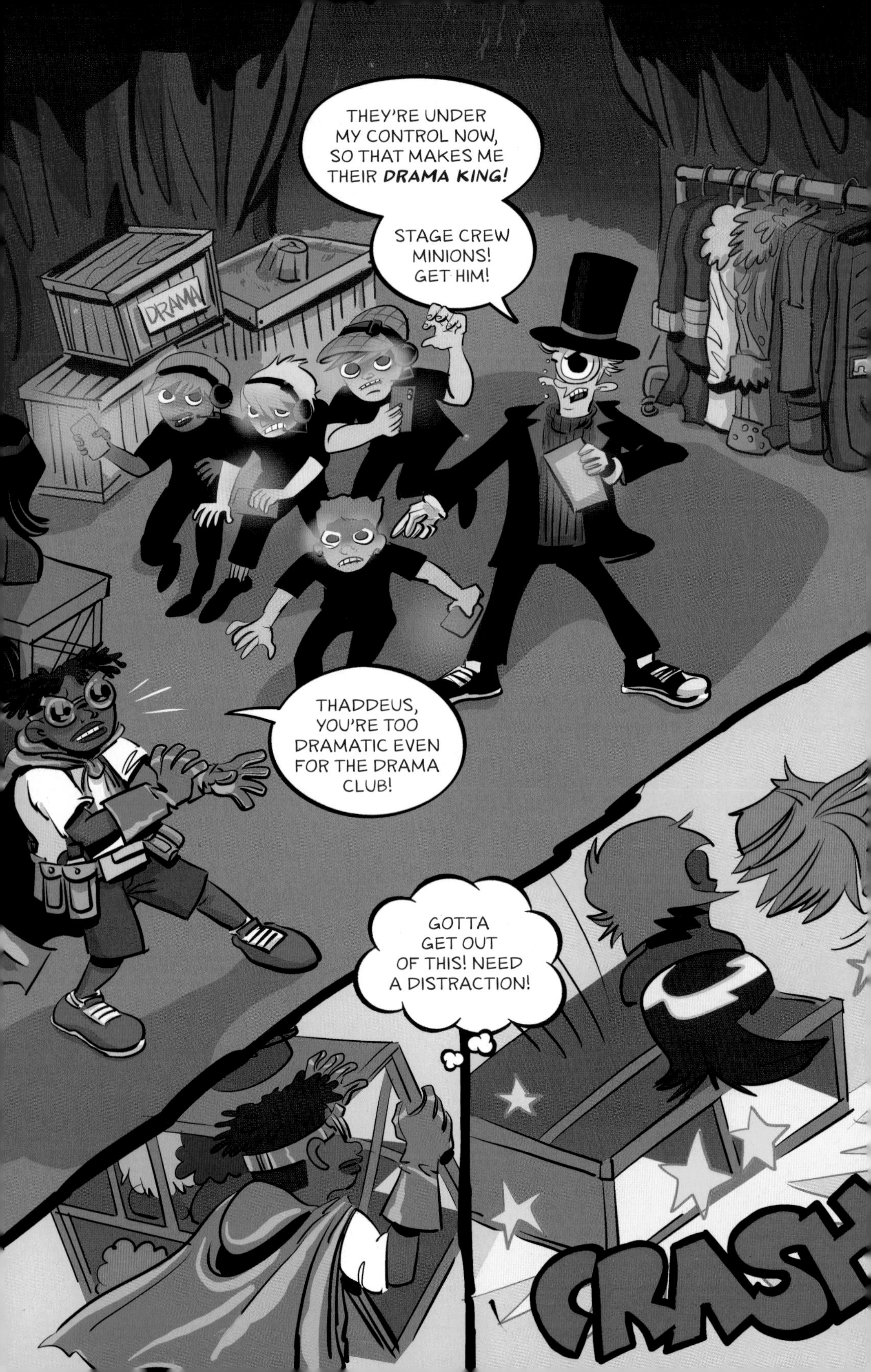

THEY'RE UNDER MY CONTROL NOW, SO THAT MAKES ME THEIR **DRAMA KING!**
STAGE CREW MINIONS! GET HIM!
DRAMA
THADDEUS, YOU'RE TOO DRAMATIC EVEN FOR THE DRAMA CLUB!
GOTTA GET OUT OF THIS! NEED A DISTRACTION!
CRASH

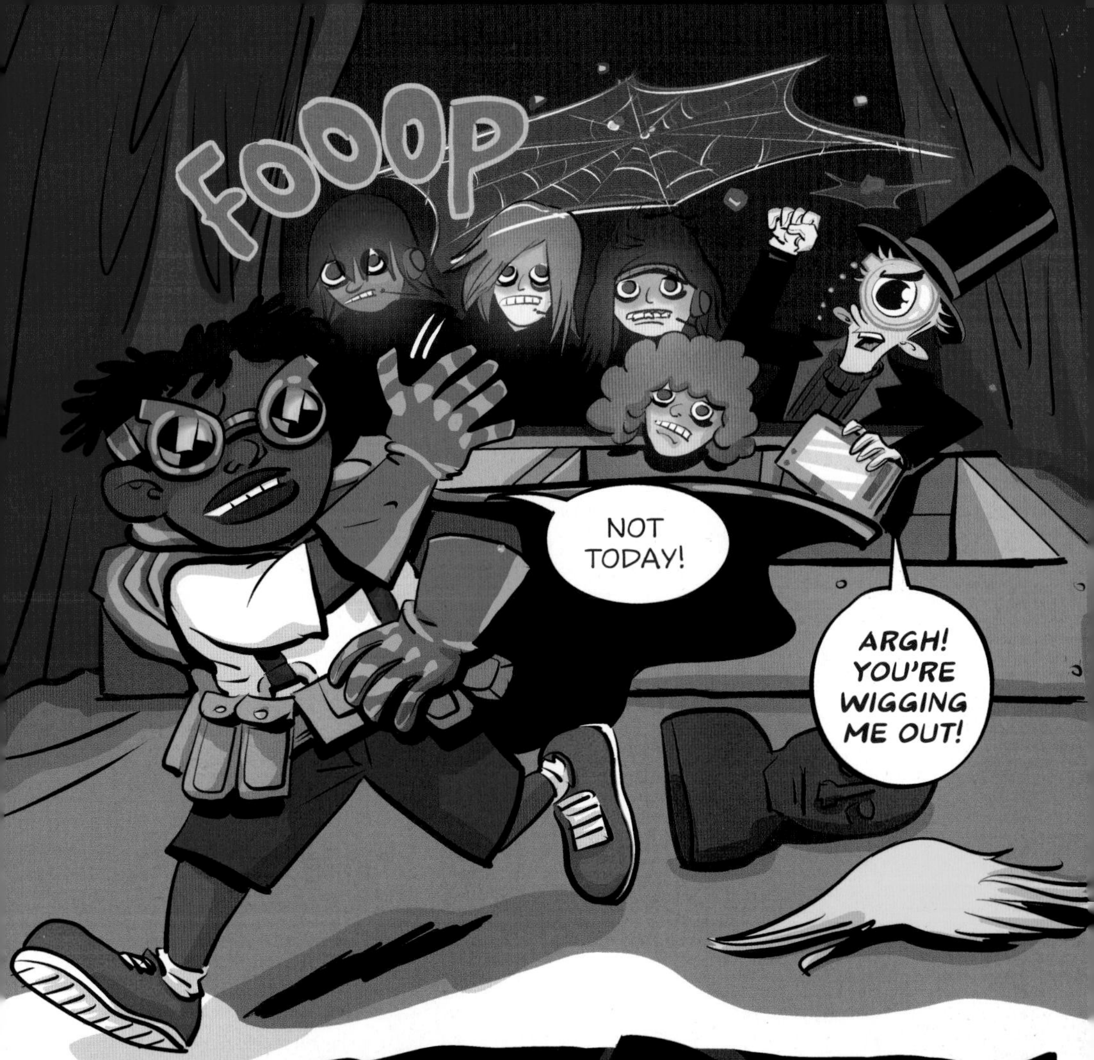
FOOOP
NOT TODAY!
ARGH! YOU'RE WIGGING ME OUT!

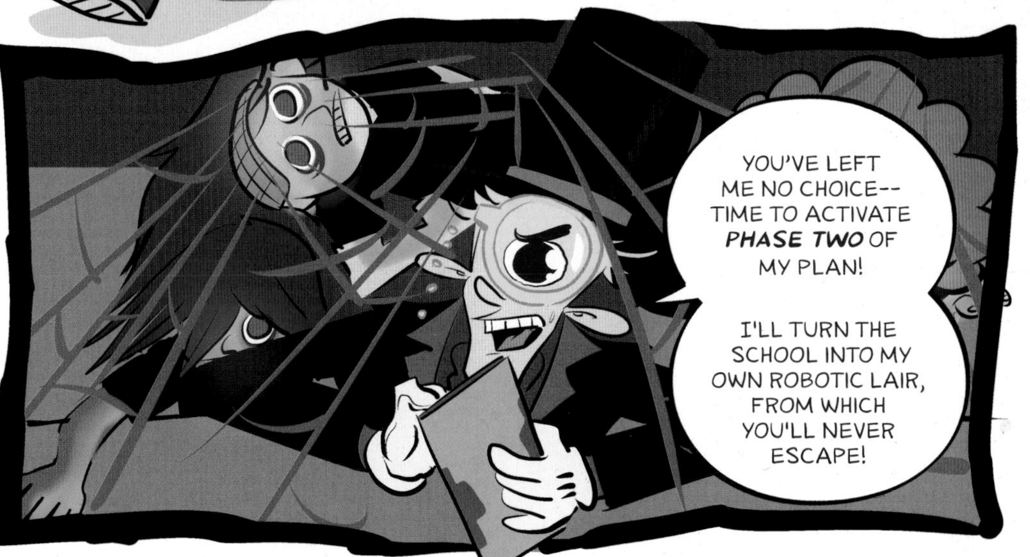
YOU'VE LEFT ME NO CHOICE-- TIME TO ACTIVATE PHASE TWO OF MY PLAN!
I'LL TURN THE SCHOOL INTO MY OWN ROBOTIC LAIR, FROM WHICH YOU'LL NEVER ESCAPE!

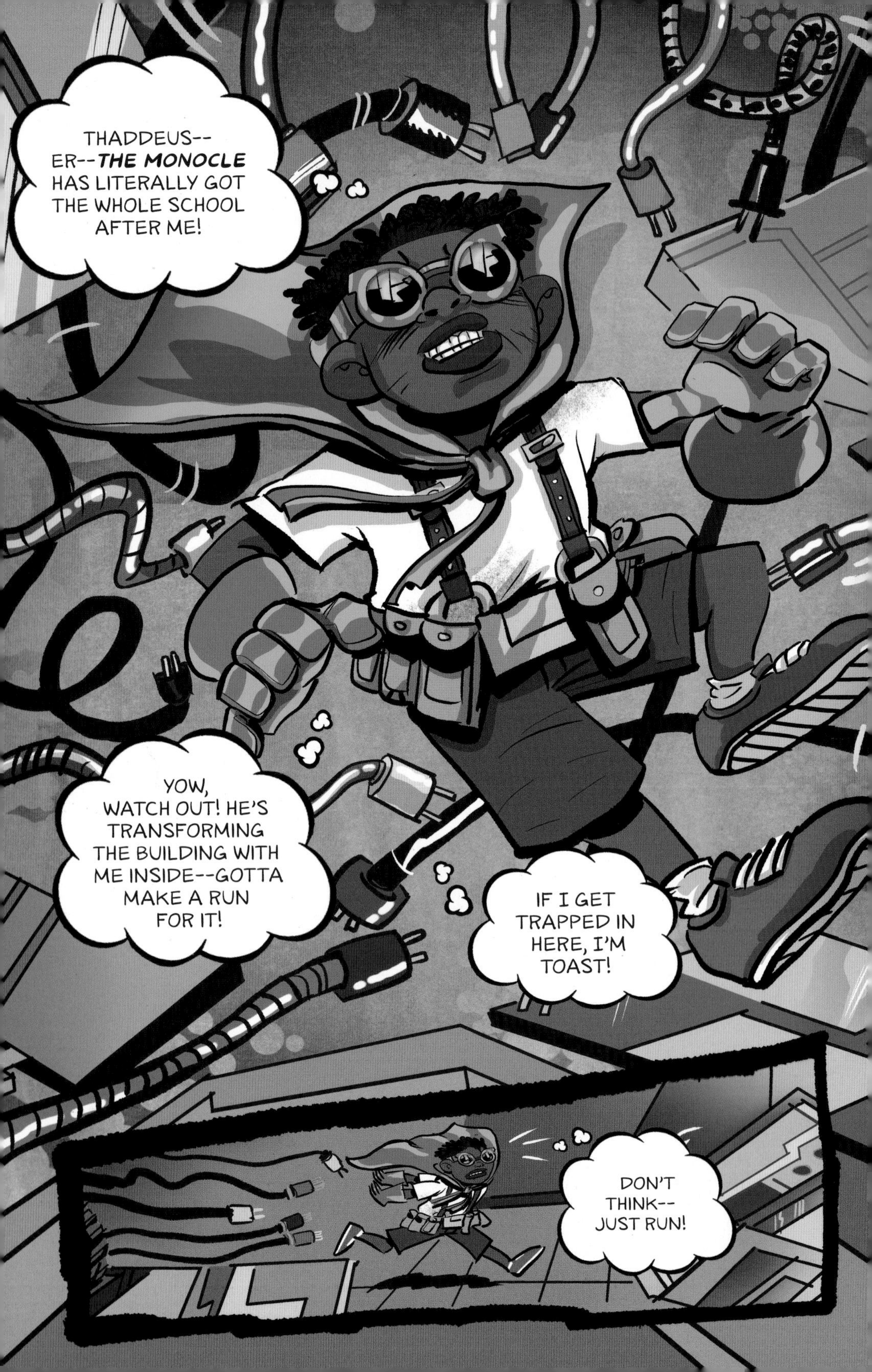
THADDEUS--ER--***THE MONOCLE*** HAS LITERALLY GOT THE WHOLE SCHOOL AFTER ME!
YOW, WATCH OUT! HE'S TRANSFORMING THE BUILDING WITH ME INSIDE--GOTTA MAKE A RUN FOR IT!
IF I GET TRAPPED IN HERE, I'M TOAST!
DON'T THINK--JUST RUN!

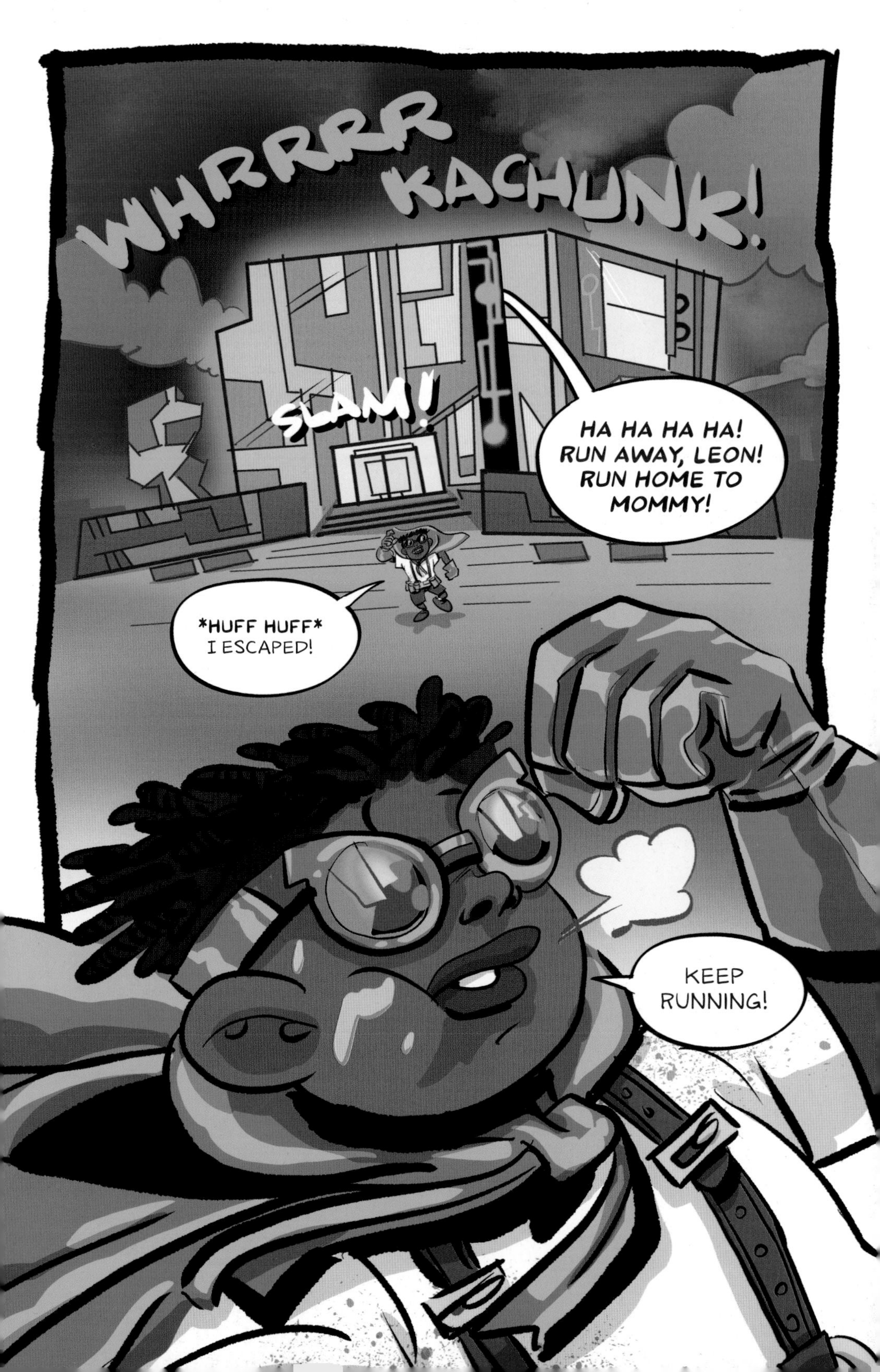
WHRRRR KACHUNK!
SLAM!
HA HA HA HA! RUN AWAY, LEON! RUN HOME TO MOMMY!
HUFF HUFF I ESCAPED!
KEEP RUNNING!

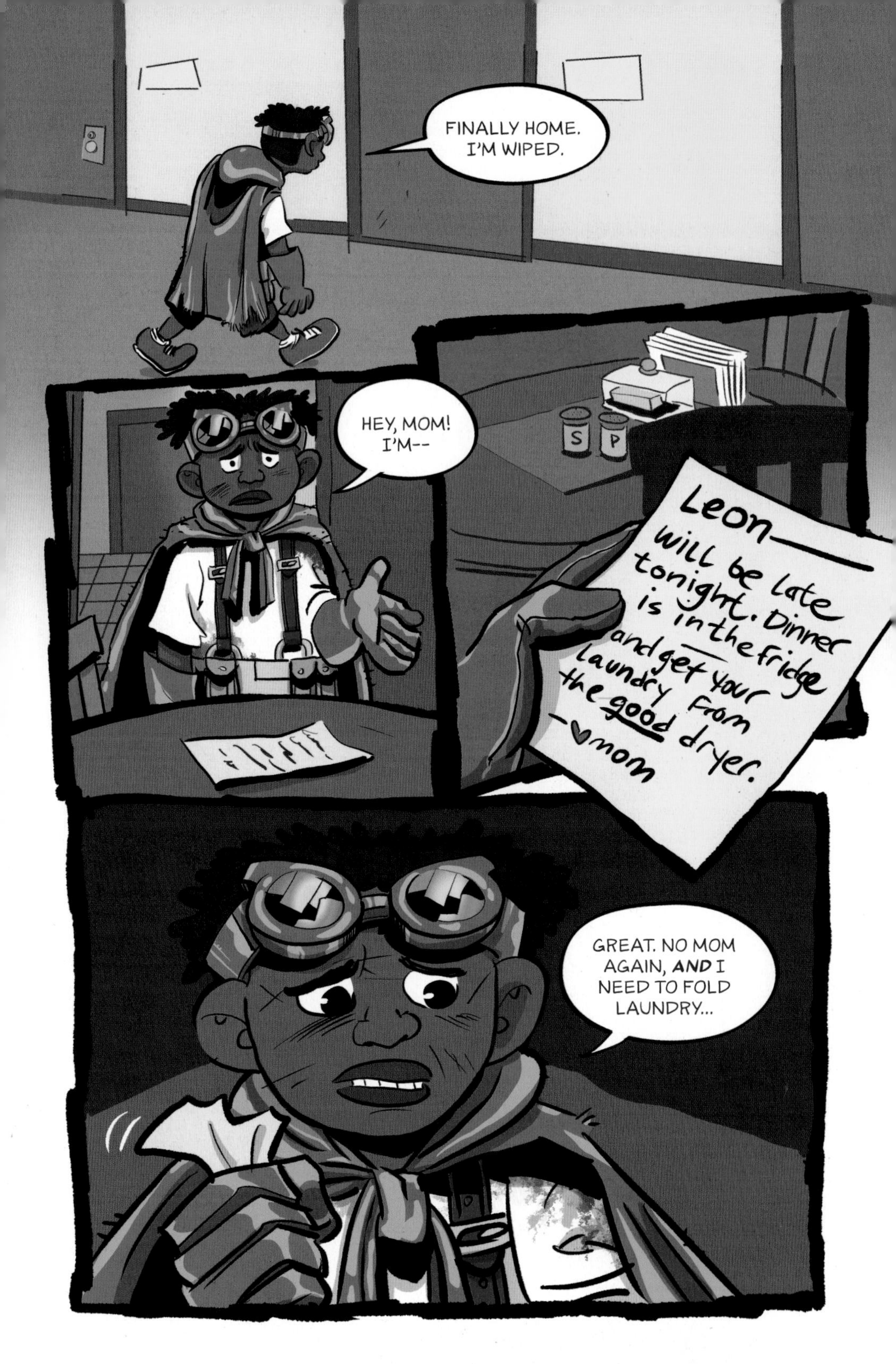
FINALLY HOME. I'M WIPED.
HEY, MOM! I'M--
Leon—
will be late tonight. Dinner is in the fridge
and get your laundry from the good dryer.
—♥mom
GREAT. NO MOM AGAIN, **AND** I NEED TO FOLD LAUNDRY...

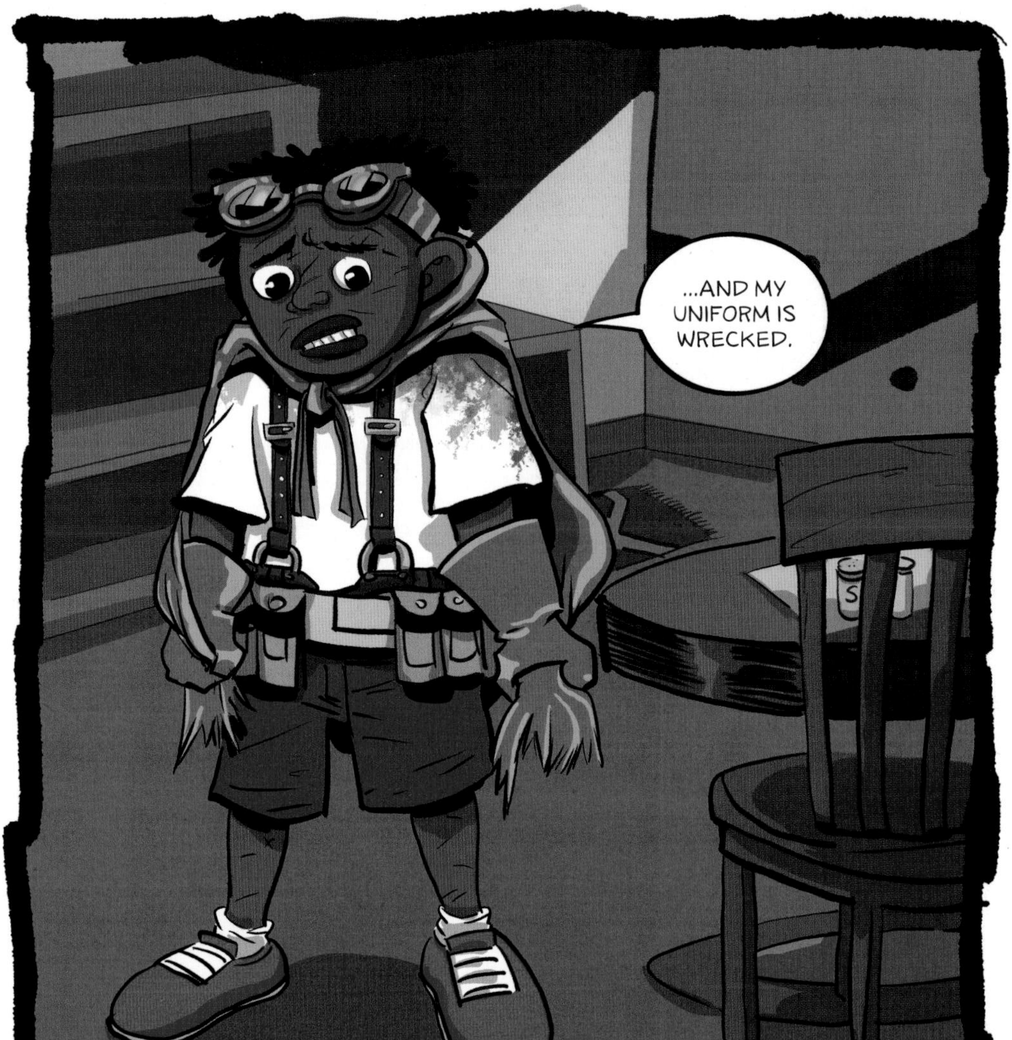
...AND MY UNIFORM IS WRECKED.

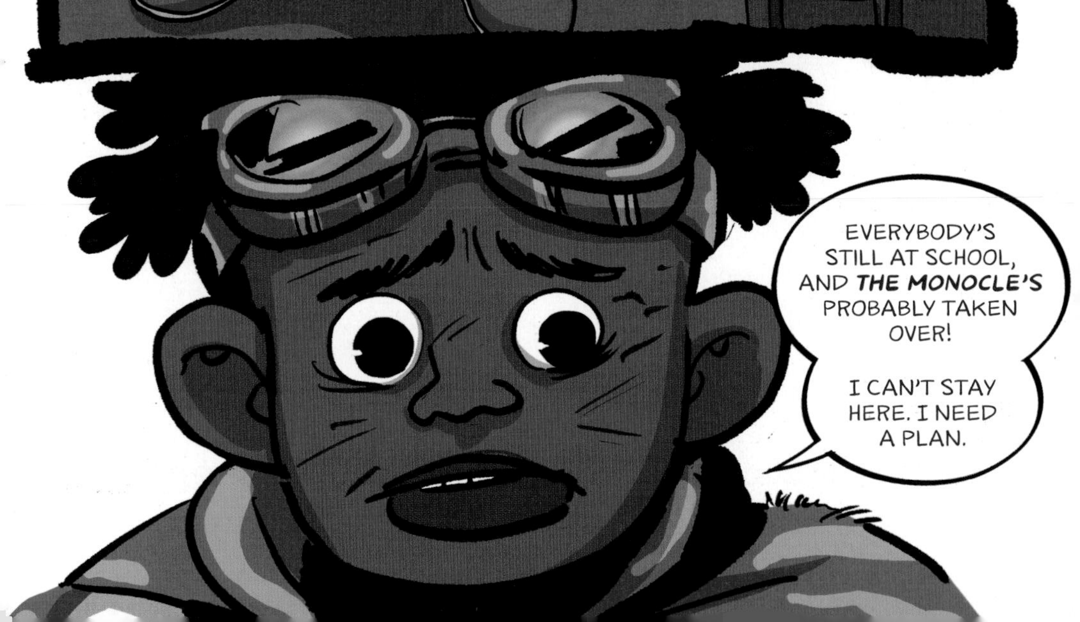
EVERYBODY'S STILL AT SCHOOL, AND ***THE MONOCLE'S*** PROBABLY TAKEN OVER!
I CAN'T STAY HERE. I NEED A PLAN.

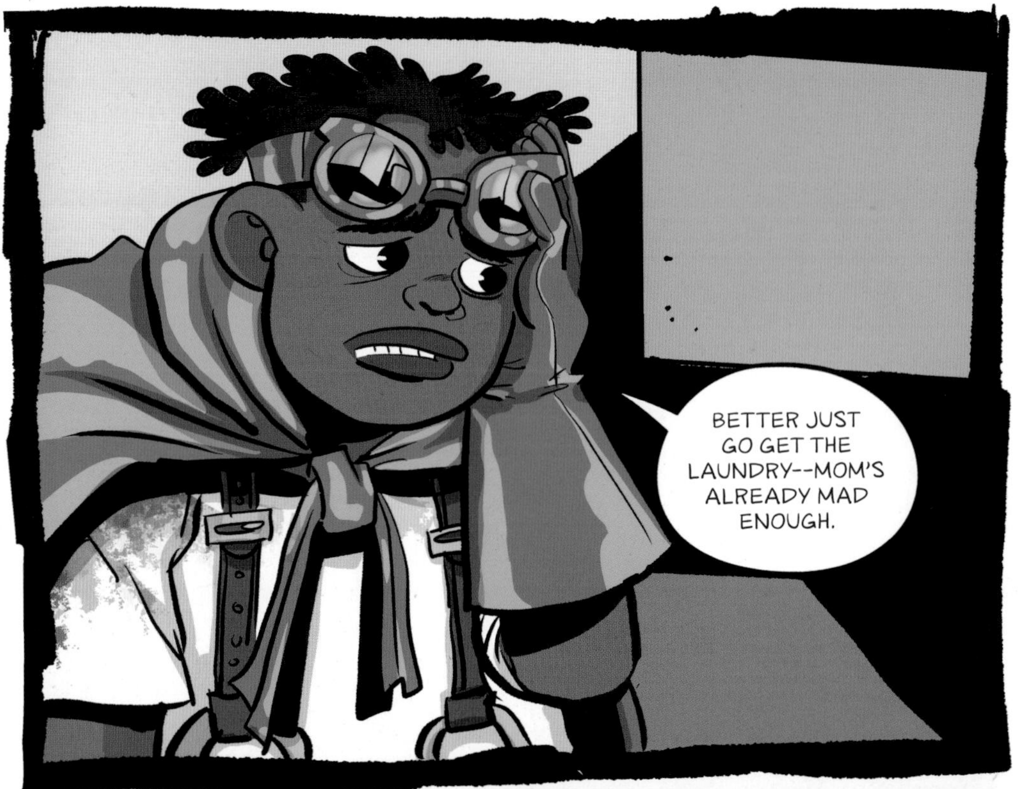
BETTER JUST GO GET THE LAUNDRY--MOM'S ALREADY MAD ENOUGH.

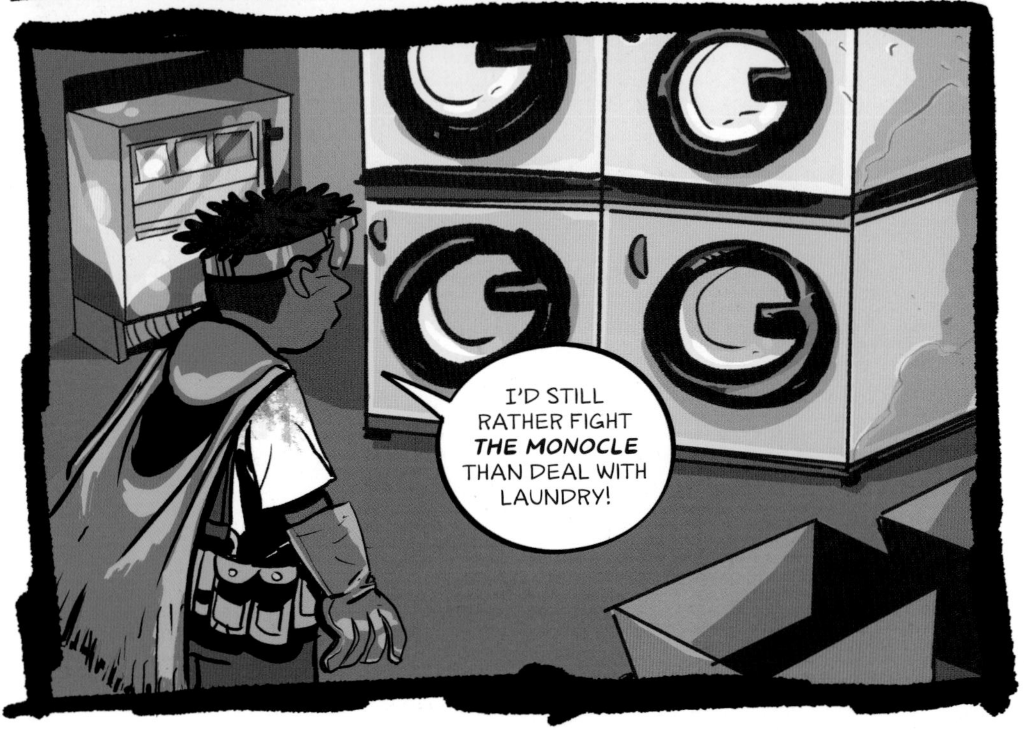
I'D STILL RATHER FIGHT **THE MONOCLE** THAN DEAL WITH LAUNDRY!

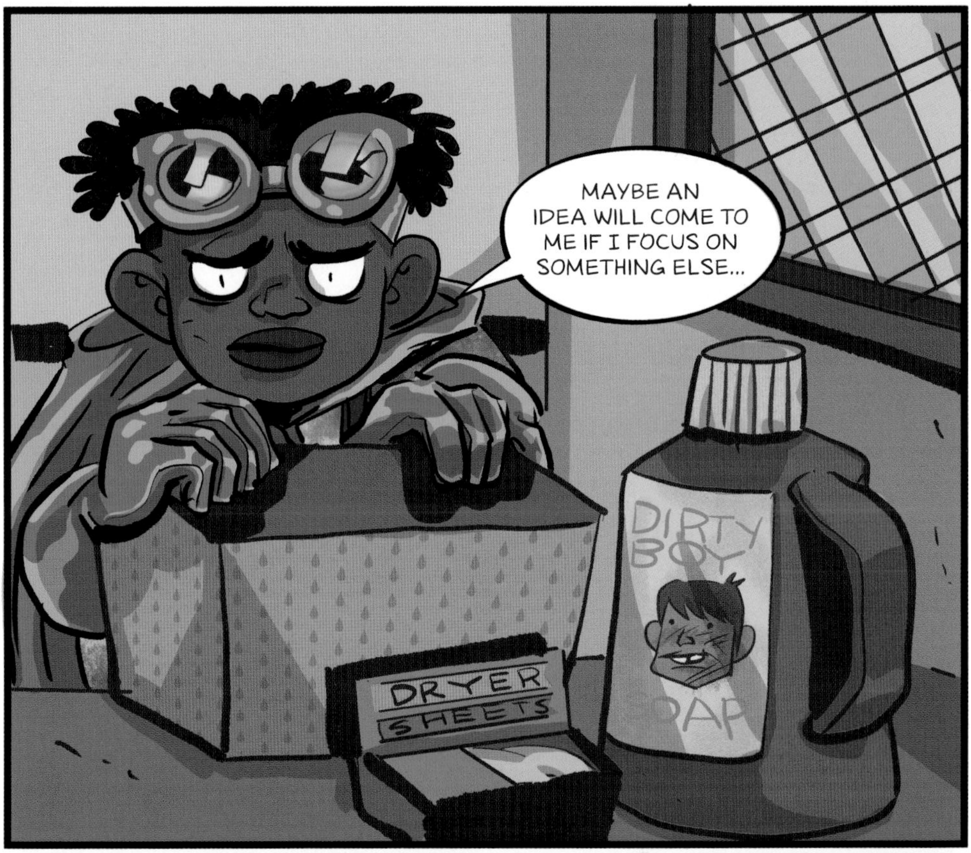
MAYBE AN IDEA WILL COME TO ME IF I FOCUS ON SOMETHING ELSE...
DRYER SHEETS
DIRTY BOY SOAP

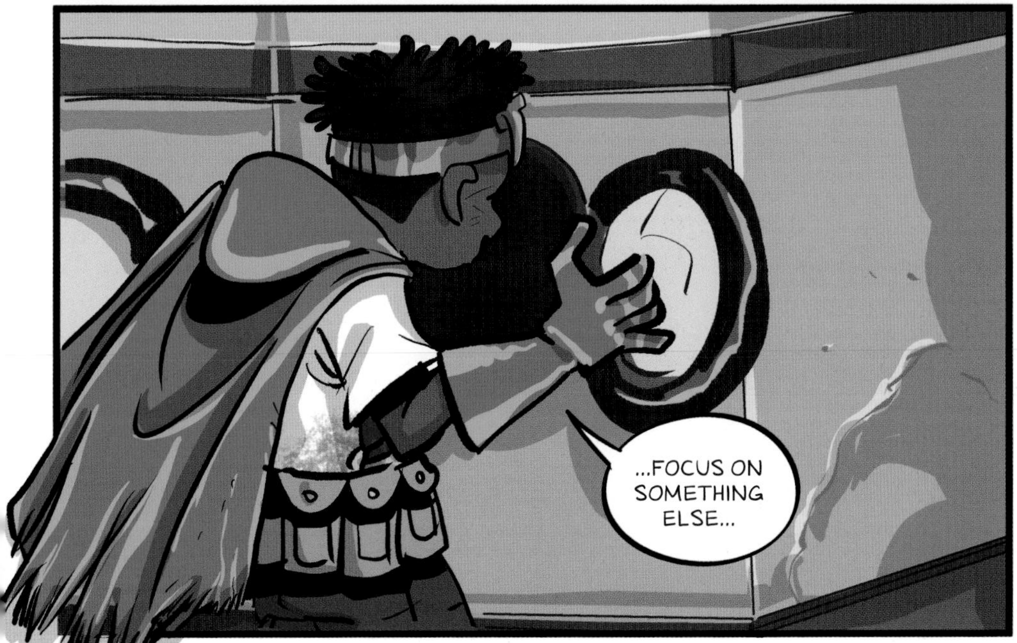
...FOCUS ON SOMETHING ELSE...

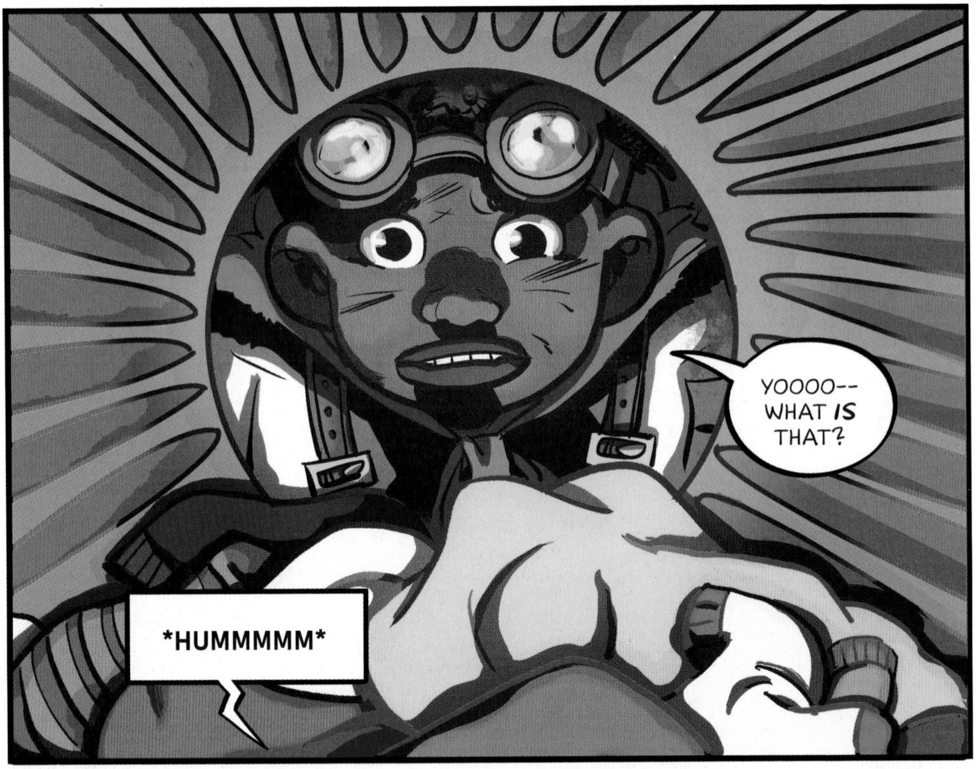
YOOOO--
WHAT IS
THAT?
HUMMMMM

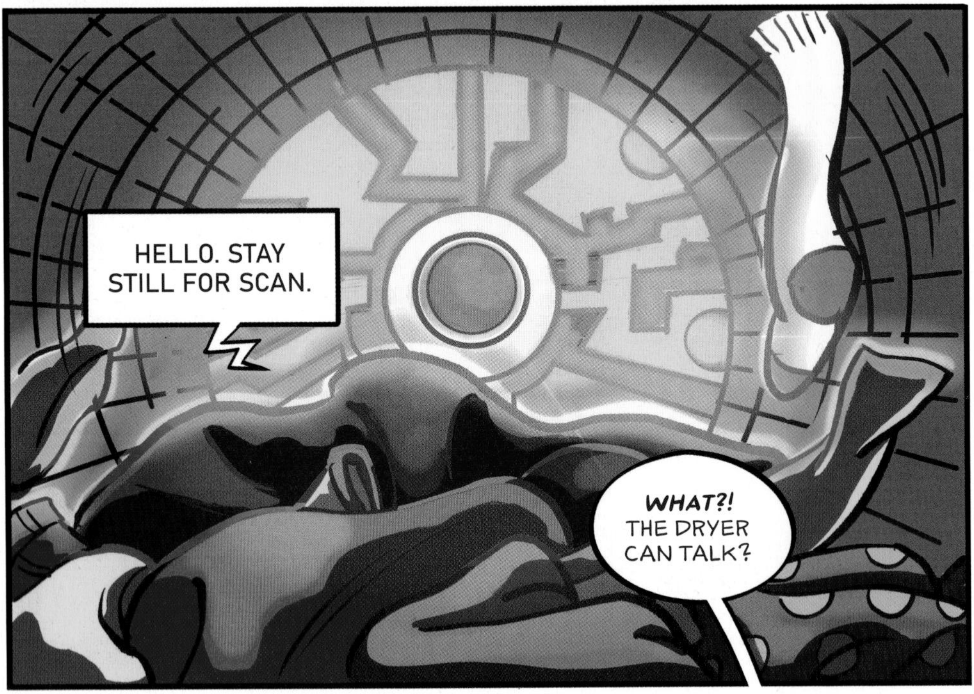
HELLO. STAY
STILL FOR SCAN.
WHAT?!
THE DRYER
CAN TALK?

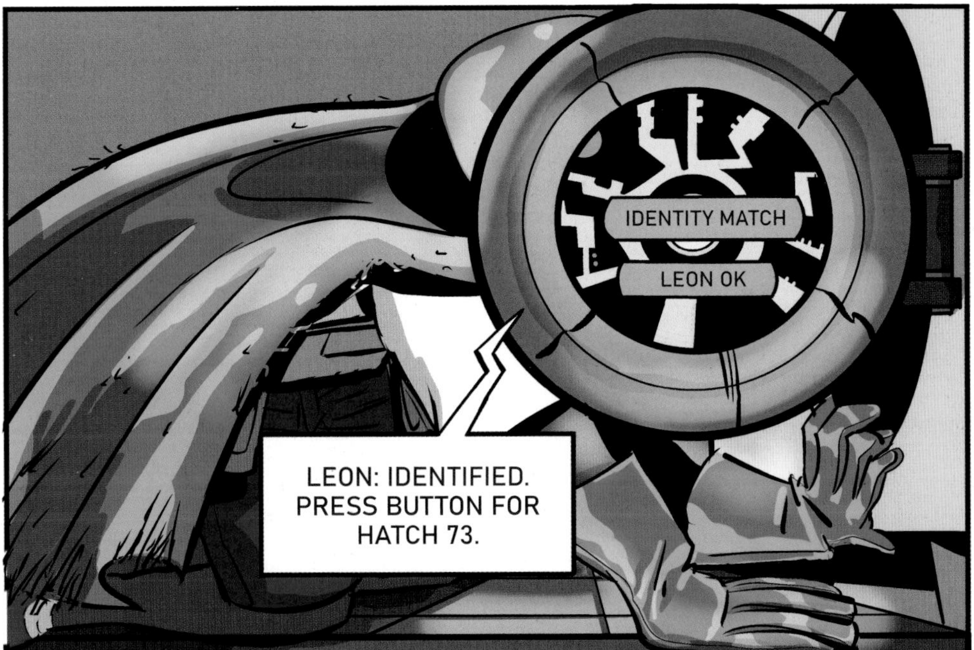
IDENTITY MATCH
LEON OK
LEON: IDENTIFIED. PRESS BUTTON FOR HATCH 73.

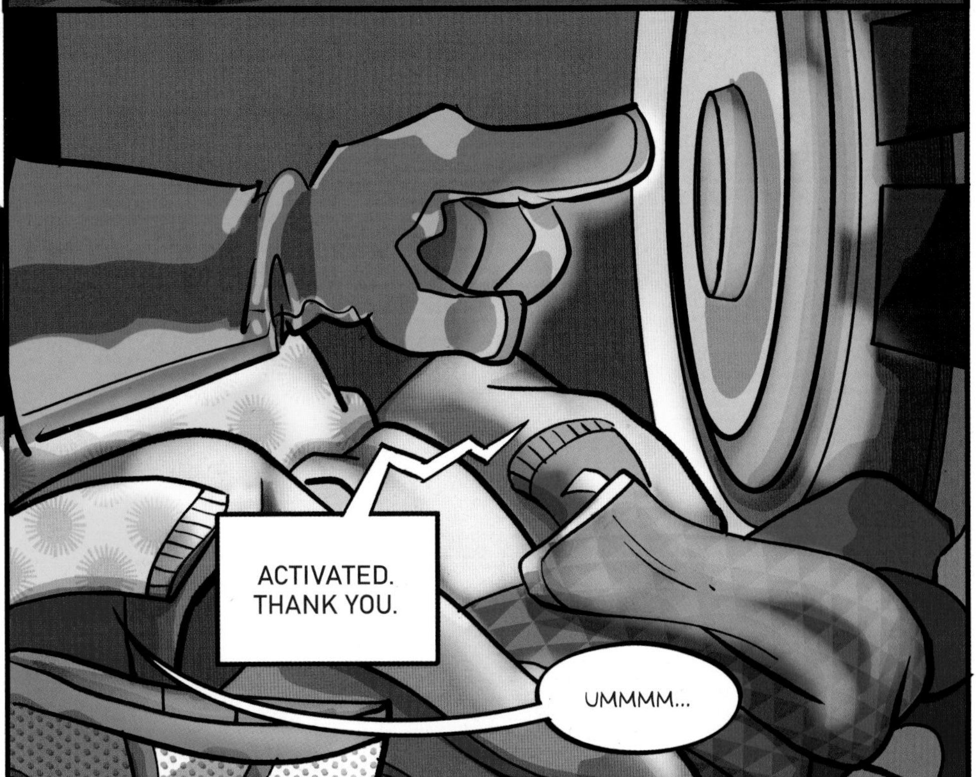
ACTIVATED. THANK YOU.
UMMMM...

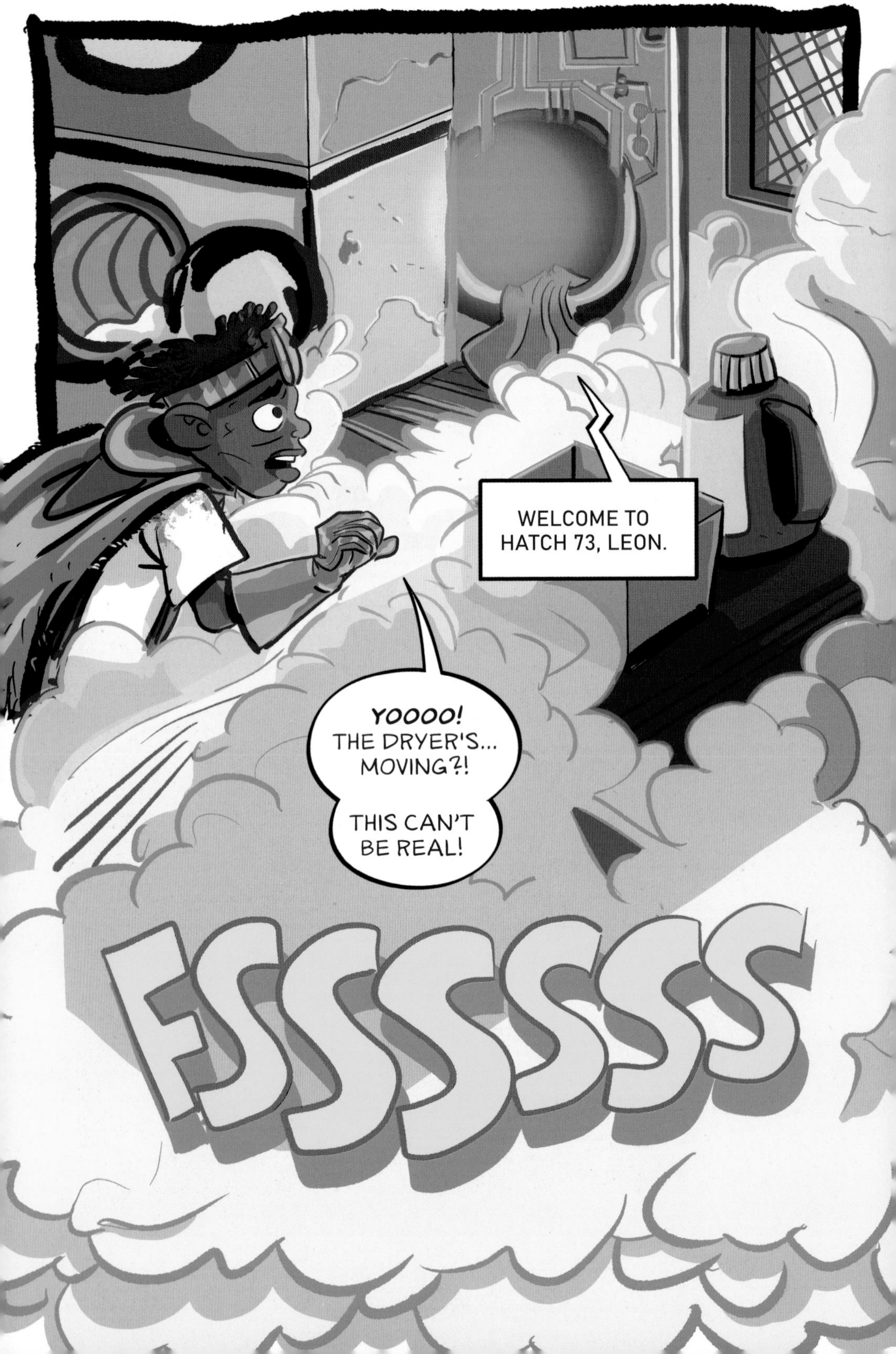
WELCOME TO HATCH 73, LEON.
YOOOO! THE DRYER'S... MOVING?!
THIS CAN'T BE REAL!
FSSSSSS

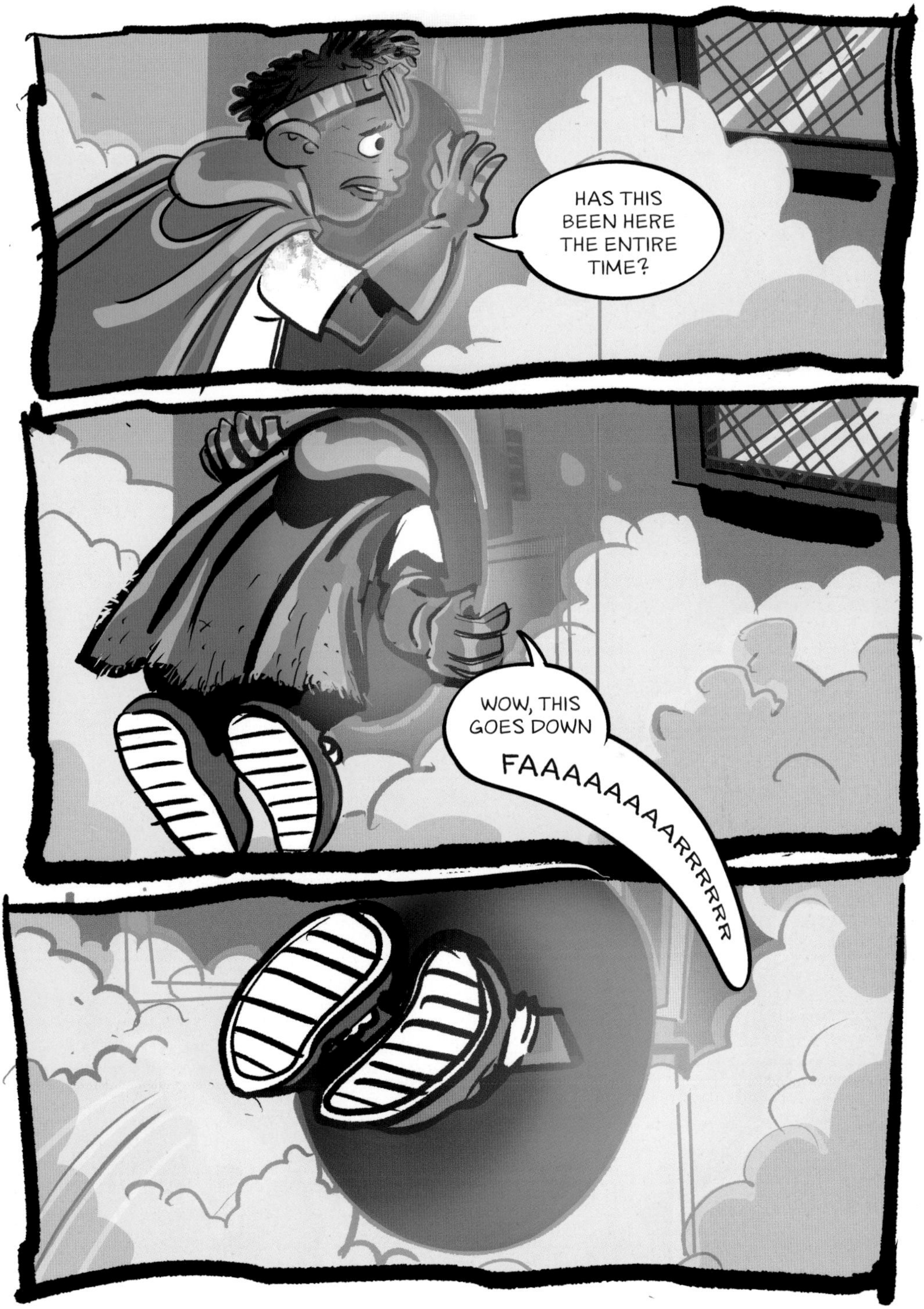
HAS THIS BEEN HERE THE ENTIRE TIME?
WOW, THIS GOES DOWN
FAAAAAAAAARRRRRR

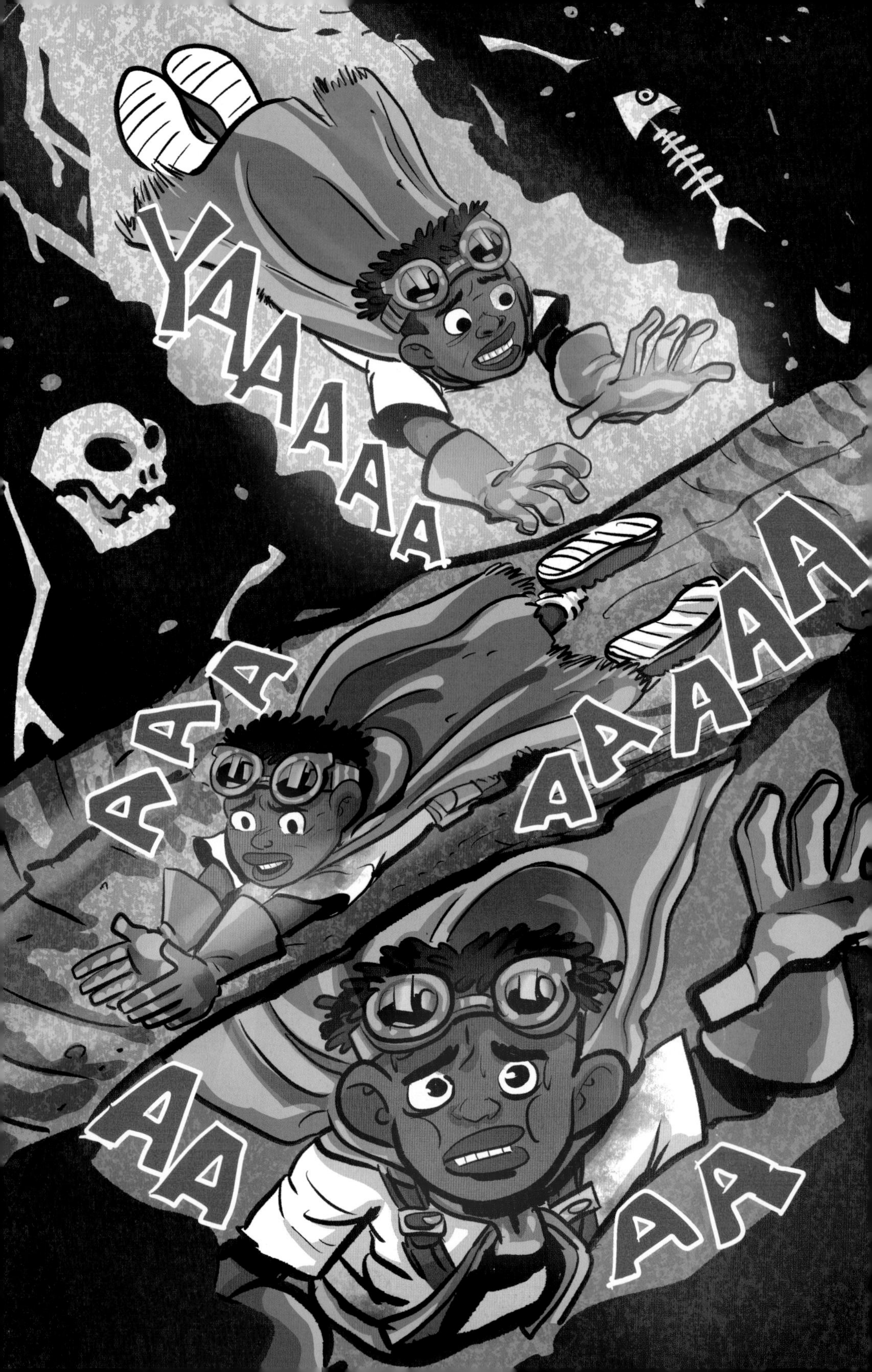
YAAAAAAA
AAAA
AAAAAAAA
AA
AA

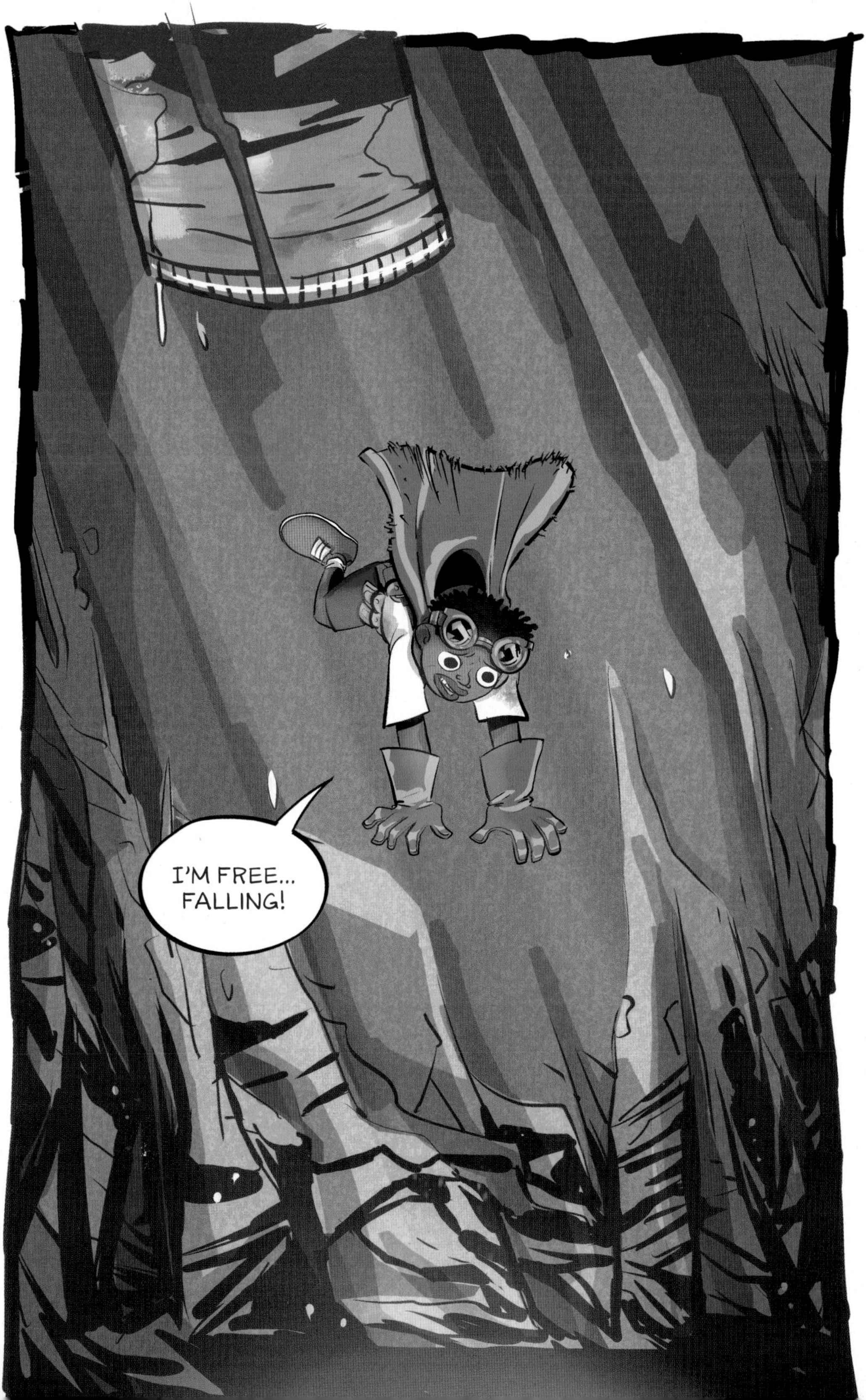
I'M FREE... FALLING!

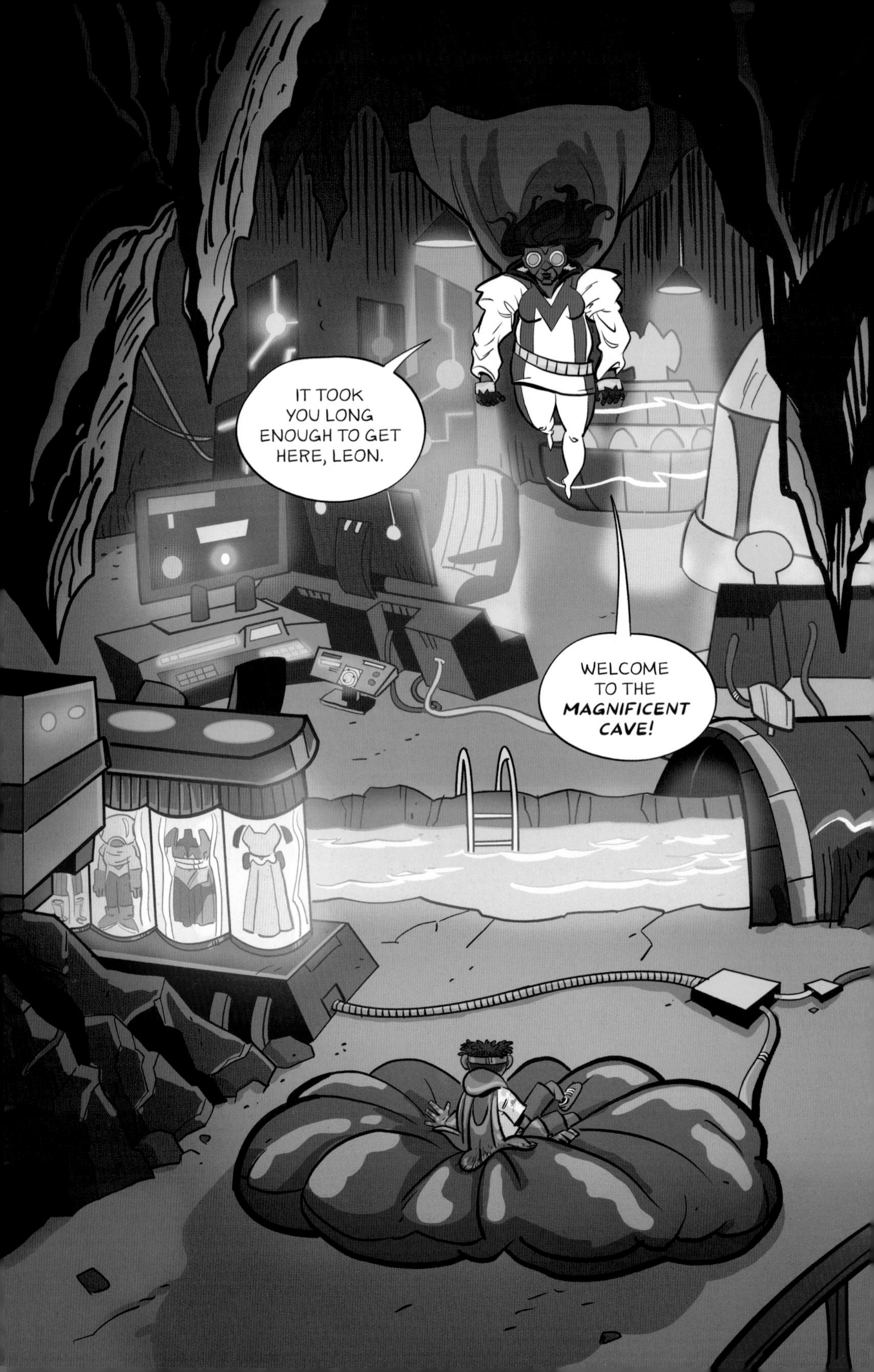
IT TOOK YOU LONG ENOUGH TO GET HERE, LEON.
WELCOME TO THE **MAGNIFICENT CAVE!**

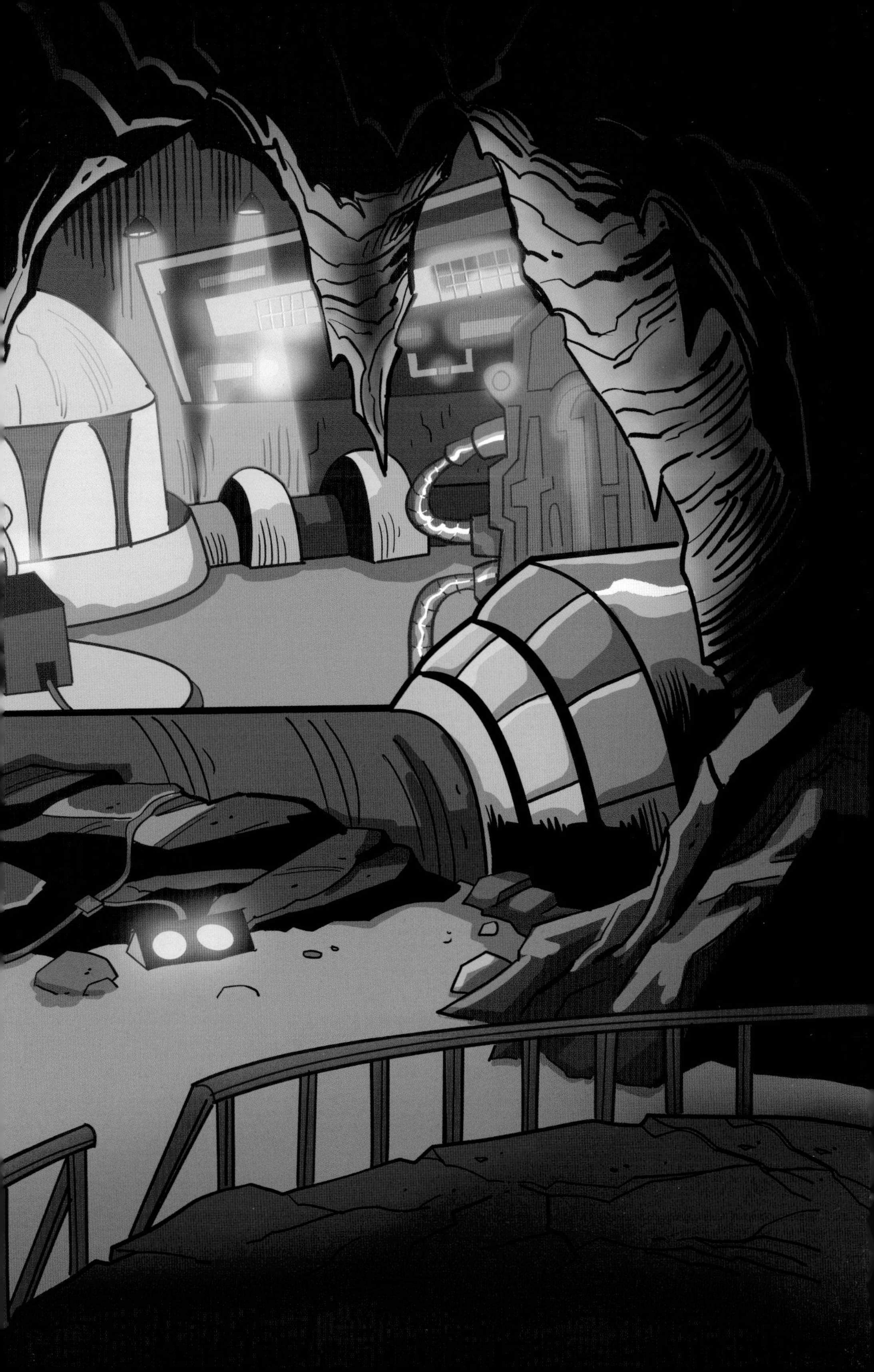

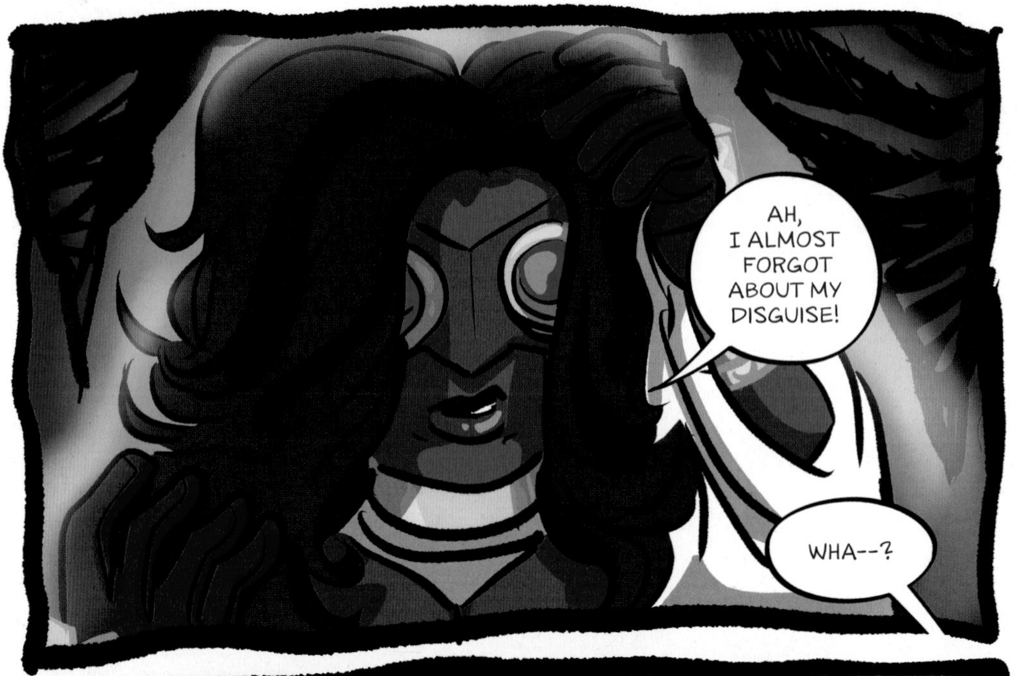
AH, I ALMOST FORGOT ABOUT MY DISGUISE!
WHA--?

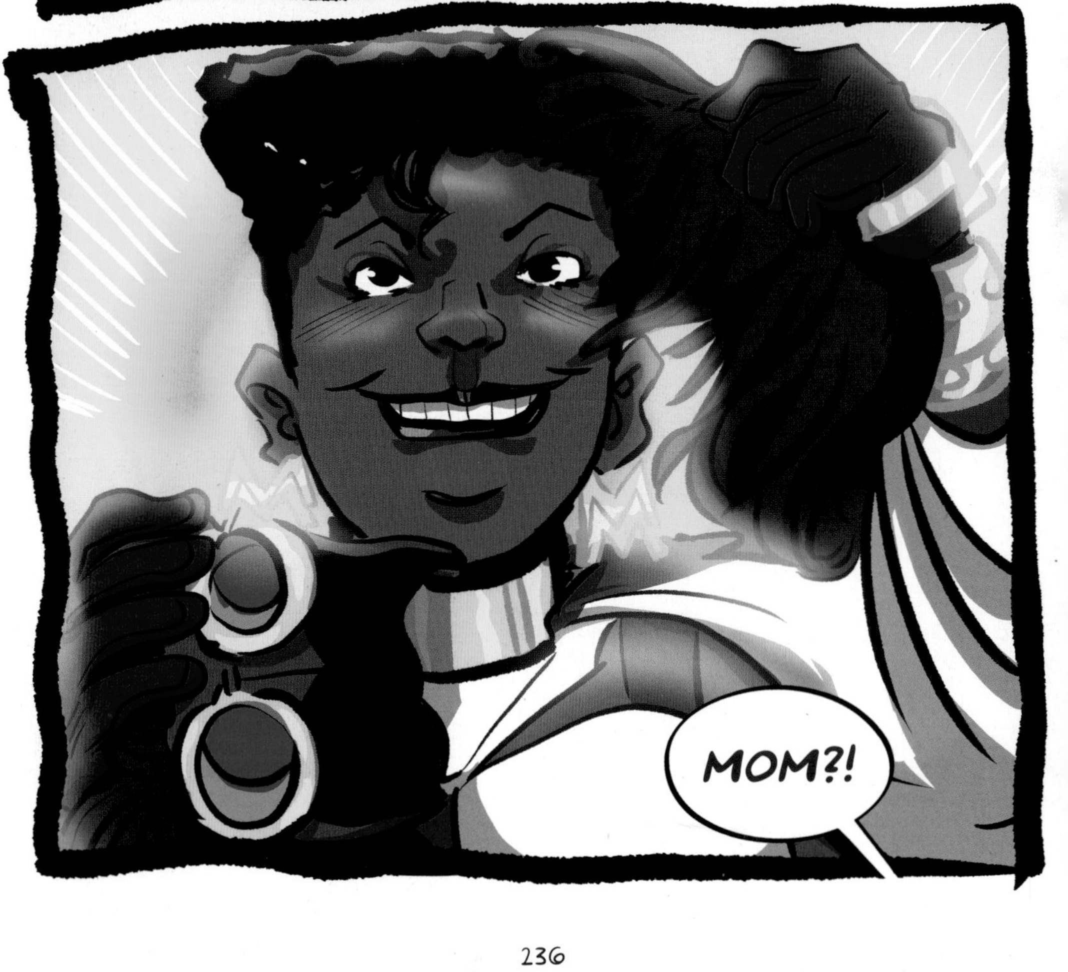
MOM?!

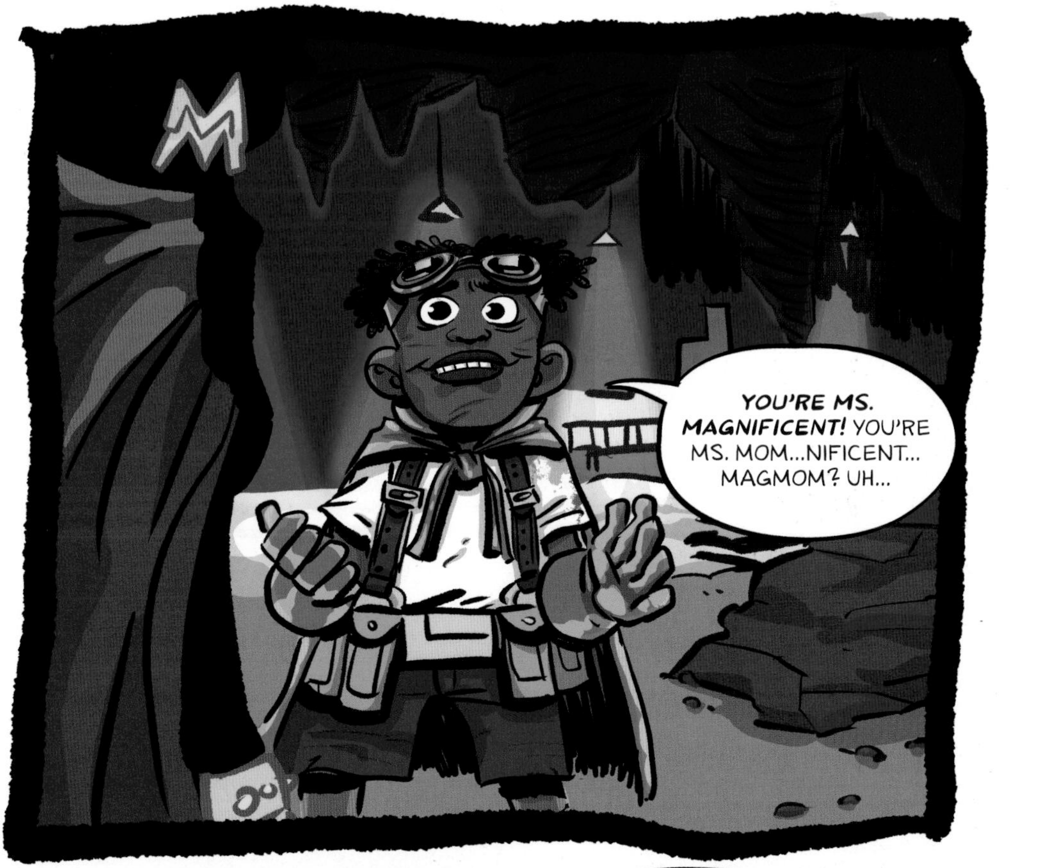
YOU'RE MS. MAGNIFICENT! YOU'RE MS. MOM...NIFICENT... MAGMOM? UH...

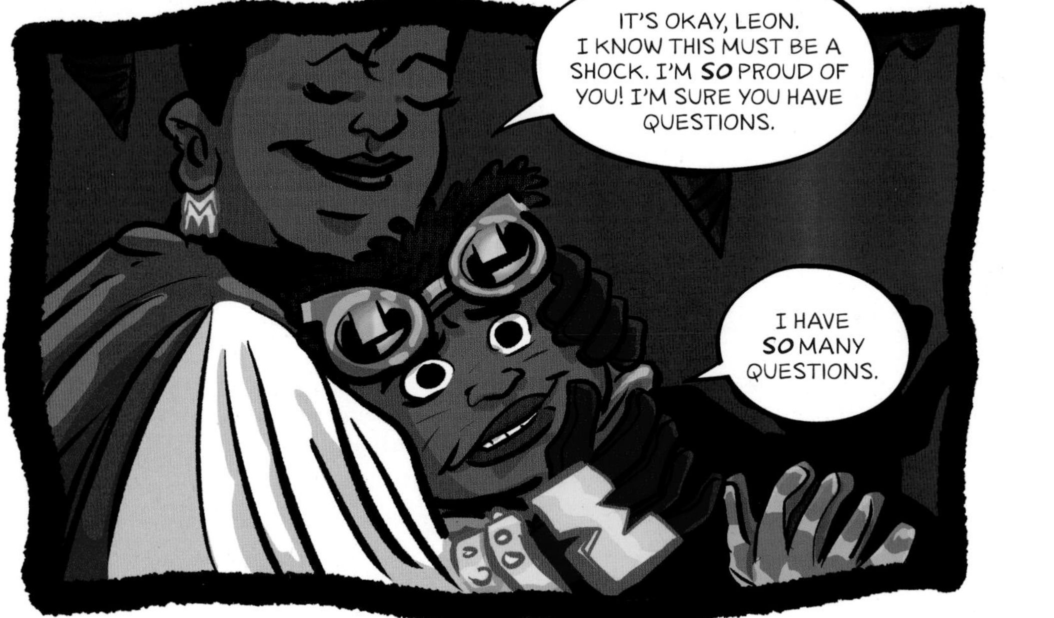
IT'S OKAY, LEON. I KNOW THIS MUST BE A SHOCK. I'M **SO** PROUD OF YOU! I'M SURE YOU HAVE QUESTIONS.
I HAVE **SO** MANY QUESTIONS.

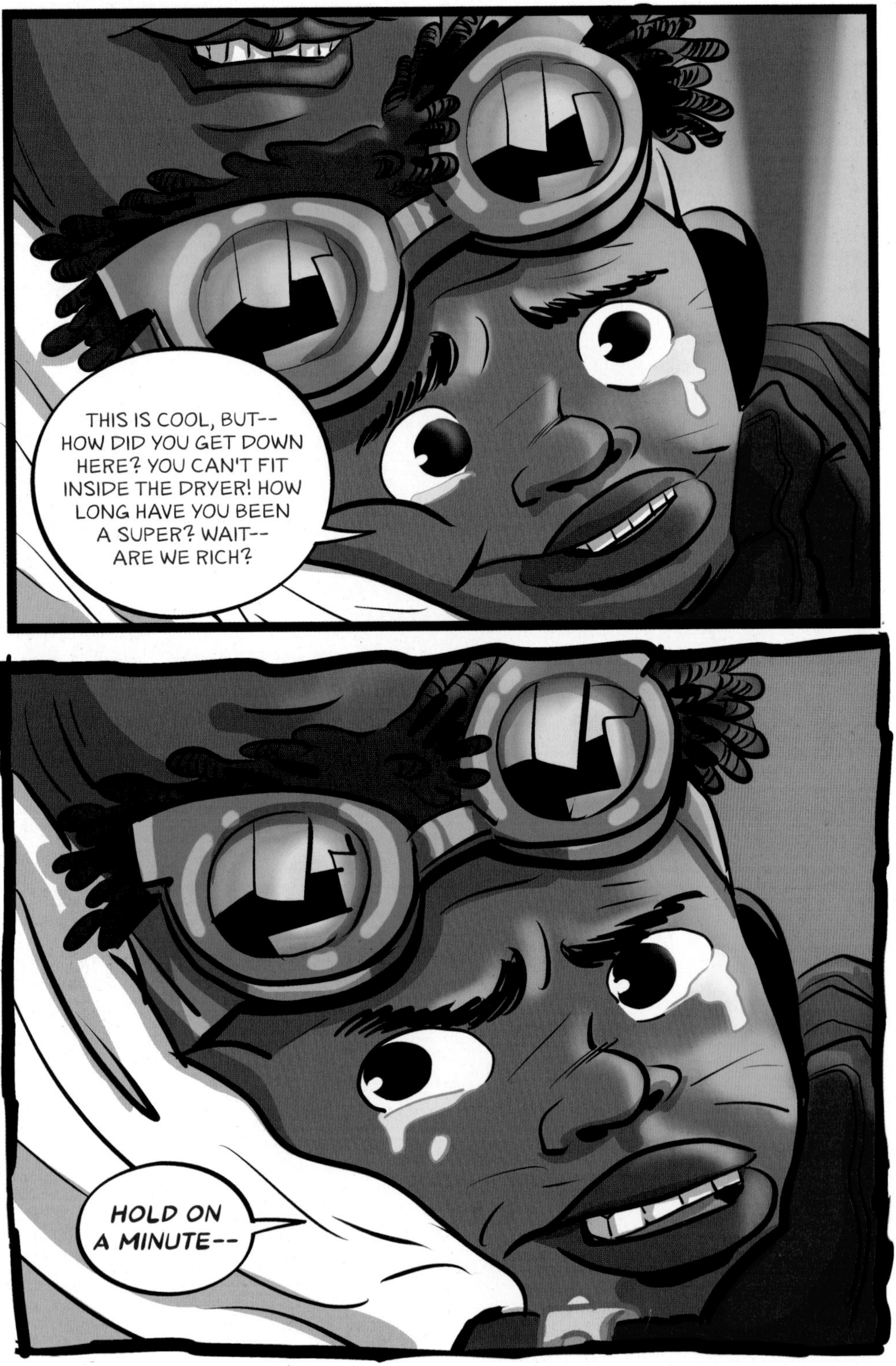
THIS IS COOL, BUT-- HOW DID YOU GET DOWN HERE? YOU CAN'T FIT INSIDE THE DRYER! HOW LONG HAVE YOU BEEN A SUPER? WAIT-- ARE WE RICH?
HOLD ON A MINUTE--

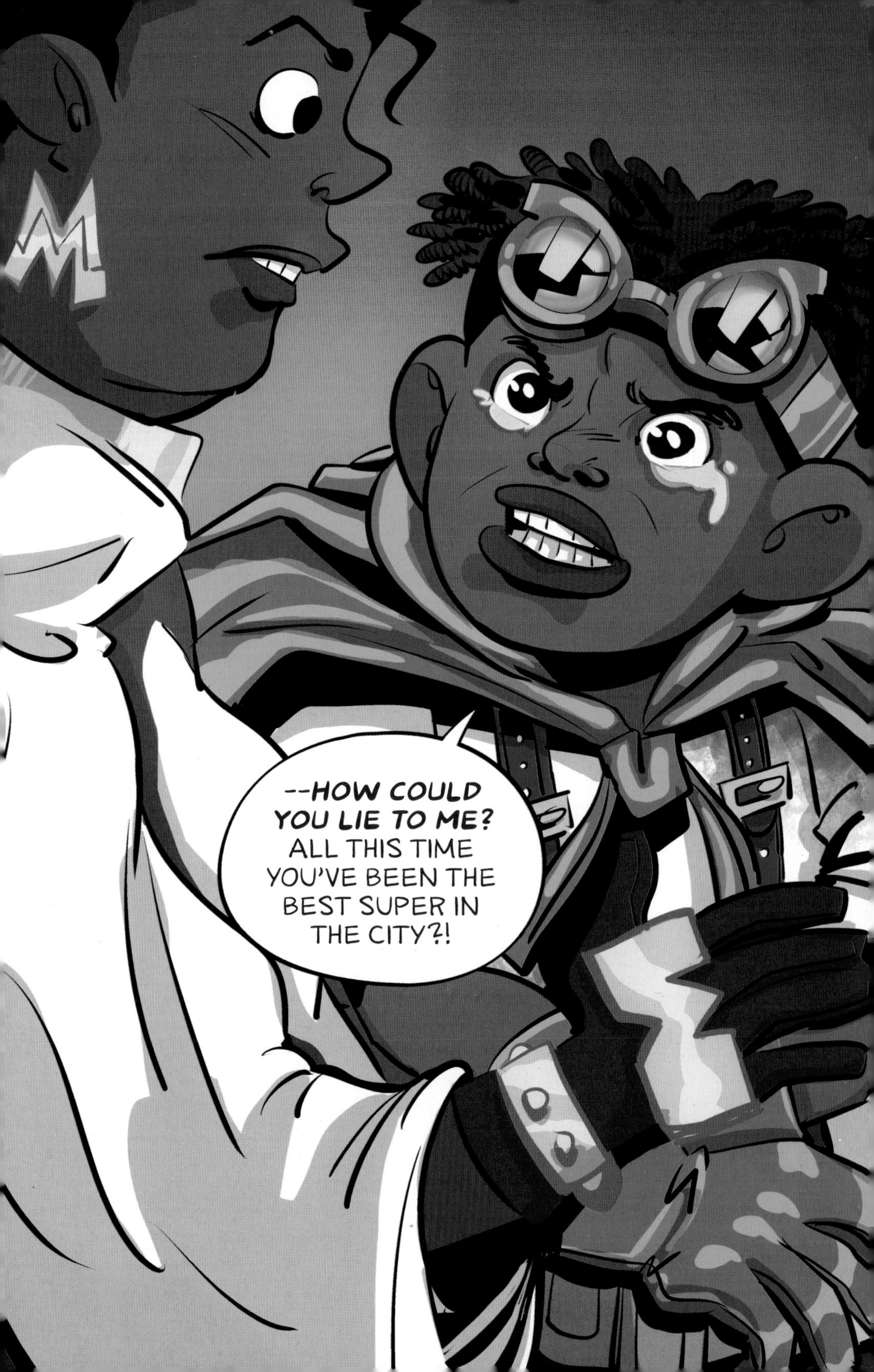
--HOW COULD YOU LIE TO ME? ALL THIS TIME YOU'VE BEEN THE BEST SUPER IN THE CITY?!

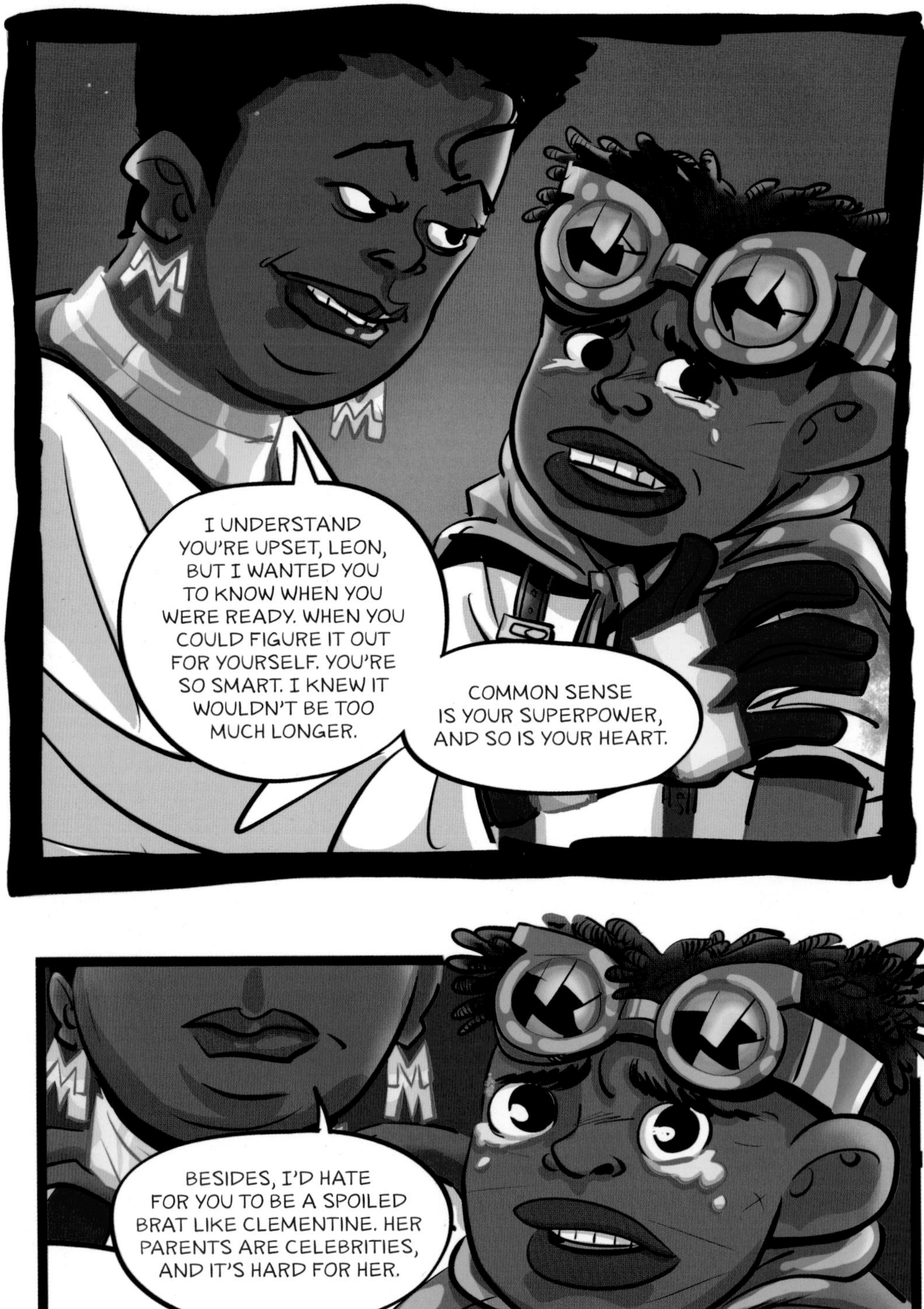
I UNDERSTAND YOU'RE UPSET, LEON, BUT I WANTED YOU TO KNOW WHEN YOU WERE READY. WHEN YOU COULD FIGURE IT OUT FOR YOURSELF. YOU'RE SO SMART. I KNEW IT WOULDN'T BE TOO MUCH LONGER.
COMMON SENSE IS YOUR SUPERPOWER, AND SO IS YOUR HEART.
BESIDES, I'D HATE FOR YOU TO BE A SPOILED BRAT LIKE CLEMENTINE. HER PARENTS ARE CELEBRITIES, AND IT'S HARD FOR HER.

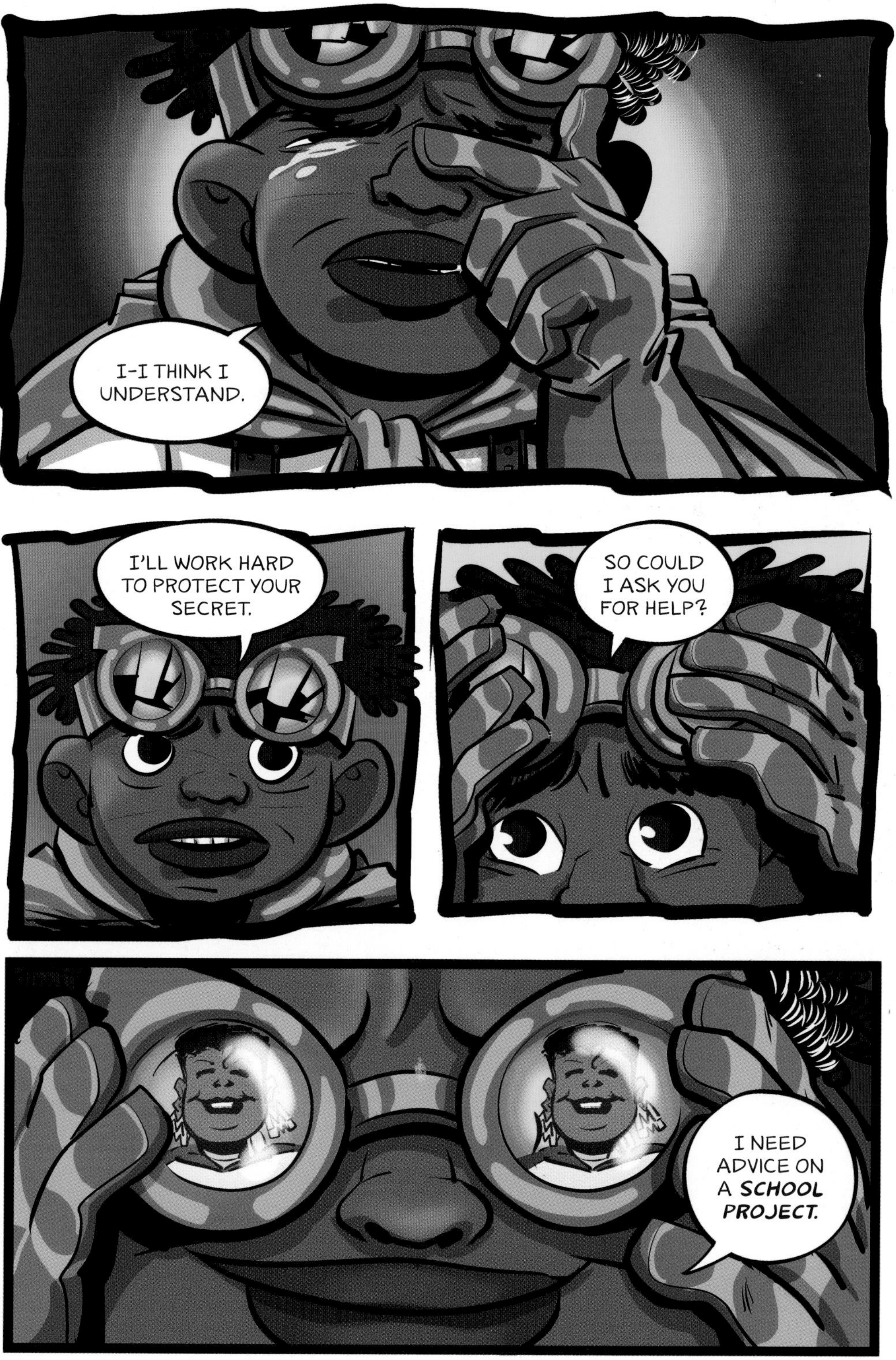
I-I THINK I UNDERSTAND.
I'LL WORK HARD TO PROTECT YOUR SECRET.
SO COULD I ASK YOU FOR HELP?
I NEED ADVICE ON A **SCHOOL PROJECT.**

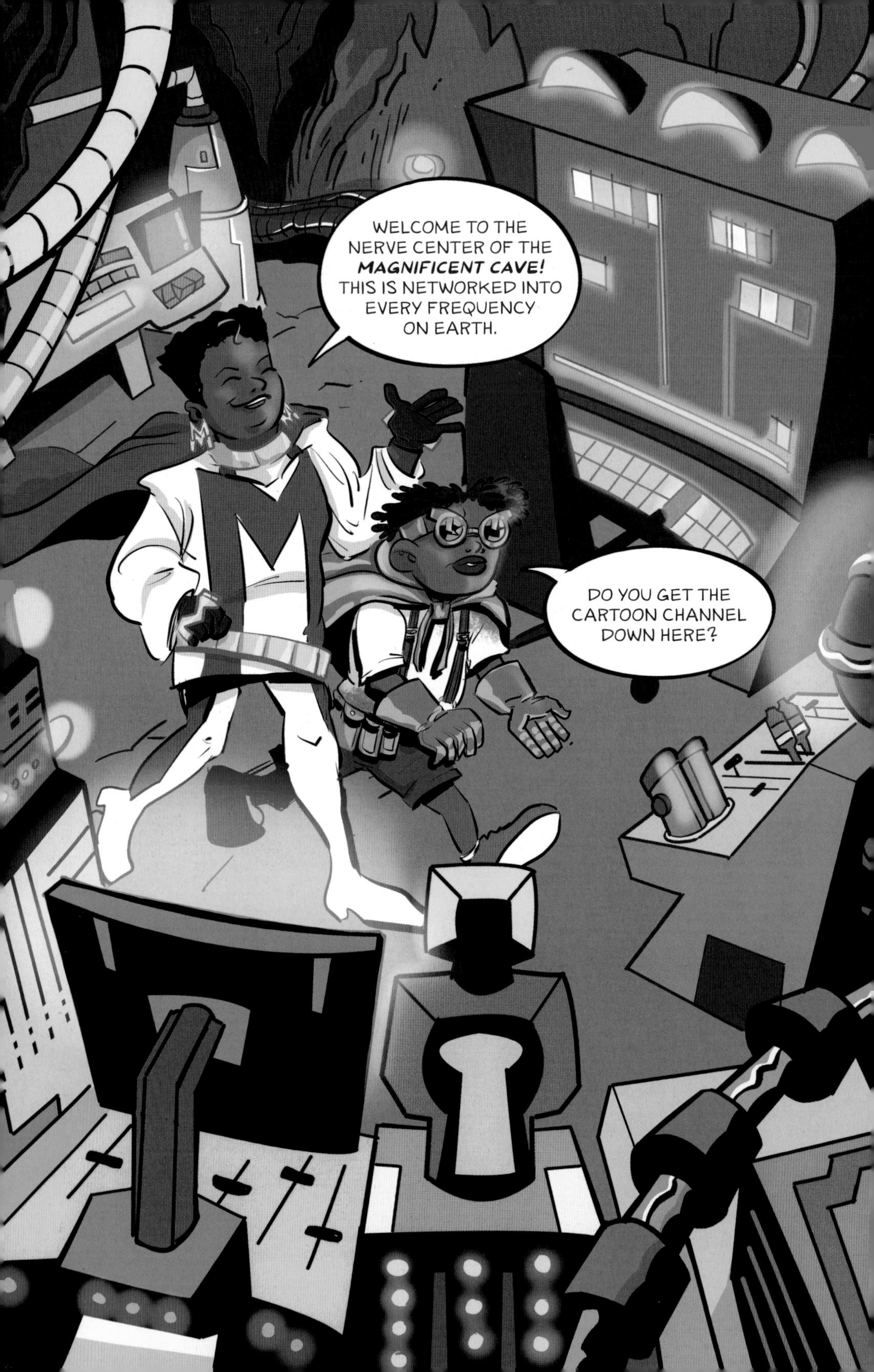
WELCOME TO THE NERVE CENTER OF THE ***MAGNIFICENT CAVE!*** THIS IS NETWORKED INTO EVERY FREQUENCY ON EARTH.
DO YOU GET THE CARTOON CHANNEL DOWN HERE?

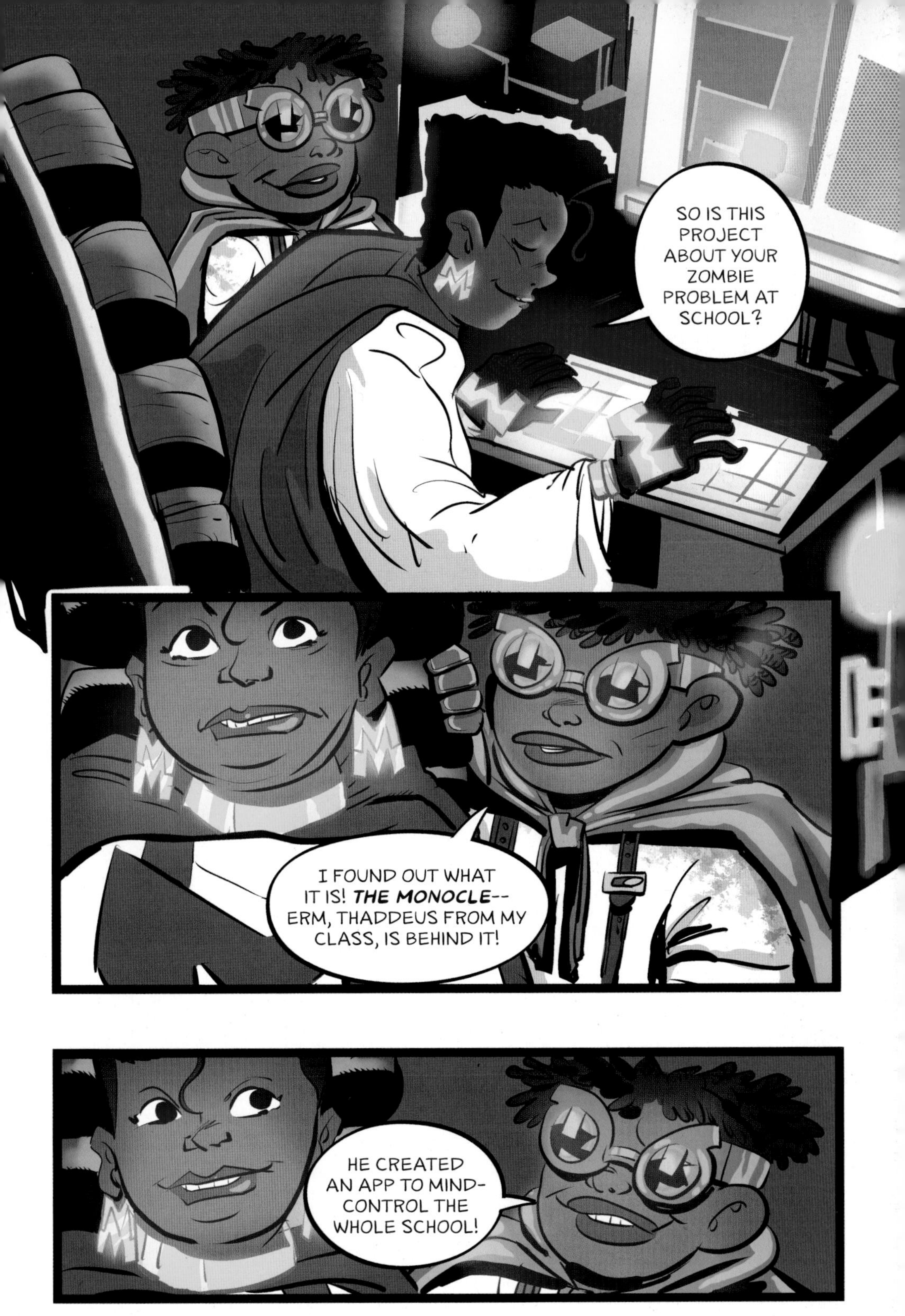
SO IS THIS PROJECT ABOUT YOUR ZOMBIE PROBLEM AT SCHOOL?
I FOUND OUT WHAT IT IS! ***THE MONOCLE***-- ERM, THADDEUS FROM MY CLASS, IS BEHIND IT!
HE CREATED AN APP TO MIND-CONTROL THE WHOLE SCHOOL!

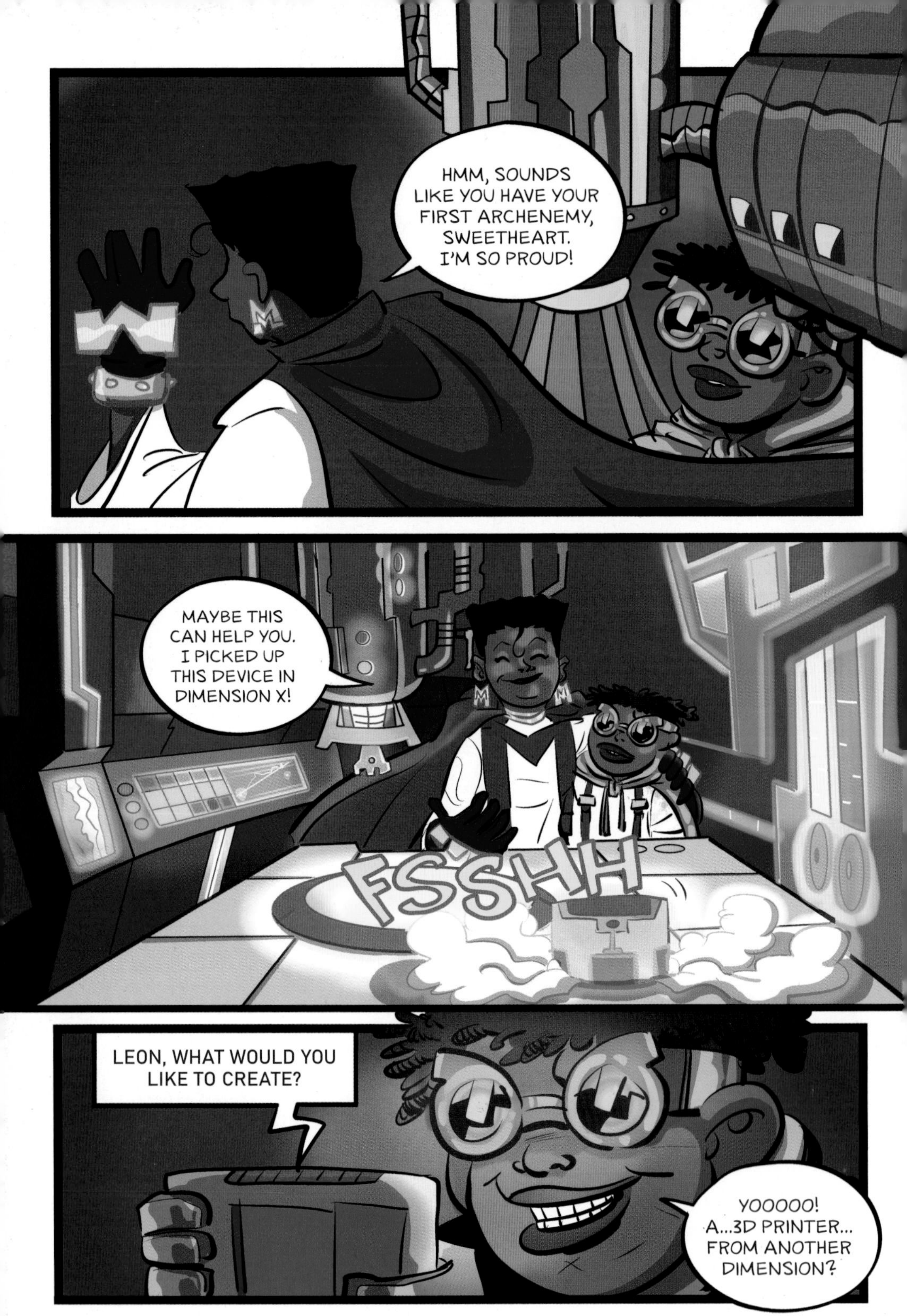
HMM, SOUNDS LIKE YOU HAVE YOUR FIRST ARCHENEMY, SWEETHEART. I'M SO PROUD!
MAYBE THIS CAN HELP YOU. I PICKED UP THIS DEVICE IN DIMENSION X!
FSSHH
LEON, WHAT WOULD YOU LIKE TO CREATE?
YOOOOO! A...3D PRINTER... FROM ANOTHER DIMENSION?

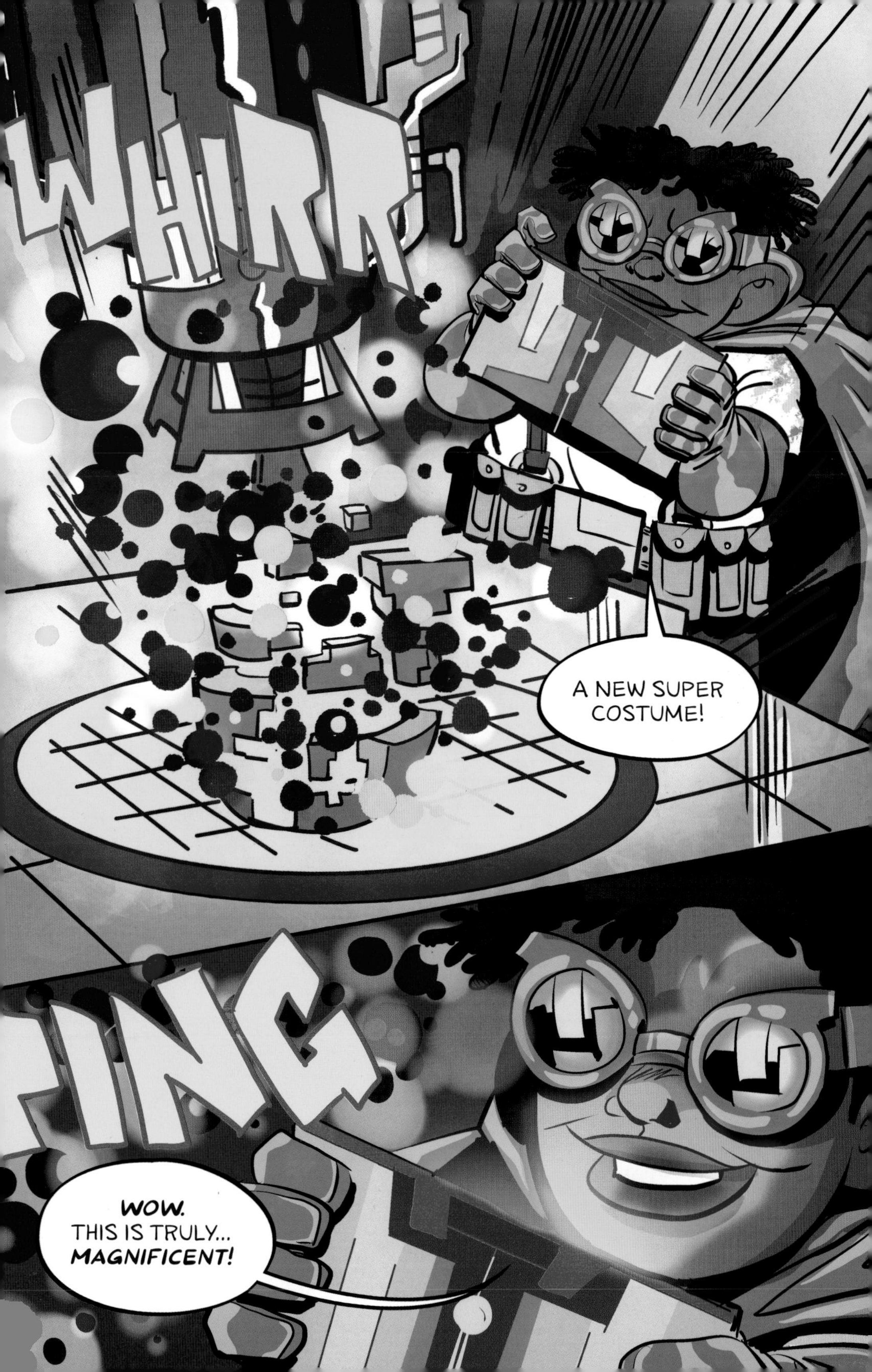
WHIRR
A NEW SUPER COSTUME!
ING
WOW. THIS IS TRULY... MAGNIFICENT!

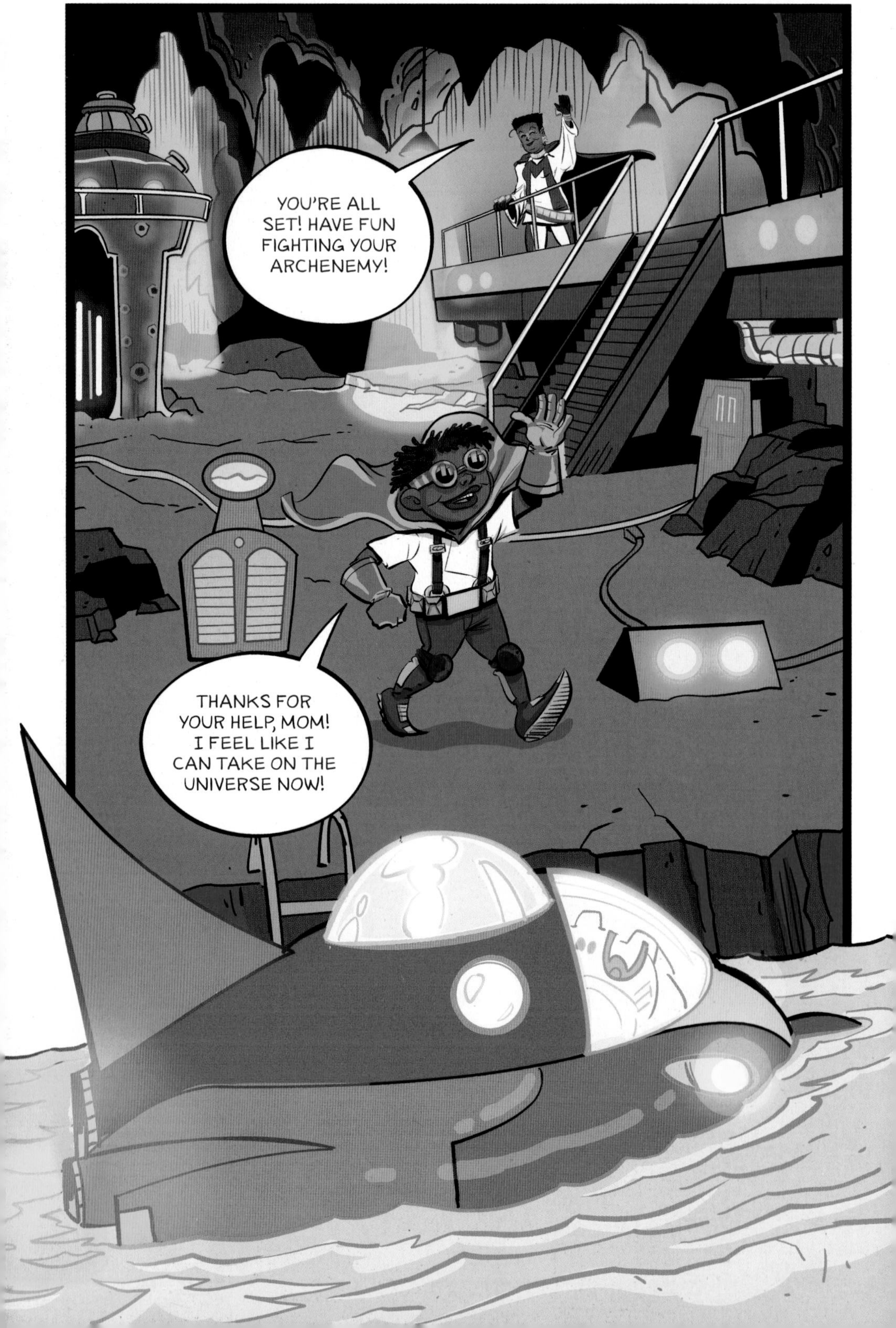
YOU'RE ALL SET! HAVE FUN FIGHTING YOUR ARCHENEMY!
THANKS FOR YOUR HELP, MOM! I FEEL LIKE I CAN TAKE ON THE UNIVERSE NOW!

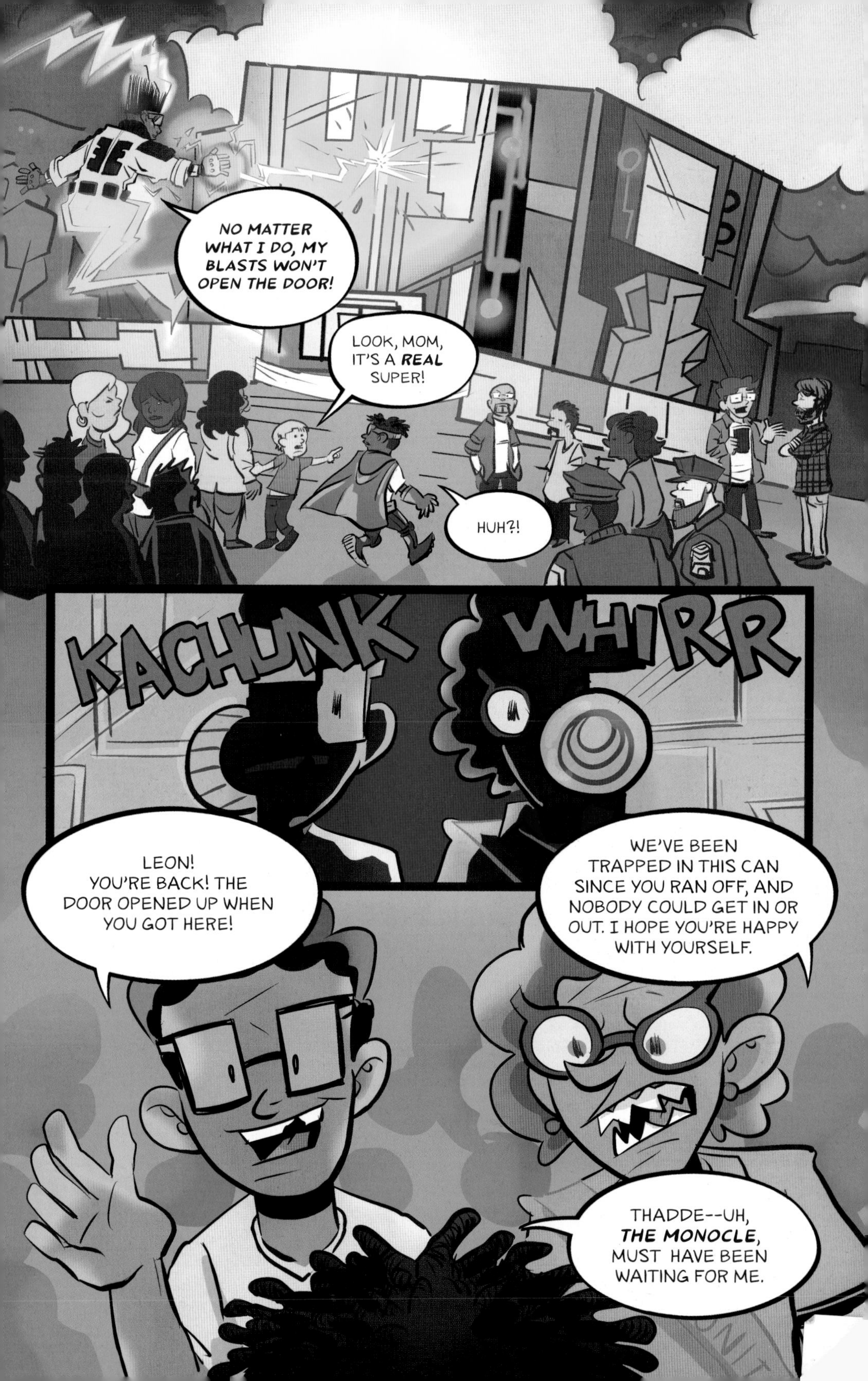
NO MATTER WHAT I DO, MY BLASTS WON'T OPEN THE DOOR!
LOOK, MOM, IT'S A **REAL** SUPER!
HUH?!
KACHUNK
WHIRR
LEON! YOU'RE BACK! THE DOOR OPENED UP WHEN YOU GOT HERE!
WE'VE BEEN TRAPPED IN THIS CAN SINCE YOU RAN OFF, AND NOBODY COULD GET IN OR OUT. I HOPE YOU'RE HAPPY WITH YOURSELF.
THADDE--UH, **THE MONOCLE**, MUST HAVE BEEN WAITING FOR ME.

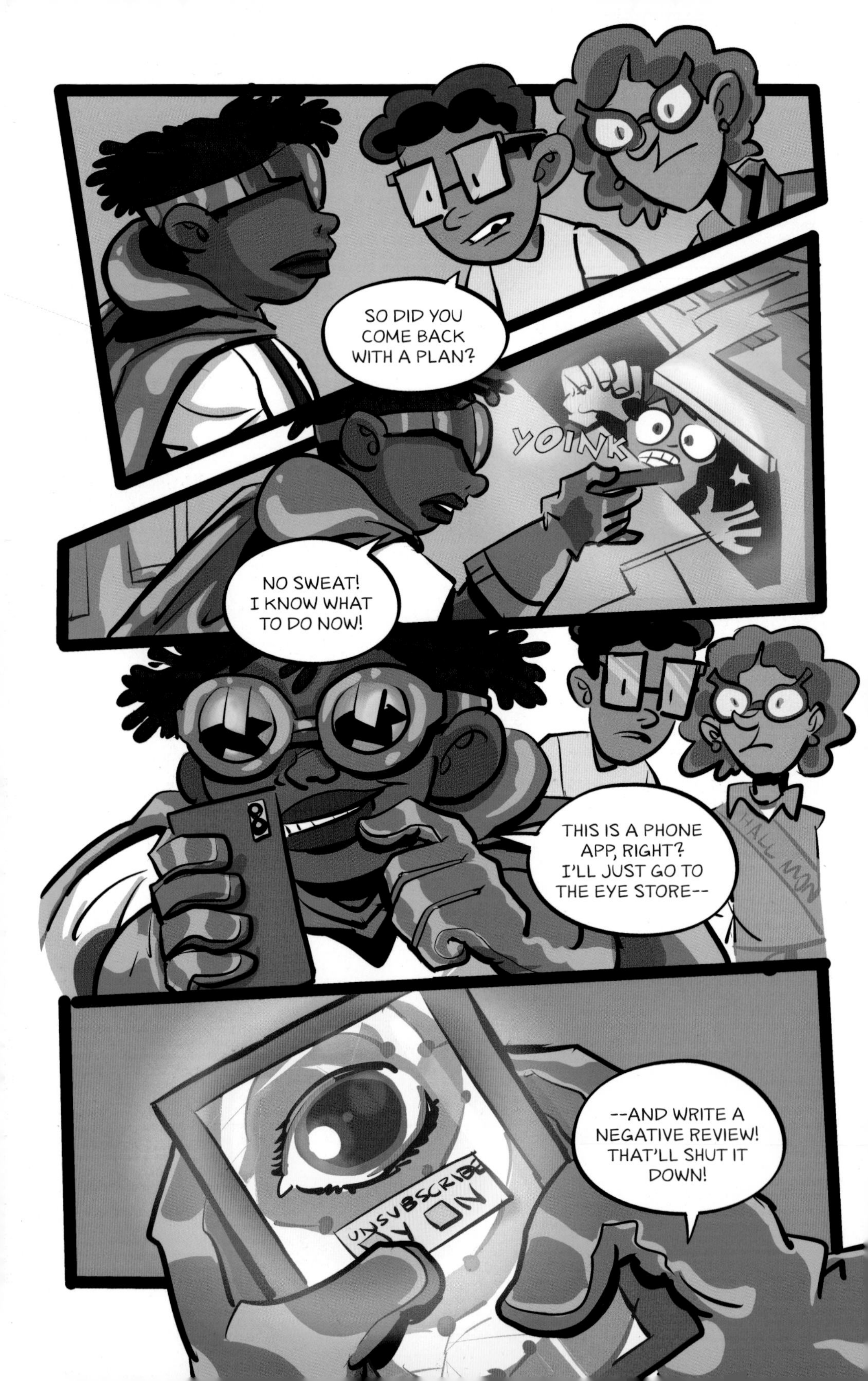
SO DID YOU COME BACK WITH A PLAN?
YOINK
NO SWEAT! I KNOW WHAT TO DO NOW!
THIS IS A PHONE APP, RIGHT? I'LL JUST GO TO THE EYE STORE--
HALL MON
--AND WRITE A NEGATIVE REVIEW! THAT'LL SHUT IT DOWN!
UNSUBSCRIBE

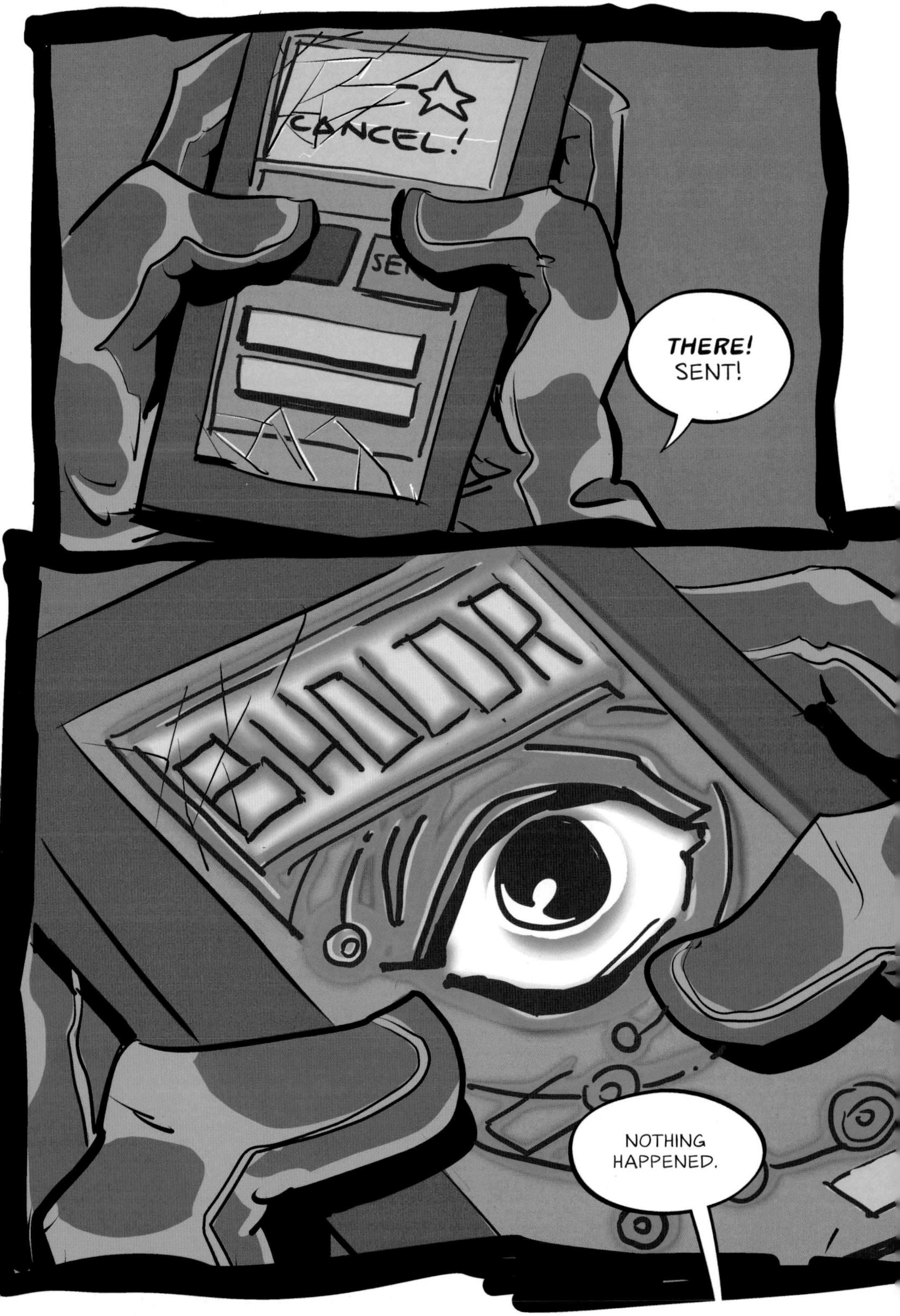
CANCEL!
THERE! SENT!
NOTHING HAPPENED.

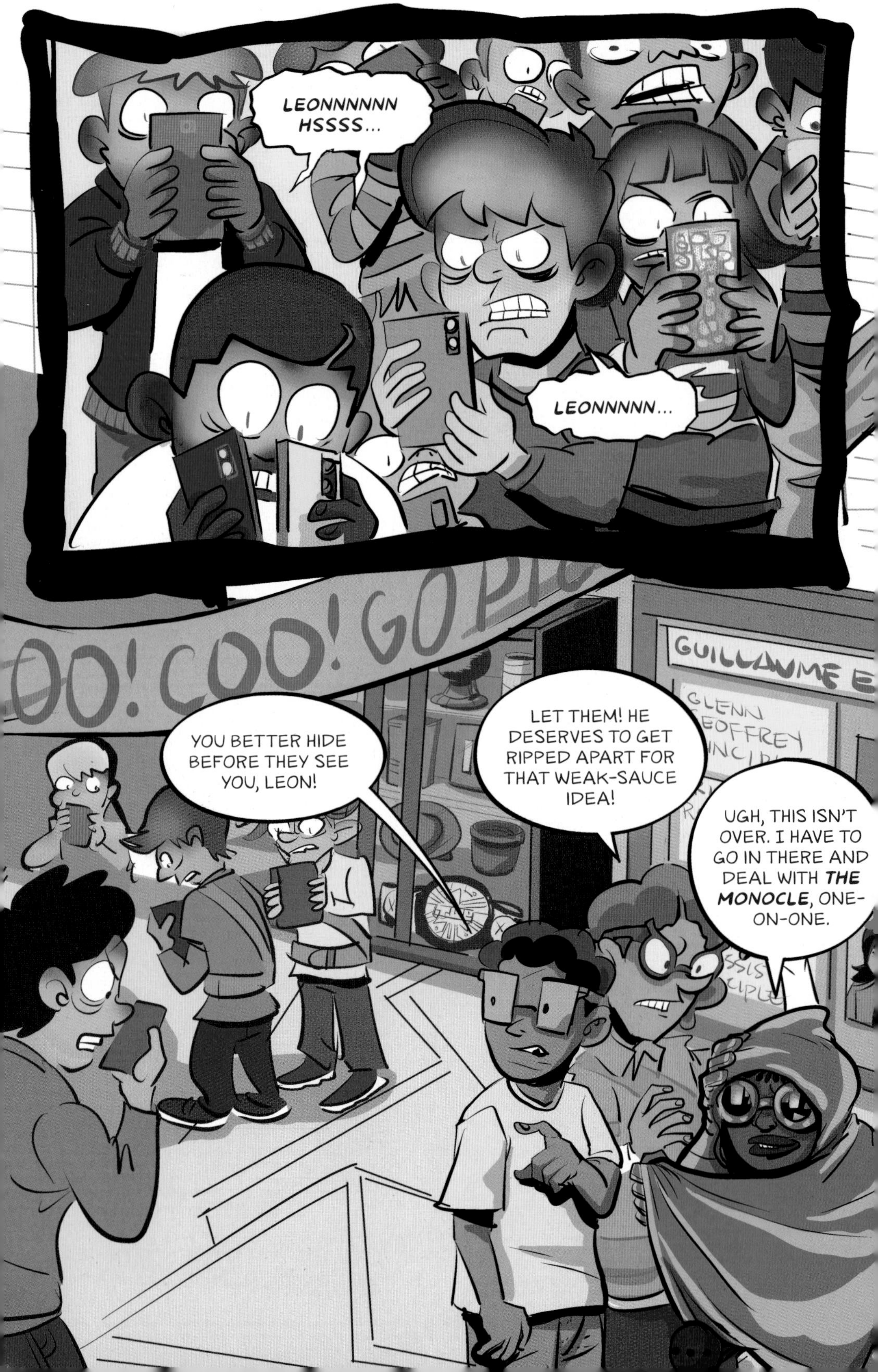
LEONNNNNN HSSSS...
LEONNNNN...
OO! COO! GO PI
GUILLAUME E
GLENN GEOFFREY
YOU BETTER HIDE BEFORE THEY SEE YOU, LEON!
LET THEM! HE DESERVES TO GET RIPPED APART FOR THAT WEAK-SAUCE IDEA!
UGH, THIS ISN'T OVER. I HAVE TO GO IN THERE AND DEAL WITH ***THE MONOCLE***, ONE-ON-ONE.

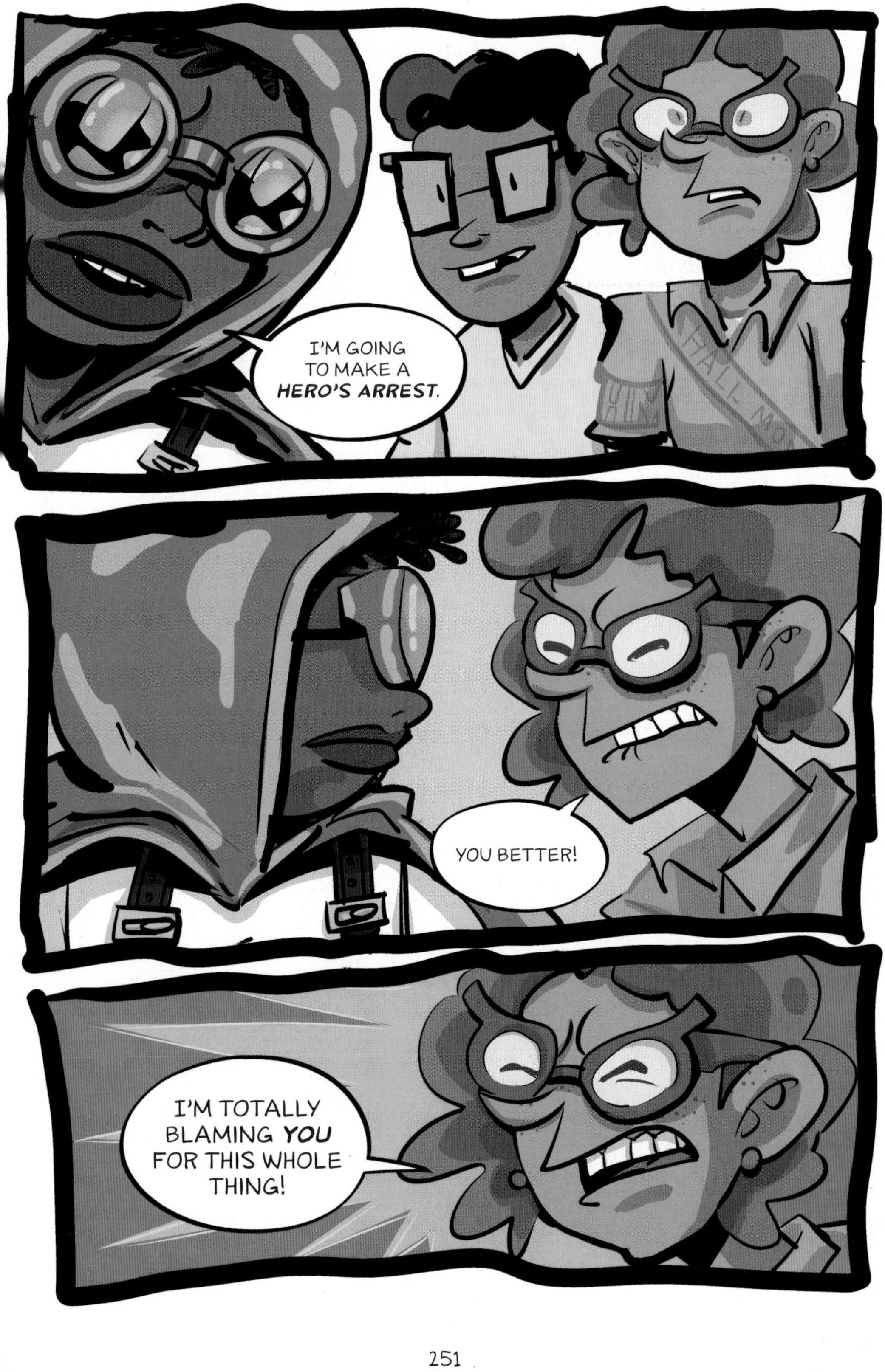
I'M GOING TO MAKE A HERO'S ARREST.
YOU BETTER!
I'M TOTALLY BLAMING YOU FOR THIS WHOLE THING!

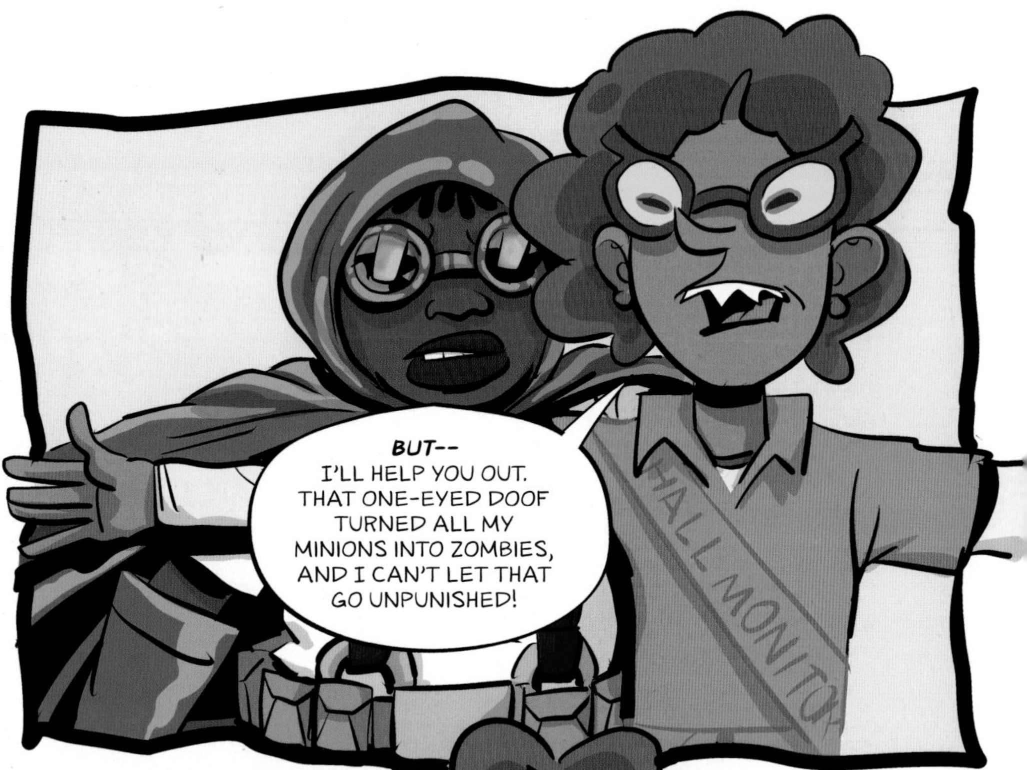
BUT--
I'LL HELP YOU OUT. THAT ONE-EYED DOOF TURNED ALL MY MINIONS INTO ZOMBIES, AND I CAN'T LET THAT GO UNPUNISHED!
HALL MONITOR

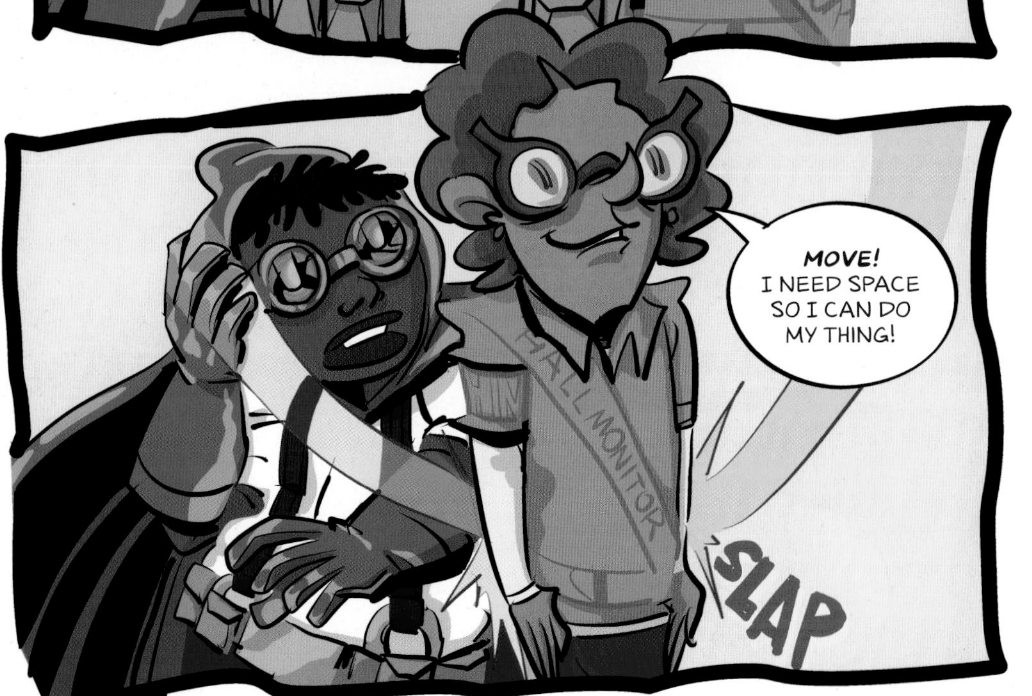
MOVE! I NEED SPACE SO I CAN DO MY THING!
HALL MONITOR
SLAP

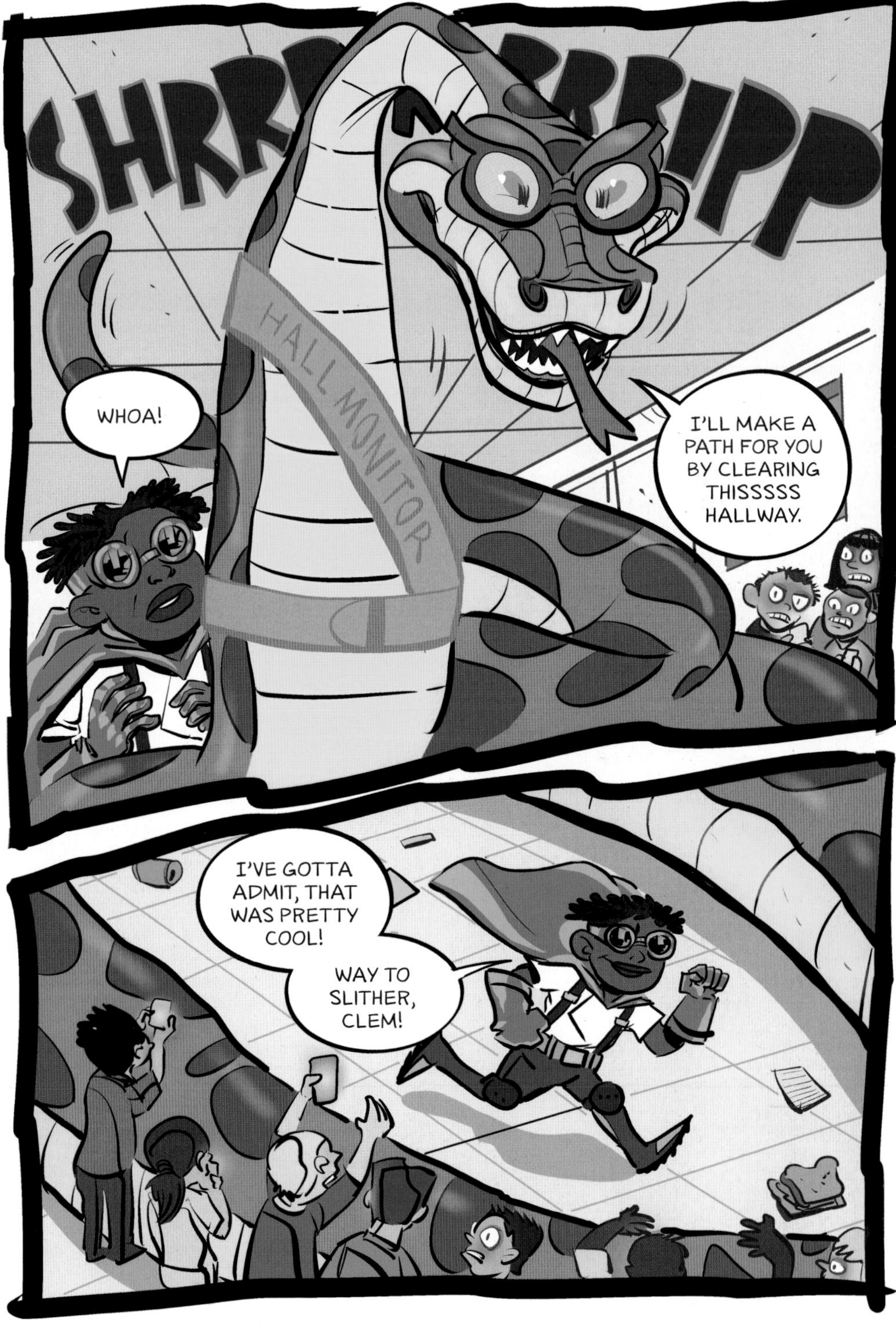
SHRRRRRRRIPP
HALL MONITOR
WHOA!
I'LL MAKE A PATH FOR YOU BY CLEARING THISSSSS HALLWAY.
I'VE GOTTA ADMIT, THAT WAS PRETTY COOL!
WAY TO SLITHER, CLEM!

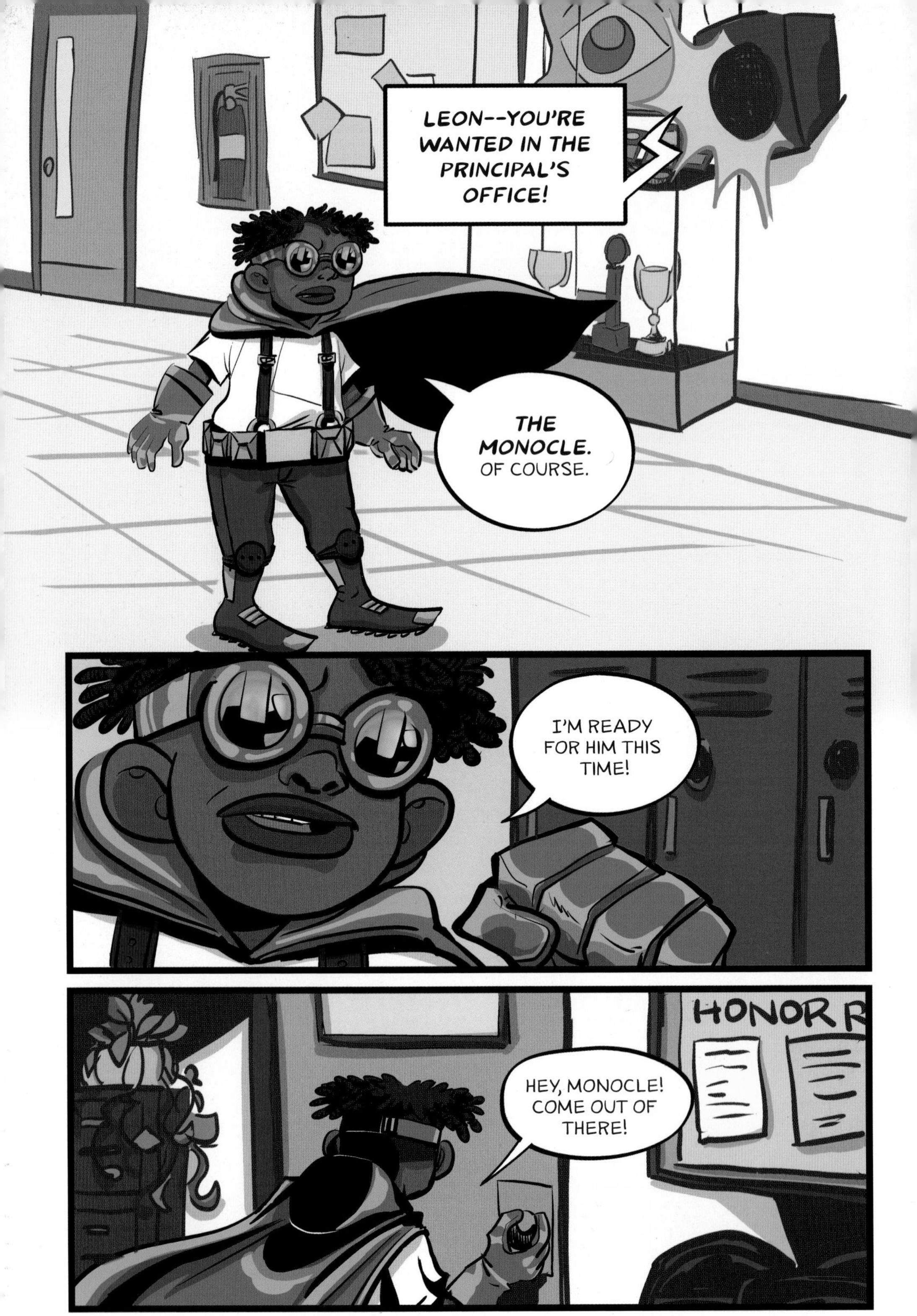
LEON--YOU'RE WANTED IN THE PRINCIPAL'S OFFICE!
THE MONOCLE. OF COURSE.
I'M READY FOR HIM THIS TIME!
HONOR R
HEY, MONOCLE! COME OUT OF THERE!

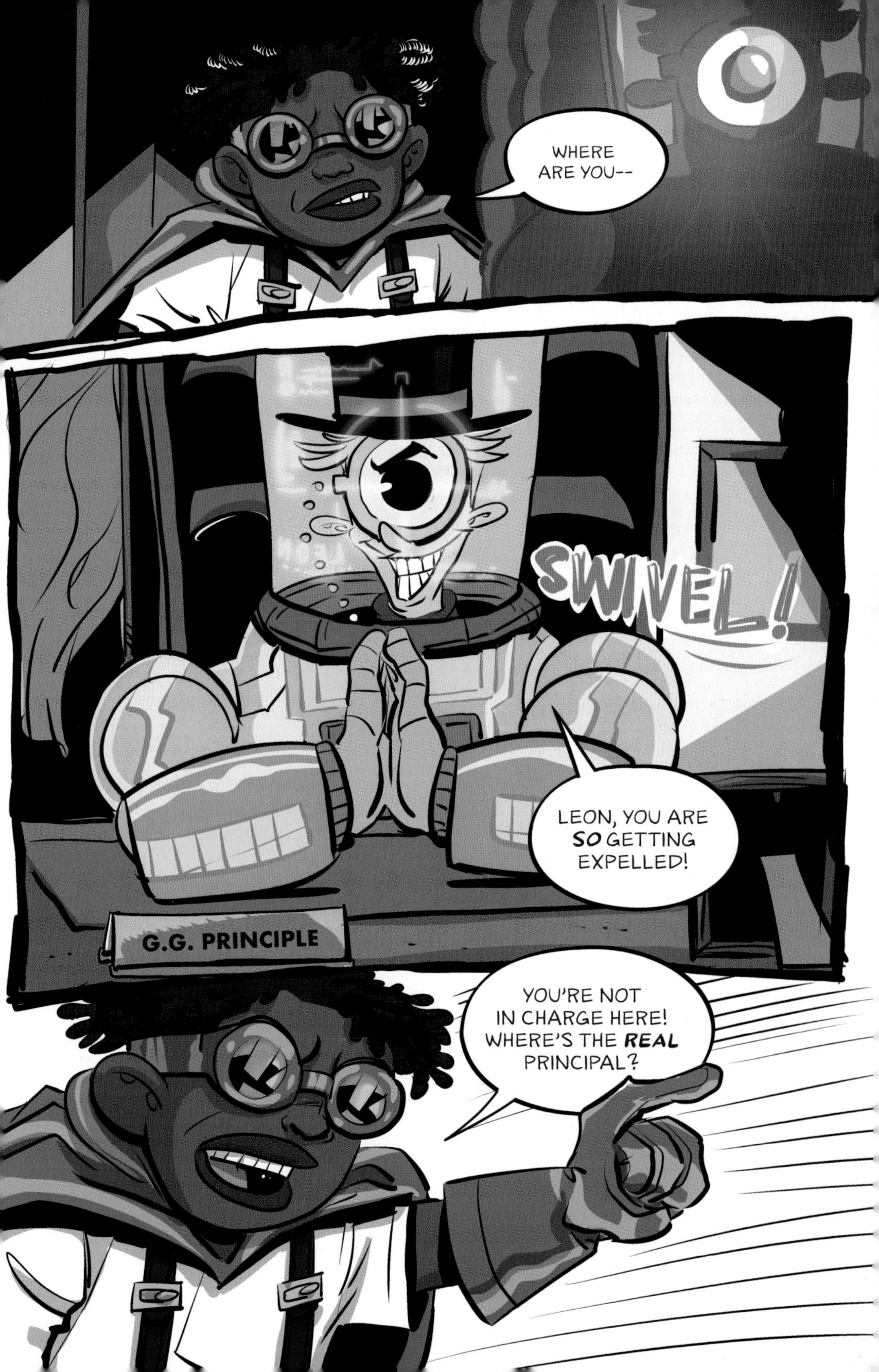
WHERE ARE YOU--
SWIVEL!
LEON, YOU ARE **SO** GETTING EXPELLED!
G.G. PRINCIPLE
YOU'RE NOT IN CHARGE HERE! WHERE'S THE **REAL** PRINCIPAL?

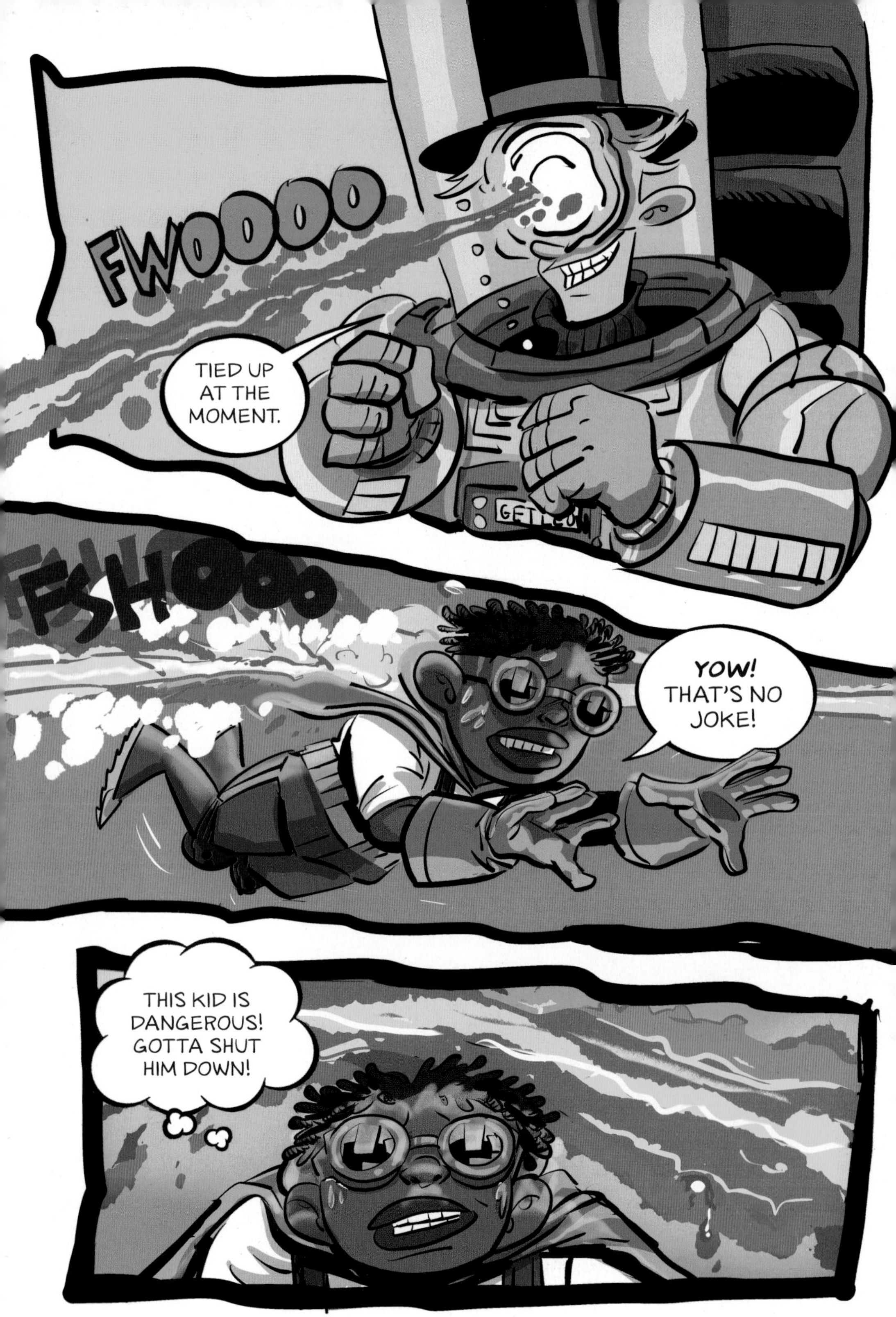
FWOOOO
TIED UP AT THE MOMENT.
FSHOOO
YOW! THAT'S NO JOKE!
THIS KID IS DANGEROUS! GOTTA SHUT HIM DOWN!

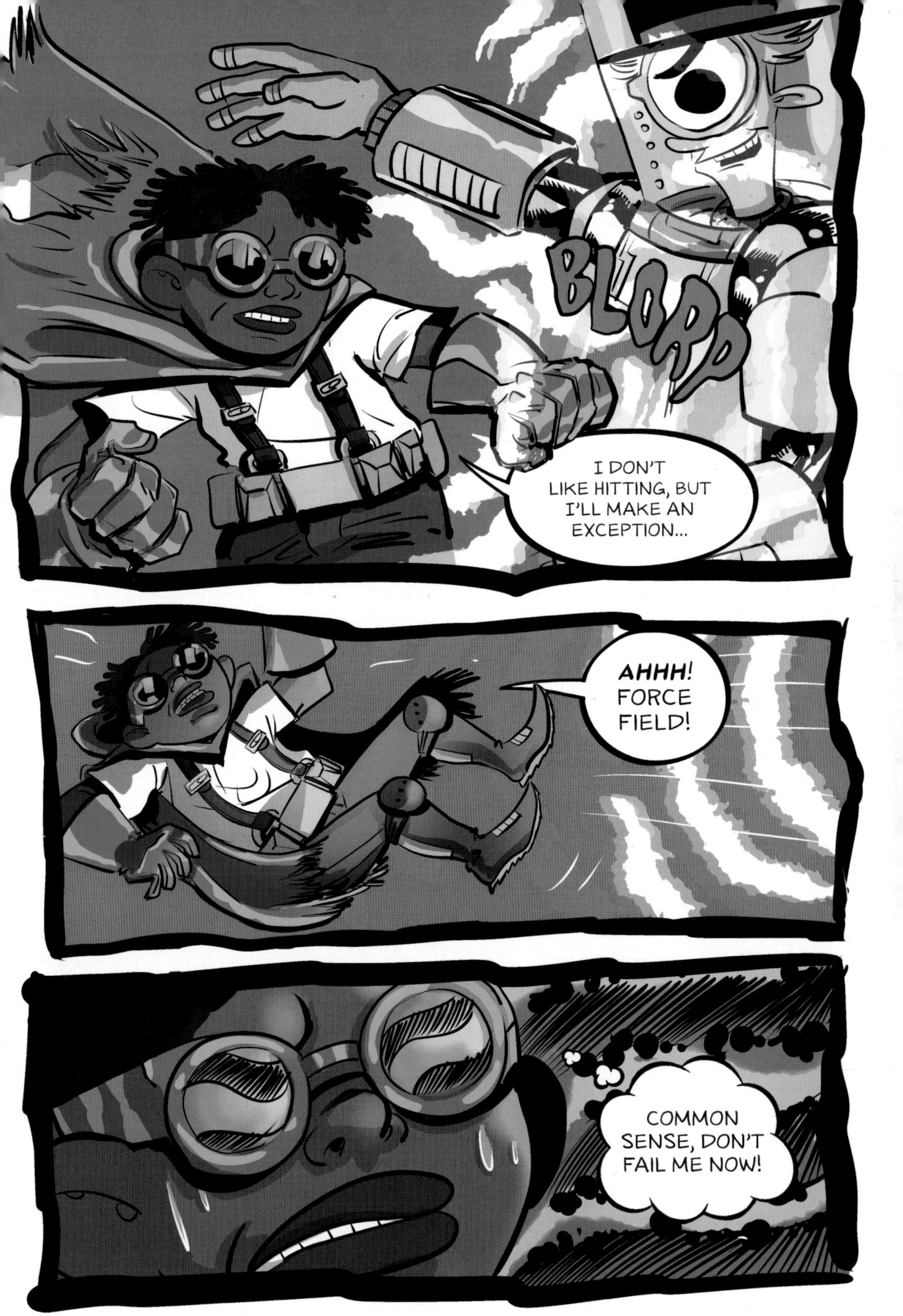
BLORP
I DON'T LIKE HITTING, BUT I'LL MAKE AN EXCEPTION...
AHHH! FORCE FIELD!
COMMON SENSE, DON'T FAIL ME NOW!

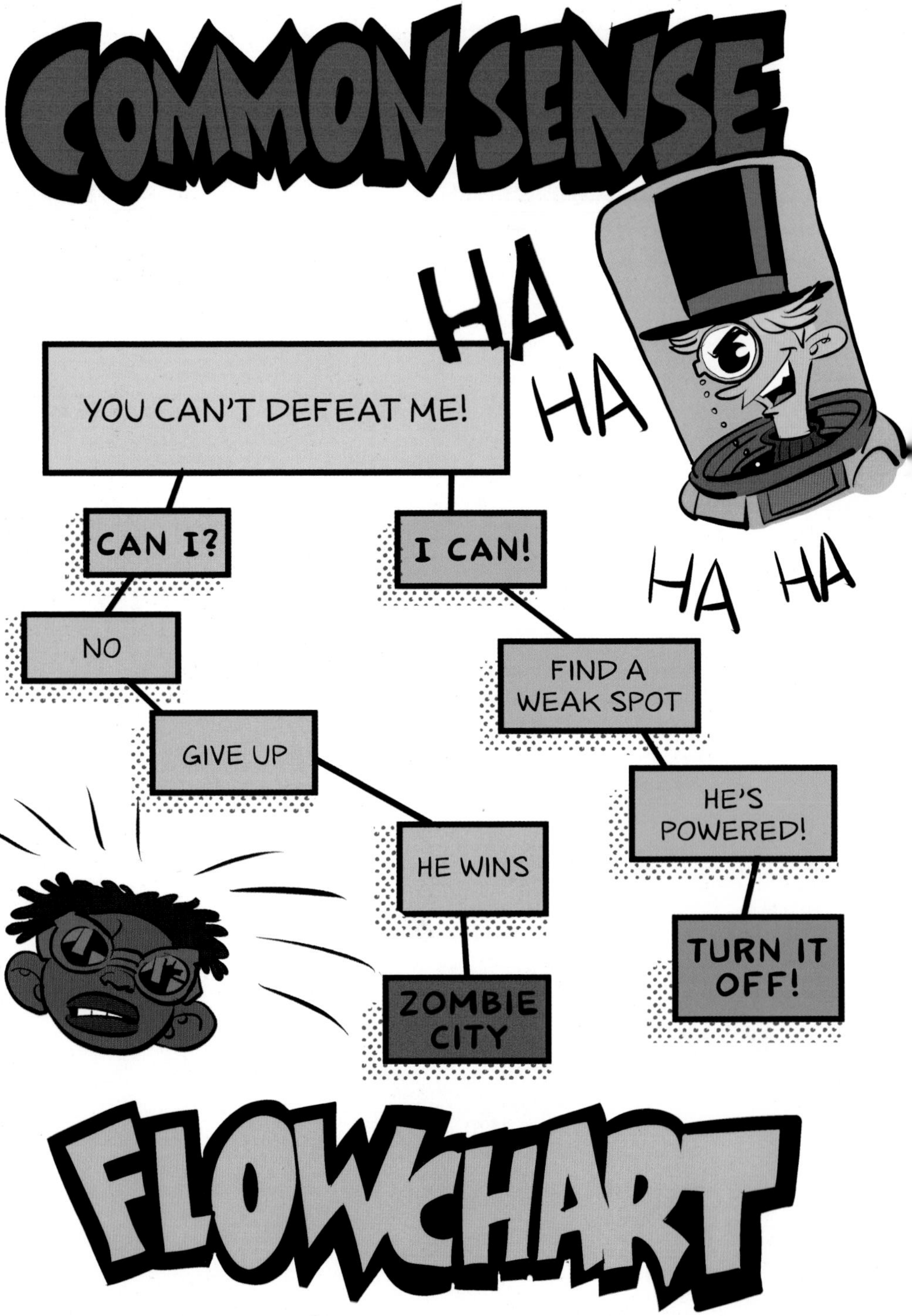
COMMON SENSE
HA HA
HA HA
YOU CAN'T DEFEAT ME!
CAN I?
I CAN!
NO
FIND A WEAK SPOT
GIVE UP
HE'S POWERED!
HE WINS
TURN IT OFF!
ZOMBIE CITY
FLOWCHART

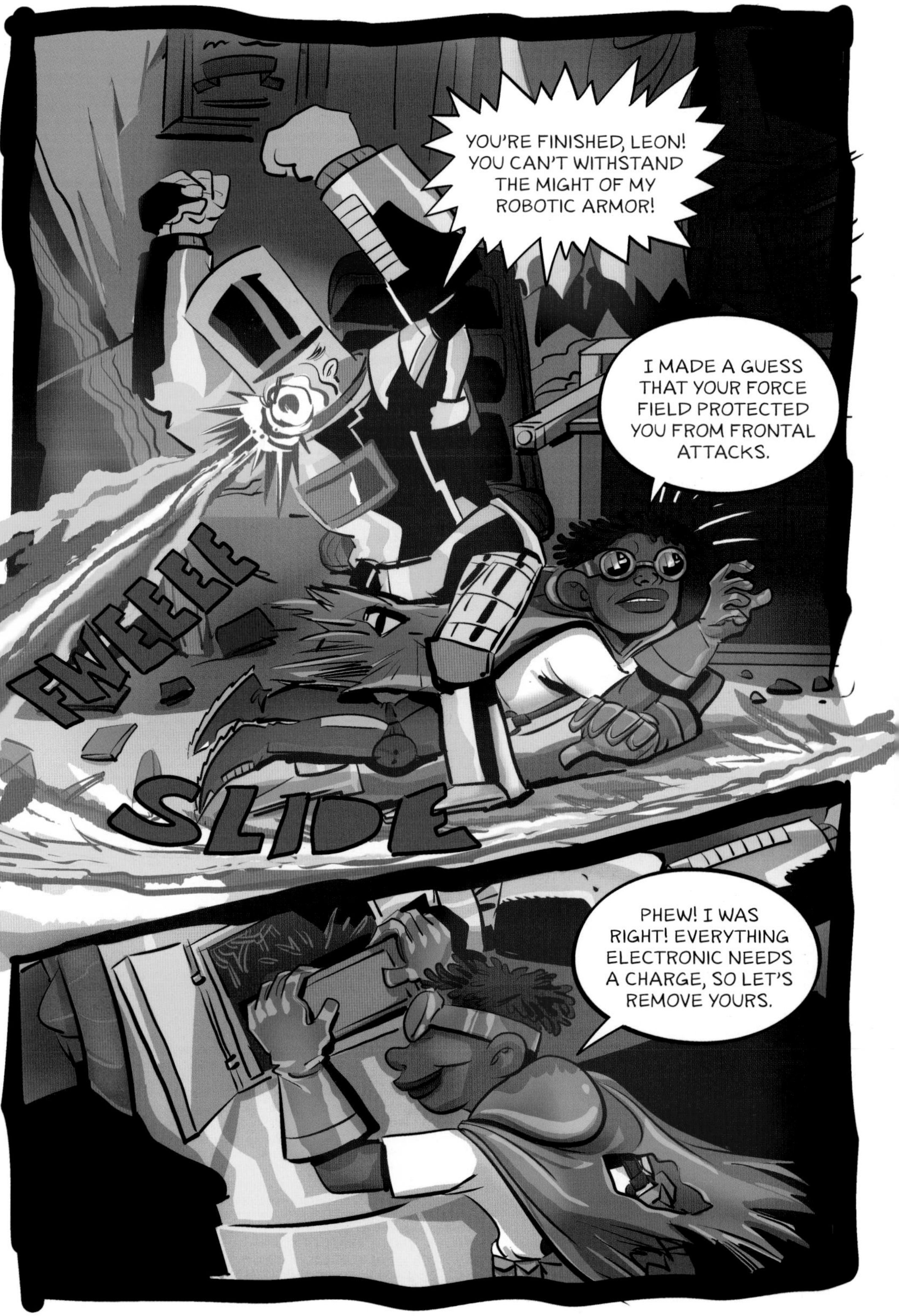
YOU'RE FINISHED, LEON! YOU CAN'T WITHSTAND THE MIGHT OF MY ROBOTIC ARMOR!
I MADE A GUESS THAT YOUR FORCE FIELD PROTECTED YOU FROM FRONTAL ATTACKS.
FWEEEE
SLIDE
PHEW! I WAS RIGHT! EVERYTHING ELECTRONIC NEEDS A CHARGE, SO LET'S REMOVE YOURS.

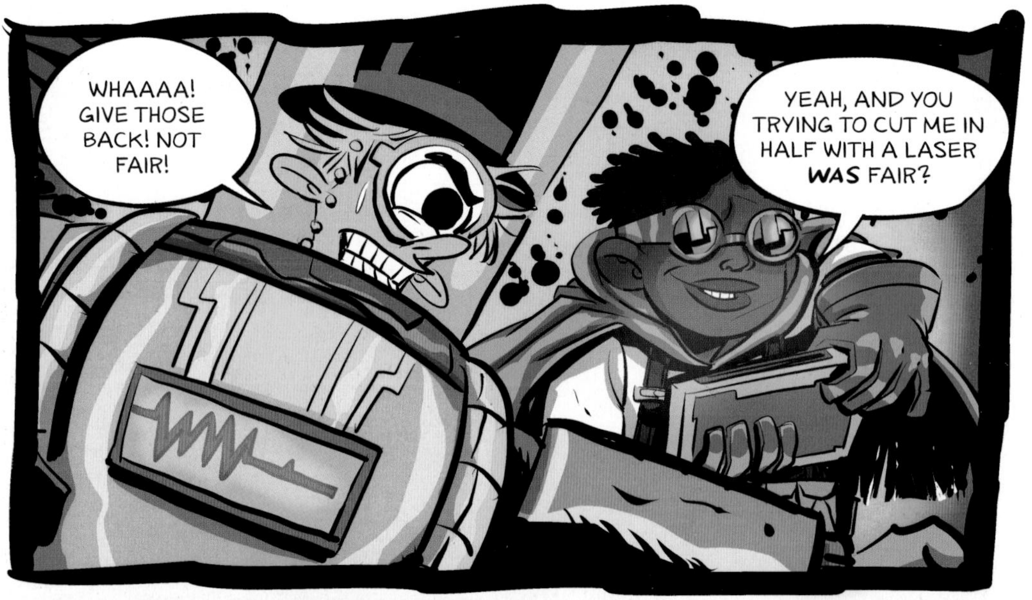
WHAAAA! GIVE THOSE BACK! NOT FAIR!
YEAH, AND YOU TRYING TO CUT ME IN HALF WITH A LASER **WAS** FAIR?

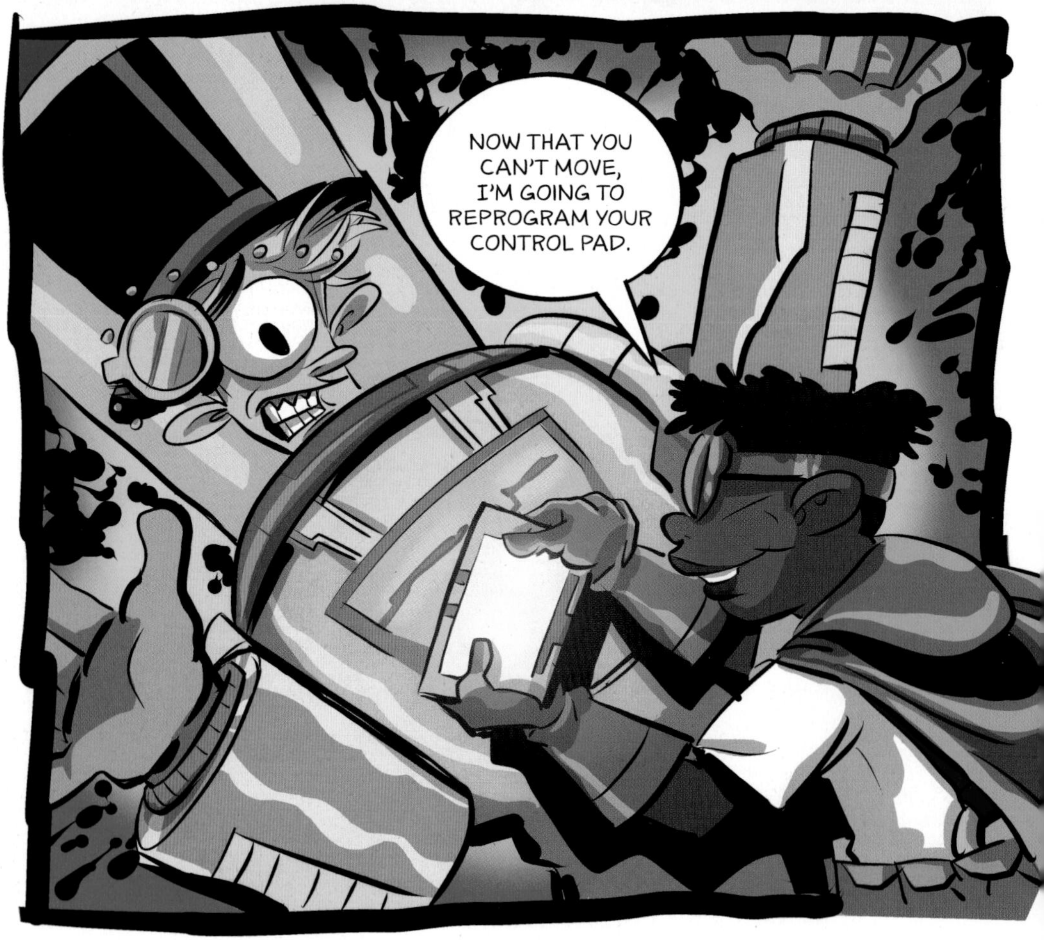
NOW THAT YOU CAN'T MOVE, I'M GOING TO REPROGRAM YOUR CONTROL PAD.

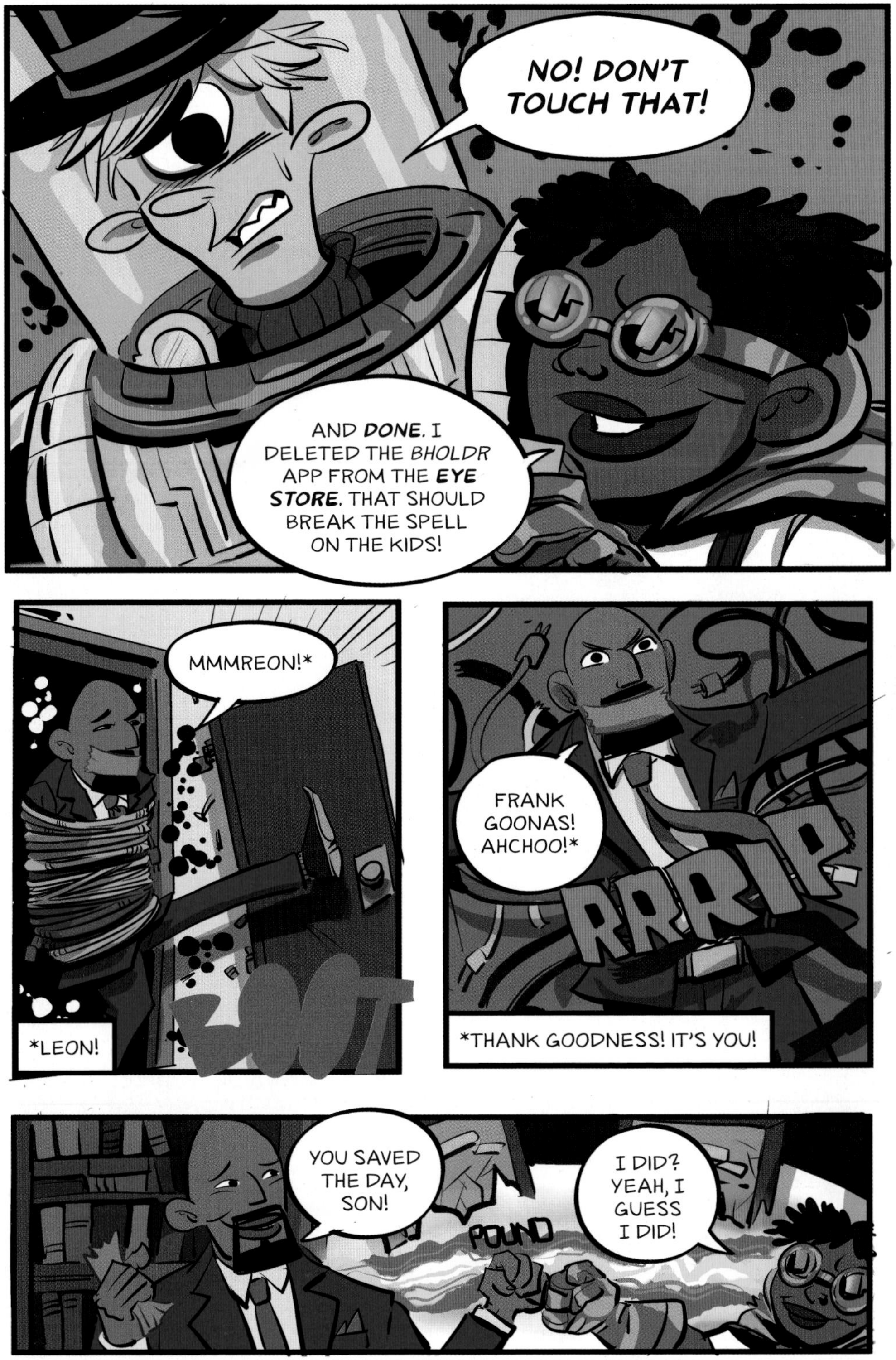
NO! DON'T TOUCH THAT!
AND **DONE**. I DELETED THE *BHOLDR* APP FROM THE **EYE STORE**. THAT SHOULD BREAK THE SPELL ON THE KIDS!
MMMREON!*
*LEON!
FRANK GOONAS! AHCHOO!*
RRRIP
*THANK GOODNESS! IT'S YOU!
YOU SAVED THE DAY, SON!
POUND
I DID? YEAH, I GUESS I DID!

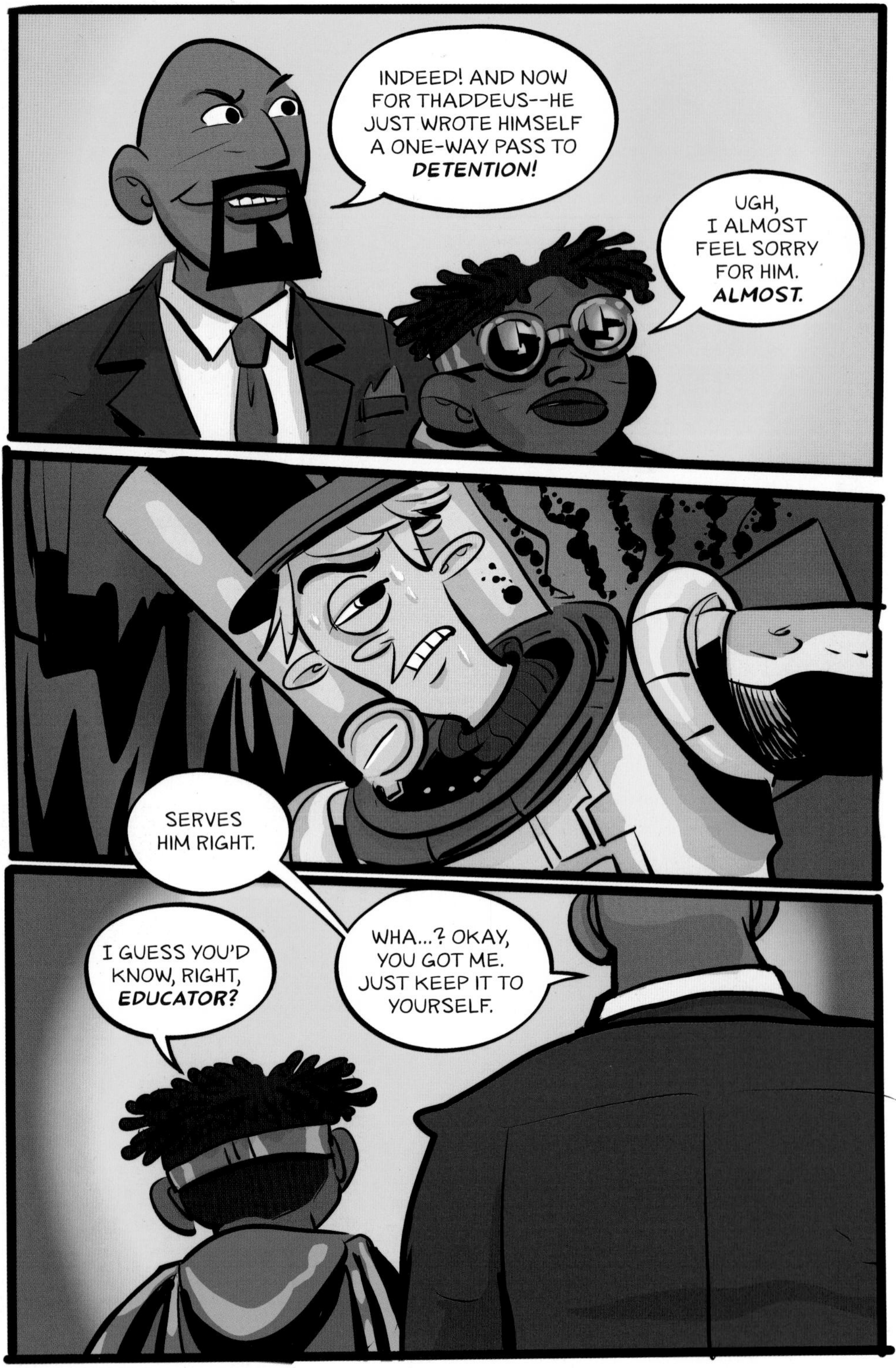
INDEED! AND NOW FOR THADDEUS--HE JUST WROTE HIMSELF A ONE-WAY PASS TO **DETENTION!**
UGH, I ALMOST FEEL SORRY FOR HIM. **ALMOST.**
SERVES HIM RIGHT.
I GUESS YOU'D KNOW, RIGHT, **EDUCATOR?**
WHA...? OKAY, YOU GOT ME. JUST KEEP IT TO YOURSELF.

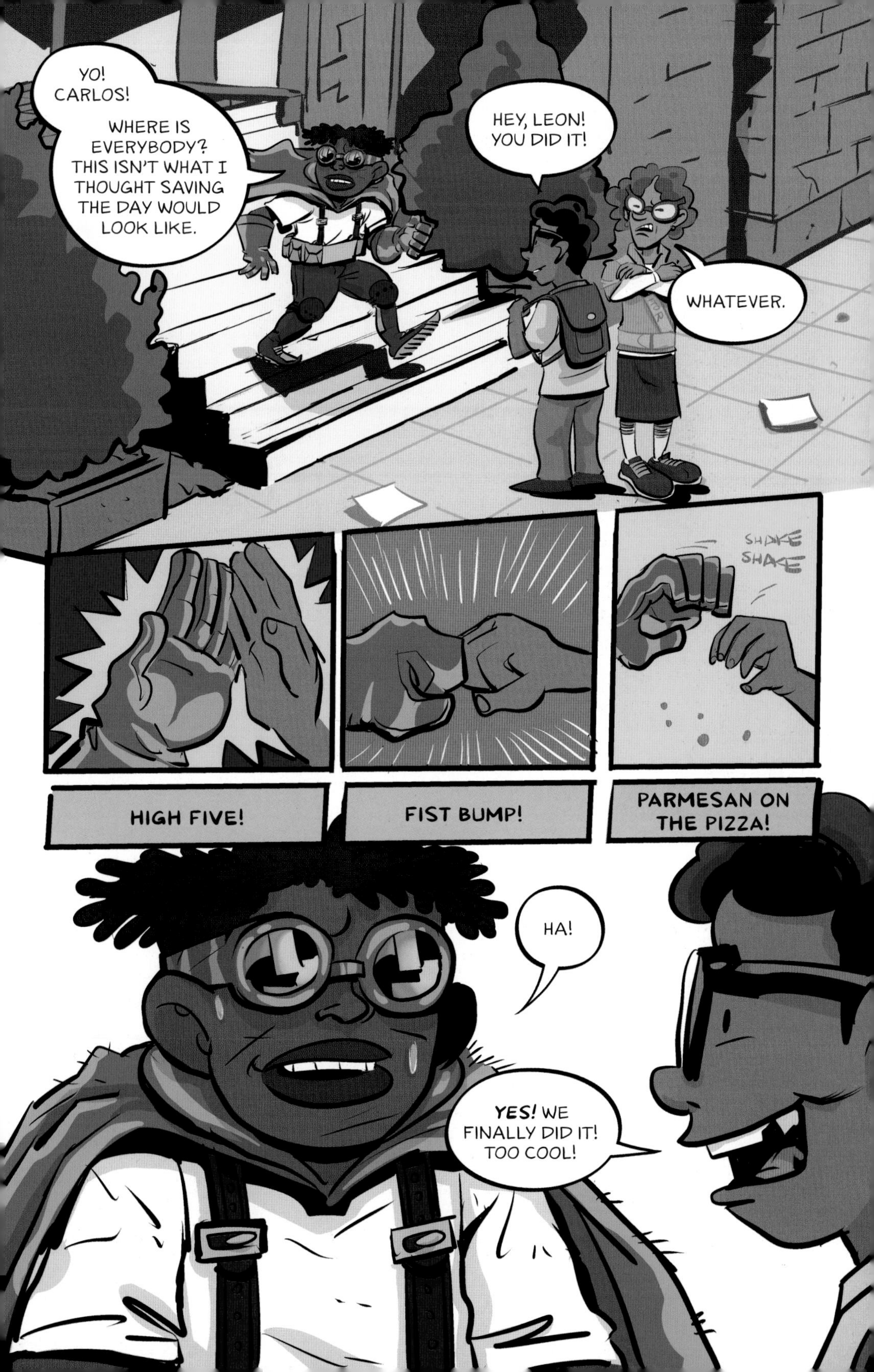
YO! CARLOS!
WHERE IS EVERYBODY? THIS ISN'T WHAT I THOUGHT SAVING THE DAY WOULD LOOK LIKE.
HEY, LEON! YOU DID IT!
WHATEVER.
HIGH FIVE!
FIST BUMP!
SHAKE SHAKE
PARMESAN ON THE PIZZA!
HA!
YES! WE FINALLY DID IT! TOO COOL!

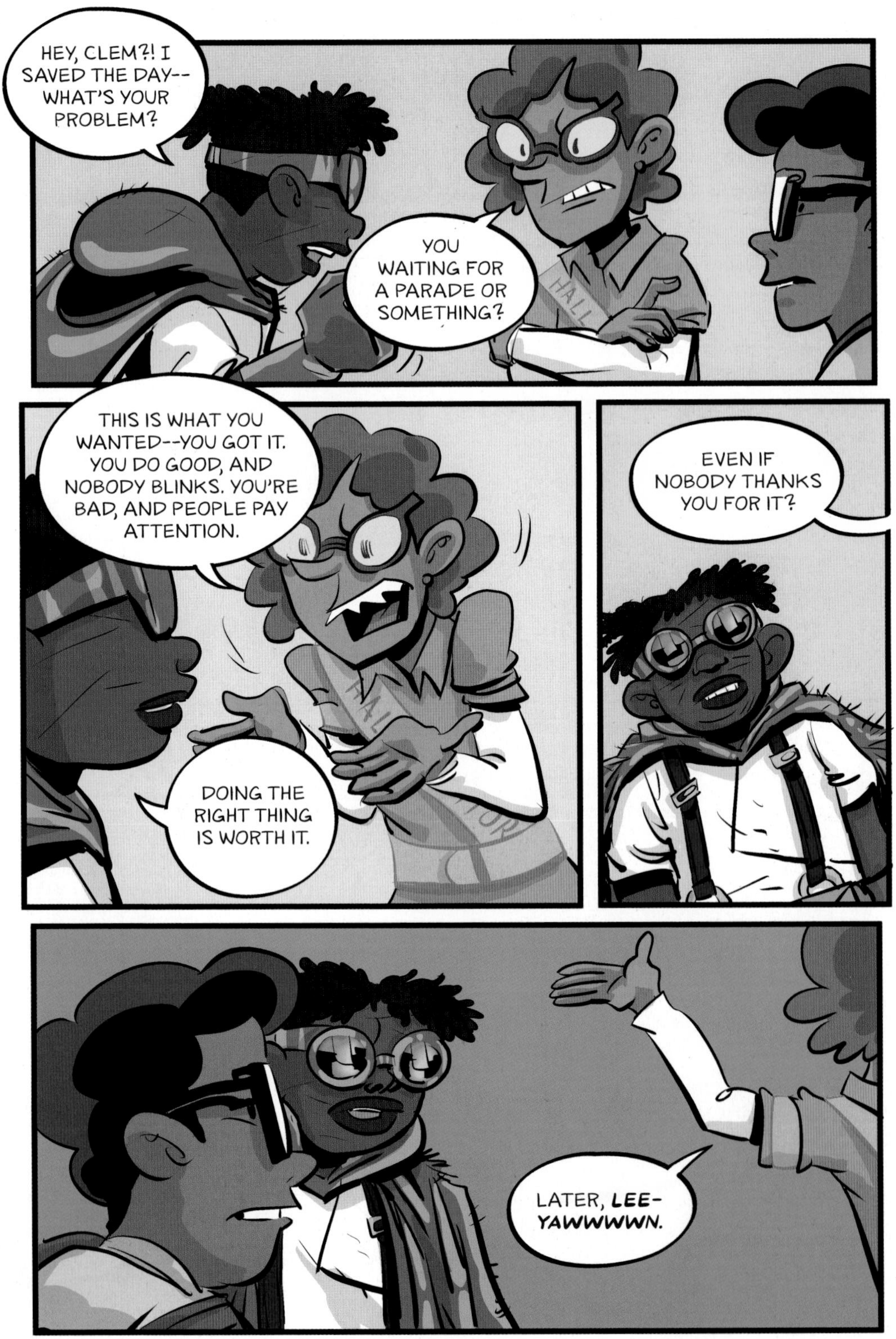
HEY, CLEM?! I SAVED THE DAY--WHAT'S YOUR PROBLEM?
YOU WAITING FOR A PARADE OR SOMETHING?
THIS IS WHAT YOU WANTED--YOU GOT IT. YOU DO GOOD, AND NOBODY BLINKS. YOU'RE BAD, AND PEOPLE PAY ATTENTION.
DOING THE RIGHT THING IS WORTH IT.
EVEN IF NOBODY THANKS YOU FOR IT?
LATER, **LEE-YAWWWWN.**

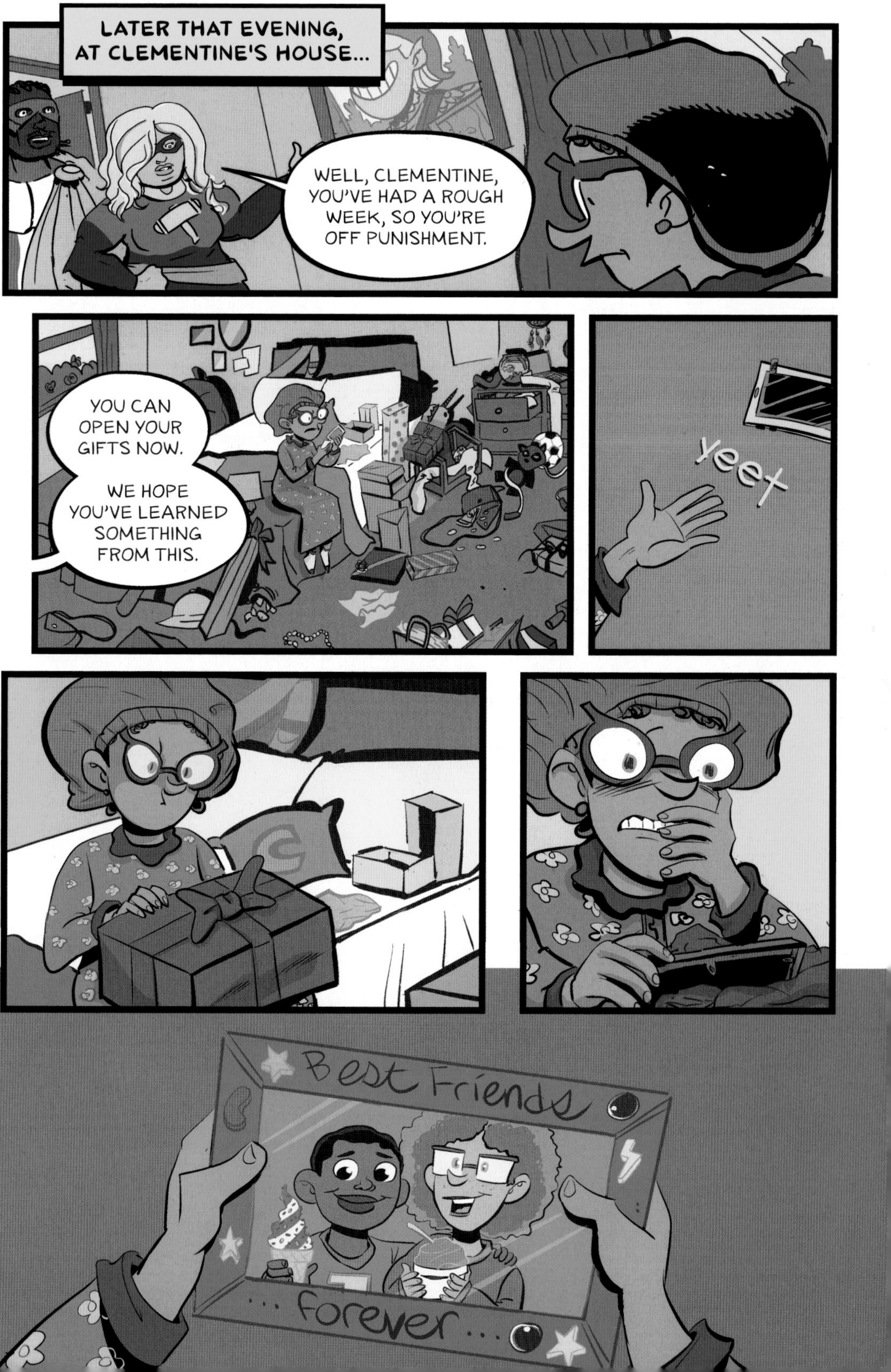
LATER THAT EVENING, AT CLEMENTINE'S HOUSE...
WELL, CLEMENTINE, YOU'VE HAD A ROUGH WEEK, SO YOU'RE OFF PUNISHMENT.
YOU CAN OPEN YOUR GIFTS NOW.
WE HOPE YOU'VE LEARNED SOMETHING FROM THIS.
yeet
Best Friends
... forever ...

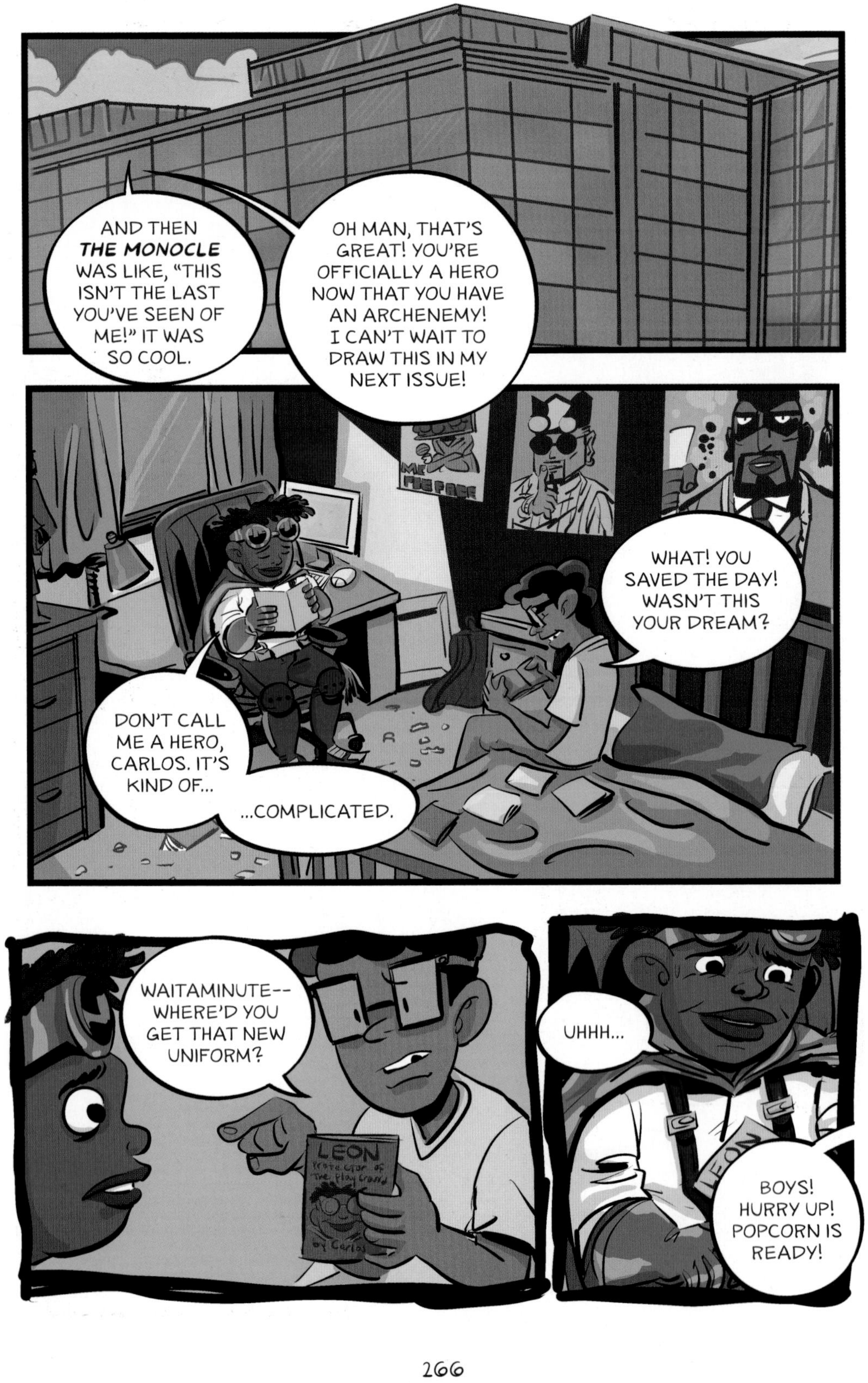

AND THEN ***THE MONOCLE*** WAS LIKE, "THIS ISN'T THE LAST YOU'VE SEEN OF ME!" IT WAS SO COOL.
OH MAN, THAT'S GREAT! YOU'RE OFFICIALLY A HERO NOW THAT YOU HAVE AN ARCHENEMY! I CAN'T WAIT TO DRAW THIS IN MY NEXT ISSUE!
WHAT! YOU SAVED THE DAY! WASN'T THIS YOUR DREAM?
DON'T CALL ME A HERO, CARLOS. IT'S KIND OF...
...COMPLICATED.
WAITAMINUTE-- WHERE'D YOU GET THAT NEW UNIFORM?
LEON
Protector of The Play Ground
by Carlos
UHHH...
BOYS! HURRY UP! POPCORN IS READY!

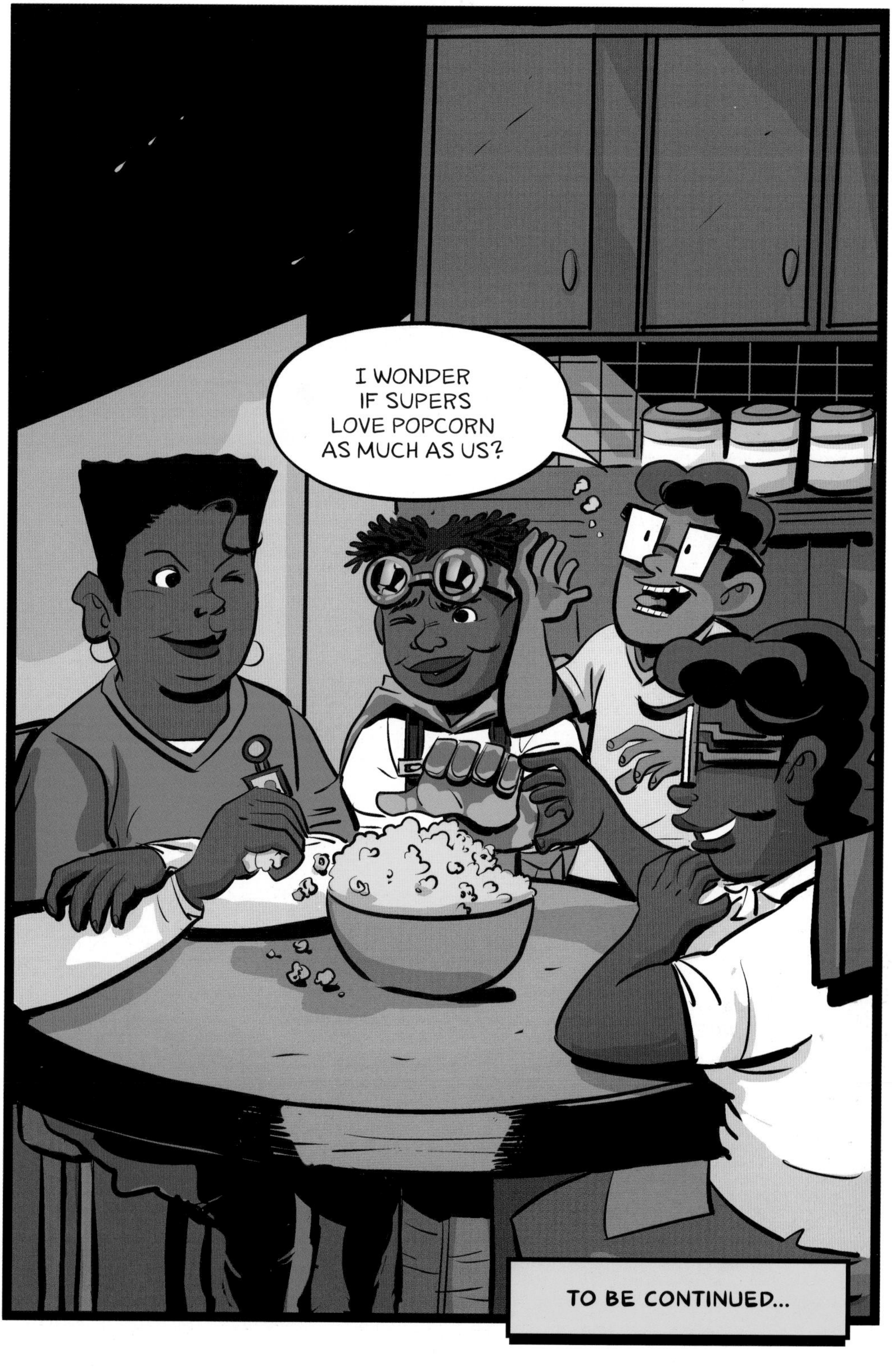
I WONDER IF SUPERS LOVE POPCORN AS MUCH AS US?
TO BE CONTINUED...

Photo by Darcy Russotto

JAMAR NICHOLAS is an award-winning artist and and educator from Philadelphia who has dedicated his career to helping young people realize the power of cartooning. Jamar aims to promote anti-bullying, healing, and kindness in his work. *Leon the Extraordinary* is the first book in a series featuring Leon and his friends Carlos and Clementine. Jamar enjoys the 1980s, podcasting, video games, and spending time with his family and pets.

BONAIA ROSADO is from Puerto Rico and graduated from the Delaware College of Art and Design. By day, Bonaia advocates and secures funding for people with disabilities in the Philadelphia area. By night, she is a colorist producing work for Sourcebooks, Mirage Publishing, TOKYOPOP, and Scholastic. You can follow her on Instagram @bonaiarosado.